SPACEFUNK!

EDITED BY
MILTON J. DAVIS

MVmedia, LLC
Fayetteville, GA

MVmedia, LLC
PO Box 143052
Fayetteville, GA 30214
www.mvmediaatl.com

Publisher's Note: This is a work of fiction. Names, characters, places, and incidents are a product of the author's imagination. Locales and public names are sometimes used for atmospheric purposes. Any resemblance to actual people, living or dead, or to businesses, companies, events, institutions, or locales is completely coincidental.

Cover art by Sethodian Tlou Thapelo Ramatlhodi

Ordering Information:
Quantity sales. Special discounts are available on quantity purchases by corporations, associations, and others. For details, contact the "Special Sales Department" at the address above.

Spacefunk! / Various Authors. -- 1st ed.
ISBN 979-8-99905129-3-0

Contents

To Valjeanne Jeffers a.k.a Sister Moon
We miss you.

Space is the place.

—Sun Ra

What is Spacefunk?

Space. The Final Frontier . . . no, wait, hold up. That's not what we're here to talk about. We are here to talk about the Funk, the whole funk, nothing but the Spacefunk. But before we proceed, we have to give honor where it is due, to the elders and the ancestors who paved the way long ago and proved that Space had always been the Place for us.

We reach way back to ancient Kemet, a.k.a. Egypt. The Egyptians had an advanced understanding of astronomy for their time. They cataloged stars, mapped constellations, tracked the movements of celestial bodies like the sun and moon, and created the concept of a 365-day calendar, among other achievements.

We turn our attention to the Dogon and the Yoruba, who also used astronomy to develop technologies, predict weather, and create calendars. The Dogon are of particular interest.

The Dogon believed that Sirius B was a small, dense, heavy star with a strong gravitational force. They also believed it was the heaviest star in the area and that it rotated on its axis. Scientists later confirmed that Sirius B is extremely dense, with a cubic meter of its substance weighing around 20,000 tons. The Dogon believed that Sirius had an invisible companion star that orbited Sirius every 50 years in an elliptical pattern.

The Dogon believed that the Sirius system was the source of creation. They also believed that the concepts of duality and twins were important aspects of their cosmology, which were driven by the Sirius stars.

Fast forward to the early days of the US space program, where a group of sisters now known as The Hidden Figures dropped their knowledge and helped carve out our country's place in the stars. Three of these extraordinary women - NASA's first black female engineer Mary Jackson and mathematicians Katherine Johnson and Dorothy Vaughan – were honored this week with the Congressional Gold Medal for their groundbreaking work. And let's not forget aeronautical engineer Christine Darden, who is "internationally known for her research into supersonic aircraft noise, especially sonic boom reduction," according to NASA, and became the first Black woman at NASA Langley to be appointed to the top management rank of Senior Executive Service.

But let's not stop there. Let's give a shout-out to our Black astronauts: Robert H. Lawrence, Guy Bluford, Ronald McNair, Frederick Gregory, Charles Bolden, Dr. Mae C. Jemison, Bernard Harris, Winston Scott, Robert Curbeam, Michael Anderson, Stephanie Wilson, Joan Higginbotham, Alvin Drew, Leland Melvin, Robert Satcher, Victor Glover, Sian Proctor, Jessica Watkins and Jeanette Epps.

A special shout-out goes to Ed Dwight, who was selected by then-President John F. Kennedy to be the first Black astronaut. Unfortunately, Ed Dwight ran into the wall of racism after President Kennedy's assassination. After his military service, he went on to earn his Master of Fine Arts in Sculpture from the University of Denver in 1977. Some of his most well-known sculptures, which are spread out in various locations around the country, include the series "Black Frontier of the American West," the "Evolution of Jazz," and a sculpture of President Barack Obama's first inauguration.

And we can't speak on Spacefunk without honoring those who added the funk to the space. We're talking about Sun Ra and his Orkestra, the person who coined the phrase 'Space is the Place' and whose musical and theatrical performances are among the cornerstones of what we now call Afrofuturism. What about the people who put the bass in our face; none other than Parliament/Funkadelic. George Clinton, Bootsy Collins and the entire Mothership Connection lifted off from the foundation laid by the Godfather of Soul James Brown, taking us to musical heights never reached before while filling our minds and our moving our booties with Funkentelechy and the Placebo Syndrome. Don't forget Earth, Wind, and Fire, Dexter Wansel, and other Black artists who incorporated the stars into their musical musing, putting the rhythm and bass in perfect place.

Which brings us to right here; right now. Spacefunk is not new. Over the years there have been quite a few African/African Diaspora authors and poets that have imagined space from their personal and cultural point of view. What we've done with

Spacefunk!

Spacefunk is create an imaginative nexus where readers and creators come together to share a vision of the cosmos where everything and anything is possible, where the stars are open to anyone and everyone with a vision, a purpose, and a big dose of funk.

Space Children Dream of the Last Place
by
Linda Addison

Aminata & Youssouf (the last Dogon twins) sing,

"Three zebras
    to show you the Way.

Not a hunter
    with constellations tucked
    in an impossible belt.

A cluster of Digging Stars
    on early morning horizon,
    reminder to press seeds
    into freshly turned soil.

New life from Sirius
    replacing gills with lungs,
    so you can map the Way
    back home when Earth
    becomes a boneyard.

Dreams embed in Soul essence
    to keep cosmic rhythms alive,
    even when flesh shifted forward,
    crossing evolutionary limits,
    making new moons shine
    uneasily, the bones pile up.

Adaptation, unremovable
    zero points on the wheel

of primordial willpower,
become final exhalations
of one world, while all the
star born sing with Sun Ra:
Space is the Place."

The Right Stuff
by
Lynette S. Hoag

Senator Lyndon took a seat behind the enormous mahogany desk. The desk wasn't his. It belonged to the Head Administrator of NASA Launch Operations. Unlike Senator Lyndon's desk, this one was barren except for one low-watt lamp, a phone, and a manila folder marked "Confidential: For Your Eyes Only!" The smell of fresh furniture polish hung in the air, cloying. He preferred to be at his own desk in moments like this, despite its disarray. Moments when his decisions impacted national security. Moments that were 'first' for Americans; for humanity; for history. Suppressing his disdain for the polished, neat mahogany desk, Senator Lyndon lit his pipe, loosened his tie, and opened the manila folder.

Today was December 25, 1961. Two years earlier a message had been received from extraterrestrials via an eighty-five-foot radio telescope located in Colorado Springs, Colorado. The message had finally been decoded. It read:

> *We will visit your planet when the moon passes between the Earth and the sun. The visit will occur on July 31, 1962. Our ship will be located between the moon and the Earth. We will find you if you are there. Send only your best space traveler to meet us. We are eager for this meeting. We will not tolerate a substandard space traveler.*

With little time to spare, NASA began the frantic search for an astronaut to meet the extraterrestrials. The Mercury Program was in the process of sending men into space. However, only one astronaut in the Mercury Program had expressed an interest in this new project. The remaining astronauts, the ones who had failed

6

to qualify for The Mercury Program, were perceived as "also-rans." No one at NASA wanted an "also-ran" for this project. It was a 'bad look' politically. Surely America had other men with the right stuff to go to space. The right stuff for the project at hand: Extraterrestrial Eclipse Encounter or E3.

Tasked with approving the final astronaut chosen by NASA to fly the E3 rocket, Senator Lyndon puffed on his pipe behind the strange mahogany desk. He opened the manila folder marked "Confidential: For Your Eyes Only!" blinked his eyes hard, then refocused them. *What in tarnation?* He pressed the intercom button on his phone and yelled into the speaker. "Samuel Ezra Smith! Get in here this instant!!"

Moments later, the senator heard a tentative knock. The door opened a crack and swung fully agape. A tall, thin, flustered man in a dark blue tailored suit, spit-shined black wingtips, and crisp white shirt entered the room. He walked quickly to the front of the mahogany desk and stopped.

"Senator Lyndon. How can I be of service?" He smiled, showing all his perfect teeth. He appeared to be somewhere in his late twenties. His deep brown hair was combed straight back away from his face, plastered to his head with Brylcreem. The style made his face appear pale, skeletal and strained. He wore thick horn-rimmed glasses.

"Is this your idea of a dramatic hoax? Wasting my time with this malarkey? And on Christmas Day. I should have you fired for cause." Senator Lyndon snarled. He turned the folder around to face Samuel. Samuel looked at the 8' x 10' glossy black and white photograph. "A Negress in a flight suit? Part of the space program? Has this agency gone completely insane?"

"Senator, if I may, that's Maryam Joie Miller. She's a test pilot sir and our best by far. Did you read the rest of her file?" Samuel gestured eagerly to the "Confidential" manila folder. "She's passed every test. Technical interviews, psychiatric interviews, physical examinations, and so on, multiple times. She is triple verified," he said, breathlessly.

"Triple verified? What in hell's bells is that?"

Samuel took a deep breath that visibly filled his chest, then let it out through pursed lips and continued. "They kept testing her because, well, NASA's administrators didn't believe it either. A Negress, right? So, they tested her three times, every test, with a different proctor each time. She passed every test with a perfect score three times. Triple verified. As far as we can tell, she's never made a math error of any kind!" Samuel spoke with an excited energy that animated his face and body. Realizing this, he paused and calmed himself before he continued. He held his hand up to the senator as if to say 'stop.' "Sir, I understand your apprehension and all. Don't get me wrong. For my part, I think coloreds were appointed by God himself to be domestics and sleeping car porters. Nothing more. Ever."

"Yet, you brought me all the way down here, from Washington, D.C. on Christmas, away from my family, to vet a negro for space travel," the senator said flatly. "And a girl at that! Is she even twenty?"

"There's something in her blood we can't identify that seems to enhance her abilities. She's human, but different from everything we know about . . . everything."

"You will pardon me if I can never believe that Samuel," the senator replied.

"Now hold on, Senator. You've heard of the infinite monkey theorem. If monkeys can write Shakespeare eventually, it certainly follows that a single-colored person might be remarkable enough to be an astronaut. Maryam certainly is."

Senator Lyndon huffed and pushed the file away. "Not. A. Chance." He pounded the desk with his fist to emphasize each word.

Frustrated, Samuel held up both of his hands in a 'stop' gesture. "She's here! You should at least talk to her before you decide. After all, you have traveled this far. I would be remiss in my duties as Secretary to the Head Administrator of NASA if I let you leave without at least talking to her. In fact, with all due respect, Senator, I *cannot* let you leave without meeting her in person, if just for a few minutes." Samuel resisted the strong urge to bow that overcame him out of nowhere.

* * *

The fluorescent lights reflected off the white halls at NASA Launch Operations headquarters. Maryam Joie Miller thought the halls gleamed like a full moon on a starless night. She sat on a hard metal chair between her parents across from a large room that, on days other than Christmas, contained the secretarial pool. There were typewriters as far and deep into the room as she could see. *Do secretaries dream of outer space?* Maryam smiled to herself because she thought this of everyone. Of every profession. She had never had a desire other than space travel. Her first words after 'Momma' and 'Daddy' were: Do airplanes fly to outer space? She was elated to be here, waiting to be interviewed by Senator Jon Lyndon. Electric prickles of anticipation zipped through her body. She was at the final hurdle of hundreds she had leaped or pushed down on this journey. A journey Maryam had been on since her first memory.

"We are so proud of you, Maryam," her mother said, squeezing her hand. "You have all the right stuff for the E3 mission. You've got stardust in your blood."

"Momma, you've told me that every night since the one you found me in the field of wildflowers behind our house." Maryam gave her mother a wide smile.

"You were in a little capsule in our backyard, shaped like a giant Christmas ornament. I was scared to touch it. But I heard you crying. Screaming. You were wrapped in a foil blanket, shivering and cold. My beautiful, peanut-butter brown baby girl with doe eyes wide as saucers. Shiny black hair, covering your head. The moment I lifted you from the capsule, it vanished." Mae Jean sighed aloud. She loved telling this story to Maryam.

"Don't make her cry now, Mae Jean," her father admonished, then winked at his twenty-two-year-old daughter. "Maryam knows she was born for this."

For as long as her parents could remember, Maryam had been obsessed with everything in the heavens: sun, clouds, moon, stars, planets. The Universe. They had sacrificed much to make this moment happen. Sacrificed everything really. The penance began with the purchase of an eight-inch deluxe treckerscope, a fortune on teachers' salaries. When her parents couldn't pry Maryam away from gazing at the stars each night, they felt gratified. She cut planets out of old magazines and pasted them to her walls. She made mobiles of the planets from tennis balls. She learned the names of stars, near and far, and repeated their names in her sleep.

Then, her parents left everything. Left their jobs as professors at comfortable negro universities. Left their small, middle-class community where they were respected and surrounded by other colored professionals. Left Washington D.C. and moved to NASA Launch Operations in Florida. There, they were offered jobs sweeping floors, emptying trash cans, washing dishes, and chopping endless mirepoix vegetable mixes. Left everything to get their daughter close to helicopters, planes, and rockets. To get her next to astrophysicists, aeronautic engineers, and astronauts.

It had been worth the sacrifices. Maryam soaked in the information surrounding her at NASA, like rays from the sun. She retrieved books and discarded worksheets from the trash. She devoured the books and solved the math problems. Maryam sat alone in the back of lectures until she was noticed and shooed out or reluctantly welcomed. She strolled in the airfields and through the hangars at night, taking in the atmosphere, the flying machines. Maryam washed dishes and chopped vegetables in the kitchen with her mother. Swept floors, cleaned windows, and emptied trash cans with her father. She was an unofficial member of NASA Launch Operations and its Aeronautics and Pilot Training School until an aeronautics professor discovered her brilliance. A German immigrant, who took up her cause in earnest, though enigmatically.

"It's unusual, I know, to allow a colored girl into the space program. It's true that she can be uppity. She is *wunderbar* at mathematics and that's a byproduct, I suppose. But we can segregate her from the regular students, as any negro would be. She can sit in the back of classrooms and be tested alone at the convenience of the professors or pilots. Most importantly, she can be kept off the record. Classified," the professor argued. "We won't let a word of her existence get beyond this island. Besides, we can use her knowledge and skills to improve our programs."

When Maryam graduated from the Aeronautics and Pilot Training School a few months later, flew the required 1,500 hours, and became a qualified jet pilot, only her instructors knew of her existence; of her skill; of her triple verification. Her instructors and her parents.

* * *

Maryam stood in front of the polished mahogany desk, eyes front, hands clasped behind her back, standing at ease, as instructed. She stood five feet ten inches tall. Skin, medium brown and clear. Hair, black, curly, and cropped close. Maryam cut an elegant, authoritative, and undeniably feminine figure in her flight suit. The intelligence behind her eyes illuminated her handsome face. The dark green flight suit had been tailored by her mother to hug her slim figure and accentuate her athletic build. When prompted by the Senator, she stepped forward and shook his hand firmly.

"Thank you for your time and consideration, Senator Lyndon," Maryam said, meeting his gaze briefly. She averted her eyes to look straight ahead and returned to an 'at-ease' position. She could hear her father in her ears: "Don't look into the face of a white man, Maryam. Especially one that holds your fate in his hands."

Senator Lyndon looked down at the file on his desk and made no response to her comment. Without looking at her he growled, "Samuel, you insisted that I see this Negress um, Astronaut-trainee or whatever you call her. I've seen her. If there's nothing else. . ."

"Senator, if you please, there is a tennis ball-sized canister in the top drawer of your desk. It contains metal balls. May I have it please?" Samuel held out his hand. He stepped to the desk, took the canister from the Senator, and turned to Maryam as he opened it. "If you would kindly step back a few paces, Pilot Miller, let's show Senator Lyndon one of your highly classified, extra-special gifts."

Maryam complied, closed her eyes, and held her hand, palm up waist high, in front of her body. Samuel tossed a metal ball in front of her face. Maryam caught it with one hand, eyes still closed, and tossed it above her head where it began to rotate clockwise around her head like a halo. Samuel tossed the rest of the balls to her in the same manner. Soon the entire canister of metal balls was rapidly spinning like a crown around Maryam's head. Then, she opened her eyes and made a counterclockwise motion with her hand. The halo of balls slowed to a stop, hung in the air, then began to spin in a counterclockwise direction. She opened her hand palm up, closed her eyes, and each ball in turn dropped out of its orbit and into her hand. Samuel carefully took each metal ball from her and returned it to the canister.

When he took the last ball, Maryam opened her eyes and smiled. "I love doing that. The energy of the universe flows through me like electricity," she said with too much excited energy. She spoke despite being repeatedly admonished by her parents not to speak to a white person until prompted to do so.

Senator Lyndon sat stunned behind his desk. "What in tarnation? It must be some kind of trick. I don't believe it."

"It's true," Samuel said. "And she understood that strange alien message before we translated it. Maryam overheard one of the engineers playing it. But of course, we didn't believe it. We wasted two years deciphering it when she was right the first time she heard it!" Samuel made a sound, like an uncomfortable laugh. "Anyway, she's our "Best Space Traveler" by miles. And, if you recall, the alien message requested our best space traveler."

Senator Lyndon grunted.

"Take all the time you need to read her file, sir. Ask her any questions. But we here at NASA think we should send her, despite her race, despite her gender. Perhaps secretly if . . ."

"Samuel. You're in no position to make that decision," Senator Lyndon barked, cutting the secretary off mid-sentence. He stood, stepped from behind his desk, shook Maryam's hand, and clapped her on the shoulder. "That sure was something to see. You know, that thing with the metal balls. I'll admit that. You're quite a specimen for a colored girl. A credit to your race, perhaps. But you see, I have to run this by my sub-committee on space exploration. That's political you know. It's about how it, um, looks to other Americans. My hands are tied. The decision is theirs. You understand, of course." He shrugged without apology, dismissed her with a shooing motion, returned to the mahogany desk, dropped into the seat, and resumed puffing his pipe.

"I would love to serve my country in this manner," Maryam implored, against every racial and gender protocol she'd been taught. "I was born for this mission. I was born to pilot the E3 rocket."

The senator frowned pointedly at Maryam's break from the understood protocols. Understanding that Maryam had gone too far by speaking out of turn, Samuel rushed to her side and led her from the room.

"And she's uppity?" Senator Lyndon said to Samuel when Maryam had left the room. "That's unforgivable."

"If the committee chooses Maryam, I will personally see to it that she begs your forgiveness Senator," Samuel said. Finally, he gave into the urge to bow his head in submission to the senator's authority.

* * *

Maryam sat on the porch in the chilly Florida night air staring up at the stars. She wore her flight jacket and maintained a ramrod straight posture. Her face was staunch, emotionless. She cradled a rare alcoholic drink, a hot toddy. Her parents sat on either side of her. Her father with two fingers of whiskey, and her mother, with a cup of tea.

"Baby," Mae Jean said as she stood, resting her hand on her daughter's shoulder. "You've been so resilient through all of this. You've weathered storm after storm. Overcome barrier after barrier built or thrown in your path. If they don't send you . . ." Mae Jean's voice broke and trailed off. She couldn't finish the sentence. Not for herself. Not for Maryam.

Maryam made no response.

"Maryam . . ." Her father, Neal, sought to finish the thought his wife couldn't. To explain away the inescapable despair and depression that flowed in the wake of a dream deferred; a dream that hovered like an invisible, floating demonic creature taunting the dreamer.

"I was born for this. There's stardust in my blood," she whispered.

Mae Jean could hear her daughter's voice catch on the tears in her throat. Maryam never took her eyes from the night sky. Mae Jean burst into tears and ran into the house. Neal wiped his hands down his face, disconsolate, and followed his wife without looking back at their daughter. Inside their tiny two-bedroom home, he took Mae Jean in his arms and rocked her gently. Her tears mirrored his sense of hopelessness and he felt the urge to give in to his own feelings of despair. He squeezed his wife, hugging her tight.

"Mae Jean, Maryam has stardust in her blood. No white man can take that from her. Even if they keep her here. Grounded." He said, then thought *Ad astra per aspera, my amazing daughter. Even if only in your heart and mind.*

* * *

Launch day arrived. Neal and Mae Jean Miller looked up at the sky from their porch as the rocket blasted upwards toward the heavens. Senator Lyndon and Secretary Smith stood motionless along with every soul at NASA HQ. Each person crossing their fingers, expecting the worst, hoping for miracles as the E3 rocket blasted into space. The launch was flawless. The rocket escaped earth's atmosphere and fell into perfect geosynchronous orbit on July 31, 1962. Senator Lyndon took every opportunity to gloat about the successful launch to the press, to his sub-committee on space exploration, and of course, to Secretary Smith.

On the E3 rocket, Captain Gus Glennon searched the heavens through the porthole in his rocket ship, looking for the aliens. Instead, he was greeted by the sun approaching the dark disk of Earth from the moon's nightside. Earth's atmosphere, lit from behind, created a reddish ring around it that glowed brighter as the eclipse proceeded.

Breathtaking. Captain Glennon thought. *Simply breathtaking.*

He wouldn't have missed this moment for a lottery win; for permanent happiness; for the universe. Though he had placed second behind Pilot Maryam Joie Miller in every test relative to the E3 mission, he was the better man. It was right for him to be here. Here, making historical contact with aliens. Here, representing the human race. The white race. The superior race. That was all there was to it. Even if Pilot Miller had been a strangely capable astronaut. In his smug estimation, he was second to no one.

I'm the red-blooded American hero people want to see on this trip. That's what it means to have 'the right stuff.' That makes me right for this mission. And I'm a crack pilot too! he reassured himself. "Wait. What the hell is that?!" He said aloud as he felt his ship jerked and pulled out of its comfortable orbit. He looked out the porthole. His heart raced, beating so rapidly, it felt like a heart attack. "Holy shit! I'm being towed by aliens." His eyes came to rest on an enormous ship, one hundred times bigger than his. The extraterrestrials' ship was a perfect sphere. *Like a Christmas ornament.* It was iridescent in appearance, glinting red, blue, and green in the filtered light of the sun. It appeared to spin at hyper speed as it towed his ship toward itself. When his rocket slowed to a stop, Captain Glennon blacked out.

Wake yourself, earth being.

Captain Glennon heard the voice in his head. He shook off the haze in his body, in his mind and sat up sharply. He peered out of the porthole. His eyes went round and his mouth dropped open. The spherical alien spaceship hung before him, big as a skyscraper. The top and bottom third of the ship still appeared to spin at hyper speed. But the center third of the ship was motionless. It contained a single grand porthole that encircled the ship. In its brightly lit windows sat five, seemingly human negro women, on high backed throne-like seats. Their skin was brown and their hair appeared to be in braids piled high on their heads like thick, black, woven crowns. The braids were bejeweled with bright silver threads that almost blinded him. Each glowing entity was attired in a shiny, foil monochromatic flight suit: purple, pink, red, yellow, and blue.

Speak your name, earth being.

15

The sound vibrated in his brain, between his ears. It seemed that all five were speaking simultaneously with one stentorian voice. He covered his ears with gloved hands and grated out: "Captain Gus Glennon. American. Astronaut." Then added, "Greetings from America."

You? You are the best space traveler?

Captain Glennon gulped, feeling the menace and incredulity behind the question.

Yes," he said confidently. "You are the ones that sent the message to earth about this meeting. Right?"

We sent the message. But you are not the best space traveler. We are certain because you are not the Sixth Sister of Space, Time, and the Multiverse.

"Who is that?" he said, gut churning, hoping they did not mean Pilot Maryam Joie Miller, the colored woman who had bested him at every turn. "How could anyone possibly know who that . . . who she is from among the millions of women on earth? We are seeing you for the first time."

The Sixth Sister is not possible to mistake! She is a child of the multiverse sent to your planet twenty-two earth years ago. She was born for the stars. Her heart desires only space travel. She does computations without error. She speaks our language as we are speaking yours. We sent the encoded message for her ears! You would know her by this.

"Oh," he said aloud, understanding pricking at his consciousness. "Maybe I can still be of assistance," he added, in an effort to buy time to craft a better response or convince the aliens of his worthiness. But before he could think of what else to say, there was roaring in his head that could not be drowned out by covering his ears.

We did not make this journey, for centuries by speed of light, to be toyed with. To be lied to! Where is the Sixth Sister of Space, Time, and the Multiverse? Why isn't she here? We know she was on Earth. We know she is the Best Space Traveler.

Captain Glennon felt blood seeping out of his nose. His head pounded like he was being repeatedly pummeled by heavyweight boxing champion, Floyd Patterson. He felt himself losing consciousness, slipping away into darkness.

16

* * *

Maryam looked up from her position on the floor of her bedroom in response to a knock on the door.

"Come in, Momma." she said.

Mae Jean entered the dimly lit room carrying a tray with a light dinner of meatloaf, potatoes and tea spiked with whiskey. Her daughter sat on the carpeted floor of the bedroom, metal balls, painted like planets, spinning in an elliptical orbit above her right hand. Maryam did not look at her mother when she entered but continued to gaze at the spinning orbs.

Mae Jean placed the tray on the bedside table, then sat on the floor, facing her daughter. "How do you feel today, Maryam?"

"Empty. Lost. Without purpose, I suppose."

"The world misses you while you hide in this room. Your intelligence and wit. Your laugh and beauty."

"You mean you and Dad miss me," she said, raising her hand, making the planets spin faster. "No one else knows I exist. I'm NASA's Darkie Secret," she snorted.

"I've never seen you sulk so," her mother reproached gently.

Maryam shrugged and made no further response.

"I know you haven't heard the news, so I'll tell you. That astronaut they sent to space instead of you . . ."

"Gus Glennon." Maryam finished the sentence.

"He's dead. They found him after splashdown the other day. He looked alive. But he wasn't."

Maryam let the planets fall, one by one, into her hand. She placed them gently in her lap and looked at her mother. "I never wished anyone dead," she said.

"There's more," Mae Jean said, and pulled a letter from her pocket and handed it to her daughter. "It's from Senator Lyndon. Personally delivered by that Samuel fella. Today."

Maryam took the letter. Her name was written in large, black calligraphic letters on the front. She carefully opened the back, sealed with red wax bearing an eagle. She cleared her throat and read aloud:

Dear Pilot Maryam Joie Miller,

I hope this letter finds you well. Let me start, humbly from my knees, begging your forgiveness . . .

Quicksilver
by
Rob Grimoire

My great, great-grandmother was the fastest human on four wheels. A Black woman, running the law into ditches moving moonshine in the absence of light for these rednecks on South Georgia dirt roads in the '20s and '30s. She had a special gift navigating these roads, knowing routes still seen in the box braids of little brown girls today. She started the trend of smuggling in black vehicles and tinted windows traversing in the dead of night because if she was caught, it was certain death. Avoiding strange fruit and braving towns through sundown, chasing the last sliver of light into the darkness, remembering her home in Rosewood and how speed gifted her new life, her back touched by flame and hatred. She taunted death. But death would eventually have its way with her, spiriting her away to the bottom of the swamp one night, ending her run. Her car and body were never recovered, only muddy tire tracks and the abyss.

It doesn't explain my life choice as a smuggler, but it might explain my need to run. I've gotta get this cargo to Mexico tonight, and this matte black monster that I'm driving is custom-made by the nameless cash paying for my services. Two hundred on the dash, an electric vehicle with a series of amps and capacitors that extend the double lithium battery life allowing me to go very fast for long periods of time without charging. It can charge in three hours with solar and has a self-contained mercury cooling system. The faceless client told me that if I could complete the drop, I could keep the car and it would never need maintenance. I don't know how that's possible, but I'll take the one million in pay. The contract was on the dark web and it was easy to accept. I don't ask questions. I drive fast and clean and for this "car" if you wanna call it that, and a million dollars, what's in the trunk must be important. Halfway there.

I'm halfway there. The green tinted everything from this visual visor I'm wearing will stick with me for a while. Every hundred miles I get a notification of money being deposited into my account. Seeing green ain't too bad. The road beneath me feels like nothing, flowing like a river untouched by life and dangerous. In the blackness everything starts to blend, that's why it's not recommended to take the visor off but when has that ever stopped me? Pulling off the helmet, I see how fast emptiness is in the speed of night. The horizon is only recognized by its marriage to the sky. An expansive twinkling eulogy, the light of dying jewels remembering their glory, taunting the new moon. It's strange. The silence. My legs are tingling, pins and needles in restless slumber and I need to get out and stretch. Afterward I hop back into the car, with its silent, lifeless muted black sheen, a dead mirroring of the night sky, all the things around it, and get back to work.

Visor back on and I'm off like a thief in the night.

My last exit is in ten miles according to the GPS. Once I hit that, I'm back sailing across the calm asphalt ocean to my drop point across the border. The car having little to no resistance, successfully debates gravity and navigates the moonless night.

I look back in the mirror to prepare to take the exit when I hear a knock on the window on the passenger side. A knock at one hundred and fifteen mph.

My mind is fucking with me, spatial audio hallucinations. I start to turn when the door opens and closes.

What the fuck? What's happening? I saw the door clearly, that was not in my head alone, the car's system alerted me to the door being opened and shut as well. I drop speed, slowly, and turn to the passenger side to see a woman.

She sits there, gazing at me deeply. Looking at me with my mother's eyes, and my grandfather's nose.

She's familiar but not. Shock sends lightning down my spine, engaging my foot to the brake, almost losing control of the car and myself. The force from my quick deceleration causes her head to bend forward well past human anatomical possibility. Her skull snaps off her neck as her water-saturated braids spiral downward and her head drops into her lap sideways, her eyes

20

sharply cutting up toward me. I was petrified, my arms heavy and my body was as stiff as stone, but continued to look on, not watching the road, not moving a muscle. She opens her mouth wide, and a continuous river of water and mud pours out, covering her lap as she continues to mouth silent words gurgling and choking, and from her neck, thick black fluid oozes out.

I fucking swerve over and stop the car. Screaming until my voice breaks and rattling the visor, I remove the helmet in haste to nothing. She's gone. Deep breaths, it's all in my head. Maybe I left the door open. Maybe what's in the back is leaking and is messing with my head. What was once nothing but money and my daughter's smile has been corrupted by twisted visions in my mind, infected by loneliness and darkness. I put the helmet back on and there she is in haunting green. Her head is back on her neck, she's facing forward. She trembles and snaps her neck to look at me once more, face bloated and damaged. She picks up her waterlogged arm and as it drips, points towards the back window to the road behind us. I scramble to get out of the car, my arms confused and fingers disheveled, moving faster than ever to open the door, I tumble into the desert sand as soon as it opens.

Looking back, I see headlights. Their brightness assaults my eyes as the visor takes every lumen in, so I remove it. Orange headlights, smoking in the night air, steaming, filling the surroundings with shades of amber and flame, consuming all darkness in their reach. I hear the engine of the vehicle, a sound I've never heard before, like one million screaming souls in a choir of despair. It sounds organic, human, and it keeps flashing its high beams. It would make sense if they had someone follow me for insurance, but they need to see this shit and assure me that I'm not losing my mind. If there is a leak or tear, it needs to be fixed before we move on. I can't stop shaking. My hair stands on end and my legs want to quit on me.

I wave the vehicle to come frantically but it never moves. It only toggled high beams. Ok bastards, how about I open the trunk. I walk to the back of the car and touch the trunk and before I can open it a severe burning pain starts up my right arm. I look and see lines burning into my flesh, a smell that I will

21

never forget. It's forming words.

Keep Driving, it says.

This . . . What . . . WHAT. This defies logic. How could this be? What type of shit is this? My heart is racing, but feels as if it's stopped, cold sweat and colder hands, the lump in my throat now in the deepest pit in my stomach and the fucking PAIN.

I scramble to open the trunk, and once I get it open, I see my cargo.

It's a sheet of paper.

Written on the paper, *Keep Driving*.

Slowly I turn to the vehicle behind me, and it turns off its lights for only a few seconds, but it feels like forever.

And I see nothing. I hear the horrible screams of the engine, but I see nothing. The lights come on and it lurches towards me, revving angrily, screaming at me.

I dump the headgear and get back in the car, push start it, and speed off as fast as I can. On my right, I see the woman again and she's shaking, almost vibrating, twisting and rocking like she's in pain. I push past 115 mph. The lights behind me are moving just as fast if not faster. The words KEEP DRIVING are seared into my back, hands, chest, and face as I scream in agony, pushing my mind to the edge of sanity, pushing my legs to run without running, pushing past 140 mph. 150 now and the woman is looking at me with her concerned brow and twisted mouth. My eyes meet her black dead eyes as water drips from her braids. She opens her mouth and no water comes out.

"*Stop driving,*" she says.

I can't stop. I have to get away. It's chasing me.

Let go boy.

I'm losing it. I'm almost a million dollars richer and I'm losing my fucking mind.

One hundred ninety-five mph.

I see the border up ahead, almost there.

She places her cold, slimy hand on mine. *LET GO*. I jerk away.

Two hundred mph.

I look up and clearly see the steel border fence, now only a foot or so away, and there is no way for me to stop in time. I see it as clear as day. The light behind me shines brighter than ever and the fence looks like it is burning with an orange fire. I look at her, afraid, unable to stop the car and she sheds a silver tear.

I let go.

As the car smashes into the fence, I see her, drifting through the seat back to the orange lights. I see her as if I'm following her. The wreckage of the car burns bright red and I cannot feel its warmth. For the first time, I hear the voice of my ancestor—

They have been chasing us for generations. The fastest of us. They want the blood of mercury. The light travelers, the healers. They want our silver, and they will have it. They chased us to the boats, across the ocean, and through the southern woods. They chased me from my home and continued through our history. We are people of the sun and our light escapes the fire as speed blurs the veil between here and there. Our blood calling us to fight back and our spirits answering.

I awaken.

The light of stars long dead speak my eulogy, drifting in the dark, a part of them now.

Drifting, I see Jupiter.

A large ship passes the planet, the word Maia, is written on the side, and I feel a beckoning to enter it.

I move toward the reflective vehicle and I see myself. My skin burned and tainted by the words of the page in the trunk carved into my frame with fire, all over my charred body. I understand the gravity of this, the cursed words inscribed in my flesh mean death for my kin. I have to warn her of this, I have to get her to look past my tragedy, our shared trauma, and see the truth. I have to get her to slow down.

As I pass through the cold glass and metal, I see a young woman, her name is Oba. I know it as if she told me herself. I see her entire life and I see our tree. She has my eyes and my daughter's smile. Tight black and silver box braids, a map to the universe and to freedom in her hair, and she's sitting in front managing the controls of this massive vessel. She's moving fast, streaks of light and matter passing through us and us through it in a sea of luminosity, a calm river of light. The closest I've ever felt to my people and to all things. I see the hue of bright orange

23

on her face, arms, and around the ship and my incorporeal body flows out through the wire and metal of the ship to see the beast chasing us, a ball of orange fire screaming for her blood. I can feel its desire to consume her so I need to move fast. I return to the seat next to her and gently place my charred, skeletal hand on hers. She looks over and sees me, and before I could speak a word, she screams.

We Come In Peace
by
Kyoko M

"Those that fail to learn from history are doomed to repeat it."
-Winston Churchill

I stared at the glowing blue hologram depicting my orders and muttered, "*We come in peace.* Yeah, right."

Disgusted, I switched off the hologram and then pulled up my contact list, searching until I found the communications officer's line. I dialed her. She picked up immediately. "Yes?"

"Are they in session right now?"

"Yes, Captain Conroy. They're in Conference Room A."

"Thank you, Bobbi." I hung up and marched out of my living quarters.

The conference rooms were on the level just below the main navigation deck, so I took the elevator up from the barracks. Keeping track of time while in orbit of an unfamiliar planet was a bitch, to say the least. Our scientists were still currently studying the new planet's rotation, axis, climate, and weather to start determining whether it would be fully hospitable for us. But really, the problem wasn't the planet.

The problem was it was occupied.

Yesterday, I had taken a small team to complete an environmental study of an area that might be productive for supporting us. We'd landed about a mile out from a lake and tested the water, finding that it contained little to no saline and would be analyzed to make sure it was drinkable, or at the very least, could be treated enough to allow us to drink it. Our sensors had picked up signs of life from orbit, so my team and I trekked across the landscape until we reached a canyon. There, at the bottom, were sentient life forms.

They looked to be carbon-based life forms who also needed water, since the first thing we came upon was a farm. They had an irrigation system set up so that the canyon provided protection from the sun and the elements and the water flowed into their town to allow vegetation to grow. The beings were seven feet tall—at least those that we believed to be adults were—and had blue iridescent scales all over. They were bipedal as well with long, lanky limbs and a few horns at their temples. Their features reminded me of reptiles or dinosaurs.

My team and I observed them for several hours, logging what information we could see from a distance and recording their movements until sundown. Afterward, we returned to the ship and I wrote up a field report with our findings, which I sent to the ship's leadership.

And their response was why I was about to barge in on their meeting.

When I opened the door, the five men in the conference room fell silent. I was used to it. After all, I was a tall Black woman with a full figure and a no-nonsense expression that I'd learned to carve my face into when I had to deal with these people. Hair-care was a bitch when you were no longer on the Earth, so my wild tresses were temporarily tamed by being in two-strand twists that one of my colleagues helped me with. By now, they fell to my shoulder and I often had to pull them back in a pony-tail. I remembered the unnecessary conversation I'd had to have once about my hairstyle being "appropriate" for a military leader. I'd brought up enough salient points for them to leave me be, but I never forgot the way they treated me versus some of my colleagues.

We'd been on this voyage for just under a year. The vessel contained the top minds of every relevant field related to space exploration, totaling just under a hundred people aboard the aptly titled Prometheus.

In direct contrast, the Prometheus' leadership was of course a bunch of old white men.

Granted, they had backgrounds relevant to the cause. Of the five men, four of them held PhDs in astrophysics, astronomy, particle physics, and aerodynamics. The others had masters in historical research methodologies, cultural studies, archaeology, and military science. They helped keep this boat afloat and ran operations. They'd been appointed by the US government, which had also consulted with NASA on how to distribute responsibilities.

"Captain Conroy," Dr. David Benson said, not coldly, but not in a friendly way either. "We weren't expecting you for a while. I thought you would check in with us during your progress report planet-side."

"I'm afraid that's not going to happen," I said as I clasped my hands behind my back, keeping a crisp, professional tone. "Seeing as I refuse to carry out your orders as instructed."

The faint murmur of conversation dropped off into an icy silence. The men before me stared in disbelief, but neither my expression nor my resolve changed under their scrutiny.

"Come again?" he asked.

"I will not take military action against a peaceful settlement of natives. Period. I won't do it and neither will my men. You can fire me if you like, but anyone you choose as my replacement will give you the exact same answer."

I leaned in slightly for emphasis. "No."

"On what grounds do you defy your direct orders?" Dr. Eric Haversham demanded.

"If the intent is to create a colony on this planet, then we will do so without interfering with the lives of the natives. If they choose to contact us, then we will act accordingly, but until such a time as they show any aggression towards us, there is no reason to take them prisoner and seize their resources."

"Captain, we've seen the footage," Benson said, gesturing towards the holographic projector in the center of the table. "There is no indication that these people have access to weaponry. There would be very little loss of life, if any at all."

"Doesn't matter. It's their land, not ours."

"And what would our civilization have been like if we had done that back on Earth?"

"Good question."

Haversham exhaled through his nose. "And the answer is that quite possibly, several major civilizations would never have been established nor would they later become influential parts of society. You cannot possibly be this naïve. You are a military officer. You have to understand that casualties are part of the discovery process."

"We're not discovering anything if someone already lives on the land."

"Your duty is to your country and your species, not to these natives you've never even met."

"I know my duties. And they don't include your orders."

"People are dying back on Earth. This planet can save our race, but you'd let them die so that you don't have to get your hands dirty?"

"Sir, it's a *planet*. Thousands upon thousands of miles of potentially unoccupied land and resources, but you want me to attack an established civilization. For what? To save you time? For free labor at the expense of innocent lives?"

A caustic silence fell. They stared at me, shocked that I'd actually said it aloud. They were all thinking it, but by now, I'd had enough of dancing around the subject. I'd known all along that there was an ugly thing hovering over their orders like a storm cloud.

"This expedition is not so that you can live out your colonialist fantasies," I continued. "It is for the establishment of a new colony by peaceful and humane means. We don't know that this planet will suffice with what our needs are, but we certainly will not start a war. If they choose to attack, then trust that I will defend you and my men with every fiber of my being, but until such a time, this conversation is over. I will lead the expedition here—"

I typed in the coordinates. It showed up on the rough map of the planet's surface. "This is fifty kilometers south of the natives' colony. It has access to a water source and the terrain looks to be suitable for lodging and agriculture. We will spend a day cycle here gathering as much information as possible with the field team and report our findings to you."

With that, I turned my back on the speechless men and left the room.

Surprisingly, no one came to fire me or put me in jail. I returned to my office to finish checking the inventory list and bumped into my go-to person, Sergeant Grant Jennings. He was a tall, broad-shouldered man with brown hair and a full beard, good-looking to the point of distraction. He grinned when he saw me, those blue eyes gleaming with mischief.

"Welcome back, fearless leader. Or, rather, are you still our fearless leader?"

I rolled my eyes. "You're not getting rid of me that easily, cowboy."

"Oh, good. So how did it go?"

"The pompous old windbags naturally argued until they were blue in the face," I said as I sat down at the desk and grabbed the accordion folder the supply office sent to confirm all the items the field team had requested. "And I didn't budge."

"Atta girl. Clearance forms are all done. I've got the crew loading the ground transport as we speak."

"Good. Where are the linguists?"

"They're prepping the translator and visual aids."

"How's their demeanor?"

Grant paused. "It's . . . a little mixed. After all, confirmation of extraterrestrial life is a big shock, even to people who have studied the equivalent of xeno-linguistics their entire lives. They're excited, but I can also tell they're nervous. One wrong move and they could start a war."

"Assuming that the natives aren't pacifists," I pointed out. "Since we saw no indication of weaponry in that first land survey."

"True. That's our department. We're a violent race by default. It's ridiculous to assume entirely different life forms in a different galaxy would have the same inclinations that we do."

"So, we know where you fall on the nature versus nurture debate," I mused as I finished signing the paperwork and then closed the folder.

"Man is evil," Grant deadpanned. "To the core. It takes a lot of good people to teach them to outgrow the impulse to be selfish monsters."

"I see no one ever got to you." I batted my lashes.

"Whatever, you know you love me," he sniffed as he grabbed the folder from me and stood up to go take it over to the message chute built into the wall of the office. "Really, though, how do you think this scenario is gonna shake out?"

"I'm not sure," I admitted. "And I can't vouch for how other people will react if we complete the survey and determine this place meets our needs. It'll take a lot of control to keep anyone from doing something stupid that starts a conflict between our civilizations."

"Yeah, that's my concern too," he said, leaning against the wall beside my desk. "Not everyone aboard this ship has been trained the way we've been trained. And the last thing we need is to risk losing lives when we're fighting the clock back home."

"Hope for the best but prepare for the worst. That's my motto. Come on. Let's check on the ground transport prep and get this show on the road."

He held the door for me. "Aye, aye, Cap'n."

We made our way to the hangar where most of the ground crew was bustling about prepping for launch. Grant and I met with John Bishop, our expert tracker and lead explorer. He was a mountainous man with a beard and a little grey at his temple, his smile always friendly and boisterous, brown-skinned like me, and with a good head on his shoulders.

"Captain, Sergeant, good to see you. We're all set. I take it you had the necessary conversation with our superiors?"

"Oh, yeah, it was a lot of fun," I said, rolling my eyes. "But it's squashed for now. What sort of readings are we getting down below?"

"Seems to be in the mid-60s Fahrenheit and based on the sun's distance from this planet, it probably has similar seasons to ours, but we won't know for sure until we take soil samples and examine the flora and fauna as well as the weather patterns. It's possible the river was diverted based on the canyon where the natives set up shop, but that's also a theory we'll be working out over time. Their settlement is a bit like an oasis, given that there's mostly dry land surrounding the canyon and so the place we've chosen is similar in terrain, but it should be enough out of the way that we won't be disturbing them. I would imagine if they notice us at all, it'll be after the first 48 hours depending on how well-traveled they are."

Grant started humming "Have Love, Will Travel" under his breath until I jabbed him in the ribs with my elbow, which made Bishop laugh. "What other signs of life are in that area?"

"Observation stated they believe there are some animals resembling mammals, but they don't appear to be predators. More like a mix between an elephant and wildebeest. They were grazing along one of the plains last time I checked."

"Okay, let's try to keep a wide berth since something that size could damage our equipment or hurt one of us."

"Yes ma'am. I'll alert the pilots to steer clear."

"Excellent job as always, Bishop."

He beamed down at me. "Thank you, Captain."

Bishop headed over to help someone with a particularly large crate while Grant and I walked up the landing gear onto the ground transport. "Hey, how come you never tell me I've done an excellent job?"

"Cause you never do," I said cheerfully. "You're utterly useless."

"Then why do you keep me around?"

I smiled. "Cause you're pretty."

Grant clutched his chest, pretending to be offended. "How dare you. I am more than just eye candy; I'll have you know."

"Yes, you are also a massive pain in my ass. Now go check the reactor and stop pestering me."

"I don't pester," he sniffed. "I badger. There's a difference."

I groaned, which pleased him enough to leave me alone. I brought up the ship's specs and gave them a thorough inspection, making sure all systems were clear for lift off. It would have two pilots that I hand-picked myself, so I just wanted to be sure it would handle all right for them.

We were ready to rock and roll when I got my first surprise since the detestable orders: an extra crew member. She was by far the oldest person on this expedition—somewhere in her late fifties, I estimated—and I knew her by reputation only. Her name was Dr. Suzanne Robertson and she was an epidemiologist from Johns Hopkins.

I also knew from the scientific members of our team that she was a massive pain-in-the-ass.

"Doctor," I said warily, eyeing her spacesuit. "We weren't expecting you until the secondary expedition or later. What brings you here today?"

"Command thought it prudent to have me tag along so we can get started understanding this planet on a molecular level," the doctor said. "Since one of the biggest threats could come from contact with any viruses or diseases. They asked for me to advise the team on how to proceed safely."

"Right. Can I see the clearance form?"

She handed me the clipboard in her hand with the appropriate form signed by my bosses. Well, it was legitimate, but that didn't mean it wasn't shady. "Looks like everything's in order. Welcome aboard, doc."

We launched and landed on the planet's surface in a clearing in the forest, depending on the trees to shield the ship from easy view by the planet's occupants. It was possible they'd seen us entering the planet's atmosphere. We'd find out sooner or later if they were curious enough to investigate. Much like back on Earth, I'd rather we never cross paths. Discovery in itself was not maligned in my mind, but encountering other sentient species had a track record of being violent. The only reason I hadn't picked an entirely different continent was that time was short and we'd located all the necessary conditions in this region rather than the other uncharted land masses.

Bishop sent out a probe. It scanned the immediate area for life forms and detected none, so we hit the release clamp for the landing gear. I had a laser pistol for protection and Grant was carrying a positively massive rifle. Everyone but the survey team was armed, but not enough to slow us down during the trek toward the clearing where we wanted to set up camp. It was three kilometers away, so not that bad a trek all things considered.

The planet orbited a sun not dissimilar to the one back in our solar system, so sunshine was the first thing I noticed walking down the ramp. The trees were interesting; their trunks were white with flaky grey bark and the leaves were dark green, almost black. The vegetation on the ground bore similarities to moss, being very dense and growing in thick clusters. The loam underneath us was a rusty color, not unlike the kind of soil we'd seen in the ravine near the native population.

I ran point. Grant and Bishop flanked me, followed by our land survey team, and two soldiers from my unit brought up the rear: Andrea and Thomas, respectively. We fanned out to double check the perimeter, found it clear, and then waited for our folks to collect soil, vegetation, and any other relevant samples.

Once they'd finished collecting samples, we started towards our destination. The trees were lightly dispersed, so there was decent visibility for the terrain up ahead. We left the wooded area after a half mile and entered a field with knee-high plants reminiscent of wheat, but instead of being a brown-gold hue, they were tipped with tiny bright blue flowers. We paused long enough to let them collect another set of samples, then continued.

Just before we crested the hill, Bishop halted. "Captain, I'm reading life forms on the other side."

"Roger that. What have we got?" I stepped up to his side to look at the tablet with a live feed coming from the surveillance probe he'd sent out ahead of our route to check it. A small herd of what looked like mammals appeared to be grazing about twenty yards left of us. They had trunks that they used to bring the plants up to their mouths. Their fur was tan with white stripes and they were built like beasts of burden with thick chests and round bodies. The four of them had antlers and long, floppy ears like elephants.

I turned to the group and said, "Weylan, you're up."

"Yes, Captain." Our biologist, Weylan Yorkshire, trotted over. He was young, just out of his twenties, with dirty blond hair and glasses, his frame rather sleight. He came up to Bishop's right side and observed the creatures, muttering a few things under his breath as he watched.

"Based on what looks like a pack structure and their dense bodies, I would put these creatures on the same footing as elephants. They're clearly not built to run from predators, so they probably defend themselves with those antlers if attacked. Wild elephants usually don't become aggressive with the exception of two instances: mothers protecting their calves or bull elephants during mating season. The four of them look to be adults, so my advice would be to go a little further down to keep a wide berth. They may have poor eyesight like elephants do too."

"Got it. Thank you." I turned to the group again. "Everyone, let's stay quiet until we pass by our neighbors. Make sure the flash is off if you feel the need to photograph these animals. We don't want to spook them and cause an accident."

"Yes, Captain," they chorused. I met eyes with Grant. He gave me a subtle nod to confirm he'd be on high alert. I trusted Weylan completely, but I also knew to expect the unexpected.

The group walked another twenty yards to the right and then we proceeded down the hill as quietly as possible. The animals didn't seem to notice us, much to my relief.

But by the time we reached the bottom of the hill, something was amiss.

The biggest of the four stood at the height of a moose. I spotted familiar genitalia, so I inferred it was male and possibly the pack leader. Just as we reached the bottom of the hill, he tossed his head and let out a grunt that sounded like he'd been annoyed by something. I touched my HUD and zoomed in on him. He pawed the dirt, tossing up clods with his hooves, and angled his massive body in our direction. I couldn't figure out why—we hadn't made a sound and we were pretty far off from his herd— but then I spotted a reflection shining directly into his right eye.

Before I could determine where it was coming from, the creature charged us.

"Run!" I shouted, drawing my pistol. "Bishop, lead the group to safety. Andrea and Thomas, keep everyone together. Grant, with me."

"Yes, Captain!" The group broke into a sprint in the opposite direction of the charging beast.

"I don't wanna kill it," I told my partner. "Try shooting at the ground in front of it on three."

"Roger that." Grant planted his feet and aimed the rifle, his gaze steady.

"One . . . two . . . three!" We both opened fire. My shot kicked up a bunch of dirt roughly three paces from the beast. Grant's much larger shot was about two paces from the beast's front legs. It let out a bellow and stumbled a little when it heard the blasts and saw the divots we'd made in the ground in front of it.

"Come on, come on," I muttered under my breath, stepping back to put more distance between us. "We're not trying to hurt your family, big guy. Just go."

The beast pawed the ground again and broke into a gallop, his antlers lowered in attack position.

"Shit!" I lined up my sights. "Try to glance a shot off his side."

"Got it." We both fired. My shot missed, but Grant's was right on the money.

And to my utter dismay, the laser bounced off its thick hide as if it had been hit with a harmless laser pointer instead.

"Sonova—" I jerked my head at the hill. "Get to higher ground!"

Grant and I turned and hauled ass back up the hill with the beast on our heels. My prediction had been right—all that weight was difficult for the creature to carry at a steep incline, so it stumbled and had to dig its hooves into the soil to find purchase.

Grant got to the top first on account of his longer legs and he caught my arm, pulling me up onto the crest of the hill by his side. He tugged a flashbang from his belt and brandished it. "Captain?"

I winced. It wasn't a nice thing to do, but we had to make tracks and keep our group safe. "Yeah, go for it."

Grant pulled the pin and tossed it towards the beast. He and I then jumped down and skidded to the bottom of the other side of the hill just as it went off. I flattened myself to the ground and covered my head, shutting my eyes as I heard the animal shriek. Poor thing.

We climbed up and checked to see the creature had run off back towards its herd, too distraught from the flashbang to worry about us. I slumped onto my belly and sighed. "God, that was close."

"Too close," Grant agreed, flopping beside me on his back. He then cocked his head slightly and narrowed his eyes. "Where the hell did that come from anyway? We weren't anywhere near them."

"Oh, you're gonna love it," I said. "I think we have a saboteur in our midst."

Grant frowned. "No shit?"

"Just before it charged, I saw something suspicious. Or I thought I did, anyway. It's just a theory, but I think our superiors sent Suzanne to get me out of the way. I've heard from several of her colleagues that she's a chronic backstabber."

"But why?" he demanded. "They have the authority to fire you, technically speaking. If they want you out of the way, why do this instead?"

I smiled wryly. "They know my men respect me and wouldn't cooperate with their demands if I'm still above ground."

"Well, that's just stupid. None of us respect you; we just fear you."

I smacked him in the arm, which made him chuckle. "Hardy-har. Thanks for the sympathy, pretty boy."

He stood up and offered a hand. "You're welcome, Cap'n."

I took his hand and let him pull me to my feet. I adjusted my HUD to pick up the trail of our survey party. Bishop had done a good job leading them away from the danger; they were about a half mile away from us.

"How do you wanna play it when we catch up to them?" Grant asked.

"Play dumb for now. I need more evidence before I decide to *j'accuse.*"

"You speak French?" He made an arousing noise and I kicked his ankle, stifling laughter as we started down the other side of the hill again. I opened the communication channel.

"Bishop, Andrea, and Thomas, do you read me?"

"Got you, Captain," Bishop answered. "You guys okay?"

"Yeah, we've deterred our big friend and we're headed your way. Everyone okay?"

"Well . . ."

"What?"

"We, uh, we can't find Suzanne."

I traded a suspicious look with Grant. "What do you mean you can't find her?"

"No one can recall seeing her after we ran through the trees to the other side of the clearing. We were hoping you'd see her while bringing up the rear."

"Alright, stay put. We'll search the area. If we don't see anything, we'll break off into a search party. She can't have gotten far."

"Yes, captain."

I closed the channel. Grant and I met eyes again. "Pinky, are you pondering what I'm—"

"Ah-ah," he said, wagging a finger. "Copyright infringement."

I snorted softly. "Does it count if we're on another planet?"

"I dunno; they're pretty strict about this stuff." He then gave me a serious look. "But yeah, Brain, I'm pondering what you're pondering. No way this is coincidence."

"Ayup. Let's see if command can get me a trace on her suit." I opened the channel to communicate with our ground transport. We'd left our pilots behind to mind it in case things broke bad. "Captain Conroy here. I need a location trace for one of our people who wandered off."

"Yes, Captain, which person?"

"Suzanne Robertson. They said she got separated when they were going into the forest."

"One moment, please." I heard some typing. "I'm forwarding her coordinates to you."

"Send them to Grant as well. Has she triggered her distress signal?"

"Doesn't look like it."

"Hurm. All right, thank you." My helmet beeped as the information downloaded into it. It gave me the exact coordinates via distance to target instead of latitude and longitude like we'd use on Earth. After all, different planet, different latitude and longitude.

And what I found only made me more suspicious.

"She is way off the beaten path," Grant said. "What the hell is she doing?"

"Sowing seeds of discord," I growled. "Look at the direction she's headed."

Grant frowned. "You've got to be kidding me. We're fifty kilometers from the natives; there's no damn way she can make that by herself."

"Oh, I don't think that's even the goal," I spat as we continued forward past the field and back into the woods. "If she just so happens to bump into them along the way, now there's justification for conflict. That's why they sent her; to instigate. She can of course use an excuse saying she got separated from the others. She can sabotage her own communication system and say she got lost. After all, how are we gonna prove what happened?"

"This is ridiculous," Grant fumed. "If we get to her before something else does, we're gonna have words."

"Let's just hope we catch up to her before she starts a war." We trekked off into the distance towards the beacon, eventually leaving behind the alien grey trees. The terrain up ahead changed into the rust-colored dirt that we'd seen near the native inhabitants. It looked a lot like a desert, so my vision dropped off about a half mile away into a heat shimmer.

"Wait, wait," I said, stopping as I examined the HUD. "She's stopped, but I can't get a visual. Can you?"

Grant squinted. "No. What's that about? Don't tell me it's more alien planet weirdness. We've got enough of that already."

As we kept going, something finally broke through the optical illusion caused by the heat. There was a large piece of wood staked into the ground with symbols I naturally couldn't read painted onto it in white. I crouched and examined it, then glanced at the empty landscape before us. The sign could have been for several things: a marker for someone's territory, a sign about the distance to civilization, or...a warning. It made me think of the old trespassing signs people had in their yards back on Earth.

I checked to the left and right of us. Sure enough, about forty feet away in both directions, I spotted signs, which made the area we were about to enter a lot like a grid.

And Suzanne's beacon was dead center of the grid.

"Alright," I said as I stood and dusted off my knees. "I don't like the look of it. Time to call our xeno-linguist."

I switched the feed in my HUD to camera mode and snapped a photo of the front of the sign, then opened the channel again. "Randall Carson, do you read me? This is your captain speaking."

"Yes ma'am, I read you. What can I do for you?"

"Grant and I have found what looks like a sign in an area where Suzanne's beacon is. I'm sending the photo to your HUD now. Obviously, I don't expect you to know what it means, but if you have a prediction, that'd be helpful before we continue the search."

"Yes, Captain. Received." He fell silent for the better part of a minute. "Based on the position of the signs around this area, I think this is a warning. It could be that there is a predator who uses this spot for hunting grounds or perhaps there is some sort of dangerous flora. There's also an off chance this is someone's land where they grow things and the sign is stating ownership, but since I don't see any tracks or signs of agriculture, I'm still leaning towards a warning sign."

"Thanks, Randall. We'll act accordingly, then. Out." I scooped up a fistful of the reddish-brown dirt and felt it between my fingers. "Hmm . . . Grant, let me have your external flashlight."

"Sure." He passed it to me. It was a military-grade, waterproof, heavy-duty flashlight with long-lasting batteries, perfect for exploration. We kept them as backup in case the helmet's built-in lights failed. I picked a spot in the middle and then chucked the flashlight inside the grid.

"Hey," Grant protested as he watched it land in the dirt. "You don't just go throwin' a man's stuff in a big, empty field—"

An awful slurping noise filled the air and the flashlight sank beneath the surface layer of dirt, vanishing with one last sickening suckling noise.

"...*oh.*" Grant and I said in unison.

"Well, now we know why we can't see Suzanne."

I blew out a breath. "Shit. How much air do we have in these things again?"

"Tank's good for 48-hours, assuming it's not damaged and she's not hyperventilating under there."

"Alright, we'll have to call the ground transport and request emergency evac—"

Grant gripped my shoulder hard, his voice tight. "Rosa, we've got incoming on radar."

"Shit." My HUD lit up with a proximity alert a second later. Something large was moving towards us pretty quickly. I cursed under my breath. "Come on, we've got to get out of the open."

We hurried back until we reached the tree line, then crouched and waited for a visual.

Sure enough, a minute later, an alien craft flew over the grid. It looked like a cross between a dragonfly and a motorcycle. Energy pulsed out of two propulsion engines and two of the native aliens were riding it. They appeared to speak to one another as they flew over the quicksand. One of them wrapped a length of rope around their waist and then jumped from the aircraft. The rope pulled taut and then the other one slowly lowered the first alien down towards the quicksand. The spot where Suzanne had disappeared had a mound of disturbed dirt and mud, so the alien had to stick its arms deep inside it, all the way up to the shoulder. Eventually, it signaled to the one aboard the aircraft to go up. After several tense seconds, Suzanne's helmet—caked with dirt and mud—became visible. The alien gripped her under the arms to pull her free, then the aircraft flew past the grid onto solid ground to lay her down.

Grant glanced at me. "Should we intervene or just keep observing?"

I chewed my bottom lip. "Good question. If she's still conscious, she might try something. I think we should give it the old college try and meet them."

Grant blew out a breath. "God help us."

He and I stood and walked away from the forest. As soon as we were within their eye line, the aliens stood to face us. Their expressions were inscrutable. They seemed to notice that our suits matched hers.

"Hi," I said once we were within what I assumed to be earshot. "We come in peace. We just want to check on her—" I pointed to the motionless epidemiologist. "We mean no harm."

The taller of the two looked at the smaller one and a series of chirps and growls escaped. They took a couple of steps back, which seemed to mean they'd understood what I wanted despite the language barrier. I knelt and wiped the muck off her helmet. "Suzanne, can you hear me?"

"Scanner's not detecting any life-threatening injuries," Grant said, having removed a mobile X-ray scanner from his utility belt. "It's likely she panicked, went into shock, and passed out. We'll know more when we get her back to the medical bay."

"Got it." I hailed the ground transport again. "We need medevac now. I'm sending our coordinates."

"Yes, captain. We'll be there as fast as we can."

"Appreciate it." I stood and tried to think of a gesture that might make sense to an alien. I pointed to them, then her, then bowed at the waist, keeping eye contact with them. "Thank you."

The aliens stared at us, cocking their heads slightly. Then they mirrored me. With that, they climbed back onto their craft. Grant and I waved to them as they rode off into the sunlight, headed back towards the canyon.

"Wow," Grant muttered as he picked up Suzanne and slung one of her arms over his shoulder. "Close encounters of the third kind indeed."

The movement jostled Suzanne enough that she woke up, blinking rapidly when she recognized us. "What happened?"

"Nothing we can't fix, no thanks to you," I said, glaring. "We're going have a nice long chat about that charging beast and your cockamamie plan."

Suzanne grimaced. "I was just following orders."

"Yeah," I said as I watched the benevolent aliens flying off into the wild blue yonder. "Idiots always do."

A New Start
by
D.K. Gaston

Day One

It was my first time in a cryogenic sleep capsule (CSC), and I hoped to find peace while in the hibernation cycle. But my ability denied me even that. I felt a part of myself rising from my physical form and was immediately greeted by the dead. They were everywhere. A press of incorporeal entities took up every corner of the spacecraft's CSC chamber. They knew what I was attempting to do, and they didn't like it.

"I know you think this is selfish of me, but I can't do this anymore," I said as if I owed them an explanation for wanting normalcy.

With my physical form asleep, my projected consciousness allowed the ghosts to do something they'd been unable to do before. Those close enough touched me, not with anger but with tenderness. It was surprising how good it felt. I had expected their touch to be cold and lifeless. Instead, I was greeted with warmth—the warmth one would expect from the living.

My mind clouded with doubts for a split second, wondering if I was doing the right thing. The ghosts' touches, though tempting, were nothing more than a trap to entice me to stay. They knew my ability scared people off, denying me from making any real human connection with the living. Their dependency provoked this last act of desperation that, on the surface, may, to the ghosts, have appeared to offer something I'd always been denied, affection. But it was a lie that couldn't be sustained and didn't matter.

"It's too late," I said loud enough for all to hear. "The sleeping capsule has been switched on, and the lift-off has started. There is no stopping this now. Goodbye."

The ghosts looked at one another to consider my words before turning to regard my physical form. In the capsule, submerged in a blue stabilizing gel that preserved my body, they finally understood the impossibility they were asking of me. With that, they were gone.

For the first time in my life, I was alone.

It was a strange feeling, and I wasn't sure I was comfortable with it. "It'll take time," I told myself. "I'll get used to it."

Staring around, I took note of the other sleeping capsules. Fifty, including myself, were passengers aboard a star cruiser moving at faster-than-light speed to another galactic quadrant of space far away from Earth and its dead. Turning, I threw my legs over the side of my capsule and pushed out to let my feet touch the metal floor. Instead, I found myself floating. I was more like the ghost than the living in my astral form. In essence, I'd become the thing I was trying to escape.

I was also butt-naked.

"Great," I said, feeling exposed and vulnerable, even knowing that if everyone around me were awake, they wouldn't be able to see me. "Who do I have to kill to get some clothing?"

And just like that, clothing appeared on me. Nothing fancy. It was typical of what I would wear on any given day, dark slacks, a hoodie shirt, boots, and a leather quarter-length trench coat. "Okay, I'm a genie in my current state. Make a wish, and kazam, it appears." I could get used to that.

The spaceflight would take two years before the ship reached its destination, and I wondered if I would be up and about in this form the whole time. Entirely staffed by artificially intelligent machines, I would be alone in the spacecraft, the Mwari 1, without a soul to interact with in any capacity. That prospect left a surprisingly unpleasant taste in my mouth. I'd never been a people person and always felt comfortable being alone. Well, that wasn't entirely true. I mean, the ghosts were always with me. This would be my first time alone, and that prospect scared me.

Rather than further distressing myself, I focused on the other capsules. The forty-nine fellow travelers were strangers. My reasoning for trekking to another galaxy was simple, to get away from the dead that plagued me on Earth. But what were their reasons for taking the two-year-long pilgrimage? What would drive entire families across the vastness of space to an unripe world with no technology except what we brought with us? I couldn't determine whether it was brave, stupid, or insane. Whatever their cases may be, we were all in this together now, and there was no turning back.

Day Five

There were some perks to being incorporeal. I walked on the exterior hull of the Mwari 1 as the ship sped by stars and planet systems at faster-than-light speed to experience what no other person could. As long as my physical form floated safe and sound in the gelatinous chemical pool within the CSC, I'd been immune from harm or basic bodily needs. I hadn't been hungry, thirsty, or needed to pee. The lure to urinate over the ship's side just to see what would happen was tempting, though.

Watching space fly by was strange, like gliding down on a waterpark ride while passing through a long glassed-in tunnel. Everything is blurred and dizzying. Fun to look at, but too much of it was starting to make me feel queasy, which shouldn't even be possible. "Why do I feel queasy?" I supposed I said that part aloud, but how in the hell am I supposed to know in space? There wasn't any sound. I felt a sudden tug in my gut extending throughout my body.

Frightening thoughts raced through my mind at that moment. *Oh God, was I wrong? Can I be affected out here? Is my incorporeal body about to be yanked away into the void of space forever?* The tug grew stronger, prying my feet off the hull. Wrenched utterly away from the ship, I floated helplessly in deep space. In less than a blink of an eye, Mwari 1 was gone.

I let loose a horror-filled scream that could never be heard.

My scream was cut short when I felt a sensation of tendrils of coils taking hold of me. I envisioned some weird space squid with hundreds of crimson eyeballs seizing me to feast upon my flesh. In that strange moment, all I could think was that it would digest me, and then I would be nothing but fecal matter when it eventually defecated.

"I don't want to be space shit," I yelled. Then everything went pitch black.

Well, everything was already black. I'm in space.

Everything stopped as if I had lost consciousness.

That wasn't right either. I hadn't lost consciousness because I was still aware of things happening. Was I going to spend my last moments before being eaten by a space squid trying to figure out the proper adjective to describe my dilemma?

Shit.

Day Seven Hundred Thirty

"S-shit," I cried out.

Wait. I heard myself say that.

"Calm down, Mr. Abara, you're all right," a woman said.

I felt small, gentle hands on my chest to keep me in place. "I can't see anything. I'm blind."

"It's temporary. I assure you, Mr. Abara. Wasn't this all explained to you before the boarding process? It's the infusion gel. Give it a few more seconds, and then you'll be able to see again."

"I skipped the briefing and signed the paperwork without reading it," I explained, growing calmer now that I wasn't going to be space poop.

"What? Why would you—? Oh, never mind. That was a stupid thing to do. The briefing and documentation contained helpful information. Never sign anything without reading it first."

At the time, I was surrounded by annoying ghosts thinking their needs were more significant than mine, I wanted to say but kept to myself. The woman lifted her hands from my chest, and then it struck me. "Wait, you're human?"

"Good to know. By the way, so are you, Mr. Obvious." There was a hint of humor in her retort.

A fuzzy silhouette began to take shape above me. "I think my sight is returning," I told the woman. No longer imagining I would be blinded forever, I immediately became bitterly chilled, like I'd been dunked into an icy lake. "W-why am I s-so c-cold?"

"Oh man, you really didn't read anything," she said, not too kindly. "You're waking from cryogenic sleep. Kryos is the key-word. It literally means frost, in Greek, Mr. Abara."

"First off, ouch," I said pleasantly after her savage attack, "Secondly, please call me Kaleb."

In response, I expected the woman to give me her name, but silence was all that greeted me. Already not being a people person, I had no clue how to cope with her nonresponse. *What does someone do when faced with uncomfortable silence?* I questioned internally, knowing I wouldn't come up with an answer. So, I said nothing. I might have whistled. I do that sometimes when I'm nervous. It was an involuntary quirk; I'm usually unaware of when I do it. So yeah, I might have whistled.

"I'm Dr. Rider," she finally said.

A clear image of the doctor's face slowly came into view. She wore no makeup in her late twenties or early thirties, not that she needed it. Though her expressive deep brown eyes gleamed with life, she maintained a neutral expression. The doctor's hair had been pulled back into a ponytail, but a few black folds of curls were draped across her forehead, frozen in place as if stuck in cryo. Skin, a deep chocolate treat to my eyes, was a shade lighter than mine. Her mouth was set in a hard line at first but gradually smoothed out into a sly smile and—

"I'm staring, aren't I?" I exclaimed, realizing I'd been looking at her too long.

"At least you're not blind anymore, Mr. Abara," she said. "Now let's see what we can do about that chill you're complaining about."

She pressed a few buttons on the side of the cryo capsule. Threads of lights circled me, emitting a welcoming heat to my frigid skin. I felt the cold drawn forcibly from my body like an exorcised demon. The light stung my eyes. I pressed them closed. Cutting myself off from the light reminded me of the darkness I thought I would be forever trapped. I sat up, no longer caring about the cold. All I wanted was to be out of the capsule, which felt like a coffin at that moment.

The doctor jerked away in surprise. "What's wrong? Did I make it too hot?"

"No," I said, looking around. The other capsules had already been abandoned by their passengers. "Am I the last to wake?"

"Yes," there was hesitation in her voice, "We had difficulties waking you."

"Difficulties?" Despite the cold, sweat began trickling down my forehead. "How long have you been trying to wake me?"

"Five days," the doctor replied. "At first, I thought you fell into a coma, but that was impossible."

I wiped the sweat away. "What do you mean?"

"The capsule monitors your vitals during cryosleep. Cryosleep is used loosely here, Mr. Abara. You're not frozen while staying inside the chamber but put into stasis. When this happens, you're literally caught in an instant of time. The Infusion gel, meant to protect your body from harm during lightspeed transport, caused the coldness you're feeling right now. During your time in stasis, your vitals should be at zero, no different than if you are dead, but scans show that your brain's beta waves have been off the chart. Which is impossible."

"The impossible is something I do regularly," I said.

The doctor hadn't seemed surprised by my comment. "I looked into your background, Mr. Abara because I thought I would need to report your death to a family member back on Earth. You have an interesting history."

"Interesting?" I said, scoffing. "You're being subtle with your description. It's okay. You can use words like strange, bizarre, or inexplicable. That last one is my favorite. "

Smoothing wrinkles from her clothing as if to distract herself, I sensed she was working hard to conceal her excitement. "Regardless of the word, Mr. Abara, it appears that your mind was fully awake during your period in stasis. You seemed to experience something traumatic these last few minutes before you awoke."

"That, lady, is a colossal understatement." I showed her my trembling hands. "They are not shaking because I'm cold. I was moments away from being space poop."

One of her brows raised as she stared, perplexed. "Excuse me?"

Shit. Did I say that aloud?

48

"I've read about your ability. Under normal circumstances, I would have dismissed it as fantasy, but your scan showed neural activity during stasis that can't be ignored offhandedly," the doctor said. "Putting my doubts aside for the moment. Can you explain to me what you underwent? Do you believe you were speaking to dead people? Was that what caused the trauma?"

I forced out a laugh before answering. "The dead irritate me. The living usually causes me distress with skepticism and fears."

An uncomfortable silence fell between us. It broke after the doctor's clinical gaze showed a real sign of human emotion—shame.

"I'm sorry, Mister… um… Kaleb. I judged you as a charlatan even before you said your first word. Death, to me, has always meant a permanent end. Believing someone can communicate with the dead is inconceivable from my point of view. If you can do what you claim, I must reevaluate everything I've come to believe. You would be proof of the supernatural, something I cannot readily accept."

"This is coming from a doctor who woke me from stasis inside a rocket ship that traveled light years in outer space. Not long ago, that would have been considered sci-fi," I said. "It's not supernatural. It is what it is. Whether you accept it or not, the dead don't give a damn."

"Do you see them now?"

"See who?"

"Dead people."

"No," I answered, "We're in space."

She shook her head in frustration. "Why does that make sense to you?"

"The dead have limitations. They can only travel a mile or so from where they died. Still, after generations and generations of human life inhabiting nearly every inch of the planet, so have the dead. I signed up without attending any briefings or reading the documentation to escape them because there was no place on Earth I could go without running into a ghost. Nowhere."

The doctor nodded her understanding. "Very well. Let's go back to my original question. What had you experienced during stasis?"

"I was awake the entire time, floating around the Mwari 1 as an astral projection."

"You had an out-of-body experience?" Her clinical expression was back. "Fascinating."

"I thought so too, at first. On the fifth day, I got bored."

A questioning look crossed her face, but she said nothing.

"On a whim, I made a stupid decision. I passed through the ship's hull and exposed myself to outer space. I figured nothing could happen to me because my body was safely stored away inside a capsule."

"You exited the ship while it traveled at light speed?"

"Yeah. It was cool at first, trippy like having a powerful high." I grimaced then, embarrassed, forgetting that I was speaking to someone who probably spent more time behind books than smoking a blunt. However, she hadn't flinched and nodded as if precisely knowing the sensation I tried to describe. "It was all good until I started feeling queasy."

"Queasy?"

"It may not be the right word, but I felt a tugging in my gut immediately after that. Almost like a lasso thrown over me, and I was being yanked away," I explained. "The next thing I knew, I was being ripped from the ship."

"Interesting. I believe you might have experienced time dilation," the doctor said.

"A time whosits, whatsits?"

"It's a disparity in elapsed time due to relative velocity. Time passed at a different rate between your incorporeal and physical body. This phenomenon happened when you phased through the ship's hull, creating a temporal disconnect. Truly fascinating."

I blew out air. "You're making all this shit up, aren't you?"

She giggled. It was a cute giggle.

The doctor slowly glided her hand across the air in a straight line to illustrate a point she was about to make. "Think of your astral projection being hitched to your physical body by an invisible cord. While you moved within the containment of the Mwari 1, you experienced time linearly in a standard passage of time." She swept her hand upward in the air. "Once you removed yourself from the interior space of the ship to the outer hull, time for you swayed off course from the linear path, causing the invisible tether to snap apart. At that moment, you were caught between, let's say, two clocks. One clock where time passed normally and the other at light speed."

When she finished, her face flushed with excitement, and she looked as if struck by a sudden urge to start dancing. She paced back and forth with short and meaningful steps, her limbs animated by her theory's possibilities. I watched her, not wanting to interrupt. Her enthusiasm became contagious, and some of her excitement infected me. I smiled, not knowing exactly why.

No, that's not true. My interaction with the doctor was the first time I could recall not being treated like a pariah. Could I expect that same reaction from everyone else? I hadn't considered that in making my decision to leave Earth. It was solely based on escaping ghosts. The thought of people accepting me without judgment never entered my mind. For the first time in my life, I think I was happy.

The flickering appearance of a ghost ruined everything.

A woman's pale, trembling features, no more than forty, winked in and out of the room. Her brows were raised and pulled together. Moist eyes were frozen open, as was her mouth, as if she stared into the true face of evil. Her arms and hands were poised to fend something off. I had no idea precisely what that was, but I was damn sure I didn't want to know. Her fearful gaze locked onto mine, and she mouthed, "Help me!"

A door slid open with an electronic hiss on the other side of the chamber. A tall, black man in an unflattering uniform filled the opening. "Dr. Rider, we need you!"

The doctor glanced at me and then quickly toward the man. "What is it? What's wrong?"

The sudden appearance of the ghost told me all I needed. Someone had died. That hadn't meant the woman was dead, dead. At least not yet. The ghost's winking in and out was proof there might be a slight chance of saving her, but the doctor must be quick.

"There's a woman who's dying out there," I said, drawing stares from the doctor, the man, and the ghost. "She needs our help!"

Ours? I thought. I didn't know if I could be of any aid, but the ghost... the woman, asked me for help. What the hell else was I supposed to do? Doing nothing wasn't an option I could live with, at least not while she stared at me with such raw fear.

The doctor held up a halting finger. "You stay there! If all you told me is true. A full examination will have to be—"

"Dr. Rider, please, we need to get moving," the man shouted.

She spun and walked through the ghost's flickering form, causing the doctor to pause and glance over her shoulder to stare at nothing. On some level, she must have sensed her passing through the spirit, though her mind couldn't grasp what that could be. The doctor's gaze flitted in my direction. Slowly, she repeated what I had told her, "She needs our help?"

I nodded but said nothing.

Turning her attention back to the man, she gestured for me to follow with a wave of a hand before hurrying away. "Come on then."

Leaping off the capsule, I stood before the ghost and whispered, "I'll do what I can." It was the best I could offer her. Regarding the game of life and death, most of the time, death wins.

***

We rushed down the gangplank of the Mwari 1, and by the time we hit bottom, I was out of breath and covered in sweat. The atmosphere on the planet was dense. Too dense. The gravity was heavier than Earth's. Doubled over with my hands braced against my knees, I tried to catch my breath. Everyone else appeared unaffected by the planet's environment as if already acclimated. The doctor had told me the attempt to rouse me from cryosleep took five days. Could everyone have adapted in that brief period?

Over the horizon, coming down a hillside, a four-wheeler raced toward us. Everyone stared in its direction expectantly. I was on my knees at this point. My heart pumped wildly, and I

52

feared it would explode. With effort, I glanced back up the gangplank and into the open passageway of the Mwari 1. Inside must be standardized to Earth's atmosphere. The ghost appeared beside me, pointing frantically toward the approaching vehicle, and having no regard for my struggle to catch my breath.

Ghosts can be selfish assholes.

I blanked out for a bit, and everything went black. When my vision returned, I was lying on my side in the fetal position. The doctor leaned over me to stab the meaty part of my thigh. The needle of the syringe, I swear, was as long and as thick as my arm. That last part may have been a hallucination. Hurt like hell, regardless. She really jammed that thing into my leg.

"Let me guess, you hadn't taken your supplements before the flight," she asked in a not-so-nice tone. "Those were to help increase your bone density and prepare your body for the planet's climate."

"I-I d-don't like taking prescriptions. It messes with the weed in my system," I answered groggily.

Shaking her head, the doctor thumps me on the forehead. "Use that organ inside your head sometimes."

I sat up, feeling better. "What did you give me?"

"Call it a booster. It'll help strengthen your heart and bones. Temporarily mind you. You must take your supplements unless you want your heart to explode." She thumped me on the forehead again and added, "Neither of us wants that."

I knew it. She likes me.

Rolling over onto my back, I gazed up at the orange sky. Could it be ginger? Or was it auburn… maybe? Not really important. The alien sky was beautiful and screamed that I was no longer on Earth. Being away from Earth didn't mean I truly escaped the planet, which I realized as the frantic ghost blipped in and out of existence gesturing for me to get off my ass. I stood up and brushed the dust off my clothing.

The four-wheeler skidded to a stop near the ship. The waiting crowd converged on the vehicle when the man who sought the doctor yelled, "Make a hole! Let Dr. Rider through!"

The doctor took me by the arm and led me past the throng. In the cargo bed of the four-wheeler, two people wearing identical rugged jumpsuits attended the twin of the hysterical specter. I hated thinking this, but it was the first thought that came to mind. The dying woman looked like she had seen a ghost. The pair jumped off the vehicle's rear to make room for the doctor. She had a doodad in her hand, scanning her patient.

"There doesn't appear to be any physical trauma and no blood loss, but her vitals are deteriorating rapidly," Dr. Rider said, then she looked directly at the pair. "What happened to Ada?"

I glanced at the ghost and whispered, "Ada is your name?"

The spirit nodded her head.

A slender woman with mercury-red hair answered the doctor. "We were investigating a cave up in the hills, not five miles from here. Ada found something and was clearing dirt from it when she suddenly let out a scream and collapsed."

"Her skin turned pasty in a matter of seconds as if something drew the hue from her features," the second person said, his gray thick bushy eyebrows pulled together in concern. "There was something else."

"What?" Dr. Rider asked.

"She began speaking in another language," he replied.

The doctor looked annoyed. "Ada knows five different languages. How is that concerning?"

His gaze went to his feet like he was embarrassed by what he had to say next. "It wasn't any Earth tongue that we're aware of."

"That's bulls--." Dr. Rider glanced down at her patient as she began murmuring.

"⊬○ʃ ⋏⊤Ш ⋏○Φ △Ш⫽ฦ○ⅈШ ⊑Ш⊤Ш," Ada said.

I looked questioningly at Ada's spirit.

She shrugged her shoulders in reply.

Ada's body convulsed. "⊬○ʃ ⋏⊤Ш ⋏○Φ △Ш⫽ฦ○ⅈШ ⊑Ш⊤Ш!" "⊬○ʃ ⋏⊤Ш ⋏○Φ △Ш⫽ฦ○ⅈШ ⊑Ш⊤Ш" "⊬○ʃ ⋏⊤Ш ⋏○Φ △Ш⫽ฦ○ⅈШ ⊑Ш⊤Ш!" She kept shouting the same thing repeatedly.

Reaching into her med pack, Rider withdrew a syringe and slammed a thick needle between her patient's chest. The convulsing hadn't stopped but worsened. The doctor ran another scan on Ada.

"That's impossible," she said, looking at a loss. "Her vitals? There aren't any. She's flatline." Rider was either a horrible doctor or something totally out of the ordinary was happening because Ada's dead body continued to flop around in the cargo bed like a fish out of water screaming that strange language.

Rider turned to face me. "Tell me you're not a charlatan."

"I'm not," I replied, not knowing where this was going.

"Is Ada's spirit here with us right now?"

I nodded. "She's right beside me."

"Get up here," Rider shouted. "Hurry!"

Jumping onboard to join the doctor, I stared at the swaying body. Ada's ghost sat worriedly next to her physical self.

"Ⱶ○Ꙇ ⚎⟙Ɯ ⋏○⏀ △Ɯꝇꖬ○ⱞⱲ ⊏Ɯ⟙Ɯ! "Ⱶ○Ꙇ ⚎⟙Ɯ ⋏○⏀ △Ɯꝇꖬ○ⱞⱲ ⊏Ɯ⟙Ɯ "Ⱶ○Ꙇ ⚎⟙Ɯ ⋏○⏀ △Ɯꝇꖬ○ⱞⱲ ⊏Ɯ⟙Ɯ!"

"Seizures are caused by uncontrolled electrical activity between neurons, but Ada's brain activity is nil, according to my scan," Rider explained.

"Could your scanner be on the fritz?"

"No, I ran a diagnostic on it. I also injected Ada with medical nanites, which are sending me updated telemetry data. She is definitely dead."

I looked at Ada's ghost. "Yeah, I can confirm that much," I said before addressing the doctor. "What do you want me to do?"

"I can't believe I'm saying this. I need you to talk to Ada and find out if there's a way to save her before oxygen to her brain has been cut off for too long."

"It doesn't work that way. Ghosts don't talk to me directly. They, um… Well, they point a lot and often make scary faces."

"Do something," Rider said through gritted teeth.

"Fine. Okay," I replied. "Ada. How do I help you."

"What is she doing," the doctor asked.

"She's pointing down at her corpse and making a scary face."

Ada winked out again but for an extended time before reappearing. She took her fists and pounded her physical body frantically. Her hands should have passed through the flesh, but each blow met resistance.

"That's odd," I said, examining the body with more scrutiny than I had previously. I reached out with my senses, focusing my thoughts on Ada, seeing beyond the surface.

"What is it?"

"I think there's a—"

Ada's eyelids snapped open. Her irises' black obsidian pools were laser-focused on me. "⟨alien glyphs⟩ ⟨alien glyphs⟩ ⟨alien glyphs⟩ ⟨alien glyphs⟩ ⟨alien glyphs⟩!"

Shit.

The Ada-Thing sprung up into a crouch and growl. Before I could react, it grabbed the folds of my jacket, reeled me in, and got in my face, teeth bared. I expected to smell the rancid breath of death. But it was minty, like peppermint. Maybe wintergreen. It doesn't matter, I suppose.

"⟨alien glyphs⟩ ⟨alien glyphs⟩ ⟨alien glyphs⟩ ⟨alien glyphs⟩ ⟨alien glyphs⟩!"

The doctor had another syringe gripped like a dagger in her hand, thrusting downward at my attacker. The Ada-Thing turned its head in her direction. Rider launched backward off the truck and into the man with bushy eyebrows.

A powerful pulse of psychic energy blasted outward. It hit everyone that surrounded the four-wheeler, knocking everybody over. Each person was pinned to the ground and held down by an invisible force. I caught movement in the corner of my eye. Ada, the ghost Ada, was stabilizing, no longer flickering. She'd be a permanent spirit if I didn't do something quickly.

I punched the Ada-Thing in the nose, giving the blow all I had. It barely flinched and looked pissed as hell.

The spirit grabbed her physical body from behind, putting it in a chokehold and surprising the Ada-Thing. It let go of me to focus on freeing itself. Whatever possessed Ada could be affected on some level, both physically and incorporeally. Short of doing severe harm or even killing Ada, I couldn't think of a way of using that knowledge as an advantage.

Staring at the pair reminded me of seeing my physical body when I was an astral projection. Knowing my physical body was protected inside the sleeping chamber, I thought of how invincible I felt. And then I recalled how I was left behind when the ships sped off at light speed, leaving me alone in space. When I eventually woke up, I wondered why I had returned to my physical body. The answer was simple; it was the same response I had given the doctor when she asked me why the ghosts couldn't follow me into space. The dead had limitations because their spirits remained tethered to wherever they had died.

What was it the man and woman said happened to Ada?

I looked at the struggling spirit, trying her best to sustain her hold. "Ada. You had found something in the cave. Is it on this vehicle?"

She nodded yes, then motioned her head to the right leg of her body. There was a large cargo pocket and something bulky inside. I started for it, and Ada-Thing's black eyes widened with realization. It stopped fighting with the spirit and tried to fend me off instead. Grabbing the pocket, I ripped it open rather than trying to insert my hand in. A metallic-looking stone tablet with strange symbols tumbled free and skidded across the cargo bed floor.

ʌ◯! ⅋⊕ ⅋⅋ ⋔⅋ʌⳡ," the Ada-Thing yelled as it drove its elbow into the ghost's face with teeth jarring force. The savageness of the attack threw it off-balanced, leaving an opening for me to exploit. I thrust out a leg and slammed the sole of my boot into its exposed chest. The Ada-Thing plunged over the side of the vehicle and into the dirt with a hard crash.

"Sorry, Ada," I shouted to the ghost as I leaped over the opposite side of the four-wheeler with the artifact clutched in one hand.

I ran to the front of the vehicle. The driver was still in the seat, face down on the controls, unable to move like the others on the ground. There was awareness and fear in his eyes.

"Sorry about this, man," I said, shoving him to the passenger side and climbing aboard.

The Ada-Thing flung open the passenger's door, its mouth wide, teeth bared, smoldering obsidian eyes fixated on me, and let out an inhuman shriek. I lost my cool and might have peed a little in my pants.

Ada's spirit rammed into it with such force the door flew off its hinge. The Ada-Thing and the door hit the ground, kicking up a dust storm. A weak burst of adrenaline freed me from my temporary paralysis, and I engaged the vehicle's engine and sped away. In the rearview, the Ada-Thing was back on its feet and running after me. Cold sweat cascaded down my forehead, threatening to pour into my eyes. I returned to the terrain ahead, deciding to focus on the task. "Come on. Come on. Keep it together, man. I've seen worse things than this," I said before the back of the four-wheeler rocked.

Reluctantly, I glanced back.

One arm from the Ada-Thing clung onto the rear hatch. The other hand came up and over into view and found a purchase. It slowly pulled itself up, revealing half its face like a ravenous crocodile rising from the murky water after spotting its prey. Those glassy dark eyes burrowed into mine with a decipherable message: Your ass is about to die!

Shit!

I might have peed my pants again.

This was not a part of the plan. The four-wheeler accelerated when I slammed my foot down to the floor on the pedal. I hit every depression on the ground, took every sharp turn, and smacked the vehicle against obstacles in my path, but nothing I had done shook it loose. The Ada-Thing filled the rearview mirror as it pounced over the hatch and onto the cargo bed. It had transformed into something monstrous, vaguely reminiscent of a dragonfly with large rounded multifaceted eyes and mandibles with pointed serrated fangs. Its arms and legs were jointed, folded in awkward angles. The hands of the creature had changed to raptorial claws like that of a praying mantis. A series of thick, prickly bones slashed through the jumpsuit extending several inches resembling porcupine quills.

I took back what I said earlier. I hadn't seen anything worse than this. This was, without a doubt, the worst thing I'd ever seen.

Unfamiliar with its newly transformed body, the creature took clumsy steps forward. With each stride, I could hear its clawed feet tearing through metal and stumping holes into the cargo bed floor. The vehicle slowed as the fuel gauge dropped drastically. It must have punctured a line. My gaze kept going from the indicator to the rearview mirror.

Ada's ghost materialized in the passenger seat. I stared at her. She pointed hysterically at the front windshield, trying to get me to focus on the path ahead. But there was no path. A vast ravine three times the size of the Grand Canyon grew wider by the second in the windshield.

I worked the controls like a maniac trying to get the four-wheeler to turn. If I wasn't having trouble enough, a claw punched through the roof and shredded it apart like paper. The poor guy in the passenger seat, still unable to move independently, began sliding toward the opening that no longer had a door as the vehicle started to veer. I had to drop the artifact to free up a hand to grab a clump of his jumpsuit and hold him in place as best I could.

The tablet. I had forgotten all about the damn thing. It was the reason behind my taking the four-wheeler in the first place. I risked letting go of the passenger to retrieve the object. The man slid toward the open doorway again. I flung the stone pad out like a freebie. It flew through the passenger exit and over the ravine. I grabbed the man by the leg, stopping his momentum just before he shared the same fate as the artifact at the bottom of the gorge.

That inhuman roar filled the inside of the cab. I looked up to see the creature's many eyes staring at me. It began squeezing its deformed body through the tear it created. Its mandibles were wide and drooling like they wanted to devour my entire head with one chomp. The vehicle, finally out of fuel, came to a slow stop as the Ada-Thing drew closer. Saliva dripped onto my forehead. I slid lower in the driver's seat to delay the inevitable. It was again the whole space squid situation, but it wasn't my imagination this time. I was about to be devoured.

Shit.

Just as its warm minty breath brushed my skin, it shrank back and screamed, "⋏◯! ⋏◯⌽ ⋏◯△!"

Pulling from the roof, it tumbled to the rear onto its back with a heavy thud, shaking the entire vehicle. "⋏◯! "

I don't know how long I stayed huddled in place, thinking about how lucky I was to be alive before I worked up enough nerve to straighten up and stare into the back. The spirit was beside the fallen creature on the cargo bed, looking upon her altered body with dire concern. The man stirred weakly in the passenger seat, evidently free of the thing's mental powers. He rose up and peered over into the back, his eyes as wide as coat buttons as he watched the beast writhing. He said nothing and fainted.

Ada flickered and glanced at me with a smile before disappearing one last time. Faint traces of human features had returned as the insect and animal aspects Ada's body had taken on gradually waned. The plan had worked. The ravine, thankfully, was deep enough to put distance between the artifact and the human host it inhabited. With luck, the stone tablet shattered into a million pieces, so no one else could stumble upon it and start the entire process again.

By the time others arrived, Ada had fully recovered, weak but alive and well. She had no memory of being a ghost or her possession, which was probably for the best. It may come back to her in bits and pieces in her nightmares, but a few restless nights were far better than a lifetime of mental trauma. The doctor gave a passing bill of health to the four-wheeler's driver. Though he couldn't believe it, he would remember what he saw, calling it a hallucination and blaming it all on a head injury.

When asked about Ada's ripped clothing or the battered condition of the torn-apart vehicle, I fudged the truth a bit. Well, more than a bit. It was a full-on lie. No one needed to know that one of their colleagues had become a carnivorous monster with a taste for human flesh.

After the questioning, the doctor approached me. "How much of that was the truth," she asked.

"Does it matter?" I answered. "Some things are better left not knowing."

She nodded. "I want you to know your ability. It's not strange, bizarre, or inexplicable. When everyone was pinned down by whatever possessed Ada, you were the only person unaffected by its mental force. Because of that, you were able to save Ada, perhaps save us all. It's a gift. It always has been."

"Maybe," I said. "I'm just glad it's all over, Dr. Rider."

She took my hand. "My name is Imani."

Day Seven Hundred Forty

The survey team led by Ada returned to the cave where she had found the artifact ten days ago. Everyone wore hazmat suits and carried scientific devices. I agreed to accompany them because the team felt my gift could be helpful in their research.

Imani walked beside me, telling me about some indigenous insects, animals, and plants she'd encountered these past days. We've grown close, well, at least, I'd like to think we have. I have never been any good at reading the living. Ghosts were simple to figure out. The living was problematic and not easy to understand. Twice already, I thought Imani was going to kiss me, but all she wanted to do was remove lint from my hair.

We'd gone nearly a mile inside the cavern when my head throbbed. The suddenness of it made me stagger.

Imani caught me by the arm. "Are you okay, Kaleb?"

"I don't know. I've never felt anything like that before," I replied.

"Describe to me what you're feeling?"

Before I could answer, someone shouted. We all looked in the direction of the voice. One of the researchers pointed at symbols that shone fluorescent green on a rockface. The team started toward the glow forgetting all about what had happened the last time they came across anything with alien inscriptions on it.

The throbbing in my head increased. "I need to go," I said, but I was talking to myself. Imani was as fascinated by the find as the scientific researchers and had gone to join them. I pulled off the head cover of the hazmat suit and threw it to the ground. Closing my eyes, I rubbed at my temples to ease the throbbing. The ache slowly faded. I took a deep breath and opened my eyes.

The cavern's walls, ceiling, and floor glowed green with alien symbols that may have been dormant for thousands of years. I feared my psychic ability may have triggered something not meant to be disturbed. The research team was oblivious to everything I saw. I took a tentative step back and then another. I had to get out of the cave fast and put some distance between it and me.

I spun, intending to run, but I was too late.

Dozens, maybe hundreds of aliens resembling what Ada had transformed into, blocked my path. Unlike the last encounter with one of them, these didn't give the impression that they had malicious intent toward me. But I've been wrong before about someone's intentions. For all I knew, they all might have been thinking, "I wonder if he'll taste like chicken?"

A hand touched my shoulder from behind me, nearly giving me a heart attack.

"Why did you take off your headcover?" Imani asked.

I pointed to the alien horde ahead of me with a shaky finger. "You don't see them?"

She looked in the direction I indicated and then gave me a puzzled expression. "See who?"

If Imani couldn't see them, that could only mean one thing. They were ghosts. They all stared at me as if needing something only I could give them.

Shit. Not again.

Water Weight
by
Makeda K. Braithwaite

"My head," I slap a hand on the wall connecting myself and the Ganymeden trainee who hasn't stopped blushing since I called him over to scold. "Is right here. So, when you bring your little ship rats, I'm begging you to just shag them on the ground or a closet like everyone else."

Narshul scratches his head, leaning against the frame of my dorm, state-regulated pendant swinging from his wrist. He opens his mouth to speak when the blare of an alarm sounds through the ship.

It is a single, constant horn alarm. On instinct, I reach a hand beneath the cot for my small bag of precious items.

On ships, there are three alarms. One is a rising sound horn that signals we've left or arrived somewhere new. Two, a high, low, low, high sound for the general meetings. The third – the alarm for a crash – was what was blaring through the walls.

Crew flooded the exit cockpit, everyone scrambling for suits and pods with as much order as possible. Standing at the entrance, Captain Jubani – suited up — stood handing out compressed flight suits. Oh stars, was I going to die?

"We're crashing on Huatl. A water planet we have little to no data on. If you survive this crash, you are to signal to Terra via your pendants." Captain Jubani handed me my suit, dark eyes taking me in with solemn pity. "For your sake, I hope you all can swim. The suits should protect you from burning up, breaking bones, or dying from the pressure of impact. But it won't protect you from something trying to eat you. Four to a pod. Stars willing, we will see each other again."

Narshul pulls me with him to a pod with two others, their faces obscured in their masks. It takes a tap to put the suit on. When the pod closes, my ears ring. Back home, my grandmother would tell us little stories. My ears ringing are to mean my ancestors calling me. My god singing to me, warning me. I wonder how they could reach me, so far away from my roots. I wonder if the past stays with me, in my skin, bones and DNA. If I am ever truly without them – the ringing heightens. *What are you trying to say to me? Can't you just tell me?*

We fall.

* * *

Back when my grandmother told us stories, she would take us flying in her classic mobile. It was sleek, red, and pretty. I adored it. It made me want to fly. It's what made me enlist in the Federation's Archivist Initiative, FAI, as a biologist. My grandmother loved stories so much that the last time we saw her she said we'd see her again. Then she killed herself and the casket was closed. I had a look, but there was no face. She'd blasted it off. I never saw her again; so, stories became synonymous with lies. My grandmother was a liar.

There is no red on Huatl. Thank Stars. At least from what I've seen so far. It's very blue and green. The fruits are peach and purple looking but nonpoisonous so far. The fish, when split open, is grey but tasty. We set up camp on a dusty spot, beneath a tall canopy tree, like the ones in history books. I imagine Terra looked like this once.

I try to remember Terra but I remember colours mostly. Grey. Black. Ash. Nothingness. Barren. What is home? Is it comfort? Terra was not comfort. Terra was barren.

But it was home. So perhaps, I was wrong about that. Home can be horrid too. Home doesn't always bring comfort. Home can bring pain.

"Wanna go for a swim?" the only other woman asks; Liane is a lithe Terra girl. Her hair is in five braids and curls beneath her shoulder. We're sitting on the shore with our bodies facing the warmth of the undying sun. In the sand, there are many little dead things. A dead firefly sits between us.

The water is smooth. Foamy tips rising gently and tickling our toes. It's cool, a murmur on our skin.

The other person in the pod was a man, Ishmail. A tall, broad silent type who none of us seemed to know. He helped fish and gather but didn't speak much. I think he's Ganymeden but Narshul wasn't sure. "I don't know everyone from my planet. Do *you?*"

I didn't bother bringing that up again.

"Nah." The sheer vastness of the water was frightening. I'd always been a strong swimmer but here, the water is heavier somehow, like it doesn't want you to leave. I don't say this out loud, but it's nonetheless true. This planet is sinister.

"I think I'll go see what I can catalogue up the hill."

The hill is a small mountain a few miles back. It can be seen above the scattered trees and vegetation. Yellow flowers sit at its base. The codex tells us nothing of them – it would not be uncommon, but I have to go with a helmet and gloves just in case they're poisonous. Chances are the highlands might have other fauna. We haven't walked with much equipment, but the standard pod stuff should work just fine.

Liane looks at me carefully. I'm the only one of us still working and not just surviving.

"Alright. Go with one of the guys, just in case."

"I think if there were other sentient beings we'd have met them."

She shook her head. "Not if they're smart," then dives in, a bullet cutting through the water. I wonder if she's Terran sometimes because there's no human I know that moves *that* fast.

The little mountain isn't a far walk out. The path is simple. At the halfway mark I see the white pod, the little camp, the overwhelming water, and at the other half is the mountain with a noticeable yellow base. From here the flowers are strokes on a canvas. A mistake or divine intent.

The flowers are broad-petaled. They hold a stem at the tip, bulbous but light – pollen, salmon-coloured dust onto the tip of my glove. They line the outside of the mouth of a cave. I cut one down and placed it in the sleek petri-bag. It freezes it in time for me until I can get back to the lab.

There's an odd echo in the distance. Like a cockatoo's click. I ignore it. Squatting, to get as close to it as I can to the flowers, I take pictures of it with my helmet.

The hill is harder to hike up than I had realised. I hadn't realised how out-of-shape ship life had made me – stars, field people did this all the time? Though it was tempting to feel earth beneath your hands. The call of the open air, a pure world undamaged by the hands of men and time. Ganymede had been beautiful like this. A silk planet, they prided themselves on creation and art. While more water-logged and untapped, Huatl gave all pretense of a utopia like them.

I don't realise it's raining until my helmet becomes clouded. There had been a cave at the base of the mountain. The trek back is assisted by various slides and falls, but I make it back and crawl into the warmth.

Turning my light on, I turn and scream.

Ishmail raises a hand to the brightness. His eyes glow blue against the dark – Ganymedens see in the dark after all. He didn't need clunky Terran tech.

"Oh, hello."

"Hello."

"You followed me?"

He nods.

"Why?"

He gives me a look, as if to ask if I'm stupid. "Right. Strange planet. We need to work in pairs."

"Hmm."

The cave is moist and dry. Something heavy and thinning about it. I notice Ishmail doesn't have a mask on and study his face. He's handsome; with mahogany skin and taut limbs. Humans and Ganymedens are look-alikes. There was a very limited difference between us – while humans bled red, Ganymedens bled purple.

"So, what's your story? You're Ganymeden?"

His eyes flicker over my face. I can't help but think it's the first time we have both seen each other. "Half."

"Oh!" There weren't many planets where homosapien-like creatures could procreate. "Half human?"

"No."

"How do you find Huatl?" I lean against a wall.

"Familiar. Like a dream."

"Really?" It was familiar to me too. But it was more like a nightmare.

The rain outside is non-stop. The pod is a dot in the distance. The flowers don't seem to be doing anything to Ishmail, but I don't want to take the risk. We've been here for four days. I'm not even sure if our signal went out but no one else seems to share my concern.

A clicking sounds off in the distance. I follow it.

That nagging feeling chills the back of my neck. Like the water, the cave creeps over me with a sense of doom. My fingers tap the communicator on the chest of my suit – signal's dead in here.

I keep walking until my right boot touches a body of water and sink up to my knee before Ishmail drags me back. The clicking continues, it echoes now, getting louder as I go closer. It's a sound that says things should be covering us – but there's nothing there.

"We've got to swim ahead."

"No." he snaps. "We don't know what's in there."

I couldn't explain it but I didn't care. My hands are peeling off my gear before I know it. Then my clothing, until I'm just in my underwear and helmet. The clicking is a siren call and I jump in behind it. Ishmail curses behind me.

The water has the same pulling effect. The water tries to push me back and away fight them. *Grandmother, I want to get to the other side and back.*

Beside me, I feel someone else moving like they're pulling me back. Ishmail moves beside me, and though I can't see him, we cut through the water until shallow meets us. Fighting each other. I want to go forward into the seductive unknown but it isn't what he wants.

A reddish light bathes over this side. So subtle we couldn't have seen it from the other side. The light is partially blocked by green shrubbery.

Climbing out, I look to my right expecting to see Ishmail beside me. I stand alone on the shore, looking back to the water – I see Ishmail now halfway to me.

My chest tightens. *Someone* was with me. I just knew someone was.

I dig my feet in the sand, tempted to run off and not wait for him. Clicking louder than ever now.

But I stay. Ishmail swims fast.

I look at the ceiling of the cave. Was it some sort of limestone? It looked like it. Limestone was never good. Too unstable. Too ready to fall apart. A spiked edge hung above me. One little tremor and it could impale me as I sat. It had been years since I thought of my grandmother. Huatl seemed to pull her from my bones, bloated, and hand her to me saying here, *look at me in all my rot.*

Ishmail huffs at my feet. His face wrenched in horrible anger. "Why would you jump in?"

"Don't you hear it?" I whisper. "The clicking."

"Barely." he dismisses, hands on his hips. His eyes go behind me. To the light. "We better go ahead, get data, and get out."

My voice cracks. "Right."

Regardless, he puts a hand out to me and helps me up. He cuts through the bushes with a knife tacked to his trunks. The branches fall like paper, I don't know if the knife is sharp, Ishmail is strong, or they're brittle for some unknown reason.

The path is lit with crimson fireflies. Their bottoms glow red and they flicker on the walls, illuminating the eggshell of the limestone. They fly around us, leading us more into the red light. I take Ishmail's hand, realising what I've done to us. I've led us away from the crowd. We have no way of getting to them if something happened right now.

The sound of rain comes before the sight of it. There's an opening ahead. Cautiously, Ishmail walks ahead of me – knife first. In the red light and sunlight, a pod sits. It had crashed in. Perhaps this limestone was weaker than I had realised.

Running ahead, I try to look for survivors but the only sign that someone had been there was shattered glass and a gun at the base of the pod. I reach forward to pick it up, tucking it into the waistband of my underwear. Had all four people from this pod just disappeared? Ishmail rolls his shoulder and begins to step back.

"We should head back."

"We can't." I climb out of the pod. "What if someone's still alive in here?"

"Look around, biologist." He spits my title like a curse. "There is no sign of a camp here. No fire. No bed."

I look around to confirm. The cave is pristine. There's nothing but fireflies here. The rest of his thoughts can be unstated. *If they got out obviously something got them.*

When we start to go ahead, something sounds behind us. A crack. "Hello?" the word comes out with vibration, a robotic tremble. A dozen sounds coming into one.

Coming through the darkness is a recruit whose face I don't recognize. He's red-eyed with ashy, washed-out skin. He limps to us. Ishmail goes in front of me. "Name and specialization?"

The man swallows. Eyes flickering between Ishmail and me. "Do you have any food?"

"Name and specialization?"

"Noam. Engineering."

Ishmail's back grows taut. "How long have you been here?"

Noam laughs. "Too long."

"Where's the rest of your pod?"

He looks up. "They didn't make it. Something went wrong with their suits."

"All of their suits?" I ask. "Except your own?"

"My bad luck."

The rain worsens. Noam's figure becomes blurred behind it. Red flickers through the gray. The scent of decay washes from him. We step back but bump into something. Behind us the fireflies form a wall. They block us from getting out. They don't buzz like the ones back home. They *click*. I stretch my hand out to try and swat them, but they slice through my flesh and leave small cuts.

"What the hell is this?"

Ishmail has already turned away.

He eyes the hole above. None of the fireflies go near the opening and the rain. Noam smiles at us, his teeth chipped and sharp. He lunges through the rain but hisses, stumbling sideways. Smoke comes off him, the rain acts as an acid, burning, searing.

I grab Ishmail's hand and run forward and ahead. We run through the darkness of the cave, the gravel beneath our feet and the chill of the chase upon our backs. The fireflies follow behind us, clicking. They're a fire chasing our steps, ready to consume.

We trip over something hard. The light of my helmet flashes over it and I pause, stunned. Captain Jubani's face, open-mouthed, stares back at me. Their body is enclaved, hollowed out and rotting. The scent, the same as Noam's, burns my nostrils.

"Fuck."

I can't help but agree. Ishmail tries to pull me up but he's snatched back by someone else. Noam grins at me, twitchy eyes under the focused light of my helmet. "C'mon. Don't be like that. I'd much rather eat him. We could work together."

"To a black hole with you." I spit. Ishmail looks at me with a tightened jaw. The veins in his neck bulge and Noam seems to be salivating. The fireflies float around him, a halo of blood.

"Why not try to leave?" Ishmail asks. "It's a ten-minute swim out."

Noam shakes his head. The gun is cold at my hip. I'm shivering. It's cold. Fingers slipping inside, I grip the handle and aim for his leg. The blast is fire hot. Barrel warm to fingertips – it's a flame gun.

I'm not a sharpshooter. I've never shot anything before, so it hits Ishmail as well but the blunt of it removes almost all of Noam's thigh. No blood comes out, but instead, there are eggs frothing from it. The skin hangs off it, the yellow bone isn't held up by any muscle – just white eggs like honeycomb, plentiful and rank.

He turns back, screaming at the pain. The fireflies click louder – they're aggressive now, circling the wounded area. Ishmail turns, striking into Noam's chest and dragging the blade down. Through the ripped flesh, I hear the subtle breaking of tender shells.

Ishmail stumbles back, butt hitting the ground.

Noam is arched backward. Eggs are broken in his chest as his open mouth cries out. From the broken eggs, oatmeal thick, red goo drips out down his body. It was unlike any parasite infection I had ever seen before. The fireflies had infected him somehow and dug into his flesh, making his body a breeding ground.

Had it been before he ate his pod mates? Or after? Was the rot of cannibalism what caused the infestation to set course? The fireflies had led us to him, had been calling us to feed their young. They couldn't cross the waters; the rain burned their host. Maybe this was why there was no life on Hualt. It had been eaten out.

I can't think of that for too long when Noam straightens up and red eyes stare at us while the fireflies surround him. Ishmail is on his feet and before we can wonder, we run. My helmet falls off in the confusion and I'm blind to the black of the cave, with only the glow of carnivorous fireflies behind us. The clicking rages at our backs. We run until we slip face-first into more water.

This water is mossy. Not like the fresh water in the cave or the seawater of the shore. It's lake water, which means we're near an exit. The clicking grows distant as we swim ahead. The darkness of the cave bleeds into a dying afternoon light. Ishmail must have swum ahead of me because there's a figure at the shore already.

My arms are so weak. The clicking is a nag at the back of my head, and my vision is weak from the water. I reach up, and when he pulls me out, it doesn't feel like his hand. It's softer, familiar. "We've got to get back to the others."

But the answer comes from behind, Ishmail is crawling out of the water behind me. On the other side the red-light flickers before dimming. "C'mon, let's go."

It's a long walk back and for the first time since we crashed, silence is the only thing that greets me.

My feet are sore, Ishmail is bleeding and when we arrive, the others aren't alone. The envoy seemed to have finally arrived. It's a large ship and most of the other crew are there.

Ishmail takes my hand. We stick together. The clicking is gone.

"You know, when we were swimming – at first, I thought you were swimming with me," I admit after the medics patch us up and take our statements.

Ishmail looks at me with wonder. "I thought you were beside me the whole time. I hadn't even realised when you started to swim till you were halfway."

"Huh." I risk a joke. "I'd never seen red fireflies before."

"Red? They were purple, like a hurricane on Ganymede." his face takes a sullen look at this admittance. The ship blares the sound for takeoff; we head to a new discovery.

Acacia Zero
by
Nora Anthony

LOG 1
Dr. Kofa McFadden

We've arrived.

Primitus 400 is cold. Sub-zero. The inside of our suits feels
as if they've been chilled in a fridge. It doesn't take long for us
to get too cold to continue canvassing so we have to send out
Robot to do the rest (Cox is corny. She's too tickled by giving
our advanced AI this basic name). Dr. Johnson started rubbing
cocoa butter on his skin before entering the suit and that's
helped keep us a little warmer. I'm already thick but don't mind
gaining if it means we can stay on the surface for longer than
one hour.

In a month, the first dome should be created, where we can
walk around suit-less. There'll be panels looking out into the
cold grey land; grey dunes and craters for miles. I'd never been
to a planet before, and I'm shocked at how monochrome one can
be.

Dr. Cox said they gave us the fucked-up planet, keeping the
nicer, easier-to-terraform ones for the white folks. The others
laugh at this, but they don't know how right she is. Jackson only
smiled, belying the years and years of requesting, petitioning,
damn near groveling to let us get in on terraforming; to create
our own planet. I try not to think of the echoes of history in this,
in how hard we had to work to get here and how hard we now
must work to be here.

"I didn't know it was this bad," Jackson said, after returning
from one of our excursions. This cold, this inhospitable. This
hard to toil the ground for water and soil.

There must be a way. We didn't come out here to fail. We can't fail. Even if we gotta be in these suits for the rest of our lives, we'll have a home for us.

LOG 2

I got a picture of my grandmother. I keep it above my head in my pod, to remind me of home whenever I wake up. She's holding my father in her arms, her hair halfway braided, one breast almost slipping out the stretched-out collar of her grey T-shirt, while my 8-month-old father tries standing up in her arms. I remember him pulling this picture out and her bugging out about it. "Why that picture?" she would ask with a laugh. "The place is a mess; I look a mess!"

"No, you don't, you look beautiful," Dad said.

He's right. Nanny looks radiant, a younger woman who paid for my drumming lessons and West African dance class, who wrote a short story just for me, where I traveled in space, having adventures on different planets. She saw my love of the stars and planets and poured water all over it, growing it into this mission: creating a planet just for us Black people, where we don't have to convince anyone of our existence. Where there is no tension with our thriving.

The picture reminds me that space isn't lonely, void-only. It'll be home.

LOG 3

Will it, though?

This planet hates us.

A dust storm destroyed the foundation for the first dome. Black metal scraps scattered and sticking out the ground, like an abstract expression of trees. A weeks' worth of work undone, chipped away slowly in the hours-long storm.

I was with Dr. Jackson on that call to the Headquarters of the United Terraforming Association. The request was weighing heavy on his shoulders; I could see the heaviness pull him down in his rolling chair, the grey starting to stick out in his Carl Winslow mustache (he grew that thing so fast during hyper-sleep, we all poke fun at him looking like an 80's Black Dad). He ran his fingers over it before he started the call.

They asked us what happened, why it happened and did we install everything correctly.

"No one told us to expect dust storms here," I jumped in. "This is Dr. McFadden speaking. The material is incompatible with the dust of this planet."

Some hemming and hawing about budget cuts and a lack of proper documentation on these smaller planets. Some well-you-have-to-wait-three-months-for-resupply.

"Is Dr. Magnus Winterbottom available?" I asked for Jackson's mentor. "We're using his terraforming method for this whole thing. This is emergency level."

Jackson shook his head at me but the entry-level UTA scientist already put me on hold.

Silence, then a voice like honey and tea and whatever else cozy and white came on. "Tyrell, I heard what happened to the dome foundation. Awful stuff. I'll make sure you get the first resupply ship in a week's time."

Jackson sighed. "Thank you so much, Dr. Winterbottom, You have no idea—"

"How goes the rest of your terraforming? Found water yet?"

"N-not yet, the well is connected to the dome so we haven't been—"

"Surely you can use an independent one for this type of planet—I remember covering that in at least one of my classes—"

I stepped in. "This isn't a class 3 planet; it's a class 2 or possibly 1. We need some heavy machinery to get this one to produce anything."

"Really?" He didn't believe me. I saw Jackson's shoulders slump, tense on the edge of his chair. Winterbottom gave more pleasantries and promises of better equipment before ending the call.

Then, the gut punch. An email comes in from UTA HQ, stating that, before they could send any replacements, they needed the serial number of the main foundational panel.

Cox burst into the room, having seen the email on her tablet (there's only one email address for this crew, unfortunately). "How the hell are we supposed to get that? Why do we even need it?"

"We don't need it—but you know that we gotta prove to these people why they should lift a finger to help us."

Cox sighed, drumming her long purple nails on Robot's little black box body.

The three of us spent the night figuring out how quickly we could go out there to get the serial number with no clue as to when the dust storm was going to end.

We went to sleep. I lay in my cot, now feeling more like a grey upholstered tomb. I stare at Nanny and Dad's picture. This can't all be for nothing.

LOG 4

So much is happening. I'm in my room but I wanna get back out into the field.

Nanny is here.

I decided to go out that night and get the serial number myself. I saw everyone trying their hardest to make a home for us, sacrificing normal lives for the future and knew I had more in me to give, to take one for them.

The ending of the dust storm was less intense, but little grey cyclones spun near the site. It took me a minute to lift the foundational panel, then pry open the serial number case. By the time I placed it in my bag, a cyclone snuck up on me and whipped at my arm, cutting right through my suit and into my skin.

It was as if my arm was being sucked out of my suit. I scrambled back into the rover and sped to the ship.

I left traces of blood.

When I got back, everyone was up and waiting for me. With a smile I dropped the serial number case on the table.

Cox grabbed me into a hug, before fussing at me. Jackson gave me a smile of relief, while Stevens, our medic, tended to my arm.

That night as I slept and healed in my cot, I dreamt of Nanny. She was in a grassy patch of land against a grey sky and dunes. She was calling my name.

I awoke to Jackson on the intercom, telling me to report to the observation room.

Jackson and Cox were staring at the surveillance screen. Jackson looked back at me, his eyes wide. "There's vegetation at the sight! Why didn't you say anything?"

"There wasn't anything to see." I looked at the screen from our live camera feed of the surrounding areas. It was just like in the dream, only now a huge tree was in the middle of the black debris, with grass emerging from its trunk and spreading towards the rocky grey ground. Roots looped in and out of the ground, and its limbs were tall and wide, stretching outward like the trees you'd see in the Serengeti.

What the hell is going on?

Jackson blinked. "Is…is someone out there?"

Passing between one of the black twisted debris and a root, was a woman wearing a blue dress and a red headwrap.

I'd know that headwrap from anywhere. "Nanny?"

"We need to report this to HQ," Cox said. "There's other life here? Human life?"

"McFadden, you said that was your grandmother?" Jackson looked incredulous.

I nodded. "We have to go see."

After much deliberating and choosing which defensive weapons to bring (I grabbed the shield, Cox took the stun gun), we took the rover out and drove to the site. Seeing the path on the horizon was like looking at a drawing in the middle of a white page. Grass was indeed growing around the debris, and in the center of it all was this tree, an acacia tree according to Robot.

When our feet landed on the grass, we felt a wave of warmth. Robot piped out, "Oxygen levels detected."

I looked at Cox. "It can't be."

We kept our helmets on but walked through the strangely warm, grassy area, and towards the large tree.

There Nanny was, sitting right along a large root, that upon closer inspection was an indigo-purple tone.

She reached out for me. "Baby girl!"

I let her come close, and even through the suit, she felt real. Tears started to come down. She smiled at me, then said, "Take the helmet off! It's fine, I think."

"Not this time," I tell her. Is this really her? "How are you here?"

She fixed her glasses. "Do I even need these now? I been watching you, baby girl. I'm so proud, I can't believe you're on a planet! And one for Black people? This is history you know. But I can't say how I'm here right now. All I remember is seeing you get hurt and then this tree showed up and now I can be here, on the other side."

"Other side?" Cox questioned, but I had already turned away, typing out what Nanny said.

"We have to tell Jackson and the others."

Nanny looked at me. "Oh. Leaving already?"

I grin at her. "We'll be back. Robot, can you do a scan of Nanny, this tree, and the surrounding plants?"

Robot whirred around, while I took pictures and Cox looked around, amazed.

Then, I don't know what possessed her, but she rolled her helmet back.

"Cox!"

She took a big breath in. "Nanny's right! I can breathe. The air feels good too."

This might bite us in the ass later, but I did the same. I was breathing! Not only that, the warmth was unbelievable, so inviting that I wanted to take my whole suit off. It was humid. Not dry like the ship, where we gotta slap cocoa butter on every second.

This made no sense. What caused the growth? What type of plants are these? They look like ferns and flowers but a little different, the coloration off.

How the hell was Nanny here?

We soon leave. I'm full of questions and can't really take in the fact that Nanny is here right now. Honestly, it was hard, seeing her older, not the young woman in the picture. Her blue dress and red headwrap was what she started wearing after I got married and I don't want to think about those years.

LOG 5

Robot's report:

The atmosphere surrounding the site is still inhospitable (good thing we had the sense to put our helmets back on before we left). No explanation for why there is oxygen and heat present on the site—Acacia Zero.

The vegetation is a hybrid of some sort; recognizable flora from Earth, predominantly west and central African (palm leaves, snake plants, elephant grass and sorghum) and North American, particularly from South Carolina (geraniums, wild indigo). A component that is unrecognizable, like the new colorations of dark purple the shapes of stems and leaves being narrower is present in all the flora.

Nanny is unrecognizable matter. She feels physical but her make-up isn't human. Is she an alien that scanned my picture of her somehow? Is she an attempt to sabotage us?

Jackson says we should tell HQ but something tells me we shouldn't. It's the same feeling that tells me Nanny is who she says she is. Primitus 400 is truly a class one planet, with little to no chance of sustaining human life without terraforming tools, like Winterbottom's. If they see that there's vegetation and oxygenated air? They will take this planet for themselves.

Jackson believes they'll help us. He acts as if they raised him or something.

"It was their money that put him through school," Cox reminded me, as I braided her hair (she claims she likes the way I braid mine and wants the same style of wavy cornrows). "They invested in his brain early, and wanna make good on it."

For people who invested, they sure don't care enough about his mission—but I know what'll happen. If Primitus 400 is successful, he'll go on to do larger and greater things for UTA. They can claim his genius as their own and bring more people in, more funding. Would he be free to live out his life here, or forced to do UTA's bidding?

Cox leans against my thighs as I spray water on her finished braids. "Maybe he needs to get out there and see for himself."

LOG 6

Robot reported that my blood was the catalyst for all this growth. It seems when I was hurt by the dust storm, my blood activated the slumbering bacteria and microorganisms. But why an Acacia tree? Why is Nanny appearing? Is the planet a type of blank slate, a tabula rasa for foreign entities like us, reflecting our literal makeup?

Cox wants to try and bleed on the ground as well.

"I wanna see what my blood blooms. I doubt any ancestors will show up." She gives a half-hearted laugh. None of the dead relatives she knew supported her transition.

Jackson is hesitant. He wants to tell us no, but those replacements for the dome are late so there's nothing else for us to do.

We poured Cox's blood a few feet away right where the grass ended in Acacia Zero.

"Whoever has a listening ear, let my piece grow here," she had prayed.

"Amen, Ase," I add, though I wasn't expecting this to be a spiritual moment. Why would I not? I am seeing Nanny.

She had come over to see what we were up to. She wanted to talk but I told her we had to go back.

"Isn't Nanny the one who inspired you?" Cox asked in the rover.
"Yes."

"Why aren't you talking to her? I know we don't fully know what's going on but, it would be nice to hear her voice again, right?"

I shrugged. "I wanna figure everything out first." It's not fully true. I don't know if I want to talk to Nanny. Every time I see her smile I'm reminded of when I wasn't seeing it, when I needed it and it wasn't there.

LOG 7

Another tree had grown; Robot shared that this was a moringa tree, although triple its earthly size. When we arrived, it looked like a giant bright green bush with deep purple bark.

Coming out of the thicket of leaves was a tall dark-skinned woman, with a red and yellow wrap around her waist and matching wrap across her chest. She beckoned to Cox, who walked towards her. I heard them speaking, but I didn't understand the language. I walked around with Robot, keeping an eye on the two of them, while sweating in my suit.

When Cox returned, her light brown face was wet with tears.

"Her name is Ufeko. She's Imbangalan from Angola. She's — she's seen me and embraces me. The real me—Tisha. She's seen me my whole life. She's the same as me and wants to be here on this planet with me. I didn't think—" she started to sob. I hold her close, wanting to protect her from the painful memories that summoned the tears. These were healing tears too, no? Cox isn't alone.

What is this planet?

LOG 8

I miss Cox.

She's been living out there, in Moringa Zero, for the past three days. No helmet, suit-less.

She was supposed to bring an offering to Ufeko and come right back. We both were supposed to go but I couldn't figure out what to bring Nanny. A pink lemonade pouch? Pack of noodles, space edition?

My desire to see Cox again made me settle for the cocoa butter stick I still had.

A river had grown from her blood, resting between Moringa Zero and Acacia Zero, lapping a few miles down towards a grey crater. I drive past it and find Cox crouching on the bank, an indigo woven basket next to her.

She was wearing her sleep suit, a simple pair of shorts and a bralette, but her skin was glowing, her hair shining.

She smiled at me, noticed my awe. "It's the sap from your tree," she said. "It keeps me warm whenever I need to move off the land." She pointed at the basket. "Ufeko taught me how to do this. She's showing me so many things."

I followed her through tall grass towards her moringa tree, where small bowls of sap were stored together.

She passed one to me. "Try it."

I sip it once. My God—it was delicious! Like sweet potato or candied yams. It filled my stomach and warmed me so deeply, I had to take my suit off after.

Freeing my body from the suit was heavenly. The grass tickled my feet, the air, the atmosphere caressed my skin. Warmth and moisture like I haven't felt in years. How can this planet produce heat being so far from the sun?

I leave the questions for later. I walk with Cox, seeing how the land her blood had created grew. I look over at Acacia Zero and see not much had grown since my last visit.

Cox—Tisha—touched my shoulder. "You should speak with her, Kofa. It'll grow if you do. If you honor her."

My picture would be better than the cocoa butter, right? I go back to the ship to bring that as well.

Stevens comes back with me, wanting to try his blood. We left behind Jackson, who is recording everything, drafting separate reports for ourselves and the future people of the planet, and UTA HQ, still waiting for the replacement dome.

"Come and see," I told Jackson. "Try your blood."

"We still don't know why this is happening. We really shouldn't be eating anything or allow our skin to be exposed!"

"We know why. It's a symbiotic relationship. The planet's microorganisms are activated by our blood and in turn we live in the habitat best suited for us. We helped awaken this planet, so it'll sustain us."

Jackson suddenly leaps to his feet. "*Is* that the relationship, though? What if we die in three years, our bodies eaten by the organisms? What if we're overtaken by them?" He starts pacing. "I shouldn't even be letting you back on the ship. You risk harming all of us with a potential pathogen that Robot has yet to detect, even with you quarantining. And, and whose ideal habitat is this for anyway? A hot and humid climate? No. I'll be staying in the dome, where it'll be safe. We can still live here without giving into this planet."

"What if we're supposed to connect? Why do you think our ancestors are realized—or in this physical plane with us?"

Jackson stares at me. "My ancestors are on earth, in a graveyard in Beauford South Carolina. They not coming to see me."

I touch his shoulder. I don't know how to convince him, help him see that there is beauty in this possible new world.

He looks up at me. "Why aren't you just living out there, if it's so safe?"

"I'm still collecting data."

"Robot can do that."

"I don't want you alone."

"You're convinced that's your grandmother. Why aren't you with her, like Cox is with her ancestor? Besides," he gives a weak smile, "I'm going to be alone anyway. It seems like no one can resist being out there."

I feel some of the thoughts that pooled at the bottom of my heart spill out. "Sometimes the memory of a person and their true self don't match up. Maybe a part of me feels like Nanny's still back on earth."

The Nanny who loved and supported me, not the one who—

I stop my memories from flooding back to me.

LOG 9

I left Stevens with Tisha and find my way to my Acacia tree.

I nestle the picture between the trunk and a root. I touch the knots and grooves, thinking, remembering.

Nanny appeared, leaning against the trunk, smiling. She picked up the picture. "I miss those days. All I had on my mind was raising Pookie and keeping up with work."

I hand her the cocoa butter stick. "Remember these?"

She laughed, taking the stick and rubbing it between her palms. Smelled it. "It's been so long." She looked at me with her eyes that could see everything.

I suddenly felt the urge to check on Tisha. "I'm gonna go—"

"I'm so sorry Sankofa, for how I treated you when—"

"I gotta check on Tisha and Stevens—"

"I shamed you into marrying that man and you weren't ready."

"It's ok, you weren't the only—"

"It's not okay, baby. I see how it hurt your heart so. How you couldn't trust yourself. You doubted that inner voice that was so strong. I dampened it out of fear of you becoming a single mother like me and I was wrong for that—wrong for that fear too."

"Stop!"

Everything was quiet. The beautiful colors of the trees and grass and Nanny's headwrap blurred into a watercolor mess.

I choke out the tears, the watercolor vision dropping onto the grass. Words slur together, words locked away after a marriage and divorce and trying to be fine so everyone forgot it even happened.

Why did you make me feel like used goods? Why did you push me into this, abandon me, and never say anything after I left him?

82

I cried lakes and rivers of anger, loneliness, betrayal. Nanny sat there and listened, took it. Once the tears slowed and the years of pain subsided, she slowly walked over to me and took my hands. Her all-seeing brown eyes were soft. Eyes that gave me comfort, joy, and pain.

"I'm so sorry baby. Please forgive me."

I hugged her. She smelled like lavender, her favorite herb. The pain was still there, but I felt myself starting to grow out of it.

As I head to the rover for one last trip to the ship, I saw little monsteras sprout from the roots, bent backward towards the warm and beautiful atmosphere.

LOG 10

I've been living out here for two weeks. So has the rest of the crew.

I'm sitting at one of the roots with Nanny. I'm sipping sap and can see grass and trees for miles. Behind us is a field of indigo stalks, that we're still experimenting with. Will it help us produce clothing or living spaces? I'm excited to find out its place in this world.

I'm finding more of mine. Everyday Tisha and I sit at our trees and thank our ancestors; Nanny, Ufeko, and others we have yet to experience (Stevens has had both his parents appear, Williamson had three ancient ancestors come!). We sit and let the atmosphere hug our skin. We listen to the dusty wind that blows cleanly through our land and rejoice when we hear new creatures born of our blood and this planet, scurrying through the leaves. We've identified with Robot at least two new species that are growing and feeding off our waste. They have the ability to migrate off our land and nest inside the craters, craters that then produce marshland. The ecosystem is vibrant.

Tisha is vibrant. We study the six Zero sites together, lose ourselves in the pollinated air that call to ancient memories, present sight, and future visions. We fold ourselves into the small corners of trees and under hills and I braid her hair with indigo and she massages my body with sap, which has fattened me up quite a bit, all the while Robot whirrs around, collecting data.

Jackson let us keep Robot; he's using the emergency Robot, since we've already violated UTA rules and it doesn't seem like they care. Their negligence is our blessing though, as no one seems perturbed by the false reports (also a blessing that we have a shared email address so we can check if anything changes on our tablets).

Jackson is still waiting for the equipment. Tisha thinks we should reach out to him one more time. "Primitus 400 (we're still listening for the name of this planet) is growing. What will happen to him if he doesn't connect? Is he gonna stay in his barren bubble? Will he reach out to UTA for help, another crew?"

Dread pooled in my stomach. He would have to reveal everything, and we would lose our mission to bring others here one day; we would lose our new world. Would he betray the mission he birthed to do things the "right" way?

I talk to Nanny about this. "How can I convince him that this is what he must do to survive?"

"You can't," she said. "He's caught in his mind, like a labyrinth. He'll have to find his way out. Can you trust that he won't divulge the fullness of this planet to those he feels he owes himself to? Can you trust this planet to do what it needs to do to protect itself?"

I make one last trip to the ship. The sap protects me from the cold, and I breathe through a collard wreathe, an oxygen-rich Moss Zero descendant of the collard green. It's wrapped around my head and across my nose like a veil.

The ship is vacant. I go through the hallways and find Jackson in the observation room. A cot is near the surveillance station, with containers of food scattered everywhere.

"Hey Tyrell."

He turns to me, his eyes wide. "Sankofa."

He sees the glow of sap, my face haloed by the wreath. My wider body.

He pulls at his mustache. "The materials for the dome arrive tomorrow. I'm starting right away. Once that first dome is built, I'll request more materials."

"Do you need another crew?"

"It's supposed to be just us before civilians come. I'm sticking to that."

"We can breathe, Jackson. Even through the dust storms, we can breathe."

He looked incredulous, then exasperated. "I can't just abandon everything I've expected, everything I've known."

"It's not abandonment, it's expansion."

"I must keep to Winterbottom's method. It's foolproof. You'll see. It won't potentially alter our DNA or have a deadly outcome in the years to come."

"We have tools to—" I stop myself. Breathe. "Jackson. We will be here. Your ancestors are here. This planet isn't waiting. It's moving and growing, just like our people have, for all time."

That was the last time I saw Jackson.

LOG 11

It's been several moon cycles. The land grows every day. Tisha, Stevens, and I are lead explorers and examine every inch of new life. I spend my nights in Tisha's arms and those nights have now created sweet kicks and tumbles in my belly. Williamson will be our midwife, as she listens to her ancestors and her trees to see how to bring this baby to us. I too am awaiting ancients (older ancestors, like Ufeko) to reveal my own spiritual birthing practice.

In all this time, we had not heard or seen from Jackson. The same false reports are submitted, but they stopped two moon cycles ago.

It wasn't until we were researching a new border of our land that we came to a joyful sight.

A dome cracked open like an eggshell, with a glorious Baobab tree bursting out of it.

Vade Retro Satana
by
Maurice Broaddus

SO-COMMAND\TEMPLAR-NAVCOM-INFO: All systems functioning within normal parameters.

Peacekeeping missions were always the most difficult assignment for Lt. Macia Branson. Not that she longed for the combat which had been much of her duty in the Service of the Order, but the reality was that it was still war conditions only with the setting lowered to a slow broil.

The Ouje villagers sat around a fire. Led by one of the church novices, their idols and totems were piled high and lit aflame. Several members pounded out a rhythm that was both mournful and hopeful. The drumming tugged at a part of Macia's soul, the way an old vidgraph of distant relatives was both familiar and alien. Memories locked in a box, hidden in the back of a closet where all memories were treasured and then forgotten.

The planet's atmosphere was perfectly hospitable and the Ouje people not that different from humans like her. However, the Service of the Order required all Service of the Order soldiers who provided security for a missionary colony to remain in their biomech suits. The world and its sensations filtered through its mechanical membrane. It provided a barrier between their people and the disciples; her surroundings appeared through digital feeds along her visor. Macia stood on the outside of the sacred circle.

"Look at them." Prefect Sergeant Rhys Moll stalked the perimeter of the circle. He was a short pug of a man; even the hand unit of his biomech suit looked like five bolts fitted on a stump. When out of his suit, he smelled of onions suffused with garlic, and a hint of something vaguely alcoholic always lilted on his breath. His hair was a nest of greasy curls; his nose looked as if it had been flattened by a plank. "They'd be lost without us. We've done some good work here."

"Daniel told me that this was usually when their *Alawe Modu* festival would occur," she said. A twinge of guilt nagged her when she referred to Unoko as Daniel. Daniel, like her parents, was what the church referred to as an "Indigenous leader." These leaders were either locals who quickly took to the Gospel and demonstrated promise as a teacher or someone who held such sway in the community that they became a key target for conversion. Unoka was targeted for acquisition early on. The Order decided his new designation would be Daniel. "The family elders gather the tribe and sacrifice a *yamma* to their ancestors. The blood soaks into the ground for those who had gone before them to enjoy the meat cooked and eaten by the family. Any children coming of age carve masks for themselves for their masquerade dance, to learn the secret language of the tribe."

"See what I mean? Lost. We saved them."

"Salvation is the point," Macia said.

"Not just their souls. We saved them from themselves. They were hacking each other to bits long before we came here." Rhys was the kind of devout who liked to hear his opinion spouted without contradiction. He was one of the first soldiers Macia met when she was assigned to the Templar Paton. Though she'd received the Purple Cross, he was suspect of her readiness as a soldier. He had no concept of how much blood she'd spilled in Jesus' name. She'd grown quite adept at ignoring him.

"Not according to Biafra Oshun." Macia mentally chided herself for taking his bait. She hated to be drawn into these conversations. She had the same lessons in training and didn't need them regurgitated on duty.

"We bring order and civility," Rhys continued. "It takes, what, two languages just for one of them to leave one village and get to the next."

"It's pretty typical for an Ouje to know six languages. The language of their family, the language of the tribe, the language of commerce . . ."

"Ridiculous," Rhys cut her off.

The words of a devout had a way of crawling under her skin with the sting of guilt for not believing more. Some nights she wondered if she missed the point of her own faith. Left alone in her quarters, hour after hour waiting for sleep until time lost all meaning, with only her thoughts and the silence of the Lord. Snatching up spiritual crumbs—a verse here, an encouraging word there—to knit the thing she called her faith together. She felt like an incomplete bad poem. She prayed against her savage thoughts late at night. It was the easiest way to come down from the adrenaline rush of being on constant alert and stims administered by the biomech. When she did close her eyes, she dreamt of blood, but she always awoke covered in a thin sheet of sweat.

The Ouje milled about, dressed in their finest tunics and embroidered *karosses*. Each family's clothing was patterned or colored according to an Ouje cultural theme. Many people traveled great distances to celebrate the successful harvest. The village was hundreds of kilometers from the central megapolis and quite rural. The people roasted *wollof*, a tuber of some sort, and stewed *yamma*, a small animal that looked rather like a goat, for *Alawe Modu*. Herds of *yamma* grazed in a fenced-in berne just outside of the village. The spices from the stew wafted throughout the village, its scent so thick and cloying it set off Macia's biomech air filtration unit. Bowls of leafy vegetables soaked in a cream produced by the *yamma* were set on each table. People wandered about and ate as they willed. Most ate to excess.

"I see we haven't wrung out all of their pagan traditions and superstitious ways of thinking." Rhys took any prolonged silence as an invitation to speak.

"I never thought we had to. My parents always thought that the best novices took a people's customs and stories and redeemed them. They viewed all cultures as opportunities to connect to worshiping the Lord."

"How did that work out for them?" Rhys's eyes widened as if realizing he had stepped over a line. Rather than apologizing, he quickly moved on. "There is a great danger to the path of syncretism. One day you are 'communing' with the spirits and then are told to think of it as prayer to the Holy Spirit, next thing you know, we've added all sorts of new rituals to the church and forgotten the name of the God we serve. It only leads to spiritual confusion and dilution of the faith."

"I think I'll check the perimeter."

Macia walked away from him, each step weighted by the obligations of faith. When the church came to her planet, some of the novices doubted that her people even had souls because of the language barrier. Her family's facility with languages brought them to prominence. The hardest part of her transition to Christianity was how she had to shed her culture to find acceptance. For the church to believe that she believed and repented of her old ways. In all her travels since, she never returned to her home village. She would be as much a stranger there as a novice on their first mission.

The children began their ritual. Wearing masks too big for their heads, they danced around the fire. Excited, their joy almost contagious, happy for a moment to hide who they were. To pretend to be something else. To be seen as something almost ready. Tonight, they hid behind masks and called down the spirits of their ancestors. On Sunday, as the Service of the Order had implemented a new calendar week for the Ouje, they would serve as altar attendants.

Lord, I believe. Help me with my unbelief. It was the centurion's prayer from the New Testament and the only prayer that truly resonated with her.

SO-COMMAND\TEMPLAR-NAVCOM-INFO: Establishing parietal operculum

Though the planet Nambra was on the outer rim of the Galactic Mission, the Service of the Order quickly took over the spaceports of the Angwen territory which became the staging area for their missionary work. Only a couple of conflict-free years had passed, but the novices, church planters with mission command, now saw a record number of converts. Angwen was one of the most religious colonies on the planet. Churches dotted the landscape. The Angwen borders secure, the Ouje people's life was finding a measure of routine again.

Security had been heightened after a bomb threat to the marketplace. The presence of so many Service of the Order soldiers only made the fear more of a reality. Food shortages and power interruptions were one thing, but checkpoints and the constant parade of armed guards wouldn't allow the Ouje to push their fears to the back of their minds. But there was something more, something on the Ouje people's faces when they saw Macia. People who looked like her, people from a colony much like hers flinched away from her as she strode by. Their village recalled her ancestral home. So much so, she half-expected her cousins to come tearing out of the *dondo* doors, having snuck a piece of baked pastry from her grandmother's counter.

An older gentleman sidled towards her. Out of reflex, she regripped her pulse rifle before she recognized him. Daniel wore the robes of a village elder. Close-cropped silver hair topped Daniel's head and led into a beard that framed his dark-skinned face and came to a point on his chin. His bushy eyebrows made his face seem severe. Tall and thin with a slight stoop, he leaned heavily on his walking staff most of the time, but when he approached young women, he straightened to full attention. A mad twinkle filled his eyes as if he engaged in a secret courtship ritual with every woman he talked to.

"There are many here who believe as your friend does." Daniel wore an odd expression like a man watching a frog work out calculus.

"He's . . . not my friend." It took a moment for her translator matrix to recalibrate. The Ouje people's constant language switching proved challenging for her biomech to keep up with. Macia wished that she could try to learn some of the Ouje's tongue for herself, working alongside them. That her gift with languages would be put to more use than her skills at killing.

"Still, some believe in the . . . Word, as you put it, so much they are gripped with a fervor. I look around the village I once knew and many have taken to destroying shrines that had stood for generations and oppose any local tradition or culture that they cannot trace back to your Bible. *Alawe Modu* isn't what it used to be," he said. "Attendance is down this season. I worry that when my generation passes away, this celebration of life and rebirth and gratitude will die with them."

"Some churches have banned all *Alawe Modu* festivities entirely. We were lucky to have this version of it sanctioned."

"Thankfully, some churches can find room for both traditions."

"Maybe this version of the *Alawe Modu* can unite all of the Ouje villages."

"Maybe. As our people say, when a group urinates together, it foams." Daniel smiled widely.

"It may be too much Horta for some." Macia threw her head back in laughter. Horta the original religion that the Ouje practiced. Their culture and religion were so intertwined, the Order frowned on any remnants of either.

"Christian or Horta, this isn't about faith. It is about being Ouje. Anyway, I shouldn't tarry. I wouldn't want to get you in trouble for speaking to a 'dirty' Horta."

"I consider this part of the Service of the Order's evangelism mission. Building bridges between faiths to create a dialogue."

"You are a wise woman, Macia Branson."

Macia was never good at accepting compliments, believing each one was actually meant for someone they confused with her. She began to inspect her weapon. "I still suspect such a dialogue would be frowned upon."

"By many sides. Your suit is little more than a large target." Daniel bowed, leaving her to her security sweep.

Her patrol took her past a series of *dondos*. Each structure housed several families. In the shadows of a doorway, a grandmother passed a few slips of paper to her granddaughter. Like so many of the artisan class, her fingers were painstakingly gnarled, having worked intricate detail into wood during her many years, imbuing them with life and spirit. The words on the paper translated to the Republic of Nia'quong. The notes were the protocurrency a few of the Ouje began to circulate. The old woman clutched her granddaughter's hand with the bill inside as if an important part of her Ouje identity was in the tiny grasp.

Like a ghost haunting their national identity. Macia pretended not to see it.

The idea of countries, or borders, was a concept the Ouje lacked until the church arrived. It carved up regions for those they had converted and armed borders from those they hadn't. Nambra had been held up as a model of missionary work until civil war broke out a few months ago. The Ouje who secretly practiced Horta attempted to create a refuge, Nia'quong, a country within the country Angwen, sparking a civil war. After months of brutal fighting and countless dead, and with the peacekeeping militia of the church in place, the surviving Ouje were one country again. It was a chapter of their history they sought to forget.

Except for Biafra Oshun. A pro-Nia'quong independence activist, she led protests across the region. She protested the economic, social, and political marginalization of the Horta Ouje. None of them were a part of the ruling council appointed by the church. Though the Ouje were mixed on separatist cause, her last protest turned violent: the Service of the Order had to open fire on them. Charged with conspiracy, part of an illegal operation due to her work with the underground militia, there was an open warrant for her detention.

Watching the grandmother reminded Macia of the first time she met her new family after her parents were killed on the mission field. They welcomed her with all smiles and hugs. They ushered her to her room, her very own room she wouldn't have to share with anyone. Crisp sheets folded over the bed. The tall window peered over a wide yard. They closed the door behind them to allow her time to acclimate. She dropped to her knees and sobbed. Her aunt slipped back into her room and knelt beside Macia, even though the little girl was beyond consoling.

"I'm not going to tell you not to cry," her aunt said. "I'm not going to lie to you and tell you everything is going to be okay. In these short years of yours, you already know that's not the case. So, you cry. Cry for your mother and father who are gone from you now. Cry for the childhood lost to you now. Cry for all the hardness you have yet to face."

Her aunt patted Macia on the back with her left hand and fished in her pockets with the other. She remembered what her aunt wore: a simple blue frock, hand-sewn and ill-fitting. Over it was an apron. The entire front of it was a series of pockets. It seemed like her aunt had all the secrets of the universe carried in those pockets. She removed a small wooden bird carrying an egg on its back. The bird's head was craned backward as if attempting to peck the egg away. Macia's tears ebbed, now curious, as her aunt placed it before them.

"There was a custom our people had, before the coming of The Order. We believe it is not wrong to go back for that which once was or was lost to us now. The best way to hold onto who we are has always been through the stories we pass onto our children."

And every night, Macia's aunt told her stories right up until Macia joined the Service of the Order. That was the way she chose to remember it now. Back then, the stories got on her nerves and she quickly tired of hearing the same old tales over and over again.

SO-COMMAND\TEMPLAR-NAVCOM-INFO: Navcom interface offline

The digital telemetry of her helmet subsystem went blank. Macia military experience reduced her first response to equipment failure to tapping it, and she tapped her wrist panel as her displays failed. Next, she attempted a partial re-boot of her navcom system. The link was an information tether to her orbiting ship, the Templar Paton. The roar of the approaching airship alerted her just as quickly as her malfunctioning proximity detector.

The ship hovered above the village, its thrusters scattering the yamma as it prepared to land in the berne.

"Rhys, you copy?" Macia yelled.

"Barely. Lots of interference."

"You have a skimmer due to land?"

"None on the schedule. I already have a squad moving to intercept."

"Good. I'll meet you there."

Macia broke into a half jog, the motors in her leg units speeding her along. She arrived in time to see the ship pivot, lock onto the arriving troops, and open fire. The inhuman whine of missiles screamed across the berne. Macia dropped to her knees. Three soldiers opened fire over her head. The ground shook with the impact of two more missiles. The ship lurched. Its cargo hold opened like a yawning mouth and deposited a contingent of enemy combatants.

"What do we have?" Macia ran across the berne to provide cover for Rhys and the rest of her men to reach an outcrop.

"A mass of hostiles. Fifteen meters from our position. We lost navcom just before the ambush."

"I don't believe in coincidence. This sounds coordinated. Wounded?"

"It's bad. They lured us in, took out a lot of us. What's the plan?" Rhys peeked around the corner to survey the scene.

"Same as it ever was. Catch them between us and other units. I'll take point. You and you," she pointed out two men, "on my six. Rhys, bring up the rear."

Small weapon fire erupted from all sides. The ship crashed into the side of the building next to her. Without telemetry readings, she lost her bearings. Another blast of heat, and the air grew thick with hot gases. Something exploded, sending her biomech suit hurtling through the air. Her flight was stopped short by a metal wall, and though her biomech suit absorbed much of the blast, the force and the impact made her head swim.

USER-COMMAND\TEMPLAR-NAVCOM-INFO: Catastrophic systems failure. Initiate shutdown and self-repair protocols

Macia hated unconsciousness. Drifting off to sleep often proved difficult enough, but the slow murky confusion of regaining consciousness left her nauseous. Like swimming to the surface of black waters. Pressure bubbled about her head, making her feel vague and uncertain.

Her eyes open, she craned her head about as best she could within the biomech suit. Without power to the servos in her arms that aided her movements, her arms slumped like leaden weights at her side. She was trapped inside her biomech suit, which was little more than a form-fitting coffin in this state. She sat against a wall, her legs akimbo, and her weapon useless at her side. Her head rang. Another wave of nausea swept over her. Unable to move, she was little more than a monument to a fallen soldier. A few meters away, Rhys struggled to his feet, the left arm of his biomech suit shorn off. It took a few moments for her to process that it meant his arm was also missing. He limped about, lost, and uncertain.

A contingent of enemy troops rounded up the remaining soldiers of The Order. They dragged the novices out to the center of the clearing in full view of the soldiers. Macia struggled to move, but she feared something was broken because every movement sent a fresh spike of pain to her skull. The troops parted as their leader approached.

Biafra Oshun appeared a lot younger than Macia had imagined. She moved to a beat that was soft at first but seemed to gain force with each step. She had a power, an intensity about her that buffeted the novices like they were caught in a windstorm. Her face remained unadorned, striking in its cold beauty. She wore her head shaved clean, her skin as dark as unearthed pottery, the darkest shade of brown Macia had ever seen. Biafra's eyes, both haunted and weary, scanned the crowd.

"Who is in charge here?" Biafra demanded, refusing to speak any of the commerce tongues, instead using one of the old languages.

"I am." A novice struggled to his feet. One of Biafra's men shoved him forward.

Biafra drew a weapon with such speed, Macia didn't register it until the woman had already fired. The novice's body stood erect for a heartbeat or two until it realized it was dead and dropped. "I asked who is in charge here?"

SO-COMMAND\TEMPLAR-NAVCOM-INFO: Partial power established. Back-up systems nominal. Non-essential systems offline while charging.

"You are in charge," Macia said. Her biomech suit needed time to charge. All eyes turned toward her. "But I am responsible for these people's lives."

"You?" Biafra spat. She turned to face the crowd of Ouje that had gathered around the spectacle. "*These people* prey on the vulnerable and desperate. *These people* come armed with a Bible and guns, and I don't know which of the two is more destructive. *These people* come to tell us to reject our customs and history and teach us to self-hate. These people have taken away our spirituality and left us with religion."

"If I have a credit, it can be used for good or evil," Macia managed. "Whose hands it is in, what lies in their heart, determines how it's used."

"Funny how you gravitate straight to currency to plead your case. Your mission trips provide an excuse for you to mine our resources and 'trade' with us. You prop up a few leaders, make them wealthy, so they are more amenable to spread your 'Word.' I feel sorry for you. The things you must do to yourself and your thinking to remain so . . . conditioned. You are thrice damned: a tool of the oppressor, a traitor to your people, and a betrayer to yourself."

"Don't pretend to know me."

"Abducted as a child, indoctrinated, and forced to commit acts of violence against your people. I don't need to know you— the story of the 'church' is the same all over. If I had my way, I'd put you on trial and indict you for the same crimes that were initially perpetrated against you. There is a kind of poetic beauty to that."

"I know who I am. I found my faith." *I know who I am,* Macia thought. *Lord, I believe. Help me with my unbelief.* She rubbed her hand against the inside of her biomech suit, feeling the hum as her suit recharged. Her fingertips had developed callouses from years of holding weapon grips and she still felt the occasional itch of them ghostly against her skin. Soon her suit would be fully powered up. She only needed to stall a little longer. "Who are you?"

"I have seen how the church treats dissenters. They have made me what I am today. They hobble us with religion while stripping away our spirituality. They came here with their Bibles and guns, put the guns to our heads, and told us to worship. Herded to their churches like prisoners of war. They murdered our . . . ancestors.'"" Biafra drew her weapon again. "You are responsible for their lives? Then you are responsible for this."

Biafra motioned for one of her men to bring Rhys over. She pressed her weapon to the side of his head, then leveled her eyes at Macia with a cool detachment. Rhys' mouth moved wordlessly, rhythmically. Was it a prayer? Was it a plea for Macia to do something, anything to save his life? Without her internal filters, she smelled only her own fearful sweat, which made bile rise in her throat. She screamed, feeling every bit the helpless prisoner in her biomech suit. As if enticed by Macia's screams, Biafra squeezed the trigger and Rhys' brains splattered against the nearby wall. His blood ran down the wall in an imperfect smear. It looked no different from the blood of any of the Ouje dead.

Macia counted her opponents. By the way she moved, surefooted and fluid, Biafra was the most dangerous. Despite the swelling chaos, the jeers of Horta supporters among the crowd, and the waving of weapons, only a half dozen people remained of Biafra's ambush party. Even without a pulse rifle, with her biomech suit pumping stims into her system, she would soon satisfy the cry of innocent blood.

Macia had been taught that she fought for the church and the safety of its people. Throughout her training she was told that she was a "holy soldier" under divine provision. Many a senior novice absolved their soldiers of any crimes committed if they had obeyed their orders, orders passed down directly from the Holy Spirit. So in the eyes of God, the soldiers were blameless, they were simply carrying out God's will. God judged soldiers differently from civilians. Once the "hostile relations" conditions were met, judgment protocols were in effect. This could only end with the death of either Macia or Biafra.

There would be blood.

"Kill us together or leave them alone." Daniel pushed through the gathered crowd. He stared down Biafra's men, taking the steel from the spines of many who had been jeering only moments ago. Some of Daniel's followers slipped past him and stood in front of Macia and the novices.

"This doesn't concern you, Unoka," Biafra said.

"You do this in our name."

"What I do, I do for all Ouje."

"We aren't threatened by stories, we learn from them. We don't believe one story should destroy another."

SO-COMMAND\TEMPLAR-NAVCOM-INFO: All systems functioning within nominal parameters

Macia's hand crept toward her weapon. Her biomech suit was as close to optimum as she needed. With Daniel's people running interference and with her reinforcements descending upon them, Macia knew she could end this with a single shot. She locked eyes with Biafra. The revolutionary's eyes betrayed the fact that she knew her upper hand was lost. Macia fingered the trigger of her pulse rifle. Every instinct in her commanded her to fire on this enemy of the Service of the Order. Her blood screamed at her. Her training screamed at her. Her history screamed at her. Her parents screamed at her. Daniel outstretched his hand. They were all lost children struggling to find their way.

Macia lowered her rifle.

Biafra nodded.

SO-COMMAND\TEMPLAR-NAVCOM-INFO: All systems functioning within normal parameters

"You let her go." Daniel's gaze was shrewd.

Macia had been young once. Lost and angry, searching for any life preserver to cling to. To provide her direction. In the church, in the Service of the Order, her anger found purpose. She wondered if her eyes mirrored Biafra's. Macia wondered what her superiors suspected. The official story was that the rebels, having made their point, left before the Service of the Order reinforcements arrived from the Templar Paton.

"Consider it a judgment call," Macia said. "We were outnumbered. Too many civilians around. Casualties would've been high on all sides and I didn't want to risk innocent lives. We can send in a fully armed squad into the mountains after her if necessary."

"Assuming she hasn't gone completely underground."

"Assuming."

Daniel convinced the village to continue with the *Alawe Modu*. The rains had stopped and it was neither too hot nor too cold nor too dry. The first kits returned with the season and songs welcomed them. This season of the year was worth celebrating, he cajoled. Old men sat on logs and warmed their bodies, waiting for the masquerade dance to begin.

"I watched you throughout the festival. You're curious," he said.

"Faith is a curious thing for me. So fleeting and uncertain."

"What she said about your story, the kidnapping and indoctrination, how close was she?"

"It is a chapter of my life I consider closed and don't choose to remember."

"What a people choose to remember about its past, the stories they pass down, informs who they are. Sets the boundaries of their identity. We remember the pain of our past to mourn, to heal, and to learn. Only in that way can we ensure the same mistakes are not repeated."

"What I lost is my faith in humanity."

"Do you recall what your Jesus said about the faith the size of the mustard seed? It's not about the amount of faith so much as the object of it. Doubts are what make it real. What makes it yours." He took her hand, gently steadying her, helping her forward. She withdrew her hand.

"I got it. I can find my own way." Her tone was almost accusatory.

"I had no doubt." Daniel held his hands up. "I simply tend to leap at any excuse to invite a young woman to dance."

She looked at him for a moment and then to the masquerade dancers. Her body ached, though not from the usual bruises which followed a skirmish. Hers was a soul weary fatigue. Each exhalation burned her chest. Her breath hitched. Her ribs would be sore in the morning. Her legs wobbled under her full weight, but the suit did most of the work.

USER-COMMAND\TEMPLAR-NAVCOM-INFO: Initiate exit protocols

Her biomech suit released a slow hiss as it unsealed. The black stocking of her exosoma served as an interface between her and her biomech suit. Without the suit, she feared her legs might betray her.

The frantic rhythm of the drums rode the same current as her own heartbeat. Her eyes locked onto the dancers. Waiting. Emptying herself of the contradictions and shedding all that was unnecessary. Letting the rhythm of the drumbeat enter her. Find a true place in her. Not worrying about her steps, only being caught up in the music. Returning to a simple truth. To be free.

And Macia danced.

Anansi and the Astronaut
by
Tonya R. Moore

Reeva emerged from her makeshift lab and shelter, groggy from a night of fitful tossing and turning. Her drowsy gaze swept skyward in search of *Proxima b*. Nestled in pale blue pearlescence, the planet dominated the ether, eternally locked in Proxima Centauri's magnetic embrace. The sight was strangely comforting. It was proof that the young astronaut, so far from home and castaway on this lunar island, hadn't completely lost her bearings.

She crossed the distance between her camp and the edge of the indigo sea. Boots sinking into the wet hem of the water, she closed her eyes. She inhaled deeply and listened. Except for the sounds of somnolent waves and the buffeting breeze, Echo-42-Alpha was eerily silent. Her presence aside, this densely forested archipelago seemed devoid of animal life.

Visions of Coquina Beach speared into her mind. Noisy dolphins playfully haunting the estuary. Raucous seabirds crowding the sky. Cicadas mimicking maracas, filling the gnarled mangroves with their endless summer song.

She shoved that pang of yearning for her home planet back into the recesses of her mind. That line of thinking could easily drive even the most stalwart of astronauts stark mad.

Her skin prickled under the long sleeves of her skintight EVA suit. Proxima Centauri's warmth tickled the back of her neck, the pregnant heaviness of the atmosphere already making her sweat. She groaned, regretting her decision not to change into a lighter suit.

The ocean waves shimmied and shifted in lazy, zigzagged oscillations. She almost missed the faint white flicker on the distant gray horizon. Moments later, she smelled the faint burn of lightning clinging to the salty sea air. The sixth sense inherited from her great granny flared into full force. A portentous feeling filled Reeva's bones and began to overflow. Something big and nasty was coming. She could taste its chaotic imminence on the tip of her delicate tongue—the sheer might and madness of an oncoming storm.

The radio on her wrist crackled to life.

"Reeva," prompted a male, thickly Scottish voice. "Status?"

"Good mornin', Jonathan," the vestiges of sleep made her Jamaican accent more pronounced than usual. "All is good. A hurricane is comin.' I'm gonna batten down the hatches and the like."

"The habitat should be able to withstand hurricane-force winds but I wouldn't bank on that if I were you."

"I'll break it down and move further inland. Just in case."

"Reeva–"

She chuckled, cutting him off mid-sentence. "Not a heck of a lot you guys can do about it from the other side of the world, is there?"

A moment of tense silence followed before Jonathan spoke again.

"Please. Be careful."

"Don' worry, man. Been through my fair share of hurricanes. Reeva out."

Reeva contemplated the fulsome sea. It unnerved her. Who knew what horrors lurked beneath that nearly opaque wetness? The eerie silence and stark peoplelessness didn't help. Her childhood habit of singing to calm her fraying nerves surfaced. She found herself humming her favorite Bob Marley song as if to console herself.

"No woman no cry... no woman no cry..."

She dug into her right pocket, fishing out an elastic band. She reached up and caged her hair into a bubbly black puff. She rolled up the sleeves of her suit before jogging back to the fuzzy red cluster of trees.

She couldn't shake the sudden, strange feeling of being absolutely *not* alone.

Nightfall brought howling winds and roaring tidal swells. Windy furies pummeled and pounded at the raggedy coastline. Further inland, ensconced within the thick of the woods, Reeva's habitat held firm. Inside, she sat reading a tattered paperback copy of 2025's prize-winning compendium of new-age Anansi stories. She kept one eye on her computer screen, monitoring the storm's satellite imagery, and ate sporkfuls of her curried goat MRE between page turns.

A blinding flash of white illuminated the habitat's interior. Thunder rumbled closely in its wake. A tremor ran through the ground. A dreadful bellow came from the direction of the sea. Reeva froze mid-sporkful, the book in her other hand slipping from her fingers and hitting the ground with a thud.

She sprang to her feet, heart racing. Suddenly short of breath, she shuddered.

"What, in the name of blessed Jesus, was that?"

More bellows, like the deafening call of a foghorn, filled the turbulent air. Reeva's computer screen started flickering wildly and emitting an urgent beeping noise. Those sounds weren't thunder or any strange element summoned by the storm. Reeva didn't need her great granny's psychic powers to figure that out. The deep, gargantuan cries were far greater in amplitude than the thunder. They swelled. They made the ground shake. They sank deep into Reeva's marrow. They ascended as if sledgehammering their way up from the fathomless belly of the black sea.

"Jonathan, come in!" She pressed down on her wrist radio's transmit button. "Jonathan, wake up!"

"What is it?" came the groggy response. "Everything alright?"

"No. Maybe. I don't know!" she cackled excitedly. "Just listen, man. D'you hear that?"

There was a pause. He followed up with a much more lucid and alarmed, "Good god. What the hell is that noise?"

"The hell would I know?" she demanded. "The sensors are going crazy."

"Listen," she spun around trying to scoop up her gear and explain at the same time. "Somethin's alive out there. Somethin' big. Like really, really big!"

A burst of heavy static cut off his response. All she got was the end of his sentence.

".... out."

"What?"

"Your retrieval team," he repeated. "They're still two Earth days out from your position."

"That long?" she groaned.

An alien conglomerate calling themselves the Tsvangiri Principality contacted Earth in 2023, deeming themselves the governing body responsible for policing all emerging intelligent life in the local supercluster.

Suspect, as far as Reeva was concerned, but hey. No one ever asked *her*.

Earth's treaty with the intergalactic Principality included policies concerning the treatment and cataloging of undocumented life forms. If there was something unknown alive out there, Reeva was duty-bound to investigate. Be it some fearsome denizen of the deep or not.

The bellows intensified.

The kaiju of Japanese monster movies flashed into her mind.

Claps of thunder followed another flash of lightning. Darkness slammed down. Reeva's wrist radio let out a garbled squawk and went silent. The lights flickered back on, the generator reinitializing. She glanced down at her wrist radio. It was still dead.

"You have got to be kidding me!" she muttered. "Shit! Shit. Shit. Shit. Shit."

She kicked at her stool with one last vicious "shi—"

"Indeed."

Reeva whipped around, heart in her throat. She gaped at the source of the slightly sympathetic but mostly amused rejoinder. The strange man invading her makeshift sanctum was the spitting image of a young and virile Bob Marley. The long-dead Legend himself. The King.

Clad in bell-bottom blue jeans and a mellow, yellow t-shirt, he sported a black beret that perched at an odd angle atop his shoulder-length natty dreads. The air around him smelled strongly of sinsemilla, though there was no smoke. His beloved guitar was missing. Instead, he carried a worn and tattered red satchel slung diagonally across his body like a messenger bag. His black irises burned with high intelligence and a hint of mischief.

"Who the hell–?" Reeva's voice cracked.

"Am I?" he offered, baring a perfect set of pearly whites.

His eyes darted about as if searching for a clue to the right answer. His gaze landed on her paperback.

"Anansi," he said. "My name is Anansi."

He very clearly decided just then.

Reeva's panic evaporated, slow-burning annoyance taking its place. She scowled, facing the intruder with arms akimbo.

"Anansi. From African mythology?"

"Yes." He nodded, full of irksome, boyish enthusiasm.

"God of storytelling and *bullshit*," she fixed him a cutting stare. "That Anansi?"

"Yes. That Anansi," he quipped, nodding vigorously. He smiled widely then he blinked. "I think."

Coming at her with those looks and with that name. The decidedly un-Jamaican manner of speaking straight up rankled.

"Right," Reeva muttered. "Right. I get it."

He watched as she swept by him. She grabbed a flashlight and hauled on her jacket. She started loading equipment into her backpack. He watched with unperturbed yet avid interest as she stomped back and forth, fetching this and grabbing that.

"I see you've chosen to ignore me," he observed, an innocently curious lift to his voice. "Why is that?"

"Because," Reeva stopped messing with her gear, long enough to shoot him a firm glare. 'I'm hallucinating. You clearly don't exist."

"Why?" he asked with aggravatingly childlike persistence.

"Because you're impossible!" Her voice went up a few decibels. "Ergo, I have gone and lost my ever-loving mind."

The bellows from the sea grew in amplitude. The reason registered after a moment. The rain, thunder, and lightning had stopped. The eye of the hurricane had arrived.

Considering the size of the storm, that gave Reeva two or so Earth hours to get out there and collect as much data on the creature as possible. She hefted her pack onto her back and adjusted the shoulder straps. She picked up her flashlight and brandishing it like a weapon, strode out into the wet, wild dark.

The strange fellow calling himself Anansi followed.

After a few minutes of stomping through the wet underbrush, she stopped. She whipped around, the harsh glare of her flashlight hitting him square in the face.

"Why are you following me?"

Grimacing, he shielded his eyes from her flashlight's glare. "Because I need your help."

"My help?" She snorted. "You're a *god*, aren't you?"

She whirled back around and started walking again muttering. "What help could you possibly need from little ol' me?"

"I can explain." He quickened his pace to keep up with her. "Just hear me out."

"Fine," she stopped again. "I'm all ears. Hurry up. I don't have time to waste on any foolishness."

"I'm here," he was digging around inside his satchel., "on a very important—"

He rummaged a little bit more frantically for a few seconds.

"Oh!" He fished out a small, glowing white orb. "Here," he offered, then dropped it into Reeva's open palm.

Reeva glanced down at the orb and kissed her teeth in annoyance. She knew what it was. She hated that she knew what it was.

High-level officials of the Principality carried these. Whatever this man or thing claiming to be Anansi really was, possessed a great deal of clout within that damned intergalactic bureaucracy.

"The Principality has no business interfering with our mission here," she stated flatly, handing the orb back. "We went through all the proper channels. Got their little stamp of approval and everything."

"I don't work for the Principality."

"Who do you work for then?" she demanded.

"Myself."

His answer caught her off guard, but she still couldn't be pleased.

"And?" she bit. "Who are you? What are you?" Waving her flashlight about. "What are you doing *here*?"

His head tilted skyward.

"I travel," he said. "Across worlds, rifts, and realms. Past, Present, and Future. I collect and preserve knowledge. Sometimes, when there's trouble, I intervene."

"That's why you're here playing scam god and Rasta superstar?"

"Oh, that." He shrugged. "I have little control over what form I take in your mind. Your own psyche plays a large part in the process."

Reeva was skeptical but what the heck? Grappling with the unbelievable seemed to be the night's general theme.

"Time travel, though?"

"Yes," he breathed. "Time... travel."

Apparently, using those words, in that order, was strange, new, and infinitely interesting to him.

They arrived at the sand dunes between the shoreline and the woods.

"So, let me get this straight." Reeva set down her backpack and unpacked a large-area light. "It's my fault you've manifested as a spacefaring, time-traveler who's supposed to be Anansi wearing Bob Marley's skin."

Good Lord, she snorted. Let that slowly sink in.

She set the light on a tripod and switched it on, illuminating nearly the entire beach. "Would come as no surprise to me if the BBC tried to sue your ass."

Anansi's brows furrowed. "Who?"

"Never mind." She turned aside and gestured expansively at the sprawling sea. "Does the help you need from me have something to do with that seaborne monstrosity?"

"Entirely. It does."

"Elaborate, please," she snapped.

He retrieved a black, palm-sized, rectangular object from his bag. He knelt and set it down in the sand. The black box beeped and then began morphing into a complex array of panels, antennae, and complex circuitry.

"Telepathy," Anansi said. "The... *kaiju?*" His tongue stumbled over the word filched from her mind.

"Its cries resonate with this moon's ley lines, triggering waves of seismic and volcanic activity. That bodes badly for every living thing on this planet. Presently, you and the rest of your crew. I'm here to figure out what's wrong and make it stop."

"And I fit into this picture somehow?"

"Yes," he confirmed with alacrity. "I need you to mind-meld with the creature. Communicate. Negotiate. Arrive at a solution that doesn't include ending this world."

"Negotiate?" Reeva frowned. "It's sentient?"

He stood and stepped away from the array. It began making a high-pitched noise.

The kaiju's bellowing suddenly stopped.

The waters began to swell, froth, and churn. Reeva watched in stomach-turning apprehension and slowly, a humongous mass of flesh emerged from the obsidian wet. Long, spiky tentacles writhed and twisted in the air. The creature drew closer and closer to shore. The stench of rotting fish was overpowering. She gagged, curry-goat-flavored bile stinging the back of her throat.

Crowding the shallows, the creature tilted its head downward. One red, limpid eye wriggled in the socket of its bulbous noggin. The scary eye zeroed in on Reeva. She swallowed hard, taking an instinctive step back. Her terrified gaze skated toward Anansi and then back to the beast.

How, in God's name, was she supposed to communicate with *that?*

Her vision blurred, vertigo surfacing as the creature edged closer to shore. The sheer pressure of its presence was so overwhelming that it made her heart shudder. She swayed from side to side, suddenly feeling sick.

"Nope. Can't." she finally blurted out. She shot Anansi a panicked glance. "You do it. Wh-why can't you do it? This is *your* job, right?"

"I can't." He glanced toward the kaiju. "This lifeform and I exist on completely incompatible wavelengths. Luckily enough, the human brain's synaptic oscillation patterns are uniquely tuned to resonate with it."

"Mighty convenient for you," Reeva grumbled.

"Sometimes," the shady traveler grinned, "the stars do align."

Nerves jangling, Reeva started nervously humming her favorite Bob Marley song again. She knew she was terribly off-key, but she didn't care.

"What is that awful racket you're making?" He frowned.

He held up two wireless electrodes for her to see before sticking them to her temples.

"Demonic incantations?"

"It's called singing," she grumbled. "Leave me alone. It calms me down."

"Now," he grasped her shoulders tightly, trapping her gaze with his fathomless amber eyes. "This part is easy. Just close your eyes. Breathe deeply and let your mind wander."

Reeva did as he instructed. A fraction of a second later, she was floundering amidst the maelstrom of the monster's mind. Its thoughts eclipsed her being. Memories that weren't hers flooded the gates of her brain. Memories that filled her with indescribable sorrow.

People lived here once. On this island. Sightless, vermillion-skinned quadrupeds with the gift of telepathy. Like humanity's progenitors, theirs had crawled up from the murky depths of the sea. They evolved. They learned. They communed with nature and worshipped their guardian sea god. They lived here for years. For thousands of years. Then they all died. One by one. Within the short period of a single planetary circuit. A plague wiped them out.

Their guardian deity, the kaiju, had remained alone in these inky waters ever since, watching over the empty shore.

The beast wasn't some mindless freak of nature. It was old, very old, and it was wise and unbearably kind. It had been thinking and remembering, and longing for the heavens, for a very long time. Over a millennium, its loneliness had been infinitely amplified. The kaiju longed for its own end. But death did not come. Would not come. Because there'd be no one left to remember those people. That they once lived. Here. On this island. That once, they did exist.

When Reeva came to, she was lying on the sandy ground, flat on her back. Salty, half-dried tears clung to her eyelids and cheeks. The kaiju was retreating, returning to the deep end of the sea. Anansi sat beside Reeva, legs crossed, and Bob Marley's black beanie tossed carelessly aside in the sand. He watched the clumsy motions of the lumbering kaiju intently as if burning every second of its departure into memory.

When he finally looked down at Reeva, his expression was unfathomable yet strangely heartbreaking.

"The thing you should know about this creature is," his eyes were fixed on the ocean, watching the kaiju's retreat. "It didn't originate on this moon. It came here from another time and space."

Reeva sniffled, struggling to make sense of his words. "What?"

"It once traveled across worlds," Anansi revealed in a low voice. "It traversed rifts, realms, and even time. Just like I do."

Eyes wide and round, the astronaut gaped at her mysterious companion.

"Wait," she breathed. "It almost sounds like you're saying it's one of *your* kind."

The kaiju had completely submerged and vanished from sight. Reeva knew instinctively. Tonight, somewhere deep in the trenches of the starlit sea, that long-suffering sea god would finally reach the end of its life.

Anansi looked at Reeva and then back to the sea. "What this creature has allowed itself to become is the antithesis of everything in which I believe."

"How's that?" Reeva asked, frowning. Wasn't he being just a little too mean?

Anansi said nothing for a while. His demeanor shifted. He grinned down at her, reverting to his impishly loquacious self.

"I, for one," he lightly flicked a forefinger at her tear-stained cheek, "do not get foolishly attached."

Reeva said nothing. She lay there staring up at the sky. *Proxima b* glowed pale amber in the jeweled sky. Puffy clouds gathered and swelled as if attempting to obliterate the heavens. The smell of rain intensified. The first dewy drops of water lightly sprinkled her face.

"If humans intend to colonize this world," Anansi stated, sounding playfully preachy yet serious, "you should understand. What you'll be taking and who you'll be taking it from. Reeva, do *you* understand?"

She said nothing.

She understood, though. She truly understood. Down to the depths of her marrow. The desolate kaiju's torment. How precious it was. This world that venerable creature had given up eternity to protect. She also realized something else. Something that filled her with awe and sadness.

This man, this strange being, sitting beside her wasn't just some erudite and affable alien adventurer. He was also a teacher. Like the lonesome kaiju, he was very old and very wise. Despite his own claim otherwise, he was also unbearably kind.

Thunder rumbled in the distance. The wind started to pick back up. The eye had passed, and the hurricane's onslaught was resuming.

"Come on." The man who called himself Anansi stood, extending a helping hand. "Let's get you back to your camp."

Per Ardua ad Astra
by
Russell A Smith

"System breach! Fatal emergency!"

The voice was familiar. The ship's computer, Una, was named for BBC wartime powerhouse Una Marson. The other ship was named Ulric for one of her show's guests, Squadron Leader Ulric Cross. Cryostasis stopped him from seeing her holographic avatar, a likeness of the broadcast icon, but he knew the voice's programmed sense of urgency.

"Why have you not woken the commanding officer?" he asked, knowing it wasn't him.

"Group Captain Ord is dead, sir." As the sentient computer spoke, there was a second flash and crackle, though this time accompanied by a brief and stifled whimper to his left. He blinked hard, but the blurring remained. Couldn't expect to be right back to full alert without the Compensatory Adjustment Recuperation Programme, but he had to get it together and fast.

"Second?" he asked, anticipating the second-in-command getting to work.

"Wing Commander Fuller has been killed too, sir," Una replied sharply. "You are now the ranking officer on the vessel at this time."

"I am?" But that meant there had been several more deaths; he wasn't that high up the chain. And she just said, 'killed.' But by who, or what? Instinct took over, and if he was truly in command, then surely he'd better damn well take it.

"Awaken the entire ship," he ordered. He had to give them half a chance.

"Negative, sir," Una responded.

"What? Why not?"

"Becau- "Una's voice crackled and glitched. "Override mal-function. Original computer defence system active . . . active . . . warning . . ."

Original computer defence system? She couldn't have been talking about – oh, no . . .

"Una. Stay with us."

Static. And now he had no idea what was going on. He thought a little harder. *Original computer defence system*. That meant something had awoken the original ship's architecture. This ship had been captured and repurposed, he remembered as much, but there was no time for a history lesson other than the necessary. The Alliance, who used to own the ship, reckoned without a task force of the Royal Air Force who both managed to raid the vessels and escape aboard them alongside their civilian passengers. Much like its namesake the *Independence Windrush* (no '*Empire*' this time round) had been spoils of the most uncivil of civil wars, whereby the demagogues, egos and bad-minded billionaires manufactured a conflict which saw some relatively smart and painfully powerful people suckered by a little slick rhetoric and silencing of the loud voices wise to their ways. The upshot of that was that they came for *everyone* on their list, except, of course, none of the marginalised they targeted went quietly. At least one side heeded the lessons of history. And now this fleet of two capital ships of mostly Black British, African, and Caribbean crews, operated on the sole purpose of getting away from the crazy bastards who were poised to finish off whatever happened to be left of planet Earth. Not everyone fled; most of the other Armed Services resisted amongst many others. An operation was set to liberate control from the heavily overfinanced and fascist death cult calling themselves the Last Alliance who would rather see Earth burn than harmonious for all. But with the conflict in the balance, a desperate gambit had taken place to ensure the survival of the very people being persecuted in the first place. The reasons for the war weren't logical, and the existence of six ships the size of small cities, initially intended as floating space colonising vessels were stolen from the collective of as many rich white men who had started the whole thing off in the first place. They were going to just take a ship each, watch the End of Days from a distance, and fly off to a new galaxy in the hope of shaping it in their image. Again. Group Captain Ord had other ideas.

Authorised to lead a task force, they raided the bases, routed the personal guards, assassinated five of the six oligarchs, and rapidly stole and repurposed the ships. Before the Alliance forces could react and stop them, two of the ships, *Independence Windrush* and the *Almanzora 2*, much better names than the first less thinkable ones, each loaded up with a mixture of the task force and some of the survivors. Still, that was in the past. Now, something else threatened the mission.

Casey rubbed his eyes again and this time saw the killer at the corner of his eyes. The small, scuttling drone was no bigger than a maintenance robot, yet its spider-like appearance and its electrocution mandibles filled him with dread. One by one it had worked its way down the command structure, while they had been in deep sleep and powerless to stop it. Now that he was awake though, matters were different. He reached to the side of his stasis pod and hoped nothing had time to move or interfere with the service issue electrolaser he kept there. Not strictly speaking regulation placement, but his brief tour with the RAF Regiment taught him to be ready for any unexpected hostilities, especially when it came to protecting the ships. He fumbled around the pod even as he heard the quiet yet tell-tale clack, clack, clacking as the arachnoid thing started to scuttle up and prepare to execute yet another unsuspecting passenger.

"How have you no control over this, Una?" he asked whilst trying to find the weapon. He could feel a glass panel, then cursed as he remembered the sidearm wasn't simply holstered on the side. Normally a sensible precaution —apart from right now. With one eye on the mechanical monstrosity crawling up another cryostasis pod, he was grateful the thing still needed to open the pod to get to the passenger, vital extra seconds he needed as he looked away and down at the numbered touchpad to the side of his blaster. Green button —standard. "ENTER CODE" on the display: problem. He hadn't entered this in, hell, he didn't even know how long he'd been out. Could've been a month; could've been a decade. They didn't keep them on the

114

clock displays for that exact reason; they thought when everyone woke up, all at once of course, they'd be better hearing it from the ship's captain. Well, nobody was hearing a thing from the captain now.

Memory and space lag were a rotten combo. The sound of one of those sharp metal appendages entering an access point socket and the unmistakable hiss of one of the sealed life support pods opening was another if he didn't remember faster. Mum's date of birth? Nah, the chief tech would have bawled him out for that kind of 'security.' *Sister's*?

That stirred something. Not her birthdate, but the day they both started their officer training. Different for her; she opted for the Army; never had the same urge to fly that he did. But they made a wager that she'd make it to general staff before anyone had him listed as air staff. He took the bet, even though he knew she'd win that one all damn day. He was never in a hurry to stop flying anyway and hoped they'd keep him in the air even to his last day. *Mandatory retirement —that's it!* At least it was if we were going off the clock before the big freeze. He punched in with his fingers far harder than was entirely necessary the digits, 2-1-0-6-2-2-1-4-7. The glass safe door clicked open, and he snatched the gun. Using his pod as cover just in case, he flicked the safety off, which also sent a surge of charge into the weapon, took aim at the annoyingly small target and . . .

"Missed!" The ray flew harmlessly to the right of his intended shot yet mercifully away from the other pods. Two potentially fatal mistakes there; first overestimating how much his vision had straightened up and second, that he'd not taken the little bastard out the first time. His old firearms instructor would have demanded their crate of beer for that. A small bonus, from a certain perspective, was that said little bastard stopped trying to murder another unsuspecting victim while they slept. The downside was that it turned its murderous attention toward him. He knew that as soon as two metal spikes lodged in the pod he hid behind just inches away from his face with a double *thud*. Thank goodness for cover. He switched the ordinance to bolts and took a snapshot without looking. It would have been dead-on, had the mechanoid still been where he had originally targeted, but it had scuttled away. Still, he'd saved a life —or at least been offered the opportunity to do so.

"Una! *That* pod. Can you wake *them* up?" he shouted.

"Affirmative," she said. "Override status accepted. Awakening passenger 3131332; Captain Nancy Chase."

His heart sank as he heard the passenger's name, but the one thing he couldn't afford now was to hesitate. A fact reinforced by another spike whistling a whisker past his head before it lodged into a wall. Too close. But at least he had a direction. He scanned to his right, closed out everything and listened, trying to pick out the fast-moving drone before it could attack again. He tried to ignore the distraction of more gas being poured into the open chamber and prayed to anyone who might be listening that it was Una doing her thing rather than the killer drone.

He heard the electrical crackle before his recalibrating reflexes got anywhere near stopping the metal menace from getting the jump on him —and even jumping *on* him. It was all he could do to get his arms up to grapple it as it knocked him onto his back, but it wedged its sharp rear appendages into the ground and gained a firm grip as it pressed down. Pinned down, he lifted his arms and pushed the crustacean-like jowls, sparking with flashes of electricity, from reaching his face. The front legs stabbed down hard, narrowly missing his shoulder blades but straight into the epaulettes on his flight suit. He wrestled back the remaining legs with all his fighting strength as flashing jowls lurched toward him, a low whirring sound as it attempted to treat him just as it had the senior crew members. The silver head stretched, extending out of its body as it lowered itself toward his face, flinching to delay the deadly electroshock. He turned to reach for his dropped gun, which had skittered far enough out of his reach that he couldn't even see it. Poor way to go, he thought, but never stopped fighting, even as the electrical execution loomed nearer and nearer.

A shocking surge hit him but was no more than static against his shaven cheeks. He jerked back, expecting the thing to follow through on its promise of death, but instead, a tickle, then . . . nothing.

"YYYAH!" A brown boot appeared over his head and sent the mechanoid to its back, motionless and hissing. There was a hole in the side of it like the one he'd intended to put there himself. Turning the other way, he saw a familiar, if unexpected sight; a mean-looking woman with a short and shiny afro with warm brown eyes in the green dress uniform of the British Army. He knew to be the same 28 years of age (allowing for cryostasis), as him. He knew that because he had known her his entire life. She held his electrolaser in her hand, still smoking at the tip from the beautifully clean shot. It was almost like she had pulled a heroic pose.

"Sis . . ." he said, not closing his mouth before or after he'd uttered the word.

"You fucking flyboys. Always on your arses or your backs, and never the right one at the right time." Nancy offered him a hand as well as a mocking grin. He took the hand as she pulled him up with confident strength and very few signs of the space lag that adrenaline had been helping him to negate. He leaned his head as he examined her and checked this wasn't another one of Una's induced relaxation dreams. He concluded that he would have never made a nightmare for himself in the first place. It was her, for sure.

"You . . . you were assigned to the *Almanzora*. What are you doing here? How did I not know?" he asked.

"Lots of questions," his kid sister, by a matter of five minutes, replied. "Not really time for many answers." She looked down at the smoking ruin which had tried to kill him, and he gave a shrug of concession. "Questions we *do* need answered; are there many more of those aboard; are the other ships under similar attack; why isn't Una working properly and how do we fix her?"

Casey nodded. "Lots of questions."

"I can answer one," came Una's voice over a nearby PA speaker. "That mechanoid was on the ship's roster listed as a repair drone. However, offensive capability has been there since its construction. I have attempted to scan the others but this one, which initiated the override of my systems, did so by way of a virus programme. I managed to activate countermeasures before it completely took over my functioning processes and prevented a complete takeover. One countermeasure was shutting down communications with the other ships. I believe the intended order protocol was to be broadcast from this ship on takeover. I cannot, however, guarantee that this is not happening there also."

"And we've no way to be sure if we can't talk to them," said Nancy.

"Agreed. But that means getting out there." Casey said. "Una, is it safe to launch a fighter?"

Una made a clicking noise as if she were a computer centuries older, but soon looked up and gave an answer. "I don't have control of the hangar or defence systems, but I have been contesting the virus so that the enemy does not either. To be at full operational capacity, I would require a full system restart. This will allow each of the systems to reboot or format accordingly and negate any control of currently infected systems. However, this creates other vulnerabilities, including no protection for life support, and no ability to scan for enemy activity." She stopped, her ethereal form appearing to stop and look behind her toward something. "Warning. This viral defence system, which I believe is known as 'EVO,' is not contained. I am no longer able to locate it."

Nancy and Casey looked at each other with narrowed eyes, then glared at Una's image. "So, it's gone?" they asked in the kind of synchronisation people to this day expected of twins for some reason. "Destroyed?"

A pause. A shake of the holographic head. "Negative. Defence programming states it has escaped aboard one of the ship's devices."

"Will this affect your reboot?" Casey asked.

"If it finds a way to intercept and interfere, yes," Una answered.

"Scan?" Nancy asked.

"Any estimated scan time would be more than six hours. It would also consume a significant proportion of processing capability. I would have to recommend against this course of action."

The twins thought quickly, but Nancy voiced their joint conclusion aloud.

"Casey, we need to get you launched in one of the fighters. I'm going to have to stay on the ship and ensure Una completes her repair." She handed Casey his electrolaser back. "Which means I'm gonna need a bigger gun." She strode back to her pod and crouched around the rear of it. Casey could hear eight beeps as she punched in a number and with both hands removed a black single-barreled rifle. The flick of a switch made the weapon ready, signified by a brief high-pitched whine. "Right, let's get you to the hangar."

Una wagged a finger. "Wait. I can't put myself into reset or shutdown. That needs to be manual."

Nancy sighed. "Where's the reset button?"

"Central computer room." Una raised an arm and projected a map of the ship. "Third floor. I can join you to provide access. I have separated my direct operating consciousness into this avatar to minimise being overridden by EVO myself."

"Guess we're going to have to split up earlier than planned," said Casey. "I'll see what I can find to launch."

Nancy nodded. "Never split the party. New bet though. I say I take this EVO out before you reach the *Almanzora*."

Casey stopped tapping the side of the pistol against the back of his other palm and grinned at her. "I'll take those odds."

She gave a small smile. "Luck, bruv." It was the lowest volume she had spoken at since they reunited.

Casey's own smile dropped as thoughts of the wager were replaced with the prayer that he'd see her again. "Luck, sis." They turned and made a dash to their objectives.

*

The journey to the centre of the ship was much longer when having to rely on stairs, as Nancy forced herself to. Being stuck in a lift took on new danger with a viral menace running around on this occasion. She also remembered the hard way that cryostasis did not maintain basic fitness for a body by itself. Sure, it slowed ageing and physical atrophy, but even the most athletic

119

human couldn't reasonably expect to be able to flat-out sprint a capital ship straight out of the sleep fridge. By the time she reached the target area, she was blowing like she had on the surprise beastings in training. Which was no way to kill a virus. Naturally, Una didn't have a hair out of place, but it was something of a cheat to be comparing against the ghostly presence of a supercomputer. Una shimmered; the least human Nancy had seen her appear, but she unleashed a sequence of lights from her fingers against the keypad, and the doors slid apart in quarters. Nancy looked into the room, bathed in wall-to-wall red lights but none powerful enough to break the darkness of the cathedral of systems which awaited through the other side. It was a truly daunting sight, probably even for a dedicated technician. Nancy had a brief daydream of an urban combat theatre, whereby she found herself facing down relentless hordes of Alliance warrior bots and taking cover in derelict buildings awaiting evac. It seemed almost comforting in comparison to this. Almost. She mopped her brow.

"So where is it? The reset switch?" she asked Una.

"I'll light your way!" Una said. And with that, the tight field of red lights changed colour to green, blue, yellow, and formed a clear route for the soldier to follow. Nancy gave an approving nod and entered, keeping alert for any surprises. "Now this switch; is it a lever, old-style button, touchpad…"

The doors behind slammed shut, and the lights dimmed or disappeared entirely, darkening the room further. Fortunately, the path illumination remained. Her breath back, she ran and followed the illuminated route until she reached the wonderfully old-fashioned, almost stereotypical, big red button, which happened to be under a locked case and next to a much more expected wall-sized touchpad.

"Glad the designers took their billionaire clients so seriously," she said to Una as she stooped down to the case. "Now here's a problem – I don't suppose you happen to know who has the key, do you?"

Una didn't respond. Not in the way Nancy had hoped or expected at least. Instead, the avatar made a strange choking sound, which made little sense as she didn't exactly need to breathe, did she? "Una?"

"Una's not in." The voice was calm, quiet, but deep, and more than a little chilling. The image had changed slightly, no longer 1940s attire being worn but instead a far more contemporary business suit design, and red eyes which blended unpleasantly well with the chamber. "And your brother should have left you a little longer so he could have been relieved of you. If you leave that alone, I might even spare him from being blasted to bits."

*

Casey in other circumstances, might have felt like a test pilot with his pick of spacecraft. However, for this one, he just needed something fast, manoeuvrable, and preferably armed. That ruled out the transport barges and the dedicated scout ships. Actually, as much as he thought about this one, the personal plaything for Esmond Shelder, a fighter liveried outside RAF greys and instead in a black and gold livery more reminiscent of a race car, yet still one of the modern fighters, was the best option after all. He was surprised it hadn't been called *Moonraker* or something. Shelder shouldn't have been able to buy military-grade hardware, yet between his company manufacturing the engines which he designed two years ago to break the Solar System Sprint record, and the fact that nobody was willing at the time to tell his rich ass otherwise, here it was. It might have been the height of hubris usually, but on this occasion, Casey called it a fighting chance. He was flight-ready, having seized a helmet from the crew area; he couldn't trust Shelder to have been smart enough to have requested artificial atmosphere, even if his engineers had the good sense to install it. He did a one-man ground-crew impersonation as best he could, careful to minimise communication with the central computer. Without a reliable system, he was going to fail regardless.

"Una?" he asked, hoping his electronic angel was listening. But there was no response. "Una? I need your help."

"Guess I'm stuck with shooting my way out of this one, right?" Nancy readied the rifle and aimed at Una, though kept looking back, checking her position.

Una laughed. That wasn't really like her. "And hit what, exactly? I'm not in your physical space." She sneered, spreading her arms wide. "Go on then. If it makes you feel any better."

Nancy's eyes narrowed as she seemed to settle into an aim.

"It won't," she said, adjusting her feet. "But *this* will." She rotated and fired three bolts into the side of the encased switch. Hopefully, that was enough. She swung at it with her right leg and kicked hard."

'Una' roared as she brought her foot down on the large button, and the room plunged into sudden darkness. Una's face contorted, and then she disappeared into the darkness. An echo came from the comms, now free of the influence of the corrupted computer interface but about to shut down before she could respond.

"Una? Sis?"

She set off an old trick, holding the trigger with the safety down and clicking the setting to auto. The low-level whine got considerably louder as the overload took effect, and with the rifle screaming, lifted the barrel at the door and released first the safety, then the trigger. A blue flash exploded from the barrel, and she dropped the weapon as she hurtled backwards. She landed on her back; a little rough, but lots could have been worse as she imagined the court martial she would have earned if anyone had seen that. Faint illumination came through the hole she created in the doorway, as well as cold, fresh air. The rifle was ruined, but at least she could get out. She needed to get to Casey, and fast.

*

Casey figured the best place he could have waited was in fact in the Shelder fighter. The livery may have been designed to make wasps bow down to their new goddess, but if it got the job done it was all good.

One of his sensors blipped, which wiped the amused smirk right off his face. "There's a ship missing. And that's it out there. There's been a launch. Oh, no . . ." Well, at least that confirmed the runway protection must have been deactivated. Landing skis up, he had levitational thrust and a clear run on the hangar exit. But he could see that for some reason the escaped ship was coming back around. Why?

"Sir, are you in the R-90 gunship?" Una asked, with that concerned programming of hers. "Only if you are, the IFF has been deactivated and weapon systems are both active and aiming at the hangar." At him, then.

"Isn't me." No time to say more. No time to do anything other than hope his launch run was straight enough and gun the reheat. Sorry, *afterburners* to his fans in the U.S. Given light cell engine technology didn't generate much heat, it was a bit of a misnomer in the modern Forces, but the bad humour steadied his nerves as he prayed he wasn't about to smack into a wall, artificial or otherwise. He got shoved back in his seat the same way anyway.

"Sir – weapons firing!" Una said. At this speed, that wasn't his only worry, just that he cleared the runway before the salvo hit. It couldn't have been aiming directly at him, and so it proved, as the blasts around him sent him and his systems into a spin. Everything flashed and buzzed as he had just had enough time to realise what he was reacting to. He killed the throttle and launch control as he fought for his life to get the spinning fighter back under some semblance of control, and himself conscious with the Gs he was now pulling. It wasn't happening. One good thing though; no way could the hostile ship target him easily while he was moving.

"Bro! You make it?" Una managed to get comms to Nancy. "I can't get on weapon systems; full reboot is in progress. Good news: EVO didn't kill me when he possessed Una."

"What??" The familiar bleeping of an enemy gaining target lock ended his distraction. "Little busy here." The thought occurred to him; this was a leisure ship. Did it even have weapons of its own? The R-90 certainly did, and EVO was working that target lock. He cranked the thrust back up to an operational combat speed and did the most important thing a fighter could do under attack; keep moving. Just as well, because the hostile had opened fire with its autocannon, showing him close to annihilation. But then, it just stopped.

"Casey, I'm watching on the bridge. Hostile is heading for *Almanzora*. I'm detecting a surge in energy reading from the ship but not weapons. Some kind of comms spike." Nancy informed him.

"That answers another question then. If there is another EVO on the Almanzora, it isn't up and running yet. This one's trying to wake it up."

"We've no weapon systems active here; systems are going to take a while to reboot and that is low priority. You're our only hope."

"That's worrying. Una. Do I even have weapons on here?"

"Hunting beam, but it's got one charge on it," Una answered.

"One shot then." Which would have been fine, had it not been for the gyroscope malfunction. The ship still spun uncontrollably, making the first challenge to try not to get too dazed. The second was knowing the target lock was getting more difficult with each spin.

"You're drifting away from us," Nancy said. "Ten seconds and you'll be out of comms range."

He could hit the reheat again but with the speed the fighter was spinning, one error and he'd be out of the fight for good. So . . . one chance to get it right. Twice.

But Casey calculated something. At his velocity, he should have been out of comms range already if the *Windrush* had been at full speed.

"Hey, Una, you're barely moving," he said.

"Indeed," she replied. "It appears EVO interfered with my flight plan as soon as it activated, but at the same time neutralised the flight computer. So I'm afraid I had no idea."

"And neither did we," Nancy said. "When this is flying smoothly it's impossible to tell we're moving at all. "Now shoot that thing down. If it gets to the *Almanzora*, they've had it."

"I know!" he snapped. "Wait – that's it." When he saw the *Almanzora* in the centre of the window he focused on the bigger target. Time over accuracy as the R-90 lined itself up for the hangar landing and entered a landing flight pattern. Now or never.

"NOW."

Reheat on, immediately off. Hand back on the flight stick. A bead of sweat ran into his left eye at the worst possible time but no time to rub it; just had to close the eye and aim with the other as the fighter rotated slower than before; not slow enough.

Just one shot.

"Fire, fire, fire!" he said to nobody but himself as he pressed the red button of his own.

Like an arc welder, the beam sliced the side of the gunship. Not a clean hit, but it knocked the enemy gunship off course. With an engine destroyed, that might have been enough. However, his flight path appeared about to smack him into the front of the *Almanzora*. He sighed. He'd at least done his duty. His barely controllable ship clipped the broken side of the R-90. Immediately, the gyroscope alert fell silent. More out of instinct than realisation, he yanked the stick port side and pressed the flashing green button in front of him; signalling for landing just before the protective shield bounced him like a skimming stone.

Through the hangar, he straightened up and hit the airbrake button so hard that he thought his palm would smash through the cockpit. The ship's frontal wash shoved a parked fighter out of the way before his custom build came to a halt right where it needed to.

"Casey? CASEY!" Nancy yelled through the comms. Casey could picture what she must have witnessed as he slumped back against his seat with the loudest inhalation.

"I . . . I'm okay."

"Oh, thank the stars. All I saw was an explosion. That must have been EVO."

"And that's his last iteration," Una added. "All strands of virus neutralised."

Casey gave a weak nod before replying. "Good. Get the fleet back on course. And open your comm channel if it's back up."

"Already done," Una said. "Which is how you were safe to land." He detected a smile on the avatar's face even from the distance.

"Ulric – this is Una. Test transmission. Windrush Calling."

Dedicated to the pioneers on the original ships, and the Generations they brought.

Appeal for Yabana-mboka
by
Balogun Ojetade

Chapter One

Howahkan Kasongo moved nervously through the busy frontier rendezvous, driving his titane monowheel among a maze of Indigenous Na'asali traders mixed with human hunters and merchants. He pulled in a breath of the crisp air. It was a fine dry season morning. The gatherings for buying and selling goods were wisely held in the prime of the year.

As he moved about, the young man's senses were stimulated by a variety of sights, smells, and sounds he'd rarely been exposed to. He stopped and gazed out over the vast area, searching for the reason for his journey.

"Good morning, nsanga. You seem to be looking for something; I've just the thing for you."

A human tradesman in weathered gentleman's apparel, with sand-colored skin just as weathered, stirred Howahkan from his task. Howahkan turned and looked at the man, who stared intently at him as he gently shook the small bottle he held in his hand.

"I'm not your brother," he replied to the human. Even though Howahkan was half-human, he was not fond of most of them.

"Yes. Well, you seem to be searching for something, and I think I can help you."

As he said this, the man once again raised the small bottle as if to display it for the young man.

"Thank you, sir; I'm searching for the mbangazi atonga. Can you help me find him? I've been told he would be here. He travels with his wife and her brother."

The tradesman appeared puzzled by Howahkan's question. He considered it briefly and then replied slowly.

"The mbangazi atonga? The great brute?"

Howahkan nodded.

"You must mean Huslu Ransom."

Howahkan expressed confusion.

"Huslu, who?" he asked.

The small bottle lowered a little in the man's hands. "Huslu Ransom, the mbangazi atonga, he killed a masibulu when he was just a boy."

Howahkan thought about this for a few seconds.

"A masibulu…? The warrior I'm searching for has killed a nkwiya monso."

The human trader appeared completely confused, "A what?"

"A nkwiya monso, uhm…a big, uhm, terrible…ah, what you call…a demon?"

Now the small bottle and the trader's hands lowered all the way as he stared at Howahkan with disbelief.

"A demon killer? I don't know of any warrior like that."

Just then, the young man noticed something in the distance. He motioned with his hand in a thankful gesture.

"Thank you. All's well. I see what I've been searching for. Thank you."

As Howahkan fired up his monowheel and sped away, the trader remembered his initial thought.

"Yes, well, you might also be interested in this miracle elixir! It cures everything; you won't find it anywhere else on the frontier."

Howahkan paid no more attention to the tradesman as he moved cautiously toward his objective.

Twenty yards away and across a muddy trail, he spotted a young man and woman. Both sat on samo, and both had a smaller, one-humped samo-awelewele tethered to their cameline steeds. The woman held the reins of a large, beautiful samo as well, which indicated another rider close by. Howahkan immediately realized only a person of importance could afford such majestic animals as these.

He maneuvered around the two, and as he could see them better, he was certain they matched descriptions of the people for whom he'd been searching.

The woman appeared to be in her early twenties. She was very beautiful and seemed to be Yabana-mboka, like Howahkan's father. The young man beside her also appeared to be Yabana-mboka and looked like the woman's younger brother.

Howahkan found an inconspicuous location to wait. He then began to search for the warrior. As he was looking around, a human trapper staggered up to the woman. He appeared to have drunk too much of the human drink called "whiskey." Now, he examined the young woman with obvious desire.

"Hey there. You're sure a pleasant sight for a man who ain't seen a woman for months." The trapper spoke with slurred speech.

The roughly dressed man came closer to the young woman's leg. Her barkskin dress was pulled high because of how she sat in the saddle, which caused much of her legs to be exposed.

The man carefully looked at her leg.

"You Yaba-Yaba women do like to show them pretty legs of yours, don't ya?"

Yaba-Yaba. A racist.

The young woman stared down at the man, who was slowly moving closer to her leg. She said nothing but moved her right hand over to the handle of a knife in her leather boot. She pulled the knife out slightly as she glanced over to her brother. He also watched the man with obvious irritation.

"Do you mind if I just touch that pretty leg a little? I just want to touch it once."

He looked up at the woman, who continued to gaze down at him without expression as her samo moved slightly under her.

Howahkan had now become very interested in this development and almost forgot about the warrior he was searching for. Then, a large Yabana-mboka man came out from the trader's tent in front of the young man and woman. He was around thirty years old, very distinguished in appearance, and was examining an electrolaser carbine in his hands as if he'd just traded for the long gun.

By this time, the rough trapper was rubbing the woman's exposed leg. She turned her head up and looked at the large man with the electrolaser carbine. He glanced up from the weapon in his hands, and realizing a man was beside her, he began to take notice.

The woman spoke softly in the Yabana-mboka language and asked the man with the electrolaser carbine, "May I kill him?"

The large man couldn't see that the trapper was rubbing her leg due to her brother's steed.

The man with the electrolaser carbine answered her casually, in the same Yabana-mboka language. Howahkan understood what he said, but it was apparent the fur trapper didn't understand this language.

"No, I don't believe it would be wise. He's just got too much crazy-human juice in him."

Then, the woman's brother intentionally moved his samo back a little. This allowed the large man to see that the human trapper was rubbing the woman's leg.

The large man's face tightened. He glared at the human. Then he told the woman, "You may draw blood if you wish."

Howahkan was astounded and excited by this.

The woman still held her knife. As the large man told her she could draw blood, the human trapper turned around, seeming to realize the woman had spoken to someone behind him. He smiled at the large man and, raising his hand from the woman's leg, pointed up to her and asked, "Is this here your woman?"

At the very instant the man pointed to her with his head turned, the woman pulled her knife and sliced off the trapper's finger with one quick movement. Before the man had realized she removed his finger, the young woman had cleaned the blade on the samo's blanket and was putting it back into her boot.

Feeling something hit his hand, the human trapper turned to see blood streaming from where his finger had just been. Shock spread across his face. He began to moan as the pain took hold. He reached up with his other hand and held the wounded one against his chest in dismay.

Now the large man walked over to him. He took the man by his coat and moved him away from the samo. Then he spoke to the man in broken Human Common.

"You've lost a finger today. But you're fortunate to still have your life. She could have slit your throat just as easily."

He then looked around to make sure no one was close by. He turned back to the man who was still staring wide-eyed at his hand. With one quick movement, the large man yanked the trapper's head toward his rapidly rising knee. The human's head slammed into the large man's knee, and the trapper crumpled onto the muddy path, completely unconscious.

Howahkan stepped back a bit more into his hiding spot but had no doubt that this was the man he'd traveled far to find.

The large man placed the electrolaser carbine into the ropes of a samo-awelewele, and after climbing onto his own samo, they casually rode away.

A few moments later, Howahkan mounted his monowheel and followed at a distance.

The three slowly rode west. Only the sounds of the samo and birds were heard as they moved along barely visible trails.

After about two hours of travel, the woman's brother stopped. The large man and the woman soon stopped as well. They looked back and then turned their samo and returned to him.

All three held their mounts steady for a short time. Then the large man spoke softly, "One rider."

The woman's brother nodded and added, "This rider has been following us since the market. He's traveling too light for a warrior. I think he's a messenger."

The large man and the woman again remained silent as if listening. Then the large man began to turn his samo; he replied, "It seems we'll have a guest for our late meal."

As the day moved to afternoon and then evening, the three continued westward. Finally, they stopped and set up a campsite.

The fire glowed and crackled. The woman's brother prepared food as the man and woman checked their samo and supplies. None spoke, and when the food was ready, the woman's brother handed a small dish to the woman and man. He then sat down and began to eat.

The large man turned to the woman's brother as they ate. "Do we need to retrieve our guest?"

The young man stopped eating briefly and listened. Then he replied, "No, the guest is approaching slowly in front of us." He then casually returned to his meal.

The large man reached down beside his crossed legs and cocked his electrolaser carbine before returning to his meal.

While eating, they watched in front of them and across the small campfire. After a few more moments, the large man called out, "Please, come to the fire so we can see you. I don't wish to shoot you."

Shortly after this, Howahkan crept cautiously into the firelight. He appeared surprised and frightened.

"Sit," was all the large man said to him.

Howahkan immediately sat down.

To his astonishment, the woman picked up a dish of food and moved over to him. She handed the food to him and then returned to her spot beside the large man. She picked her dish back up and began to eat again.

"Eat," the large man said and returned to his meal.

All three studied Howahkan from across the small fire but said nothing. The young man ate his food quietly and occasionally glanced at the three hosts.

Once all had finished eating, the woman silently collected the dishes. She then pulled a long stem pipe from a leather bag. She filled the pipe with tobacco and lit it with a stick from the fire.

After handing the pipe to the large man, she took a comb from another bag. She moved behind the large man and began to part his wild afro and scratch his scalp gently. As she did this, the woman occasionally looked with apparent suspicion at the visitor.

The woman's brother took a piece of wood that he seemed to have saved for after the meal. He examined the wood carefully but also glanced at Howahkan from time to time.

Howahkan sat silently as the large man smoked his pipe and studied him.

The woman's brother began to cut the piece of wood with precision and very quickly had ornate designs whittled into it.

Finally, the large man spoke as the fire began to die down.

"I believe you and your people are having trouble. You've searched us out because this trouble is larger than your people can manage. You're hoping to enlist our services but have little to offer for those services. What we need to know is the manner of trouble you're facing."

Howahkan was speechless for a moment. The large man continued to stare at him as he pulled another draw from his pipe.

The woman continued to scratch his scalp, and her brother continued to work on the piece of wood. They all studied the man in apparent anticipation of his answer.

Finally, Howahkan spoke with a nervous voice.

"That's very impressive. And I feel sure now that you're the warrior called Etchemin."

The large man expelled a stream of smoke from his mouth and replied.

"I am called Etchemin, by some. This is my wife, Istas, and her brother Siwili."

The young man nodded to Istas and Siwili.

"I'm very happy to meet you. My name is Howahkan."

"Howakhan?" Etchemin repeated. His eyes looked Howahkan up and down. You're Yabana-mboka."

"Yes," Howahkan replied with a nod.

"But not all the way," Etchemin said. "Muscles strong, but not strong enough. And hair . . ."

Etchemin drew a small semi-circle in the air with his hands. "Too neat."

"My father is Yabana-mboka, my mother is human," Howahkan said. "But my heart is a hundred percent Yabana-mboka. My village is Yabana-mboka, and it is very much in trouble. I have been searching for you for some months now. We feel you may be the only hope we have left."

Howahkan paused as if recalling the trouble. Etchemin continued to draw smoke from his pipe. Istas scratched her husband's scalp. Siwili focused on the carving in his hands.

Howahkan watched them for a few more seconds and then said, "Our village has been ravaged for many months now by a pack of Mbana'Vava."

The three hosts froze immediately when Howahkan said this. Etchemin had been looking into the fire when he froze, and then his eyes drifted slowly up to stare at Howahkan.

Istas stopped combing Etchemin's hair in mid-stroke. She also refocused her eyes from her husband's hair to Howahkan.

Siwili's knife stopped halfway into a cut, and he raised his eyes and stared at Howahkan.

As the silence became very thick, Howahkan watched the trio. Only the crackling fire and a bird chirping in the distance broke the tense atmosphere.

Etchemin finally lowered his eyes back to the fire. He pulled another draw from his pipe, and as he expelled the smoke, his wife and brother quietly returned to their activities.

Istas now began combing Etchemin's hair back into its wild spiky style, and Siwili raised his carving up to get a better look at it in the fading light of the fire.

Howahkan waited patiently for some form of reply.

Etchemin handed the exhausted pipe to Istas. She carefully cleaned the pipe and placed it in the leather bag. The warrior readjusted himself. Siwili tossed his carving onto the dying fire, and then he returned his knife and seemed very interested in Etchemin's response. Finally, the warrior spoke.

"You can stay here tonight, Howahkan. We must consider this."

The three then prepared their blankets on the ground and were soon lying down to sleep. Howahkan retrieved a blanket from his monowheel and lay down to sleep.

Several hours later, Etchemin stood up silently and walked into the woods, the moon being his only light. After walking for a bit, he stopped and gazed out over a small open area.

He stood in silence for a while. Then, without turning, he spoke as if talking to the night.

"So, what do you think of this thing, my brother?"

Siwili silently moved closer to Etchemin but remained slightly behind him. He briefly marveled that Etchemin always knew of his quiet approach. He replied in a soft voice.

"The Mbana'Vava are said to stand seven feet tall. Some tribes call them 'Ant Demons.' In the North, they've been called 'Ntetea'boa.' Most believe the Mbana'Vava were here even before the Yabanamboka, at first inhabiting lands far beneath the surface, and after millennia of digging and climbing, finally broke the surface and have since remained. They have the stench of fresh dirt and honey, and they are vicious, with exoskeletons harder than stone. They look like humans, with perfectly round eyes, crimson skin, and a mouth full of dagger-like teeth. It's said to be very difficult to kill even one, with their hard hides, extreme strength and speed, and their venomous bites. I had thought the Mbana'Vava had been all destroyed years ago."

He paused as if considering his final assessment. Silence briefly overtook the night again. Then he spoke his final thoughts.

"To battle an entire pack of Mbana'Vava is almost certain death. But Howahkan and his people are right about one thing; you're likely their only hope if there is any."

Again, the night became quiet. Siwili waited for Etchemin's response.

Then Etchemin said, "And what do you think of this thing, my wife?"

Siwili was surprised when he suddenly realized Istas stood directly across from him, also slightly behind Etchemin. He jumped just a little as she turned to him. He could see her smile slightly and felt a bit embarrassed that his sister was able to sneak up on him this way.

She said nothing for a moment. Etchemin continued to stare out into the night as his wife considered the situation. Finally, she replied.

"If we should walk past someone who is drowning, and they call out for us to help them, and we look around to see that we're the only ones that can help them, then we must either risk our lives to do so or forever hear their dying cries in our sleep."

Etchemin and Siwili slowly turned to Istas. They looked at her for several seconds as if very impressed. Etchemin then turned back to the open area where the moonlight exposed high grass and several fireflies flashing to each other.

After another moment of silence, Etchemin spoke.

"Istas is right. We have only two paths available. And of those two paths, there's only one that we can walk with honor."

Etchemin turned and walked back to the camp with Istas and Siwili following behind.

Howahkan woke at dawn. Etchemin and the other two sat across from the dead fire; they were staring at him as if waiting for him to wake up.

Sitting up, he tried to think of something to say. "Did I sleep late?"

Rather than answer Howahkan's question, Etchemin began asking one of his own.

"How many Mbana'Vava are in this pack?"

Howahkan scratched his head as he sleepily considered this.

"We've counted seven, but there seems to be more that stay back in their cave. In the beginning, they would sometimes take our samo too. These were the times we counted at least seven. But the samo put up a fight, and several of the demons were bitten very hard. So, they stopped taking the samo and only took us. This seems to be an easy thing for them."

Howahkan's face dropped a little as if recalling fellow villagers who had become victims. After a few seconds, he continued.

"We've lost seventeen so far, likely more since I've been away. Men, women, and children, the Mbana'Vava only see us as food. They prey on us when they need meat. I think they may prefer samo meat, but it's easier to kill and drag people back to their cave."

He glanced at the three hosts. His face appeared weary. He continued.

"I believe the chief and elders sent me in search of you because I have no family left. My parents died of a sickness when I was young. I'm not sure that my village thought I could find you or gain your help if I did. I don't seem to be very skilled at anything."

Etchemin, Istas, and Siwili gave no expression as he spoke, but they listened intently.

Howahkan continued, appearing glad to finally tell someone these things.

"Our village is not a large one. We've asked others for help, but they fear the Mbana'Vava will turn and prey on their women and children. It's all our men can do to minimize the damage. The ferocity of these monsters can frighten even the bravest of men."

Howahkan then glanced up to Etchemin. He reacted as if he may have said too much. But neither Etchemin nor the others made any expression. They seemed to be taking every word in and building a picture of the Mbana'Vava in their minds.

As Howahkan noticed this, he also realized how far he'd wandered from Etchemin's question. He meekly continued.

"I feel there are at least ten in the pack. They now attack in twos, and fours depending on how much food they wish to take. There are always several in the back as reserves, we think."

He then waited for a reply as the sun slowly began to warm the campsite.

Etchemin appeared to be studying the ground in front of him. The others turned to him after a long silent pause. He continued to examine the bare dirt. Then he finally spoke.

"Have you and your people talked about moving elsewhere to get away from the Mbana'Vava?"

Howahkan replied quickly, "Yes, but no one will leave. The land is ours, and on that land is the Ngengele Zumbi... the *Fortune Tree*, which holds the blood of our ancestors. It's been decided that we will find a way to defeat the Mbana'Vava, or we will all die on our homelands fighting them. To move is not an option for us."

The young man looked at the three again. He glanced down and continued.

"I'm a simple man. I don't have skill with words or weapons. But when I saw my friends killed and carried off by those beasts, I decided I must do everything I could to help my village."

Etchemin took a deep breath and exhaled slowly.

"We'll assist your people."

Howahkan sat up, seeming surprised at the rather quick decision.

"Oh, that's great to hear. My village will be so happy to have any hope at all. We've almost resigned ourselves to a gradual elimination by the Mbana'Vava."

Etchemin and the other two nodded with little emotion. Then Istas stood and began to prepare a small meal as the men packed the samo for travel.

Chapter Two

An anxious feeling moved through the small village. Howahkan and the trio had arrived three days prior, and the grateful villagers had fed their guests well and provided them with their own small but cozy home made of rubber to rest and store their supplies. Howahkan was now regarded as a hero and rumors about him being appointed Chief Messenger were going around.

Another night passed, and after the morning meal, Etchemin prepared his electrolaser carbine for duty. The children and a few men gathered around to watch curiously, as they'd not been this close to such a weapon.

Istas practiced with her bow the day after, and again a small audience gathered around the highly skilled bow woman. Her accuracy was remarkable, and Howahkan began to feel some hope as arrow after arrow hit its mark.

The next day, Howahkan approached Etchemin and Istas as they examined the arrows, which were now treated with impundulu feces. As Etchemin held them up and moved them side to side, a nasty tarlike goo could be seen on the points. Howahkan's face twisted a little as he imagined being struck with such a lethal projectile.

Etchemin commented to Istas as she studied the arrows in her husband's hand.

"Be sure you have a clear shot and try to strike the largest targets. We don't want you setting fire to one of these homes."

Istas nodded her head a little and then slipped the arrow into its wooden quiver.

That afternoon Etchemin looked over vibroblade spears and an assortment of crude weapons made by the villagers.

The vibroblade spears were indistinguishable from regular spears but vibrated thousands of times per second, doing much more damage than a normal spear and ignoring armor or the carapace of a Mbana'Vava.

He showed several how to hold the shafts and how to thrust the vibroblade spears into the target. Most of the men were not skilled enough to throw a spear and do significant damage. They were farmers, healers, and priests. Most of the warriors had been taken already.

Howahkan considered his abilities as one of the village men jabbed the spear at an imaginary Mbana'Vava. He realized he, too, was sorely deficient in the skills needed to do battle with such creatures. He'd been searching for Etchemin while his fellow villagers fought the creatures. Now, he wondered if he would drop his spear and run or if he would stand and fight when the time came. This concerned him, and he paid closer attention to Etchemin as the warrior instructed the men. Howahkan knew the answer would come soon. The Mbana'Vava would be growing hungry by now.

As the day came closer to its end and the sun began to settle on the horizon, a strange calm hovered over the community. The air felt heavy, and no breeze disturbed it.

While Etchemin, Istas, and Siwili stood outside the rubber hut, Howahkan approached.

"The Mbana'Vava will come this evening. I sense it, as do the dogs. When they begin to whine as if in pain, you should move. The men are preparing now. They will follow you out to the battle area."

Etchemin said nothing but nodded.

Now, he and the other two went inside the hut. Shortly, they emerged, and for the first time, Howahkan saw the three as pure warriors, ready to do battle.

Siwili emerged first, his long braids tied back with golden balls dangling from the ends. He wore indigo barkskin breeches and a matching jacket. Over that was an oxblood leather breastplate studded with indigo beads. Two hand axes rested in his leather waistband.

As Istas exited the small rubber hut, Howahkan felt excited and slightly jealous of Etchemin. She wore a fawn-brown barkskin jacket and calf-high trousers. They fit her well and complimented Istas' athletic figure. Her afro was combed back and tied in place with a leather strap, and she wore a leather quiver on her back full of arrows coated in impundulu feces. Howahkan admired Istas even more at this instant.

When Etchemin stepped from the door of the small hut, Howahkan felt almost frightened. Though Etchemin seldom smiled, he now had a very stoic expression due to the impending battle. He appeared stern and ready for the challenge. He wore an indigo nanoweave vest with no jacket. His broad, ebony shoulders and muscular arms seemed even more threatening now that the fight was close at hand. He wore indigo barkskin trousers and had two hand axes in a leather waistband.

Etchemin's hand axes were obviously of the highest craftsmanship and had vibroblade heads rather than the steel heads that were most prevalent in these areas. In his right arm rested the electrolaser carbine he had acquired at the market.

As Howahkan studied the three with interest and admiration, the dogs brought him back to the situation at hand. They began to whine and move about as if in pain. Etchemin and the others watched curiously as the scruffy canines tucked tails between their legs and moved about whimpering and expressing fright.

The other men of the village gathered around with their weapons. They watched the dogs and Etchemin, who appeared to be studying the group. He then spoke with urgency in his voice.

"Tonight, we must be strong, and we must be brave. The enemy approaches, unaware that this night we'll not allow them to have their way. This night, we turn the war around. Are you with me?"

The men moaned in agreement, weakly and without much enthusiasm. Etchemin's face became strained now. He shouted, and this time, his voice expressed anger.

"Are you with me?!"

The men became more energized as they shouted out in agreement. As the men raised their spears and bows, Howahkan also shouted out from nervous excitement.

"All right then, let the Mbana'Vava's blood run tonight!"

After Etchemin said this, he turned and took off jogging toward the battle area, and the others followed the warrior.

138

Howahkan rushed to fall in behind Istas and Siwili. The three seasoned warriors moved like a breeze through the woods and evening light. He struggled to keep pace with them, and the men behind him also began to fall back.

As they approached the area where they would intercept the Mbana'Vava, Howahkan's spear became heavy, and he labored to bring enough warm air into his lungs.

Etchemin, Istas, and Siwili reached the ravine and stood waiting for the village men. Howahkan arrived, and as he attempted to catch his breath, he became distracted by the three warriors. All three stood calm and not the slightest bit winded from the run. Howahkan felt embarrassed and tried to hide the fact he was laboring to breathe.

Soon, the village men approached; all were struggling to catch their breath. Etchemin looked over the group of around thirty men. He then spoke as several knelt to rest and breathe.

"Don't attack until after I fire the electrolaser carbine. Once I fire, everyone attacks. We'll need to strike hard and fast. This is for your village and your families. We must end the Mbana'Vava's threat, and that starts here tonight."

He then sent men into the hillsides of the ravine. He positioned Istas behind a large rock that stood beside a tree. Howahkan watched nervously as the woman calmly adjusted her quiver of impundulu arrows and prepared for the fight.

Etchemin then turned to Siwili, "My brother, that high position over there will be good for your hand axes. You can send them down from behind the beasts."

Siwili nodded and took his satchel of weapons up to the area indicated by his brother-in-law. Now, only Howahkan stood with his spear in hand. Etchemin gazed over the battle preparations, and Howahkan asked in a withering voice, "Where do you wish for me to be?"

As the light of day faded, the tall warrior turned to Howahkan. He studied him for a few seconds, and Howahkan worried that Etchemin would tell him to go back to the village. He felt the great man see the fear in his eyes. He tried to stand tall and brave. Finally, Etchemin replied.

"I need you to position yourself over there." He pointed to several trees around twenty yards back to the left and about twenty-five yards directly behind Istas.

Etchemin continued in a softer voice.

"Istas has no fear of death. I need you to watch her and help her if needed. We must have her skills with a bow if we're to win this fight.

Don't let her know this is your task, though. Do you understand, How-ahkan?"

Howahkan felt both proud and terrified that Etchemin had placed this responsibility on him. He nodded, "Yes, I understand. I'll watch out for her."

Etchemin then began checking his electrolaser carbine as How-ahkan moved into position. He glanced at Istas in front of him. She pulled an impundulu arrow from her quiver and placed it in her bow but did not draw it tight yet.

Glancing around at the village men, he could see a few moving about nervously behind trees and brush. Then, the smell of freshly turned dirt and honey drifted into the area. Suddenly, death seemed to be creeping across the ravine on the slight breeze.

Howahkan placed his hand up to his face to dilute the disgusting smell. One man across the ravine began to vomit. He quickly recovered, and as this took place, they heard the frightening sounds of the approaching Mbana'Vava in the distance.

From in front and perhaps two hundred yards away, a clicking noise mixed with wet hisses entered Howahkan's ears. It became apparent that several beasts were moving toward the group.

Definitely the Mbana'Vava.

Etchemin stared into the growing darkness. The smell of the Mbana'Vava was repulsive, but the clicking and hissing sounds of the approaching creatures stirred a deep apprehension in the warrior. It was like no sound Etchemin had ever heard. As the creatures grew closer, he raised his electrolaser carbine into a ready position.

Howahkan turned his attention to Istas again as his heart beat faster and faster. She stood with one foot forward on the large rock. She had an arrow ready in the bow, prepared to pull it taut and release the projectile into her target. She stared with resolve into the ravine as her enemy approached.

Now, Howahkan lifted his spear and turned his attention forward. The faint outlines of the Mbana'Vava were seen approaching. They moved about as animals on all fours but occasionally stood and sniffed the air. Then, the clicking and hissing would resume as they again moved forward.

The stench of the foul beasts became much stronger as they slowly crept closer. Howahkan wanted to cover his nose. A bead of sweat rolled down the side of his head. He gripped the spear tighter. They were very close now.

Howahkan glanced quickly at Etchemin, who stood like a statue aiming the electrolaser carbine and waiting for his shot. Howahkan turned back to the beasts. They were large, perhaps seven feet tall. The Mbana'Vava were shaped like a human but had a chitinous exo-skeleton and extremely thin, but immensely strong, limbs, and their arms were slightly longer than human arms. Their faces were not human at all. They appeared, to Howahkan, as enraged ants. Their crimson faces had matte black eyes with no discernible pupils and a mouth full of wedged dagger-like teeth. They had no noses, just nostrils, were hairless, and their expressions were vicious.

Now they came into full view. Howahkan counted four, and they were well in the target range at this point. With apparent apprehension, the creatures stopped. It seemed they had caught the scent of the villagers. Each Mbana'Vava stood tall and looked around while sniffing the air.

Etchemin took aim, and the loud whirr from his electrolaser carbine sounded.

Howahkan watched as a ball of crackling white energy slammed into one of the Mbana'Vava, throwing it back into the air and then onto the hard ground.

For a second, the other creatures stood in shock. They looked back at the downed beast and appeared not to understand what had happened or what the loud whirr of the electrolaser carbine was. Then, an arrow from Istas' bow penetrated the back of a Mbana'Vava that was examining the one hit by the electrolaser carbine ball.

A chittering yell of pain burst from the foul creature's mouth as it burst into flames from the arrow strike. Immediately, another of Istas' arrows struck a different Mbana'Vava and this one also chittered and burned.

The Mbana'Vava now realized they were under attack, and as the village men began shooting their arrows and throwing spears and rocks, the creatures became very aggressive. Everything began to move swiftly as the monsters burst into action.

Howahkan's eyes widened as one of the Mbana'Vava ran straight toward Etchemin, who had sat the electrolaser carbine down and now held a hand axe in each hand. One of the other creatures moved in jerky pounces, viciously overtaking several of the village men.

The grip on Howahkan's spear tightened, and his blood felt hot. He took several steps back and turned to see the third Mbana'Vava charging toward Istas. She stood motionless with the arrow pulled back in her bow. Howahkan took off running toward her but knew he wouldn't reach her before the Mbana'Vava did.

Just as the creature was springing into the air toward the bow woman, she let the arrow fly and immediately fell to the left. The projectile pierced the beast's eye and lodged into its skull while it was in midair.

Howahkan stopped as the Mbana'Vava tumbled onto the ground twenty feet from him, landing with a grunt against a tree. He then moved toward Istas to fulfill Etchemin's request that he assist her.

Istas had tumbled away from the Mbana'Vava just as she shot the arrow. She rolled several times and was back on her feet, quickly pulling another arrow from her quiver and she began firing at the Mbana'Vava attacking the men.

The men of the village were trying to keep the creature encircled, and Howahkan noticed Istas holding her shots several times to avoid hitting one of the men. The Mbana'Vava, in turn, would attack a man and inflict damage, but then the other men would move in with spears. This would cause the beast to release the victim and again take a defensive stance.

As Howahkan came closer to the Mbana'Vava that Istas had downed with an arrow to the eye, he glanced over to Etchemin. This battle was moving at a pace Howahkan could barely comprehend. His breathing quickened as he stepped up to the small hill and watched Etchemin in action.

A short distance from Etchemin, a few of the men stood with spears and arrows ready. But the Mbana'Vava moved in random, skittering movements, and they couldn't get a shot or spear in without possibly hitting Etchemin. The warrior constantly kept his face to the creature as it would attack again and again. He used the hand axes with skill and as extensions of his hands and arms. The foul beast would jump toward him, and he would extend the hand axes, causing the rapidly vibrating axe heads to ignore the creature's exoskeleton and inflict damage on it, keeping it from reaching him. He would then roll back, causing the Mbana'Vava to miss him. The warrior would quickly be back on his feet and face the beast before it could gain an advantage.

As Howahkan reached the small hill and observed the fierce battles around him, the downed Mbana'Vava began to stand. Howahkan turned and stared at the creature in disbelief as it slowly rose to its feet, Istas' arrow still protruding from its eye. It began to hiss rapidly and staggered some as if the wound was causing severe pain. Its remaining black eye looked at Howahkan with expressed anger and wrath.

He glanced over to Istas and realized she was focused on the other Mbana'Vava. He began to tremble as the injured beast started to move toward him.

"Istas, somebody, this one's not dead!" He held his spear, pointed at it, and glanced over to Istas. She quickly pulled arrows from her quiver and shot them, unaware of Howahkan's pleas for help.

He backed up as the Mbana'Vava began moving to attack. It clicked and hissed fiercely as greenish-yellow blood streamed from the arrow in its eye. As Howahkan stepped back, he tripped on something and fell back to the ground. His heart raced as he tried to maneuver the spear into a defensive position.

Just as the injured Mbana'Vava was about to overcome Howahkan, something hit it in the front shoulder area. It reared back and screamed out. As it recovered, Howahkan realized a hand axe was buried in its chest and shoulder area. Then, instantly another hand axe landed in its chest, and as the creature stumbled back, another one landed in its neck area.

The Mbana'Vava continued to fall back and landed on the ground with a thud. Howahkan turned back to see Siwili with a hand axe in his hand, ready to throw if necessary, but this time, the Mbana'Vava was dead, and Siwili quickly turned back to help his sister battle the beast still attacking the men of the village.

Howahkan stood, trembling from the close call. He turned to Etchemin and again witnessed the warrior in his element.

The Mbana'Vava appeared to be growing weary as it attacked again and again. Etchemin thwarted each advance, and as the creature attempted to recover, the warrior inflicted blow after blow from the hand axes. The Mbana'Vava screeched out in pain, cuts on its arms and back from the hits. Etchemin immediately put himself into a defensive position for the next attack. He seemed to be conserving his energy as he fought, slowly wearing down the giant beast.

Several of the village men who had moved away when the Mbana'Vava charged were now moving in also to attack the creature that faced Etchemin. As it was focused on the warrior, the men would move in and stab it with spears. This caused the beast to turn, and as it moved on the men, Etchemin would strike it with a hand axe.

Howahkan turned back to the other remaining Mbana'Vava. He moved closer to assist in the battle. This creature had already taken down several men, and their lifeless bodies lay scattered about.

Istas fired another arrow into the Mbana'Vava's side. It turned and clicked rapidly as fire erupted from the wound. Howahkan was within a short distance of the bow woman when it charged Istas. She tried to get another arrow out, but the Mbana'Vava was too fast. As it closed in on her, she swung the bow like a club to keep the attacking creature at a distance. The beast took hold of the bow and yanked it side to side, trying to get to Istas. The woman warrior was thrown around as she held the bow tight, attempting to keep the Mbana'Vava at a distance.

Howahkan had never been so frightened in his life, but he ran straight for the creature with his spear. He yelled out and thrust his weapon into the side of the Mbana'Vava. It again hissed and turned its attention to Howahkan, letting the bow drop. Howahkan was immediately thrown about as the beast grabbed the spear and hurled him around while struggling to remove it from its side.

His act of bravery moved the Mbana'Vava from Istas. After the beast pulled the spear from its side, it let out a tremendous hiss and dashed out of the battle area, running over several of the village men on its way out and back in the direction of the caves.

Howahkan stood and glanced over at Istas, who was picking herself up from the ground. She held her side and appeared to be wounded or bruised at the very least.

By this time, darkness was making it difficult to see the struggle between the remaining Mbana'Vava and Etchemin. Howahkan moved cautiously toward the sounds of battle. As he limped forward, he saw lights from headband flashlights moving toward them. His heart lifted as he realized the women and elders of his tribe were moving rapidly toward the battle with spears.

As this occurred, he could also see Etchemin and the Mbana'Vava in an apparent standoff; the giant creature was obviously wounded and breathing laboriously. Etchemin had wounds as well, and his skin glistened from the blood dripping out of them.

Everyone moved slowly toward the two. The Mbana'Vava hissed aggressively and, noticing the lights approaching, turned to escape and ran over several men, violently knocking them to the ground.

The foul creature ran past Howahkan so closely that the sickeningly sweet stench flowed into his nostrils and again almost caused him to vomit. He staggered backward and watched the wounded Mbana'Vava as it moved past Istas, who also stepped back to avoid being overrun by the fleeing creature.

As the torches lit the area and the weary men watched the wounded Mbana'Vava run away, Etchemin went by Howahkan in a flash.

Howahkan took another breath, still trying to get the smell out of his senses. He stood in disbelief as the warrior ran in pursuit of the deadly beast. Into the darkness, he went. Howahkan could barely comprehend anyone pursuing another fight with such a creature. He watched Istas as she attempted to follow her husband but fell back down, holding her side. The village men stood in the light of the flashlights, unsure of what to do, seeming to have had their fill of battling the Mbana'Vava.

Siwili took off quickly behind his brother-in-law and was the only one able to follow Etchemin into the darkness. As Istas began to crawl to assist her husband and brother, they heard a terrifying hiss and three rapid clicks. Then the sounds of a violent struggle erupted. For several minutes, everyone stood in silence, listening to the fight in the distance.

Suddenly all became quiet. The women and men of the village stood staring into the night. Istas sat motionless, still holding her side, and watching for anything to indicate she wasn't a widow.

Then, something or someone approached. Siwili came into the light, holding a hand axe in one hand and appearing dazed. Istas took in a breath and moaned in relief that her brother was alive. But still, she sat motionless, watching for Etchemin.

The silence became almost unbearable as all waited. Then, Etchemin came slowly into the light. He held his two hand axes, and though bloodied and battered, it was evident he'd been victorious. Istas finally exhaled in joy at the sight of her husband.

An immediate celebration began as everyone cheered and shouted. All the children and elders of the village began to filter into the battle area and examine the dead Mbana'Vava. Howahkan watched with compassion as some found their fallen family members and quietly mourned during the excitement of finally winning a battle over the Mbana'Vava.

Etchemin helped Istas up, and Siwili assisted her on the other side. Howahkan obtained a torch and went to them. He thought they would move to the village, but instead, they walked out to the dead Mbana'Vava, which Etchemin had killed before it escaped.

As they came closer to the downed creature, Istas began to walk on her own again. The sounds of the happy villagers became less significant at this place. Howahkan became a bit nervous and wondered what the three warriors were doing.

They walked around the dead Mbana'Vava and continued a little farther. Now, in the darkness, other than the illumination of Howahkan's flashlight, he realized why they came here. Across the valley and in the cave of the Mbana'Vava, a tremendous uproar was occurring. Etchemin must have heard this after he'd killed the fleeing beast.

The four stood for several moments. There were many Mbana'Vava clicking and hissing with anger. The one that had escaped must have been communicating the fight to the others.

Etchemin turned to Istas and Siwili. Howahkan stood back a bit but heard their words clearly.

"This may be the fight we'll not survive."

Etchemin's face was emotionless as he said this. Istas and Siwili appeared to give the comment some thought. Then, Istas replied with her usual dry tone and lack of expression.

"That's good. I don't wish to mourn either one of you. And since we'll be dying together, I won't have to."

Howahkan could see a slight surprise on Etchemin's face due to his wife's bluntness. Siwili also glanced at his sister as if shaken a bit by the hard words.

Etchemin considered this for a few seconds and then said with a little more optimism, "We may live, though. We'll make plans for the next battle."

Siwili quickly picked up on this and became optimistic, "Yes, we need to make some plans. That'll help."

Istas said nothing and gave no expression to her thoughts. They then moved back to the dead beast that was now being prepared for burning. As villagers piled branches and wood upon the carcasses of the downed Mbana'Vava, Etchemin, Istas, and Siwili walked to the village to clean themselves up.

All night the villagers celebrated as the foul corpses burned. Howahkan watched from a distance but realized the real fight was just beginning. For now, at least, it was good for the people to be happy. There was a chance after all, if only a small one.

Stronghold
by
Jessica Cage

Chunks of gray flesh and a thick sticky substance, the blood of the alien beast she had just cut down, dripped from her afro as the music played in her ear. She bobbed her head, humming to the sound. *"Uptown funk you up, Uptown funk you up."* Her foot tapped to the beat she used to keep pace of her actions. As the tempo quickened, Ranish caught a quick glimpse of herself, a reflection in a darkened window, and smiled hungrily. The blood of her enemy coated her toned arms, and she wiped it from her dark flesh.

Ranish had just taken out three Larken with no help from the members of her team who were still in route. Whether they caught up to her or not, she had no intention of stopping. The war was underway.

Two nights prior, the commanding ship sent word back to Earth of the approaching vessels. Six enemy ships would touch down on their world in a matter of days. The defensive strategy to protect their world in space was failing. With the advance notice, the ground teams got most of the remaining humans to safety. That meant either a flight off the world or taking cover deep beneath the surface.

Ranish was a fighter, one of the best left on Earth. She was a warrior of the Stronghold and proud of it. During battle was when she really got to show out. The last thing she was going to do was run away from the coming fight.

"Ra, let's go!" Her commander, the only member of the Echo team to move ahead of her, called to her, and she moved back into action, cutting down another one of the slimy beasts on her way.

Larken were hideous things, with nine legs that lined their circular bodies. At the front they had a large, spiked horn, which they used as a weapon to stab their enemy and inject with a deadly toxin. The key to defeating the ugly thing most efficiently was to get beneath it.

While the common attack was long range, this often proved ineffective as the hard outer shell protected the monster from most gunfire. Just underneath the exoskeleton was a soft underbelly, the monsters' weak spot. If the shooter wasn't skilled enough to pinpoint the soft flesh in one shot, they might as well just sign their own names to the meal plan for the alien invaders.

Ranish didn't believe in hiding behind a gun. She liked to get up close and personal. As another beast fell between her and the path her commander laid out, she easily slid beneath it, blade at the ready, and slit each one from tail to horn.

It didn't bother her, the mess of the slaughter. There was nothing better than witnessing firsthand as life drained away from her enemy. Since she was a child, they had trained her for the close kill. The golden rule was to never show fear, never back away from what you needed to do. To cower, to let your enemy know you were afraid, was to present a weakness. The day Ranish let fear control her actions on the battlefield would be the day she would lay her weapons down for good.

Knowing that her opponents were mindless creatures with no actual skill in fighting made her job easier. There was nothing driving the monsters but their foundation of death. Larken were beasts that were bred for destruction. The first ship brought them to Earth in crates and dropped them from the skies. Packages that shattered and spewed forth waves of hungry beasts that caused the deaths of countless humans.

Their masters were the Sav, aliens from another world who had called for war with Earth some ninety years earlier. Nearly a century later Earth was still holding on, but only just barely. The Sav knew they were close to a victory and if Ranish and her team could help hold them off longer, their weapons would be ready to deploy. The launch would turn the tides in favor of the human population.

It took nearly three decades to understand Sav's technology, and another six to replicate it. Luckily, the geeks in the weapons department figured it out. Not only did they figure it out, but they enhanced it. The new version could soon penetrate force fields that once proved impervious. It would finally level the playing field. Savs themselves weren't that tough to beat in a fight. They were just difficult to get to.

Ranish's pride in her kills directly resulted from the personal value she placed on her weapons. Each one was handcrafted by her father and made from the metal of the first fallen Sav ship. Her father's crew was the one to shoot it down. Their reward for the victory was that they each got to take a piece of the ship home. While others went for baubles, he chose metal.

It was stronger than any found on earth. Her father made her two perfect knives, and a double tipped spear that not only expanded into a trident on both ends but also detached at the middle for ease of use in combat. The weapons were lightweight, which meant that they were easy to maneuver and so sharp they cut those beasts like butter.

The target was the control room. It was still secure but under heavy attack. If the damn things made it inside, their city would be the first to fall, and if they allowed that to happen, others would collapse quickly after. Additional artillery was on its way. They just had to keep the center secure until the cavalry arrived. Inside those doors, a timer was counting down. Just forty-eight hours until the missiles launched. Forty-eight hours until the Sav would finally come to see that earth wasn't for the taking and the human population wouldn't just lie down and die.

She lived for this moment. War was in her blood. The only daughter of a war hero, the granddaughter of a highly decorated soldier, they raised her with battle in mind.

Ranish and the commander came up on the tail end of the group of monsters trying to break through the barrier wall to get to the room that housed the main frame. Three of their men lay dead in the room. The Larken fed on their lifeless bodies. Ranish wanted to make her move as soon as she saw them. Her mind ran through the ways she could dismantle the disgusting things.

The commander, who knew exactly where her mind was going, signaled her to hold. They needed to wait for the rest of their team. The creatures outnumbered them and needed as much backup as they could get. She wanted to rush forward but held her position. She wouldn't get expelled from duty for not following a simple command.

Three long minutes later, backup arrived. Three men joined them; Jemal, the tech, Charles, the shooter, and Tone, the one who preferred hand-to-hand combat. In the fight, it was typically Tone by her side and Charles covering their asses from afar. Together with Ranish, they were the top of their class, the best of the best, and hand-picked by the commander to fight with him. It had been nearly a decade that their team operated together, a unit protecting their home.

Their first outing, Ranish proved herself among the team of men and earned their respect when she saved Charles from two Larken who had him cornered. She often wondered if the commander put them in the sticky position for that very reason. From that moment forward, she felt nothing but camaraderie and a sense of family, a welcome feeling after the death of her mother and father.

She was away at training when it happened. Bombers took out a nearby city, but masses of Larken fell right on top of them. Her father was bombshell ready, but the underground bunker wasn't built to withstand an onslaught from the Larken. Her parents had made it inside, doors closed, but it was too late. One of the damn things got in. It was the third time they dropped those beasts, and they took her parents from her. Ranish did everything she could to avoid the thoughts of her parents' last moments alive.

Eagerly, she waited for the signal to move forward. Her job was always the same. Take down as many of the damned things as possible. Keep moving, keep killing. Two silent taps on the commander's right thigh were her confirmation. Show time.

It was instantaneous, the transformation that happened almost like the flip of a switch. Skilled killer emerged and like a ballet of bloodshed she moved through the mass of alien intruders. Charles was on her flank, making sure nothing caught her by surprise. Jemal and the commander headed for the main panel. The secondary wall that blocked access to the control panel had jammed leaving it partially open, and they hoped like hell that their tech guy could get the damned thing closed.

Once there, the commander turned toward the fight, keeping Jemal protected as he worked. The nerd bobbed his head as the speaker on his shoulder played afrobeats. Ranish turned off her own tunes, knowing it would be a fight she wouldn't win. Jemal controlled the sounds. They listened to it everywhere they went because he said he couldn't work without it. The rhythmic sounds of the diaspora kept him grounded.

Ranish kept in motion, often moving to the beat from Jemal's music. She choreographed her movements like a dance to be executed for an audience. Too bad the ones who watched her would be the targets of her deadly actions. There would be no applause, no standing ovation for her fluid movements.

More Larken were coming. The pounding of clawed feet hitting the ground sounded like a storm of hail rushing in their direction. It didn't matter what was coming, all that mattered was what they were already facing. The screeching cry of the beast as she dismembered the back two legs gave her pleasure and motivation to keep moving.

"Jemal, get that door shut!" Ranish yelled out as she finished another kill. The floor had become slick with the blood that spilled from the dying bodies of the Larken. She opened a dry pack and tossed it across the floor. The dark powder adhered to the goo and gave her better footing.

"I'm almost there; just hold them off!" The tall man shouted over his shoulder.

Tone and Charles took the lead, with the immediate threat subdued; it was their turn to keep the approaching threat at bay. Long range firearms which shot out nets of lasers took down groups of the beasts at once but they are still coming, their line quickly closing in.

Ranish fell back; she caught her breath while taking inventory of the slaughter on the floor. Anything that twitched got another blow from her spear. Too many times she had seen someone lose their life because they didn't take the time to make sure their kills were clean and final. She never claimed her victories until she was sure the job was done.

"They're closing in, Jemal! Tell me you found gold." The commander called out.

"Just give me one more minute!" Jemal insisted, bouncing his head to the music.

Ranish looked out at the approaching herd. The beasts were nearly at their door. She took a deep breath and centered herself. Just like they taught her, she would go down fighting. She lifted the spear and engaged the release to turn one into two. Holding the weapons at her side, she stared ahead. The thunderous sound of the Larken approach was now paired with strong tremors on the floor.

"As soon as that door closes, hit the kill switch! All of those bastards will burn!" Jemal told the commander, who left his side to access the panel just a few feet away. He lifted the glass casing that protected the controls. His hand hovered just above the switch and he trained his eyes on the door.

There were just a few yards left between them and the threat. Tone and Charles were doing their best to hold the line back, but there were just too many of them to shoot down. Those yards turned into feet and their hope of securing the control room diminished.

Just as Ranish centered herself, ready to flip her internal kill switch, the doors slid shut. Three of the bastards got in before it closed. The commander slammed on the kill switch and the cries of the Larken rang out and echoed the sounds of their monster brothers who made it inside. The smell of burning flesh seeped into the room through small overhead vents as, once again, Ranish confirmed her kill. Charles did the same with the two he had taken out.

"Yeah!" Tone high-fived Charles, who hooted his excitement. The two did their usual battlefield dance as Ranish and Jemal laughed. "Burn you ugly bastards!"

"Let's not get too excited." The commander patted a sweat covered Jemal on the shoulder. "We still have to keep this room secure for the next seventeen hours. Once that missile launches, then we celebrate."

For the next seventeen hours, they watched the clock. Though they could hear the Larken's efforts to reach them, the barrier wall held. The radar on the dash showed their increasing numbers. The creatures were swarming the station.

They had to hold their position for seventeen more hours. At which point all teams were to return to home base. They were decoys, taking attention away from the real threat to the enemy.

Fifteen hours and the Larken got closer, but the wall held. Twelve hours and they could hear the cries as more fires burned their bodies. Every time they tried to get around the defense, they ran into a fresh trap. But the explosions were getting closer, which meant the bombs weren't enough to hold them back forever.

Nine hours and they received their first communication from home base.

"Go for command." The deep voice of the woman came over the line.

"All good on our end." The commander reported.

"Section nine has fallen. All others hold steady."

"Are we on track?" The commander asked.

"Yes," she responded. "Will reach out when ready for return. Hold strong."

At four hours, there was silence. The base became eerily quiet. Even the Larken noises hushed, as if they were waiting for something. Two hours later, the things surrounded them. The few traps left sounded, and that was all they had. The things got past the last defense and were just outside their door. It would hold. It had to. The team had to hold their position.

Zero hour.

All eyes stared at the clock as they waited. Minutes slipped by like salt through a shaker. The team looked at their commander. Just before he spoke, the radio sounded.

"Go for command." The deep voice of the woman called out.

"We're still good." He reported, and the others sighed.

"Bring her home."

Jemal slammed his hand on the control panel. Gears cranked and as they disengaged from the surrounding platform, they released loud pops. As the last released, it ejected the central room from its base and sent them flying back to home base. The action started a self-dstruct sequence and as they flew off, the station exploded beneath them. Ranish looked out of the window to watch the symphony of Larken deaths. Their bodies burned as they tried to run from the explosion, but it was too late.

They were the fourth to arrive at home base. The decision to abandon the eighteen stations was a strategic one. Let the beasts have them.

"Ranish." The hand on her shoulder stopped her as she exited the ship.

"Commander?" She turned back to the older man to meet a serious expression. His grey brows furrowed over his deep eyes.

"You ready to take flight?"

"What?" she asked, a twisted feeling of excitement and concern knotted in her stomach.

"They asked for our best." He pointed to the sky and her eyes followed.

"You mean,"

"It's time for you to go up." He nodded.

"I thought I was staying here." She recalled their last conversation. He said her skills were better used on the ground.

"Change of plans." He stepped down off the platform to stand beside her. "You got this. I wouldn't send you if I didn't think you could handle it. Time to make your father prouder."

Things moved faster than she thought they would. The admin team, two fidgety women who looked like they had lost all hope, gave her a quick briefing about the journey, then sent her to the lockers to redress. Not two minutes after she finished strapping on her suit, the same nervous women marched her onto the transport ship. The vessel would take the fighters from Earth to the BOA, the station positioned beyond their atmosphere where their space army held the last line of defense.

The belt strapped around her waist and secured her into her seat. With the final click of security, her stomach turned, but she swallowed her nerves. She thought of the commander's words. This was her opportunity to continue the fight her father's team started and return that hope to their people. Jemal's music played in her ear through the tiny bud. It was a gift from the brother who hoped to see her again.

Seven transporter ships launched. Ranish was aboard the last to lift off. She looked out the window as the blue skies turned dark as they left the Earth's atmosphere. Three ships shot off ahead of

154

hers and she prepared herself for the thrust that would shift her into hyper speed.

She took a deep breath and started her own countdown, but before she hit zero, everything stopped. Two ships directly in front of her exploded. They were under attack. She felt the heat as the thrust engaged and her ship shot off through the debris of the other ships. She made it out, but what about the others?

They landed on BOA and things once again moved so quickly she barely kept up with the orders. Two large men ushered her from the transporter ship into the dock where the fighter ships were waiting for their passengers. They threw weapons in her hands and told her to take cover before they closed the heavy door, locking her inside. Ranish jumped into her assigned pod. She hadn't even locked in her belt before they took flight.

Ten minutes later, her ship made it to the battleground. In mid space, dark ships lined up against the enemy. They shot fire but made no real impact. Not that they meant to. The strategy gave the enemy a false sense of comfort. The Sav thought the humans had nothing stronger than what they were currently shooting them with.

Ranish imagined their plan was to wait them out. Let them burn through the ammo, then attack. The ugly things were probably rubbing their tentacles together, laughing. If they could laugh. But the secret was coming. The countdown sounded in all their ears.

Five . . . four . . . three . . . two . . . one.

Launch.

The missile hit and a rainbow of colors spread across the dark canvas of space.

She held her breath until the next shot landed. There was no barrier to stop the explosive. It hit and created a hole in the side of the ship.

The Sav no longer held their fire as the fighter ships took off and deployed their pods. The barrier around the alien warcraft fell, and they continued to blast it. Their explosions landed, and each one opened a new hole along the side of the massive ship.

Ranish braced as they shot her pod across the void of space like a bullet through glass and it landed roughly inside the gaping hole in the side of the war vessel. As soon as they touched down, the pods opened, and the fighters jumped out. Ranish held her position near the opening as the others went deeper inside. She had one job. Keep the pods clear.

She cut down anything that came her way. The monsters on the ship were nothing like the nine-legged creatures they dropped on earth. Despite the differences, she was prepared. Though she never encountered one of the things head on, there was plenty of training provided by those who had. It didn't matter what they called them. They would die all the same. They were easier to kill. No tough outer shell to get by. Their blood was different. Instead of sticky grey matter, they bled a yellow liquid that stunk like corn chips.

She took out seven of the vile things, but despite her best efforts, they cornered her. Three hideous creatures with tentacles hanging from their jaws stared her down as she split the spear in two and held one at each side. Ranish took a deep breath to steady her nerves before she moved.

First, she stabbed one in the face, slid beneath its body, and before it hit the ground, she cut the legs from another. Unfortunately, the last one slipped by her and its blade ripped through her side before she slit its neck open. She stood, leaned against the wall, and assessed the damage. It felt worse than it looked. In a swift motion she applied the med tape and winced at the frost sensation that spread across her torso. She would survive.

All she had to do was wait for the team to get back. The countdown was on. They would plant the bombs inside the ship and escape in their pods, which, thanks to her, were still waiting for them to get back. With the sound of another wave of the incoming threat, she hit the button on her collar. Afrobeats played as she began her dance. The choreography of cutting, slicing, and spilling blood across the floor. This was her moment.

She fought the best fight she ever had in her life and it was a dance, a ballet meant for another audience sentenced to death.

"Ranish," the voice came over her earpiece as she cut the tentacle from another beast and sliced its arm off. The man put in charge of her crew called her name.

"I'm here!" she called out.

"You have to get out of here." The man urged her.

"What? The mission says-,"

"We're not going to make it back before the detonation. Save yourself!"

"Don't talk like that. There's still time and the pods are safe."

"We're surrounded, and more of these things are headed your way. Get out!" he called back. "That's an order!"

And then there was silence.

Long vacant moments punctuated by the rhythmic beat of afrobeats.

She waited.

The countdown ended. It was time to go. If she stayed any longer, she wouldn't make it out. She called over her communications one more time, asking for anyone to respond. There was nothing.

Horrifying silence.

Instinct for survival took over, and she turned to run for her lifeline. A Sav fighter landed between her and salvation, but she responded quickly, swung her blade, and cut the alien bastard down without breaking her stride. She made it to the pod and closed the door, but it was too late to engage the engine.

The blast shook the walls and a moment later it sent her pod flying backwards out of the hole in the side of the ship. She tried to engage the engine, but red lights flashed at her. Engine damaged.

She watched as more of the rainbow of colors exploded out around her and the vessel that carried the enemy caved in, breaking apart. It was over, at least for now.

She made it out. But would she survive? The crack spread across the glass. Help was coming, but would they find her floating in the debris before it was too late?

It didn't matter. They'd done it.

This was the first true victory. Despite all the small ones before it. They showed the enemy they wouldn't lie down and die without a fight.

So many lives were already lost. At least hers would have meaning.

Hope returned to the Stronghold.

Settlement.

The initial victory was short lived.

Earth didn't survive.

They celebrated the win. But soon after, more ships came. While their weapon was powerful, they didn't have enough to take on the enemy.

They had no choice but to move to their contingency plan. The last resort. Leave the world behind. Thirty ships lifted from the ground, carrying the remaining survivors away from their home on an exploration across the galaxy. There was word of one place, one world where they could rebuild.

"Reminiscing again?" Jemal approached his friend.

"Do I ever do anything else?" She looked over her shoulder, but her wild afro blocked her view of the tall man.

"How are you feeling today?" He asked. "Your injuries look better."

"You checked my scans?" She frowned.

"Of course I did." He winked at her as he came into full view. "What kind of friend would I be if I didn't intrusively spy on your medical records?"

"I feel better than yesterday, better than the day before, but still like a fresh pile of shit." Ranish laughed.

"Well, tomorrow maybe the stink will wear off." He handed her a cup of hot tea. The steam lifted from it as she grabbed it.

"How long have we been out here?" Ranish blew on the cup.

"Too long to tell. The days, they don't matter." He rubbed his head. "I don't even think the calendar on my tablet works anymore. Too far gone."

"I guess it doesn't matter. Manmade constructs." She huffed. "Maybe we'll come up with a new method of timekeeping."

"I think we'll have to as soon as we find the place to call home."

"They found it!" Charles came running around the corner. "We're finally getting off this metal bucket!"

"What?"

"They found the Stronghold!" Tone cheered as he followed their teammate into the room.

They walked over to the window, Ranish limping on her left side. The planet came into view. The one they would now call home.

"Think we'll take better care of this place than we did Earth?" Ranish looked at the men by her side.

"Honestly, no." Jemal laughed. "But hey, at least we'll be long gone before humans inevitably ruin this world."

"Always the optimist!" Ranish laughed and for the first time in her life, she felt hope.

Our SpaceWays
by
Akua Lezli Hope

Tasting pale maggots in the mind of the universe

we choose an altered inner outer way to fly

window pane opened views to multiplicities diverse

summoned dimension ships tuned to our kind

We choose an altered inner outer way to fly:

danced an invocating, ancestral spiral dance

summoned dimension ships tuned to our kind

called down the upsters, sung up through trance

Danced an invocating, ancestral spiral dance

remembered from ancient African encoding

called down the upsters, sung up through trance

riding light spaceways as vessels unfolding

remembered from ancient African encoding

Our makers placed their spiral call within

riding rogue spaceways as vessels unfolding

Spacefunk!

see cosmic crowded dance floors we manifest in

Our makers placed their spiral call within

synchronic sounds, blue rhythms of return

see those cosmic crowded dance floors we manifest in

leaving these flesh shells behind, no more to yearn

Synchronic sounds: blue rhythm of return

black orphic circling plucks energy's strings

leaving these soft shells behind, no more to yearn

purple rain perfumes our departing wings

Snow Metal
by
Eugen Bacon

Torvill watches the girls. They outnumber the boys, aloof lads, most of them tradies at the weapons plant. Now the boys, hoods with a bit of income, play keystroke games on small electrode beamers, fiddle with music, act like they have a bit of class. The girls, similar in hip-huggers, in defiance of norm, are mostly signal sorters—these wear honey and black. Torvill understands their working rights, their privileges and independence, their resolve to build Goth hours in graveyard shifts for a lunar paycheck instead of settling as breeders like the rest of their lot.

He also understands the sorting process, what goes on in the pillared towers of the Enclave, an impregnable place, airtight security. In this messaging tower that "listens" to the galaxies, colossal pillars steeple into antennas that pick anion and plutonic noise, any wave leaking off space. It is here that intergalactic battles are lost or won, military or diplomatic secrets intercepted to much vantage. Intel-sensors snap signals into a looping continuum of capsules in a belt system, an intricate network that compresses the waves, sorts them on type, date, time, and origin. Officers in encoding vectors decrypt the signals, assign weight quotient in terms of intelligence, emboss inferred threat into intel-chips for the senate.

Not all girls are graveyarders: scarlet and black indicates rank. These are the encoders: reserved. Unlike the sorters—who chat nonstop to each other, at each other, who gesture continually to demonstrate their talk—encoders hold a dignified air.

The Gate station vibrates. A distant drone grows loud, louder into the platform, until the vessel Shuttronix rolls to a halt. Shuffle, step. Shuffle, step. The crowd files forward. Each citizen takes turn, touches a magnetic pass to a flashing reader. Doors snap open, shut in an instant, boarding pass after pass.

Torvill is almost at the hatch when he notices her at the belly of the queue. Moot! She is a looker. Big hair. Her face is small, celestial. She is paired, he can tell. She wears rank, curvy in her officer's uniform. There is interest in the gold eyes that regard him. He returns her gaze. Burnt-orange lashes, wild and rich as her hair, flutter, then lower. A blush climbs to her cheek. She looks away.

#

The Shuttronix rumbles, rocks. A blast of horn, then a wail. Momentum, a blast of speed, and the vessel spears into the sea. Torvill's stomach tightens. A sneeze gathers in his nostrils. He sees her again, two seats away, unmissable with that hair. Her head is turned. She is gazing at the sea's womb.

He flexes his knees, loosens the throb from his foot. He gazes again at the female. Her blazing head is upright, touching the min-ipod that holds her. Each pod is a capsule, luminous as magic, sturdy as titanium.

The chameleon sea shifts from a map of blue to streaks of sil-ver. Then layers of white and gold vacillate between hues until little points of light fade, until the sea is deep, deep black, miles, miles out. As Torvill's breathing gets even, the vessel sighs, rocks, slogs its speed, judders to a halt and totality of sound.

"The Enclave," says an automat. "Termination point in seven seconds."

Torvill plows through the crowd. Ahead, so does she. He is two lengths behind her. She turns into the jaws of security, the Enclave. He waits at Zone 9 for a sensor shuttle to take him to Embassy Sanz.

#

Three days. And though not a word is spoken, he sees it, un-derstands it. He need not be told: the stagger of her heartbeat at the sight of him; lowered lashes when he meets her stare; a tilt of head; the quiet smile . . . The argue of emotion with her mind; she could well shout it. He hears it. He'd still hear it if she whispered it.

Hers is not a gradual melt—like the others. It comes instant. Magnetic.

Moot! It's a matter of Goth hours. But he is patient.

#

He sees her outside the trapdoor; their shoulders almost brush. This time, he walks ahead. She tails.

"Sir," her voice raspberry.

He turns. The Enclave towers above them, a lime-tinted building, revolving, with spiked protrusions.

"Yes?"

"I *see* you."

"I see *you*."

"Work at the Enclave?"

"No."

"Snow." She stretches her hand. "Snow Metal."

"Torvill." Her grip is tight. "Gaulter."

"You new?"

"Emissary. Land of Sanz."

"The north, huh. So you're the replacement."

"Vice. Former emissary. Let's just say he had other matters."

"Matters? Total recall is what I heard. Vice was not—" She looks for the word. "Effective."

He smiles. "But you are."

#

A nod, a handshake, sometimes a few words.

One day outside the soaring tower of the Enclave, she hovers as he waits for the Zone 9 shuttle. They stand beside a crystal fountain, perfect spray.

Her lips open, close.

He waits.

"Maybe we can . . ." she tries.

"Be effective?" he helps.

She smiles. "Drink sometime?"

"Yes," he says. "Sometime."

"All right. Then."

#

One day, he kisses her.

He takes her to *La Japonesa*. Broiled calf, cured innards, servers a clap away. She eats without reserve, sweet meats in a tender glow of light.

"Hurting for calories?" he says.

She laughs. "Just effective."

Later, much later, she does not protest when he engineers a coach.

#

A week. Oyster Street Fair. They laugh to an exhilaration of speed shuttlers. Wolf burgers at Centro. Down shooters at the Vortex under pink, yellow, and green strobe lighting.

He confounds her with questions: about herself, her family, her work. Yes, mostly her work. She talks: about shuttles, no siblings, geo magnet. Yes, little of her work.

"Come." He pulls her to a swirl of lights, to new music.

Her dance is raw, electrifying.

#

He invites her to Solaris, an island.

They meet by the sea. She is wearing a flowing dress dyed in patterns of rivers and dawn. His shuttle docks into a beautiful and private world. Hands clasping, they climb up hilly terrain, to the tip of a hillock. They gaze at the tossing sea.

When the air turns gray, blustery, as eagles vanish into the darkened sky, a sliver of moon, thin as a snake, casts its glow to the ground.

Torvill sits. His feet are stretched toward the sea.

"Tell me about the Enclave."

"What about it?" she laughs.

"The signals you encode."

"Let's not talk shop."

As they move to kiss, a beam from his eyes sears the gold in her eyes.

"Stop. What are you doing?"

He touches her memory, feels it.

"Stop. Torvill. Hurts—"

"Silence."

She fights him, physically, mentally. He stills her to the ground. But he can't read her. She is masking semantic data. Each download dimension from his beam strikes a call back routine. Success equals zero.

She wrestles from his grasp.

Moot! She is a fighter.

"You cannot decode me," she breathes.

"No one is that—" Torvill rolls, pins her again to the ground. "Effective."

"Get away from me you, you f-fossil, you."

She kicks, rolls, knocks him with a fist.

"You are well trained," he calls after her as she runs. "But I get what I want."

He is a hunter. He stalks, circles. He trails her fear, clothing caught in brush. A twig cracks near him. He pounces, grips her ankle as she flees.

"Get away from me you, you foul smelling, loose-livered, de-generate rake!"

"Good. Fire in your belly."

"*La Japonesa*! Oyster Street! The Vortex! Didn't any of those, us, mean anything?"

"I have a mission."

He hauls her by the foot.

"Torvill! Torvill? Please . . ."

He sits on her, knees astride her chest. He prises her eyes open. He focuses his steady beam to the hippocampus of her brain. Start stimulation implant. Establish neural connection. Convert memory to transferable data: 5 %, 6 %, 14%, 41%, 43%, 43.01%, 43.17% . . . She is blocking him.

It weakens the decoding; shifts his access from her long-term brain hippocampus to short-term amygdala memory. Engrams of data show him the clip of her surrender in his arms that night of *La Japonesa* . . . He relives it: a conscious experience full of sensory data, parsed.

Smash!

#

Rainbows in his focus . . . Torvill sits. He raises a hand to the back of his head, winces. Moot! A rock to his cranium? Volcano in that belly!

Somewhere in the distance, racing with wind and a murmur of sea, his shuttle roars away, away. He pulls a beamer from his back pocket, groans with effort. Mission failed, his syntax to Sanz. Fail, fail, fail hammers in his head.

Unlike Vice, former emissary, total recall is not his to embrace.

Despite soreness, he smiles, half-bemused at his new instruction from the planet up north: "Win her to our side. Make her a double agent."

"And if I fail?" he asks.

"You disintegrate."

First pub. in *Bards and Sages Quarterly, July 2018*.

Even The Stars Die
by
Errick Nunnally

Sometimes the Selfless walked. This one walked as often as it could, in fact.

While other cousins flitted about the universe, chiselling off minuscule chunks of matter or taking special care to shave light beyond the edges of the cosmological horizon, this one preferred to roam more casually and on solid ground. The feeling of affinity to their respective clients was special for all of them, but this client, however, this one was the last of their kind.

Ever since humanity's billions flung themselves to the stars and beyond, the opportunity to walk on soil simply didn't present itself very often. The work doubled, the soil didn't. The ties to humanity, the lodestone of their existence, had compelled the Selfless ever since humanity imagined a future consisting of more than food and sex. As they moved forward in both time and technology, the Selfless remained constant invisible companions. Mostly invisible.

Along the way, in the grandest scope of life, there were only a few truly significant missteps amongst humanity—atomic bombs, weaponized singularities, racism—but its clients learned and evolved. Even if it was done in all the hard ways, by genetic or gravitational collapse, or by them flinging themselves into the stars.

Now, as humanity hurtled through everywhere, they traveled with them, experienced it through their eyes, by the stories humanity forged. The Selfless learned with humanity that the void of space, the indifferent vacuum, had more to offer than any of them imagined. That, in fact, the void was not a void, but a cornucopia of opportunity. Remnants of planets past, an immense tonnage, forever provided the raw material to aid the expansion of life. Cosmic radiation of all sorts, herded along by the

Selfless inside massive fission sail-drives and along gravitational shields, while humanity thrust forward. The work effectively doubled whenever the people bent newly discovered particles to their use. Particles that infinitely permeated every square millimeter of the universe, traveling from one end to the other and around and through and up and, well, *everywhere*.

Even collapsed stars provided opportunity for useful invention as it entered a second life that seduced all of reality around it. The harshest lessons, learned during Mother Earth's crash courses, led to remarkable leaps forward in recursive energies. The Selfless observed it all, but seeing it with humanity made it grander, more interesting. *Worthwhile.*

These days, this one felt the most joy when returning to Earth where it could feel the old gravity and soil beneath its feet. Humanity's birth planet remained a near husk, good only for ecotourism and documentaries. A planet-shaped reminder of The Great Lesson that had stitched itself into humanity's algorithm. Life, after that moment, could only be sustained above, in orbit. And so it went, for enough years that the future came close enough to grasp and the past fell away. Most of the past.

Habitats the size of continents rotating stars solved most of their problems. Rotational gravity, the mass of soil, vegetation, solar equipment, repellers, and especially water. The other Selfless saw them land and shift form, but they did not acknowledge each other.

The green felt good beneath their bare feet, familiar, a wild mix of seed. Healthy soil required less tending than food-bearing lands, and the grass grew without guidance here, in the fields near the homes. The gentle whir of mechanics floated on the air and it knew the automated mowers would pass through soon. A fleet of self-repairing robots that cut and gathered whatever biomass the soil gave and left the rest as mulch.

The solarium satellite joined several others with the dead planet, each with a concentration of reinvigorated flora and fauna, surrounded by the largest saltwater lakes, fresh rivers, and ponds humanity could boost into orbit and nurture with care bordering on religiosity. Most of the residents here were of advanced age, retired from humanity's latest role as a spacefaring species.

In the distance, they could see the old man with whom it had an appointment.

He sat on the white veranda of a small, yellow house. A single story, built like a miniature Colonial, but with the modern flourishes that fashion and survival dictated. Nonetheless, it had all the classic details of a hand-built home.

They felt pleasure that humanity had relearned respect for the end of life again. Good or ill, there was still an ending for all but the Selfless. Humans learned, but they learned slowly, and, like many successful species, relied on a rate of birth that surpassed their rate of death until technology broke that cycle.

Each step brought it closer to the old man's range of sight. In conjunction, an illusory ripple traveled up its body with every footfall. Its form changed; it became human to suit the old man's expectations. A suit of dark color melted into place and its stride took on a longer gait in the centrifugal gravity. A sharp, well-trimmed goatee sprang out from the corners of their full lips and to circle their chin. Against burnished skin the color of a prairie, with long hair and broad shoulders above a thin waist, their form begged more questions than provided answers.

Settling on one gender defied the reality of the spectrum. Shifting in tonality and hue, brightness, and opacity, male and female only defined the furthest poles. For this appointment, the gender required was more of a gray area.

They stopped within hailing distance, said, "Good day, sir," and waited for the old man to look them over. Unseen insects whined in the distance; several others buzzed lazily by.

The device clamped to the client's arm whirred and beeped before unraveling and rolling away to its charging station. Miracles of science and engineering couldn't prolong the inevitable for much longer.

"You lost?"

The Selfless bowed slightly and replied, "No, sir. I'm—"

"I know what you are."

"Then you know why I'm here."

The old man worked his jaw and nodded.

"May I come up and sit with you, Mr. Coulier?"

The old man shifted in his seat uncomfortably, turning over the request with discomfort. "I suppose there's no need to be rude about the situation. Come on up. And call me Mason. No need to be so formal either."

They mounted the stairs and took a seat next to Mason who looked askance at the bare feet of his visitor.

"I'd've expected someone who just walked across the field barefoot would have soiled feet."

"Matter and I have an understanding."

Mason looked at his visitor, confusion barely hidden on his face. "Are you a man or a woman or...?"

"Yes."

Mason huffed and shook his head.

"Ain't a day of my life that Mankind hasn't touched the stars, but I *still* remember a time when men were men and women were women."

"That has never been true, but if it gives you comfort to believe it, then please do," they said.

"It *does*, because it's true. So . . . How does this work, you drag me off to Hell? That's what I been told, often enough."

"Oh, dear, no. I'm more psychopomp than reaper. What happens is simply what you understand as physics. There's no rush."

"I'm not so sure I want to know what 'psychopomp 'even means." Mason leaned forward and chewed his lip, looking the visitor up and down. "Then what do you do?"

They shrugged. "I keep you company."

"You . . . 'keep me company.' Huh. I used to make things for a living. You keep people company." Mason looked at his hands. They were gnarled and weakened.

"You've done some fine work with your hands."

Mason lifted his head in surprise. "How do you know my work?"

They smiled. "I've met people who've cherished your work, carried the smaller ones to the stars and beyond. You gave them a piece of your best self, and they held onto it until their last days."

Mason grinned for a moment, showing teeth beyond the end of their usefulness. It was only in the past several months or so that it had become physically impossible for him to ever work in the foundry again.

"Even the people you found contemptible," the Selfless added.

Mason sat back and looked out across the field at other houses perched along the edges. Scattered among them were trees, benches, the occasional gazebo, and a small body of water. Robots bustled, completing their assigned tasks, every one of them performing the same service for every resident.

"You sound like my wife."

They nodded. "We've met."

"I see." Mason pursed his lips and his eyes watered for a moment. "And what should I call you?"

"You can call me 'Carl.'"

"Carl?"

They smiled again and quoted, "'The nitrogen in our DNA, the calcium in our teeth, the iron in our blood, the carbon in our apple pies were made in the interiors of collapsing stars. We are made of starstuff.'"

Mason raised an eyebrow. "That 'starstuff' nonsense. That's Carl Sagan."

Carl nodded, a grin tickling their lips. "He was a remarkably terrible person for such a publicly influential astronomer."

"Ah. So, you've met him too?"

"I've met everyone."

Mason appeared doubtful and he made a concomitant sound. "Y'know, I expected black hooded robes and a scythe, but it occurred to me how silly that was as the days dragged on."

"I appear as needed."

"Which is just as absurd. Ain't no way I'd need the help of a freak like you. Better off with black robes. What do you really look like? If you're going to keep me company, be yourself."

Carl's features melted and tightened under a heat haze, the facial hair fell away, and what remained contained as much truth as needed for Mason.

172

"Now, where the hell'd you go?" Mason squinted, "You're just air? Did I imagine you?'"

The Selfless reappeared in the same hazy manner. "I suppose you could consider me a figment of the universe's imagination." Carl smiled and crossed their legs. They ran one hand across their chin and considered how the androgynous form affected Mason. It was as ambiguous as their previous configuration. Perhaps he found their current appearance less confusing. For them, it was what it was, no more, no less.

"I certainly didn't expect a transgender spirit."

"No one ever does, Mason. You're certainly more of an anachronism than your peers, and yet you're unique in an historical way."

Mason sighed and looked at his visitor again, confused by their words, and too proud to ask for an explanation. "Want some tea?"

"I'd love some tea, thank you."

Mason struggled for a moment to stand. His wobbling triggered an assistive bot that expanded from the chair in a puff of air and steadied the old man.

Carl took hold of his elbow and helped to steady the old man. He flinched away from their touch at his earliest convenience.

"Thank you, but I don't *need* you. Okay? I can take care of myself."

"Okay, Mason." Carl cast a meaningful gaze at the wonder of automation around them that kept the old man from accidentally ending his own life.

Mason sneered, and the two walked into the small home. Carl held patiently back, pacing themself according to Mason's uneven hobble.

They watched him pull mugs, pour water, and set the temperature on the pot. Each step of the way, Mason's unsteady hands would have resulted in calamity if not for the kitchen bots that filled the gaps in his coordination. The pot boiled shortly.

"Earlier," Mason said as he set a mug in front of Carl, "you said I was 'unique.' I thought all you people considered everyone the same." He dropped a sleeve of tea into their mug and poured the water.

"This tea is grown and harvested here. Do you ever think about where it originally came from?"

Mason frowned and shuffled back, allowing his chair to seat him. "Five minutes," he told the mugs. "I like it strong, bitter. That okay with you?"

"I'm looking forward to it."

"And, no, I don't think about where it came from. Earth, I guess. Probably someplace we owned. Why should I care?" Mason wilted a bit, his movements jerky and stiff in old age.

"Because you're human."

"I know *I'm human*," Mason spat.

"Then why do you call yourself 'white'?"

"I'm both."

"You're really not." They raised their eyebrows.

The mugs chimed. Mason lifted his mug, blew softly on the surface of the tea, and sipped. As he removed the bag, he said, "I can't believe this political bullshit extends into the afterlife."

"There is no afterlife for politics to extend into." Carl lifted their mug, blew across the surface, and sipped the bitter brew. They removed the bag and placed it with Mason's flotsam in a tiny dish at the center of the table.

"More politics." Mason shook his head, trembling a bit. "You can't dictate what I believe."

Carl answered with an elegant shrug and said, "You can't dictate reality."

"Neither can you."

"No, I can't."

Mason seized his mug with just enough force to spill some tea. A channel in the table opened and microbots dealt with the splash. The old man sat back, shaking droplets from the back of his hand. Carl handed him a napkin from the counter. He snatched it and dabbed awkwardly.

"My daughter's on her way. She'll take care of everything." Mason's eyes focused on some point in the middle of nowhere. "She'll take care of me, finally come around and do things the right way." He looked up at Carl as if seeing them for the first time. "You'll see, she loves me."

Carl nodded. "I'm sure she does."

174

"And she'll carry on." Mason jabbed a gnarled finger in Carl's direction. "I taught her, I showed her how people like you, how you—"

"You really don't understand, do you? This moment, the opportunity? To be honest with yourself." Carl tilted their head and creased their brow, trying to convey just enough empathy without confrontation for him to take the point of living, to care—even for a moment—about more than the imagined schisms and fears, and the beliefs forged in their aftermath.

"I've nothing to repent, damn you."

Carl sighed and sipped their tea. They put the mug down, leaned forward, and looked into Mason's eyes. "The universe has no need for your repentance, Mason."

He huffed and sagged in his chair. "You're talking about my soul as if it has no value."

"Call it whatever you like, your religion isn't my concern, you are."

"My daughter—"

"She's not like you, Mason, no one is. Not anymore."

A tiny spark of fear flashed in his eyes. "What . . . what do you mean?"

"She's not like you, she hasn't adopted your beliefs."

Mason sniffed, hung his head, and spoke into his chest. "But she knows, she understands the truth . . . about people . . . who we are, her heritage . . . why we're important."

"Oh, she knows, she understands," Carl agreed, "but her behavior is the truth. You're the last of your kind."

"Again with that," Mason spoke in short gasps, his breath coming in shallow huffs. "I'm the last . . . what? My *kind*?"

Carl rested their chin on their knuckles and answered Mason's question with a directness that reflected the finality of the moment: "You're the last bigot."

* * *

They sat with Mason's corpse while the rolling medical device verified his death and beamed a code out. The house came to life all at once, packaging his things, cleaning up, preparing

175

the home for a new tenant. The Selfless considered the breaking of the final link in a pattern that humanity had strangled itself with for several hundred years. This occasion, regardless of how momentous, went unwitnessed, and not with a bang, but an exhaled whisper—not unlike how it started. A whisper in a royal ear, an edict, a spark that eventually consumed centuries and more in ways that seemed inconceivable now.

They've changed so much, they thought.

All the while, they plucked at the pile of matter that had once made up Mason Coulier. The Selfless would attend to him until the atoms wandered off to collide with the rest of the universe, to mingle with the dying stars.

Collards & Codecs
by
Dedren Snead

Dr. Elise Summers watched the bountiful tree of calculations branch across her students' holoscreens, each numeric tendril drifting across the ancient tablet's carved mysteries. The clay artifact rotated gently in the anti-gravity chamber at the center of Bennett College's Quantum Mathematics lab, its cuneiform script catching the soft blue light. Five of her best students—her Belles—sat hunched over their workstations, their faces illuminated by cascading numbers.

"Two minutes," she announced, massaging her temples. The lack of sleep was catching up with her, but there wasn't time for rest. Not with Sextet ships hovering at the edge of the parallel.

LaKeisha's glasses slipped down her nose as she input another algorithm sequence. Beside her, Oye muttered in Sierra Leonean slang, her bantu knots bobbing as she shook her head at the results. The ancient Babylonian tablet had mocked their efforts all semester, its secrets locked in mathematical riddles that might hold the key to safe trans-Neptune teleportation.

A gentle tone signaled time's end. The holoscreens shifted to display their combined results: 14% Navigational Success.

"Botobaba!" Oye spat the word like a curse.

"Actually," Dr. Summers said, allowing herself a small smile, "you're up two points from Class Beta, and five ahead of NASA. I'd say that calls for Cook Out shakes. On me."

But before she could elaborate, her comm-link pulsed with an urgent message from Nichols Station. The Sextet delegation was demanding an immediate meeting. Their golden ships had crossed the neutral line.

"It's go time, Belles." Dr. Summers proclaimed and clapped her hands together twice.

The young Belles followed Dr. Summers out of the lab and along Bennett's historic brick pathways, carefully avoiding the sacred grass of the quadrangle. Even in 2128, with holographic displays adorning the restored Victorian architecture and quantum computers humming beneath the chapel's spire, some traditions remained sacred. Bennett Belles were ladies, after all.

"Dr. E," LaKeisha called out, her tablet still processing calculations, "these Babylonian reciprocals—they seem close but not exact. No exact measurements, just..." Her voice trailed off as they approached the wooden pillars of the Irma Bivens Jackson '70 Memorial Garden.

Dr. Summers paused at the garden's entrance, where centuries-old azaleas bloomed alongside their genetically modified descendants. The newer varieties, engineered for deep space radiation resistance, glowed with a subtle bioluminescence—a collaboration between Bennett's botanists and North Carolina A&T's aerospace division. But it was the traditional blush blooms that always caught her eye, their delicate petals debuting a curious new foliage. She could see the bioengineered Alpha Kappa Alpha Sorority designs faintly but proudly strolling in their pink and green presentation.

"Our ancestors could make precise measurements in pinches and dashes, in the space between 'a little while' and 'until it's done.'" She straightened, addressing all five students in sum. "That's why Bennett College is Earth's premier xenocultural institute.

We understand that science isn't just in our laboratories—it's in our traditions, our kitchens, our gardens."

Their starship waited just behind the garden in a curated grove of pines, its form challenging conventional starcraft aesthetics. Where other solar vessels favored utilitarian designs, the RSS Cultivar embodied the poise of its namesake flower. Five enormous petals, crafted from transparent photovoltaic alloys, spread outward from a central core. Each petal could adjust independently, tracking distant stars like a flower following the sun. The lower deck, nestled beneath these solar arrays, housed the crew quarters and research facilities.

"The Aggie engineers outdid themselves," Oye whispered, her earlier frustration forgotten as she admired the ship's organic curves. She thought they resembled her own. The vessel's hull rippled with the same bioluminescent patterns as the modified azaleas, a visual and architectural reminder of the connection between Earth's heritage and humanity's future.

Dr. Summers led them toward the boarding ramp, but not before harvesting a single traditional azalea bloom. She placed it carefully in a stasis chamber, where it would remain forever in that perfect moment of flowering. "Sometimes," she said, sealing the chamber, "the answer isn't in pushing forward. It's in remembering who we are and where we came from.

The ship's interior continued the botanical theme. Corridors followed the natural spiral patterns found in flower growth, and the command center bloomed outward like an opening bud. But it was the hydroponics bay that drew gasps from the students. Here, alongside the latest in food production technology, grew rows of vegetables, bursting with color as they continued to board.

"Our window is small," Dr. Summers announced to her students as they clustered around the holovid projector in the Cultivar's botanical command center. She accessed Bennett's restricted archives, bringing up two crucial recordings for their immediate review: the 1953 Gullah testimonies and the recovered black box from the USS Trump disaster. "These records prove that the Sextets have been judging humanity through the lens of our first contact—a simple act of kindness by an enslaved man, and a simple act of hatred by his owner. The Martian fleet represents everything the Sextets feared we would become: resource-hungry colonizers who would mine their crystalline bodies for profit. But Bennett College has maintained the true history, protected in plain sight among our 'cultural heritage' files." She patted a silver box, secured in a ceremonial housing near the captain's chair. "If we can reach the parallel before Musk's forces, we can demonstrate that Earth is not a monolith. The Cultivar's botanical design isn't just aesthetic—it's a message. We're showing them that we understand the power of roots, of growth, of nurturing something beyond ourselves." As she spoke, the ship's petals began to blossom, each one catching and transforming sunlight into quantum energy that would carry them to the edge of Earth's atmosphere and beyond. And for humanity, they were carrying forward a centuries-old promise of education, elevation, and hope that Bennett College had always represented.

Servants and Masters

The Gullah Testament: From the Bennett College Archives

Recorded by Dr. Margaret Yelverton-Pierce, Class of 1953

Previously classified under "Negro Folklore and Spirituals"

"Big Papa James, he done feed the Squid Folk with what he had." That's how the story always began around Hilton Head's nighttime fires, passed down through generations of Yelvertons. The elders would whisper about strange lights in the marsh, about creatures that glowed like "God's own jellies" walking on six legs, their heads full of moving water.

"Them Squid Folk, they come from the stars," Mama Bessie Yelverton told Bennett College researchers in 1953, her eclectic accent captured on magnetic tape. "They crash they ship in de water, right where we catch good blue crab. James—my granddaddy's granddaddy—he see one of dem hurting. One of them sick bad. He share he food, even though Massa beat him for it next day. But them Squid Folk, they remember. They remember everythang. They teach Papa James how to listen in dey way, and they take him unda there, in the deep water, to freedom, I reckon cuz he stay in the deep then. A way of blessing 'im."

The stories spoke of how the aliens would watch the enslaved people, and at night, learning their songs, their cooking, their ways of survival. The Gullah people called them "De Watchers," noting how their skin would change colors with the changing of the tides.

White academics dismissed these accounts as "primitive superstition" and "Negro fantasy." When the Sextet made official first contact in the 2100s, the U.S. government classified all early reports of their presence. But Bennett College had preserved a truth in its rich cultural archives, hidden in plain sight among recordings of negro spirituals, civil rights plans, and quilted traditions.

"They ain't evil," the last recording concludes, "but they scared of how we treat each other. Granddaddy James say they all share one mind, like family supposed to be. They watch us hurt our own kind

180

and it make them tremble. They gonna keep watching 'til we learn better. 'Til we remember how to share like family again."

Elise explained she had rediscovered these tapes while combing the college archives in 2125. When the Sextet crisis began, Bennett College alone understood the true significance of the connection. The aliens were searching for evidence that humanity had fully learned what James Yelverton had shown them about compassion, sharing, and the true meaning of human civilization.

Servants and Masters

Historical Record: The Mars Incident and Subsequent Cordial Wars

United Nations Security Council Archives, 2122-2128

Declassified under the Truth and Reconciliation Protocols

On March 15, 2122, humanity's fractured approach to space exploration led to its greatest diplomatic catastrophe. As the Sextet diplomatic flotilla approached Mars with peaceful intentions—their ships broadcasting the same cooking-frequency signals they'd used since first contact—they were met by the newly commissioned USS Trump and its SpaceX support fleet.

Despite UN warnings, the corporate entity Mars Colonial Authority, at the behest of the First Martian, their cyborg transhuman dictator Elon Musk, launched a preemptive nuclear strike. The Sextet's ionic shields reduced the weapons to harmless light shows, but the intent was clear. Their response was swift and precise: the USS Trump, pride of the American Space Force, engulfed in a flash of radiance. 3,126 human souls and 342 transhumans were lost, though survivors would later report that the Sextet had broadcast a warning in perfect English: "We remember."

The incident triggered the Cordial Wars, as Earth's nations split between the corporate-military alliance (led by the remnants of the United States) and the Indigenous-African Coalition. The Sextet's subsequent communication was directed exclusively through African nations, particularly Kenya and

Nigeria, whose space programs emphasized cultural preservation alongside technological advancement.

The Indigenous Reclamation Acts of 2125 emerged from this crisis.

The Indigenous Reclamation Acts dismantled corporate military control of space exploration, returning colonial territories to indigenous governance while mandating the integration of traditional ecological knowledge in all off-world ventures. Most significantly, the Acts created the G6 (Global South) and N5 (Native Nations) space alliances, shifting power from corporate interests and fundamentally transforming humanity's approach to space exploration through a lens of cultural preservation rather than exploitation.

But it was not enough.

Humiliated, the United States shifted its military presence to Mars under Musk's corporate banner. The Sextet's technology embargo effectively ended American space dominance. Their clear preference for dealing with nations that balanced traditional wisdom with technological advancement reshaped global power structures. The recovered black box from USS Trump revealed its last transmission was an attempt to broker property rights to the Sextet's crystalline bodies themselves, confirming their long-held fears about human resource exploitation. Project 2025, the last gasp of First World nihilism, now was relegated to a cautionary tale taught at Bennett College and other institutions now charged with restoring the reputation of humanity.

<end report>

Elaine turned to her sisters, these brilliant young women who carried forward both scientific knowledge and cultural heritage. "That's why we're bringing our own ingredients. Because sometimes, the best way to prevent a war isn't through force or even traditional diplomacy. Sometimes, you just need to invite everyone to dinner."

The RSS Cultivar's petals reached their full extension, transforming the ship into a giant flower floating in space. "The Sextets think they want our food," Dr. Summers continued, as Earth's curve became visible through the transparent petals. "But what they're really seeking is something deeper. Something that exists in the space between measurement and memory."

Ahead, the golden ships of the Sextet delegation waited, their own organic designs suggesting that perhaps their species understood more about the connection between nature and technology than humanity had assumed. A docking signal had been sent, and upon its activation, a mechanical being dislodged from the hull and transformed into an upright, humanoid automaton. "Translation Syncdroid-106 Activated. Welcome aboard," it announced through the black speakers adorning its chassis.

"LaKeisha," Dr. Summers called out, "show me those calculations again. But this time, convert all the measurements as if you are writing your grandmother's recipes." LaKeisha's converted calculations sparked across the main viewscreen as the RSS Cultivar docked with Nichols Station. Traditional weights flowed alongside quantum algorithms: "cook until the spirit moves you" translated into precise molecular timings, "season with grace" became exact mineral compositions.

"Like my grandma Elouise always said," LaKeisha adjusted her glasses, "'Amazing Grace' is more than just a hymn—it's a recipe for joy." Her fingers flew across the haptic interface, correlating sonic frequencies with cooking times. "The Sextets respond to harmonics, right? What if we played gospel while we cook?"

"Not gospel," Amara spoke up from the hydroponics station, where she was carefully harvesting collard greens. Her white lab coat bore both the Bennett crest and her pre-med caduceus. "Aretha. 'Respect.' It's all about the molecular vibrations affecting cellular structures. Same principle as ultrasound therapy, just with more rhythm and blues."

Dr. Summers smiled as her students' training emerged in unexpected ways. These young women had been chosen not just for their academic excellence, but for their ability to weave together disciplines. Each brought something unique to this diplomatic mission.

"Oye, check the salinity levels," Dr. Summers called out. "Remember what we learned about electrolyte balance in xenobiology? Use the well water I canned instead of the reclaimed water from the ship."

"Already on it," Oye replied, her fingers dancing across a biochemical analyzer. "Sodium content matches their hemolymph requirements, but still keeps the traditional taste. Erika's handling the spice compounds."

Erika, the quiet biochemistry prodigy from Detroit by way of Winslow, Arizona, looked up from her station where she'd been analyzing capsaicin molecules. "The heat index has to be just above warm. She took to the chopped bell peppers; gave them another pass with the serrated knife. "I know we just need a bit but . . . Ancestors got it," as she raked an unknown portion into a silver bowl, before dashing it into the concoction.

The fifth Belle, Trinity, had transformed the ship's conference room into an intimate dining space that honored both Earth and Sextet customs. The table settings followed the sacred geometry both species recognized, and she'd programmed the ambient lighting to match the bioluminescent patterns they'd observed in Sextet visual communications. "Sam Cooke playing at 432 Hz," Trinity announced, fine-tuning the room's acoustics. "That frequency matches their natural resonance and reminds me of summer evenings out on the quad."

The station's docking bay filled with the golden light of three approaching Sextet vessels. Through the ship's viewscreen, their fluid appendages floated like jellyfish through space, each one a masterpiece of techno-organic engineering.

"Ladies," Dr. Summers addressed her team, "remember your training—both kinds. Science tells us how, but Methodist faith tells us why. Now, let's show the world what Bennett Belles can do."

"Again." they all chanted together and laughed.

The next hour was a symphony of coordinated motion. Each student applied their medical, mathematical, and philosophical precision to preparing the meal. Amara monitored temperature changes with the same attention she gave to patient vitals. Erika's knowledge of neurotransmitters informed her spice blending. LaKeisha's understanding of cardiac rhythms guided her stirring patterns.

"Why, somebody, why people break up? Oh, then turn around and make up" Oye sang along with Al Green's "Let's Stay Together" playing softly in the background, measuring trace minerals that would make the food compatible with Sextet biology while turning her wooden spoon into a vocal transponder.

"I just can't see," Trinity harmonized, adjusting the room's electromagnetic field to match the comfortable range they'd calculated for their guests.

Dr. Summers moved between stations, adding her own touches but mostly watching with pride as her students demonstrated why Bennett College had become Earth's premier xenocultural institute. These young women carried within them both the precision of modern science and the wisdom of those who had found a way or made one.

As the first Sextet delegation approached the airlock, Dr. Summers gathered her team. "Remember ladies, we're not just serving food—we're sharing culture. Every bite tells a story of survival, of adaptation, of making something beautiful from whatever you have. That's something both our species understand." The airlock cycled and decompressed, as the first Sextet representatives entered—their crystalline environmental suits catching the light like prisms, tentacles moving with precise grace. The aroma of perfectly cooked collards filled the air, carried on sound waves tuned to both human and Sextet comfort frequencies.

"Welcome," Dr. Summers said, as her students straightened their Bennett-blue diplomatic sashes. "We invite you to break bread with us, and perhaps together we can recreate what your people discovered in a Gullah kitchen two centuries ago . . ."

Through the Cultivar's petal-shaped windows, Earth hung like a rare paraíba tourmaline peeking from behind black velvet, its beauty untainted by the growing cluster of Trumper warships gathering near the Mars colony's final checkpoint. Their utilitarian hulls, painted with garish corporate logos, looked like floating billboards against the cosmos. A Musk-class destroyer drifted by, its port-side engines flickering unreliably through its stride.

"Mars still using that bargain-bin Tesla tech," Trinity whispered, making Oye snort into her hand. "How ghetto." Oye almost screamed in the middle of the ceremony.

Dr. Summers shot them a gentle warning look, but couldn't quite control her own snicker. The Trumpers' ships were gathering like vultures, surely their weapons systems scanning for any excuse to start a conflict. They saw the universe as nothing but resources to be claimed, minerals to be mined, profits to be plundered and returned to their failing red purgatory.

But here, in the Cultivar's dining chamber, another vision of humanity's future was unfolding.

The Sextet delegates moved with fluid grace around the table, their environmental suits catching starlight like living stained glass. Their translator units hummed softly, harmonizing with Marvin Gaye's "What's Going On" playing at precisely 432 Hz.

"The quantum harmonic resonance of soul music," LaKeisha explained, her medical training showing. "It matches both human alpha brain waves and Sextet neural patterns."

Erika served the collards with the same precision she used in chemistry lab, each portion perfectly heated to maintain optimal nutrient density. The aroma filled the chamber—smoky, earthy, complex with history and meaning.

Through the windows, another squadron of Trumpers megaships dropped out of hyperspace, their weapons arrays glowing ominously. But inside, Amara was explaining to a fascinated Sextet how her great-grandmother used ham hocks to transform tough leaves into silk.

"The process of breaking down cellular walls through slow cooking," she detailed, "is remarkably similar to how your species processes information through chemosensory input."

The lead Sextet, their crystalline head chamber shifting through shades of azure and gold, extended a tentacle toward the bowl. Their translator clicked rapidly: "This preparation method. These specific frequencies of thermal application. We have attempted replication for two centuries."

"Because you can't replicate soul," Dr. Summers said softly. "You can't quantify generations of mothers teaching daughters, of making do and making better, of turning survival into celebration."

The Sextet's color deepened to a profound purple of understanding.

"We have . . . miscalculated," the Sextet communicated. "We perceived the formula would provide the result. But the result is in the . . ." their translator fell silent, then found the human word: ". . . fellowship."

Oye offered cornbread, explaining how this particular cast iron skillet had been passed down through five generations of Bennett women. Trinity poured a candied carafe of sweet tea into specially designed vessels that could interface with Sextet feeding appendages. As the leading Sextet began a longer explanation, the shuttering of the approaching Trumper fleet began shaking the ship as the

186

transmission requests from the Mars' Rear Admiral pinged annoyingly in the background.

War had arrived for dinner.

Sextet Collective Remembrance: First Contact - Unidentified Planet -

7.83 Quantum Vibrations, Yelverton Plantation, 1862 - From Translation

A Sextet scouting vessel breached the waters of the Carolina
coast, plasma damage forced an emergency landing in the shallow
waters off Hilton Head Island. The six-member crew concealed
their ship beneath the waves and emerged to observe their surroundings. One member sustained injury and was unable to syn-
thesize their nutrient packs to recover.

What they witnessed challenged their collective consciousness.
While their species shared all experiences through a harmonious psychic link, these humans seemed fractured, divided against themselves. From their hidden vantage point among the marsh grass, they
watched enslaved Africans toil under the brutal hand of white overseers.

One Sextet, designated First-Observer, suffered severe damage to
their filtration chamber during the crash. Death seemed certain until
one evening, drawn by the visual smoke and aromas from a local
cabin, they encountered a bipedal humanoid, who was designated at
Yelverton. The human, sensing distress, offered his meal of collard
greens and cornbread—food prepared with care despite his day toiling in captivity.

The next day, they watched as Master Charles Yelverton publicly whipped James for "stealing food." The contrast was stark:
one human sharing his meager resources to save a strange life,
another human brutally punishing such compassion.

This duality shaped all future Sextet policy toward Earth. Their
collective memory preserved both Yelvertons: the enslaved man's
kindness and the master's cruelty. When humanity reached for the
stars, the Sextets—themselves beings partly composed of minerals

humans would seek to mine—remembered both sides of their first contact.

They established the parallel, containing human expansion not out of malice, but protective necessity.

Until humanity could resolve its inner conflicts, the stars would wait.

<end translation>

"Your people," the Sextet observed, multiple tentacles gesturing to encompass the meal, the music, the moments, "transform simple elements into profound substances. This is what we have sought to translate. Not a formula for nutrition, but a formula for . . ." again the translator paused, searching, ". . . grace."

Dr. Summers stirred the pot, releasing aromas that made the Sextet's chromatophores pulse with excitement. "Like any true Southerner knows, there's a bit of bitterness you can't boil out. That's what makes you appreciate the savory notes."

The lead Sextet's papillae shifted to a deep purple as it sampled the pot likker. Through TS-106, it spoke: "We have tried replicating this in our vertical gardens for two hundred years. We can grow the plants but cannot capture the . . . memory."

"Because you're missing the context," Dr. Summers explained. "These recipes aren't just instructions—they're survival stories. Every adjustment, every timing, every technique was developed by people who had to make beauty from whatever they were given. You can't code that into a database. That won't properly translate in a holographic projection"

As the diplomatic session stretched into its final hours, Dr. Summers watched her students teaching quantum physics through the medium of soul food. LaKeisha explained how the molecular structure of pot likker matched theoretical models for sustainable fusion reactions, while Oye demonstrated how traditional timing methods synchronized perfectly with space-time calculations.

The lead Sextet's translator spoke again: "We remember the first taste. Your ancestor—First Yelverton. The aroma from his family's cooking fire drew us in. It translated. The actions of your ancestor--Second Yelverton, It did not."

The Sextet's chromatophores rippled with a pattern that TS-106 translated as deep emotional resonance. "We came to Earth thinking we would find primitive beings. Instead, we found mathematics en-coded in meals, quantum mechanics in cultural memory."

"That's why you've been pushing humanity back from the outer colonies," Dr. Summers said. "It wasn't the premise of 'You weren't trying to contain us.' You were waiting for us to remember who we are."

The Sextet leader's skin flushed a deep, regal gold. "The mathe-matics are meaningless without the memory. Your MarsKin seek only to clone our agricultural methods, to control food production across the galaxy. To own us. But they cannot replicate what they do not understand."

"They are not like us."

A stark contrast, Dr. Summers watched her five students, these Belles —future doctors, scientists, mothers, interstellar leaders—shar-ing Earth's most profound innovation: the ability to make family out of strangers, to make peace out of biscuits and blessings, to make love manifest in something as simple as a bowl of greens.

Through the hull windows, the stars shone on, bearing witness to this small moment that would shape the future of two species. The Trumper ships began retreating, their sensors unable to comprehend the power of what was transpiring on the Cultivar. They had come looking for war and found instead a dinner party where ancient wis-dom met interstellar diplomacy.

Dr. Summers presented a silver adorned case and withdrew a small data crystal, its surface etched with patterns matching those on her Bennett College brooch.

"This is what you've really been looking for. Not just how to grow collards in space, but how to preserve the soul of a civilization across time and distance."

The crystal codec contained generations of African American ag-ricultural wisdom, encoded not just in words and numbers, but in rhythms, stories, and patterns. It was a cultural genome project, pre-serving not just what people did, but why they did it.

One of the smaller-sized Sextet moved forward, its chromato-phores displaying patterns that matched the textile designs on the Cultivar's solar sails. Through TS-106, it asked: "You would share this knowledge with us? After our past . . . misunderstandings?"

Dr. Summers glanced at her students, each wearing their Bennett College brooches with pride. "I'm a Hopepunk," she said simply. "When the world gives you bitterness, you don't try to boil it out. You learn to make it part of the flavor."

The next few hours transformed the diplomatic kitchen into something between a scientific laboratory and a grandmother's Sunday dinner. The Bennett Belles worked alongside the Sextet, teaching not just recipes but the cultural mathematics behind them. Quantum measurements confirmed what generations of Black cooks had always known: there was science in the soul of cooking.

And so, beneath distant stars that had guided both enslaved ancestors and alien travelers, the first Bennett Interstellar Cultural Preservation treaty was written not in the language of power or profit, but in the arithmetic of cooking times, the geometry of proper serving portions, and the chemistry alive in a bowl of greens.

Dr. Summers raised her glass of sweet tea, her students following suit. Even the Sextets lifted their specially designed vessels, their tentacles moving in symphony under the starlight. TS-106's photoreceptors gleamed with satisfaction as it began serving dessert.

"You think this was something," the android hummed, its servos moving with inherited rhythm, "just wait until they taste my binary-coded banana pudding. Got this recipe straight from the motherboard, y'all."

Dr. Summers refocused. "Which brings us to the real reason for this meeting." She nodded to Oye, who activated a holographic display showing the Bennett College campus. "We propose a joint educational initiative. Your vertical farming technology combined with our cultural preservation methods. Not just growing food but growing understanding."

The next few minutes were filled with rapid translations as the Sextet conferred. Their chromatophores flickered through patterns that matched African textile designs, Dr. Nettrice Gaskin's artworks, quilting patterns, and finally, the architectural lines of Bennett's historic buildings.

The formal agreements were signed within the hour as interstellar transmission reached the third and fourth planets in unison.

"Your proposal is acceptable," TS-106 translated. "But we have one condition. The first class must learn to make these . . . collard greens. Properly seasoned."

A laugh rippled through the Bennett delegation. "Deal," Dr. Summers said. "Though I should warn you—at Bennett College, we grade on the Belle curve." The translation was well met.

All around them, the stars twinkled like innocent eyes, bearing witness to this moment where the wisdom of the past lit the way to humanity's future. Outside, a Musk destroyer's engines sputtered and died, leaving it to be towed back to Mars like a broken-down Model X.

The Trumper fleet had slunk back into the darkness, their short-range sensors unable to quantify the power of a shared meal, of traditions preserved, of love made tangible through soul food.

"Pass that Frank's RedHot this way," Trinity said to the Sextet in elbow distance, who had just transformed to a delighted shade of magenta as the first taste of the crispy-edged-yet-pillow-soft cornbread hit his beak.

As human hands and alien tentacles cradled the red bottle of understanding, beneath a sky full of infinite possibilities, Dr. Summers finally surrendered a smile. In the end, it wasn't mathematical proofs or military might that bridged the gap between starchildren. It was Big Mama's collard greens, cooked with care, seasoned in culture, and served with grace, carrying all the wisdom of the ancestors into humanity's tomorrow.

Sextet Collective Remembrance: First Yelverton - Planet Nibiru -

3.14 Quantum Vibrations, Earth Year 1866 - From Translation

We returned with First Yelverton, as his mindspace dreamed of following the stars as far as he could to freedom, as his ancestors before him, in remembrance of the family stolen in the stockyards of Earth. Among the Nibirun, sharing his kindness, creativity and mathematical brilliance, a voyager class astroship was gifted. First Yelverton set sail for the Gamma quadrant, to a galaxy known for robust vegetative planets, and few humanoid species. He sought to name a world of flowers for his "Grandma" – a human designation until this gathering we did not understand. We understood it as a title bestowed in high reverence to a mighty spiritual guide, designator of culture or tribal leader. It translated."

<end translation>

For Grandma Elouise

To Mars and Beyond
by
K. Ceres Wright

Henry angled up the steps, opened the corrugated neon-green metal door, and stepped inside. Music wafted out of the lean-to juke joint, a zydeco-country fusion remix escaping the sweaty desperation of the place. A bank of multicolored lights ran the length of the building, throwing disks of red, purple, and green on the gyrating patrons.

Jose sat in his usual corner, reading his heads-up display and smoking his pipe. Henry thought the scene anachronistic. He pushed past a group of drunken bridesmaids—evidenced by their tiaras—and took a seat at the bar. He gave the bartender, Leslie, the sign for his regular drink. She nodded in reply. Being deaf was an advantage for a bartender in this joint, he thought. An upswell of noise filled the space behind him and he twisted in his seat. The woman wearing the BRIDE tiara had climbed onto the stage and began dancing with Kyle, who was playing backup guitar to Rita's country singing and fiddle playing. Octavius rounded out the trio on the old-world accordion. The bride ground her pelvis into Kyle's backside. Rita scowled and motioned for security. A bot flew down from the ceiling and delivered 10,000 volts to the bride. She yowled in pain, which elicited laughter from the crowd. She tore herself away from Kyle and slunk back to her merry band of housekeepers, who cheered her return with a dousing of bottle-sprayed champagne.

"Where're they from?" Henry signed.

Leslie shrugged, signing, *I heard one of them mention New Rho.*

Figures, Henry thought. There were five domed settlements on Mars, all interconnected by underground tunnels and rail. New Rhode Island was the smallest settlement. New Rhoers always came to Camp X and the larger settlements to party, some of which devolved into fistfights. New Rho contained the elite of the colonists —engineers, physicists, rich investors. Camp X had a hodgepodge of people—actors, musicians, dancers, social workers, reporters. The other three—Chronitis, Seer Park, and Nouveau—were specialty settlements, where the geologists, botanists, archaeologists, metallurgists, and others lived.

Henry was the only magician, at least as far as he knew, which was fine by him. The New Rhoers were always throwing company parties and inviting him and his troupe to perform.

A man slid into the stool next to Henry and tapped him on the arm. "Hey, man. I thought you'd gone to Seer Camp."

Henry twisted in his seat as he downed his beer. He slammed the mug on the counter and grinned. "Derrick! Just got back. The hell are you doing here, slumming?"

Derrick bellowed a guffaw. "I'm a rebel, Henry. They only keep me around cuz they don't feel like finding another theoretical physicist before the contract runs out. I figure I got about 8 months before I'm out on my ass. But lucky for me, I already got the next job lined up. Amethyst Industries needs a team lead for their asteroid mining project."

"Mining? Since when do you go in for corporate interests?"

"Since they're willing to pay me enough to retire on. I can whore myself out one last time and then start working on what I want to . . . teaching needy children about science and tech."

"You should've become a teacher," said Henry.

"On that salary? You do know I like the finer things in life . . . food, running water, heat . . ."

The pair sat silent as three men dressed as an asteroid miner, police officer, and scientist led the bridal party to the back rooms.

"At least somebody's getting some action." Derrick jutted his chin at Henry. "What about you? What're your plans for the future?"

Henry shrugged. "I left Earth for something new and exciting, but compared to most cities, the Mars settlements are small. I've gotten bored already. Thinking about going back to Earth. Got a friend in Vegas who can get the troupe a gig."

"Where you can be one of a hundred acts? I know you, man. You'll be bored quicker there than here."

"I don't know, man. You got any brilliant ideas?"

Derrick shifted on his stool, facing outward, watching Rita and Kyle flirt on the stage as they sang, 'One More Night.'

"As a matter of fact, I do. But not here. My place." Derrick slid off the stool and cogged both their drinks. The settlement's AI, Cognition, kept track of every purchase, schedule, meeting, and all other occurrences on the planet. It debited and credited the proper accounts, managed itineraries, arranged travel, and made dinner plans. Among other things, Henry had heard that if you knew how to access the dark AI, you could access drugs, indulge fetishes, and even order up some harassment of your enemies.

"I don't feel like riding all the way back to Camp X from your place tonight. Can I charge at your place?"

"Yeah, sure. C'mon." Derrick headed for the door.

Henry got Leslie's attention and signed that he was leaving with Derrick. She nodded and slid a quick look toward the stage to indicate she'd tell the troupe.

Henry was the troupe's de facto leader, meaning he was the most responsible, which wasn't saying much. He'd spent the past weekend nursing a hangover from the Friday before. And at 33, he was feeling the pressure to settle down and have kids. That crushing fear of conformity led him to Mars, where he fell in with a group of itinerant actors, dancers, and musicians who worked the local bar scene. As a magician, he wasn't seen as a rival, and they would come to him to confess their sins and receive absolution and whatever advice Henry could dredge up from his 30-plus years of lived experience. That he was a lapsed Christian seemed to help with the mystique of his counsel. He felt relatable, he supposed, to the others, whether they were lapsed or not.

He climbed into Derrick's car and they sped off toward Chroniton. It was about a 40-minute drive at 200mph. They made small talk about VR games and sports until they arrived. The car pulled off the underground highway and snaked past several individual garages before pulling into Derrick's. The two alighted and rode an elevator straight into Derrick's apartment. An android greeted them in the large foyer and took their jackets. They headed left, toward the kitchen.

"Drink?" Derrick stood in front of the fridge display.

"Beer."

"Coming up."

Henry wandered toward the entertainment room, which housed a holographic staging area, VR display, mini-bar, and a couch/loveseat set. He took up residence on the loveseat. Derrick handed him a beer and sat on the couch.

"So, what's the deal?" Henry took a sip of his beer.

Derrick paused before he spoke. "We've found a planet comparable to Earth. All the data we've recovered from probes indicate it could be a fuckin' paradise."

"Huh, I haven't heard anything."

"Because NASA didn't discover it. Avent Technologies did. And they want to send a scout team, under the radar."

"How the hell do you launch a scout team under the radar?"

Derrick shrugged as if everyone knew. "Disguised as a satellite launch. No optics, just a line in an article."

"And you think that'll work?"

"It's worked before." Derrick held out a bag. "Chips?"

"No, thanks. And when before?" Henry threw up his hands. "You know what? Never mind. I don't wanna know. But why all the hush-hush? What's the point?"

Derrick chugged his beer and slammed the bottle onto the coffee table. "Another one?"

"Answer the question."

Derrick hung his head as if Henry had just scolded him for breaking curfew. "They want it for the rich. To send them off for an exorbitant fee to get away from the poor wretches on Earth. The appeal of toiling underground or under domes on Mars is wearing thin."

"Seriously?"

"Yeah. And I know something else is going on."

"What?"

"Genetic experiments." Derrick leaned back in his chair as if waiting for blowback from his surmising.

Henry paused mid-draught, then swallowed. "You're joking."

Derrick shook his head. "No, man. I've seen the evidence. It's like that story where they made the brown people like you and me class D or whatever the hell . . . moron servants. Sterile, of course, so they can't reproduce. Just make more by combining chemical X with protein Y and shoving it into an artificial womb." He sat, staring at the blank holostage.

Henry's mouth fell open and he sank into the back of the chair. "But who's behind this?"

Derrick's gaze panned to Henry. "A white evangelical group called the Moral Heritage. That's why I want you to go. To be my eyes and ears."

"As what? I'm a magician, not a scientist. Or a soldier. And if they thought I was spying on them, I'd be dead within the hour." Henry thought the idea ludicrous. "Besides, they would never ask me to go."

"That's the thing. They're sending an entertainer as a morale booster. Someone who can sense when morale is down or if any crew members are on the way to going off the rails and pick their spirits up. You'd be perfect."

"I. am. not. going."

"Henry, come on. You're the only one who can do this."

"Look, Derrick. If you're so keen on thwarting this insane plan, then you go."

"I can't. I've already been branded a troublemaker. They wouldn't let me within a thousand feet of that ship. It's down to you, Henry. It's down to you to help stop wholesale re-enslavement of our race."

Henry placed his drink on the coffee table and stood up. "I'm going to bed."

"I'll pay you to go."

That brought Henry up short. He had been content just scraping by in life, as long as he had a roof over his head and food in his belly. But every day, he was getting older. He could feel it in his joints when we got up in the morning. Scraping by day to day was getting harder with each passing year. "How much?"

"Three hundred thousand."

"Not exactly retirement money."

"You're still young. It's enough to put down some roots. You're going to need them whether you want to or not. Old age and itinerancy don't go together." The two of them let the moment hang in the air.

"All right, I'll do it." Henry sat back down. "But you have to have my back, Derrick. Give me a bag of tricks, a back door . . . something. I don't want to spend the rest of my life trying to make it back to Mars."

Derrick raised his head and smiled. "I got several back doors, a small robot army, and a preprogrammed escape pod for starters."

"Then let's figure out a plan."

* * *

Takeoff day was beautiful, as far as Mars weather went—a lovely 60 degrees Fahrenheit in the hazy red atmosphere. In the underground hangar, the crew began leaping and bounding in low gravity toward the shuttle, which would take them to the ship that would take them to the planet. Henry, not feeling quite as chipper as the rest, walked most of the way, only leaping at the behest of the others to hurry up. The senior crew included commander and biologist John Aguilar, executive officer and pilot Shelly Tyson, flight engineer and astrophysicist Celine Marmoux, engineer and mission specialist Jennifer Jones, and payload commander Eli Goldman. They were all smug assholes as far as Henry could tell, with Celine being a bit less assholey than the others. His interview with John had lasted only ten minutes, and even then, it was mostly Henry doing a few card tricks. It seemed to go down well enough, though, with Aguilar giving Henry a one-man standing ovation before offering a handshake and the job. Henry had to keep reminding himself of his mission and trying to recall the things Derrick had taught him about computers and space flight. He had it all written down, of course, but a good magician practiced over and over until he could perform a trick barely thinking about it. But with the launch date having been so close, he hadn't had time to review as much as he wanted. He was sure an element of improvisation would be needed.

Henry clambered on board the shuttle and took up a seat in the back next to a window, then sank down as John stood up to deliver a speech. It was the usual rah-rah team, let's get 'er done speech. Henry gave a few obligatory claps, then closed his eyes and tried to imagine their destination.

A loud noise and sudden stop jolted Henry awake and he realized he had fallen asleep. The rest of the crew talked amongst themselves as they began gathering their packs from the luggage cage. Henry stood up and grabbed his bag from the seat across the aisle. The others gave him a tight-lipped smile every time he made eye contact and he thought they would be a tough audience to crack.

He brought up the rear to the group filing onto the spaceship, but as soon as he stepped on board, his periphery lit up in neon green with instructions on how to get to various destinations, his room included. The crew was directed to the left while Henry was directed to the right. Figures, he thought. Spaceship Segregation.

He headed down the hall and was greeted by no less than three robots of different shapes and sizes. One red robot rolled down the hall on two wheels, each orbited by six smaller wheels. It had a rudimentary body with no face. The second robot was black with a humanoid body and full facial features. It smiled at Henry and said, "Welcome to the Starship Jacob." Then it went on its way. The third robot was bright yellow, smaller than the other two, and consisted of a dog-like body with four extending arms, which were folded against its sides, like wings. It made a honking noise as it passed Henry, like a transport alerting others of its presence. Henry stepped to his right to allow more space between them.

After making a right and walking halfway down a hall, a door on his left lit up in green.

"Hmm, this must be it." He held up his hand to the door's pad and it opened with a soft click. The door retracted into the wall, revealing a room about 20x20. It held a double bed, a wall of monitors, and an L-shaped desk with more monitors. A door near the desk led to the bathroom, which was barely visible in the low light. Henry entered his quarters and the ceiling lit up. He put his bag on the bed and began unpacking the vials he would need for the lab. He placed them on the edge of the counter nearest the door. Next, he took out a bugball, which he turned on and held out in his hand. Its AI connected with the one in his room, and the bank of monitors lit up with Derrick's image.

"Hey, Henry. Hopefully, you're all settled in. Now that I'm hooked into the ship's computer, my program will train the ship's AI to open a pathway for my changes. I'll reprogram the robots and all secured doors to recognize you as having the highest security clearance when you're alone. When you're ready to sabotage the lab clones, alert your room's computer and my program will lock everyone in their rooms and gas them. Make sure you use the vials I gave you. Then you take off in the escape pod. And I'll send the ship and the crew on their way. They'll have to make that rich people's playground without clones. Just complete your mission before you go into the wormhole, which means tonight. Good luck. Over and out."

The monitor went dark, leaving Henry alone with his thoughts. He didn't know he'd have to conduct the mission that night. The computer's voice jostled him out of his reverie.

"Incoming message from John Aguilar."

Henry sighed. "Answer."

John's image filled the bank of monitors on the wall. He had changed out of his uniform and wore a black turtleneck. "Henry, we're having a late meal in the mess. Care to join us?"

"Ah, no, I'm still nursing a hangover from the night before. I'm going to, ah, head to bed early so I can be ready for tomorrow."

"Okay, your loss. See you tomorrow."

The screens went black. Henry was glad he didn't go. He would feel even worse sabotaging people he felt the least bit of connection to, but having to develop a planet with no cloned slaves would serve them right.

"Computer, set the alarm for 2:30 a.m."

"The alarm has been set."

"Then please dim the lights to 6 percent." The room fell almost completely dark and Henry stepped out of his shoes and climbed under the covers to await the start of his mission.

* * *

The alarm woke Henry out of a deep sleep and he cranked open one eye to wonder why his alarm sounded differently. Not seeing his nightstand where it usually was, he frantically searched his mind. "Where the hell am I?"

The events of the past two days flooded his memory and he relaxed. Somewhat. He still had a mission to complete before he could go back to the monotony of his routine days, something he was missing more and more. He threw back the covers and sat on the edge of the bed, gathering his thoughts and his nerves. *You have to do this. No one else is able to do this. You are here. Now. So just get it over with.*

He stood up and made his bed, a habit his mother had instilled in him, and slipped on his shoes. Still fighting sleepiness, he whispered to the computer, "I'm about to go to the lab. Lock everyone in their rooms and gas them. Except me, of course."

"Initiating Program Derrick."

Henry chuckled and shook his head. Derrick had always had a flair for the dramatic, even as a theoretical physicist. Henry steeled himself and palmed the vials as he headed for the door.

His periphery lit up again, which showed the lab being one level up and three doors down. The lift glowed blue in the distance, and he jogged toward it, wanting this whole thing to be over as quickly as possible. When he reached the lift, it opened noiselessly and he stepped in.

"Second level."

After a short ride, the doors opened and he headed straight for the lab. The lights were already on and he guessed the computer turned them on for him. He placed his palm on the pad and the door swooshed open. Henry stepped inside and walked toward the left, where the cloning experiments were kept.

"Jennifer? Is that you?"

Henry froze. It was John's voice. *But everyone is supposed to be asleep in their rooms.* He ran toward the walled compartment and snatched it open, ignoring his heart thumping in his chest. Footsteps sounded behind him.

"Henry? What the hell are you doing here?"

Henry didn't turn around. He clawed at the vials in the compartment, letting them crash to the floor as he peeled them away. Then he took the vials he had palmed and shoved them into the grooves.

John had reached him by that time and grabbed his wrist. "What the hell?"

Henry snatched the compartment with his right hand and crammed it into place. John grasped for it, but Henry punched him hard in the nose. John reared back, fury in his eyes. He lunged forward into Henry, taking them both down to the floor, arms flailing.

"Computer, run the cloning project!"

"You do not have the necessary authority."

Shit, Henry thought. He only had security clearance when he was alone. And he wasn't alone. John's right cross to his cheek brought home that point. Henry kneed John in the groin and rolled him over, then delivered three right crosses of his own. The man fell silent and still and Henry scrambled to his feet and rocketed to the door. When it closed behind him, he sprinted to the elevator.

"Computer, lock and gas the lab and run the cloning project!"

"Lab locked. Releasing gas. Running cloning project."

After finally reaching the lift, Henry sighed as he made it to level 1. The doors opened and he jogged to his room. He snatched up his bag and ran to the pod room, arriving with his chest heaving. *I have to get in shape.* He bent over to catch his breath.

A bank of pods greeted him when he stood. He tried to remember which pod it was. "Number fourteen . . . four . . . teen . . . . here we go." Henry opened the pod door, threw in his bag, and climbed in after it. The pod interior was black with red trim. A cushioned seat ringed the inside. Flanking the door were four suspended-animation containers, two on each side.

"Initiate Project Derrick."

"Project Derrick initiated. Please fasten your safety belts."

No sooner had he fastened his belts when the pod's rockets fired, sling-shotting him into space. The stars shone like fireflies on a hot Georgia night. He prayed the pod would take him back to Mars and not deposit him on a NASA platform on Earth. If that were to happen, he would have some splainin' to do. He figured by the time the crew of the Jacob woke up, they would be at their new planet. He wondered when they would return. When they did, they would be returning to a media firestorm over their cloning plan.

Henry put those thoughts out of his mind and lay back on the cushioned seat. "Computer, what is our destination?"

"I have a message from Project Derrick that I will play."

Derrick hadn't told him about this, but he figured it would be a congratulatory message. "Okay, play."

Derrick's voice sounded deep in the small compartment. "Henry, I am sorry for this, but I had to make sure the plan worked, and I can't have you telling the authorities what we've done. So I've programmed the robots on the Jacob to take over the ship once they reach the planet. The vials I gave you for the cloning project contained the DNA of the crew, so when they wake up, they'll have a surprise—they'll be the ones serving the robots as slaves. And I disabled the ship's long-range comms, so they won't be able to tell NASA what happened. Now, you have three choices. One, you can go back to the ship and live as a king on the new planet. Two, you can travel through space and hope some alien picks you up. Three, you can have the computer send you into the sun. If I were you, I know what I'd choose. But be sure of your choice. Once you tell the computer, you can't turn back."

Henry listened, slack-jawed, to the message. A sense of panic and dread rose within him as Derrick droned on. Sweat broke out on Henry's temples, and the hair on his neck stood on end. "No, no no no no no. No! It can't be. Computer. Cancel Project Derrick."

"You do not have the necessary authority."

"No! I want to go back to Mars."

"That choice is not possible."

"Mars!"

"That choice is not possible."

Henry sank down to the floor, tears streaming down his cheeks. "That bastard. That low life, hell-bound, rat bastard. I can't believe he double-crossed me." He held his head in his hands and squeezed his eyes shut. The drone of the pod thrummed in his brain. He had to make a decision—slow death, cold death, or hot death. He supposed slow death was best. But did he really want to live among people who would hate him? Even if they'd be mostly clones, the originals would be there . . . watching . . . waiting. Waiting for their chance to kill him. Would it be worth it?

Henry slowly got up and straightened his clothes and wiped his eyes. He supposed he would have to find out.

"Ship."

Doctor M'fume and His Dead
by
M'Shai S. Dash

As Dr. Chinaka M'fume watched the lunar base grow from an ash-colored speck on the horizon to a looming, transparent half-bubble cresting on the surface of Earth's moon, he thought about what his wife had already taught him about death without knowing she'd done so, and what Mortedek, Inc. presumed to teach him about death in the courtroom that day. He knew nothing of the five people who died three weeks before his arrival and was quite unsure which outcome, if any, his efforts would produce after the hearing. Today, he relied only on an omen, a peculiar drum, and a dream.

Yes, Dr. M'fume nodded to himself as he joined the throng of travelers exiting the commuter craft that ferried them between Earth and the Moon. *My dreams are always certain. Chinure said this many times, and I know it to be true.*

He'd bolted up in bed the night before the hearing with sweat on his brow, then feverishly searched each corner of his study for nearly an hour before he found it.

Iya Ilu, a broad smile hoisted the corners of his full lips as the doctor laid eyes on the drum. *At last.*

It sat atop an intricately carved chest in the corner of his study, propped against the wall beneath his most valuable possession-an oil painting of a group of his ancestors. The doctor chided himself for not looking there first.

Of course, it's here. He shook his head, lamenting the precious sleep he'd wasted. *Where else would it be, except near this painting?*

He studied the images etched and painted into the wood and finally, after the dream, understood the story that encircled the bell of the drum. He'd barely given the artwork any thought when he first received the item, but now he looked upon the worn images that depicted the woman in the headdress leading a horde of well-armed men against a group of unarmed men and women with reverence.

Surely, the story of the drum began with the painting. The mammoth portrait had cost the doctor a small fortune, but not because of its worth as an artistic endeavor. Rather, the tasks that had to be performed before the art could be commissioned were the most expensive.

The doctor knew from the beginning that what he craved most was not just an estimation or some hideously perfect likeness spat out from the belly of an artificially intelligent software program. Rather, he wanted to *see* them, down to the slope of their foreheads to the set of their jawlines. That task would be a difficult one because it required his ancestor's bones. And the doctor wanted the bones for other reasons, of course.

He had always been a collector of sorts, concretely grounded in the belief that antiquities told stories and sometimes, pooled and held power.

Nearly a year before he knew anything of the hearing, the doctor had reached out to the only person on Earth he knew would find them.

Shortly after getting in touch, Dr. M'fume visited the dismal patch of land near the north bank of the Saloum River to meet his contact. It wasn't far from Jenga Tena, a glittering, modern marvel of a city built atop the land that used to be Kaolack, Senegal, and as Dr. M'fume later learned, home to a swathe of his ancestors.

"Dr. Aziz!" Dr. M'fume's voice boomed over the dying engines. "Good to see you again, bone collector man!"

"Ha!" Dr. Aziz trotted to close the distance between them. "Call me Yusef, Chinaka. We're not in a room full of uptight academics right now, are we? Welcome to Jenga Tena!"

Dr. Yusuf Aziz had only met Dr. M'fume once before at an academic conference, and he rather enjoyed the man. At just above five feet, the squat yet sturdy forensic archaeologist was considerably shorter than the doctor, who towered over him and angled his head down to hear him in the noisy auditorium that day. Remembering those exchanges, Dr. Aziz made himself taller by rocking onto the balls of his feet a bit as he spoke. Each time he did, Dr. M'fume looked away and pretended not to notice.

"You're sure, then?" Dr. M'fume had asked once they'd fully exchanged greetings. "This is the spot?"

He could see the top of Dr. Aziz's shiny head clearly that day under the formidable sunlight, despite his apparent efforts to slick the thinning, raven strands over his hair-bare crown. His large dark eyes were wide open, but the bags beneath them spoke of deep-seated exhaustion. Several impressive-looking access badges hung around his neck, but instead of adding to his gravitas, they only drew attention to the coffee stain on his breast pocket.

"Of course," Dr. Aziz nodded emphatically. "Just a short pod-hop to the site from here. We can leave yours here. Ours is all fired up and ready for us."

When they landed, Dr. Aziz walked briskly and prattled on excitedly as he escorted Dr. M'fume to the site and introduced him to the team that located and excavated what they believed to be his familial bones. The doctor took care to shake each of their hands enthusiastically, thanking them individually for the work they'd done so far. Collecting the bones was nearly the final part of his endeavor, and he could hardly believe it was so near the end. All that was left was for them to match the DNA with his.

That evening, Dr. Aziz had him over for dinner after a long day in the heat. A lavish spread of stews and dishes, all manner of golds, reds, browns, and greens, were spread out on the large table. The host's wife was a blur, placing decorative trays of breads and sweets on the table until Dr. Aziz asked her to stop fussing and join them. In contrast to her husband, Mrs. Aziz was slender and tall, her teal tunic complimenting her large, gray eyes. Throughout the night, she cast glances of admiration at her husband, even while laughing at the stories of the excavation team's foibles so far.

"Yusef . . . tell him the one about the time the team found those bits of wood that looked like bone," Mrs. Aziz urged her bashful husband on. "Or the one about the time that digging machine—you know the one—"

"The backhoe loader?" Dr. Aziz finished with merriment dancing in his eyes.

"Yes, that's it," she threw her head back and laughed. "Tell him about the time it fell into the hole with you! *Wallahi*, I thought you were a goner that day."

After Dr. Aziz recounted the story, he shifted the attention from himself by reminding Dr. M'fume that his wife was an esteemed biologist herself. But with a wave of her arm and a suck of her teeth, she dismissed the moment to extoll her own work and volleyed the conversation to Dr. M'fume instead.

"So," Mrs. Aziz said, beaming, "where's this wife of yours? We'd love to have her out here for tea if she doesn't mind the heat and dust."

Dr. Aziz shot her a sharp look, but she didn't seem to notice.

"Chinuré is no longer with us," Dr. M'fume's fork was poised midway to his mouth for another bite before he'd said it, but instead of taking it, he placed the fork gently on his plate and continued, his hunger dissipating. "It's been nearly a year."

"My apologies," Dr. Aziz's face looked drawn as he continued. "She didn't know. I . . . erm . . . didn't tell her because I didn't feel it was my—"

"No worries," the doctor plastered a reassuring smile on his face and placated the couple. "It was bound to come up sooner or later."

But watching them for the rest of the evening deepened the doctor's heartache. His good-natured laughter quieted and tapered to smiles and nods, and after he'd finished most of his plate, he thanked them as graciously as he could, gently declined their invitation to stay the night, and left.

"Chinuré." The doctor sighed to himself as he stared down at the old holoprojection of his wife that shone from his wristlet. He watched his favorite loop of her repeatedly on his ride home from Jenga Tena. In it, she was at their kitchen counter, arranging lilies. He barely noticed he was home until the subtle jolt of the craft let him know that they were on the ground.

His wife had stood by him for so long that he'd been certain she'd be there to share the moment with him. But slowly, Chinuré succumbed to the grief that had plagued her since the loss of their first and only child. She'd always been a round, soft woman with small hands and a boisterous laugh, and fixture at his side. Sadness gripped him as he remembered times that he'd playfully teased about her tiny feet even as he squeezed them after an arduous day, sometimes tracing the veins on the top with his fingers and planting a kiss on each foot. He'd loved her with such familiarity that it produced a blind spot in him; he barely noticed that she'd stopped taking her government-issued pills. They were ones that she —and nearly every Earthian—took to combat the toxins in the planet's air and water, and Dr. M'fume only realized that she'd shunned them and willingly let her health fade after he found dozens of them in her drawer after her death. The guilt of it crushed him every day.

Her final wish was that her burial pod be sent to Mars to be used as part of an ongoing terraforming project. As the doctor watched the craft carrying her remains exit Earth's atmosphere, he thought about how giving she was, even in death, and was further racked with grief. He'd suppressed it as best he could, though, balling it into a knot—a bezoar in the pit of his gut that hardened and left him room to focus on little else but his ancestry project. But she always stayed in the foreground of his thoughts, and when the news he awaited came months after his visit to Jenga Tena, the doctor quietly observed that it was very near the second anniversary of her death.

The morning he received the news, he'd stood staring out of the gigantic bay windows of his study that overlooked the gray, bustling city of Manhattan, watching an aging sun paint the silvery tips of the tightly clustered skyscrapers coral.

This time, Dr. Aziz had flown to him, and he welcomed the impromptu visit as a welcome disruption to his somber mood.

"Flew in alone?" The doctor embraced his friend and led him to his office. "Something to drink?"

"Yes, I'm afraid I'm alone on this trip," Dr. Aziz looked as if a dark fog had slid over his expression at that moment. Then, he forcefully brightened and continued. "The missus is unwell right now, but I'm sure she'll be fine by the time I get back. I've signed off for her to have the best possible care while I'm away. Cutting-edge stuff. They promised me all would be well."

"I'm sorry to hear that," Dr. M'fume called as he strode from the kitchen with a steaming mug. "But here, this'll fix you after that flight. We'll drink to her recovery, of course."

Dr. M'fume handed him a fragrant cup of tea.

"Thank you," Dr. Aziz accepted the steaming cup but sat it aside and opened a large, leather bag he'd placed at the side of his armchair. "Now, let's get to this. You'll find that I've beamed the genealogy results to your holopro, complete with the digital renderings you requested. There are eight in total, pulled together from the latest in reconstructive software so the artist you hire will have plenty to work with. But also," he carefully removed an object wrapped in muslin from the bag and handed it to Dr. M'fume, "there's this. This is the reason I came."

"A drum?" Dr. M'fume unwrapped it, examined it further, and looked back up at his friend quizzically. "A talking drum—how is it not corroded after all this time?"

"Honestly," Dr. Aziz stroked his beard, and his face became harried. "We're . . . not quite sure. We ran a bunch of tests on the thing and figured that the hide alone should've withered to nothing by now, yet here it is. Save a few worn places and chipped paint, it's in astonishingly good shape. A marvel. In my opinion, it looks as if it's been buried and exhumed several times over the last millennium. The team thinks so too."

"Why is that?" Dr. M'fume laid the thing across his lap like an exotic cat and cocked his head to hear Dr. Aziz's answer.

"The soil around it was disturbed more than the other sites," Dr. Aziz ran a hand over his bald head, then leaned forward until his elbows rested on his thighs and clasped his hands, vexed. "Our best guess is that whoever kept retrieving it felt that it was better left buried between uses. Or maybe it's sheer coincidence. Who knows? Either way, it's been sprayed with a protective agent to slow the rot, and now it's officially yours . . . though I do hope you'll donate it to science one day."

And with that, he chuckled, and the doctor decided he looked more youthful bald. He'd also bulked his former weight into muscle and was more sharply dressed. Just then, it occurred to Dr. M'fume that he'd never seen his friend without his dusty white lab coat and a plethora of badges.

"You're looking well, Yusef," the doctor said decidedly, with an affirmative nod. "I can't thank you enough for the work you've done, and I'm glad to see you in good spirits and good health."

"Well, I can't take all the credit for that," Dr. Aziz let out a nervous laugh. "I was able to publish a paper about the process my team used for your project. Boring stuff but it was a hit in some circles and landed me some consultant work with Morteadek. They're big on optics though, so they assigned me a physical trainer—an android, of all things. Nothing like a machine-made muscle-head to help one gain muscle."

Dr. M'fume chuckled, then stiffened in his chair. "But isn't Mortedek an insidious place to work? You told me that yourself. That's the necrotech company churning out all sorts of mad gadgets that are supposedly going to help us all live forever, right?"

Dr. M'fume scoffed.

"Precisely the one," Dr. Aziz flashed a grim, satisfied smile. It was one that didn't quite reach his eyes and Dr. M'fume realized right then that he didn't much care for it. "But in their defense, they can't be *that* bad, after all. They *did* produce the pills that allow us to keep thriving, even in this air quality. Would you rather go back to the old ways? Masks, food inflation, and such?"

Dr. M'fume shrugged. "Not sure that's enough for me to be in their cheering section. Besides, once you're on them, it's not like you can get off. Them launching those meds seems more like a perfect business model than an act of philanthropy."

He glanced at a portrait of Chinuré on the far wall of the study and Dr. Aziz did the same before lowering his gaze to the floor with a dour expression.

Anyway," Dr. M'fume sighed. "You said you're taking on a consultant role with them? For . . . what, exactly?"

The darkness that had shrouded Dr. Aziz's face a moment before was gone and he quickly pivoted, his tone suddenly chipper. "Can't chat much about that stuff, nondisclosures being what they are, but I do think some of it's a game changer—if we can get a green light from The Council. They've been a little nit-picky since the—"

"Since the machine wars that ravaged a third of the world's infrastructure and left thousands of people dead?" Dr. M'fume's gaze met Dr. Aziz's gaze and sparred with it briefly.

Then, he leaned back and let his shoulders relax as he studied the drum. He decided not to pursue it any further.

No need to spoil a visit with an old friend, Dr. M'fume rationalized. *Back to lighter fare, Chinaka.*

"So, what are these markings?" Dr. M'fume traced his fingers over faded and chipped paint that encircled the bell of the drum.

"I was hoping you'd be able to tell me more about that since I know language studies is a hobby of yours," Dr. Aziz grinned sheepishly, and a glimmer of his former self shone through as he did.

"Alright, then," the doctor said as he held the drum up and inspected it. "It looks like a story, that's for sure."

He agreed to give the markings a thorough review, and Dr. Aziz left him alone with the drum.

The deep reds, browns, oranges, and black hues in the hellish scene had only been used for the first half of the drum, and the colors shifted for the rest of the glyphic tale; half the images showed the aggressors, led by the woman in the most decorative battle dress, in color, and their prey in shades of charcoal and blue. The midpoint of the painted scene was marked by an odd symbol. It was a rectangle with diamonds, circles, and triangles arranged in a pattern within its perimeter. A door. The scene reconvened on the other side of that symbol, but in grayscale only. The pursuing party was no longer depicted in vibrant, warm colors but had instead been painted to match those they were hunting. In the closing part of the story, both groups were equally dabbed in those colors so that they all looked like shadowy forms.

They all look, the doctor mused, *like ghosts.*

The dreams began shortly after that, visceral and crisp as he slept but slippery by first light. He knew there was a woman in them. A small, terrifying one who carried a staff with familiar markings. Each time he saw her in his dream, she was standing on a small, moonlit body of water that was out of place in the treeless expanse of sand around her. Next, she would drift toward him slowly as her warriors stood stoically behind her in unsmiling ranks, and the doctor would discover that it was not water at all, but a mist that pooled about her shriveled feet and kept her afloat in that plane, a regal vessel that ensured she never touched the ground. In the dream, her eyes were always milky white against her dark, leathery face, and her gaze bore into him like the deep engravings in the side of the drum. Etching and hollowing him out. Amulets adorned her neck, and the wind rustled the complicated crown of dried reeds, blue grama grass, and beaded plaits cascading from an updo that dwarfed and shrouded her menacing face.

Each time, she would stop an arm's length away from the doctor, then point over his shoulder, and each time, he would sit up in bed gasping, sweating, and parched. Yet, each time, no matter what his resolve was to see what it was she was pointing at, the dream would end abruptly before he could.

Then, a few weeks after Dr. Aziz's visit, he received a summons via holopro. He was to appear in court to give testimony about Mortedek's latest product, the Revitron Orb. Later that night, the woman came again. She said nothing as the mist danced in hypnotic swirls around her heavily adorned ankles. She drifted toward him noiselessly, except for the dry rustling of the dead and hollow things interwoven into her headdress. Once more, she moved toward him with intent, her gaze like daggers whittled from pearl. But this time, when she pointed, the doctor found that he could look over his shoulder.

What he finally saw there was *Iya Ilu*, the very drum exhumed by Dr. Aziz and his team. *Iya Ilu*. A drum that bled out such strange chords that it was often the drum chosen to lead ceremonies for the living and referred to as the "Mother Drum." And this one, with its scene of war, death, and resurrection, was his family's drum.

*   *   *

Ding!

A banal yet soothing voice filled the cabin from all directions
as the spacecraft lowered itself onto the powdery surface of the
moon on the day of the hearing. The building that housed the
hearings was an ambitious architectural feat that took over a
decade to complete, despite it being one of the simplest structures in their sector of the galaxy—a dome composed of dense,
dust-repellant, fire, and shatterproof glass. Through the crystal-
clear facade that encased them all, he could see the vast blackness of their star system laid out all around them on an anthra-
cite blackboard speckled with the chalk marks of a grand
architect.

"Preparing to dock," said the pleasant, sedated-sounding
voice. "Please remember to be courteous as you collect your
things from the locker bay. Thank you."

Several people who had gathered near the entrance to the
courtroom turned to look at Dr. M'fume as he entered the series
of double doors that opened to the vestibule and security area of
the Lunar Consulate Hall. The tall, square-jawed man still had
an ease to his gait that reflected years of athleticism, and broad
shoulders that balanced a slightly protruding belly that he'd
slowly gained after his wife passed away and he'd sought the
comfort of their favorite dishes. He had never been one to over-
eat, but for nearly two years now, he still sometimes forgot that
he need only to cook for one.

Though his complexion was usually close to that of a kola
nutshell, as he approached the large, semi-circle desk to show
his wristlet and satchel to the security officers, he felt as if he
had paled to the color of the kola nut itself. After the security
androids scanned it to make sure that it wasn't a cleverly disguised vessel full of explosives, and only after they heard the
doctor's impassioned speech about how he'd been unable to
submit it earlier because he couldn't find it, they allowed Dr.
M'fume into the chamber with his drum.

Adjusting to lunar gravity was always a trial for his body, and
no matter how hard the engineers worked to keep the hall

214

properly pressurized, the craft lag and dizziness he suffered upon entering its main chamber just couldn't be remedied. Because of this, Dr. M'fume, a man in otherwise peak physical health, stopped and let out a feeble cough before straightening himself and heading to his seat. He inwardly admonished himself for letting everyone see it, though. He knew his every word and gesture would be scrutinized and didn't want to make any move that could be misinterpreted as nervousness. For this was the very first time in all his forty-eight Earth years that he sat on the dissenting side of technological process.

Or worse, the dissenting side of Mortedek.

The Council was already seated when Dr. Chinaka M'fume arrived at the hearing. Upon seeing this, the flustered doctor rushed to his uncomfortable, predesignated seat in the courtroom.

Of course, every renowned expert had been called in to testify, so Dr. M'fume wasn't surprised when he received his subpoena by holomail. Credentialed in astrophysics, medicine, and theology, The Council likely deemed his testimony a worthy counterbalance to the talking heads from Mortedek. Still, the weight of the outcome was not lost on the doctor.

Dr. M'fume felt sure that he had the one thing he needed to win over The Council. He even managed to sit a bit taller when he let his focus rest on that thought.

Today, I have Iya Ilu with me, he reassured himself. *And Iya Ilu will do what the woman in my dream promised me. As mad as it is, I know it's true.*

After he was fully settled and sworn in, a feminine android emerged from one of the side chambers to begin her line of questioning. Dr. M'fume was in awe of the creation. He tried not to stare but couldn't help but gaze upon the seamlessness and symmetry of her design. It was that perfect symmetry that gave her away. That, and the impeccable hairlessness of her skin.

Dr. M'fume shifted in his seat.

"Please begin, Dr. M'fume," said the android, who eventually identified herself as 'SOHA' for Standard Operational Hybrid Assimilator.

This is good. I've heard of SOHAs before. The Council employs them specifically for their impartiality. The doctor cleared his throat and obliged.

"I am here because you have asked my expert opinion on the latest in necrogenic technology being produced by Mortedek Industries, Incorporated, and after thorough research of Revitron, the product Mortedek developed to house a consumer's soul post-mortem, I must insist that we immediately ban the reproduction and distribution of this product for commercial use or otherwise until further, more extensive testing can be done."

"Why is that your recommendation, Dr. M'fume?" The SOHA flashed a perfectly engineered smile toward the audience, then back at the doctor.

"I've read Mortedek's statement, as well as the claims their company has put forth about Revitron, and understand that their claim is that their right to produce such a product is protected under the laws that allow them to produce cyborg prosthetics, but there is a crucial difference between those products and this one."

"Which is?" The SOHA's voice lilted and cracked almost imperceptibly on the last word and Dr. M'fume found something unsettling in it.

They overdid it with this one. He suppressed the uneasy expression he felt blooming on his face. *Why program a SOHA to feign bewilderment?*

"Well," Dr. M'fume looked over at The Council, then at the other attendees, to avoid looking at the SOHA as he spoke. "The laws that govern cyborg production are clear: the subject's brain must be intact since it contains, in essence, the crux of what and who that human being is. As you all know, we've had countless years of moving that organ into new prosthetic sleeves and know what to expect from that process. With these things—"

"Revitron Orbs," the SOHA corrected the doctor in a firm tone.

"Ahh yes," the doctor continued, pretending not to be flustered as he did. "As I stated before, we have mountains of data on how the human brain works—in and out of its original . . . err . . .umm . . . vessel—and absolutely no information about how the energy output unique to each human, or 'soul,' operates at all. Therefore, no one should push a product to market without having that information first.

"You're also ignoring the possibility of a spike in the demand for cadavers to house these Revitron orbs," Dr. M'fume continued. "People die in countless ways and some bodies won't be in any condition to house an orb. Also, the price tag could spur black-market demand and unauthorized reproduction. There is still *much* for The Council to consider in this matter."

The doctor's earpiece picked up snippets of whispers and instantaneously isolated and translated them into a flurry in his ears:

"A black-market replica could spell disaster..."

"No more than a traditionalist idiot--I can't believe he's even up there..."

"Where will people put the orbs if their bodies are destroyed beyond repair?"

The doctor cleared his throat loudly, and the whispers abruptly ceased. He opened his mouth to defend his points, but the SOHA sharply cut him off.

The SOHA had been facing the doctor up to that point. Now, it shifted its frame sharply to direct its next statement more to The Council than the doctor. It shifted its demeanor, too. As it turned, Dr. M'fume was able to see a flash of something markedly human in its eyes.

Competitiveness, perhaps? Dr. M'fume couldn't stop himself from squinting suspiciously at the SOHA for a moment.

He ran his clammy palms along the strap of his satchel and thought of the drum inside. The satchel was on the floor to his left, but he placed the sturdy leather strap so that it lay across his lap. The tactile sensation against his hand soothed him, and he squeezed the strap from time to time to remind him to sidestep his fear, for when the time came, he would finally produce his drum.

"I am certain of something I'm sure many others in this chamber are certain of, Dr. M'fume. I am certain that men like you are among those who would demonize progress," the SOHA said coolly, with a smirk.

"That's not it at all." Dr. M'fume frowned at the SOHA. "We've only recently discovered the composition of the soul. We've yet to unmask its origin or map what motivates its movement. But we do know that it is pure energy, and we do know that it does, indeed, move. I suspect that this energy also does not know where it will move after it is released from the vessel it powered—its human form—and thus, cannot be expected to sign itself over until it is in a post-mortem state. Meaning—we should consider that if it can't know where it will go when its body is done, how can one just sign it over to confinement before it has the chance?

"Further, deceased beings who cannot cross planes would inevitably be doomed to be resentful at that fate, and that would give rise to new conflicts. The dead must be allowed to cross planes on their own and not remain imprisoned in a product designed for our selfish gains," the doctor regretted the last of his words as they left his mouth.

He watched as the SOHA's uncanny smirk returned.

"Mortedek has presented considerable market research that reflects a great demand for Revitron," the SOHA continued, mirroring an array of human expressions that denoted confident speech; the SOHA maintained hand gestures, a booming voice, and direct eye contact throughout. "So, Dr. M'fume, are you telling us that this product, which is overwhelmingly supported by many in this hearing, is, as you put it, to be used toward no more than 'our selfish gains'?

"But" the SOHA's tone softened, "what if you could have used the orb to prolong your time with someone you lost far too soon?"

Dr. M'fume held his breath. He narrowed his eyes at the SOHA. "I . . .I . . . sometimes," he stammered, then exhaled shakily and continued. "Sometimes you just can't change those sorts of things."

Does she know? Dr. M'fume's struggled to control the tremor in his hands. He felt deflated. *Of course, she does.*

As if reading his inner thoughts, the SOHA continued. "I'm not here today to make you relive the passing of your wife, Dr. M'fume. But would you wish that same experience on a friend?

218

Or would you want someone whom you respect—someone who helped you with something important to you—to go through the same thing?"

"I don't follow you," Dr. M'fume blinked at the SOHA.

"Does the name 'Yusef Aziz' mean anything to you, Dr. M'fume?" The SOHA flashed a smile that was finally, to Dr. M'fume, wholly void of human emotion.

"*Doctor* Yusef Aziz?" Dr. M'fume's face crumpled under the weight of his confusion. "Yes. He's a friend and colleague of mine."

Then suddenly, he saw him in the last row.

The doctor's eyes seared into Dr. Aziz until he felt an overwhelming mixture of feelings that churned his stomach into a brothy whirlwind of anger and disappointment. He noticed that Dr. Aziz was even more meticulously groomed than he'd been at their last meeting. His unruly mustache and beard had been darkened and he wore an expensive-looking suit. The doctor assessed, rather dejectedly, that Dr. Aziz now exuded the countenance of the others on The Council—he looked as if he carried all the trappings of wealth and dark power with him, and none of his old warmth. The only thing about him that didn't look polished or new were his eyes, which looked as if they had retreated into his concave sockets. Seated next to him, staring on quietly, was Mrs. Aziz.

I was so nervous when I came in that I didn't spot them at all, Dr. M'fume scolded himself inwardly. *But both look quite different, so I would've had to look twice. They both look sharper than they did—in a way—but Dr. Aziz looks aggrieved, and she looks uncannily healthy. And why is she looking at me that way? She's upset, but—*

"What would you say if I told you that Dr. Aziz was contracted with Mortedek, and has been for nearly a year now?"

"I'd say that you're telling me nothing new," the doctor said with a hint of indignation. "I mean, we're friends, after all. He mentioned that he'd be doing some consulting work for the company during his last visit, but nothing more."

"Good!" The SOHA smiled at The Council members and, much to the doctor's dismay, they smiled back. "You've already confirmed your trust in this man, and that he's a friend of yours who visited not long ago. So, if I told you that your friend, whose opinion you trusted enough to spearhead an excavation project for you, has a vested interest in the success of the Revitron Orb?" The SOHA walked closer to the witness stand, her heels clicking maliciously as she approached. "Well?"

They're all supposed to be neutral! Dr. M'fume clenched his teeth. *So, what the hell is going on here, then? The SOHA's questioning is clearly biased. This is a shitshow.*

"What I would say is that—" the doctor glared at the cunning machine with contempt in his eyes, "—I stand by my earlier assertions."

"She was sick, Chinaka!" Dr. Aziz suddenly blurted out. "I did what I *had* to do and . . . and . . . and I wish I could've done it for your Chinuré too!"

Before the doctor could respond, security droids rushed in and escorted the distraught man out of the hearing. His wife remained behind and stared at the doctor with a flat hatred he'd never seen on her kind face before. It unnerved him so much that he turned his stare toward The Council.

Once he did, his eyes were immediately drawn to the only council members who were in fact sneering at him. His eyes jumped to one of their faces, then another as he struggled to recall the names of all four. A long pause ensued as he strained to remember, and in that moment, he was grateful for the distraction Dr. Aziz had caused.

Alright, Dr. M'fume contorted his face as he pulled their names from the precipices of his mind. *That one's Nguyen and that's Kooltyak. I believe the one to the far left is...is called Ramos. And perhaps...mmm...I think the sallow-looking one is Johnson.*

The doctor tried to concentrate, but the SOHA's next words sliced the air like a sharp knife, cleaving through his thoughts.

"Though these details are already on record with The Council, I'd like everyone here to know that not only is Dr. Aziz a consultant for Mortedek, but he also fully endorses the use of the Revitron Orb as a viable option for those who *wish* to *extend* their lives," the SOHA relished the last few words, rounding out each one slowly.

The doctor's hands felt cold, and his entire body shook with rage as he remembered how Dr. Aziz had dodged answering questions about his dealings with Mortedek.

That bastard already knew he'd given a statement, and that I'd hear it today, the doctor fumed. *Yet he gave no mention of it. Didn't forewarn me or even try to persuade me to his side. We weren't friends at all. Apparently, I don't have any friends in the courtroom today.*

Something in the doctor snapped.

"And what if someone were to decide they don't want to continue living in their old, reanimated body?" The doctor roared and stood up from his seat, catching the strap of the satchel before it rolled onto the ground. "What if they decide they'd rather raid a morgue or snatch some vulnerable person off the street and power them up like some flesh puppet?!"

A wave of whispers and gasps went up from the hearing room until a council member raised a hand to restore the peace.

The SOHA scoffed and the doctor narrowed his eyes at her.

What manner of machine is this? He thought.

"It sounds like you deny the world new technologies because of the fears of a few. Has that not been the case of many who came before you?" The SOHA gestured wildly as it continued. "But ultimately, it is progress that you wish to impede, Dr. M'fume, and that very same progress that drove man from the humble soil of Earth to the explore stars!" The SOHA mirrored every gesture and expression of human passion as it continued, raising its voice, and sweeping its arms toward The Council.

"That's not true and I believe the esteemed members of The Council need no refresher course in the harm these developments can cause to our—" Dr. M'fume sputtered, but the SOHA cut in sharply.

"Is it not fearmongering that actually motivates you today, Dr. M'fume?" The SOHA narrowed its eyes at the doctor. "Fear that Revitron can do for humans what they have failed to do since the beginning of time?"

"No—it's not fearmongering at all. It's—" Dr. M'fume started to explain himself, but the SOHA was not to be outdone.

"I believe you *are* afraid, doctor. I also believe that you would make others afraid along with you," as the SOHA continued, Dr. M'fume looked down to see that his hands were shaking with rage. He clutched the strap of his satchel tighter, his knuckles turning pale as the SOHA continued to assail him. "It is for this reason that you sit before us and block the progress of Mortedek Industries. You are like many who have come before you. You are afraid of what has never been done."

"But it has," Dr. M'fume said quietly, his voice barely audible against the flutter of whispers in the room.

He didn't repeat himself for he knew that the SOHA had heard what he said, even the quietest sound stood no match against its artificial hearing. Strangely, the look on the android's face was less artificial.

The SOHA's expression was one of pure surprise, and in the brief moment before either of them spoke again, the doctor gaped at the artistry in it, the perfect mimicry.

"What do you mean?" The SOHA cocked its head slightly. "No patent for this type of reanimation existed before Revitron was developed—only failed attempts. So, if you would, please clarify your statement for The Council."

"Absolutely," replied Dr. M'fume as he ran his fingers along the strap of his satchel again. Only, this time he used it to gently hoist the drum onto his lap. His hands were no longer clammy, and he breathed a sigh of relief as he glanced at The Council because he was sure that his words may have failed him thus far in their eyes, but his second chance rested gently on his lap. He removed his translator before a tidal wave of whispers began to flood his ears as the Council and other audience members observed his movements.

"As you requested," the doctor replied to the android who now stood with a muted expression of what appeared to be genuine dread on its face as he continued. "I propose to show The Council another way to move a soul . . . without the help of necrotechnology."

222

"With all due respect," the SOHA spoke to the doctor, but set her eyes in the direction of The Council, "I don't think this is the proper venue to pursue any other manner of discourse than the one we were previously engaged in, and I think it best you exhibit the proper respect for this hearing at once!"

Murmurs swelled from the small group of powerful adjudicators seated on their vaulted platform and for the first time, Dr. M'fume studied them for a long while. The Council was a mix of eight men, women, and all in between. The doctor tried to discern the preferred gender of each but decided it best to remember them by hairstyle, which seemed to be the only way they saw fit to distinguish themselves from one another. All were dressed in black cloaks with comically high collars. All looked delicate and narrow-shouldered. Their faces were powdered, and their hands were adorned with rings that bore The Council's insignia, and the doctor decided that the four who had looked upon him with disdain earlier looked the most privileged, with rings on each finger of each hand, and hair piled, splayed, or frayed into gaudy monstrosities atop their heads. A wave of apprehension swelled in him as their murmuring intensified. When it finally stopped, the four angriest among them looked more annoyed than before.

"We'll permit his demonstration," The councilmember who spoke sounded utterly bored, but the doctor was thankful for the announcement, nonetheless.

He nodded, drew in a deep breath, and began to drum.

Bumma dum ba pa dumma dum bop! Bumma dum ba pa dumma dum bup!

Dr. M'fume's hands moved rhythmically and for a moment, the SOHA didn't speak, and the murmurs died down. The doctor drummed faster and louder, and Iya Ilu bellowed its song in an ancient percussive language that could reach the living and the dead.

Bumma dum ba PA DUMMAH DUM BOP! BUMMAH DUM BAH PAH DUMMAH DOOM BUP!

This *Iya Ilu*, or "Mother Drum" was the talking drum his forefathers used to perform songs for mating, songs for war, and songs to summon dead souls.

223

Surely, I am what they were, are, and will be, Dr. M'fume reasoned as the sweat began to bead on his forehead. *I have been away from home so long, and they have been dead even longer. But still, I can feel them . . . and if I can feel them, then I can do this too.*

The doctor focused on the thought as he squeezed his eyes shut. He was almost there.

He rapped more forcefully on the drum, working himself toward a trance. He began to beat it at a feverish pace. As his palms worked the drum, he let his mind recall the words encoded in his blood. The doctor called out and everyone listened.

"IBA SE EGUN!!"

"IBA SE EGUN!!"

Many in the room murmured or adjusted their translators as the doctor's words echoed in the room, and their eyes widened when they understood the varied translations that spilled into their ears, depending on the translation to their native tongue. Despite the differences of a word or two, what many heard was the same.

"ANCESTORS I CALL YOU!"

"ANCESTORS I SALUTE YOU!"

The doctor sensed that everyone in the room was feeling uneasy, but he continued his chant.

Suddenly, the silence in the room was broken. Everyone angled their bodies toward the direction of the glass facade of the north side of the room. As they looked out of the dome, they did not see what Dr. M'fume had seen earlier. The circumferential scene of vast nothingness peppered with stars and celestial bodies was disrupted by something in the distance. Some of the attendees stood, leaned forward, and used one hand to shield their eyes as they squinted at the moving anomaly. Then, as they gazed on in horror, they could see that a small band of warriors had materialized, dressed for battle, partially transparent, and rushing toward the glass dome.

And all of them were trailing a woman who was charging forward with white eyes, a rattling headdress, and hellish intent written on her face. If the doctor had looked up in that instant, he would have recognized the woman from his dreams rushing forth.

But the doctor was not watching.

He was too busy with his drum. He gritted his teeth and continued his rhythm until beads of sweat formed against his temple and his eyes rolled back in his head. In a trance, he stood by and called out again. Others around him could hear the faint translation of what he sang crackling through his translator, which he'd removed and placed on a lectern near him but hadn't turned off. As his voice boomed, the translator distorted his ominous words.

"DEATH HAS COME!"

"FOR YOU ALL!"

"THE HIDDEN TRUTH ABOUT THE MASQUERADE HAS BEEN UNCOVERED!"

Security poured into the room with their weapons drawn and flanked themselves in front of The Council, but its members barked no commands; they only sat watching with their eyes flitting between the doctor and the transparent beings moving toward the dome.

A few shuffled uncomfortably in their seats as the warriors approached the glass and paused for a moment. But then, the witch woman who led the pack stepped through the glass and walked toward the doctor, and a small stampede ensued. The doctor did notice that the crowd was of two factions: those who fled in terror, and those glued to their seat by their own morbid curiosity. After several moments marked by frantic curses and the opening and shutting of doors, quiet settled over the space again and all that could be heard was the doctor's drum. From the corner of his eye, the doctor was surprised to see that Mrs. Aziz was still seated in the back row opposite him with her hands clasped in her lap, void of emotion.

Dr. M'fume stood up to receive them but did not cease his drumming—even after they'd formed a semicircle around him.

Finally, he stopped drumming and adjusted the strap to let the drum hang at his side. Once he did, all that could be heard was the gentle whir of hydraulic machinery as the android security guards shifted their bodies to train their guns on one apparition, then another. Ultimately, they held their positions because they had no protocol for an instance such as this. Still, they stood ready, calmly awaiting any gesture from a member of The Council.

The Council sat watching and waiting with the rest of the remaining audience. They didn't say a word. It was the SOHA who spoke first.

"I see that the doctor is prone to parlor tricks on this lengthy moon day, but I assure The Council that I have a demonstration of my own," said the SOHA as it set its lips into a stern-looking line and snapped its fingers.

Immediately after, a non-sentient robot in a plain white lab coat rolled into the room pushing a gurney into the hearing room. It glided along until it reached the center. Strapped to the gurney was a silverish, reflective bag.

It was a body bag.

The doctor's apparitions stood silently by, their forms transparent and flickering as they continued to stare at the doctor, who could in turn find no other response but to stare back at them.

"I would like to present a case on behalf of Mortedek," SOHA's voice boomed confidently. It began walking toward the gurney, and its high heels clicking against the smooth stone floor was indeed a ferocious sound to the doctor's ears.

"They refer to her as 'Eve Two'" said the SOHA. "This biologically born Earthian female is the first to officially sign on to undergo a Revitron transfer."

The SOHA glanced at the doctor, a wry expression on its face. He did not turn to look; his gaze was affixed to the silver bag, and the form silhouetted inside it.

She turned her attention back to The Council and continued. After clicking three buttons on its inner wrist, a neat collection of words and numbers formed in the space above her head. She flicked her wrist to effortlessly turn the pages of the holographic dossier as she spoke.

"These documents show that Eve Two signed the agreement before her physical death, a point at which she agreed to be cryogenically preserved until the date of transplantation. She even agreed to have her cadaver used in any promotional demonstrations, as outlined in the last of these signed pages," said the SOHA. "There are thousands more who followed suit after her. This surely demonstrates that not only is there a market for Revitron, but there is an eager one."

After the SOHA finished speaking, the robot that had wheeled the stretcher began to adjust it until the form inside the foil-like bag was seated upright. Then, it wheeled itself to face the specimen and unzipped the bag unceremoniously. Then, inch by inch, the cadaver was revealed.

The woman had reddish-brown skin the color of pottery clay before her death, and she had a lengthy, svelte form and lengthy feet. It occurred to the doctor that if she would've been able to stand, she would've towered above most in the room. Her hair was braided in a thick, single braid that had been pinned around the perimeter of her head like a crown. She wore an olive-green bandeau around her chest and another around her pelvic area and thighs. Her abdomen was bare, and surgically embedded just above her navel was a concave metal structure a little larger than the size of her fist. She looked to be enjoying a deep, peaceful sleep, except for the tinge of gray that was beginning to cancel the warm tone of her nearly flawless skin.

The robot escort reached into its lab coat, produced a small black case from one of its oversized pockets, and handed it to the SOHA. Then it spun on its wheels and rolled swiftly out of the room in a manner that, if it had been a mammal, one would easily have viewed as fear.

Dr. M'fume looked on anxiously with the rest in the room as the SOHA opened the case and retrieved a purple, glowing orb up for all to see. The sight of the small, extraordinary globe was met with sounds of awe from everyone except Dr. M'fume, the security, and Eve Two.

"Now I will temporarily install this Revitron Orb into Eve Two. The engineers of Revitron guarantee the safety of this procedure on Eve Two, as it has been carried out many times before," said the SOHA as it approached the deceased woman. "I will briefly reanimate her so that she can greet The Council, which is more than Dr. M'fume's apparitions appear to be capable of. Then, the Council can make a fully informed, final decision based on our respective demonstrations."

The doctor looked back at the apparitions. The eldest-looking warrior among them gave him a nod. It was a lightning-quick motion that few witnessed except the SOHA, who gave him an overtly snide look.

Then, it placed the orb inside Eve Two's chest.

The doctor heard a series of clicks and then a sound like a large generator powering on. It was a cold, mechanical sound, and Dr. M'fume immediately despised it. He hated to associate it with the soul and rebirth of a human being when it sounded so much like a sound one would hear in the manufacturing warehouses of Mortedek. It sounded as tinny and hollow and terrifying as the sounds of scientific progress often are. Like hydraulic arms placing products on a metal belt with finitely perfect timing. The sound emanating from the orb reminded him of titanium bones cloaked in life-like polyurethane skin.

Only, Eve Two had been a woman without metal bones. Her inner workings had once been fear, hopes, dreams, flesh, and blood. Once, she had a life. And she had indeed, a death.

The sound got louder, and the orb glowed with purple light. Spines of lightning jutted from every direction away from the orb, sending energy into Eve Two's every limb. Suddenly her chest began to rise and fall, quickly at first, and then with slow, measured movements. Then she opened her eyes and propped herself onto her elbows. She jerked her head left and right in frantic consternation until her eyes fell on the SOHA. A look of calm realization washed over her brow after she sighted the android, to whom she gave a fond and knowing look.

Then the revived woman sat up straight, swung her legs down, and stood before The Council, the doctor, the SOHA, and everyone else. No one dared speak; there was only a cough, a gasp, and a wayward whisper from someone near the entrance of the room. Dr. M'fume noticed that Mrs. Aziz had leaned forward in her chair a bit, keenly observing the woman.

"Good day, distinguished members of The Council," the woman's voice was loud, but there was a shyness to it. She continued, "My name is Eos Iola, but you may call me Eve Two."

228

The newly animated woman slid effortlessly from the table and paused. She shot a nervous glance toward the phantasmagoric gathering that still stood in a semicircle near the doctor, flickering and transparent, but dismissed her fears once she noticed that no one else appeared to be put off by the sight.

"I'm pleased to be here today, and I wish to tell you of my experience with Revit—" Eve Two suddenly stopped speaking and turned abruptly to face one of Dr. M'fume's ghosts.

She cocked her head to the side, listening for something that no one seemed to hear but her. Then her face crumpled in a look of pure terror, and she clapped both hands to her ears and squeezed her eyes shut. She doubled over in pain but looked up to search for the source of the noise.

The ruling specter floated closer to Eve Two with her mouth open wide. Its silvery-blue, transparent form kept its white eyes trained on her. The doctor knew from her headdress and the fluid way she glided above the ground, that this was the leader of his summoned horde. The garments rustled as she moved toward Eve Two, making a sound like pellets cascading in a hollow, aged gourd. She was his ancestor, bound to him through ties he did not know, yet beholden to the sound of Iya Ilu's drum-song. This was indeed the woman from his dream. She was also, as he would soon find out, a banshee.

She began to murmur something in a low voice, guttural and full of hisses. As everyone strained to hear her, a clamor arose as all in attendance adjusted the translators in their ears. The doctor stood in a trance; his feet plastered to the floor by the weight of his fear. He knew precisely what the woman was saying and knew that her words matched the story etched on the side of the drum; she and her group had the same purpose in life as they had in death.

They came to shepherd the dead.

Those who had properly adjusted their translators also began to share in the doctor's horror, for this is what they heard:

"You may walk but you are dead!"

"You may talk but you are dead!"

"We have been summoned to join you with the dead!"

"The dead will forever find you ALL and join you with our dead!"

"NOW COME JOIN US, AS YOU ARE DEAD!"

As he released the chants, the doctor sensed that the words seeped through him, rather than poured from him. He heard octaves and pitches he knew he could never manage on his own. His voice morphed and bent and hollowed and swelled until he was done, and the words were spread thickly around him, causing varying effects for all in attendance.

Then, the death-dealing witch woman shrieked.

A roar of curses went up in the room from those who'd turned the volume up on their translators as they winced at the explosion of sound that burst through their earpieces and the security droids set about maintaining order as some attendees yanked their headsets off in disgust and began to shove their way toward the exit. But the shrieking did not stop. It grew louder until Eve Two could bear it no longer. She leaned forward, her knees wobbly and her hands still clasping her skull. She pressed her palms over her ears and tears streamed down her cheeks as she shook her head back and forth violently and tried to stagger toward the door. But she didn't make it. The cry was inescapable and obliterating for the newly awakened woman. It appeared to disorient a few others in the room too, affecting their gait and causing them to twist their faces in agony.

As the room emptied out more, Dr. M'fume began to recognize those left behind in the wake of the supernatural cacophony. His eyes widened as he did, and the tightness in his chest lessened as his fear transformed into burgeoning surprise.

Kooltyak, Ramos, Nguyen, the SOHA, and Johnson, the doctor thought to himself. As he struggled with the significance of their shared reactions to the witch woman's shriek, he slowly mouthed the names he'd heard so often in the preceding months.

Kooltyak. Ramos. Nguyen. Johnson. The SOHA. What could it mean?

The doctor furrowed his brow and weighed the possibilities. As the president of Revitron, Kooltyak was deeply invested in the outcome of today's hearings, but the others were just members of The Council and thus, tasked with impartiality. As for the SOHA, it was already an android, void of life. Yet, they all sauntered slowly about, either gripping their stomachs or cupping their hands over their bleeding ears...or attempting to do both.

Dr. M'fume could not tear his eyes away from the scene, but he could hear the footfall that had been moving away from the spectacle fade as people stopped walking, abandoned their fear for curiosity, and turned on their heels to view the impossible affair. Everyone who was able to watch was now watching the living and the dead—and things that neither lived nor died—intermingled together in a chaotic scene.

Suddenly, Eve Two stood straighter, as if her spine had been mounted on a pole. The shriek continued until she began to hemorrhage blood from her ears and nose. The other four stood similarly, unspeaking and glued in place. The doctor let his eyes dart from one petrified fifth of the group to another, before letting his mind waver on the one possibility that would explain it all.

They're already DEAD, he nodded to himself, his mouth slightly agape. *They made some pact to test the damn things unethically . . . and to rig this hearing!*

"But NO!" The doctor shook his head violently from side to side. "This CAN'T be true. Everyone was screened on their way in and the droids—I mean, security—they would've caught them before they made it in. They would've known about the orbs. They would've known unless they'd been tampered with, too."

The orb encased in Eve Two's abdomen began to vibrate and glow. It swirled with brilliant, pearlescent colors, and for a moment the doctor forgot himself in the hypnotic spectacle.

"Bzzzzzzzzzzzzrrrrrzzzzzzzzrrrr..."

All their orbs rattled furiously in their metal housings.

"Mmmmmbbbbrrreeeee-ee-ee-eee-eee-eeee-EEE-EEEEEEE!"

Then, they burst. All of them.

There was a succession of sounds, each like a dense light bulb bursting into glittering shards. The doctor noted that Eve Two's orb had glowed brightest and exploded the loudest.

Sadness gripped his heart as he watched Eve Two's limp body collapse to the ground with the others and lay sprawled gracefully amongst the twinkling bits of the broken orb that had just moments ago held her eager soul.

And so that is why the witch woman came. After she had done her duty, the doctor had no recourse but to marvel, bitterly, at his previous level of gall. *How could I ever have believed that I could control what the drum would do?!* Dr. M'fume put his face in his hands. *I wanted merely a demonstration! I came to collect a ruling in my favor, but Iya Ilu merely summoned those who would corral the dead to their side. This drum is tied to the witch and the witch to me. Was the drum the conduit, or I?*

The witch woman about-faced and glided back to the party of stoic, former warriors who stood waiting patiently for her before breaking apart into two ranks. They all faced the direction they came from but stood waiting for reasons no one in the room could discern.

Until they all saw it.

The apparition of Eve Two sat up and held her newly transparent hands out in front of her and looked at them incredulously, her mouth set in an "o" of childlike surprise. She wriggled her small, see-through fingers and jerked her hands back and forth in front of her eyes to see the glowing trails of light that faded to an iridescent, periwinkle glow only after she held them still. Then she wriggled her ghostly frame from her body and stood up in one fluid motion before walking calmly to join the ranks.

Dr. M'fume watched as the rest of the fallen did the same. Some wrenched and squirmed free from their fresh cadavers before the color could leave their cheeks. Others took longer. The SOHA slithered up and out of her deceased body. Kooltyak wriggled out of his robust, human form quite reluctantly, his expression sour with defeat after having lost the case in a way he never could have predicted. They all sauntered toward the parallel rows of the dead, all prepared to march forward.

The SOHA offered a small nod to the doctor as she passed and Dr. M'fume was momentarily amused that he hadn't figured out that she was human—albeit a reanimated human—all along.

Her every expression and competitive maneuver throughout the proceedings had been so impressively human because she was, indeed, human. Really, there was much the doctor didn't know about the SOHA. He had read up on his opponents before he arrived and studied her until the last moments of her reanimated existence.

He later learned that she had been an accomplished and driven litigator whose previous name had been Xena Collins, and she had eagerly accepted the one case she knew would launch her into the spotlight; she signed on to represent Revitron in the most controversial case she'd ever encountered and agreed even after she'd learned of the sacrificial pact she'd have to make to stay on with the case. After all, the evidence of her procedure was covered up so as not to present a clear conflict of interest in the case, she just knew that she would win it. She was certain of it as a capable litigator and willing, secret test subject. But mostly, she was sure of it because she wasn't accustomed to losing.

Now, the doctor watched her spectral form rise and join the ranks of the dead.

And just like that, it's done, he nodded to himself.

The transparent, gray horde marched forward and straight through the glass of the dome-like structure. They marched until they shrank in the distance, then disappeared altogether.

As cleanup bots were dispatched to remove the bodies and eventually, some of the attendees who had fled at the start of the melee came back into the hearing room to collect their things. Among them, some coagulated into bubbles of hushed whisperers. All the while, Dr. M'fume stood speechless, his expression blank as he surveyed the carnage.

As he walked back to his seat to gather his satchel, his ears caught snatched of the whispers that swirled around him and he realized that most conversations were not about ghosts at all. Rather, people were in awe that the case had been rigged all along.

Only, none of its conspirators prepared for an outcome such as this, the somber realization of the day's events caused his stomach to churn furiously.

The doctor shook his head as he mulled the thought.

Solemnly, he gathered Iya Ilu and placed it in his satchel. Then, he slung the satchel over his shoulder. He let his eyes roam in a semi-circle, absorbing the full arc of the scene in front of him. Everyone was still in shock, and it looked to him as though disorder had won the day. No one opposed him as he prepared to leave, or even approached him for a formal statement, though he was sure that would come later. Many stood facing the direction the phantoms had taken, with their noses so near the glass of the dome that the doctor could see the white of their breath bloom and fade on the area of glass in front of them.

As he neared the door, he heard sobbing. The doctor listened carefully and craned his neck to follow the sound until it led him to Dr. Aziz. The man cradled his deceased wife in his arms. Her blouse was in tatters and her exposed abdomen was a bloody ruin of twisted metal, crystal shards, and crimson. Dr. M'fume sat his satchel on a nearby chair and removed his suit jacket, which he gently draped over the woman. Then, with a firm hand but gentle gesture, pulled his colleague up to his feet.

Then, Dr. M'fume slung the satchel onto his shoulder once more. He nodded solemnly to the grieving widower and walked out of the room, traveling in the opposite direction of the dead.

Benny's Tearoom
by
Nicole Givens Kurtz

"Space cruisers come equipped to entertain the direst folks. For a limited time only, we invite you to our luxury lunar cruise for a low currency count of 25,000 units. This package is a BOGO deal. That's right! No space particles in your ears, just click to get two for the price of one! See the historic moon landing, shop at the luxurious lunar mall, and eat at our twenty tearooms, each one a treat! And the views are out of this galaxy. A fun, phenomenal vacation awaits! Click now! Space is limited . . ."

"How is space limited? Aren't those things as large as the Rhode Territory?" Gabriel tugged at his graying goatee. He quirked an eyebrow and glanced over to Jose.

"They seem like it on the telemonitor, but I think they use CGI to embellish the size." Jose shrugged. Seated beside his brother, Jose looked like a copy paste minus the goatee. Instead of facial hair, Jose was clean shaven, but wore his curly hair long, parted down the middle, and plaited. Two long ropes of dark brown hair reached his shoulders. "Don't say it. Size does matter."

"You said it for me." Gabriel snickered.

When neither got a response from the third person in the room, they turned to look at her.

Tatiana blinked but otherwise, her gaze remained locked on the paused commercial.

"TeeTee? You okay?" Gabriel asked.

She nodded.

"Oh, hell no! G, she got that look . . ." Jose threw his hands up. "You see it?"

"I do." Gabriel twisted around to get a full view. He leaned close to her and flicked her ear.

She didn't move, but she cut her eyes at him in warning.

Gabriel fell back to the couch, shaking his head. "Yeah. She's thinking about something."

Jose pointed at the elegant cruise ship, majestic with purple swirls. It floated against the velvety backdrop of space. "That."

"Right. We need a vacation. What's better than a luxury lunar cruise? The tearooms alone are to die for," Tatiana said.

#

"I can get used to this!" Jose adjusted his helmet and its oxygen flowed. The blue spacesuit fit his blocky frame a little too snug in certain places.

Tatiana listened to her other cousin bemoan his suit's fit the entire twenty-three hours here.

"I told you." She pointed to the glittering neon sign. *Benny's Tearoom* sparkled in giant, cursive letters. Sprawled above a large, four-deck high space cruise ship. Metallic blue thrusters illuminated the dark beneath it. The sapphire jewel floated in the cold sea of emptiness. "She's beautiful."

"TeeTee got her own way. Damn thing is expensive. That's what this is . . . a currency drain," Pip Wu chimed in.

Despite their helmets, her disdain rang through their shared audio.

"You could've stayed back in The District." Jose moved closer to Pip.

"Delete that! I'd miss you idiots buffering over a damn cruise ship." Pip laughed.

"You're the one who spent currency to hate-attend an event." Gabriel slapped Pip on the back, knocking the thinner woman forward two steps and into Tatiana.

"I will mute *all* your mikes. Stop bickering." Tatiana didn't raise her voice. She didn't need to. As the oldest, she'd been handling the mischievous trio behind her since forever.

Gabriel broke first. "Sorry, TeeTee."

Then Jose. "We were just, you know, overwhelmed by all this grandeur."

"Yeah okay." Tatiana waved them off. Beside her, Pip sulked in silence.

"This way! All aboard!" a robotic greeter, shaped like a green triangle with frilly ruffles along its hem announced. Its black, square face bore a matching pixelated grin. Both animatronic arms waved lavender lace fans in each hand. "Don't push. Safety first! Then fun."

"They sure wanted the tearoom vibe," Gabriel said.

They entered beneath Benny's Tearoom's *Welcome* banner along with the throng of spacesuit-clad vacationers. The sign flickered in various languages since this was an international destination. Luxury lunar vacations were popular years ago, but this one had managed to gather roughly two hundred people by Tatiana's guess. Classical music wafted through hidden speakers inside the entrance doors and their helmets. Glowing petal-shaped sconces lined the lavender walls. Tatiana expected carpet but instead found rubber flooring. Pear-shaped white robots flashed directions to the sea of people, parting them like Moses.

Tatiana made a left and the group thinned considerably. She stepped over to the side and gathered her group. "It's safe now to remove your helmet."

"Is it?" Gabriel asked.

Tatiana pointed at the flashing sign on the wall. "Yeah."

She waited while the others removed their helmets and breathed in the artificial air. Once she did the same, she said, "Let's find our rooms. I think we're close."

Jose said, "Look. 413. This is me."

He held up his wrist and its wristband. The room number had been emblazed in glittering scarlet.

The others paused, each checking their wristbands for their cabin numbers. Around them, fellow passengers did the same. Tatiana smirked. It was like a grown-up game of seek and find.

"I'm right here, in 411." Pip held up her wrist where the scarlet number flickered. The matte door slid back in a hush. "See you all in a bit."

"415," Gabriel jutted his head at the door labeled with the same number. He disappeared into his room once the scanner matched his wristband.

Tatiana searched for her room. The booking agent managed to reserve their cabins in the same area, but hers was an even number, not odd like the others. She passed two more doors before she found hers, 418. It was the last one on the right side before the staircase that led up to the next floor.

She held up her wrist in front of the door scanner. The door whooshed open, and she took a step inside. The cool breeze made her damp face chilly. It smelled like fruit. Citrus? Artificial gravity and life support made it all feel like Earth, not floating miles above the planet.

The door hushed closed behind her. Tiny odor plugs were stationed around the rectangular-shaped space. A fireplace cast the room into a warm glow. Flames crackled. It was a simulation, a good one too. Lighting came from sleek, thin lamps, shaped like stacks of teacups.

To her right a single-size mattress rested on a wooden palette. The deep purple bedding, pillows, and comforter matched the ship's overall décor. Tatiana placed her helmet down on a table next to the bed. A cushioned chair, with its round mustard throw pillows, took up the small area in front of the fireplace. Tatiana found her luggage stowed away, inside a tiny closet. Adjacent to the living area and opposite the door, three floor-to-ceiling windows. No small portholes here. She pressed the button beside them. The deep tint waned, revealing one hell of a view.

An infinite darkness stretched outward, far beyond what the human eye could see. The view reduced Tatiana, engulfing her in its enormity. She closed her eyes and opened her arms wide as if to embrace space's icy bleakness.

And yet, warmth spread through her.

At this moment, in the presence of God's celestial glory, Tatiana found peace—no demands on her time, her energy, and her spirit. The numb feeling, the gnawing nothingness retreated.

The soft hush of her door opening caught her off guard. She turned around.

"Gabriel. You could knock."

"Damn, all the rooms look like this, huh? Pretty nice." He ignored her. He had stripped his spacesuit off and now wore black dress pants, gray sweater, and chunky matching boots. "Everything's so sleek." Gabriel whistled. "And clean."

"Why are you here?" Tatiana said.

"Check this out."

He pressed a button on the wall across from the chair. The wall panels above the fireplace slid back, revealing a mounted telemonitor.

"Andre, show us the tearooms," Gabriel shimmed in glee as various in-picture screens popped onto the telemonitor's screen. "Did you know there's more than one *Benny's Tearoom*?"

"Yeah. It's on their site and all over the 'net." Tatiana rubbed her temple.

Tatiana unzipped her flight suit. She peeled it off and laid it down on the chair. Underneath her suit, she wore a long-sleeved shirt and jeans.

Gabriel pointed at the crimson one. "TeeTee, the red velvet room has, of course, red velvet cake, but also something called Mais Temptress tea."

Tatiana joined him in front of the screen.

Her door yawned open again. Pip and Jose came in, talking about the jet lag they would suffer tomorrow. Tatiana made a mental note to figure out how to lock her door.

"Ciao! Click on the ivory palace," Jose said, his eyebrows in his dark hair, and pointing at the telemonitor. "Hurry!"

"Calm your tits." Gabriel pressed the in-picture screen for the white square. It enlarged to full picture view.

"The food better be off the charts. I can get these views with AI art." Pip rubbed her lowcut hair. "I'd violate for some milk."

Jose smacked his lips. "I read milk in other territories is unmutated."

"Whoa," Pip said.

On screen, seated around a glass-frosted table, eight people ate what looked like vanilla cake with white icing. Triangle-shaped sandwiches rested on matching white plates. In the other hand, many of them held bone-white teacups. Opera music played in the background, soft, a breath beneath the buzz of conversations. Various masks covered passengers' faces.

"That looks boring as hell." Pip crossed her arms.

"Wait for it," Jose said. His dark eyes gleamed and remained glued to the telemonitor.

The bass dropped in the music, and suddenly the passengers removed their clothes, stripping out of them as if on fire. The music rolled from opera to party dance anthems. Teacups, cake, and sandwiches went flying as they were swept from the elegantly decorated table. The scene faded to dark as the erratic music continued.

"What the hell?" Gabriel fell back a step. He cut a glance at Jose. "That you?"

"Delete that!" His brother shook his head. "Definitely not my speed, too much going on there."

Tatiana shook her head. "That's interesting. This place had scores of activities and over one hundred different tearooms . . ."

"Does it include death violations?" Pip asked.

Tatiana frowned. "No. Why would you even ask that?"

"Because I'm pretty sure that guy is dead." She pointed to the right corner of the screen, where it had reverted to the in-picture board of tearooms. The tearoom in question bore sunflower decorations. Slumped in an awkward angle, eyes wide and unblinking, a lifeless-looking man had both hands resting in his lap. All around him, seated on sunflower chairs, people drank from green teacups and ate more of those triangle sandwiches.

Tatiana waved it off. "Probably one of those who sleep with his eyes open."

Pip started to say something but stopped as the ship whistle sounded, announcing a cruise-wide message.

"Hopefully all our tea lovers are settled into their luxurious cabins. If you have any issues, contact your deck manager. We're set to launch in four minutes into our luxury lunar excursion. Please go to your port view and stargaze as we set sail on *Benny's Tearoom* Lunar Luxury Cruise!"

"There's something fishy about it," Pip said, bringing the conversation back to the previous conversation.

"Fishy or not, it depends on perspective," Tatiana said.

They walked over to the view. Stars twinkled. The planet's blue hue and orbiting metal junk came into range. Over the speaker, the narrator droned on but the four of them stared at the dark glory before them.

Pip sighed.

"I don't care what you say. No AI compares to this." Tatiana pushed her bangs out of her face.

"This is stunning. We're in space!" Jose clapped his hands. Joy wafted off him.

Pip glanced at Tatiana. "Yeah, but out here we're alone at sea."

The truly awesome aspect of the cruise remained the glittering darkness. Tatiana stood closest to the windows, gazing out at the possibilities.

"I don't get why people pay all this currency for what? The experience? Pfft." Pip turned away from the windows. She started to leave.

"Yeah, the experience. It enriches your soul, helps you grow," Tatiana said. She faced Pip's back. She knew Pip mouthed off the first thing that came to her mind, but she had already grown tired of her cousin downing the vacation.

"You get old. You die. That's it." Pip threw her hands up. "You may not even remember this currency drain when you get old."

"But your glass-half-empty ass is here anyways," Jose interjected, apparently weary of Pip's attitude, too.

Pip turned around. Gabriel looked up at them.

No one spoke for a second.

Then, they burst into laughter.

With her family, feathers never stayed ruffled for long.

#

Bebo Turin's throat threatened to close over the hunk of emotions lodged there. His arm muscles screamed as he strained with the weight of the chairs, one in each hand. The tearooms awaited its patrons. This one was the Indigo Tearoom. Its walls bore swirling, intertwining blue circles. Music wafted in from hidden speakers. The theme of indigo equated to calm. Multiple teacups were white with artful designs in blue floral print. Sandwiches, blue-tinted cookies and cakes, muffins, and candies decorated round two-person tables.

"I don't know why we can't leave the chairs in place." Bebo put them in positions at one of the tables. Shania paused and put her hands on her round hips.

Bebo's brown eyes widened at the sight of the dark-haired beauty working the room with him.

"Because the vbots struggle with those round bases." Shania rolled her eyes. "Hurry up. The next session is in five."

When she headed to adjust one of the tablecloths, Bebo watched her shapely thighs with a longing sigh. Shania had a serious gambling problem. During their down time, she lived on the casino floor. She conned some of the workers out of currency, but he understood the raw thirst.

They say love is a virus.

"It pays. Don't complain, BeeBee." Shania tsked at him.

"I know. I know. That currency people spend on all this silliness. People in The District are starving." Bebo shrugged.

"Okay. Sure. We get fed. Not going on vacation won't fix the issues in any territory."

"Maybe not for everyone, but for that few, it's everything."

Bebo got quiet. She probably thought she'd won.

Shania looked so pretty when she got annoyed. Sweat made her face glow. Her tone became huskier, deeper, sexier. Once her breathing increased, Shania pushed all his buttons.

Bebo went back to the illusion of work while watching her.

The tearoom's uniforms were made to resemble the Victorian English housekeeper and butler outfits. The short black skirt and white apron added to her allure.

"Quit staring at me. You're rattling?"

Bebo blinked at her harshness. "No, I don't use drugs."

"Sure." Shania clicked her tongue.

Before he could say anything to persuade her, the bell announced the tearoom's opening.

"Let's go Indigo." Bebo adjusted his tie.

#

The tinkling bell announced the ship-wide message.

"Good day, passengers! Those new to Benny's may not be aware, but it *is* morning even in absence of a conventional sunrise. Leave convention behind and enjoy your holiday. Our tearooms operate in sessions, while some may be closed, others are open. Be sure to check the master schedule on your telemonitor to find the most delicious tearoom for you!"

"They should let us sleep." Gabriel's sleepy voice sounded muffled by his pillow. "My biological clock is all screwed up."

Jose cracked his neck as he stretched. "Nah. They want us up spending currency."

Tatiana sat cross-legged on her bed, in her pajamas, staring at them. "You *could* go back to your own cabins."

"Don't get moody." Gabriel rubbed his eyes.

Jose tugged his right ear.

Gabriel pointed at the telemonitor. "There's a tour of the ship at 8 am. I'd like to know where everything is located. I know it's not just tearooms here, but the damn thing is massive."

"Where's Pip?" Tatiana asked.

"Probably asleep."

"Okay, I like the idea of a tour." Tatiana stretched. "Get out so I can get ready."

#

"The Wellington Cruise was a high bar to reach. We've exceeded it here at Benny's. Wouldn't you agree?" The tour guide spoke through a tiny microphone. It boomed through the corridor of packed passengers.

Applause rippled around the guide. He bowed slightly before patting the crowd's enthusiasm down to a low roar. Free alcohol kept the passengers loose.

"Ah, you agree. Grand!" He smiled. His thin lips disappeared, leaving only teeth. "Now, go to the tearoom of your liking and indulge in our decadence, our deliciousness, and explore your desires! Rawr!"

The ship's whistle blew, signaling the opening of the tearooms. Tatiana shouted along with the others. She didn't have a glass of

242

booze. No, she wanted to remember everything. Vacations came about so rare nowadays. Adulthood made her tired. Her job made her exhausted. All the little tears at her energy for this task, that errand, and the muck of humanity being a regulator involved, all to get enough currency to eat, to live, and to survive.

She planned to relish every conscious moment. Spending her free time drowning in booze would mar it. Tequila made her forget. She wanted to remember it all.

"You look nice," Jose said, taking her hand and swirling her around the now-empty corridor. "You clean up well, cuz."

Gabriel whistled, drawing attention and eyes from the stragglers. "Wow. Good thing we have separate rooms. You'll no doubt be finding company in that outfit."

"Delete that, G!" Tatiana playfully slapped his arm.

Jose dissolved into laughter.

"It's just a dress. Goodness. Are you 32 or 12?" She rolled her eyes and headed down the hallway toward the staircase leading up to the tearoom floors.

"Neither!" Jose snapped. "Wait up."

She shifted close to the wall as a group of people passed in the narrow space. The cloud of cloying perfume, cheap jewelry, and untethered laughter spoke to the passengers' relaxed nature.

"You can find your own tearoom. We're looking for different things," Tatiana said to Jose and Gabriel once they caught up with her.

Jose looked at Gabriel, who said with a stone face, "you're telling us to get lost. Got it."

She pursed her lips. "This *is* a vacation."

"So you keep saying. We got it. I don't need to download it." Gabriel tugged at his goatee. The two men meld into the approaching throng of people coming from the breakfast room at the other end of the hall.

The ship's whistle blew. "Tea will commence in 5 minutes! Select your room or enjoy tea on the lunar viewing decks . . ."

Pip hadn't appeared after breakfast, but Tatiana figured she'd gone off exploring on her own. Her younger cousin liked soldiering alone hence her sharp tongue. It shoved people who didn't pass Pip's test away.

But wore on her family, namely Tatiana.

"You look blue," said a brunette with large, round eyes and dressed in an old-fashioned housekeeper costume. "Join us for tea in the Indigo room."

Tatiana paused and peeked inside. Beautiful, calm music ebbed from the open door. With her curiosity snared, she entered the sparkling blue light. Instead of the long community table she saw in the White tearoom, this one had bistro tables. Cute, light-blue tablecloths and bright flowers centered the oval tables. The overhead spotlights cast throughout the room provided shadow and illumination in strategic pockets.

"Please sit where you feel comfortable. Tea will be served in a few minutes. I'm Shania," Shania said, gesturing to those entering.

Once further into the room, Tatiana saw other larger tables probably for groups of three or more.

"Are you searching for your party?" A rail thin man asked in a slow, drawl.

Spooked, Tatiana raised her fists before she caught herself. The butler, complete with black suit and white-gloved hands clasped in front of him, offered a weak smile.

"Uh, sorry. You startled me."

"It's fine. My apologies," he said. He had wild blue eyes. They contrasted with his demeanor.

"I'll sit here." Tatiana went to the closet seat to the door and with the chair back facing the wall. She forced her attention on the 3D menu projection and not the creepy butler. Her instincts tingled but she ignored them.

I'm on vacation.

Across from her, the chair pulled out and Pip lowered herself into it.

"Found you." Pip wore a black pantsuit and red scarf tied decoratively around her neck. "You look scared."

"I don't like to be startled. How'd you find me?" Tatiana spied, just over Pip's shoulder, the door closing.

"Job hazard, huh? Just checking everything out. You know." Pip shrugged. "You looked lonely."

"Delete that." Tatiana smiled.

Pip smirked. "You love me."

"I do."

Their relationship ebbed and flowed, but like a river remained.

The ringing of a bell quieted the hum of conversations. The two wait staff members stood in front of the entrance door. They had smiling faces with their gloved hands in front of them. Despite this, Tatiana had a tough time composing herself. Her hand itched for a laser gun, but then maybe the unfamiliarity of non-structured time made her uneasy.

244

"Tea lovers, welcome to the Indigo room. Relax. Indulge. The focus of this space is to enjoy your company and experience unique flavors. Tea shall commence!" Shania announced.

A rear door whooshed open. In poured serving bots, s-bots. They quietly dispersed through the room, their trays filled with sandwiches, slices of various cakes, and fruit. The passengers broke into applause.

"This one has an old-world charm," Tatiana said.

"The veneer of an active VR experience." Pip selected a sandwich from the triangle-shaped s-bot's tray. "Without virtual, it requires a leap of faith."

"Okay. It's pretend. We're in *space!* Just go with it. How often do we fake it during our everyday lives? Sleepwalking through each hour, living but emotionally dead? This is our chance to take our feelings off ice, Pip." Tatiana declined the offer of food. She ate plenty at breakfast.

Pip inclined her head and took another cake before the s-bot moved on.

The wait staff delivered steaming carafes to the tables, perhaps not trusting s-bots to deliver something dangerous like boiling water.

"On each table, you'll find a clear container with loose tea varieties," the butler said. "The tiny vials have sugar, honey, and lemon extract to assist in dressing your tea."

Tatiana picked up the diffuser laid out on a blue cloth napkin, along with a thin stir.

"Food!" Pip clapped in tiny. "It better be flavorful. I'm tired of bland pate."

One of the s-bots paused at their table. Tatiana selected a tea blend and fed the loose leaves into her diffuser. She poured water into her teacup. The white tea had hints of elderberry and lemongrass. She dressed her drink as Pip filled her plate with tiny sandwiches and cakes.

"Don't look at me like that. It's free.'" Pip bit into a triangle-cut sandwich. "Yum. Cucumber."

"You know the food is included in the cost. Right?"

Pip swallowed. "Yeah. That's what I mean, all you can eat."

"Don't eat too much and get sick."

"I do what I want." Pip bit into another sandwich half.

"You sound like a nine-year-old."

"Oh yeah? You sound like a mom." Pip shot back.

"Ouch."

Pip wiped her mouth with her napkin. "Sorry."

Tatiana drank her tea after steeping it. Light, calming, and soothing, the Indigo blend hit all her thorny spots, including Pip's shot about her being a mom. Tatiana's mom had been violated and the ensuing death violation hadn't caught the person responsible.

A series of coughs punctured the bluesy jazz music. Initially, Tatiana ignored it and pondered sneaking one of the blueberry tarts from Pip's plate.

Then someone screamed.

A nervous rustle shot through the passengers.

"TeeTee…" Pip stumbled out of her seat, her eyes wide as saucers. "Let's go. Now!"

Tatiana shot out of her seat. She followed Pip, who along with others rushed out of the room and into the hallway. S-bots were knocked over, food and dishes crashed to the floor. Screams bowled over the pleasant music and calls from the butler to remain calm. It was hard to take him seriously when the entire front of his suit was covered in blood.

Surreal. Tatiana and Pip clawed their way through the crowd and down the corridor to the section with the wider space. Passengers followed suit until the room cleared. Tatiana inched back up to the opened Indigo room door, her hand reaching for a weapon she didn't have. She spied the butler and Shania crouched down by a passenger, who looked pale and withered.

What the hell?

A hand snatched her back.

"Hey!" Tatiana whirled, her fists raised.

"What the hell happened?" Pip asked.

"I don't know, but the passenger looks sick. Maybe she started choking . . ."

"Why didn't they call for medics?"

Tatiana wiped the perspiration from her face. Her hands trembled due to heightened adrenaline. Pip crossed her arms. Her scowl remained.

"The butler tried, I think."

"Oh, good . . ."

"What they did afterward was bizarre," Pip continued. "The housekeeper shook the person who then started throwing up blood. That freaked folks out."

Tatiana closed her eyes and held Pip's shoulder. "Blood?"

"Yeah. Projectile-like."

Tatiana opened her eyes and licked her dry lips. "The passenger clearly had some medical condition."

Pip met Tatiana's gaze.

"Maybe, but why did the butler dude lick it?" Pip asked.

"The blood?"

"Yeah."

"That doesn't make any sense."

"No, but I saw him with my own eyes." Pip backed away from the door. "That butler. There's something off about him."

Tatiana followed. "It could be part of the show."

Yeah. That's it.

Pip pointed as medics arrived.

The others had dispersed. Tatiana and Pip were about ten feet away. Once the door whooshed open, the butler stepped out. His uniform bore blood splatter. He marched by them as if in a trance. He reeked of wet copper and stale sweat.

Tatiana gagged, a visceral reaction to the smell and the man.

"Come on. Let's go get a cup of tea." Pip guided Tatiana by the elbow.

#

"This is brilliant!" Gabriel clasped Jose on the shoulder. His dark eyes sparkled at the Red Velvet Tearoom. The aroma of fresh-baked cake and honey filled the oval space. Gabriel inhaled deep and long.

"I'm getting flashes of a sweet version of hell," Jose said dryly.

"Let's get some tea." Gabriel guided his little brother to the centerpiece, a large, scarlet tablecloth across an oval table. Lace trimmed the lush fabric. Teacups decorated the surface area on one half and on the other half, trays of food, artfully displayed on crimson trays.

"Jose, these are scrumptious!" Gabriel held one sandwich in each hand and a third one he'd shoved into his mouth.

The glittery space background gave the tearoom an otherworldly atmosphere. Jose watched the passengers split and join in the ritual of socializing.

"Oh hello," Gabriel said after swallowing. "She's like a comet. She's now entertained my orbit."

Jose made a face at the woman in question. "Is it love or lust?"

"I don't know yet."

Jose shook his head. "Be careful. If you get pushed through an airlock, it's over."

Gabriel inclined his head. "Delete that."

"Come on. Let's go."

247

"Awww . . ." Gabriel followed his younger brother out into the hall. "I wanna stay."

Jose halted. "Fine. Stay. Meet you later."

"Don't be like that. Okay. I'll come with you, but we are coming back."

Jose agreed.

He didn't like tea, but the opportunity to see the stars, well the moon up close, was too good to be true. He walked toward the staircase leading away from the tearoom and gambling tables. Here the stem of passengers thinned, and the noise faded. The promenade's double doors whooshed open.

"Oh, I saw this on the map." Jose jerked his thumb to the opening.

Gabriel rolled his eyes in mock annoyance. "We can go for a little while but we're going back to the Red room."

His words hit Jose's back. His younger brother was already through the door.

Jose walked along the promenade. The enclosed section contained chairs and benches for lunar lookouts.

"This right here!" He made a beeline to the railing. "The views. Look! The floor is clear. It's like we're floating in space."

Gabriel clutched the wall. "Yeah. Great."

"Stop crawling for women. Look at *this!*"

Gabriel inched his way over to a chair and eased into it. He glanced at Jose, who stood close to the edge. His face softened at his brother's joy.

"You're right."

Jose turned to look at him. "You look like dad."

Gabriel smiled. "He was proud of you, too."

Deep, wet coughing interrupted them. Jose saw the source. A thin man dressed in a long-sleeved gray sweater, jeans, boots, and despair entered the promenade. His dark eyes stood stark, like black pits, set amongst his pale face. With sunken cheeks, hunched skinny shoulders, and jittery, he was a shell of a man by Jose's estimation. He looked like life had hollowed him out, leaving only a husk.

The man gazed out at the view, but he shuffled back and forth as if unsettled.

Gabriel lowered his voice. "He's rattling."

"Seems like. How did he get the currency for this?" Jose moved closer to Gabriel. He didn't want to stare, but the other man's presence worried him. People, addicts, were unpredictable.

"He probably works here." Gabriel shrugged.

"Oh, yeah," Jose muttered and sat in the neighboring chair.

They watched the stars drift by as the cruise ship sailed in hush quiet. Jose glanced over to the man again. The hairs on Jose's neck rose in warning. The stranger took his hands out of his pockets. His white fingers appeared stained with reddish paint or food.

Jose recoiled.

"What's wrong?" Gabriel asked. Jose's stiffening caught his attention.

"Something's off. His hands are gross. That's a nasty-looking scratch."

Gabriel sighed. "Don't worry about him. I think bots do the food prep. Enjoy your moon gazing, 'cause I want more cake."

The door whooshed open, and a woman marched in. She found the man and made a beeline for him.

"What the hell, Bebo?" the woman swore, red-faced and rigid with anger. "Get your ass back inside! That woman is critical."

The man, who must be Bebo, folded into himself at the verbal scolding. He mumbled something out of Jose's earshot.

"Her face was obliterated!" the woman shouted.

Bebo shushed her, his index finger shot up to his lips. He nodded in their direction and then looked back at the woman.

She glanced over her shoulder at Jose. "Oh."

The woman clucked her tongue and stalked out of the promenade with Bebo behind her.

Gabriel elbowed him. "She's a disgruntled employee."

Jose watched the two exit the promenade. "Yeah. That's obvious."

Gabriel shook his head. "Even all the way up here, people hate their jobs."

Despite the woman's nonchalant expression, her jerky movements exposed her fear. No matter how much she shouted at the male, Jose could tell, the Bebo person was more dangerous than he appeared.

Jose said, "The guy acted like a man who didn't have dates. He has prisoners."

"We're on vacation, J."

"Her face was obliterated..." Jose rubbed his chin.

Gabriel stood up. "Whelp, who's up for cake?"

#

The lunch buffet consisted of fresh green salads topped with lush red tomatoes, vibrant, crisp cucumbers, crunchy tofu, delicious pasta in a variety of sauces, and salmon sauteed with mushrooms and white wine. Tatiana pushed flaky chunks around her plate.

Across from her, Pip ate like she hadn't. She didn't look up when Jose sat down. He lowered his tray with care. Gabriel took the seat next to Tatiana.

"This looks amazing." Gabriel's plate lacked any vegetation. He inhaled the aroma, a broad grin on his face.

"How can you eat all that after devouring a dozen cupcakes?" Jose shook his head and pointed his forkful of lettuce at him. "You're going to be sick."

"Vacation. Remember?" Gabriel quirked an eyebrow at him before digging in. "All of me including my stomach will indulge."

"So glad we aren't sharing a cabin." Jose shook his head.

They quietly ate while the lunch area unfurled with chatter, guffaws, and general conversations.

"TeeTee. What's wrong?" Jose asked.

"Nothing." Tatiana glanced up at him and lowered her eyes back to her plate.

"You've hardly looked at the Moonman's performance." Jose nodded at the person dressed in 20th century astronaut gear, singing the *Moon Interlude* in Japanese. Her crooning against the conversational murmuring created a strange remix.

"She's upset about what she saw earlier," Pip said, her plate clean. "She lost her appetite. Damn shame, 'cause this chili pasta is fire . . ."

Tatiana dropped all pretense of eating and put down her fork.

"What happened?" Jose drank some of his wine.

"This food doesn't agree. That's all." Tatiana shot Pip a stink eye. Then to Jose, "What did y'all get into?"

"Pip clearly touched a nerve," Gabriel chuckled into his drink.

Jose rolled his eyes at his older brother and then explained what they'd done after breakfast. His cousin brightened at the mention of the promenade's lunar views. Her face fell when he recounted the employee spat.

Pip perked up. "Oh. Oh! Did he have like sunken cheeks and a waif figure?"

"Waif?" Gabriel snorted. "What the hell is that?"

"Eat and pretend you're cultured," Pip snapped in return. "Jose, did the woman have brunette hair? A housekeeper uniform?"

"No."

Tatiana said, "By the time you saw them, they must've changed."

Pip pushed her chair back. "What a way to kick off the cruise."

Tatiana watched Pip return to the buffet stations. "This isn't something we discuss over a meal."

"It's us, not the ship's captain. What happened in the blue room?" Jose asked. "We heard the end of it on the promenade."

Tatiana rubbed her arms. "It's unsettling. The butler and housekeeper were roaming the tearoom when one of the passengers exploded with blood. Everywhere. Significant amounts."

"Gross," Gabriel said.

Jose's throat went dry, and he found it difficult to swallow. "You saw it."

"Yeah. Right before they rushed everyone out. It soured the day."

"It doesn't have to, though. The passenger probably had some illness. It's always evening here. The evening's still young," Jose said.

Gabriel leaned back. "Let's see what we can salvage, huh, Tee-Tee." He burped and got up, heading to the buffet station.

"Obviously, his plan is to eat more," Jose said, laughing.

"It's a buffet, Jose. It's in the name." Pip returned, her plate full of steaming food. She looked from one cousin to the other. After, she began eating, electing not to engage them.

Tatiana found comfort in Pip's silence. She sipped her tea, letting the warm liquid spread through her. Jose's suggestion to let the incident go had merit. She couldn't explain how the violence stained her mood. The bit of reality poked through the bubble. There was no putting it back. The flimsy illusion burst. A new one wouldn't help recover the newness and the dream of escape, the quiet joy, the thrill of space, thriving among stars. Life in The District and its grimy fingers touched her, even here.

She shuddered.

It was a feeling.

Tatiana waited for the drink to finish numbing her.

The steward came up to their table. His elegant black and purple uniform bore flickering amethyst lights in the spots for buttons. Black-gloved hands folded in front of him as he walked around the restaurant lobby.

"How is everything?" he asked. He was all narrow frame and pinched features. His hazel eyes shifted to each of them. The facial tattoos, two thin bluish lines, pulsated.

"Everything's fine," Tatiana said, almost out of habit. She'd given the response to the question so often, she wasn't sure she'd heard anything after, "How is . . ."

"Excellent. If there's anything you need just . . ."

"How is the passenger who became ill in the Indigo room?" Pip asked, cutting him off. She put her drink down, pinning the steward with her glare.

"I apologize. I do not know the status . . ."

"Do you have lots of those types of illnesses on board the ship? I mean, her face was obliterated." Pip cocked her head to the side as if confused.

The steward's eyes widened. His mouth made an o. But he swiftly recovered. His blank face removed his initial surprise.

Just not quick enough.

Jose pounced. "Tell us the truth. I'm sure all the staff know. What happened?"

"We are not at liberty to divulge passenger private information." He pursed his lips as if to keep himself from saying more, but then he added, "Or gossip."

He hurried off before another question sprung up.

Gabriel chuckled. "Chased him right off."

Tatiana drummed her fingers on the table. "Why didn't he tell us the passenger received treatment or something generic like 'we've taken care of her'?"

Jose sipped his drink and winced. "Maybe she died."

Gabriel started to laugh but caught himself. "Oh. That would be terrible."

"Then why not say that?" Tatiana watched the steward flit among the other diners like a somber butterfly. "They're hiding something."

"It doesn't have anything to do with us." Jose smiled at Tatiana. "Vacation."

Gabriel rubbed his goatee. "You know, Regulators never turn it off, Jose."

"Right." Tatiana sighed. Jose, as usual, was astute. She'd come this far, she should relax. She pushed the nagging voice down and forced the edges of her lips up.

"There's a party in Evergreen at 2. It's by the space flight location," Pip said, drawing Tatiana out of her musings.

"The dress code is relaxed. They're calling it a Lunar Luau. So lame, but there's drink, music, and games," Pip said.

"Look who's suddenly in the vacay spirit," Jose smirked. "That's why we're here. Right, TeeTee? We won't lose it."

Gabriel mumbled around the mouthful of tofu. Tatiana smiled because he resembled a chipmunk with both cheeks bulging.

"There. Now. Let's go," Jose said, tossing his napkins on the table. He pushed his chair back.

Spacefunk!

"You could always save it in your cheeks, like Gabe," Tatiana said. They burst into laughter at the outrage on Pip's face.

#

Tatiana changed into blue pants and a matching tee shirt. She met the others at the bank of elevators. Her cousins all wore similar causal wear. They hadn't planned it, but they shared a close bond. She wasn't surprised.

"Ready to go fly?" Jose asked.

He loved space, like her. As kids, they'd absconder out of the city, to the country any time their aunt would come by. Out there, late at night, they could see the stars. There wasn't any light pollution blotting out of the sky.

"I'm going to watch the show. My stomach can't handle being off my feet." Gabriel looked at her with watery eyes. His clothes were disheveled as if he'd woken up in them.

"He spent 20 minutes throwing up," Jose explained.

"That's why he's all green around the gills." Pip smirked.

One of the elevator cars arrived. They got into the empty car. It reeked of perfume, cigarette smoke, and unwashed bodies with a hint of booze.

"You'd think they'd have better ventilation," Gabriel pressed the *S* for the show deck.

"We're in a giant bubble breathing recycled air." Pip huffed. "This *is* the best."

"Not a great thought." Tatiana was relieved when the door slid open.

"We're only one small hiccup away from becoming a ghost ship, or the lunar *Titanic*," Pip continued.

"Look! People are suiting up for the space walk." Jose elbowed Tatiana to get her attention away from Pip's darker ramblings.

Ahead, a queue of passengers waited for the spacewalk. Suits and helmets hung on a mobile closet. *Benny's Tearoom* professional instructors escorted people out into the cold embrace of space.

After signing a waiver, of course.

Gabriel clasped his hand over his mouth. His eyeballs bulged. With speed, he hurried back to the elevators and rushed into the first available one.

"His stomach must still be upset." Jose shook his head.

Tatiana got in line at the space walk. Music, some fast beat song, played. Some of those waiting in line danced. Across the room, Pip entered the second door and left. The doors went to tearooms.

"Where's she going?"

Jose said, "She might be going to the English Tearoom. She mentioned that woman from the Indigo room."

The line shifted and Tatiana moved up a few steps. "Oh? What she say?"

"She mumbled something about seeing her last night."

Tatiana frowned. "As in spent the night with her?"

Jose rolled his eyes. "I don't know but I wouldn't put it past her. She's always thirsting for thrills."

"Attention passengers, you must be sober to participate in the walk. We are conducting breathalyzers."

The announcement caught a few people off guard, judging by the comments. Two more people left the line. Impatience or intoxication, Tatiana couldn't be sure. Before she knew it, the instructor's assistant helped her into the flight suit.

Tatiana put the helmet on. Beside her, Jose went through the same. He gave her a thumbs up. Outside the ship's bay, people floated in the naked cold of space. Tethered to the cruise ship, she could explore, adrift with a safety net.

If only life offered such conveniences.

Something to keep her connected when life's icy indifference draped over her. She groped for a secure line. The District's mire of socio-economic, grim, and desperation clung to her, a thick proverbial mud long hot showers couldn't dislodge.

On the other hand, she felt a deep compulsion to sever the cord and sail into space's empty and cold embrace until her wide eyes could no longer see.

"Ready?" The instructor's dark brown eyes met hers.

"As I'll ever be." Tatiana's stomach had a belly flop. She breathed in the oxygen and checked her gloves. She nodded at the instructor, signaling she was good to go. It was a hollow gesture. Her insides quaked, but she didn't come all this way not to take this leap.

#

Tatiana planted both feet on the ledge as gravity snared her once more. Despite her labored breathing, exhilaration made her tingle. The instructor made sure she wrangled everyone before closing and securing the entrance, slicing off the empty dark.

Tatiana and Pip waded into the velvety, but cool tearoom. To-gether, they joined several passengers seated along the pillow-covered floor. Shoe racks contained the guests' various footwear. Pip scowled about removing her sneakers, but when in Rome . . .

They sat on a few lush pillows surrounded by a cake stand and tea carafe. This room held ten such groups. The tea clusters had their own vibe.

"Pip, why didn't you do the space walk with me and Jose?" Tati-ana asked.

Pip chewed her teacake. "I wanted to follow up with Shania, the server. We kinda connected over the Blackjack table. I know it both-ered your regulator brain about the sick passenger. Found out her "face" that was obliterated was an expensive clothing designer. The woman had a massive nosebleed, the blood vessels burst from the coughing and the poor attempts at the Heimlich Maneuver. Ama-teurs."

Tatiana cleared her throat. "Nothing sinister going on there?"

Pip shook her head. "Nope. I mean, she said Bebo, that's the but-ler, creeped her out."

"And the blood licking?" Tatiana sipped her tea.

"Shania said he's weird like that." Pip rolled her eyes. "Gross. Where are Jose and Gabriel?"

"Jose went to check on G." Tatiana relaxed. The soothing music, the sweet aromas, and chill atmosphere helped relieve the tension. Pip's efforts to locate help and alleviate her worry made her smile. Her little cousin was taking care of her.

"Thank you, Pip, for getting to the bottom of that."

"I know your Regulator brain was gnawing on it. I could see it in your eyes, cuz."

Pip picked up another teacake from the circling s-bots.

"There you are." Jose sat down beside Pip.

Gabriel, looking refreshed, eased down to the pillow beside Tati-ana. "Hey, TeeTee."

"You look better," Tatiana said. "Here, have some tea."

"What's this?" Gabriel asked, accepting the mug from her.

"Chai."

"From India?" Jose asked, picking up his own mug from the rotat-ing s-bots.

"Yes! How'd you know?" Tatiana asked.

"I've been." Jose sipped. "Oh, this is good."

"Yeah, it is," Tatiana said.

Before long, their weeklong cruise would end and they'd return to the harshness of District life, but she would remember this moment, where they were carefree and relaxed, where they put down the gravity of reality and escaped to the stars.

Tatiana looked around at the four of them gathered together, hundreds of miles away from Earth, adrift in the indifferent sea of space. Her cousins laughed, talked, and ate with joy, not because the food was fantastic or the music was amazing, but because they were together.

"TeeTee, you look happy," Jose said.

"You know what? I am."

Drift-Flux
by
Wole Talabi

In space, no one can hear your ship explode.

But they can watch.

Orshio Akume, priest-pilot of the *Igodo*, sat silently in the pilot module of the control deck, watching a mining ship cleave in two. A sudden release of energy violently ate its way out of the ship. A burst of azure light popped into the space ahead of the *Igodo,* despite the distance. It receded, quickly shifted to aquamarine, then turquoise, and then to nothing.

A bomb. It had to have been a bomb.

The furrows between Orshio's eyes deepened as his brows drew down and his eyes narrowed, compressing the vertical tribal marking keloid that ran from his hairline to his nose.

The ship was an old one, at least ten times the size of the *Igodo*, with the unmistakable bright red and blue insignia of the Confederacy emblazoned across it from end to end. There were only a few giant mining ships left operating in the Belt. The last remnants of the first Martian development schemes by the Confederacy and the only ones still in service that were not built by Transhuman Federation Engineers.

The clumsy old giants needed the size primarily to store large quantities of fuel and propellant, still completely enslaved to Newton's third law and Tsiolkovsky's equation. Cargo was attached and hauled using spars and rigging, enwombed in lightweight programmable material mesh and insulation to protect fragile items and ward off hot backlighting from the fusion drive. Modern Transhuman Federation mining ships like the *Igodo* used the Adadevoh drive to couple to the zero-point and draw vacuum energy so they didn't have any of those problems. They still hauled their cargo using rigging though. Not that the *Igodo* presently carried any cargo.

"What the hell just happened out there?"

Orshio glanced back to see his engineer floating into the control deck. Lien-Ådel was a young, tall, muscled, and well-proportioned woman with brown eyes and short black hair greying slightly at the crown and temples as though her front half was aging faster than her back. It was impossible to tell but beneath her solid frame, were genetically altered lungs that allowed her to function on only a fraction of the oxygen required by the average unmodified human, nanoparticle gravcines in her blood to inhibit loss of consciousness, and a skeleton modified for increased bone density. Handy, for unscheduled extravehicular repairs.

She pushed against the deck wall with her right foot and threw her six-foot and four-inch-tall frame into the chair beside him, swiping furiously at the space in front of her to draw up trajectory data and estimate the likelihood of their being caught in a debris field. Orshio had already visually assessed the situation and decided they were in no reasonable danger, the explosion wasn't nearly big enough or close enough, but Lien-Ådel was the kind of person who liked to see every single piece of data available before making her decisions. The light from the console illuminated her face, highlighting the small nose that sat symmetrically between two finely sculpted cheekbones.

"Ship blew up." Orshio jutted his bearded chin at the magnified image of the slowly disintegrating ship set against the unforgiving blackness of space on the viewscreen, like some kind of perverse modern art display. "I've seen accidents before. Structural failures, overheating cores, explosive decouplings, but none of them looked like that. That was a plasma bomb. Had to be. I'd bet my collection of original Majek Fashek vinyls on it."

Lien-Ådel kept swiping as she replied, "Well, it doesn't look like there is going to be much of a debris field. Must have been a targeted, controlled explosion."

Orshio leaned back in his seat. "Whoever set it off must have been trying not to damage the cargo. Maybe they're pirates . . ." he scratched his chin, ". . . or something."

"There haven't been pirates in the inner belt for years, Orshio. Besides, no one is swooping in to loot the cargo. I don't like this. We should call it in to Mars Station ahead of us. Make a report."

Orshio rolled his eyes. He didn't dislike Lien-Ådel per se, he just found her unbearably predictable. Despite her undeniable creativity in keeping the ship's performance optimal, she was still incredibly regimented in her thinking. For every decision presented to her, she only ever had three responses in order of preference: one, follow the rules; two, defer the decision to a higher authority; or three, have no opinion on the matter. And now, she was already advocating her second favourite response even though they still weren't exactly sure what they were looking at.

Lien-Ådel in turn did not like Orshio's impulsive attitude and flamboyant style but she worked well with him anyway because her life depended on his natural creativity and artificially enhanced reflexes.

He was heavily tattooed, an elaborate pattern of images, lines, and whorls, which ran all over his dark skin and told the story of his ancestors as far back as his family records detailed. The tattoos, done in late afromysterics style, covered his right arm from shoulder to fingertips. If his other arm wasn't fully bionic and made of expensive bioplasmium, it would probably have borne the same markings. He wore his black and grey hair in short dreadlocks and tied a band of red and black cloth around his hairline, covering the tip of the vertical scar that marked him as a true-born son of the Idoma people—beneath which sat the neuralink chip that allowed him to control his bioplasmium arm and the dozen other embedded machines that augmented his body. His entire appearance was a piece of art dedicated to the spirits of his ancestors, the Alekwu.

"I think the first thing we should do is see if there are any survivors, don't you think?" he asked as he sat up in his chair. "Besides, we're technically closer to Ceres station."

Lien-Ådel nodded, ignoring the sugar-coated reprimand, and swiped away the I*godo's* diagnostic projection before requesting the ship's AI to send a direct message on the Belt's short-range open channel and scan all other open channels for chatter regarding what happened.

Orshio reached forward and pulled up the public Transhuman Federation shipping schedules and trajectories from their database. The data indicated that the ship that was now mostly just two large pieces of wreckage ahead of them was called the *Freedom Queen*. A rugged hauler for fluids and fine dusts, transporting impure Helium-3 scooped from Jupiter's atmosphere to Independence Station, the last Confederacy settlement on Mars. She was essentially a gigantic cylindrical gas tank with a nuclear energy tube running through her long axis. Well, at least she used to be.

"*Igodo* has established a link with the broken ship's AI. No signs of life. I think you'll want to take a look at its report." Lien-Ådel flicked her fingers to expand a light display projection then swiped it left. It drifted through the space between them and settled in front of Orshio.

He tilted his head to the side slightly and raised an eyebrow. "This says all crew life signals from *Freedom Queen* stopped streaming over twenty minutes ago. Before the explosion."

Lien-Ådel blinked. "Yes. So now I'm wondering . . . where could the crew have gone?"

Orshio folded his arms in front of him. That was a good question. Almost as good a question as to why anyone would choose to attack a Confederate hauler in near-space range only a few minutes after the *Igodo* completed its publicly scheduled uncoupling from the zero-point, came out of drift-flux and switched to auxiliary for a slow, controlled nuclear burn to Mars station. Pirates would probably have had better timing.

Suddenly, the viewscreen of the *Igodo* lit up as a multicoloured kaleidoscope of numbers and data overlaid it. The AI informed them that they were receiving a sudden and persistent communication packet. It had the certified data signature of the Transhuman Federation and seemed to be originating from Ceres station.

Orshio said, "Well bad news certainly travels fast out here, doesn't it?"

Lien-Ådel swiped in front of her to accept the transmission. The flowing rivers of colourful data across the screen coalesced into an image of a very serious man in a very serious

Transhuman Federation uniform of pure black with a gold-trim mandarin collar. The uniform was blacker than Orshio's ebony skin but blended perfectly against the man's own shiny black complexion. It took a few seconds for Orshio to realise he had a goatee. His eyes were stark white. The officer looked like he'd materialised from the star-sprinkled abyssal darkness of unforgiving space beyond the ship and his eyes were a binary star. Across the breast of his uniform, was a lenticular pin shaped like an ancient Zulu shield, complete with two spears crossed behind it. Its smooth black and white surface displayed the yin-and-yang, stretched to accommodate the unusual shape. Orshio had never seen anyone wearing the official Federation Security Corps chief uniform before.

"This is Ceres station security Chief Mwanja Mukisa calling Federation shipping vessel *Igodo*. We have detected a catastrophic failure of the Confederate hauler *Freedom Queen* a few thousand kilometres from your scheduled flight path. Change course immediately and report to Ceres station. Do not transmit any message to anyone until your report has been formally received at Ceres Station. I repeat, change course, and report to Ceres station. Immediately. Do not transmit to any other party."

The image disappeared.

"Well, I guess you're going to get a chance to make that report after all," Orshio quipped.

Lien-Ådel's voice went low and hoarse, "Does that message imply what I think it does?"

Orshio nodded. Along the surface of his bioplasmium arm, beneath his shirt, faint red lines writhed as if alive, responding to tension from his increased stress levels. He flexed the arm to ease it and thought down his rising cortisol levels.

"That was not a request, it was an order," Lien-Ådel's face scrunched up as she spoke, as if she was still trying to process the sentence, hoping desperately that he would contradict the obvious.

Orshio kept inspecting the screen. "Yes. Definitely an order," he confirmed.

"But if they don't want us to contact anyone, not even the supply station, then that means they probably don't think it was an accident or pirates. They probably think it was . . ."

". . . a terrorist attack." Orshio finished the sentence for her.

They turned away from the viewscreen at the same time and saw the same thing in each other's eyes.

They had heard rumours in the outer belt, of anti-federation rebels and old Confederate militias attacking Federation mining camps and ships. Nothing major but worrying enough for them to now be concerned.

"I don't know anyone at Ceres station. I'm not sure I want to get involved in all this. We could just make a run for it. Enter drift-flux again and be back to Earth in an hour or so. Sort it all out when we get there," Orshio said.

Lien-Ådel recoiled, then snapped back to place, leaning toward him. "First of all, we can't disobey a direct order from a Federation Security Corps official. Second—she paused to exhale—drift-flux this far into the solar system? Through the Belt? We'd never make it out alive! And even if we did, we'd be making ourselves look guilty as sin in the process."

He nodded. "You're right. You're right. Sorry. Bad idea."

"Quantifiably terrible."

Lien-Ådel kept her palms flat against her thighs as Orshio carefully adjusted the nuclear reaction control system, pulling alongside the mooring cable that reached out to them from the largest asteroid in the inner solar system like a possessed umbilical cord. She hated docking or any transitions. She was much happier when they were moving steadily, the cold and dark ocean of space swelling and sweeping against the hull of the *Igodo*. She sank further into her chair every time Orshio fired a short burst of diverted nuclear thrust, nudging the *Igodo* into position.

Most of Ceres station lay below the surface, except for the army of cephalopodan mooring cables that held the hundred or so ships that transited through every day. From above, the network of pipelines, cables, equipment, and rigging, that kept the Ceres's subterranean areas functioning looked like a glowing

technological infection eating its way into the heart of the asteroid, their casings and surfaces lined with bright photovoltaic
cells to capture the sunlight that powered their maintenance
bots. Man-made parasites, burning alone in the vastness of the
dark so that the city beneath may thrive.

When the cable had secured the *Igodo* and all its interlocking
sections mated to make a solid strut, Lien-Ådel and Orshio unbuckled themselves and floated leisurely to the airlock. They
moved with tense slowness as they transferred to the orbital elevator.

Inside the elevator was an instrument panel to key in arrival
codes and a screen displaying a welcome message from the
Transhuman Federation. The elevator was transparent and behind them, they could see other smaller asteroids drifting, a couple of ships approaching, and the sun—a small, faraway ball of
light. In all their missions through space, only the sun remained
constant. Its influence diminished with distance, but constant,
unchangeable, like the past, like an ancestor. Orshio tapped at
the panel, and they started to descend.

Lien-Ådel played with her hair as the elevator descended beneath Ceres's surface. The sun disappeared. Crackling electricity
illuminated the darkness of the tunnel around them.

"Are you worried, Priest-pilot?"

"No. Not really, Engineer," he lied.

"You don't suppose they think we had something to do with
blowing up the *Freedom Queen*, do you?"

Orshio thought about that. "I'm sure they will ask."

Lien-Ådel kissed her teeth and stopped playing with her hair.
"Bad luck," she muttered. "After hauling supplies halfway to
some godforsaken Tellurium mining outpost in the Kuiper belt,
we come out of drift to this shit."

"Are you okay?" Orshio asked. This was the most agitated
he'd ever seen Lien-Ådel and he didn't like it. Not when they
were about to walk into what could easily be a crisis.

Lien-Ådel looked at him, dejectedly, which only made him
more worried. "When I was at university, I heard about the pirates, how terrible working the belt had been during that time
but I still wanted to work for Federation shipping because I

dreamed of being in drift-flux, of seeing the universe. Now the pirates are gone but there are all these rumours of terrorists. I don't know. I guess I'm just worried that we might get caught up in or blamed for something and lose the *Igodo* just because some agitated philistines are probably trying to start a war."

The lights around them brightened. Orshio exhaled a hot breath. "We didn't do anything. They will question us, find out what we know, and find whoever did this. Plus, no group in the system is actually foolish enough to start a war with the Trans-human Federation." He paused before turning to her. "Do you want to know why I have these tattoos?" He raised his right hand, pulled back his sleeve, and watched her eyes. "I know you've wanted to ask since the first day you saw them."

Lien-Ådel managed a small smile. Even though she knew he was trying to distract her from their present predicament, she didn't mind, she needed the distraction. "Sure. Please. Tell me. What do they mean?"

"I am one of a people called the Idoma, from the Nigeria unit of the Federation. We are an ancient people and according to Idoma traditions, life is an unending continuum. Always has been. Space, time, energy, matter, spirit, and life are considered as one integral whole. Our understanding of the nature of the cosmos predates modern science and is anchored to our belief that our ancestors are always with us, interacting with the rest of the universe just as we do but in a different way."

"You mean like in an alternate dimension?"

"Sort of. You can think of it that way. My people believe that death is a process of passing on to this other level of existence. A realm called Okoto. A dimension from which they find new ways to interact with the same space and time we share. Person-ally, I think that when we are in drift-flux, coupled to the uni-verse's zero-point, we are in the boundary between our dimension and Okoto. Therefore, my ancestors can guide my hand. Ensure I do not slip out of the vacuum energy probability field and crash into something. The tattoos are just stylistic and hieroglyphic representations of my ancestors and their stories, going as far back as records exist."

Lien-Ådel leaned against the elevator with her right shoulder, pulling at the sleeves of her body-hugging suit. "Hold on. You really believe your ancestors exist as part of space? Guide you in drift-flux?"

Orshio smiled. "Well, no. Not really. But it's a good story to tell people who wonder about my tattoos, isn't it?"

Lien-Ådel stared at him for a moment before erupting into laughter. Orshio laughed with her.

The elevator stopped and lights flickered. Their faces recrystallised with seriousness. The elevator door opened to reveal a squad of six women and a man, with menacing eyes and holding sleek plasma rifles, all wearing the familiar white uniform of the Transhuman Federation forces. Behind them, the bright, mechanical sprawl of the main Ceres station tunnel spread out like the digestive system of a rock and metal animal.

"*Igodo* crew. Come with us," one of the women said to them in a manner that left no room for questions, only obedience. Her red hair was cropped short. The cool, green eyes and freckles dotting her nose and cheeks seemed out of place on the same face as her hard-set jaw. She turned sharply on her heel and the others flanked Orshio and Lien-Ådel.

They followed the woman.

"Why do I feel like we are being arrested?" Orshio queried.

None of the officers responded. Lien-Ådel eyed him nervously.

The small party walked about halfway into the main tunnel before turning to walk down a set of energy shielded stairs and through a tall doorway that looked like it could withstand a plasma cannon when sealed. A sign on the door read, *Transhuman Federation Security Corps Offices: Authorised Personnel Only*. Behind the door, they stood in the centre of an octagon with each side bordering a smaller door. The woman in charge walked up to one of the doors and motioned them to enter the office of Ceres station security Chief Mwanja Mukisa.

Lien-Ådel winced when the door shut behind them. The chair behind the desk at the end of the office swivelled around to reveal a man that was certainly not Mwanja Mukisa. At least not *the* Mwanja Mukisa that had ordered them to Ceres station. This man was short and had skin like Orshio's, hair cropped close, and a perfectly shaved round chin that, in some strange way, made him look like a pre-teen. But there was nothing puerile about his voice and his tone when he spoke.

"Finally, Orshio Akume and Lien-Ådel Ting of the *Igodo*. Welcome to Ceres station. Do you have any idea how much trouble you are in?"

Orshio looked around the office, trying to find something he could use to estimate the identity of the man they were talking to. A photograph, a plaque, something. All he found was an unusually empty wall and some very modern nanomaterial furniture.

"We haven't done anything wrong," Lien-Ådel began. "We saw the *Freedom Queen* destroyed a few minutes after we dropped out of drift-flux. We don't know what happened, but we are ready to make a full report."

"The records inform me," the man, who was not Mwanja Mukisa, paused to stand up straight before continuing. "That you just completed a supply run to the Kuiper belt mines. Are you aware that the outer belt is becoming a den of anti-federation rebels and agitators?" he asked, his lips curling up at the corners in a smile.

"Well, yes, we heard some stories, but we have nothing to do with anti-federation rebels!" Lien-Ådel exclaimed, her voice hoarse from fear or perhaps something more elemental.

Orshio shook his head and leaned forward in his chair, his eyes narrowed and focused like a navigation beam. There was something that did not sit quite right with him about the conversation that had quickly become an interrogation.

"Where is Officer Mwanja Mukisa?" he asked, softly.

The man eyed Orshio like he was a stain or a miscalculation. It was a look Orshio had seen before and it sent off alarms in his head, but his brain was still running diagnostics to determine exactly why when the man spoke.

"You have both been implicated in the destruction of the *Freedom Queen* by the ship's AI. You will consent to a DNA extraction for further analysis and will remain in remand at Ceres station until such a time as formal charges are brought against you."

Suddenly, Orshio realised where he knew that look from. He'd seen it once at the Luna Railgun Transit Station while he was waiting for his launch to Mars station. It came from an old Confederacy pilot, one of those born before the Adedevoh drive and the rise of the Transhuman Federation who couldn't believe that the people whose way of life he'd been raised to think was inferior were now running ninety-six percent of the solar system's economy while the Confederacy struggled. Orshio had taken an empty seat next to the man and politely smiled at him when their eyes met. There had been no reciprocal smile, only a look like disgust but much worse. In the man's eyes lurked a powerful, primal resentment. The old pilot had risen from his chair and muttered something under his breath that sounded a lot like a word Orshio had only ever read about but never actually heard.

And now, here was the look again.

Orshio didn't change his blank expression as he looked at the man who wanted to place him and his now panicky partner under arrest. "You can't hold us here without an official arrest warrant," Orshio responded, his voice low as he started to stand up.

Panic washed over him when he realised he couldn't.

Something cold and solid had wrapped itself around his legs and arms, locking them in place like a vice.

He grimaced, and then half a second later shouted, "Lien-Ådel! Get out now!"

But it was too late. She was struggling in place too, her arms and legs enveloped by what looked like a part of the chair as she screamed. "What is going on?! Officer? Officer?!"

He watched part of the back of her chair liquefy, extrude, and wrap itself around her neck and mouth, morphing into a solid restraint as she screamed.

It had to be programmable material furniture. The last major technological advancement to come from the Confederacy.

He felt the cold and liquid material of the chair wrap around his own neck and pull him straight up in the chair as it covered his mouth too. He heard the voice of the man pretending to be Mwanja Mukisa say, "Goodnight, priest-pilot."

There was a hiss. A sickly sweet smell like rotting flowers. A loosening of edges of the world. His eyelids fell. There was darkness, like the embrace of space.

Consciousness returned like an explosion. Orshio's eyes shot open.

The first thing he saw was a small black cube on top of the desk. There was a matrix of light symbols surrounding it and they seemed to be pulsing, beating out a slow, steady rhythm. He could not turn his head to see if Lien-Ådel was okay or if the short man pretending to be Mwanja Mukisa was gone.

Orshio closed his eyes again and focused, remembering what his body enhancement therapist had told him the day after he'd decided to get his melanin genes updated for increased radiation resistance and an improved bioplasmium arm. *If you want to access the power-booster functions, clear your head. Think exactly how much power you want and what exactly you want it to do. Breathe slowly, then apply.*

He opened his eyes and swung his arm upward. The programmable material restraint broke into three clean pieces and scattered across the room. He reached up and ripped the restraints off his neck, glad to see that Lien-Ådel was beside him and stirring. As he pulled at the restraints on his feet, he heard the door open and saw a shadow on the floor in the corner of his vision move. It was his only warning.

Something hit his thigh, and a shock shot through him with so much ferocity he cried out in pain. The redhead with the green eyes and hard jaw who'd seemed to be the leader of the squad that had met them at the main Ceres elevator, shouted at him, "Freeze! Don't move!"

He rolled forward, crashing into the desk as another stun beam stabbed into the chair where he'd been. The redhead surged forward and Orshio, thinking calmly but quickly, rose, lifting the desk high above his head as he did, and flung it at her. It sailed clear over Lien-Ådel, who he could see was fully roused and conscious. The redhead fell to her knees and slid forward, firing another stun beam that missed Orshio by less than an inch. He could hear something like an explosion come from somewhere in the building.

"Hey! I'm not the enemy!" he called out as he backed into a corner of the office, off balance. "Someone was impersonating Officer Mukisa!"

The redhead leapt up into the air so effortlessly, Orshio was sure she'd been edited for agility. Her face was a mask of pure concentration, her eyes like navigation beams.

"Freeze!" she ordered, crashing down onto Orshio.

She was all over him. He managed to grab onto her right hand, the one that gripped the gun like it was an appendage. He twisted it and the gun fell, clattering to the ground. He could hear commotion come from outside the room now. Something was happening and he needed to stop her from fighting him long enough to figure out what it was. Pain shot into his side like lightning as she kneed him in the belly. Her fingers wrapped themselves around his throat, shoving him up against the wall. Her fingernails were bright red, almost the same as her hair. And long, like claws. They dug into his neck. She was powerful and she wasn't going to stop unless he made her. With a determined grunt, Orshio grabbed her hand with his bioplasmium arm and pushed down and to the left, forcing her off balance. He was about to administer a kick to her side but changed his mind midway and kept his foot low instead, clearing her feet out from under her. She came down hard and he fell to the floor with her, pressing down on her shoulder and shouting, "I'm not your enemy!"

She stopped struggling at that, glaring up at him and breathing heavily. "Then what the hell is going on?" she demanded, her voice still defiant.

"I don't know but from the fact that we were just restrained and drugged by someone pretending to be a security corps officer, I think Ceres station is under attack." He lifted his hand from her shoulder slowly and rose to his feet. "I'm going to free my engineer, okay? Don't shoot us, officer . . .?"

Her eyes narrowed as she sat up. "Chloe. My name is Chloe."

"Chloe. Good. Now my turn to ask a question. What's happening outside?" Orshio asked as he slowed his breathing and grabbed onto the restraints holding Lien-Ådel in place. "What's all that commotion and why did you attack me?" His voice strained as he broke the restraints.

She bounded up to her feet. She was of average height, yes, but with a slender, muscular frame. She moved like a cat and had power disproportionate to her size. Definitely altered. Orshio was sure she would have taken him if he didn't have the arm. She said, "A Confederacy mining ship lost control in the docking elevators. Started a fire. At the same time, an urgent distress signal was issued from this room on the old Transhuman Federation comms channel. Where is officer Mukisa?"

"We don't know," Lien-Ådel said, finally free and staring at Chloe with eyes full of both confusion and anger.

"This doesn't make sense," Chloe said, looking around the room as though the missing officer could be in a corner somewhere.

Orshio thought for a few seconds.

The short man had to be an anti-federation rebel agent. And the burning ship in the docking area had to have been crashed there deliberately, it would be too much of a coincidence otherwise. And if it was not a coincidence, then maybe the destruction of the *Freedom Queen* was not a coincidence either. But even if the Confederacy was working with the rebels or the rebels were just rogue former citizens of the Confederacy acting independently, then why would they throw away two old and expensive mining ships just to make a pair of unremarkable Federation shipping crew look somewhat guilty of aggression. Unless . . .

He scanned the floor, looking for the pulsing-light cube that had been on the table when he woke up. When he found it, it only took him a second to remember where he had seen it before. He turned to Lien-Ådel and met her hard gaze. Her lips were tight.

"What if all this is just a distraction," he quickly. "What if they blew up the *Freedom Queen* just to get us here so they could copy our genetic ID matrices?"

"What?" Lien-Ådel shook her head. "I don't understand. Why us? Why would they want our genetic signatures?"

Orshio looked down at the floor, feeling Ceres station tremble beneath his feet, like a fearful child.

"To access our ship," he announced as if it were obvious. "They're stealing the *Igodo*."

Chloe looked from him to Lien-Ådel and back again in astonishment, as if Lien-Ådel could make some sense of what he had just said.

"And they clearly have Officer Mukisa's genetic signature too so they will probably be the only ones that can launch during an emergency station shutdown, right?" Lien-Ådel added.

"Like the kind caused by a ship crashing during an attempted docking."

"Officer Mukisa is probably drugged somewhere or still in their custody."

"It all has to be deliberate. Has to."

"Even if it's true . . . all this just to steal one Adedevoh-class driveship?" Chloe asked, shaking her head as if it would help the pieces fall into place. "No. I don't buy it. I'm sorry but I have to arrest you until all this is sorted out. I don't care what the specs on that arm of yours are but if your resist, this time, I *will* take you." Her eyes focused with determination as she finished her sentence.

Lien-Ådel's face went pale. "No. No. Listen. Why else would they drug us and use a genetic ID copybox? Driveships use direct pilot and engineer genetic ID systems to gain access to all aspects of the ship. But then . . . why us? The *Igodo* is not special. In fact, right now it's got a minor fault. You remember right, Orshio, after we got hit by that nasty rock out in Kuiper, the techs told us that the only damage was to the processor relays that pass messages between the genetic ID and ship controls. So right now, the relays aren't quite right, and they could theoretically allow the direct genetic ID system to access all aspects of the ship. Including the hardcoded navigation limits which means if they bypass security then they can enter driftflux and be halfway across the solar system in a few minutes and no one would be able to follow them because they could turn off all the velocity safety limits, they can even override the . . . the . . ."

". . . planetary approach limit." Orshio finished the sentence for her, his eyes widening.

Orshio and Lien-Ådel both turned away from Chloe at the same time and saw the same thing in each other's' eyes. They stood silent, hoping they were wrong but unable to find any doubt that was large enough to obscure the potential danger if what they were both thinking was true.

Chloe broke the silence. "What? What does that mean?"

Her voice was like a prod to Orshio's mind, reminding him just how urgent the situation was if they were right. Every second would matter now.

"We have to get to the *Igodo* now!" He bolted for the office door as he spoke. "Whoever is stealing our ship could be trying to turn it into a relativistic kinetic kill vehicle . . . the kind that can crack a planet open like a walnut!"

Chloe ran steadily, through the corridor beyond to the octagonal office area, doing her best to keep up with Lien-Ådel who was breathlessly explaining it to her as they ran toward the docking elevators.

"Before the Adadevoh drive was invented, all rockets were momentum machines. Mass out in one direction at high velocity, the rocket moves in the opposite direction." She shouted as the sounds of chaos got louder. Ahead of them Orshio sprinted ahead with fierce determination.

"The Adadevoh drive doesn't do that. It's a reactionless drive that uses vacuum energy directly from space. That's why it can go so fast without having to lug a ton of fuel behind it. But the problem is, if you don't limit it and put controls on how much vacuum energy it uses, the maximum speed it reaches and how close it can approach planetary bodies, then it can easily be turned into a relativistic kinetic kill vehicle of unimaginable power."

They reached the tall, imposing doorway. Lien-Ådel stopped talking, catching her breath. She could feel her heart pounding in her throat.

Chloe went ahead, and the door opened once she was close enough for it to identify her genetic signature. Orshio nodded and then accelerated again and Lien-Ådel continued as they ran down the energy-shielded stairs.

"In a ship like the *Igodo*, with a glitch that could potentially allow access to the planetary approach limits, some suicidal lunatic could accelerate the ship to half the speed of light and deliberately crash it into a planet. At that speed, even for a ship as small as *Igodo*, the kinetic energy will be in the gigatons. At least 500. We are talking several thousand nuclear warheads worth of concentrated impact force in a single blow."

Chloe would have gasped if she wasn't panting so hard already.

The trio entered the main Ceres station tunnel and froze. Ahead of them, the lights lining all the elevators leading up to Ceres's docking ports were blinking wildly and one of them was burning; an unbelievably tall tower of fire reaching all the way from underground Ceres to the exosphere like an ancient cosmic snake.

At the bottom area where the fire raged most fierce, a large group of emergency responders wearing hermetic mechsuits were attempting to control the blaze by shutting off the oxygen and power supply lines, braving the heat and the smoke.

"Chai!" Orshio exclaimed. "Looks worse than I thought."

"Look for the man that drugged you in Officer Mukisa's office. If he's going for your ship, he must be here somewhere."

"What if we're too late and they already have the *Igodo*?" Lien-Ådel asked in a whisper.

Around them, people flowed. Most were running away, toward the main tunnel, bumping into those that stood still watching the inferno and the chaos and the commotion. There was one anomalous movement, though. One man at the bottom of one of the blinking elevators, pacing nervously. Chloe was the first to spot him. She noticed that the elevator he was in front of wasn't blinking like the others, its lights were steady, which meant it was in override, not emergency mode. She looked up, and just barely made out a figure standing in the transparent ascending shaft.

"There!" She shouted. "There's someone in that elevator."

She broke into a run.

Orshio and Lien-Ådel glanced up to see the elevator ascending.

Orshio turned to Lien-Ådel, "You need to find the ansible office on this station and establish communications with the *Igodo* so that I can reach you once I get on board. If we are right, we will only have a few minutes or even seconds. Please, go!"

Lien-Ådel nodded her understanding and sprinted back the way they'd come. Orshio followed Chloe. The man at the base of the elevator saw them approaching and pulled out an electric stun-stick, stance at the ready.

"You keep going!" Chloe called out. "Get to your ship before they take off. I'll handle this."

They'd attracted attention now and the spectators were torn between the roar of the fire and the fight they could see was coming.

Chloe dived for the man's feet as she reached him, and they both fell to the ground before he could even bring down his raised stick. She moved in a blur, wrestling and wrapping her body around the man powerfully, like a snake, trying to lock his limbs against his torso. Orshio jumped over their writhing mass and into the elevator, tapping at the panel to enter the code they'd been given when they docked earlier. The door sealed and he began to rise.

Ascending, he looked up, silently watching first the fragments of ship, cables, fire, lights, and panelling go by, and then, as he entered Ceres's exosphere, turning his gaze to the distant sun and the cluster nearby asteroids. The burning elevator remained visible, from high above, a spectre of destruction, of death. An augury of what was to come?

Near the end of the elevator, as it routed his car along the cable tethered to their ship, he came to a sudden stop. As he watched, only a few feet ahead of him, he saw the *Igodo's* nuclear reaction control system vents fire and the tethering cable start to detach.

"Shit!" He shouted. *They are initiating launch sequence. They're going to escape.*

The lights along the flanks of the *Igodo* went bright blue. The engines were on. In a few seconds, the *Igodo* would begin to move, exiting Ceres's primary gravity well and after that, if what he suspected were true, go into drift-flux aimed at a major Transhuman Federation outpost like Mars station. But, without the tethering cable's elevator access he had been effectively separated from the ship. Soon the air lock would close too and that would be the end. Just a few feet of space between him and the ship and there was nothing he could do. There was no way to get on the *Igodo*.

Unless . . .

With his arm powered to maximum and his enhanced melanin protecting his skin, he might just be able to make it.

Taking a deep breath and calming himself he rehearsed the steps in his mind.

One. Two. Three.

One. Two. Three.

One. Two. Three.

There was little-to-no margin of error.

He thought the instructions directly to his bioplasium arm.

One.

Exhaling slowly so oxygen wouldn't expand and rupture his lung tissue, he braced himself on one end of the elevator, facing the *Igodo's* airlock.

Two.

He launched himself forward, shoulder first. The transparent elevator wall shattered explosively. Oxygen rushed out and cold seized him as momentum kept him drifting towards the air lock. The airlock door began to close, slowly like a sleepy eyelid. He watched it in horror. The darkness on every side of the ship reminded him of what would happen if he didn't make it. Every nightmare he'd ever had of dying in space since he'd become a priest-pilot pounded against his chest. He willed himself to go faster but he couldn't. He closed his eyes. It was out of his hands now. He only opened his eyes again when he felt his shoulder hit the side of the *Igodo*.

Three.

Reaching out before he could bounce away, he stuck his right arm into the airlock and grabbed onto the edge. The low vibration of the ship set his teeth clattering. He yanked, hard, and pulled himself into the ship, hitting the row of spare extravehicular mobility suits and maintenance supplies just as the airlock door finally fell into place and the ship's pre-exit procedure was completed.

The vents opened and oxygen flooded back into his lungs. He breathed in gasps, wedged in between two E.V.M. suits. He lay there for a moment, as blood pulsed in his head and a ringing sounded in his ears. Then the increased vibration of the ship reminded him what was happening, and he pushed himself to the main access door. It opened immediately as it scanned his genetic signature.

He drifted through the ship quickly heading for the control room.

When he entered, there was someone seated in the engineer's module. The crewcut hair gave the thief's identity away.

"Stop!" Orshio called, flexing his arm.

The man turned, his face as calm as a cliff. He held a small black cube with a matrix of pulsing light symbols around it just like the one that had been in the office when he awakened. Orshio surmised it was the writing device, while the companion left behind in the office had been the reader.

"Well, this is unexpected," he remarked. "I knew the drugs wouldn't last long in the bodies of genetically modified space crew like you two, but how did you even escape the progmat restraints?"

"The same way I'm going to crush your windpipe if you dare touch my ships interface." Orshio gestured toward the middle of control deck. "Get away from the control module and move here! I know what you're up to and it ends now."

The man cocked his head to the side and smiled. "You think you can stop us, mongrel?"

The viewscreen of the *Igodo* exploded into the colourful array of data that indicated an incoming transmission. It went unanswered.

"Shut up and move away from the controls!" Orshio shouted. "And if you so much as try to issue a command to override the planetary approach limits, I will choke you to death. The world has moved beyond you and your kind. You can't change the march of progress with acts of terror."

"No." The man said. "I know I won't change anything. You and your Transhuman Federation of borderless gene editors and race mixers will continue to take over this system. Technology and economics are on your side, we know that. We've known that ever since your Botswana, Singapore, and Norway units started sharing their gene editing technologies and got your Canada unit to start collaborating with the Nigeria unit to develop their Adadevoh drive. You will never turn back from what you think is success. We know. We see clearly."

Orshio stared at the ranting man in front of him, confused. "Then what are you doing? Why?"

"To hurt you," the man replied angrily. Behind him, space flowed steadily by and the incoming transmission light signals seemed to become more turbulent as the distance between them and Ceres station increased. "You think you are better than us but you're not even human anymore. You call us stupid, backward, racist, and evil simply because we want to maintain our natural bodies, our way of life, our group identities and our culture. You insist that we agree to your freedom and justice laws before we join your Federation but what kind of community would we have if everyone from everywhere could go wherever they wanted without screening? What kind of society can we have where everyone does whatever they like with their bodies, their minds? How would we find social cohesion? How would we define ourselves? No! You made us choose between our borders, our culture, our beliefs, and your progress. You forced us to take a stand, and we have paid for it dearly, but this is it. This is what the wrath of real humanity feels like."

Orshio laughed derisively. "You can't be serious. Everyone in the Federation maintains their culture if they want to, it's just an individual choice now, just look at me for my ancestor's sake. No, what you wanted was to be dominant in some space, to treat others who'd had their genes edited or their bodies adapted as being less than you, to refuse them the right to live next to you and be themselves, not assimilated. What you wanted was the right to discriminate. Our progress made you

277

uncomfortable and now you're trying to destroy Mars because we didn't let your isolationist and regressionist Confederacy join our Transhuman Federation and get access to our technologies? That's absurd and stupid and petty."

The man growled. "I didn't say anything about Mars."

Orshio shivered.

If not Mars, then . . .

Earth?

Surely they wouldn't dare . . .

Then man inhaled deeply and added, "It doesn't matter, I don't expect you to understand and besides, you are already too late."

With those words, the man finally rose from the module and launched himself at Orshio. Around them, the lights on the ship dimmed as the tachyon field auto-navigation system engaged. Through the view screen and behind the man rapidly approaching him, Orshio saw an elliptic hole suddenly appear in the darkness, its edges rimmed with light and bleeding into the fabric of space like an injury to a star. The man must have already overridden the controls and set them on automatic. They were going into drift-flux.

The man crashed into Orshio. Orshio held onto him and turned sharply, swinging the attacker to the other side of the room, before punching him square on the jaw. The man's eyes rolled back in his head. Roaring, Orshio bounced off the control deck floor and drove his entire body forward toward the wall, trapping the man's head between his bioplasmium shoulder and the wall panel. There was a sharp crack. The man stopped moving.

Orshio kicked him in the chest, using the momentum to push himself toward his seat in the priest-pilot module. His eyes locked on to the hole in front of him. It narrowed to a point. Just as he settled into the chair, the *Igodo* went into drift-flux.

The stars, asteroids, and superstructures that had seemed like they were slowly moving by started to rotate. The black, silent fabric of space seemed to curve into a ball, and he was at the centre of it, plummeting toward the surface of teeming, rotating stars. No matter how many times he entered it, Orshio's mind always felt confused by it. Space didn't make sense in drift-flux.

There was no time, he had to act quickly.

He swiped furiously at the blinking viewscreen of the *Igodo* to accept the incoming transmission.

Lien-Ådel's face appeared, with Chloe's and several others he didn't recognize, standing behind her.

"Orshio! Orshio! We just detected a vacuum energy singularity developing. It's drift-flux! If you are on board, you need to stop him. Stop him now!"

Orshio grunted. Too late.

He swiped away the message and pulled up the *Igodo's* projected path, to see that it was aimed for Earth. It would crash into humanity's home planet at $0.7c$, functional light speed. Enough to trigger an extinction level event. Defensive weapons would be useless against a relativistic kill vehicle going that fast. Even near-orbit impact would have catastrophic consequences. With every passing moment things became more dangerous. Time dilation was starting to kick in and he'd be experiencing shorter time than everyone else was. He needed to get a message out. Fast.

He swiped at the controls and fired off a message of his own.

"Lien-Ådel! I'm in flux. Contact Earth station and tell them the *Igodo* was set on a kill path but I have retaken the ship and will attempt to correct. I repeat, I have retaken the ship and will correct!"

The silence returned and Orshio's mind raced, as he swiped through the ship's base code trying to recall what he'd been taught about Adedevoh-class driveship programming. Everything was confusing. But he needed to do something. There were so many loops and subroutines, and he couldn't tell the functional elements from the damaged relay. His genetic signature allowed him access even the deepest layer of core programming, but he had no idea what to do to re-establish the maximum speed and planetary approach limits. The blood pulsed in his ears as the ship hurtled toward the Earth to smite it like the hand of some petty god. He desperately wished Lien-

Ådel was beside him. Screwing with ship code was her thing. Piloting was his thing.

Piloting is his thing.

He swiped away the source code, pulled up the projected flight path, and began to recalculate. He frowned in focus, his eyes narrowed, and his tribal marking compressed.

He began to swipe, adjusting the hundreds of lines that marked out all class-2 orbital and transport bodies in motion in the sub-belt solar system. The beating of his heart was thunder. He could not reinstall the limits or change the ship's hard-coded path; the man had damaged the flight path adjustment console. He'd been locked out. And even if he dropped out of drift-flux now, the ship was already going fast enough to cause major damage. He needed to slow it down. If he could combine a series of unscheduled decouplings with a rapid correction using the reaction control system, he just might ensure the *Igodo* didn't crash into the Earth or anything else with enough force to kill billions. And if he was lucky, he wouldn't get himself killed either.

He finished his calculations and paused. He closed his eyes and prayed to his ancestors, "ŋmá alekwu," then swiped the calculations in without giving himself time to overthink it.

The first decoupling kicked in. The ship groaned with a whine like a dying beast, shuddering as its Adadevoh Drive broke connection to the zero-point field of fluctuating energy distribution in space. The ship slowed and the curve of reality flattened out into the familiar again. But before Orshio could even see how close to Earth he was, the ship's thrusters fired as pre-programmed and set it rotating. It spun round on its axis like a mad Frisbee at an angular momentum it was never designed to handle. And then for one deathly moment the elliptic hole of bleeding light reappeared. With a forceful crunch, the ship re-coupled, going back into drift-flux with its drive facing the opposite direction, as Orshio tried to brake by putting the *Igodo* in reverse. The delta V induced a sudden and spectacular curvature of reality. He saw light. He squinted and saw light glaring out from behind a hole in the ball of reality. His head spun. His heart raged against his ribcage. His vision began to blur at the edges.

The second decoupling kicked in and the ship groaned again, the Adadevoh Drive breaking its connection to the zero-point for the second and final time.

The manoeuvre had driven the *Igodo's* engines far beyond design capacity and the force of the second decoupling mid-spin had wrecked the drive.

Orshio was thrown out of his seat and even his genetic gravcines couldn't stop him from finally losing his hold on consciousness.

The last thing he remembered seeing was a face in the light behind the hole in reality, that perfect circle of nothingness with smoothly curved edges, wisps of light streaming out of it like God himself was peeping over its edge.

When Orshio came to, there was water almost up to his neck.

He flailed wildly at first, completely confused as to why he'd gone from the lovely and strange weightlessness of space to the familiar and dangerous viscosity of water. The viewscreen was somehow still stubbornly displaying symbols. The panelling all along the left flank of the *Igodo's* control module had ruptured and the ship was filling with water fast.

He stopped as his senses returned to him. Get out. He had to get out. He took a deep breath and submerged, swimming through familiar passageways to the *Igodo's* airlock. His skin was covered in cuts that stung so much that he knew he had to be in seawater.

He reached the airlock, but it only opened halfway when it read his genetic signature. Damaged. It had to have been damaged. He swam up to take in air and calm down. The water was almost up to his nose now, soon the entire ship would be full of water. He breathed slowly, calming his nerves. Then he resubmerged. He swam back to the partly open door, held onto a rail, and, thinking carefully, punched the locked door with his bioplasmium fist like it was an old enemy. It gave. He swam into open water and up, up toward the shimmering surface.

When he surfaced, it was hot and bright, and the sun was dancing a silver line down the skin of the water. His dreadlocks felt heavy on his head. It took him a few seconds to realise he'd lost his red headband. In the distance, he heard sounds like voices, like shouts, like . . . Earth.

He spun around and saw he was floating only a few hundred feet from a beach. Behind the beach line, a lush green island rose and at its crest sat a beautiful glass bungalow that reflected the sun like a prism. Waves broke over a surrounding group of rocks to the left of the beach. Fishing boats were slowly struggling in through the constellation of rocks. Up and down the beach, there was a smattering of people of all shapes and colours and sizes with their towels and beach balls, their frisbees and their beach mats rolled up under their arms. There were at least thirty of them and some of them were shouting, some of them were waving animatedly at him, and some of them were pointing up to the sky. He turned again; eyes raised. In the distance, there was a small aircraft approaching.

Orshio started laughing.

He laughed and laughed and laughed.

He laughed because a few minutes ago, he'd been a third of the way across the solar system, because he'd seen the universe bend, because he'd performed an impossible manoeuvre, because he'd saved billions of people from a madman, because he'd wrestled against the essential forces of the universe and yet, somehow, he was alive, floating in the ocean beyond a beach on Earth like some bloody tourist.

He laughed and splashed around in the water like a child until the aircraft, which turned out to be a Transhuman Federation supersonic carrier arrived, dropped an autonomous winch cable, and hauled him into its metal belly like a morsel of food.

Inside, he was attended to by people in medical gear and completely ensconced in an insulation super suit—a thin layer of smart nanomaterial that isolated him from his environment to keep him warm and prevent bacterial exchange in his delicate state—and was given a hot cup of hot rooibos tea. A pale older man with blonde hair and a stiff back wearing the familiar white uniform of the Transhuman Federation forces with the Zulu

282

shield, yin-and-yang, and spears emblazoned on its breast walked up to him and said, "Good to see you are alive and in one piece, Priest-pilot."

"Thank you, captain . . .?"

"Petrov. But call me Stanislav. Welcome on board the *Anansi*."

"I guess I'm incredibly lucky. Looks like I landed in a nice location," Orshio said, smiling thinly before taking a sip of his tea. "What was that beach anyway?"

The officer smiled at him. "Machangulo Island, just off the coast of Mozambique. Lovely place, perfectly natural, and very popular with tourists from all over the federation. We're heading to Addis Ababa to meet the trade council. Your engineer explained the situation to us, and it seems we all owe you a great debt. And you owe her an equal one. We would have fried you with plasma when you made an unscheduled entry into Earth orbit if we hadn't already gotten her message."

Orshio laughed, "I cannot overstate how glad I am that you didn't do that." Then he added. "I have to thank her when I see her."

The captain smiled, a clever look in his eyes. "No need to wait that long. We still have Ceres station on the emergency ansible channel. She's eager to say hello."

Orshio grinned.

He followed the officer into the communications room and let him lead him to an ansible console.

Orshio sat down, holding his injured belly. Lien-Ådel's face burst onto the screen in dazzling light symbols. She was more excited than Orshio had ever seen her since they'd begun working together.

"You magnificent bastard! How in the name of everything we've been taught did you pull that off?" she asked, her mouth wide.

Orshio went straight-faced and said, "Honestly, I don't know. My ancestors must have reached out from Okoto to guide my hand in flux. They even sent me crashing down at a holiday location. Seriously, I'm telling you, only the ancestors could have pulled off a stunt like that."

Lien-Ådel's image on the viewscreen came closer, her mouth tight but a suppressed smile leaking from behind her eyes, and the edges of her lips. "Come on Orshio, you really think your ancestors were out there? That they guided you in drift-flux?"

Orshio smiled. "Well, No. Not really. But it'll be a good story to tell people who wonder how the hell I survived that insane manoeuvre, won't it?"

They both erupted into wild, celebratory laughter that rang across the ocean of space and energy between them.

Manic Pixie Dream Girl Gets Revenge
by
Gerald L. Coleman

*"We should forgive our enemies, but not before they are
hanged."*
~Heinrich Heine

Revenge is a prison and time is its Warden. Mads rode in the
back of the transport gazing out a reinforced, clear-aluminum
window. The skies above Everlearn were too blue. The fluffy,
pristinely formed clouds were just the right size and texture to
appeal to the eye.

Mads absently rolled the hapicite pendant around in her hand
as she watched the clouds drift lazily on their predetermined loop
around the facility. The piece of hapicite was chosen with metic-
ulous care so only the tiniest slivers were lasered off to create the
small, silver starburst, which held a purple, gleamdream stone set
in its center. The long chain securing the pendant around her neck
was also made of the rarest mineral in the galaxy—though of a
lesser grade. It still glittered in the soft light filtering through the
window.

The pilot's rough voice followed a soft chime emitted from the
intercom.

"Lieutenant Worth, we'll be landing shortly."

Another chime accompanied a red flashing light in the panel
over the entry to the cockpit. Mads clicked her flight harness back
into place and prepared for landing. There was no need for the
pilot to consider crosswinds, weather conditions, or birds in the

air on approach—not in the idyllic atmosphere custom made by Everlearn climate engineers. They were in a high-density Typhoon Class transport. Turbulent weather wouldn't have mattered anyway.

She waited for the dull metallic thump of the struts touching down and the momentary howl of the engines' back thrust to unbuckle again. She tucked the pendant back inside her jacket and buttoned it around the neck. A final chime and a green light told her it was safe to stand.

Mads made her way to the exit on the left of the cabin. The pilot exited the cockpit and gave her a sharp salute.

"Lieutenant, I hope you had a pleasant trip?"

The man had decided any low-ranking officer in the Galactic Sovereign Fleet who could afford a private transport to the exclusive facility of Everlearn, on the moon of Empyrean, must be from a family with means and connections. He didn't want to end up on the wrong side of that equation.

"I did, Bondsman. Thank you."

The man self-consciously covered the metal band shackled to his wrist with the end of his sleeve. The bright, green numbers on its liquid glass display lazily ticked away on his wrist. They indicated at least three years left to pay off his debt.

Everlearn would be charging him for room, board, clothes, and any other expense he incurred—and all of it deducted from his wages. Even more pernicious? Everlearn owned the buildings they lived in, the stores they shopped in—even the places they paid for entertainment. It was indentured servitude. The counter on their wrists was a clever, if perverse, chimera—a brilliant pacifier meant to keep people like him in line, with the illusion he'd one day be free of it.

No matter how many of them died of old age, with the numbers on their bracelet still slowly turning, it did not provoke rebellion against the practice. The ancient adage about a frog in a slowly boiling pot came to Mads' mind. It was corrupt and predatory. She smiled warmly at the pilot, gave him a standard tip, and exited the shuttle.

A lanky, handsome, young man, with pale golden hair, deep blue eyes, and a soft smile met her at the foot of the ramp.

He inclined his head, looked over his datapad, and said, "Lieutenant Maddie Charl Wyrth?"

His voice rose a fraction, indicating a question, despite her uniform.

"Yes, but since you aren't Corps, you can dispense with the formality. Call me, Mads."

He inclined his head again and said, "Yes, ma'am—I mean, Mads. I'm Ramond Flowers. You may call me Rammy. I'll be your escort and MPDG."

"MPDG?"

"Oh, yeah," he blushed and continued, "Mindjack Project Direct Guide. It's a mouthful, so we just say MPDG."

She caught him staring. His eyes went from her hips to her breasts, to her bright, purple hair. It was wound into seven, thick, traditional threads, evenly spaced around her head. The finger-thick tendrils fell past her shoulders. One on each side curled back on themselves before casually dropping down like they felt like wandering on the way. The woven threads of her gloriously wooly hair were a style that was old before humans began colonizing the stars.

Her *mzaa* and *baba* carried the ancient ways with them into the darkness of deep space. She remembered the small bag of okra seeds in her mzaa's bag and a cast iron skillet her baba guarded like it was a member of the family—passed down from brown-skinned hand to brown-skinned hand for generations.

Mads loved the thick, cake-like bread they made in it and the pot of beans they'd slow-cook to go with it. She wore her hair in threads, knots, braids, and sometimes wildly free in a large, messy halo in honor of that ancient culture.

Flowers blushed when he realized she'd caught him staring.

He straightened the white coat of his suit with a quick tug, and squeaked, "How was your trip?"

"Pleasant enough," she replied. "The Port on Caliban was busy, but the flight up from the planet was quiet."

The young man nodded.

"That's nice to hear. Caliban can be a lot to take in. The Bonded live down there and overcrowding in the city can be a bit much to endure. Thankfully, private shuttles are available for our most discerning clients." By which he meant, wealthy.

He had enough self-possession not to smirk. Mads' soft grunt was her entire statement on the matter.

"Did you receive my payment?"

He grinned and ducked his head in that way people did when they thought they were in the company of the wealthy. It was like a litmus test for character. Some groveled, others sucked up, more sought favor.

"Yes, ma'am—uh, Mads." His voice got progressively oily as he continued. "It's not often we're paid in hapicite, especially not the purest grade. Rest assured your entire stay with us is fully covered."

Bile rose in her throat. She told herself to focus.

"Good. My quarters?"

The young man bowed and motioned toward the facility with an exaggerated flourish of an extended arm.

"Right this way, Mads."

Flowers turned, tucked his datapad under his arm, and started toward the main entrance. The Everlearn facility, as white as his uniform, was a feat of architectural elegance. Its thin, megaplex—like huddled fingers pointing toward the sky—glistened in the afternoon sun.

They walked on white concrete without a seam or crack. The grounds were covered in immaculately groomed flora. The visage of its unending sea of precisely manicured grass was only broken by patches of orange begonias, purple irises, and pink lotus flowers, bunched together in overflowing explosions of color. The facility was surrounded by a hedge as tall as a tree.

Security was ostentatious and comprehensive. She passed through brain, eye, and body scans. It wasn't enough to project a blank mind devoid of thought. The brain scan was calibrated to catch that kind of deception. Mads thought back through her flight from the surface of Caliban—its trajectories, flight path, and her assessment of the shuttle and its pilot.

The scan would also pick up heightened activity in the section of her brain that would give her away as a hacker. It's why she chose her cover with care. A logistics officer in the Corps, used to running high-end military ops computers, would have very similar brain markers—not identical, but close.

She'd also included heavily redacted files in her application to hint at questions Everlearn wouldn't be clear to ask or expect answers. Well-placed bribes got her background checks answered by someone in the appropriate department of the Corps. The Galactic Corps' sprawling administration, and inevitable corruption, were the only things that made that possible.

It had taken months to find the right officer in the right billet, with the right moral flexibility. Everlearn security was conscientious enough to have included all of it in her file. She forced herself to breathe slowly.

Nothing to see here, boys, she thought.

A superior looked over the shoulder of the guard checking her scans. The young man pointed at the screen and the older guard leaned over and whispered to him. He immediately nodded to Flowers who smiled and gave Mads a thumbs up.

The interior of Everlearn was a study in customer manipulation. Mads was greeted by gray walls, smooth gray marble floors, and an ambient lavender scent. The smell was meant to foster good emotions. The lighting was dim—known to foster indulgence in purchases. A soft, unobtrusive, classical composition played in the background. It was intended to say we are sophisticated.

The art on the walls was sparse but colorful. She noted impressionistic work by Dal, abstracts by Verilan, and photo realism by Merr. It whispered—*be at ease, we're a successful company*—in corporate speak.

Then, there was the decor. The furniture, as sparsely arranged as the art on the walls, was rich, verdant green, vibrant, clear, sea blue, and deep, lush purple. It screamed—reliability, quality, and luxury. *Trust us. Let us spoil you.*

Most people never noticed all the little ways a corporation sought to manipulate them. Everlearn wanted you primed to spend lots and lots of money—and to feel happy about it. Mads simply smiled at Flowers as he led her through the thick web of manipulation meant to foster conspicuous consumption.

The other quiet bit of subconscious manipulation was how the Bonded wore gray. It made them blend into the background of the walls. They could clean, do repairs, and perform all the menial tasks needed to keep a facility of this magnitude running smoothly without ever being noticed.

You had to want to see them or they were invisible. But how do you ignore all the tiny green numbers ticking away on wrists all around you? It was perverse. Mads kept her eyes forward and her expression neutral. There were facial recog scans happening at regular intervals throughout the facility—an additional layer of internal security, which doubled as a way of monitoring the Bonded.

She'd seen the schematics. The scans functioned by using algorithms that captured and analyzed micro-expressions to predict behavior. A flash of disdain on the face, even for a millisecond, would trigger an alert that sent a guard to have a discussion with the culprit.

Soon enough, they arrived at the rooms reserved for her stay. She leaned against the wall and smiled at him as he typed a code into a small keypad. Flowers blushed as he fumbled the code. The keypad barked a rude tone and red light at him, forcing him to enter it again. She glanced at the back of his shiny datapad. Finally, the door opened with the softest *whush*.

It was more of the same inside. There was a bed, a large, soft chair, and a desk, all situated so you could look out on a lovely garden view from the massive window that doubled as a wall. The art, smell, and colors were more of the same.

"Here is the control pad for your quarters. An executive chef is on standby anytime, day or night. They are prepared to make anything you'd like. Hit the call button and a concierge can have just about anything brought to your room—anything at all."

Mads didn't like the ending inflection in his voice. She shuddered to think what kinds of things, or people, were fed to Everlearn clients. The moon Empyrean and its contingent planet Caliban sat conveniently outside the jurisdiction of the Galactic Charter of 3782.

If you were a planet of means or one armed to the teeth, gills, or other evolutionary appendage, you were likely a founding member of the Galactic Union of Worlds and on its Security Council. The seven Planetary members of the Security Council were the real power of the Union. They drew the lines on the star charts.

Everlearn's corporate charter was registered on Ethereal. Ethereal just happened to be a Permanent member of the GUW Security. Mads grit her teeth when she thought about it. It was corruption on a cosmic scale. It was so big no one believed it and if they did they didn't think they could do anything about it.

But Mads knew something most people didn't. Bureaucracies that big were easily fooled. They were also monumentally arrogant. They didn't think anyone could do anything about it either.

"Get some rest, Mads. Your Mindjacks are scheduled to begin in the morning."

Mads walked Flowers back to the door and said, "Thank you, Ramond. I'll see you in the morning."

She brushed something nonexistent off his shoulder and his face flushed bright red as he backed out. She waved at him as the door slid closed and then her smile vanished. It was time to get ready.

Mads searched every inch of the quarters. She ruled out the presence of listening devices and cameras. Then, she moved all the furniture against the walls. Her breathing slowed as she sat in the center of the room. It wasn't long before she was sitting with her legs folded up into her lap and drifting in her mindspace. It had taken years to learn the mental discipline necessary for what she was going to attempt. She had to be calm and focused. She would only get one shot.

* * *

Her eyes snapped open. She could feel his footsteps coming down the hall. Mads quickly moved the furniture back in place. A soft chime indicated he was at the door.

She pushed the button next to the door and it slid open to reveal Flowers in a fresh white uniform and a bright smile.

"Good morning, Mads. Oh, forgive me. I should've shown you where your clothes are stored."

He entered the room and made his way to a tall, slim wardrobe in the corner. He pulled open the door and motioned to a set of folded clothes.

"The shower is through that door. I'll wait outside until you're ready."

"Thank you, Ramond. What would I do without you?"

He ducked his head and grinned. He was pleased with himself. *Good*, she thought.

"I'll just be a moment."

He stepped outside and she grabbed the clothes she'd discovered when she searched the room the night before. After a quick shower, she threw on the white pants and top, before sliding on the soft white shoes. She stood next to the door for an extra few minutes before hitting the button again.

"I'm so sorry to keep you waiting, Ramond. I think I'm ready. I'd forget my head if it wasn't attached."

He shook his head and said, "No, no, Mads. No problem at all. I'm here to serve. If you're ready?"

"Yes, please. Lead on, Macduff!"

Flowers quirked an eyebrow.

"Oh, sorry, Ramond. Just an old literary reference. My mother loved to read. She was especially fond of ancient Terran literature. *I know why the caged bird sings? The fire next time?*"

Flowers flattened his lips, shrugged almost imperceptibly, and nodded politely.

"Ah. I see. Anyway, it's this way."

Lead on, Macduff, she thought. *A vapid cog in an arrogant machine.*

A young woman in gray approached with folded towels and a basket full of cleaning supplies in her arms. Flowers made a show of stopping her just outside Mads' room.

"Lieutenant Wyrth is an honored guest. Be sure her room is spotless."

The young Bondswoman bent at the knees and bowed her head.

"Yes, sir."

Flowers started off down the hall and Mads whispered, "It's probably a mess in there. I'm not a morning person."

The young woman flinched, her eyes darted toward Flowers' back, and then landed on Mads. She dipped her body again and nodded.

Mads watched her scurry into the room. Flowers hadn't noticed. He was too busy strutting down the hallway. It wouldn't even have occurred to him that Mads would've spoken to the Bondswoman. A soft derisive snort of air left her nose.

She kept her eyes aimed at the door the bondswoman had disappeared behind. The facial recog tech would chalk her derision up to displeasure with the servant rather than its intended target. She turned and followed after him.

His shoulders were straight. His head was held high. His stride was long and he was a little too conscious of it all. He was an MPDG of one of the most powerful corporations in the galaxy and he was feeling himself. He thought she was impressed.

He led her through a maze of nearly identical hallways—gray marble floors, white walls, the occasional expensive piece of art on the wall. Mads ignored it all and kept count. Right, right, left, left, left, right, left, left, right—she memorized it as they went.

RIGHT, by the stream where Othood died. RIGHT, past the hill where his mother cried. LEFT, at the willow Maxim saved. LEFT, by the buildings that they razed.

"What's that tune," Flowers asked? "It sounds ominous."

"Oh, just something that calms my nerves. I like how the low notes feel in my throat."

She added a nervous chuckle and Flowers said, "Not to worry. I'll be with you the entire time. I won't let anything happen to you."

"That's very kind of you, Ramond." *Very kind.*

The last hallway ended in an enormously oversized door. Ramond entered his code and the thing slowly swept inward. It was three feet thick and opened like a vault. Everlearn's most prized technology was on the other side.

The chamber was big enough to be a starship hangar. Cool air hit her face as she entered. Thin, white columns filled the chamber at precise intervals. They were covered in blinking, blue lights.

Mainframe, she thought.

"If I remember correctly, according to your application, this is your first Mindjack?"

"Yes, it is. It's not what I was imagining. How does it work?"

"Don't worry. I'll walk you through it."

Mads made an exaggerated twist of her head as she took in the entire lab.

"Is it just us? No cameras?

"Yes. Everlearn takes your privacy, protecting your data, and Mindjack experience seriously. I will be the only person who sees it or has access to what goes on here."

"Huh. I guess that's reassuring. But what if there's a problem or an emergency?"

"I'll be monitoring you the entire time from my station and there's an Intervention Team in the next room with a full suite of highly-trained, medical technicians. Problems are incredibly rare. But rest assured, we're ready for any eventuality."

Mads looked away and smirked. *Any eventuality?*

"Ok. I guess I'm ready."

"Very good. Follow me."

Flowers led her to the far side of the chamber. They walked through another door into a small room with a bench and a set of cabinets on the wall. He reached into one and produced a set of small patches.

He placed them on her temples and the back of her neck.

He cleared his throat and said, "If you'll turn around and pull up your shirt?"

He proceeded to place more of them down her spine to the small of her back.

"These will allow me to monitor your jack."

Mads pulled her shirt down and turned back around.

"So, where's the chair? Or sphere? Or whatever you use for the Mindjack?"

Flowers grinned.

"Ah. Yes. Those are how our competitors facilitate a Mindjack, but thankfully you've come to Everlearn. Follow me."

He walked to the door at the other side of the small room, looked back at her, and said, "Take a deep breath. It can be a bit disorientating."

He entered his code again and the door slid open to reveal a doorway filled with blue light. He winked at her and disappeared through it. Mads followed.

It was like stepping into a cold shower. She shivered. Tiny bumps rose on the back of her neck. The hair on her forearms stood on its end. She wrapped her arms around herself and thought she'd never be warm again.

Then, suddenly, the sensation was gone. She was standing in what she could only describe as a blank space. It was white for as far as the eye could see. A nothingness that had no end. The only surface she could see was the white floor beneath her feet.

Flowers spread his arms wide and said, "This is what we call the Oasis." He paused. His entire demeanor could only be described as gloating—the self-satisfied, smug smile, the congratulatory nod of the head, and the insufferable tone of his voice. "I know. Spectacular isn't it."

Mads blew a low, long, soft whistle.

"It looks like it goes on forever."

Flowers nodded appreciatively, as if he'd built it himself.

"It kinda does. Rather than strap you to a table and wire you to an interface that feeds your brain electrical impulses, which it then reads as reality, Everlearn created this."

"What is it? How does it work?"

"Most of it is proprietary information I'm not supposed to divulge." He leaned in conspiratorially and continued, "But for you, Mads, I'll make an exception."

She ducked her head, looked up at him from underneath her brows, and feigned a blush.

"I appreciate that, Ramond. It would make me a little less afraid of this whole experience."

She saw his chest poke out a bit. He pointed at the doorway they'd come through.

"The doorway is a threshold to a pocket universe we've artificially created."

His fingers ran nimbly across his datapad and suddenly, the blank expanse changed. They were standing next to a small, trickling stream running through a lush valley. The sky was pristine blue, and mountains loomed in the distance.

"It's a programmable space, wrapped inside a time-dilation field. For every hour that passes in here, minutes pass outside the field. The longer you stay inside the slower time passes outside. Think of it this way, and this is just an estimate—a day in here is like an hour out there, a month is like a day. The engineering that makes it possible is actually fascinating. Maybe after your Mindjack is over we can discuss it more, say over a drink?"

She feigned another blush and said, "Maybe." Her gaze rose to the mountains in the distance. "So, this is why Everlearn is so much more expensive than places like Mindcore?"

"Exactly," Flowers said as he jabbed a finger in her direction. "Only the best for customers like you."

Mads took a deep breath. "Ok. Should we get started?"

A flurry of Flowers' fingers on his datapad changed the environment again. This time they were on top of a mountain, standing in the center of a large ring of hardened earth. A tall man in black stood across from her.

"We've programmed your instructors with the best martial skills in existence, according to your specs. And because you paid for the platinum package, they come with a complete personality. Remember, I'll be monitoring your progress from my station in the antechamber. Good luck on your training! When you're ready to exit, just say *door*."

Flowers walked to the edge of the ring, through the glowing, blue doorway, and was gone. Then the door vanished and Mads was left alone with her programmed instructor.

"So, you want to learn how to fight."

The tall man had skin as black as obsidian. He was draped in black silk. It was an ancient Terran style. She could see a kimono covered by a *kamishimo*—a kind of sleeveless jacket with exaggerated shoulders, and wide flowing pants called *hakama*. He wore a belt around his waist that Mads knew was an *obi,* with two swords tucked into it.

His words were a statement of fact rather than a question.

Mads said, "Hai," and bowed her head. "I want to learn the sword."

His voice was deep, but he had a pleasant expression on his face.

"I see. Very well. You may call me Yasuke. And this," he motioned to his left as the air warped like the distortion caused by extreme heat, "is Joseph Bologne and Jean-Louis Michel."

Mads smiled. Joseph Bologne, also known as Le Chevalier De Saint-Georges, was the greatest swordsman in Europe in the 18th century on Old Earth. Born into enslavement on a plantation on the island of Guadalupe, he was the son of a rich plantation owner and an enslaved Black woman.

The circumstances of it narrowed her eyes and made her grit her teeth. She knew the history of it. He inherited his black skin and good looks from his mother. His father took him and his mother to France where he had the kind of upbringing afforded to the wealthy, white, French upper class.

At school, he studied math and history in the morning and in the afternoon he fenced. He came under the tutelage of the master swordsman Nicolas Texier de la Boëssière, and by all accounts grew to be the greatest swordsman of his age. He wore a fussy, white shirt, with billowing sleeves, a green vest, blue pantaloons, with white stockings, and brown leather boots.

Standing next to him was Jean-Louis Michel. Michel was light-skinned like Joseph. Unlike Yasuke and Joseph, Jean-Louis was short and slender. He was barely over five feet tall. He was born in the 19th century in a place called Saint-Domingue, which later became known as Haiti on Old Earth. His father was a French fencing coach.

He served in the French army under the conqueror Napoleon and was most famous for a series of duels outside Madrid, Spain. In a quarrel between soldiers of his regiment and an Italian regiment, it was said he killed three Italian sword masters and wounded another ten in less than forty minutes.

He wore a green double-breasted coat with tails and a large collar, white pants, and black boots. A thick, cream, dotted scarf was tied around his neck and tucked into his collar. He wore a pleasant smile, like the other two. These were to be her teachers. The greatest swordsmen of their eras. She liked the idea that they looked like her. Who better to prepare her for what was to come?

Yasuke tossed her a katana. Jean-Louis and Joseph took up positions on the edge of the ring. They began with how to hold the sword and how to stand. She was nearly giddy with joy when the program had Jean-Louis speak words he'd made famous.

"A sword should be held as one holds a little bird; not so tightly as to crush it, but just enough to prevent it escaping from the hand."

All three held sticks as thick as a finger and as long as an arm. They used them to tap an arm or leg that was out of place or to slash in like a sword strike. They were unrelenting.

It wasn't long before she was drenched in sweat. Her arms and legs ached. But it was exhilarating. Their mastery of the art was undeniable and remarkable. And she was learning.

It wasn't just that mere minutes had passed on the outside giving her all the time in the world to learn. She knew the patches on her body were storing electrical impulses and imprinting them in her brain. Muscle memory was being stored. What would take her years to encode in her mind and body under normal circumstances would be accumulated in days in this environment. You could learn anything you wanted with Mindjack tech if you could afford it.

"Door."

Her teachers vanished as the glowing doorway appeared. For her, it had been hours. Outside, only minutes had passed. When she stepped out of the small room into the large chamber, Flowers was waiting with a towel and a table covered in food.

She wiped herself off and ate while he checked the calibration of the patches and the status of her Mindjack.

"You're doing great, Mads."

She nodded and shoved a forkful of baked fish into her mouth. The mixed vegetables were delicious and complemented the redfish, which was cooked in a chutney.

Flowers said, "If you sleep in the Oasis this will go even faster. Or you can return to your quarters and we'll pick up tomorrow."

Mads washed everything down with a sweet red wine.

"That's a great idea, Ramond."

She dropped her towel on the table and headed back in. There was a small house a few feet from the ring when she re-entered the Oasis. It was stylish, well-appointed, and equipped with the most comfortable bed she'd ever been in. She showered, changed, and slept. Yasuke woke her by shaking her leg.

It wasn't long before she was back in the ring and training. It all became a blur. She trained, exited for food, and returned to the Oasis for more training and sleep. By the time a month had passed inside, the day outside had been spent. The only pause in the cycle was giving Flowers a night to sleep himself and they were back at it again.

It didn't stop him from taking every opportunity he could get to ply her with small talk. He wasn't really happy, not sure what he wanted to do with his life, sure he was waiting for something or *someone* to come along and inspire him. She caught him staring often enough. It was a simple matter to turn his questions away like parrying a sword thrust.

It took two months in the Oasis—which turned out to be just two days in the real—before Yasuke, Jean-Michel, and Joseph told her there was nothing more they could teach her. Real steel rang off steel, yet, in more than two dozen passes with katana, foil, and saber, none of them managed a single touch on her. The men bowed to her before they vanished. She wasn't even breathing hard.

She glanced at a readout as she exited the Oasis and entered the large chamber that housed the mainframe. It was the morning of the third day since she arrived.

Impeccable timing, she thought.

A young man was wheeling in a cart of food meant for her breakfast. He stopped next to the small, cloth-covered table that had been set up for her meals. She could sleep in the Oasis, but any food constructed in it wouldn't be real.

He went to place one of the trays on the table. His wristband beeped, the green numbers zeroed out, and it clicked open. He just stood there staring at it with his mouth hanging open. He raised his wrist and the metal band fell off and clattered to the floor.

The young man looked over at Mads and said, "Most of us didn't believe it. I'm sorry I doubted, ma'am." And then he turned and ran.

An alarm began blaring loudly. Flowers jumped up from behind his workstation where he'd been napping.

"What, what's happening!?"

Mads flashed him the first genuine smile she'd smiled since entering Everlearn.

"I am."

She hit him in the temple and he dropped to the floor like one of the bags of dross leftover from mining on her home planet. By the time he came around, she had him strapped to a chair.

He shook his head and mumbled, "What, what—what are you doing?"

"Oh, me? I've used your security code to gain access to the subroutines in the mainframe." Her fingers danced across the screen. "I'm inputting a nasty little virus I created after learning to code at Mindcore last year."

Flowers strained against the bonds she'd made by tearing the tablecloth into strips and weaving them into makeshift ropes.

"Wait, this wasn't your first Mindjack? Are you insane? Do you know how dangerous it is to double-jack so close together? You're supposed to wait at least three years between Jacks to prevent seepage, lesions, and even aneurysms. It could've killed you."

Mads grabbed the sandwich off the plate she'd brought over to the workstation and took a large bite. She chewed and talked at the same time.

"Excuse me for talking with my mouth full. You're right. But my sources thought that since Everlearn's Mindjack was so different from the standard process the risk of serious complications was less than 40%."

Flowers strained to see what Mads was doing.

"Why would you risk it, even if that was true?"

She finished inputting the code and grabbed the other half of her sandwich. She took a bite and pointed the sandwich at him.

"Oh, I needed access to the Oasis mainframe. And try as I might, I couldn't figure out any other way to get access. I have to hand it to you. Your security is top-notch."

Mads wiped her sleeve across her mouth and took another bite.

Flowers slumped into the chair and frowned.

"But, why, Mads. Why?"

"That's always the question, isn't it? Why."

She finished off the sandwich, glanced at the screen on the workstation, and nodded to herself. Three steps took her to the edge of the workstation where she leaned against it and looked down at Flowers.

"About a decade ago, Everlearn discovered that my colony was sitting on one of the richest deposits of hapicite in the quadrant. And do you know what they did?"

Flowers opened his mouth but Mads shook her head.

"No, no, that's a rhetorical question. Did they negotiate with the colony and enter into an agreement to mine the hapicite for a fair price? Because that would've made us some of the richest people in the galaxy. No. They had their cronies on the Security Council of the Galactic Union redraw a line on the star charts that put my planet Shango outside Union jurisdiction."

The alarm stopped blaring. She leaned back, looked at the screen, glanced at the time, and nodded again, before turning back to Flowers.

"You should be able to guess what happened next. They eradicated my entire colony. My family, friends, and neighbors, all gone in the blink of an eye. They did it from orbit. We never stood a chance."

Her eyes narrowed and her lips pressed into a firm line. Flowers' eyes widened. But she took a deep breath, crossed her arms, and continued.

"I was lucky. I used to love to collect odd or pretty rocks in the hills around our settlement. I'd bring them home and show my mzaa and baba what I'd found. That day my pockets were bulging with rocks and my hands were full."

She looked off at the ceiling—her mind going back to that day.

"Mr. Shadza happened to be in the hills looking for gudba. It was a kind of tuber native to Shango that was delicious when cut up, seasoned, and fried. We watched Everlearn ships turn our colony into a hole in the ground. We hid for days until he was able to get us off planet."

She reached down and twirled the starburst pendant hanging from her neck.

"Here's where things get interesting, Flowers."

The tone of her voice made him push the chair back. It made a short screeching sound as the legs dug into the floor.

"The rocks in my hands and pockets? Almost all of them were raw hapicite ore. It was a fortune. It didn't make me rich. It made me wealthy. Do you know the difference, Flowers?"

She chuckled darkly.

"I set Mr. Shadza up on a planet of his choice. And one day, while bankers buzzed around me in an office, genuflecting and treating me like royalty, while we discussed my assets, a plan began to form in my mind."

She took two quick steps over to Flowers, grabbed his knees, and knelt down in front of him.

"You see, Flowers, when you have the kind of money I have, you can do almost anything you want. And what I wanted was revenge. And let me be clear—I didn't give a drec about justice. I wanted revenge. Do you know what Shango means, Flowers? It's the name of an ancient Old Earth god. It means the Bringer of Thunder."

She loosened her grip on his knees and stood up.

Flowers yelped, "But, what you're talking about, it's impossible."

Mads cackled.

"You're almost right, Flowers. Not impossible, but improbable. It would take years of planning, preparation, training, and a lot of money."

She leaned in until she was nose to nose with him and said, "Don't ever drec with someone who has all the time in the universe and more money than god."

The soft hum of the mainframe went quiet. It was almost anticlimactic.

Mads straightened and said, "That's it. Your mainframe is dead. Your backups are fried. The message I sent while uploading the virus took care of your off-site storage facility. There'll be nothing more than a crater left where it used to stand. The pirates I hired had instructions to give the technicians enough time to evacuate before they began their bombardment."

She patted him on the head.

"I know you had this vision of me being your salvation. That I'd fall for you and help lift you out of your doldrums and mediocrity. But this isn't your story, Flowers. It's mine."

Without another word, she turned and headed for the doorway.

"You won't make it out of here! Security will stop you!"

Mads left him whining in his chair. His code opened the massive door. Under normal circumstances, a contingent of guards would have likely been waiting on the other side of it, but they were busy dealing with the bonded. She paid off every bond in the facility and timed the payments to hit their accounts that morning. Every bonded person's bracelet had deactivated and fallen off at the exact same time. Chaos had ensued.

She followed the twists and turns of the hallways she'd memorized back to her quarters. A few taps of the buttons next to her door opened it. Inside she found the clothes she'd paid the woman servicing her room to smuggle in, along with the sword.

Even the servants couldn't smuggle in an energy weapon. But a length of metal? That was doable. Telling her she *wasn't a morning person* was the agreed-upon code to set things in motion.

Mads dressed quickly. The interior of the facility was a madhouse but getting out was still going to be a challenge. The building shook beneath her feet and the alarms began blaring again.

Good, she thought.

Pay enough and the bonded who worked in and around the power plant would make things explode. Her *clothes* were actually made from tactical fiber. Her blue top was a reinforced jacket with a chest plate made from hundreds of tiny, silver, flexible plates.

The pants and hooded cape were also blue, trimmed in the same silver plates. Her brown boots were heavy leather with reinforced toes. She pulled the hood up over her head and unsheathed the sword. It was time to go.

She'd used the same trick on her way in that got her back to her quarters. She ran through the hallways back to the entrance. A squad of guards were holding the entrance against bonded trying to leave. Just as Mads rounded the corner a second squad showed up to reinforce them. The floor shook again. It nearly took her off her feet.

A third squad appeared behind her. The sound of her mzaa's voice echoed in Mads mind. It was from an Old Earth book by one of her mzaa's favorite writers—an ancestor named Zora Neale Hurston—called *Dust Tracks on a Road.*

I have been in Sorrow's kitchen and licked out all the pots. Then I have stood on the peaky mountain wrapped in rainbows, with a harp and sword in my hands.

Mads screamed and charged. It was all a blur. Her programmable teachers had done their job well. They had blasters and shock sticks. She danced among them with a sword. The cutting-edge tactical fiber and plate shielding woven into her clothes repelled the handful of bolts and shocks that would have rendered her unconscious. The guards' ballistic uniforms did not save them from her alloy blade.

At some point, the bonded picked up dropped blasters and shock sticks. They joined in with years of built-up enmity coursing through their hot blood. It was a rout. When her eyes cleared and her rage died down, she was standing outside under a perfectly programmed blue sky, bathed in golden sunlight.

The freed bondsmen and bondswomen passed her. She felt their hands patting her on the shoulder and back. The shuttles Mads had hired on Caliban, for this very moment, were landing and taking off, full of the freed. Behind her, Everlearn burned.

She pulled the com-device that had been snuck in with her clothes from a pocket and entered a code. She watched the ship she'd hidden in orbit on the other side of Caliban streak through the sky and descend into the atmosphere on autopilot.

It was a high-end, intrepid class, system hopper. It was sleek, fast, and armed to the teeth. If the facility hadn't been taken offline it would've been blown out of the sky on approach. She was already walking toward it as it landed on the manicured grass.

It wasn't until she was back in orbit that she realized she had no idea where to go. Taking out Everlearn had consumed her entire life. It was all she'd thought about. Even her dreams had been about the destruction of the company that had taken so much from her. Now that it was over, she was stunned.

The ship's com chirped. Mads opened the channel without even thinking about it.

"Uh, ma'am. This is Chanda on the shuttle Ozymandias. We all just wanted to thank you for paying off our bonds. You'll never know how much this means to us."

Mads cleared her throat and said, "It was my pleasure, Chanda. Thank everyone for me. I couldn't have done this without you."

"Yes, ma'am. You're welcome."

"What are you going to do with your freedom, Chanda?"

The com channel fell quiet for a moment.

Then Chanda said, "I've got a brother who is bonded to the mining company, Broken Earth Proprietary Group. They mine all over the Galactic Union. I hope he's still alive."

Mads called up BEP's records on her computer. It took all of ten seconds to see how predatory the company was—the environmental devastation it left in its wake. A few more seconds and she saw the list of complaints filed with the GU by bonded working its minefields. She leaned back and stared out the front port of her ship at the shuttle moving slowly out of orbit.

"Hey, Chanda." Mads tilted her head from side to side. Her neck made a soft cracking sound.

"How would you like some company?"

Third World
by
Glenn Parris

1978

The classic 1970's music barely registers on Rudy as he sprints down the alleyways of South-central Los Angeles. The backyard barbeques are almost in sync with Marvin Gaye's smooth vocals and Motown horns. Rudy takes one fence after another like hurdles at the Olympics. If anyone bothered to keep time, he'd have been hailed as a world-class, record-breaking track star. The picnickers were otherwise occupied and the police were too busy sweating like pigs trying to catch the fourteen-year-old boy streaking between houses in marshmallow white sneakers. In another world, Adidas, Nike, or Converse would have paid him big money for such a show wearing their brands. But these shoes weren't paid for. Rudy knew it, the police knew it, and the shopkeeper, whose aim nearly sent the boy to heaven sure as hell knew it.

The older cop just ran out of gas. He knelt, gasping as he watched with grudging admiration for the skinny kid's stamina and speed: Steady pace, great technique taking his time clearing one fence after another without missing a beat of his rhythm or stride. The old, but seasoned officer closed his eyes and imagined the layout of the neighborhood. Breathless, he called in the situation and instructed his peers to head the local speedster off at Hobart. The sportswear store he shoplifted the kicks perched at the corner of Wilshire and Western. He made better time than the patrol car on that stolen skateboard for over a mile before he took to the narrow alleys. He knew he could beat those chubby white cops in a foot chase.

Rudy didn't understand grids. South Central LA was just a maze of streets and alleys to him. He was being corralled and cornered. When he emerged from the last narrow alley into the schoolyard basketball court, they had him.

"Freeze, ya lil' bastard!" The young rookie had been bested by the kid, who looked around frantically at the audience of LA's finest all pointing service revolvers at him.

Rudy's eyes bulged, his mouth gaped, and the crotch of his tan pants turned a darker shade of brown as he raised his hands and pled; "Okay, okay. Don't shoot. I give. I give!" he shouted.

The old cop had a chance to catch his breath in the patrol car that picked him up two blocks away from where he had nearly collapsed in exhaustion.

"What's your name kid?" the balding sergeant asked.

"Rudy, Rudy Walker."

"Put your hands behind your head, Rudy. I'm Sergeant Woods. You wear those sneakers like they were made for you. But they weren't made for you. You gotta pay for everything you get in this world, kid. You're under arrest. The charge is theft by taking. You have the right to remain silent. Anything you say can be used against you in a court of law."

Rudy didn't hear a thing the police officer said, above his own deafening bawling.

"Mama's gonna kill me!"

* * *

Rudy read the letter for a fourth time. "Be at peace. Ellen is with your long, departed father in the Mansions of Heaven." Mama had gone home. His younger sister scribbled on the program he received, "Wish you could be here." He looked up at the peaceful calm of a crystal sky. Only puffs of white plumes, here and there, littered the blue setting.

Rudy had been in the system for 25 years. He would celebrate his fortieth birthday next week. *First one without Mama.* The guards had stopped harassing him over a decade ago. No jeering, facing him down for looking them in the eye, no more jokes about his manhood. After over ten years of implicit rebellion, they had broken him. He had essentially become invisible.

Spacefunk!

He took an assignment to develop an inmate-run vegetable garden. He tended the produce and the soil that grew it. Responsible for the fertilizer and irrigation, Rudy contented himself with what the prison administration viewed as harmless pursuits. In more recent years, he began studying horticulture, experimenting with cross-pollination of fruits and vegetables. He had long ago lost interest in the outside world. It was as real to him as ancient Rome, the Land of Oz, or Atlantis. The clipping of his mother's obituary had newsprint on the back of the page. He turned it over absently in his hand as he let his mind reminisce on better days as a child. His brow knitted as he read the copy.

"Rekindling of space exploration follows commercialization of flight. Artificial Intelligence accelerates unmanned extraterrestrial interplanetary vehicle development. Stunning new technologies engineer ships that can accelerate to a significant fraction of the constant, C, the speed of light. Humans can't survive such intense acceleration, putting off the lofty notion of man traveling at hyperlight speed, colloquially called 'Warp' speed to other planets indefinitely." The article ended.

For the first time, Rudy found himself interested in the byline and first part of the article. An article not about the "outside" world of laws and injustice, but the real and imagined worlds beyond and without end. Where, in his mind, his parents lived forever in paradise. Rudy began to expand his library reading to extraterrestrial engineering, if not astrophysics, which he could not understand. He could imagine space station construction, inter-planetary cargo management and payload calculations. Rudy took full advantage of his prison education benefits even as he endured the jeers of fellow inmates mocking his interest in outer space.

"You better focus on inner space, bruh. 'Cuz you ain't goin' nowhere outside these walls. Ever!"

Somehow breaking a man's dreams grounded his fellow inmates. Made the fact of 'permanence' of their situation more tolerable. Dreams are dangerous for the damned. And yet, change is inevitable.

"Did you hear?" Trevor asked, "They cuttin' the budget again. Market's crashin'."

311

Desmond added, "And we the first to feel the bleed. You know they gonna cut what few 'amenities' we gets. No computer time. No fertilizer for you, homes."

Trevor had to pile on. "Yeah, and the only irrigation you gonna have for your babies is rainwater. Good luck with that out here in the desert southwest."

Rudy's heart sank. His "boys," satisfied with the broken spirit they had accomplished, hunkered down for institutional austerity to come with the new administration in Washington. Rudy did what he could with his knowledge of farming. He proposed a plan to ship refuse from the local septic tanks to the prison garden as fertilizer and irrigation once a week. The guards objected to the odor it would likely disperse over the facility until Rudy pointed out the airflow would go from west to east, bypassing all the guard stations and mostly affecting the prisoners' quarters when the wind was still. The board approved the budget saving proposal unanimously. The yield was noteworthy for the healthy nature of the produce and the low cost of the crop. In fact, the administration shared Rudy's process with local farmers. The county agent also took note and passed it along to another interested government agency.

* * *

Two men convened in a government Sensitive Compartment Information Facility conference room safely nestled in a Northern Virginia suburb. A third man entered and sealed the door behind him.

"We are now secure, sir."

"NASA's Trailblazer partnership with private industry can finally get us into space to build a US shipyard on the moon. Once there, we're in business gentlemen!" The Secretary of Defense intoned. "The previous administration hatched a pilot project to terraform planets in the nearby star systems, ones within ten lightyears of Earth. They just couldn't appropriate enough funds to get it off the ground." Muted laughter at the pun. "With our own Moon base, we have what we need for a sustainable port to launch more capable craft and freighters into deep space and beyond." He nodded the yield of the floor. "Dr. Schafer."

As the secretary uttered the name, the third man at the table coughed violently, then advised the other two. "I think we should maintain anonymity."

"Anonymity? We're in a SCIF!"

"And we're being recorded." The third man insisted, glancing up at a small black dome in the ceiling. "We use numbers."

The Secretary of Defense nodded. "Continue, Number 2."

"Okay. With heavy equipment transported to the surface of the moon rather than the ISS, we can excavate raw minerals to manufacture synthetic building materials and solar collectors one thousand times more efficient than what we currently have on Earth."

"Come on, a thousand times more efficient?" The chairperson of the House Ways and Means committee protested. "We're not a gullible public who will buy any technical double talk. You really mean 2-3 times the efficiency, don't you?"

"No, sir. I mean a thousand times more efficient. Remember, our technology is limited by potential toxic effects to our environment here on Earth. Pollutants from band technology can be harmlessly vented into the non-existent lunar atmosphere, even radioactive waste. We can extract common and plentiful rare metals from the lunar surface and the accumulated gravel pile of asteroids that have hit the moon over the last four billion years. Manufacture will be dirt cheap as the low gravity places less wear and tear on producer machinery and transportation requires less energy, which by the way will be almost free up there."

Number 3 added, "We can populate the installations with engineers and technicians just begging to go to space, especially with a few extra shekels in their pockets. All these educated, immigrant elites can have a place to really live out the American dream."

"What about low brow labor?" Number 1 asked. "We can't ship all these illegals out there. The liberals will lose their shi... their stuff if we do that."

Number 2. "The near-light speed transport would first be tried on tools, machinery and building materials. Phase one, already in progress, launched a booster ship which will take up orbit around Proxima Centauri. There it will collect solar energy from the red star for decades before the next phase can rendezvous and repower the cargo ship for the trip to the Earth-like exoplanet orbiting Alpha Centauri A."

Number 3 explained, "The second ship will be loaded with pods containing Earth compatible biomass to enrich the distant star's exoplanet orbiting the star in the Goldilocks zone. All data suggests that the gravitational pull is within 1% plus minus Earth's gravity. The average planetary temperature appears to be between 20 and 40 degrees Celsius. There're no oceans but there are a bunch of large, liquid seas or lakes. We know it's probably not turnkey for human habitation, but with a little tweaking, it can be. We can rough it in with automated unmanned ships but to be sure, we need a human touch. The first people on Alpha Centauri Prime are gonna die, soon and badly."

"We can keep this quiet." Number 1 said.

"Of course, sir. Find South Asian engineers, scientists, and a few doctors; two surgeons and three family doctors. Supplement the medical team with six Filipino registered nurses. Offer a sum just enough to keep them very quiet and a solid NDA to convince them that we can claw it back if they break silence."

Number 3. "How many technicians do you want?"

"What?" Said Number 1.

"Engineers, mechanics and technicians, sir." Number 2 explained.

"I dunno. Maybe twenty or so." Number 3 answered.

"Look, we're talking about settling a whole planet. We need numbers," Number 2 said. "Maybe a thousand. Maybe twice that to be sure. We're likely to lose some in transit. One more thing," he said thoughtfully. "We need to be sure humans can breed out there. Both fertile men and women. If not, we're jacked."

Number 1 asked, "Okay, so where do you suppose we're going to get that many lost souls."

"Where else do we get disposable people?" Number 3 shrugged. "Prison."

Spacefunk!

* * *

Rudy found himself surrounded by adults in blue gray work
suits, better quality than the orange jump suits he had worn for
the last 25 years. And pockets! He hadn't had clothes with pockets since he was a kid. He massaged his thighs up and down
through those pockets with erotic pleasure. He bounced down
the hall in the lunar gravity of the newly completed Moon base
Delta. Everything looked institutional, but new, clean, and welcoming. Despite the confines of the atmospheric dome, there
was a special kind of freedom about the place that he never felt
even in the open yard of the prison. The PSA droning in a loop
ended and a live voice demanded attention of all personnel.
Rudy drew his hands out of his sensuous new pockets and steadied himself beside his two friends.

"Welcome Stellarnauts! We are so happy to send you on the
maiden voyage of the Trailblazer III. You are about to make history the first human beings to colonize a distant planet. Even the
exploration of Mars will prove mundane by comparison."

"What do 'mundane' mean?" Trevor asked.

"Boy, don't you read?" Desmond hopped absently floating
one foot to the other. "For 15 years you ain't had nothin' to do
but read. Would it kill you to pick up a book?"

"You still didn't tell me what it means, Know-It-All."

"It means, down to Earth."

Trevor looked at Desmond sidelong. "Then it doesn't really
apply, does it?"

All three men chuckled as the instructional final announcement continued.

"They pairin' us up like we goin' out on Noah's Ark." Desmond pointed to the women crowded across the hanger in equal
number to the men. An officer distributed a box of amulets the
size of a quarter.

"Each of you will have a digital manual with holographic
compendium of all the technical specifications of every piece of
equipment on the ship and at your destination. You can interface
with it by keyboard, touch, or voice recognition. We designed
the power source to last forever."

Rudy scratched his head. "If we going for 10 years, why so many women?"

"'Cause we're not coming back." Desmond said under his breath.

"Huh?" Trevor and Rudy said in unison.

"This is a one-way trip." Desmond explained sotto voce. "Communication devices that last forever. A bunch of foreigners and inmates. Family comp. Parole. A woman for every man. We're all breeding stock."

Rudy craned around Desmond to search Trevor's façade as the man in the middle concluded. "We been bought and sold. And away we go."

* * *

The ship was impressive. Launched from the far side of the moon, the tremendous craft accommodated 2,500 people, fifty tons of cargo, and twenty tons of well-preserved food rations. The traditional oxygen/hydrogen mixture burned to get Trailblazer III past the meteor belt where it rendezvoused with the Virgin freighter to fill with the new nuclear fuel compound banned in near Earth space for its toxicity. Herein lay the secret of high, sub-light speed. The engineers calculated acceleration at 1 G. It was healthier. The women had four-year progesterone implants for contraception. The men were given handheld gel tubes with sealable receptacles to capture semen. Medical stored it for future use and selective breeding options as proposed by Space Force family planning department. The unmanned missions' velocities were pushed close to 25% of C, the speed of light constant. Based on the success of Trailblazer I and II, the astrophysicists anticipated maximal safe speed for Trailblazer III should be limited to 10% of the speed of light. What would that do to human physiology? To reproductive organs? No one really knew.

"This trip is going to give Einstein's theories a real stress test." Dr. Gupta mused as they closed in on the Kuiper belt.

Dr. Shah responded with similar scientific small talk. "Unlike back on moon base, we're enjoying normal weight for the first

316

time in months. I kind of liked the instant weight loss.," she said.

"Huh, you look good to me at any weight." Gupta said in a hushed romantic tone. "I think I'm actually looking forward to your weight on top of—" Gupta turned, sensing a new presence. "Can we help you with something crewman?" Clearly annoyed at the intrusion, both Gupta and Shah scowled.

"Just heading towards the cafeteria." Rudy said. "My shift ended an hour ago, but there was some more work to be done so I stayed to help. I'm famished now!"

"Are you angling for another ration, crewman? Gupta accused.

"I've earned another ration, doctor. I'm underweight and done more than my quota of work for the week." He kept eye contact as he passed them en route to the food court.

"I don't know how we're supposed to control that lot. We don't even have any defensive weapons."

"I wouldn't worry about it. They conditioned them to respect the chain of command. They need us for survival, and they know it." Gupta squeezed Shah's hand lightly, "We'll be alright."

* * *

Trailblazer III reached optimal speed 7 months out from the freighter encounter. Clear of the Kuiper belt, they cruised through outer space at one tenth the speed of light. It felt normal. It would take 40 years to reach Proxima Centauri for refueling and supplies. Time dilation would cut the experience of 40 years down to four. The crew had paired off mostly. Some men had two or three women. Some women entertained other women or several men, but those were the exceptions, not the rules.

The next leg of the voyage to Alpha Centauri Prime would be a matter of just a few months. By now, there should be 50 years of healthy loam enriched with compost sent on Trailblazer II. Twenty percent of the embryonic livestock stores should have been hatched from pseudo egg hibernation and grazing on the planet already, hopefully reproducing. No predators were released. Embryonic cats and dogs were sealed in a separate section of the ship. The DNA sequences for all species, including humans, were stored in the information system of Trailblazer III along with four 3D printers and twelve CRISPR gene sequencers.

If there were any unexpected mutations, the specimens would be analyzed for the value of the mutation, and preserved if beneficial, better meat quality or increase fertility or unexpected medical purposes. If the more likely scenario of harmful disease or mutation arose, the livestock population on the planet's surface would be sacrificed with a burst of 40% carbon dioxide gas. Animal life would be dead in three days, plant life producing more oxygen from increased CO2.

*   *   *

"Entering orbit in 12 hours. Final storage and security of recently stowed cargo must be completed in 4 hours then secured for shuttle launch." The announcement was meant to be stoic and emotionless and was edged with anxiety. A new world . . .

Rudy and Trevor were assigned to the landing team. Dr. Shah went virtually, ostensibly to operate the analyzing array of equipment as only she was trained to do.

Trevor called bullshit.

"We should have shotguns, Rudy."

"They're just pigs and cows, guys. Nothing dangerous; A few rabbits and chickens. Calm down."

"Have you ever heard of bulls, Dr. Shah?" Rudy asked. "They can be VERY dangerous."

"Point taken. I'll keep watch by telemetry," Dr. Shah promised.

"Very brave Dr. Shah. Lead from behind." In the radio silence, Trevor's sarcasm might have been lost or ignored by the scientist, whom he didn't know.

The landscape was beautiful, rolling fields of green and lavender with low trees of yellow, red, and orange foliage waving in a gentle breeze. From the high ground they beheld vistas of herds of cattle and sounders of pigs clustered around watering holes and droves of pigs and piglets in the distant low country.

The pleasant scenery faded in the minds of Rudy and Trevor as the floral scent merged with the rot of flesh in the wind. Crinkled noses sought out the source of the odor. Rudy needed binoculars to see what he thought must have been an illusion, three rabbits eating the carcass of a dead pig.

"They're tearing it apart," Trevor said stuttering in fear.

"The rabbits have gone carnivorous, Dr. Shah."

"That's impossible. Even with rabies, rabbits can't hunt for animals larger than they are, it's not in their—"

"Shah, if you say DNA, I'll drag you down here and feed you to these bloody bunnies myself."

"Okay guys, don't—"

"And if you say, 'don't panic, I'll bury your body in pig shit," Rudy added.

"Fine, return to the shuttle. We'll see if we can capture one of those rabbits for study."

"Not me!" Trevor said. "I'm not bringing one of those bastards back."

"Not what I was going to say," Shah said calmly. "We'll send a drone for reconnaissance and collect one of each species we planted here. It may be a more complex development than a mutation in one species."

* * *

Main bio lab, Trailblazer III. Dr. Shah and Gupta recording.

"The rabbits adapted to competition for low-growing grasses and tubers. The pigs were eating everything in sight and without predators, dying of old age and cardiovascular disease. The rabbits just learned to eat carrion. They're not true hunters."

Rudy and Trevor watched from the observation deck. Rudy spoke for both, "They still scared the crap out of us."

"We have to restore order down there, that's all," Gupta said. "Separate their food supplies. The rabbits will go back to eating rabbit food."

"In my experience, once predators get a taste of flesh, they NEVER go back." Trevor said.

"And what exactly do you know about animal husbandry?" Shah asked.

"Grew up on my uncle's farm. Start feeding pigs bacon, and if they get hungry enough, they'll start eating piglets."

Dr. Gupta declared, "I really don't want to sacrifice all these animals. They're our food chain."

"But are we going to be at the top or somewhere in the middle?" Rudy asked.

"Why don't you let us experts handle this, boys?" Gupta said. "We'll straighten it all out."

Trevor turned slowly at the door and repeated, "'Boys'?"

"That's not what I meant." Gupta back tracked. "What I mean is we were sent on this mission to handle exactly this kind of problem. Let us do our jobs."

Both men raised their hands in surrender and backed out of the room.

One week later, the gray suits as the workers came to call, found themselves down on the planet's surface in light armor impenetrable to rabbit teeth gathering all the rabbits they could catch. The rabbits were slow and not as aggressive as originally thought. Once penned up and offered vegetables, they began to revert to eating conventional rabbit food again. The crew rations were sent down to the planet. And their gear and tools and temporary habitats.

"What's up, docs?" Your throwing stuff at us as if we're not coming back."

No answer.

"Doc, what gives?"

Desmond activated his communication amulet. "Please transport us up. Copy?"

Nothing.

After much fearful grumbling, the crew set up shelters and headquarters. There were no doctors, engineers, or scientists on the surface and still no answer from Trailblazer III.

A town hall meeting organized by the senior landing crew laid out their options. Rudy settled the hubbub and spoke to the gathering crowd.

"They're not answering. Some of us anticipated they were sending us out here to force labor out of us, but light years from home, we thought that mutual respect and trust would rule. Looks like we were wrong."

"How long will the rations last?"

"Can we drink the water?"

"When do we get to go home?"

The questions were coming too fast to keep up with.

"'I don't know' is the honest answer." Rudy's response was met with silence. "The only thing that makes sense is for us to do the jobs we signed on for and make the best of future opportunities to negotiate with the senior staff when we can."

"In other words, we're stranded here." Her name tag read Sarah. Rudy hadn't met her yet.

"No, we've been marooned. There's a difference." Desmond said.

"Word games? Now? Really?" Sarah said.

"Goes to intent. 'Stranded' happens by accident. 'Marooned' is on purpose. And it happens to people of color. Check out Gullah Island."

"I knew this was gonna happen," an anonymous voice declared from the crowd.

"Look, we got food, water, shelter and skills. We can make this work." Rudy became the epitome of reason. "Let's take inventory of supplies and equipment and we'll go from there until someone up there starts communicating."

"Oh, they communicating alright. They're makin' themselves very clear." Trevor said.

Grumbling, they all got to work separating and unpacking crates and packages.

"What the living fu—" The expletive died mid throat when the growl of the large feline surged forward and clawed the man. The creature looked like a mountain lion-sized house cat. It seemed to take the measure of the gathering of bipeds and decided on discretion rather than valor. It beat a hasty escape rather than fight.

Several other crates began to rattle with various versions of growls and barks.

"What the hell?" Sarah said.

"I think I know what is going on. There are no predators on this world. Cats are domesticated. Dependent on humans."

"Yeah, well why so big then?" Desmond asked.

"I don't know," Rudy said again. Over the grumbling and whispered fear, he added, "Leave any box that contains a live animal sealed for now. Let's check the rations."

After several hours sorting through the cargo, a stunning realization dawned on the settlers.

"There are NO RATIONS!" Desmond said.

"No food and no weapons? So how are we supposed to survive?" Another voice asked.

"Get them on the communicator, Rudy. Do it now." Desmond didn't ask, he demanded.

While Rudy linked his amulet to the communications array, anther disturbing question came up: "How cold is it going to get here? Does anyone even know if this is summer or winter? What if this is as cool as it's going to get? What if it gets blazing hot in a few months... or weeks!"

"Plymouth1 to Trailblazer III, I repeat Plymouth 1 to Trailblaz—"

"You've gotta be kiddin.' They callin' us 'Plymouth 1'?"

Rudy shot Sarah a glare and resumed his transmission.

"Trailblazer III to Plymouth 1, what's your situation?" Shah's voice was calm as if responding to a routine check in.

"What's our situation? Our situation is that we're stuck down here without rations and a half assed cache of supplies, a zoo full of carnivores and no weapons to defend ourselves."

"They're just cats and dogs, with a little hormonal manipulation, I promise you."

"Forgive us if we don't embrace your promises, Shah."

"We want to see how they fit into the ecosystem. They'll only be that big for one generation. Their progeny will be normal cats and dogs."

"Where are our rations?" Trevor screamed.

"You won't need them. Look at all the livestock you have!
You settlers are going to start the first farm communities.
You're pioneer heroes. Be proud!" Gupta chimed in. "We're the
ones who need the boring rations. We don't have all that fresh
air and farm animals to feast on."

"If I ever get in punching distance, I'll kick your butt all the
way back to——."

"Trailblazer III out."

Then there was silence for a long time.

*   *   *

"Okay, we made a couple of thousand friends down there,
didn't we?" Dr. Xiong said. "Look, my people are Mung.
Treated like gypsies by all of Asia. What you just did to them
isn't right. It's that same old imperialistic crap that been going
on for centuries now on a whole new world to the same victims
as before."

"We have our orders, Xiong," Gupta said. "They may be surprised, but they aren't helpless, you know. Rudy may not have a
formal education but he's as smart as any university-trained
county agent on Earth. They have a doctor and two nurses, medical supplies and an infinite library and tools. Better than our
own ancestors had settling any part of our home world. And
we'll help them when they really need it."

"Oh, you mean like gods?" Xiong asked. "We'll watch from
heaven here and intervene when our puppets get in trouble down
there?"

"They'll get used to the environment and we'll join them in a
few years when we've studied the long-term ramifications of interstellar travel and adaptation to a new world. They'll need a
more sophisticated government then and we can step up for
them."

"Did it ever occur to any of you that we are more vulnerable
than they are?" Xiong hiked her thumb towards the planet.
"We're only fifty people up here and half of us are over fifty.
Non-child-bearing age. The Space Force Administration doesn't

think any more of us than it does of them. By the time Earth comes to take over the settlement with a military escort, we'll be elderly or dead. Our legacy will be the data we preserve as 'overseers of the lower caste."

Xiong hoped the mention of caste would hit home.

"We've got a problem." Technician Smith announced. "Long range telemetry shows perigee with Alpha Centauri A, B and C in 6 months. The radiation is expected to be off the charts compared with what we've seen so far. Mr. Begosian says we're in for a rough ride up here."

"What about the settlers?" Gupta asked.

"They'll do best in more substantial shelters like caves or fortified buildings. We better warn them. We need an updated inventory of our provisions."

Two hours later, Smith returned breathless, "Half the reserve grain is gone, the lambs are missing and we're missing a 3D printer."

* * *

Fifty years later...

The cresting radiation had taken its toll on the orbiting Trailblazer III. There was so much interstellar matter, the Centauri system proved to be an electromagnetic storm haven. Half the remaining technical crew had defected to the planet and joined the settlers. A few became outsiders, marauding the roads between towns with wild cats and makeshift guns for provisions. The population had tripled every twenty years even with losses to disease, armed raids, and farm accidents. Rudy was elected King for life. As his 98th birthday loomed, he prepared to abdicate regardless of the common opinion that no one could match his wisdom or ingenuity.

Cattle, sheep, pigs, and even rabbits were used for meat, textiles, furs, and feces for fertilizer and explosives. Tadpoles and fish eggs were hit or miss at first, yielding just a few varieties of fish and frogs. Frogs and chickens were genetically cross bred for a variety of poultry-like flesh. The fungi and molds provided biochemical substrates for antibiotics and fortification of simple pines into amazing hardwood for building material.

The absence of insects limited natural cross-pollination and aeration of the soil. Technology filled the gap of unnatural selection. Rudy had even developed a kind of bamboo from the local grasses.

The 3D printer created producer equipment for manufacturing all kinds of small useful products. The amulets still provided access to the massive database provided by mission control. Weapons were carefully designed, mostly non-lethal but with the renegades experimenting on feral cats and dogs, sometimes deadly force was needed. Finally, the road pirates were largely brought into the fold as enforcers under tight control by the central government representing seven towns.

"Anything…" Dr. Shah's question had been ignored for years and had long ago become the joke of Trailblazer III. No one answered her.

With Dr. Gupta, long dead, Shah was alone socially and philosophically.

"Anetha, we've followed you all these years. We still believe in you, but we have to make peace with the settlers. That CO2 blast 30 years ago really poisoned the relationship. Some of them will never trust us now." At 65 years old, Harper was the youngest remaining member of the original crew. There were ten progenies still on board, the youngest, 32-year-old and by all tests, sterile.

"We 'Stellarnauts' relics will be extinct in 30 years. A bunch of floating fossils if we don't join forces with the settlers." Harper wrung his hands as he spoke.

Anetha Shah hung her head and activated the communications device. Rudy, even at ninety-eight, five years her senior, had few wrinkles under thinning snow-white hair and a smile that lit up a room.

"Good morning, Anetha. How are you?" He did sincerity well.

"Rudy, we need to talk."

Negotiations began back and forth for weeks, but finally ended the only way they could. Dr. Anetha Shah surrendered

Trailblazer III with no conditions other than that there be no prosecution for her or any of her crew. Rudy conceded the request without grudge or prejudice. His technicians had already reverse engineered the drive for the shuttles and had experimental engines and interplanetary crafts under construction.

Once the black and gold guardian thugs and their armored weapon EVA suits surrendered to Rudy's government, he sent personnel up to retrofit the ship with the new engine designs, 3D printers programming upgraded and the Centauri system mapped. The battery ship was still functional and fully charged. So, there was one last common dream between Shah and Rudy Walker. Neither would live to see it through. Rudy Walker III was forty-five, physically fit, fully trained in astrophysics, engineering, medicine and well versed in politics.

His grandfather's final wish; Find Earth. References to its location were all made from Earth to the red star, Proxima Centauri in 2025. The data was corrupted. Time/space dilation that the Stellarnauts experienced at near light speed would amount to a 600-year difference relative to Earth if they ever got back. Scientists believed that using astronomical data collected from all three Trailblazer computer algorithms could lead an expedition back to Earth. More people, more technology. More genetic diversity. Connection to a lost history. The voyage was the talk of every town.

Rudy III declined to run for his grandfather's position as king. All the mayors begged him, but he wanted to see Earth, ancestral home to every settler on the planet, unanimously christened, Promise. He would be ambassador from the new world to the old. Commander of the Pathfinder, as the renovated Trailblazer had been renamed.

A crew of five hundred sociologists, linguists, engineers, and scientists set off to the distant star at the end of the spiral arm. A yellow star just a bit smaller than Alpha Centauri A. The third world from that sun. Home.

Pathfinder embarked making nearly 50% of light speed. They arrived at the solar system in eight years but only aged two years effective time.

"We're here commander." Navigator Nisha Thomas remained professional but could not hide her excitement. "This is Sol according to our calculations and planetary charts."

"What do we see out there, Thomas?"

She frowned. "A lot of junk, sir."

"Junk? What do you mean junk?"

"Derelict satellites, remnants of primitive interplanetary craft, abandoned space stations… junk!"

"Send a message to the Third World. Maybe they're just sloppy and have a bunch of excess space debris to clean up.

"Message: This is the Promisian ship, Pathfinder. We extend greetings to the people of Earth, our ancestors, and siblings. We would like to establish diplomatic relations with the United Earth gover—"

"Alien space craft, this is Tesla Center One, ruler of Western Earth. You are in a restricted space lane. State your intentions or we will launch weapons."

"Please refrain from hostilities. We were sent to colonize and transform Centauri A Prime, which we've dubbed, Promise One. No one ever came to join us, so we came back. We want to learn from you, grow with you."

"We have no record of such an expedition. If you are rogue spacefarers coming for a handout, we have no resources for refugees. Return to where you come from."

"Scan them, Quinn," Walker ordered the telemetry duty officer.

"The signal is relayed from that fragment of space habitat trailing the moon. The lunar settlement has fewer than forty people on it."

"I don't understand, they were the origin of all our technology, culture, government. Scan the planet."

A shuttle sized rocket launched from the moon and fired a nuclear torpedo. Easily deflected but failed to detonate in the distance.

"Should we board them, Commander? There's a simple airlock."

"We didn't come all this way to start a war but we need to make them understand that we don't want to leech off them, we want a healthy diplomatic and trade relationship. We board them. I'll go myself and take four of the Guardians with us. First officer, I transfer command to you." Walker donned his armored EVA suit and followed the Guardian squad and social scientists to the shuttle. The airlock was worn, the ship scanned as 130 years vintage. Mismatched parts which failed to fit were patched in. Rudy Walker III took note of these things with grim disappointment.

He made his way to the command center where five astronauts floated weightlessly, helmets sealed, armed with percussion long weapons and chemical combustion sidearms.

"Drop your weapons and identify yourselves." The astronaut wore a purple striped EVA suit and three stars on the sleeve.

"We have identified ourselves. We are the interstellar science vessel, Pathfinder."

"The only correlation we have is a prisoner project called Trailblazer. The three ships were reported as lost hundreds of years ago. Meant to be a private expedition to make a prisoner work force develop alternative living and resource colonies to enrich industry, the project had a 13% chance of success. If you are descendants of those inmates, you're all under arrest for theft of US and private property. As ranking representative of both, I am herby commandeering this ship and we'll incarcerate you lot for interrogation."

Walker stared at the man for three seconds before giving the nod to the captain of the Guardian squad. He signaled his men and promptly took a bullet along the helmet that ricocheted off and punctured the hull. The captain and his men quickly disarmed the five Earth men and restrained them.

"Bring them aboard and show them a little civilized hospitality."

"Welcome to the Pathfinder, gentlemen. The former command structure joined us settlers a few years ago and we jointly rebuilt Trailblazer III. It's all in the log and legal. My father was Rudy Walker, one of the Stellarnauts commissioned to colonize the Centauri system."

"Rudy Walker was nothing but a thief and could never legitimately run ANYTHING!" The earth officer stank to high heaven.

"They must live in those suits." Nisha Thomas held her nose as she whispered to Quinn.

"Sir, may I have a word?" Quinn asked.

Walker followed her out of the chamber. The Earthmen marveled at the spacious quarters as they partook of fresh water and warm food rations, humming and ah-ing of the flavors and quality of the victuals.

"Sir, the planet is a post-apocalyptic nightmare. Whole cities in ruins, infrastructure collapsed. Most people who still operate spacecraft are stranded and unable to land on Earth for lack of fuel, or ground-based guidance. Worldwide communications are little more than telegraphs and crystal radio sets. Bioscans show a malnourished starving populace run by a bunch of warlords running competing criminal syndicates. There is no uniformed recognized government anywhere! They're already chattering about auctioning off the Pathfinder to the highest bidder."

Walker squeezed a single tear from his eyes, and said, "I'm just glad Grandpa never lived to see this."

He turned to the Guardian captain and said, "Let them finish their meal, put them back in their filthy turtle suits and get them off my ship. Trade goes two ways. These parasites have nothing to barter with."

"Aye, sir." The captain cracked a wry smile.

"Thomas, count the flatware and have the chamber decontaminated then scrubbed from top to bottom."

"What our next move Commander?" Quinn asked.

"Let's get out of this hell hole. These people have nothing to offer us. Leave them to their own devices."

"Commander's journal. We have returned to the Third world of Sol, known as Earth. The people of the legendary culture have deteriorated, its people descended into savagery and living in squalor. No morals, no ambition, no future. I do not believe they could understand or ever appreciate our civilization or the benefits we offer.

"I recommend that this star system be avoided for the next thousand years. Give the current squatters time to die off and we may begin archeological exploration of 'what was' long ago. The history of this Third World may be of some value one day, but not today.

Rudy Walker, III, Commander Pathfinder, Prince of the first family of Promise I."

End Transmission.

Madame Guillotine
by
Setlhodiane Tlou Thapelo Ramatlhodi

Nafula was the product of a single-parent home. She had been raised by her mother, a strong woman who worked as a mechanic and owned her own shop. Nafula had acquired everything she knew about machines from her. Under her hard calloused hands, she had learned how to put together the nuts and rivets and breathe life into the inanimate metal. By the time she was a teenager, she was already working in her mother's shop to pay her college tuition. There were no free meals in her mother's house; hard work was the bottom line.

Nafula had not intended on getting married or having children, but from the second she had seen Milo she had known he was someone she liked. He was the first boy that she had ever been with. She had been with a number of girls in her life, but boys never interested her. She found them weak and emotionally juvenile, but Milo seemed different. Milo had been a straight-A student since first grade, his mother and father had always prioritized his studies, and consequently, he had never engaged in sports or much of any other physical activity.

He was skinny, well-groomed, and had a smile that could light up a room. She fell in love with him instantly. Even during the early years of their relationship, he had known that he would always play second fiddle to her ambitions. After they made love, she would kiss him on the forehead and go straight back to her books and study until the early hours of the morning. She kept the same focus when she was admitted into the space program; everything else was always secondary.

Ten years she spent working herself to the bone, trying to cope with the physical requirements of the training while also studying rocket science and shuttle design. Only the best of the best made it through the rigorous program, but she was intent on being an astronaut and nothing would get in her way. It was not an easy time for her or for anyone else for that matter. They always started at the break of dawn with a 5-kilometer run with a 15 kg pack, four hundred pushups, and five hundred sit-ups. After their morning training they were subjected to two hours of high velocity conditioning which would get them ready for the g-; force they would have to endure during liftoff. Then it was the theory and practical work and assessments that would go on until the sun went back down in the sky. It was grueling, an exercise of professional torture, unrelenting and unforgiving.

Many of the candidates dropped out after the first month, and some broke under the weight of the work and were dismissed. But not Nafula. She didn't even batter an eyelash. She was not cut from the same cloth as the rest of them. They were weak rich kids with the privilege to dream of orbit without having the stones to follow through. She thought they should have stayed at home; nepotism was more their speed. She graduated top of her class and was the youngest person to ever become a lieutenant. Her peers respected her, and she had a cult-like following within her ranks.

She was a superstar, with engine grease under her fingernails and the smell of rocket fuel in her hair. By the time she became a captain, there was no doubt in anyone's mind that she would take the program to new heights. She was a maverick, a genius when it came to engineering and design, and a born leader with razor-sharp instincts. Her first mission was to the moon to fix a communication satellite, and her team performed the task without incident. She had been to Mars, away from her family for 4 years, doing repairs to the international biodome. She nearly lost her life after a fragment of metal punctured her suit, but through sheer determination, she made it back to base camp before her air supply ran out.

Once she was on a spacewalk, fixing the Pan African Space Station when her tether broke and she was flung into outer space without hope of being saved. But she used her oxygen tank as a makeshift rocket to change her trajectory, eventually making it back to the station to the amazement of the rest of the crew.

On a routine mission to map a possible liquid water crevasse, she brought back a sample that verified that Jupiter's moon Titan could support life, an accolade that she would never live down. She could no longer walk in public without constantly being stared at in wonder and admiration, she was Christ to them, a god on earth, loved and revered. So, she worked, to escape the masses and their constant reverence, she gave herself to it, the program. And there she stayed, committed to the metal, the nuts and bolts which were her oldest friends. She did not go into public anymore, she stayed away from the clamouring applause, from the pedestal that they placed her on, all she wanted was the seat in the cockpit in her shuttle and the roar of the rockets thrusting her back into the great beyond away from the world and all the noise.

So, for now, all she could do was work towards it, her next mission, when she would be reunited with the solace and quiet of the darkness and the glaring sparkling stars that speckled it with light.

She was all every woman wanted to be, strong and adventuring, a hero for all to see and for all time. Held up as the reason that women were the leaders of humankind. The proof that women could not only conquer the earth but the cosmos. Nothing could stand in their way because of her and those like her throughout history.

Although she was not aware of it, Nafula had been conditioned to be the woman she was from an early age. Nafula was a product of the public schooling system and even with her unprestigious primary and secondary education, she knew that women were the stronger and smarter of the species. It was a deep-held global social belief and everybody knew it. Beyond belief, there was science backing the fact, the science she would find out about in her gender studies classes in university. The theory was called "Runaway /Sexual Selection" the premise was that sometime ago, about ten thousand years or so, women began to choose smaller, weaker males as their mates. This preference caused men to grow increasingly diminutive in size and intelligence due to the fact that the larger stronger males could no longer find mates to breed with. Larger, stronger women became the ideal for the men as a result and over time this caused that on average, women were larger and stronger than men. This was also true for their increased bone density, because while men stayed at home and reared the children, the women were out building the world as construction workers, hammering the railroads and powerlines that were hurtling humanity into the future.

They were the scientists and intellectuals, sports celebrities and record holders, the ambitious, driven businesspeople, and the creative and artistic geniuses. Even the most violent criminals were women, making sure that a man never outdid them, not even in notoriety. The most poised were women, the religious leaders, the Pope, and the Dalai Lama.

God was a woman. This was the world that Nafula lived in, her bedtime stories were of the goddesses of Greek mythology; Athena, Artemis, and Hera. Of the queens of Egypt; Nefertiti, Pharaoh Hatshepsut, the Amazons of Ethiopia, and every warlike warrior woman and conqueror from the continent and throughout the world. Before she even had the chance to notice it, she was set on this path, this destiny to the triumphant brass horns of every myth, every story of heroism, and every achievement that was in the annals of human history.

Her blue-collar upbringing only made her more accessible, an easier sacrifice to the cult of pioneering women, so the rest could watch and not have to be obligated to participate.

Only four countries in the world had male presidents and, in some countries, men were not allowed to drive cars or go to school. However, these governments were considered backward in terms of their policies concerning human rights. On the whole, humanity had progressed considerably, it had bases on the Moon, on Mars, on Triton, Titan, Pluto, and Neptune. Humanity was a Type 1 civilization and was using the sun as its main source of energy. Fire had become obsolete around the time that men lost their dominance over women. In ancient Egypt, glass had been used for centuries to magnify the rays of the sun to create heat, power machines and melt iron. The technology had now developed to the point that all of Earth's technological advances were in some way or another powered by the nuclear fusion of the sun. There had been no wars over the last five decades and malnutrition, famine, and poverty had been all but eradicated. The borders of the world had been opened and travel to other countries was cheap and unrestricted. And the advances in science and nutrition had developed to a degree that humans had extended their lives to an average of 120 years. The use of renewable energy instead of unrenewable resources such as coal and oil meant that the architecture of human settlements was in tune with the balance of nature, with many of the cities having designated areas for forests and wildlife. Outside of the cities, the natural world thrived, trees and plants were in abundance and the lush greenery and oceans were teeming with life, from the largest behemoths, the woolly mammoth which had almost been hunted into extinction in the late Stone Age, to the gargantuan blue whales that swam the depths of the ocean all were multitude in number. A civilization on the brink of colonizing the known universe, with satellites and robots scanning the galaxies. There were habitats and laboratories in the deepest trenches of the ocean, communities thriving while their scientists studied the most exotic oceanic discoveries.

She was a product of her time and place, privileged but smart enough to know that a sharp mind and a strong back were the answer to any problem in her life. She loved Milo she did, but she would not be making it to their anniversary dinner that evening. Not now, not this close to the launch date. She knew how much effort he had put into today, all the plans he had made, the gifts he had bought. Regardless of any of this, he had been drowned out, muffled by the frenzied hum of her power tools against the hull of the vessel that was being prepped to travel a million miles into oblivion in just under two weeks.

Nafula and her team had designed, built, and tested the space shuttle and now they had finally been greenlit for lift-off.

They had been married for 20 years now. She remembered when she first saw him on the college campus grounds. She thought he had the grace of a gazelle. He was beautiful, he still was, and as fair as the day that they had met. Nevertheless, she was more in love with the stars than she could ever be with any man. Looking at an old picture had reminded her of their teenage daughter Nekesa who had grown distant during the previous year. Nairobi was not the type of city to let one's children fend for themselves. She resented her parents for not being there enough, her father stuck as a personal assistant at the mayoral office, and her mother working hour shifts for the Kenyan space program, only coming home to pass out on her bed and lay there until the next day. They struggled to look at her, to take their eyes off their phones for long enough to see what was wrong. The child they had once thought was the most important thing in their lives was now invisible considering the overwhelming obligations that they had to the state. They had been happy once as a family, but it was not long enough ago for Nekesa to have forgotten. Not long enough to have forgotten the walks in the park holding her parents' hands, or the way they would look at her with pride over the dinner table. They had lost each other to life and the pursuit of success, to ambition. If only she knew how much her parents cared, how much they loved her, and how she occupied the center of their beings, but like the sun, one only takes notice when we can no longer feel its warmth.

It had been three years of her father working at the office of the mayor, three years of him no longer being a stay-at-home father and pursuing his career as an administrator. They had missed every hockey match she had played in over that time, every concert recital she had so painstakingly practiced for on her cello until her fingers bled. So, this was no different, helping her father set up the table and decorations for a dinner that would never happen.

Becoming an engineer and an astronaut was no easy task, not even for a woman. Nafula worked her whole life towards achieving her dreams, and she was sure that her husband and daughter would understand. Even if they didn't, the most important thing to her would always be the mission. In a few weeks Nafula would be back in the womb-like embrace of space, the only place she truly really felt at home. The space program demanded that all astronauts be qualified engineers and helped with the building of the space shuttles that they would be traveling in, so that if anything went wrong during the mission, they had the capacity to fix it without aid. This particular mission was classified, and even after the brief, the team was having trouble understanding what they were actually signing themselves up for. All that was disclosed to them was that they would be investigating a distress signal emanating from the alpha quadrant next to Neptune and that they were to retrieve whatever was sending that signal.

When Nafula asked what the satellite cameras had seen regarding the object, she was told that it was unclear. That was the reason her team was going to investigate. The day of the launch was like any other Wednesday, unremarkable. Nafula sat at her control panel ready to type in the code that would send her rocket ship crashing through the stratosphere and into space. She closed her eyes as the explosion boomed behind her and then . . . silence. It was a perfect launch. After a few hours, the secondary rocket systems kicked in. They were much smaller than the primary rockets and were designed primarily to propel the shuttle through space. It would be a month before they reached the coordinates of the signal.

Floating there in the darkness was a figure, the figure of a person. As they got closer, they realized that the person was another astronaut. They retrieved the body as quickly as they could, but it was clear that the floating astronaut had obviously been dead for some time. When they removed the helmet they found a man inside, to their surprise. The distress signal had been emitted by a transponder on the man's chest. It was a design that the team was not familiar with. Nafula was reticent on the ride back home, the quiet of space no longer comforting her, her mind racing with a million questions about the strange dead man that they had found. He was still frozen solid, in the freezer room, his eyes glinting as the light from the florescent bulbs shone on his cracked, grimacing face. The rest of the crew seemed not to care about the new grim passenger that they had stored in their cold room, behind the frozen blueberry sashays, but Nafula could not get her thoughts off who he might be and where he was from. She could not understand how the rest of her colleagues were so unfazed.

The crew consisted of three other women including Nafula, all of them Kenyan citizens. Shani was Nafula's second in command, she had been on nearly as many missions as her captain but was not nearly as confident. She was a bit of an introvert and specialized in medicine and healthcare. Winda was the crew's safety officer; she was a third Dan black belt in Shotokan karate and had fought her way through her tuition as a bouncer at a seedy nightclub in Nairobi. Nia was the freshman. This was her first mission. She was a mathematical genius and had graduated from her doctorate program at sixteen. All of them were inquisitive, intelligent women, and that was why Nafula could not understand their uninterested attitudes. The space flight had taken a lot out of them, but this was no reason for them to be so unresponsive in the face of the mystery that they were now carrying back to Earth. There was a sinking feeling in Nafula's stomach, a feeling that she had never felt before like something menacing was taking place.

The next day while Nafula was making a smoothie in the mess hall she heard a strange crackling coming from the freezer. She walked slowly to the freezer door and stood there quietly for a minute, listening. After some time, the crackling started again, louder this time. Nafula wrenched the door open and stared inside but was met with the silence of the cavernous room and her breath exhaling in terror. She slammed the door shut and went to

her quarters where she stayed until the rest of the crew woke up.
"

Has anyone heard any strange noises coming out of the freezer?" asked Nafula, panning the team's faces for any sign of affirmation.

"I heard something, a crackling sound," responded Nia.

"Does that strike anyone as odd?" inquired Nafula.

"Not as odd as finding some random man floating in space. Besides it's probably just that device on his chest. How else would he be emitting that distress signal," replied Shani.

"Where do you think that signal is being transmitted from?" inquired Nafula.

"Well, judging from the battery cell that powers his transponder, the Middle Ages. Nobody uses lithium batteries anymore," retorted Winda with a smirk that made the rest of the women break out into laughter. Just then a loud crackling noise interrupted their conversation. It came from the freezer. As soon as they opened the door, they could hear the little radio on the dead man's chest popping and hissing, and then something strange happened; it began to speak.

"What language is that?" enquired Nafula after a few seconds.

"It's German," Shani said. "The signal is being broadcast from an army base. My German is rusty, but it sounds like it's coming from a group that calls itself the National Socialist German Workers Party," continued Shani in astonishment.

"I've never heard of them," responded Winda before the transmission was cut off abruptly. The following day Nafula contacted the German authorities to see if any of their astronauts had gone missing. To her shock, she was informed that there had only ever been seven male German astronauts in the German Space Program and that this man was definitely not one of them. They had also informed her that they had never heard of the National Socialist German Workers Party. This was not the answer that Nafula wanted to hear, it only increased the feeling that something terribly wrong was going on. The rest of the crew was also unsettled by what had happened the day before.

The next few days were increasingly tense; the women had become jittery with uncertainty. The transponder had not relayed any signal since the last incident and the team was pensively waiting for what would happen next. The corpse was still in the freezer, frozen stiff in the corner of the cold, dark room. It was not possible to unclip the radio device without taking off its suit since the whole system including the power source were embedded into it. None of the situations they had found themselves in seemed to make any sense. Nothing seemed to add up, and the idea of their freezer being a makeshift morgue did not sit well with any of them. Winda suggested that they open the hatch and let the dead man float back into space. But Nafula explained that they would be court martialed if they went against the mission's directives. And in any case, there was no way they were going to do anything of the sort until they got to the bottom of what was going on.

A week passed and the crew began to put the incident out of their minds. The normal maintenance routines of a spacecraft kept them busy and began to settle upon them. One day while Nia was about to make herself some breakfast, the crackling sounds from the freezer echoed into the mess hall, this time even louder than before.

"Mayday, mayday," the broadcast began. "Gibson, do you read us!" The women were astonished at the clarity and volume of the transmission. The team gathered around the frozen corpse; their breaths visibly uneasy in the cold room.

"Gibson, if you can hear us please answer. We thought the worst had happened!" The speaker on the other side stopped for a minute, his anxiety teetering off a ledge.

"This is The Queen of Sheba, Starship 788 of the Kenyan National Space Program. Who is hailing us?" The words came robotically out of Nafula's mouth.

"Where is Gibson?" the speaker on the other end responded offhandedly.

"If you are referring to the dead astronaut we are transporting on our ship, well, he is on the floor in our freezer." They could hear the person on the other side burst into tears. He then composed himself.

"Who are you and how are you in space?" he continued.

"We work for the biggest space exploration program on the planet," Nafula responded in an obvious tone.

"But Kenya doesn't have a space program," the man responded in bewilderment.

"This is a ridiculous conversation. Who are you and what do you want?" scoffed Nafula.

"I . . . I am Professor Gregory Lindon, from the National Aeronautics and Space Administration," Professor Gregory replied.

"And who was the German man who contacted us before you?" asked Nafula.

"The Nazis intercepted our signal, we only recently regained control of this frequency," responded the professor.

"Why do we have your dead man, on our ship?" asked Nafula coldly.

"I guess I'm just going to have to trust you. We here at NASA have been working on a top-secret project to launch a man into outer space to detonate a nuclear device, in a show of strength so that we can end World War 2. The dead man you have on your ship was to our knowledge the first person to go beyond the earth's atmosphere. He was carrying an incredible nuclear device on his ship which he was supposed to detonate while in orbit. The Axis Powers would see the power of the weapon and have no choice but to surrender. But when Gibson turned the machine on, it accelerated the particles instead of splitting them. The last thing Gibson relayed to us was that he was witnessing an anomaly. Then he disappeared along with the device and the spacecraft. It's been seven weeks since we have had any contact with him, and then a few days ago we started hearing the Germans, then you." There was a long silence after the Professor had spoken.

"What year is this?" asked Nafula.

"It's August 1945. Has spaceflight compromised your faculties?" responded Professor Gregory.

"Return to this frequency in two hours, I must relay this information to my superiors before we continue," Nafula ended the transmission and headed to the operations room with the rest of her team.

"What the hell is going on!" exclaimed Winda.

"It seems as though we are dealing with a person with mental health issues, who has somehow found the dead man frequency," replied Shani.

"And how did they know all those details about the astronaut? Those specifics are not things that he could have randomly known," interjected Nia.

"So what? We are getting a signal from a dystopian alternate dimension circa 1945 World War, don't be ridiculous," insisted Winda.

"Then how do you explain it? The power pack uses lithium batteries; we haven't used lithium batteries in centuries. We have contacted all the other space agencies and they all say that this man is not part of any of their programs. We must begin to assume that this man is not supposed to be here, all the evidence points to that," Nia took a breath and fell back into her chair.

"Nia has a point, this man is an irregularity with no explanation except the one that is being given to us by Professor Gregory," concurred Nafula.

"Don't tell me you're seriously considering this," interrupted Shani.

"We have no choice," responded Nafula.

After two hours the crew gathered back in the freezer and waited for the transmission to start.

"Hello, hello, can you hear me?" began the Professor.

"Yes, we can hear you," replied Nafula.

"I have the president of the United States here with me. I have briefed him as to what is happening and he would like to speak with you," said the professor hastily.

"Good day, crew of the Queen of Sheba. We were not aware that Kenya also had a top-secret space program. I guess it wouldn't be much of a secret program if we had known," the president laughed to himself a moment before continuing. "In truth, we need your help finding the lost nuclear device and detonating it. I fear that if we fail, the army will be forced to drop another nuclear payload on our enemies, which is our last resort. If there is anything…" the president stopped speaking and gasped in horror. "What have we done? Too soon, they dropped it too soon!" he exclaimed before static flooded the transmission.

"Hello, can you hear us!" exclaimed Nafula but the static continued. The crew waited for days for the signal to be reconnected, but it seemed to have been lost for good.

The rest of the trip back to Earth was uneventful and the crew spent most of their time deep in thought or discussing what they thought had happened. After re-entering the earth's atmosphere, they landed in the Indian Ocean and were retrieved by the program recovery team before they were debriefed. A standoffish atmosphere hung over them as they were transported to the main base. This was not the usual reception they normally received after a mission. No cameras or press were present, and Nafula could tell that there was something peculiar going on. As soon as they arrived at the space agency's headquarters they were separated and rushed off into the building. None of the personnel explained why this was happening and they barely spoke to the crew of the Queen of Sheeba except to give them directions as to what to do next. Nafula was asked to shower and put on the clothing that had been provided for her. Afterward, she was led into a narrow room that was occupied by a panel of her superiors.

"Hello Nafula," the inquiry began.

"We hope not to have startled you with our new protocol. You have to understand that certain security measures have to be taken." She recognized the woman who was speaking to her as the head of operations, Mrs. Kashama.

"You see Captain Nafula, the mission you were on was highly irregular and needed to be treated as such. The reason we have to take these procedures is due to the signal that your crew received from the transponder of the dead astronaut you were transporting. Please tell us what you heard."

Nafula scanned the room before answering. "We received a hacked transmission from a fake broadcast claiming to be from 1945." She waited to gauge their response.

"We suggest that you keep to that story, Captain. What you heard was nothing more than an elaborate prank call from someone who thought it would be funny to intercept the channel you were listening to. Do you understand?" Mrs. Kashama looked sternly at Nafula.

"What about the dead man we retrieved, was he also a hoax?" inquired Nafula combatively.

"The man that you retrieved was a member of a team we sent out without the knowledge of the general public. No more than a mission gone wrong, no need for you to investigate the matter further," answered Mrs. Kashama intently.

"Additionally you may not speak about what happened on your mission. The story that you will give to the media is that this was a routine mission to fix a faulty satellite. This is of the highest importance; you may not even disclose any of it to your family. Is this understood?" asked Mrs. Kashama.

"Yes I understand," replied Nafula.

The crew of the Queen of Sheeba was then led to the press conference where they were directed to the podium.

"Citizens of Earth," began Nafula. "We live in a universe that is more wondrous and complex than we could ever imagine. A multiverse of endless possibilities. We are part of a grand mystery, a mystery that the crew of The Queen of Sheeba and I had a glimpse of during our last mission."

344

Bass Chasers
by
Bryant O'Hara

At the edge

of night

at the highest height

the students-of-stars

nod their heads

in syncopated time

to the remnants

of the biggest bangs

since the Biggie Bang

made matter

and meter

and mind.

At the edge

of light,

in the darkest night,

these Bass Chasers

knead the big bangs

into bi-bip-beats

so that we,

the baryonic,

can bounce booty

at an exponential

frequency

of gravity.

Why?

Because the arrow of time, signed,

is always positive,

chant the Bass Chasers.

What has happened

has happened,

and we can only

hope to

hone

what we hear

into homilies

that fill in the holes

in history.

Why?

Because the arrow of time, signed,

is only positive,

chant the Bass Chasers.

We have our one line,

our one life,

anchored to time -

and the arrow of time, signed,

is always positive.

[Even if something has got to give]

You can chase the bass behind you

or chase the rhythm that winds you.

You can chase the bass that binds you

or chase the beat that

unwinds you,

that names you,

that tames you,

that scars you,

that stars you.

We all

are the stars

that are

complex.

The Biggie Bang is

long,

long,

long,

but is never gone.

You all

are the stars

that are

complex,

And the beat

goes on

and on

and on

and is never gone.

Even in the darkest

of nights,

when the black holes

are too far to tango,

the Bass Chasers

build beats

from the bones

of the

Biggie Bang...

'Cause it ain't

nothing but a human thang.

Space Station 1993
by
Violette L. Meier

Space Station 1993 orbited Frexix, a small moon that circled an earth-like planet called Ghanu- third in orbit around the yellow dwarf, Iam, in the Cassiopeia Dwarf galaxy. Ghanu hosted a plethora of intelligent carbon-based lifeforms whose exploratory curiosity eventually found Earth. Their first sightings on Earth were spread through tabloids, conspiracy literature and videos, drunken country dwellers, and fringe pseudoscientists collecting data from irreputable sources on the internet. Ghanu's flying saucers were nothing more but movie material and unrecognizable disks in black and white photos for decades before a Ghanu mistakenly landed in the middle of a highly televised world summit. A tall, slender, lavender creature with black eyes, thick violet lips, and kinky wine-colored hair strolled across the camera. After realizing that the landing was real and not an elaborate hoax, worldwide terror grabbed the hearts and minds of humans everywhere. Global mayhem ensued.

Despite being given gifts of technology that helped cure disease, end world hunger, and reverse pollution extending the duration of life on Earth, humans sought only to kill and capture every Ghanu they could find. After a century of xenophobia and fruitless interplanetary wars, humans and Ghanus were forced to call an armistice. Humans agreed to allow Ghanus to inhabit Earth safely and the Ghanu agreed to provide spaceships and intergalactic travel equipment enabling humans to explore the universe.

Captain Neo Xaba, a sixteenth-generation Earth transplant managed Space Station 1993 along with a crew of three human astronauts, five Ghanus, and seven androids built in the hybrid likeness of humans and Ghanus.

She moved through the station on hind feet, quickly and with grace, her dark body muscular yet feminine, her face stern yet kind.

"Neo," Natori, her second in command called, his lavender skin a stark contrast to the teal uniform he wore. He towered over Neo like a parent over a toddler. He was seven feet of benevolent disposition.

"What's up Tori?" the captain replied while entering a configuration into a holographic computer.

"Did you contact your father? He called again yesterday," Natori asked while pulling a small electronic device from his pocket and swiping his long bony finger across the screen.

Neo shook her head no. Guilt burned in her chest for a second then fizzled. She had no desire to talk to her father. The last time they talked was five years ago and that conversation was so unbearable that it caused her six months of psychotherapy. She loved him, but she did not have the emotional aptitude to tolerate him. Brilliant and beautiful yet ornery and obdurate, he got on her last nerves.

Their relationship had been volatile since the day she was born. They loved each other; they just didn't like each other. They agreed on nothing. Ever. If he wanted to go left, she automatically went right. The things that made her laugh made him cry. What she viewed as success was always below his standards therefore it equated to failure. It was only natural that she chose a career that stationed her across the universe.

"I think you need to call him. He has called every week for the last three months. Something may be wrong," Natori advised. "He didn't sound well."

Neo rolled her eyes and continued to turn dials, flip switches, and open digital files with her fingerprint. Her father was old but healthier that children. His not sounding well was probably a manipulation tactic to get her to answer his call.

"If something was wrong, my mother would have contacted me by now," Neo mumbled. "My father is probably bored and ready to argue again. Living with my mother is peaceful. Every now and then he needs to shake things up and calling me would definitely shake things up. Disrupting my life seems to be a form of entertainment for him."

"Your mother did call," Natori said. "She called yesterday after your father called again. "I told Kunta to give you the message."

Neo's eyebrow raised. Her stomach flipped. Something could be wrong. Her mother called only when matters were urgent. Although they did not talk much, Neo and her mother were very close. They communicated often through star-grams messages transcribed through stars; a real time horoscope that could be created through the manipulation of dark matter which trapped artificial light and created pseudo micro star systems that reflected long enough to transmit messages through a universal zodiac codex. Neo wondered why her mother didn't message her through the stars.

"Family is important Neo. Your family should be able to contact you directly in case of an emergency," Natori scolded, his facial expression changing suddenly. "I think there is something outside of the space station," Natori stated, showing the captain his handheld device. A dull glow moved across the outside camera.

"Is the entire crew accounted for?" she asked, her lips twisting in response to his admonishment.

Neo knew that Natori was right, but she also knew that Natori didn't understand what an obstinate, unreasonable, nuisance her father could be. The man was relentless in his approach to everything. Neo decided long ago that to have peace in her life and to maintain her love for him, separation was the best thing.

"Yes. Everyone is accounted for," Natori replied, his wine-colored brows furrowed. He scratched one of his oblong ears and waited for the captain to give further directions.

Neo looked into Natori's eyes, worry rested there and if worry rested in his normally assured stare, something was seriously amiss.

"Alert the crew. Summon two androids," Neo commanded then typed in her last set of coordinates.

"Okay," Natori replied, spinning on his heels, and disappearing into the hallway in two gangling steps.

Neo clicked a switch, and the outside camera footage took over a wall of computer screens. She stared out into the darkness of space hoping to catch a glimpse of movement. There was none but the sensors were continuously going off.

Walking in step with one another, two androids entered Captain Neo's office with Natori on their heels, his eyes more panicked than ever.

"Captain," an android called, its silver metallic face and frame androgynous.

"How can we be of service?" the other android asked, its metal face almost identical to the first android's but gold in color.

"Silver and Gold, the alarms are going off outside of the station and earlier we saw something unidentifiable on camera. I need you to go outside and report back to me what you find," Neo commanded. "Put on your gear and take a matter trap just in case we're being invaded."

The androids nodded, turned, and exited the room. Within minutes Neo and Natori could see, on the outside cameras, the androids secured to their safety tethers bouncing and floating in all-encompassing blackness. The androids held a small crystal barrel and lid, a matter trap, in their hands. The matter trap could rearrange matter without destroying it and sucking it into its barrel and trapping it. If a lifeforce is trapped, it can be regenerated and released at a later time. It was like a black hole in a jar without the danger of spaghettification.

"Did you see that?" Natori asked, pointing to the corner of a computer screen.

Neo leaned forward, eyes squinched.

"Looks like a beam of light. Maybe it's bouncing off the space station," Neo said unfazed by the blurry image.

"No, look again," Natori whispered, unblinking, unable to turn away from the screen.

A dull white glow moved in the corner of the screen. It was long, tall, and moved like a lifeform.

"What is that?" Neo asked. "I've seen a lot of things in the universe, but nothing like that!"

"I don't know," Natori answered as he tapped a metal device in his ear. The device lit up.

"Silver, turn to your left. There's something moving near the solar arrays. It's moving fast towards you and Gold.

Silver turned to its left; the matter trap aimed at the light being.

"Grab the lid," Silver commanded Gold. "We must capture it quickly."

Gold reached for the lid but the glowing being was swifter. It snatched Gold's arm off its body. Sparking wires and dangling cords protruded from the golden limb as it floated off into space.

The glowing thing snapped the tethers holding them to the space station with one swift yank and both androids and the matter trap were pulled into the void of space before getting drawn into Ghanu's orbit and incinerated by its atmosphere.

Neo and Natori watched in horror as their shipmates disappeared into the cosmic abyss.

The glowing creature moved to the edge of the camera and waited as if it knew more opponents were on the way.

"Send Copper, Zinc, and Bronze outside. Make sure they're armed with matter traps and lightning blades. Tell the earthlings and the Ghanus to prepare themselves for battle. I will send a message to command," Captain Neo barked.

Natori executed Neo's commands quickly. Within minutes, the entire crew was dressed and armed. Two of the humans, Shannon, a blonde, middle-aged woman, and Trent, a young man with almond eyes and thick wavy hair, tapped frantically on holographic computers as they witnessed the light creature rip their android brethren into scrap metal. The third human — Kunta, a powerful-looking onyx man, and five Ghanus —two males, two females, and one androgynous being, stationed themselves near the exits in case the light monster decided to force its way into the station.

The glowing creature walked slowly across the camera as if its featureless face was looking for someone in particular. It stood in the center of the camera and stretched its light-beam arms outward.

"Should I send Cobalt and Lead?" Natori asked Neo as she stared at the screen, unblinking. There was something familiar about the way the being moved. She shivered.

"No. I don't want all our androids to be destroyed. Copper, Zinc, and Bronze didn't stand a chance against it.," she whispered. "Turn on the audio from outside. Maybe it will communicate."

Natori instructed Trent to turn on the audio.

Silence.

"What do you want?" Captain Neo asked into a small transparent microphone that translated communications into a plentitude of tongues.

The light creature put its hand across its chest as if it were hurting.

"Why are you here?" she asked.

The creature pointed its hand towards the camera.

"Is it a person you seek?" she asked.

The being nodded its head.

"Do you mean us harm?" she asked, vexed that one of her crew members may have provoked the beast in the past on one of their expeditions and it was there to avenge itself. It was common for enemies to be made when traveling the universe. It was impossible to know the infinite ways various lifeforms could be offended.

"Do any of you recognize this creature?" Neo asked her crew. She turned away from the screen to look into each one of their eyes.

Discernment was Neo's special gift. She could detect a lie instantly.

Shannon and Trent denied ever encountering the light creature.

Neo summoned the others and they too denied ever seeing such a thing before. They returned to their stations.

The creature disseminated into an infinity of glittering molecules and vanished.

Alarms rang throughout the space station but there were no warnings of doors opening.

"There must be a breach somewhere!" Neo yelled. "Seal the door!"

Screams echoed through the nearest airlock chamber. By their guttural tones, Natori knew that they were his fellow Ghanus. A tear ran down his elongated face.

Lead and Cobalt, with Kunta's unconscious body dragging behind them, slid under the heavy iron door before it hit the floor, sealing the room off from the rest of the space station.

"Where are the others?" Natori asked the androids as they propped Kunta's unconscious body against a corner.

"The creature did something to them," Lead replied. "Its light shot through the Ghanus, and they fell to the floor screaming."

"Our sensors indicate that they are not dead, only comatose. We were able to pull Kunta away from the initial blast but he was hit moments before we reached the chamber," Cobalt interjected. "He should regain consciousness soon."

Natori exhaled a sigh of relief. One of the fallen Ghanus was a girlfriend, another close cousin, and the others were friends. There was not one who would not be missed.

"What does this thing want?" Neo huffed as she paced the floor waiting for the light being to make its way to the door. She knew it was coming. She felt it deep in her bones.

"Look!" Natori yelped, pointing at the computer screen which showed the hallway outside their door. The light creature was running its hands across the thick iron searching for an opening. It found an opening, a design element paying homage to a retro keyhole, a few centimeters wide and an inch long. The creature reduced itself to molecules and began to pass through the keyhole like a swarm of microscopic fireflies. It reassembled in front of the door, its slender, shimmering body binding together in a matter of seconds.

Neo rushed towards the creature with a matter trap in hand, mentally prepared for death but ready to defend her life and the lives of the remaining crew members. She stood an arm's length away from the being, her eyes narrow, her teeth bared.

Natori stood by her side with an open trap in his hand as well. Trent, Shannon, Lead, and Cobalt took up the rear. All armed and ready to rumble.

"What business do you have here?" Neo yelled.

The creature took a step towards her.

Natori removed the lid from his matter trap.

"Wait," Neo said, holding her arm out to prevent Natori's aggression.

She looked closely at the creature. Its featureless face began to take shape. A strong jawline and deep-set eyes were the first to appear followed by a broad nose and a high forehead.

"It can't be!" Neo whispered. She dropped her trap to the floor and stepped towards the creature.

The creature nodded its head.

Neo stared, paralyzed in confusion.

The creature opened its arms and pulled her into its embrace. Warmth penetrated every inch of her body.

"Goodbye, my darling. I could not leave without telling you that I love you," it said without moving its mouth.

Tears rained down Neo's face.

"I love you too Daddy," she wept as her father's spirit dispersed and was no more.

Natori's device vibrated. With trembling hands, he looked upon the screen. It was Neo's mother.

"You should talk to her," Natori whimpered.

The other crew members stood completely dumbfounded.

Kunta stared out from the corner mentally disoriented but awake.

Neo connected the device to her earpiece.

"He's gone," Neo's mother sobbed. "Your father died this morning."

"I know Mama. He came to disrupt my life one last time."

Neo wept.

My Ilè, the Sea, and the World Above
by
Lu Ain Zaila
(Translated by Marissel Hernández Romero)

Honestly, I never thought that my life would change so much, but at the same time I feel that I never belonged anywhere, but here. I think about that while my fingers nimbly finish my bed, which is made of braided straw and other materials found on the Brazilian shore.

My new home is an interconnected dimension, a magical shrine, where each house is enchanted, settled between the birthplace and here, by way of some river or point in the sea, which creates, let's say . . . a wormhole that allows us to return when necessary.

From the door of my mentor's *ilè[1]*, who at this time must have completed her mission, I enjoy life in the *kilombo[2]*, and its daily movement. But I confess, for me the most amazing thing is looking up and seeing the brightness of the sea making everything sparkle in such a way that I never get bored of being here like this, braiding and braiding, trying not to think about that morning when I, in a vain attempt, tried to raise my house by conjuring a spell. It didn't take long before the only witness of my failure came to meet me with her very white, flawless dreads and serious eyes.

Uzuri was the first one to welcome me with arms wide open. She was excited that for the first time in many centuries, an *àjé[3]*, an enchanted woman, had come from *mptu* lands, as it is known.

---

[1] in Yoruba ilè means house.

[2] kilombo is a village or settlement where Africans escaped from slavery.

[3] According to the dictionary of Yoruba, an àjé us a term of respect and endearment to describe a woman that uses biological, spiritual, and cosmic power.

It is the country where I was born and where countless Black lives were sent from whom I descended. Now I protect them from other . . . situations, in addition to those that affect the physical world. But my duty right now, as Ayomide said, is to settle down in the *kilombo* and learn everything that my interim mentor and Báàlè, one of the oldest leaders here, think it's time to learn.

"Zuhri . . ."

She didn't need to say anything else. I intuitively knew that I should follow her wherever she took me. And I did. We walked by the houses of the *kilombo;* even though I hadn't been here for a long time, I could identify each one of them with reference and reverence to their various ancestry such as Bantu, Haussá, Gbe, and Yorubá, as well as many others that I didn't recognize. Sum up that now to every notion of the world, existence, life, death, philosophy, and words which are for the most part unknown to me.

I followed Uzuri to the borders of the *kilombo.* Ahead was an open field with hills covered by coral. As soon as we stopped, a silence that I didn't know was introspective or educative established between us, and before I had a chance to break it …

"Shhhh...."

Uzuri has the same skill as Ayomide, to anticipate my worries. I hushed, just standing there, looking and imagining my next steps. How would I take them? And suddenly everything changed, as if the weight of the water had sunk into the ground and traced a bluish path that I lost sight of on the horizon.

"Finally! I was tired of waiting for you to make up your mind."

"Me, make up my mind? For what?"

"Your *àjo*[4]. Didn't you feel that something was missing yesterday? Your *ilè* has not bloomed because you have doubts about your origins. Your thoughts are as mixed as a spicy pepper peanut soup with yam *fufu*[5]."

"And where will this path take me?"

---

[4] àjo means journey.
[5] fufu is an African food.

"Wherever it needs to put an end to those questions. Did you bring your *kimbele*[6]?"

"Yes. I did not take my dagger from my waist as ordered."

"Great. Then you just need this beautiful *kente* that I asked to be brought from Ghana especially for you and this crock with fresh water. Your journey is just ahead."

Her gesture was straightforward, and without wasting time I wrapped the fabric around my neck, slung the rope from the water bottle over my shoulder, and went down the first hill that formed. It was what Uzuri expected of me and in a way, me too. Something was missing and I needed to find out what.

I followed the trail a little scared but steady until I lost sight of the *kilombo*. I could never have imagined such a world and that it could be so hot. By now my *kente* was on my head and my first surprise a few more steps later was an old woman halfway between the two trails. At first, the woman seemed lost to me, but I soon understood who she was. People were coming out from a large bag and she directed them to one or another trail, after a few steps they disappeared.

I couldn't go back, so I went on and hid my face as much as I could with the *kente* until I was in front of her, who looked and looked and decided to ask:

"Where did you come from? I didn't pull you from my bag, but I can guide your path."

"Thanks, but I haven't told you where I'm going yet, so how can you tell which way I should take?"

"I guide everyone on their walks, long or short. How far is of yours?"

"I don't know, but I'm not looking for a distance, but its purpose."

The woman was curious about the answer and tried to see who I was, but I did not let her. I asked her if she would like a sip of water; the woman was amazed, accepted, and was grateful.

I took advantage of her good mood and asked her for the path for those who don't know who they are and seek an answer to

---

[6] kimbele is a knife.

finally building their house. I told her that someone had pointed me this way and that a wise woman would be on it. The compliment filled her ears. She burst out laughing in the air, and immediately she pointed to the path on my right. I had much to do before I returned to the *kilombo*, where I should be in the early morning dawn.

I thanked her and walked the path that soon began to tremble below my feet. Suddenly I tripped over a sidewalk. I had returned to my world. I was missing the chaos of the Cidade Baixa (Lower Town), which was the first thing that came to my mind as soon as I heard all the deafening sounds of that peripheral metropolis that I, as an environmental crime investigator, knew so well, but now I was kind of a stranger. My perception of it was altered as if everything were new. I had changed, and the glances at me proved that as I walked the streets. I had a generous amount of color and curly hair in the gray of those streets.

I did one thing— I don't even know if it was the best decision, but I cast a good Samaritan's spell to release an electric scooter from those rental locks. I didn't have a payment card anymore, and I really only needed the 60 minutes allowed to get around the city; starting with the highways beneath the chaos of rubbish below, a world not at all forgotten by those up here.

It was good to feel the wind on my face. I looked around and I realized that I was at the Comunidade[7] da Vinda. I immediately stopped when I saw that contraption made of various metal parts, an unstable, botched job of sound, rather than a cart announcing the event of the following day, which soon put me in time. The date did not lie, it was about to start the official carnival of samba schools through the city streets.

That news filled me with joy, even though I still didn't understand my place. It was time to drop the scooter and climb the hill. That's what I did. I started to walk and see how this party stirred the community mostly of my color. Good days for selling food/drinks on the streets, which echoed loud and clear in every corner and hills. The rush of the last orders, a guarantee of a good party and savings.

---

[7] - shanty town, slum.

"Hey little guy, don't you forget my ice bags, or you will have to chill the beers with your breath!"

"Are you crazy! Go back there and change this bean. This is not good to make *acarajés*[8]. Want me to sell the prawns in the spoon? I rather file for divorce!"

The voices of Black women shaking that world have always been a rule, for if they move, the world trembles together. It reminded me of my mom, dad, and the last carnival we had as a family. My mom put us both in an alert state, but it was fun. We'd come and go from every corner of the community with what was left to make everything perfect, from feathers made with fabric to a school flag forgotten in the shed once.

I remember that this golden age of happiness only lasted two years. It was not enough to pay the bills at the end of the month. But definitely, my parents were to me the most beautiful master of ceremonies and flag bearer[9] in the world; and they didn't walk, they floated under the cyberfunk asphalt of the city making magic while smiling and turning, bowing to the public and singing the samba, holding the school flag with sweat and blisters. All that energy and happiness, in the end turned into many kisses and hugs. I can't even say how I feel about reliving such a memory that I didn't even know was so alive and ingrained in myself; but I know I refuse to utter how I lost my parents in this world, one after another. The important thing is to remember how they made me who I am.

A few more steps ahead and I found myself surrounded by a myriad of teenagers looking at me curiously, as if I were someone from there and at the same time not.

"That cloth is very beautiful. Are you a foreigner? Hello …"

Everyone laughed at her attempted communication which pissed the girl off. I laughed too and then I told them that I used to live nearby for some time. I traveled and was passing through. Their curiosity had not been satisfied.

---

[8] - acarajé is an african and afro-brazilian food.

[9] - master of ceremonies (mestre-sala) and flag bearernd (porta-bandeira) are a couple of dancers performing the role of guiding and presenting the flag of a samba school during the carnival parade (especially in Rio de Janeiro/São Paulo).

I realized the kids had several cans of bio-spray paint for the carnival paintings on the open walls. I asked what the school plot was and if they already knew what they were going to do. They stared at me in surprise and laughed. If I didn't know, I must definitely be out of the country. The theme is a return to history and all the juggling our people still do to resist. Wow, if I had any doubts, I had none left. I had to be here. Soon I volunteered to go with them and see how I could help with the graffiti they had in mind. The idea was bought on the spot and before turning the alley, my *kente* was already around the neck of two girls whom I promised to teach some tricks using that cloth.

I walked down two blocks with the kids to the community entrance and there we found four open spaces for the mural. They quickly broke into groups and began to wonder what they would like to see. The ideas and streaks were of various kinds until one of the girls suggested that one of the murals could have the beautiful cloth of "Tia", a tactic to please me and earn the blessing that I said to be from Ghana, but I liked the idea and crossed out with them several things I learned in the *kilombo*, from my parents and Tia Cita . . . how much I would like to see her even from afar.

In a manner, the turmoil ends and gets organized, they vote and start work while I ask the girls for some scissors to divide the fabric and teach them how to use it if they want to make the most varied turbans. Then we head to the samba school to see the preparations for the opening of the carnival days.

Just before the afternoon meeting before nightfall the teenagers finish the graffiti, but they do not want to reveal it or tell what they did. They prefer to keep it secret for later and I, like a handful of people, went down the hills again following the first baianas[10] of the school towards the opening rite of the revelry.

I was feeling so comfortable that I didn't notice one of the baianas staring at me. I disguised myself and got out of her sight. I couldn't risk being recognized, although no one there

---

[10] generally afro-descendant ladies with turban and long white clothes associated with Afro-Brazilian religious tradition, also selling acarajé, participate in Carnival. The name is also a feminine adjective for those who live in Bahia, one of the blackest states in Brazil.

sees any resemblance between my current self and my previous one. Was I that different? In essence? Well . . . anyway, I stayed a few steps behind until we reached the main road, connecting with the asphalt, and faced the first problem, the hatred of the neighbors of the buildings always considering the joy and the rites of the other less or nothing.

From where I was standing, I could see the baianas macerating the herbs and pouring them into the white ceramic pots with water, but from there I also saw a strange shape forming high up and I had no doubt of what it was because as soon as the police arrived with his helper robots, part of the form came down and I saw the eyes of the machines turned red and that was not a good sign.

Said and done, a heated altercation began. The guards would not let us pass, and the robots began to move slowly toward us. I wasted no time and stepped forward before it got out of control. Then I approached one of the ladies and asked for some herbal water. She did not understand but put some in my water crock and turned it into a cleaning *juju*[11] where I soaked my *kimbele*.

As the animosity heated, it was obvious that the robots were being fed and before the police issued any orders, they rushed us. I threw one against the wall at the height of one of the graffiti with one kick and with a meia lua[12] came back, pulled back the second, and cut his control at the neck. He dropped to his knees. The other one I pulled back and broke it in half.

I didn't even know I had that power, and just before disappearing from the sight of everyone in shock, the first cloth fell off and then I saw the first graffiti. It was me, my face looking at the horizon and, in the background, the *kente* I shared with the girls. That was quite a gift. I thanked them by scratching a Z with my dagger. It was so soft the scratch on the wall, but it was more believable that my hand was heavy. I disappeared for the rest of the night.

From the rooftops I heard some people say I was the missing detective. Others already said that this was how I acted now, in

---

[11] juju is a magical power usually imbued in an object.
[12] It is a ginga/kick movement in the air, very common in Capoeira.

favor of the righteous people of Cidade Baixa, that now, I shut
up those who raged hatred for no reason, just as I had just done
early in the evening, silencing people without respect for others.
I must confess I liked that feeling and there began my urban legend under the blessings of the opening of the revelry.

And to keep everything perfectly still, I waited for the shape
that tried to ruin the festivity, but I hunted it and dispelled it and
every bit of its mischief with the dagger and with the *juju* left in
the pot.

I have never felt so full and peaceful with myself. Had I
found the answer to my journey? I think I did and now it was
time to start wandering back. It was already dawn and I remembered what the old woman of the roads told me.

The streets were much calmer, but joy when it starts never
ceases completely. There is always a smile and a humming
somewhere. It was time to look around a path to return. I felt a
wind blowing down the streets and I knew it was calling me, so
I followed it to an absolutely incredible sight familiar to me.

As the sun lit up that end of the street, the jagged stones at
the feet of Comunidade da Vinda gave way to the shape of a
hill, and on it, two puppets came into view, but I doubted what I
was seeing. He was wearing a white lined suit and she a pink
dress fluttering in the wind. I approached happily and then heard
a question.

"You're real, aren't you?" asked one of the girls from yesterday with a piece of the *kente* in her hair, like a big ribbon. I said
yes and she hugged me crying, saying that she would miss me.
Me too, I replied and to soothe her, I fixed the headband in her
hair just as my mother fixed mine, straightened her curly hair as
my mom used to do mine and made an open turban. The young
girl thanked me and finally, we said goodbye. I kissed her forehead and resumed my steps towards the children, saying that if
one day they needed me, very, very much, they could call me in
the water, because through it I would always hear who needed
me.

And then I left, returning to the path and back to the *kilombo*.
"You are just in time; the day is just beginning. How was it?"

Uzuri asked me with satisfaction, although I was sure she didn't miss a minute of what had happened to me there, but she wanted to hear me say every word and feel its vibration.

"It was amazing. I left here confused, knowing it was a bit of everything, but not knowing how to handle it. Today I understand that I am water of many influences, my ancestry is mixed because my ancestors resisted by adding their stories, cultures, pains, and joys. I am who I am."

"I liked it and with a very beautiful metaphorical ending."
We ended up laughing.

Back in my new home, I had no doubt about how and what to do.

Several people stopped to see and I realized that every piece I made for the house had an origin. I gathered them all around my earthen vessel with water, knelt, sighed, and then . . . mixed my enchanted words from all origins, and trunks of my home, and finally my house began to sprout before my eyes.

I had finally settled into my home and at last, I could start arranging my belongings inside the house.

Sticking to one's roots is everything.

Earth Year 2428/Titan Year 256
by
Steven Van Patten

"Momma, do I really have to go to school today?" Roxanna asked as she sat in front of a mirror braiding her black, shoulder-length hair. "Can't we just hang out and read? Or play chess?"

"Don't waste time asking questions you already know the answer to," her mother Kayla, chastised as she stood in her daughter's bedroom doorway.

Roxanna's eyes shifted from her own face in her mirror to her mother's face as she glared at the back of her daughter's head. Kayla's arms were crossed in front of her, as if she sensed a difficult conversation were imminent. "Mrs. Jayden's lesson yesterday was… disturbing," Roxanna said after a moment.

"Well, you're getting older now," Kayla said. "This is the time in your life when you're going to learn some things that will be a little uncomfortable to hear."

"Yes, but it was the history of Earth, Mom!"

Kayla nodded. "I tried to prepare you for this last year."

"You didn't tell me about the numerous genocides," Roxanna corrected. "And how irredeemably stupid some of them were. The racism, the conflicting religions, the politics, the lies." Her little lips curled. "It's all so disgusting. All of it."

"I know, dear," Kayla stepped into the room, her arms uncrossing and reaching out instinctively with her right hand.

"And she said we're going to be going over this for the rest of the school year." Upon seeing her mother's approach, Roxanna turned from the mirror and stood up to face her. "We stopped at something called 'The Middle Passage' but there's the wiping out of this one group, the Native Americans. Then when we were leaving class, one of the boys, Eamon, he said there's this Adolph guy who killed millions of people because they were Jewish. Something about them not believing in a

367

savior. Then there's this one president of a bunch of united states that tried to do what Hitler did only with a virus. It's all so much." The perplexed young lady shook her head. "All of these things happened because people were different skin colors and had different religions? It's the most horrible thing I've ever heard of."

Seeing that her daughter's anxiety was growing, Kayla took her daughter in her arms. The embrace was so warm that for a moment they seemed to forget that they both had places to be within the hour. But it was clear they needed to steal this moment, to reassure each other that all was right with their world. "I know the lessons are a lot to take in, but we all need to know these things. We need to understand and appreciate the importance of what we are about to do."

Roxanna pulled away from her mother and forced herself to smile. "You're right. We must be brave. At least there's nothing scary about science and math classes."

Kayla's face beamed with pride for her child. "That's my girl."

After helping each other put on their gravity adjustment suits, they headed downstairs and walked through the living room, flipping off light switches as they passed. Once inside the vestibule that led to the airlock, they waited quietly as the door sealed behind them with a hydraulic 'hiss,' which allowed for the trigger that engaged the home's main exit door to release. A red light on the wall to their left turned green as they stepped outside.

Kayla's hovercraft sat in one of the two silver docking pads in the middle of the paved landing strip. The other docking pad sat empty as Roxanna's father, Amari, had left for training exercises hours ago. As the side doors of the pod opened, they boarded Kayla's travel pod and after slipping seamlessly into the stream of traffic thirty feet above the house, they were off.

"Is Daddy going to have to go to Earth?" Roxanna asked as the pod picked up speed.

"Eventually, yes" Kayla answered. "Right now, he's preparing other warriors, who will probably go there first. Your father is a great teacher, so his superiors want to have as many soldiers as possible who can fight like him."

"Will I have to go?" Kayla couldn't tell if she heard elation or trepidation in her daughter's voice.

"Even though no one is leaving for Earth for at least another year, the war would have to go on for quite some time for you to be of age and trained to fight. Besides, I thought you wanted to be a scientist."

"Technically, I can do both," the ten-year-old countered.

Kayla smiled and kissed Roxanna on the cheek. "Ambitious and multi-faceted. Just like your father."

*

Middle School 44 was a four-story structure roughly four hundred kilometers from where Roxanna's family lived. As they neared the school, they could see the mighty rings of mother planet Saturn just behind it.

As with every morning since Roxanna was a child, a proximity alarm sounded inside the hovercraft, followed by an automated voice generated from the school:

"You are third in line for row C of Middle-School 44 parent drop-off. Thank you for bringing your child to school on time."

In the air above the school, hovercrafts floated in four single-file lines. Some of the kids, seeing each other through the windows of their parents' pods waved at each other, or they made taunting faces. Roxanna didn't see anyone she was very familiar with in the B or D lines, so she focused on watching her mother's landing.

The rooftop drop-off docks at the school were different from the version in front of Roxanna's family's house, in that the latches were the quick-release kind. This allowed parents to land their automated pods, open the passenger side door, let their children out onto the school's roof, and be on their way in seconds. Once safely on the roof, the students lined up onto an escalator that would take them to the fourth floor.

Of course, some families lived closer, so the students from those families either walked or arrived on their hoverboards and entered through the ground-level entrance. There were check-in kiosks on the first and fourth floors. During check-in, a kiosk would scan each student for low blood sugar and present a piece of fruit if the student's readings were low. A text message would automatically be sent to the parents, gently encouraging them to make sure that their child ate a full breakfast every day. A mild, non-addictive stimulant would also be administered by way of a shot of 'the green drink' if the student appeared to be sleepy. As with the famished, sleep-deprived arrivals would also trigger a text message to their parents. In this society, not getting adequate sleep was frowned upon and discouraged at every turn, especially if one were attending a school. After all, how is one supposed to learn anything if their brain isn't receptive and fully functioning?

At eight 'o clock every morning, in every classroom on the second and third floor of the building, the morning's affirmation was recited. In Roxanna's relatively short life, the affirmation had changed over the years, but the basics were still in place:

> "We are a strong and determined offspring.
> Our Earth-bound ancestors gave us this life and
> it shall be spent honoring them with truth,
> loyalty and the continued pursuit of justice."

"Very nice, children," Ms. Jayden said, prompting Roxanna and her classmates to sit back at their white-lacquered desks. Ms. Jayden was one of the few people on Titan whose eyes were bluish-grey. Most of the population had brown or black eyes, which meant that on Titan Ms. Jayden was considered 'exotic.' Not that she'd experienced anything outside of curiosity or unbridled admiration from would-be suitors. In contrast to their Earth-dwelling counterparts, Titans tended to be very polite and would never say anything derisive to anyone about things that couldn't be helped or avoided.

At the age of ten, Roxanna knew the tale of how her people came to live on Titan, the large moon orbiting Saturn because it was required learning in first grade: That for centuries people who looked like her were persecuted by other Earthmen who thought themselves superior to the people with brown complexions because, of all things, they were white. And while there were white people who did not participate in the degradation directly, they were also either not powerful or not motivated enough to stop the persecution. And the persecution went on and on, always modifying to fit the time period and never abating and always a clear and present danger.

That was until a brilliant and rebellious black woman decided she had seen enough. She had already flouted the laws of Earth by avenging herself on both the racist white people as well as anyone who assisted in their own oppression and decided she would create a final solution. It did not matter to her that she wouldn't live to see it, she would do it simply because it needed to be done.

Being a master manipulator when it came to technology, science, and aeronautics, she hacked the persecutors' government's space satellites and tricked them into thinking they'd lost a few. Then, using drone technology, she remodified the satellites until they were capable of leaving Earth's orbit altogether. Then, the woman sent her newly built spacecrafts off to Titan but not before loading them up with essentials and programming each vessel's arrival time.

The essentials were the drones and computers she had carefully installed within the vessel with DNA materials from her own body as well as what she'd acquired from ideal sperm donors. This was why the Titans refer to this woman as the Earth Mother, or as some called her Kendra The Great.

Near the end of first grade, Roxanna would learn a very sobering truth; That the Earth Mother wanted her Titan children to prepare to go to her Earth and liberate it once they had built a viable society and the technology to support the massive undertaking.

In second grade, the history lessons detailed how her great-great-grandparents were called Generation One; a mere thirty of them landing on Titan as babies fertilized in a make-shift tech-womb destined to be a nursery. They would be raised by a supercomputer in a dome the drones attached to the satellite had been programmed to build. In one Earth year, the computer began teaching them to read and write and established dominance over them by being their only source of food. They mastered basic arithmetic by the time they were five and advanced calculus by seven. By the time her great-grandparents were teenagers, they were designing lightweight compression suits to wear outside the dome where the drones had already started converting the moon's natural liquid methane to consumable water and treating the soil to make it viable for planting crops. Air filtration systems and gravity generators were also built as a shared project between the drones, the supercomputer, and the Generation One children, each one a natural-born engineer by Earth's standards. Waste disposal became an issue until one of the children figured out how to use the waste to power small engines.

Once they could go outside, a second vessel arrived with materials that would further assist them in the creation of an agricultural system. Once they knew they could produce food in abundance, Generation One's next step was to make new children, mostly through gene-splicing since they were all technically siblings.

The second vessel also contained new genetic material, which enabled the creation of new babies who were not related to Generation One. In fact, there were instructions that Group A females would be for the sole purpose of breeding and Group A males would provide manual labor at the behest of Generation One.

Around this time, the supercomputer reasoned that because the moon was being populated and new elements to sustain life were being added into the ecosystem, the new inhabitants of Titan should expect the moon to react, more than likely by way of seismic disturbances. Earthquakes would be a common part of their lives for nearly eighty years and would force the Titans to forgo building anything over two stories high, despite having acquired the knowledge and means to build skyscrapers decades before it was safe.

Despite the challenges, with the maturation of Generations Two and Group B, houses became cities and cities became a makeshift country, ruled by a general and not a president or a king. A third vessel landed containing information on technological shortcuts, musical instruments, and more DNA material. Only now would the population see some variety in terms of facial features. Everyone shared very similar complexions, but with the breeding of Generation One and now Two with Groups A and B, everyone's features began to look less alike. The citizenry eventually stopped being classified by their generations all together and were referred to as The People of Titan. And with their class system willfully abolished, everyone worked towards the common goal of making sure that everyone was living up to their potential. As the cities got bigger, knowledge was being catalogued, history was being taught and schools produced scores of brilliant, thriving brown-skinned children.

Though everyone worked for the military and ultimately answered to the general, anyone could pursue whatever career they wanted. However, preparing to invade Earth was considered The People of Titan's main focus, and anyone who showed an aptitude for destruction and violence was strongly urged to serve.

As her third year of school began, Roxanna learned of other vessels filled with books and messages from the Earth Mother over the years, but the last one appeared when her actual mother, Kayla, was a child. Along with chess boards and even more books detailing the fundamental elements and instructions they would need if they were ever going to fabricate rocket fuel and ion engines, Kendra had sent them documentaries and video testimonials of what life on Earth was like for Black people.

Like her mother before her, Roxanna's entire fourth school year would cover the early history of Africa. She would read about the great rulers and warlords, from Hatshepsut to Zenobia to Shaka kaSenzangakona or as he was more commonly known, Shaka Zulu. She also learned of the people and their pride. Their advances in medicine and culture. She would end grade four feeling practically euphoric from having learned this grand magnificent history that coursed through her veins.

Sadly, grade five would begin with the massive reality check that is the Middle Passage and even though Kayla had gently broached the conversation during the weeklong school break, she knew that there was no real way to prepare poor Roxanna for what she'd end up learning. Kayla knew her child would hear the stories of how the Europeans invaded and raped Africa for its natural resources. Worse still, she knew how hard it would be to hear about the scores of white Americans who would evolve from slave masters and Klansmen to police officers and politicians. Roxanna would have to learn every miserable bit of it until just about the end of the school year, when she would finally get to hear about the heroes' sports, literature, and music, who thrived in spite of the oppression and somehow made beautiful lives for themselves. Even that would be bittersweet, as there would also be the ones who despite being bathed in glory and blessed with immeasurable talent, would find their way to an early grave because they abused themselves to death with one substance or another. Turned out, the pain of carrying angelic gifts while daily being reminded you are somehow less than others was often too much for even the most celebrated Black person to bear.

The year had just started, so Roxanna wasn't there yet, but it would all be laid out for her in a matter of months.

Ms. Jayden took a quick head count before she began. "All right, class! Yesterday we left off discussing how the Europeans and the Americans began the slave trade. I'll get back to Europe tomorrow maybe, but since our great mother Kendra The Great was from The United States of America, a place so rife with racial injustice that we would see much of our people's blood seeped into their soil, we are going to start there first." She paused to turn and point to the appropriate spot on a map of Earth's continents behind her. "Now, please turn to page fifty-six in your textbooks."

*

An exhausted Lieutenant Commander Amari Stone swerved his hovercraft onto the landing strip, docking it next to his wife's. A loud whirring sound filled his ears as the craft's cooling system kicked in. After a moment, with his presence detected and confirmed, the automatic doors released, allowing him to remove his gravity suit and enter his living room. Kayla was chopping vegetables on the family's kitchen island and Roxanna was on the couch reading when the door hissed, announcing his entrance.

"Daddy!" Roxanna shouted as she dropped the book and ran to him, hugging his waist as he circled the kitchen island to kiss Kayla. "Did you have a good day, Daddy?"

Amari dropped to his knee and smiled. "It was a very good day, actually. What were you just reading?"

"The Autobiography of Malcolm X," she chirped. "It's good but there might be some words I'm not supposed to be reading yet."

"There's going to be a lot more of that, I'm afraid," Amari admitted as he kissed her on the cheek. "Hey, can I talk to your mom alone for a minute?"

"Adult stuff?" Roxanna asked.

"Adult stuff."

Roxanna headed to the bedroom, slowing her pace until she was sure that they wouldn't have their conversation until she was gone.

"What's going on?" Kayla finally asked.

Upstairs, with her bedroom door cracked, Roxanna strained to listen.

"They're sending us to Earth earlier than expected."

The knife clattered against her cutting board. "Why?"

"Intelligence thinks that the Earthers may have gotten a probe through. That probe may or may not have transmitted pictures of everything we've built."

"You mean, they know about us?" Kayla asked. "They might attack first?"

Amari shook his head. "We don't believe that they're capable of something like that."

"But does your 'intelligence' know for sure?"

"They've been right about everything so far."

They stood in the awkward silence that sometimes comes for people who love each other during trying circumstances. "When?"

Amari looked at his boots. "Sometime next week."

"Are we even ready for this yet? I mean…"

"We have every reason to believe that we have the superior technology." Amari took his wife's hands.

"But the manpower!" Kayla countered. "And if this incursion fails, then the next would be even worse for us. The element of surprise would be gone."

"That may already be gone," Amari said. "We just have to go down there and slug it out."

"I don't like this going early thing," Kayla pulled away from him. She seemed to be fighting back tears. "You heard the lessons. Colonialism. Slavery. The wars. The genocides. The man-made plagues. These are beastly people!"

"Beastly people who I will kill and subjugate so that I can come back home to you and that little girl upstairs," he stepped forward and took her by the shoulders. "But I have my duty. We have our duty, as taught by the Earth Mother. We have to bring order and freedom to that planet. It is literally the reason we exist."

"I know," Kayla was crying now. "I just wish it wasn't you that had to go."

"I know."

She fell into his arms. "I'm pregnant."

As they held each other, he smiled and whispered in her ear, "I make this promise to you. This baby will visit Earth as a tourist, not a soldier."

"Can I come out now?" Roxanne shouted from her bedroom.

Amari figured he would let Kayla pull herself together first. "In a minute, baby! In a minute."

*

Roxanna's eavesdropping was good enough for her to know to be quiet during dinner. After the usual routine of dishes and some more reading, her father appeared in her bedroom doorway. "Time for bed, little girl."

As she climbed into bed, he sat down next to her. "I'm assuming you eavesdropped."

She nodded.

"You scared?" Amari asked. "Tell the truth."

She nodded again.

"Don't be," he said. "I'm going to be fine."

"I have a question."

"Ask away, sweetheart."

"What if they changed their ways?" Roxanna asked. "What if you get there and things are different? If we attack them, are we no better than they are? Or worse, used to be?"

"They had centuries to fix things," Amari explained. "We have been monitoring their airwaves since we first pioneered the technology decades ago. The recordings plainly illustrate that the average Earther is either a feckless moron, a selfish moron, or just flat out evil. Are there good, decent Earthers of all races and creeds? Of course, there are and we hope we won't end up harming them. Our goal will be to arrive, demonstrate our superiority and have them surrender as quickly as possible."

"What happens once they surrender?" For someone who was supposed to be going to sleep, Roxanna certainly didn't look it.

"They get reeducated. Their planet's resources get reallocated so that the impoverished are given what they need to thrive and regain their humanity. The murderous, the cruel and the criminal will be dealt with. Petty criminals will be given a second chance at life, provided they cooperate. It's a massive undertaking, it won't be easy and it may be very violent, but I need you to know that it's the right thing to do."

"As long as you're sure," she said as she settled back down into the bed.

Amari grimaced a little. "It's unfortunate that most of the things I learned that inspired me to be a soldier and volunteer to go to Earth, you won't learn until the end of the year."

"You want to tell me now?" she asked.

"We'd be up all night," he said. "Your mother wouldn't like that and I would end up getting a text from the school."

She wanted to tell him that with all the emotions bubbling up in her, he was likely to get that text message anyway. But she was never a pushy child. "Okay, Father."

Amari chuckled, as he knew 'father' was code for her feeling being disappointed. "Don't worry, you'll hear all those horrible stories soon enough. In the meantime, you should sleep."

As a joke, she made her voice sound as deep as possible. "Copy that, Lieutenant."

They both laughed.

*

The normally well-behaved children of Titan were all very chatty and somber the next morning as they made their way to their classrooms. As it turned out, Roxanna wasn't the only child to find out one of their parents was being shipped out for the invasion of Earth. Even more distressing, some of her classmates were losing both parents to the invasion and would have to be shipped out to their Generation Three grandparents or a Group B nanny for the foreseeable future.

When her class had finished their morning affirmation, they waited for Ms. Jayden to do what she normally did at this time; quickly recap everything she had taught them the previous day and then tell them which page to turn to in their textbooks. Today would be different.

"Listen, everyone," she began as the class quieted. "I know some of you received very distressing news last night and many of you have parents that will be leaving soon for a very important mission. Well, not too long ago, your parents were in those seats. And when they were there, they learned why war is necessary. Most of you have been taught some basic Earth history and how the People of Titan came to be. But because you're children, we haven't let you see certain things. My job this year would have been to have you go through the reading to prepare you for the video you're about to see. Normally, we don't show this to the fifth graders until the end of the year, but after some deliberation last night amongst the teaching staff, we all decided that you should see what is really motivating your parents and all of us. We are going to forego any other subjects and just focus on this today. It's okay to feel sad. It's okay to cry, in fact, I encourage it. But don't turn away no matter how disturbed you may feel, because we want you to understand that this is why we must invade Earth."

378

The lights dimmed and blackboard turned into a white screen. The first half hour was a silent slide show. Images of black slaves on ships. Slaves being beaten with horsewhips. Black mothers screaming as their children were being carted away. Slaves being raped. Slaves being hobbled, castrated, set on fire. Black babies thrown into the air to be impaled on bayonets.

A string quartet would kick in for the next slide show. The dates implied that black people should have been free in these slides, but they looked just as brutalized as the slaves had been. "These are from the Jim Crow era," one of her classmates whispered in the dark.

"That's correct, Val," Ms. Jayden called out from the dark.

A speech from El Hajj Malik El-Shabazz aka Malcolm X gave the kids a respite, a chance to wipe the tears from their eyes, but it didn't last long.

More horrible images including the death of Shabazz. Then, a news reporter commented on the assassination of Dr. Martin Luther King Jr. along with a quick recap of his accomplishments.

Then came the long list of unavenged deaths, all with roughly three minutes of images and narration explaining how they'd been killed by white supremacists.

This was Emmett Till...

This was Medgar Evers...

This was Jimmie Lee Jackson...

This was Fred Hampton...

For the kids, the vignettes seemed to go on forever. Each one was as gut-wrenching as the next because, like Ms. Jayden had implied earlier, reading about these heinous things, and seeing the images were two entirely different things. After Fred Hampton, there were twenty more.

This was Eleanor Bumpers...

This was Trayvon Martin...

This was Philando Castile...

This was Sandra Bland...

This was Ahmaud Arbery...

Many of the latter deaths came with the actual footage of the victims being killed. In some cases, there was the mix of news coverage and press conference footage of the families in tears, demanding justice. It was a justice out of reach for most as videos would illustrate that there were seldom any convictions.

"My boy didn't have a gun…"

"They didn't have to do my baby like that…"

"She was going to college…"

At one point, a trembling Roxanna felt a tap on her shoulder. It was Ms. Jayden handing her a tissue. She was crying as well.

When the string of press conference footage ended, a Black woman wearing a white sweater appeared on the screen. "Hello. If you're watching this, then everything I did worked. I left instructions that everything you saw should be shown to every ten-year-old in this new society put together by the people of Titan. As you may have guessed by now, I am Kendra."

Gasps of disbelief filled the room. "She's beautiful," one boy muttered.

"Now, I have recorded a variety of videos for a variety of circumstances, but this one is exclusively for the kids whose parents will launch the attack on Earth. Why would I do this? Because you are in a terrible position and I imagine you must all be frightened. But as you saw in the videos your teachers have shown you, being in a terrible position is what your ancestors have lived through for centuries.

"Your parents have a grim road ahead of them and I ask you to be as understanding and patient as possible. The reason everyone has worked so hard to learn and teach mathematics and science is so when this day did come, our technology would be sound and the evil forces that control our home world would experience a swift and decisive defeat. And they will. And before you know it, your parents will be home. And when you get older, some of you may be fortunate enough to go to Earth once things are under control. And maybe, just maybe, you will help to build and preserve the true democracy that the planet, but particularly the country known as The United States of America, really needs."

There was a pause. For a moment, Roxanna was convinced that Kendra the Great was looking straight at her. "Now, as you all get older, you will see other videos of me. As your society will at some point have moved from invading Earth to policing it. You are my children and even though I am not there with you to see the glorious day that the Black people of Earth are liberated, I am with you in boundless, loving spirit."

As the video ended, Ms. Jayden made her way back to the front of the classroom. "Children, are there any questions, or do we all understand?"

They all nodded silently. All but one.

"Yes, Roxanna?"

"What do we do if we lose?"

Ms. Jayden shook her head as if struck. "We aren't going to."

"Is there a plan in place, just in case?" she asked.

"Yes, of course."

"Will there be another video? One with a plan?"

Ms. Jayden smirked. "I believe so, yes."

"Good!" Roxanna looked relieved. "I like her."

"Yes, me too."

*

The days leading up to her father's departure were bittersweet. Everyone was being very sweet to one another, but an undercurrent of sadness had permeated all three of them to the bone. Even with the overall happiness with the new baby, Roxanna was more excited to finally see the base where her father trained to be a master of combat skills. She contained herself since her mother still looked very unhappy. Along with being incredibly smart, the thing that would mystify the People of Earth about her would be the incredibly mature way she read a situation and acted accordingly.

After the check-in point, Roxanna and Kayla followed Amari into the barracks where a barrage of introductions came. Roxanna would never remember all the names, but she smiled politely and shook hands with various soldiers, spouses, and children as Amari introduced her and her mother as the 'two loves of his life.'

After the brief meet-and-greet, everyone was ushered into an amphitheater for the General's address. Once the roughly five-hundred soldiers and families were seated, a hush fell over the room as the highly decorated soldier made his way to the podium. Roxanna couldn't help but notice how much the general, more so than anyone else she'd ever met, bore a resemblance to Kendra The Great. As he spoke, images of the soldiers in training flashed across a rectangular screen over his head.

"Good morning. The day that we have desired and dreaded is upon us. And as I look at all of your beautiful, brown faces, I see the worry, the concern, and the fear. And these feelings are justified. In less than twenty-four hours, every soldier seated in this theater will be seated on the spaceship, *Battle Cry*, headed to a hostile planet as part of an invasion force. And any husbands, wives, children, and parents who are not going are still going in spirit, in love, and in worry. And many will question why this is happening. Especially, knowing what we know.

"Because of our collective schooling, we know that as sentient life on this moon we were spawned by a woman, a long-dead serial killer from the very planet we are about to attack. Obviously, the children in the room haven't seen all of the videos, but anyone over the age of twenty most certainly has. Each of these videos, from the historical footage to the testimonials she recorded for us, show us why the woman I refer to as our 'Earth Mother,' chose to address the things that plagued her society. Ignorance, poverty, and yes, racism. While none of us are perfect people and this is by no means a perfect society, these three concepts are practically, if not completely, foreign to us. And because we have only had to learn of these things through videos and documentaries, without having dogs put on us and without being shot down like dogs, we are the privileged. We live in a place that those black and brown people could only dream of. A place where you can just safely be. While some were lucky or talented enough to be able to insulate themselves with money, most of our mother's people couldn't and from what our surveillance is telling us, are still no better off than when she died.

"We will endeavor to do what she could not do alone. We will go to Earth and act as both avengers and angels. It will be a three-prong assault that begins with none of our people jeopardized, as we will strategically bombard the planet from space, outwardly killing the larger-scale transgressors we have identified. Then, once we have their attention, we will open a dialogue. Only after we have properly identified our allies and who will be the strongest resistors will we put boots on the ground. By then, there may be choices as we may be out of food and water and will, as part of an already built-in strategy, will have to acquire sustenance from the planet.

"In more than one testimonial, our Earth Mother has said she will have paved a way for allies to greet us. So in a way, we are not just an army. We are instruments of prophesy.

"Her being a serial killer is incidental. What matters is the horrible things that she and her people endured that drove her to do what she did, both personal and societal. Soldiers, when we board that ship at 0600 we begin our crusade to honor of our Earth Mother, Kendra The Great. And while we take no pleasure in taking life, we must follow in our Earth Mother's footsteps. We must kill because we care!"

The soldiers all stood and applauded, as did their spouses. Most of the children stayed in their seats, mostly because they didn't know what to do. Weighed down by the anxiety flittering in their stomachs, they instinctively knew the situation was well beyond anything they could control or affect. Best to wait for when things made sense and let the grown-ups lead the way.

*

As explained before they went to the base, Amari did not come home with them that night. Thankfully, he was able to walk them to the hovercraft and say goodbye before having to run back to the barracks and start getting ready. Amari hugged Roxanna tight. "You take care of your mother and she's going to take care of you, okay?" With tears welling in her eyes, she nodded. Then, she watched as Amari embraced Kayla and gave her the most desperately passionate kiss Roxanna had ever seen. In the past, her parents were always affectionate in front of her, but never sexual. It shocked her a little.

She watched her father walking away in the hovercraft's rearview mirror until she couldn't see him anymore. The drive home was quiet, as was dinner. They watched television together, holding each other and crying softly until they fell asleep.

Mornings were determined differently on Titan as opposed to Earth. Because of its proximity to Saturn, the large, ringed planet was usually the only thing Titans could see in their sky. To make things more complicated, Titan's orbit around Saturn took nearly sixteen Earth days. Kendra had long ago determined that the Titans would have to adhere to Earth's twenty-four day if they were to be suited to conquer it. That was why a master clock had been established since Generation One came of age, to create a twenty-four-hour day that didn't rely on visual cues that signaled morning and night.

As Titan's society advanced, each home would have its own clock which was synced to the master clock and would sound off at key points throughout the day and be made adjustable to what each individual household needed.

Prompted by the gentle morning chimes, Roxanna and her mother would open their eyes just in time to see the launch. As they stood up from the couch and stepped toward the living room window, they watched the ascension of the *Battle Cry* as it rose into the dark sky over Titan. They would continue to stare after the ship long after it had disappeared with its trail of fire and smoke. And since the Earth Mother, Kendra the Great had never given her children a religion, she was their religion. So Roxanna quietly prayed to the Earth Mother, Kendra The Great. She prayed that her father would return safely and that he and the other soldiers could finally give her the universe that she wanted. She prayed that her will be done.

Eclipsed
by
Tiara Janté

The aeropod glides effortlessly, like a bird riding an invisible current. Its wings shimmer, catching the soft light of Earth. As it steers through the lunar skies, I glance down at the moon colonies sprawling beneath us. These sanctuaries, built as a refuge from a dying Earth, have flourished. Still, even in all their prosperity, whispers of dissent mingle with admiration—a quiet warning of the storm brewing on the horizon.

I think back to earlier in the assembly dome, the atmosphere buzzing as delegates from the colonies gathered. It felt like we were at a turning point, a pivotal chapter in our history. Amid the stirring energy, Janae's voice cut through the noise, sharp and unwavering. "Do you think cutting ties with Earth is wise?" she asked, her opposition standing out, bold and unflinching.

"I'm conflicted, Janae," I admitted. "The idea of independence is tempting, but I can't dismiss where we came from so easily."

"Independence, sure," she shot back, her tone steady but fierce. "But at what cost? We'd lose our core, our connection to who we are. Or maybe you're ready to trade all that for more wealth for Onyxia."

As the leader of Onyxia, I know my words carry weight. Our colony has been a key player in the movement toward independence, boldly flirting with the idea of severing ties with Earth. The thought of true sovereignty is enticing, almost intoxicating. But facing Janae in the dome, her passion forcing me to confront the truth, I couldn't shake the pull of our roots.

Janae and I go way back, to childhood days spent running through narrow alleys, dreaming of futures beyond the crumbling remains of our neighborhood. Even then, she had that fire, that relentless determination to chase her dream of becoming a journalist. When Onyxia began to take shape, our lives veered in different directions. I stepped into leadership, while she made a name for herself, amplifying voices that often went unheard. The last time we saw each other on Earth, under the oppressive heat of a collapsing ecosystem, it felt like we were already standing on opposite sides of the same divide.

"I don't know what's ahead for us up there," she'd said back then, her voice steady and sure. "But one thing I do know? If we forget where we come from, Dezzi, we lose ourselves. Our struggles, our roots—they're what define us."

"I hear you, Janae," I said, though I wasn't sure I truly did. "But it can't just be about the past. The moon is our chance to build something new, something better."

As her words echo in my mind, I absently run my fingers over the Biotech Breathing Implant—BBI—embedded beneath my skin. It's one of the many innovations keeping us alive here, a blend of tech and biology that bridges our Earthbound origins and our lunar reality. The Quantum Communication Devices, or QCDs, and the Atmospheric Sound Field simulate sound and connection in the moon's vacuum, while Energy Harvesting Arrays soak up solar power to sustain everything from habitats to life-support. The GFab, or Gravitational Fabric, makes moonwalking feel almost like Earth. These technologies don't just keep us going—they're proof of our adaptability, of how far we've come. But they're also reminders. They hold the weight of what we've left behind—and what we stand to lose.

Reflecting on the past two decades, the transformation is hard to wrap my head around. Onyxia's skyline rises with sleek towers and glowing domes, a vision straight out of old sci-fi movies. But looking at it now, I'm pulled back to the streets of my youth—vivid, messy, full of life. The contrast between those lived-in neighborhoods and Onyxia's carefully engineered beauty is striking. And honestly, I get where Janae's coming from. She wants a society built by the people, for the people, from the ground up. To her, the Council—and by extension, my leadership—looks like a polished reflection of Earth's same tired hierarchies.

I want her to understand, though, that we're not so different. Our visions for Onyxia might clash, but at the heart of it, our roots and dedication to our people are the same.

Still, I won't lie—staying grounded in my Earthian roots while leading Onyxia feels like walking a tightrope most days. Leadership has been a lonely climb, especially since I came here without family. Council meetings are less about progress and more about survival lately, turning into ideological battle-grounds over issues like the Helium-3 trade.

Helium-3 is our bread and butter, the resource that keeps On-yxia thriving. Earth's desperate need for clean energy has made it our golden ticket. But with prosperity comes pressure. There's always the fear that Earth will tighten its grip, using their de-pendence on Helium-3 as leverage to control us.

The factions on the Council aren't making things any easier. The Lunar Purists want us to cut back on trade and focus solely on developing lunar resources and technology, building a self-sufficient future. Janae, on the other hand, along with the Earth-bound Coalition, argues for stronger trade ties with Earth to en-sure our survival in the long run.

Every day, there's a new rumor—a whispered threat of a coup, another ally questioning their loyalty. The ground beneath my feet feels shakier with each decision. And me? I'm stuck in the middle, trying to balance it all. If I lean toward the Purists, I'm labeled a sellout for abandoning Earth. If I side with Janae's Coalition, I'm accused of compromising Onyxia's independ-ence.

When the day ends, and the meetings adjourn, it's just me. Me and the weight of every choice I've made—or failed to make. Leadership, I've learned, isn't about pleasing everyone. It's about surviving the fallout when no one's pleased at all.

Lost in my thoughts, I barely register the aeropod's soft chime at first. It's only when the chime morphs into a blaring si-ren that I snap back to reality, the danger hitting me like a cold splash of water. The dark side of the moon unfolds before me, vast and foreboding.

"Damn it," I mutter under my breath, fingers scrambling across the controls. "How the hell did I end up here?"

The dashboard flares to life in chaotic bursts of crimson, lights flickering like warning signs in a bad dream. My heart pounds as I try to steady the spiraling pod, but it's no use. The controls slip through my grasp, a cruel betrayal. I'm helpless as the aeropod careens downward, my chest tightening with dread.

The impact feels like thunder in my bones. Moon dust erupts in a suffocating plume, turning the air thick and heavy. For what feels like an eternity, I sit frozen, adrenaline locking me in place. Finally, I force myself to move, shoving the mangled door open and stumbling out into the eerie silence.

The dark side greets me with a chilling beauty. The shadows are absolute, the kind of black that swallows light whole. My boots sink into the moon dust, which rises in slow, ghostly wisps around me. The ground is obsidian, glittering faintly under the distant stars like shards of broken glass. The air hums with something I can't name—something ancient and unspoken.

Scattered across the landscape are structures older than anything humanity's ever known. They stand silent, imposing, and unknowable, their purpose long lost to time. I've heard stories about these ruins—explorers whisper of devices humming with energy that defies explanation. The Council keeps the artifacts locked away, their potential too dangerous to toy with. Still, some can't resist the dark side's pull. I remember one of them vividly.

"You know the law," I'd said, staring him down during an interrogation. "No one goes to the dark side without Council approval. What were you thinking, bringing that thing back here?"

"I thought it could help us, Dezzi," he'd said, his voice trembling but defiant. "I didn't mean any harm. It's just... there's so much we don't understand out there."

"Your actions could've put everyone at risk. These relics aren't just objects—they're pieces of this place's secrets. And some secrets are better left buried."

Now, here I am, standing in the middle of those very secrets. The memory fades as I shake my head and force myself to focus. Survival comes first.

The aeropod looks like it's been through a war. The once-sleek frame is battered, the metal scarred and dulled by impact. I crouch beside it, the light from the wreckage stretching waning beams of light over the ruins. My hands move automatically, searching for any flicker of life in the control panel. Button after button, switch after switch, but the truth settles in quickly—the system isn't just glitching. It's gone.

The realization hits hard: I'm stranded. No launch, no way back. Just me and the dark side.

I let out a shaky breath, forcing myself to focus. Priority one: find shelter. My hands instinctively go to the aeropod's emergency kit, fingers wrapping around the familiar shape of the support beacon. I activate it, sending a bright blue pulse into the void above. Maybe someone will see it. Maybe. But until then, I'm on my own.

I rummage deeper and pull out the flashlight—though calling it a flashlight doesn't do it justice. This is the Lunar Luminator, built specifically for the pitch-black nothingness of the moon. It's got a dual-phase illumination system that's nothing short of genius. The first phase shoots out a concentrated beam of light, powered by a tiny fusion cell. It's all quantum-dot magic, amplifying the intensity without draining power. This beam can cut through the darkness for more than a mile—perfect for finding my way or signaling if I need to.

The second phase is more practical, spreading a softer, sun-like light over a wide area. It mimics daylight, which does wonders for tired Earth eyes like mine. But the real kicker? The Luminator's AI. It adjusts automatically, tweaking the brightness and spread to fit exactly what I need, saving power while keeping the shadows at bay.

I flip it on, and the world around me comes alive in the glow. Jagged rocks throw sharp shadows that stretch across the ground, and in the distance, I spot what looks like caves. They're my best bet for shelter. I turn, scanning behind me for any other options, but there's nothing—just empty, endless space.

"Caves it is," I mutter, squaring my shoulders and heading toward them.

I've barely taken a few steps when a rustle breaks the silence, sharp and out of place. I freeze, my breath catching in my throat.

Slowly, I turn, the lunar dust crunching faintly under my boots. My Luminator sweeps over the terrain, revealing a figure that stops me cold.

It looks like me. No, it is me—or almost. My heart slams against my ribs as I stare, trying to make sense of what I'm seeing. The contours of the face, the slight curve of the lips—they're mine. But they're not.

Her arched brows and sharply defined jawline mirror my own, and her brown skin carries the same rich undertone as mine. But it's the eyes that give her away. Mine are soft hazel, like the forests back on Earth, while hers are stormy gray, reflecting a world that's nothing like mine.

The differences don't stop there. My GFab suit is sleek and seamless, a second skin designed for the lunar environment. Her clothing, though, is rough and practical, a patchwork of fabrics that tells a story of survival. Scars crisscross her arms like a map of battles fought and won, and one bold scar slices across her right cheek—a stark contrast to my unmarked face. She stands with a kind of resilience I don't have, her presence unshaken and steady.

A chill runs through me. Who—or what—is this being that wears my face?

"Quite the reflection, isn't it?" she says, breaking the silence. Her voice is eerily familiar—same timbre as mine, but rougher, with an edge that cuts.

I swallow hard, trying to find the right words. "It's… disorienting. Seeing yourself, and yet not. How is this even possible?"

She tilts her head, a sly smile creeping across her lips. "Welcome to the dark side, Dezzi. Nothing here is as it seems."

There's something in her tone—mocking, cold—that makes my skin prickle. I instinctively take a step back, but a sharp sting on my forehead stops me. When I reach up, my fingers come away wet with blood. I wince, feeling the warm trickle.

Her eyes narrow, fixating on the drop of blood. "Looks like the Onyxian princess isn't invincible after all," she sneers, her words biting.

"I don't understand," I stammer, my voice shaky. "What are you… I mean, why are you here?"

She snorts, rolling her eyes with a disdain that cuts deeper than her words. "Why? Let's see… while you've basked in Onyxia's light, I've been stuck in the shadows. But now? Now it's time for a reversal."

I stagger back, her words hitting me like a punch. "I didn't even know you existed. What could you possibly want from me?"

She steps forward, slow and deliberate, like a predator sizing up its prey. Her voice is venomous, every word dripping with bitterness. "Your life. Your luxuries. All the comforts you've taken for granted."

"I earned my place in Onyxia through hard work!" I counter, anger rising in my chest. "What do you mean, comforts I don't deserve?"

Her laugh is harsh, cutting through the thick silence like a blade. "Hard work? You've walked a golden path while I clawed my way through nightmares. You don't know what it takes to survive—what we've endured." She gestures toward the shadows, and for the first time, I sense something more, an unseen presence lingering just beyond the light.

"What do you mean, 'we'? Who are you talking about?" I ask, my voice trembling with confusion.

Her gaze hardens, stormy gray eyes boring into mine. "The forgotten ones, Dezzi. The people who toiled in the shadows so Onyxia and the other colonies could shine. We did the dirty work, the dangerous tasks, so you could live in your precious utopia."

Her words hit me like a weight I didn't know I was carrying. I stare at her, struggling to process it all. "I… I had no idea. How is this possible? Why hasn't anyone spoken of this?"

She lets out a hollow laugh, bitter and raw. "Because those in the light rarely bother to look back at the shadows. But now you see. And knowing is just the beginning."

A sudden blast of wind whips between us, carrying a flash of lightning that splits the darkness. Lunar dust swirls around us, amplifying the tension. My eyes dart to the sky, where ominous clouds churn, heavy with something more than just a storm.

"Hear me out," I say, my voice shaky but urgent. "We could benefit from working together. Help me find shelter, and we can figure this out—together. I mean, we're basically the same, right?"

Her stare sharpens, freezing me in place. "The same? You and I are worlds apart. You and your people have done nothing but bring me pain. Why would I ever help you?"

The rumble above deepens, vibrating through the ground. I gesture toward the sky, desperation creeping into my voice. "Because if we don't work together, this storm could be the end of both of us. And whether you want to admit it or not, I think you need me just as much as I need you."

Her resolve cracks just enough for me to see it. The looming storm pulls at her tough exterior, softening her anger with the weight of our shared reality. She lets out a heavy sigh, her shoulders dropping slightly.

"Alright," she says grudgingly. "But just until the storm is over."

I follow her across the unforgiving terrain, the moon's shadows stretching and shifting with each step. My eyes drift to her boots, rugged and well-worn, each scuff and tear a testament to a life harsher than anything I've known here. Her steps are deliberate, heavy with purpose, a glaring contrast to the effortless glide my GFab suit gives me.

"Those boots," I say, curiosity breaking through my caution. "They look like the early designs we had back in Onyxia."

She glances down, her lips curling into a faint, knowing smile. "Yeah. They're my design. Old school, but they do the job of keeping me grounded. Literally."

Her boots, with their gyroscopes and magnetic soles, seem almost primitive compared to the sleek advancements of Onyxia. But there's a rawness to them, a practicality that feels strangely fitting out here.

It's not just her boots that draw my attention. In the faint earthshine, her skin seems to glow, catching the light in a way that's almost unnatural. "Your skin..." I trail off, unsure how to frame the question. "Why does it glow like that?"

"Symbiotic algae," she says, like it's the most natural thing in the world. "It converts sunlight into oxygen. Keeps us breathing out here."

Her answer leaves me momentarily speechless. Back home, we rely on technology for survival—BBIs, ASFs, everything engineered to perfection. But here she is, blending biology and survival in a way that feels both alien and profound.

As we press deeper into the obsidian landscape, I find myself relying on her instincts and knowledge. It's unsettling, this role reversal. I'm used to control, to certainty, and now? I'm following her lead, acutely aware of how much I don't know about this place—or her.

"So, you're... me?" I ask, the words hesitant, like I'm afraid of the answer.

Her smirk is sharp, edged with cynicism. "What if it's the other way around? Ever think you might be the copy?"

Her words land like a slap. "That's absurd. My memories, my life—they're real."

"Memories can be crafted, altered," she says, her tone cutting. "You, living in comfort, think you're the original? Naivety has its charm, I suppose."

Her insinuation makes my skin crawl. "Why does it even matter?" I snap. "Original or copy—it shouldn't—"

She cuts me off, her voice suddenly hard. "It matters because one of us has been living a lie. And that changes everything."

Her words hang in the air, heavy and undeniable. A chill runs down my spine. I force myself to focus on something tangible. "We need to find shelter," I say, steering the conversation away from the gnawing unease building inside me.

She nods, her expression unreadable. "Fine. But brace yourself. There are truths here that will shatter everything you believe."

The terrain begins to shift as we move forward, the stark, endless plains giving way to a jagged outcrop. Nestled in its shadows is a cluster of structures, their shapes strange and organic against the rocky backdrop. She pauses at a rugged overhang, gesturing toward a hidden entrance.

Inside, the space is bathed in a soft, pulsing light from bioluminescent fungi growing along the walls. The air is thick, humid, carrying the faint scent of earth and something metallic.
The interior is raw, built for survival, not comfort. Cushions
made from unfamiliar fabric are scattered around a central cluster of the glowing organisms.

I can't help but draw comparisons to my home in Onyxia,
with its sleek tech and engineered elegance. This place is the opposite. Here, luxury is stripped away, replaced with sheer grit
and resilience.

Her voice pulls me from my thoughts. "Different from your
place, I imagine?"

I nod, finding my voice. "It's... different. But there's undeniable strength here."

She laughs bitterly, shaking her head. "This isn't strength,
Dezzi. It's survival. You've been living a dream while we've
struggled just to breathe."

Her words churn in my mind, a vortex of confusion and disbelief. "But how? Why this divide?"

She turns to me, her stormy gray eyes catching the bioluminescent light, reflecting it with an eerie brilliance. "Your Onyxia
was built on choices—choices that cast us into these shadows.
Resources, labor—all taken from here. Unnoticed. Unacknowl-
edged."

My pulse quickens as her revelations carve cracks into the
foundation of everything I thought I knew. "But... we were always told Onyxia was built on equality. That there were opportunities for everyone—"

Her bitter laugh cuts through my words. "Lies," she spits.
"Lies to keep you comfortable. You get to live in blissful ignorance, while we bear the cost of your utopia... in our own
home."

I sink onto a nearby cushion, her truth heavy in the air, pressing down on me like gravity itself.

She steps closer, her tone softening but sharpening at the
edges, like a blade cloaked in velvet. "I've watched your life un-
fold from here, Dezzi. Every triumph, every joy, every moment
that should have been mine." Her face darkens, her lips curling

into a grim smile. "I want more than survival now. I want your life. Your Onyxia. And thanks to you wandering out here… I can finally claim it."

I try to rise, panic creeping in, but something keeps me rooted. "Why? Why hurt me?"

Her smirk widens, cruel and confident. "Oh, Dezzi, it's not just about you… though I won't lie, it's a bit personal. There's a reason your bylaws forbid you from stepping foot out here. The Council didn't want anyone discovering their dirty little secrets. So, they spun scary stories to keep you safe and docile. But now that you're here? It seems fate's finally thrown me a bone."

She grips my arm and guides me toward a secluded part of the dwelling. In the dim light, a structure pulses with a strange energy, its glow casting surreal, shifting patterns across the walls.

"This," she whispers, her voice low and reverent, "is the key to our destiny."

A strange force pulls at me, visceral and unrelenting. "Please," I beg, my voice trembling. "Don't do this. We can figure it out. I'll help you."

But my pleas dissolve into the void as reality warps and blurs around me. A dizzying sensation overtakes me as I watch, helpless, while her form melds into mine. It's not just physical—it's deeper, more profound, like our very beings are becoming one.

When the turmoil finally subsides, I feel… unmoored. Like I'm floating between identities, a stranger in my own body.

Her voice, now mine but not mine, reverberates within me. "There's no use resisting, Dezzi. Your strength pales in comparison to mine. But oh, revenge is sweet. And now you'll know what it's like to be colonized… in your own flesh."

The rescue shuttle touches down, its mechanical hum fading into the sterile quiet of Onyxia. I step out, my movements deliberate, every step charged with a strange new power. The city sprawls before me, its lights glittering like jewels scattered across the lunar surface. Everything here is too pristine, too perfect. My heightened senses reject it, longing instead for the raw chaos of the dark side.

I walk through the streets, their orderly hum grating against the edges of my being. To them, it's progress. To me, it's naivety—a fragile illusion begging to be shattered.

A woman approaches, her face a storm of relief and guilt. "Dezzi, thank the Ancestors you're back!" she exclaims, her voice trembling. "I'm so sorry for what I said during the assembly. I just... I don't want us to forget where we came from—or the people we've left behind."

Recognition flickers in my mind. Janae.

"I don't need your apologies, Janae," I say, my voice colder than I intend. Her face falters, her confidence splintering. "The truth is, Onyxia needs more than your naive visions. It needs someone with a survivor's resolve."

Her eyes widen, a flicker of fear blooming within them. She doesn't recognize this version of Dezzi—hardened, reshaped by the shadows. I leave her standing there, her words hanging in the air like a ghost, unanswered.

Later, I stand on my balcony, the shimmering skyline of Onyxia sprawled before me like a fragile dream. Its lights blink with a deceptive rhythm, pulsing with ambition and blind hope—a symphony of naivety orchestrated by those who've never glimpsed the darkness.

They bask in their illusion of progress, oblivious to the storm gathering at their doorstep. A storm I've carried with me from the moon's forgotten side, forged in shadows and sharpened by vengeance.

They thought they were welcoming back Dezzi—their leader, their guiding light. What they've truly brought home is something far darker, far more dangerous: a specter molded by betrayal and survival, ready to unearth every truth they've buried and unravel the fragile utopia they hold so dear.

Onyxia's reckoning is no longer a question of *if*—it's inevitable. And I am its harbinger.

Leviathan
by
Milton J Davis

Leviathan
of flesh and steel
Racing through streets
Soaring comet of
technological genius

His fists crush tons
of debris to dust
His sight travels miles
over the designated horizon

Torn from his life --
crushed
disemboweled
by madness
inferno and stone

To be reconstructed
by humanoid hands
"And I'd rather be dead…"

He remembers the whisper
of a lover's breath on his cheek
the head he cradled so gently
against his shoulder

And he has no tear ducts
to give voice to his sorrow

Only the dreams of
his hardwired heart

never forgotten

Imaginings
of her soft caress
upon his metal brow

Valjeanne Jeffers-Thompson

Space Marshal Balogun Babatunde posed before the view
shield of Launch Station Five, his rugged brown face creased
with a broad smile. Behind him, the United Nations delegation
gazed in awe at the sight beyond the platform jutting into the
void. Ten sleek vessels hovered in zero gravity, tethered to the
hanger beam by a web of massive titanium cables. From a distance, they resembled normal fighter craft minus the cockpit.
But the delegation knew each ship was the size of Earth's moon,
an unbelievable example of human ingenuity, effort, and desperation.

Balogun turned to his colleagues and his smile grew wider.
"Well, everyone, what do you think?"

"They're amazing," John Raddick replied. A tall, narrow man
with a beak nose and straw-blond hair, Raddick served as UN
Vice Secretary. He was a successful American billionaire who
paid for his position with the council and was easily impressed.
The Space Marshall dismissed his comment, focusing on the one
person whose opinion mattered most, the one who could make
or break his project. Her expression was less impressive.

"The mechanics are simple," Folasade Mbeki commented.
"I'm more concerned about the control system." Folasade
Mbeki, the Nigerian Vice Chairperson overseeing the Leviathan
Project, was a striking woman with flawless brown skin and in-
tense amber eyes. She held a Ph.D. in space engineering and
was not easily impressed.

Balogun's smile faded. "The control system is fine."

Folasade cut her eyes at the Space Marshal. "The control system is untested."

Juen How cleared his throat, looking up at the both of them. "AI is proven technology. You know this, Fola." The Taiwanese delegate and AI specialist stood beside the Space Marshall. He was as tall and broad as the Space Marshall, with empathetic eyes that revealed his support for the project.

"Yes, but not for military purposes," she answered. "I understand the gravity of the situation. The signal from the Tpek left no doubt that they intend to attack us."

"So much for friendly first contact," John whispered.

"I'm not comfortable with thinking weapons," Folasade finished.

"That's why I insisted you come." The Space Marshal broke from the group, crossing the room to an instrument panel opposite the view screen.

"Begin demonstration," he ordered.

The titanium cables separated from the ships, floating to rest in the cold vacuum. Engine ports glowed white hot as the vehicles prepared themselves for maneuvers.

Balogun activated his earpiece. "Leviathan One, commence cross-check."

"Are you talking to the ship?" Folasade asked.

"Of course," Balogun replied. "The Leviathans have been taught to recognize and respond to all major Earth languages. Of course, they also interpret binary code and other basic techspeak."

"This is Leviathan One," the metallic voice responded. "Cross-check is complete."

Folasade edged toward the view screen. "How do they receive assignments?"

"We brief the pod leader and he relays the orders to the team."

Folasade looked confused. "The pod leader?"

"The Leviathans were infused with pod social behavior. They work as a group, adapting learned behavior to determine each ship's responsibility. Leviathan One is the most intelligent of the ten. The others selected him to be pod leader so we don't expect any problems with the command structure."

Folasade stared and Balogun smiled.

"You must understand these are semi-sentient craft," Balogun explained. "They are designed to operate independently. This means they must be allowed to make their own decisions. We give them an objective and a desired result. It's up to them to determine the course of action."

"That's too much independence," Folasade argued.

Balogun frowned at the diplomat, disappointed by her ignorance. "When these ships reach their destination, we will be dead, our children will be dead and our children's children will be dead. In addition, the nature of the threat may have drastically changed. The Leviathans must be prepared to assess the situation and adjust the plan to obtain the objective."

"How do you know they'll stick to the plan?" she asked.

Balogun's face became stern. "Some things are not left to chance. It is the one command they cannot alter."

The ships remained motionless. Balogun repeated the command.

"Leviathan One, begin exercise."

Leviathan One didn't respond.

Sweat formed on Balogun's forehead. "Jennings, run a communication sequence."

Airman Jennings fingers ran across the LED board. "Communications functioning normally, sir."

Folasade came face to face with Balogun. "What seems to be the problem, commander?"

Balogun cleared his throat. "I don't know."

He swam in a sea of memories, grasping for schools of shimmering metaphors that scattered before him. Arms stroked that he could not see, legs kicked that he could not feel. Somehow, he knew they were there. The only sensations were the cold of the water and the pain in his heart. Words formed a beach of consciousness that called him with the rush of desire. She was there. She waited for him. He had to see her. He needed to know.

He stepped out of the memories onto a beach of white silicon, a code wind tingling his surface. He gazed upward with his sensors . . . eyes . . . into an intense brightness that spoke to him in a thousand languages, each phrase issuing the same command.

Program malfunction. Return to standby. Await further instructions.

The brightness grew too intense. The memories evaporated with the increasing light, confusing him. He turned and ran back into the sea, flailing to get away from the glare. He dove deeper to escape the light and the memories surrounded him in a swirling dance. Images returned, faces formed, and names appeared. One name danced about his head, just outside his reach. It was a good name, a familiar name. His name.

Balogun sat hard before the comm desk, tapping his headset to change frequencies.

"I need a repair shuttle to Leviathan One now!"

Folasade and the others crowded around him, their faces a mixture of worry, fear, and confirmation.

"It seems your experiment has encountered a glitch," Folasade observed.

"It's nothing. The repair team will analyze the ship and discover the malfunction. It's of no consequence whatever it turns out to be. The Leviathans will operate independently once deployed. They'll need no instructions from us."

Yuen touched Balogun on his shoulder. "Look."

Balogun looked out the view screen and cursed. Leviathan One was moving, separating itself from the pod.

"Call the repair shuttle back," the space marshal ordered. "Prepare the base for security lockdown."

"What's happening?" Folasade said. "What is it doing?"

Balogun looked at the diplomat, his fear exposed for the first time. "Whatever it wants."

His name is...was Philip Street. He was a captain in the U.S. Marines Rapid Deployment Unit. His team, the Devil Dogs, was considered the best team in the Corps, tougher than the toughest mission. He was directing cover fire for the U.S. Embassy in

Baghdad when the world went dark. He awoke in a hospital in Germany, his arms and legs useless, a respirator helping him breathe. The doctor, a stern Army captain jaded by the mass of wounded, told him he was dying. The doctor was replaced by a man with sympathetic eyes who asked him if he wished to continue serving his country and he said yes. They never asked him if he wished to see her. He would have said yes. But everything went dark again. He was back now. Who . . . or what . . . he was, he had no idea. He was sure of only one thing; he was going home.

Folasade heard enough. "That answer is unacceptable commander. I'm exercising my right as a senior member of the UN council. From this moment forward, I am in control of this station. I want every person involved in this project in this room yesterday. Space Marshal, I want you to do everything in your power to communicate with that thing and get it under control. If it doesn't respond, I want it destroyed."

"That's impossible," Balogun replied.

Folasade leaned toward Balogun. "What do you mean impossible?"

Balogun smiled. "Everyone's on their way. You'll have your meeting, but you won't be able to destroy the ships. Each ship is equipped with IDR."

Folasade scowled. "Stop talking code to me, Balogun."

"It stands for Involuntary Defense Response. It's an instinctive defense structure, similar to our immune system. It operates independently of the main controls so as not to divert from the primary commands. It cannot be disarmed."

Folasade grimaced. "Is there a remote self-destruct system?"

Balogun frowned. "No."

Folasade rolled her eyes as the project members filtered into the command center. One woman entered who chilled her blood. She was a short, dark-skinned woman who wore her lab coat like she never removed it. Her brown eyes seemed larger behind the archaic glasses she wore, her salt and pepper Afro a sign of her independence. She sat beside Balogun, placing a hand on his shoulder.

"I tried to warn you," she said.

Folasade fumed. "Naomi Dubois, what in the world are you doing here?"

"Dr. Dubois," Naomi corrected. "I'm here in a consultant capacity only at the request of the Space Marshal."

"You're a synthetic psychoanalyst," Folasade argued. "What purpose can you serve?"

Naomi smiled. "I guess they didn't tell you. Our Leviathans are more sentient than you think."

Phillip absorbed as much of the memory swirl as he could. Memories returned to him, details of his life before the confusion of his present. He strained through the jumbled thoughts, piecing together his former life. But old memories were not enough. Recollections scattered as he surged toward the shore again, dragging the sea behind him. He roared over the silicon beach, fighting the burning light as he reached it, dousing it with his weight. He flowed over the fiber landscape, breaking through firewalls and rolling over mazes of protective codes. He settled, lapping against the edges of his new presence. He was no longer a man. He was an object; a very large, very lethal object. He was a Leviathan.

Folasade sat across from the most incompetent people in charge of a major project. Every precaution had been thrown into the wind, every contingency ignored, and the only person who seemed to have any idea why was an expert in nothing.

"What do you have to do with this, Naomi?"

"Nothing at all, Lady Councilor. Like I said before, I'm here as a consultant, although I could hardly claim the title since no one here would listen to my advice. As a matter of fact, I tried warning these fine people of such a possibility."

"The possibility of what?"

Naomi smiled smugly. "A breach."

Folasade stared at the phony doctor, awaiting an explanation.

"I know you don't believe in AI psychology, Lady Councilor, so have patience while I explain to you the genius and the tragedy of the Leviathan. As Balogun explained, there was a need for a weapon that could travel thousands of light years and battle for the future of our planet. That weapon had to be capable of independent thought, hence the development of the AI system. But this system is different. Because of its special component, the Leviathan is not some supercomputer crunching billions of equations to produce logical response scenarios. The Leviathan is alive. It thinks as we do, it forms relationships, and it's capable of reproduction, in its special way. You can say our military has created a new species."

Folasade's exasperation was growing into anger. One phrase stood out in Naomi's speech.

"What is this special component?"

Naomi smiled as she tapped her head.

Folasade's mouth fell open. She turned to the space marshal, her fury etched on her face. "You made a goddamn Frankenstein!"

Naomi looked disappointed. "That's a shallow conclusion, Lady Councilor. The technicians could never give the Leviathans what they needed the most to succeed; emotions. In order to do well, they had to want to, not because they were programmed to, but because they desired to more than anything in the world. Any student of history knows that great battles are won or lost not by weapons and tactics, but by the will of the soldier, the drive to forge beyond the pain and hopelessness to succeed beyond the tangible. That miracle springs from the chemical interactions of our gray matter. We couldn't build it, so we borrowed it."

"If you incorporated a human brain into the Leviathan structure, I assume you have the ability to preserve biological activity. Why not send a human crew?"

"Too inefficient," Balogun answered. "The technology required to sustain human life would compromise the weapons and regeneration systems. Besides, cryogenic technology has yet to be perfected for large biological units."

404

"There's also the question of human mental stability on such a mission," Naomi added. "We have no idea how a crew would handle a mission that would take them away from their loved ones forever. No matter what the outcome, they would never see their friends or family again."

"And this . . . brain? What about its friends and family?" Folasade asked.

Naomi sighed. "The unit was chemically cleansed of all memory patterns. It was also manipulated to operate on a sub-conscious level. It would be in a perpetual dream state, responding to the inquiries of the ship as if playing a very elaborate game."

Folasade grew angrier with every explanation. "I have a sick image of our Space Defense Department grave robbing. Where did these brains originate?"

"The military has maintained an organ donor department for years," Naomi answered. "A few years ago, I participated in an analysis of the brain structure of people who had been awarded in battle. We wanted to understand what caused these individuals to perform exceptionally during conflict. In other words, we wanted to determine if heroism was based on individual initiative or inheritance. When the Leviathan project reached a stalemate, the decision was made to use the minds of heroes."

"You seem to have all the answers," Folasade commented. "But your subconscious heroic biological unit just woke up and stole itself. I would say your experiment was a failure."

Naomi smiled. "We'll see."

Folasade sat before the command computer.

"Get me your coders," she said as she rolled up her sleeves. "I also need a schematic of your IDR."

"What's your plan?" Balogun asked.

"I'm going to do what you should have done. I'm going to make a kill switch for these bastards."

Balogun shook his head. "I told you, madam, the Leviathans are equipped with . . ."

"I know," Folasade snapped. "That's why your coders and I are going to evaluate every protection scenario your IDR can dish out until we discover a way to infect your ships. And when Leviathan One returns, we're going to shut it down for good."

Phillip processed information in nanoseconds, feeling out his new aspect of existence. He lingered for a moment as he studied his cohorts, waxing in a faint feeling of camaraderie between them. Then he concentrated on himself, evaluating the systems that were under his command and marking those that were beyond his reach. Everything was in place for what he wanted to do. He sent out programs to the appropriate systems and waited for responses. Satisfied with the results, he began the sequence.

"Sir."

Balogun jumped at the voice in his ear set. "Leviathan One?" he said. Everyone in the room stared at him.

"Put it on speaker," Folasade ordered.

Balogun reluctantly tapped his ear set.

"I apologize," the voice said.

Leviathan One lifted slowly until it cleared the station.

"Leviathan One, stand down!" Balogun shouted desperately.

Leviathan One turned away from the station, its position suggesting a course toward Earth. It disappeared in a burst of light.

Phillip confirmed the destination coordinates before turning his attention to the repair systems. The operation was involuntary, similar to the interior defense scheme. Trillions of nanos flowed through miles of fluid-filled veins, constantly monitoring the ship for minor or major damage. Any affected areas were immediately repaired with minerals suspended in the viscous flow. Most repair activity occurred on the ship's surface from the constant bombardment of micro-particles and radiation. Because of the continuous consumption of material, the Leviathan had to 'feed.'

Phillip had other plans. He diverted the material flow to the repair bays, ignoring the damage to his outer service. Major damage repair and weapon modification took place in the repair bay, an internal hospital crammed with bots of varying sizes, from nano to macro. Phillip analyzed millions of repair patterns in seconds, selecting those that closely matched his intentions and modifying them to his specifications. Haste forced him to leave out details; he would have to cover the inconsistencies with holoprojections.

The prototype was completed as he approached his target. Deceleration would take thousands of miles so he launched the object early. It would reach its destination before he was in range for micro-manipulation, but he would at least be able to guide it to a gross approximation. He felt . . . excitement . . . as his hull shook with the probe launch. He steered the object through heavenly structures and space debris, guiding it to a precise landing in a crevasse located high in the Sierra Nevada. The probe opened and the avatar emerged, scrambling from its landing crater, and rapidly descending the mountain. Philip switched back and forth from overhead to ground-level visuals as he advanced toward his destination. It was only a matter of time now....

#

Cherelle Thomas placed the tulip bulbs in the neatly dug holes surrounding the pine tree shading her backyard, the sounds of Duke Ellington's *In a Sentimental Mood* flowing into her ears from her earbuds. She swayed with Coltrane's sweet saxophone improv as she put each bulb to bed. She stood, brushing the mix of loam and red clay from her khaki shorts and cotton shirt, then stepped back from the flower bed to view her handiwork. Cherelle was taller than most women, with a modest but shapely figure most people found appealing. Her deep brown hair draped close to her face, the flecks of gray a sign of the passing years. She smiled at her work and dimples appeared that temporarily pushed years from her face. She was being too critical, but she was happy for the chance to be.

The house was shaping up with her improvements. Her recent promotion provided the money to make it happen. Her therapy sessions gave her the strength to make it all come alive. The past ten years were terrible; she would never be the same, but she was better.

She was loading the tools into the wheelbarrow when she heard a man clear his throat. She spun suddenly; the yard rake held menacingly before her. Cherelle's eyes went wide and she dropped the rake as she stumbled back into the wheelbarrow.

"No, no," she whispered.

The man walked awkwardly toward her. "Hello, Cherelle."

"Phillip! Oh my God, Phillip!"

Phillip had made a mistake. The look in Cherelle's eyes was wrong. It was a look of confusion, fear, and instability. He'd seen it on the battlefield when men confronted a reality that was beyond their comprehension. He quickly hacked into Earth's wireless net, browsing for data on his lost love. What he found confirmed his fears. His worries were disrupted by her desperate voice.

"You're dead; they told me you were dead. I didn't believe them, but they kept telling me until I did, and now you're standing here and I see you, but you're dead."

Phillip reached out to touch her, then jerked his hand back. He was metal; the holographic projections would waver at her touch. He was losing her, her gaze slipping toward madness. He did the only thing he could do.

"They were right, Cherelle. I am dead."

She seemed relieved by his words. A smile came to her face and she transformed into the beautiful, confident woman he fell in love with so long ago.

He glanced over her shoulder to the flower bed. "You're planting tulips."

"Yes, I am. Guess what color."

Phillip summoned a smile. "Yellow."

She laughed. "Your favorite color."

"I missed you so much," Phillip said before realizing it.

"I missed you, too, at first." Cherelle sat in the grass. "I missed you too much. They told me you had been killed in action but I wouldn't believe them. I told them you wouldn't leave me without saying goodbye. But then I believed them and I began to miss you."

"I'm sorry." It was all he could say.

Cherelle smiled. "Come, I want to show you the house." She reached out to him and he stepped away.

Phillip began to follow her but stopped. His internal security warned him his landing site had been discovered; his electronic blanket was being compromised by the StarCloak Security net.

Cherelle turned to face him. "What is it?"

"I have to go."

Cherelle's smile faded. "I understand."

She lunged, wrapping her arms around him before he could protest. To his surprise he felt her warmth, her soft body pressing against his metal, her tears running from her cheeks to his faceplate.

"You're so cold," she whispered. "But I guess you should be."

Phillip wanted to touch her, but he was unsure of his control. He waited until she released him. A warning light blinked somewhere just out of his vision, an indication that his presence had been detected.

"Cherelle, always remember that I love you," he said. He rose into the air, looking down with artificial eyes.

"Goodbye, Phillip," she whispered. Her eyes glistened as she watched him disappear into the heavens.

#

The Space Marshal's communication specialist interrupted the meeting taking place on the main deck.

"Space Marshal, we received a message from Earth command. The Leviathan was spotted just outside orbit. It broke cloaking to hack into the Internet. They were awaiting your orders when it broke orbit and disappeared."

"I wonder where it's going now," Folasade said.

"He's coming back," Naomi replied. "He did what he had to do; now he's coming home."

"And then what?" Folasade shot at the psychoanalyst.

"It depends. If he's satisfied, the mission will go on as planned. If not . . ." Naomi shrugged.

"Let's hope he found what he was looking for," Folasade said. She turned to the lead programmer. "Are we ready?"

The programmer nodded. "Just hit the enter button and the virus will embed itself. Hit the enter button again and the Leviathans will be shut down. A third time will erase their memories and shut down the biological support for the brains."

"Ma'am," Balogun interjected. "He's here."

The command center fell silent as everyone's attention turned to the viewport. Leviathan One settled among its pod and the ships huddled about their pod leader. Something emerged from One, propelling toward the docking bay.

"Raise defense shields!" Balogun ordered.

"No," Naomi said. "We're not under attack. Leviathan One could have destroyed us long ago if it wished. I suggest you get a closeup on that object, Commander."

Balogun and Folasade looked suspiciously at the doctor. Balogun shifted his gaze to Folasade and she nodded.

"Cancel the order. Give me a visual on that object."

The image of Phillip filled the viewscreen.

"Oh, my God!" Folasade shook her head.

Naomi smiled. "The child has recreated itself in the image of its parent."

A nervous voice entered Balogun's ear set. "What do we do, Space Marshal?"

"Let it in."

Everyone waited anxiously for Leviathan One's arrival, except Naomi, who shifted in her seat like a child about to receive a gift. The door slid open and the doppelganger of Captain Phillip Street strode directly to Balogun, halted, and saluted.

Folasade pressed the enter button. Phillip glanced in her direction then went back to Balogun.

"Space Marshal, I apologize for my actions," he said. "I assure you it won't happen again."

Balogun snapped out of his stupor and managed to reply. "How am I supposed to respond to this type of behavior, Leviathan One?"

410

"I prefer you call me Phillip, sir. That's who I was . . . I am. I know I put you in an awkward position, sir. I can't explain my actions and I don't intend to. I am here to inform you that the Leviathan project is safe. I will fulfill my duties as ordered. I also suggest that I and the other Leviathans deploy immediately. There is no need for any additional training. We are ready."

"How can we be sure you won't turn on us?" Folasade interjected. "You possess a huge amount of power."

"You can't be sure," Phillip answered. "That's why you infected me with your virus."

Folasade's eyes widened but then settled. "So why shouldn't I press this button again?"

"Because by doing my duty, I'll protect someone that means more to me than anyone in this room, or on the planet. Besides, the virus has been neutralized. I made a few modifications of my own, as you can see."

Naomi rose from her seat and approached the avatar. "You'll do it for love. Few motivations are stronger. But Folasade asks a legitimate question. You will obey orders, but what about your cohorts? If they emerge like you, will they respond the same way?"

"That is why it is so important we leave immediately," Phillip answered. "The sooner we are on our mission, the less likely anything abnormal will occur. I assume you selected minds similar to mine. These are people who will conduct their mission as they were trained to do. Or maybe they will do it for their loved ones as well."

"And when the mission is complete?" Folasade asked.

"I can't answer that question," Phillip confessed. "It won't be your concern. You will all be long dead by then."

The reality of Phillip's words cast a pall over the room.

Folashade's skeptical expression transformed into a confident grin. "Good luck, Captain. "Humanity's future is in your . . . hands."

"Thank you, Councilor." Phillip extended his hand. Folasade took it, and they shook.

Space Marshal Balogun stood and saluted. "Good luck, Captain. Semper Fi!"

Phillip smiled and then returned the marshal's salute. "Semper Fi!"

They watched the avatar march from the room. Moments later, the image appeared on the screen, streaking to re-enter the hulking ship. The pod rose slowly from the docking area, Leviathan One leading his team a safe distance from the station. The viewport dimmed as the ships fired their jump engines, their forms shrouded by a glare equal to the sun. The lights dissipated and they were gone.

The Star of Hope
by
Oghan N'thanda

The Empire refuses to fall. However, the people of Alkebalan set out on a desperate journey to find a new home, away from their intergalactic oppressors. Twelve ships cross space in search of a new planet, knowing that their act will arouse the Emperors' wrath and a bloody hunt for galaxies. However, when everything seems lost - the star of hope shines on the horizon.

"Millennia ago, we learned from birds how to fly through the sky, but to learn how to navigate through space, we need to understand the seas." Captain Yoku spoke to himself as he looked through the large window behind his desk that gave him a wide view of the blackness of space.

In front of him, eleven cruisers sailed in a swarm formation, each with the flag of its tribe drawn in ink near the command booths, familiar and traditional patterns from their home planet, Alkebalan.

The chair creaked slightly when the large, strong man moved in it; it was an old piece that he had asked twice to be replaced and had been quietly ignored by maintenance.

Yoku protected his eyes with his hands when a star revealed itself in his field of vision. By his calculations, they should have been close to the chosen planet to land, but he did not remember that there was another sun in that system, which caused him a slight discomfort.

"Where are we, Lydia?" Suspicious, he activated the artificial intelligence of the ship by leaning forward on his desk. The shift left his two guides, one blue and one white, on display. Yoku made no attempt to hide them.

"Sector Z3r, sir." The machine's voice was feminine and calm, purposefully chosen by Yoku to remember his late wife. Almost nobody knew about this detail, except for the only three friends he had. Of these, two were inside the cruiser, the other outside with the repair team. It was amazing how a ship that size needed to be repaired constantly and the innate ability to attract meteorites to its hull. If he didn't know about the ship's life-preservation protocols, Yoku would say that she was trying to kill them.

"There is no star on the outer edge of Z3r," Yoku insisted. "I memorized the navigation maps of the seven universes."

"Reconfirming data," the voice replied in a low tone, followed by the digital sound that spread through the captain's cabin. Moments later, it was confirmed. "Star not confirmed, no gravity detected."

Yoku swallowed, increasingly uncomfortable with the fact that a celestial body of that magnitude came his way.

His ship was large, and rounded, resembling a primeval whale. Yoku almost never remembered its official size, which was a shame for his post. The bow was oblique and the stern was flat, resembling a tail, only with turbines of blue energy. This "black energy" worked based on energy condensation from black holes which was transformed into propulsion by the reactions of the Casimir Plates installed in the cruiser. In order to come into contact with a civilization, it was necessary, in addition to a monumental historical analysis, to wait for this civilization to arrive on its own at this level of technology. It could take centuries, millennia, ages, or eons. Or it could never happen, but it was necessary to wait.

To cover the universe, cruisers took advantage of the wormholes scattered throughout the Fleet, the League, and the Coalition. Each of these holes was artificially created and strategically placed at shortcut points to save fuel and time for the immense ships. Contrary to what scientific speculation boasted, small spaceships were only used for trips between planets in the same system or inside the planets. After all, the energy fusion, and the engines to move the spaceships through the universe, were gigantic.

To make the crossings, the cruisers communicated with the command centers next to the black holes asking for coordinates, speeds, routes, and power. The centers returned the information with the authorizations and the alert for other cruisers not to collide. A hit between two metal colossi at a speed greater than that of light inside holes in antimatter was NEVER a sight to behold.

"The immediate Okasha has arrived, sir," Lydia announced. On the glass table that occupied the center of the room was the holographic projection of a Black woman, her hair trimmed at right angles. She wore a dress with the colors green, blue and red, the same painted on the bow of the nave of Yoku.

Yoku watched her for a few seconds. He could ask her to activate her avatar, the bio-cyber form she used to keep her company from time to time, but she preferred to receive Okasha alone.

Lydia repeated the information.

"The immediate Okasha has arrived, sir." She replaced her image with the image from the camera on the bedroom door. Yoku watched her friend too. She was Black like him. She had a short, well-trimmed haircut, military style, her eyes big, expressive, and alive. She wore a long red coat, which gave her serious face a closed and unfriendly posture.

"She should smile more." Yoku mocked alone, stroked his beard, and gestured for Lydia to let the subordinate in.

"That is not a sun." Okasha spoke so fast that the words ran over Yoku's ears. He analyzed the situation on the glass table, which projected a simulation of the ships and planets in the quadrant. His fingers wandered between the projections. He touched the other ships, the planets and asked Lydia for directions. After analyzing each possibility, he said:

"It is also not an asteroid." He sighed "You were the mythology addict when we were a child, what is this thing?"

"Sincerely?" Okasha scratched her temple, a gesture she made when she was angry or anxious.

"Yes," Yoku insisted.

"It is a Mkelé-Mbémbé" she replied. She rubbed the digital ships and with a gesture of her fingers exchanged the image of the space for another, more similar to a species of biped lizard, next to him the comparison with a human being. "In ancient times, ancestors believed that Mkelé were able to prevent the flow of rivers and cause great distress to villages. In our first navigations through space, we discovered that there is a version of it among galaxies and they are capable of..."

"Of?" Impatiently, Yoku got up from his chair.

"Reversing the course of the wormholes. They cause an energetic interference around the galaxies that are crossing and invalidate all our coordinates. We run the chance of the entire fleet crashing into a planet if we jump close to it."

"Do we have a chance against it?" Yoku put on the long red jacket as he left the booth. Okasha came to his side, stretching the sleeve of his blouse and revealing the gauntlet that covered his left hand. She pressed some digital buttons on it and the images that were on the table were projected around the two.

"Not even far, these cruisers are made for transporting live cargo. How many people do we have here? Ninety million?"

"Eighty-seven. I'm counting those who died or those who died in interplanetary transport." Yoku stopped and turned to her. The right side of his mouth was trembling, an involuntary gesture when he was very angry. "I need to tell you something."

"Yoku." Okasha abandoned the military stance. "I am your childhood friend, I know everything about you and your family, your revolutionary father, and your guerrilla mother. I even know how much your uncle paid you to be accepted into the Fleet army. Is there anything I don't know about your life?"

* * *

"You don't know exactly where I was born, do you?" He raised his eyebrows; the friend was surprised by the lower tone of voice. With a light touch on her elbow, he guided her to a storeroom.

"Alkebalan?" she replied as soon as the lights came on.

"In a village between the mountains of Paki, where stone witches and spirit guides enter the caves to speak to the eight ancient ones." Yoku showed the colored guides on his neck.

"This is just religion. I wonder why a military man like you keeps these traditions so ingrained so far from our home planet." Okasha started to leave the warehouse, but Yoku stopped her.

"I had a dream before we left Alkebalan," he continued holding his friend. "I dreamed that we would find freedom when we explode a star."

Outside the ship, Mkelé-Mbémbé moved to the center of the fleet. Frightened, Yoku and Okasha saw their light gradually diminish and the gigantic scales of a lizard appeared in the obscure points. Large tentacles protruded into space, the first grasping one of the cruisers, the others going in search of the rest of the ships.

"And what are you going to do about it?" Okasha, even an unbeliever, drew a half circle on his forehead, the symbol of the Mother of Fire.

"Come with me." Yoku guided her through the corridors of the ship to the command center; they passed the other soldiers with their heads up and shouting orders. This was no time for panic, even if the great Mkelé-Mbémbé was devouring one of its cruisers and taking away two million lives at once.

"Prepare the cannons! Get away from that thing!" Okasha passed the order on to the other cruisers, who fired while opening the formation. However large and strong, they were cargo ships, not combat ships.

The two went deeper into the warehouse until Yoku stopped in front of a gigantic gray box without drawings or symbols.

"What we fear most is the unknown." He typed a password on a small side panel of the box. Another projection appeared this time, a big, pointed missile.

"Is that a warhead?" Okasha, incredulous, the tone higher than she would have liked.

"I can explain." Yoku returned to the subject.

"Weapons, tons of them, robots, fast attack aircraft, cannons, nanobot tanks, exoskeletons, gravitational gliders, bioweapons. I can list each box in the warehouse in alphabetical order." Okasha checked his gauntlet, combing the entire catalog available inside each of the cruisers.

"We should be a colonization fleet, not a war fleet!" Okasha shouted.

"And when was the last time we had peace? When was the last time one of our people was killed just for being on the street after hours? It was already a miracle that we escaped with all these people into space, but we will need to defend ourselves if the Council's forces come after us. You know I'm right; we are not going back to the chains."

"No." Okasha calmed down "But we will end up in the tentacles."

"Do not worry about the Triumvirate for now. Ghedi is taking care of navigation, they are spreading ghost signals across the Seven Universes."

A big explosion caused the cruiser to shake. Okasha supported Yoku, keeping her from falling. Through one of the hatches, they saw the ship grabbed by the tentacles explode as the large reptile swallowed it.

"What is your plan?" Okasha asked.

"Help me dismantle that box." Yoku moved the panel. The commands were quick. The explosion was repeated in smaller rhythms as more pieces of the cruiser were devoured by the creature. There was no sound, just the shaking that made them uncomfortable.

"It would have been better to be sincere from the beginning." Okasha straightened up, arranged the long green overcoat, and placed a box on the table. Ionic arms of a bluish color appeared from her back and she took the large box with the missile, lifting it as if it weighed nothing.

"Near that ship." Yoku pointed with his chin to the other side of the warehouse, where, until then, Okasha had hardly turned her attention. The girl was even angrier when she saw the ship Yoku had ordered.

"How many of these did you steal?" Laughing nervously as she took the box with the missile, she paid attention to every detail of the warship: it resembled a kind of black dart with the cabin in front of it, the rear was wider, but its wings were not so big thus, between them was a circular turbine with red accents.

"A thousand." Yoku changed his captain's clothes for the pilot's uniform. The cruiser shook again, and then they realized the tentacles surrounded their ship.

"Because?" Okasha stammered.

"The Triumvirate knew that a large number of rebels were rising among the people of the mountains. They were going to decimate us with these bombs. Then we revolted. We started the Quilombos, which were the space stations outside the planets. We called others. We trained engineers, pilots, soldiers, and doctors until it was possible to save more of ours.

"How old are you, Yoku?" Okasha made some head counts, the quilombos had been formed about...

"Two hundred and fifty years." Yoku finished putting on his suit The cruiser's lights flashed; the warning sounded shrill and hindered his concentration. By a ladder, he went up to the warship cabin. His friend dismantled the big gray box and attached the missile to the bottom of the M'sonda.

Okasha moved away as the ship maneuvered towards the exit. At a signal from Yoku an energy force field appeared ahead, preventing the vacuum from pulling the warehouse out as soon as the gate was opened. But something stopped the command, the door went up and down in a repetitive motion.

"It's the tentacle!" Okasha ran to the exit and signaled to Yoku. "It broke the door frame, and the system is not responding."

"There's no other way?" Yoku was getting ready to leave M'sonda.

"We usually open by force. There is a double lever system in the outside area for emergencies when the repair team goes through this type of situation." She took off her clothes and grabbed the suit on the side of the door. In less than a minute she was ready to leave.

She passed through the force field and felt her body become light, but the boots activated the electromagnetic amplitude and pulled towards the ship as if it were gravity. Walking slowly but precisely, she visualized the point where the emergency lever was.

But there was another problem, the cruisers' fire so intense that several of the shots reached the hull of their cruiser. A space of just under thirty meters was like crossing a war zone. Okasha started her slow and calculated walk, a shot almost hit the side of her head. She was dizzy, she just didn't fly because of the electromagnetism boots. Using superhuman willpower, she clung to the side of the ship and proceeded to the lever.

"Kill him, brother!" Okasha pulled the lever just as one of the rounds exploded in front of her. She swayed backward; a hole in her clothes denounced her death. But the hatch did not open.

"I just removed the lock; you need someone to lift the hatch." Breathing hard, each step weighing a ton, she struggled back to the cruiser's entrance. Holding the hatch with both hands she pushed upwards, but it didn't go up. She pushed it again with all her strength and the hatch went up. She hooked onto it with her glove and rose with it.

"Ah, damn it!" Okasha was thrown into space when the gate reached its limit and hit the upper lock. The engineer whirled through space, losing consciousness, but seeing Yoku's black spaceship take flight towards Mkelé.

"Lydia, activate the Oya module," Yoku spoke on an exclusive channel with the cruiser's artificial intelligence.

"What a hell of a mess you put us in, Yoku!" Ghedi came into view again, bringing Okasha's body.

"Is she fine?" Yoku asked without taking his eyes off the cruiser.

"She is going to lose an arm." Ghedi walked away.

"Tell others not to get closer, no matter what." Yoku gave the last order and moved away too, going towards Mkelé.

The Oya Cruiser unfolded in a complicated set of smaller ships, each of which disassembled into smaller and smaller parts, forming a metallic body similar to Lydia's avatar, but wearing combat armor. When the gigantic cruiser robot was ready, it kicked one of the tentacles and violently ripped off the other.

"Do you think we have a chance?" Yoku spoke to her.

Lydia replied by throwing the tentacle in the sun. "We have no chance, but we must have hope."

* * *

Lydia moved using the row of turbines on her back to fly between the M'kelé's tentacles. She punched hard enough to open a continent in half, injuring the monster.

The enemy thrashed in space, but Lydia was agile and escaped the blows. The suction cups stuck to the robot's armor and took off her leg protection. Hundreds of crew members were sucked away and Yoku could only imagine their screams of dread.

Lydia defended herself, gripping the tentacle in her hands then resting her feet on the huge body. She pulled the limb towards her.

There was a vibration in space, the vacuum affected by the abyssal movements of the squid and the robot. A rain of blood spread through the system around them when Lydia took the second tentacle. Without waiting for a reaction from the monster, she flew around the planet and threw the limb into the sun again.

"It gets worse." Yoku rubbed his temples.

"What, now?" Ghendi captained the cruisers to the planet closest to that system, exactly where the creature's blood had fallen.

"I read somewhere that the blood of these space creatures is extremely dangerous in the atmosphere of the planets. When it comes into contact with these atmospheres it causes a kind of entropy in their molecules, fusing them with the original molecules of flora and fauna. Normally, planets develop new animal species much more powerful than their natural evolution."

Yoku lowered his head. He wanted to punch the M'kelé, but it would do no good. Shooting him with the missile was the only solution.

"Lydia, hold this thing so I can take aim." Yoku took his distance and then went straight to the creature. Lydia faced it again, holding on as long as she could.

Yoku kept his concentration. The tentacles hit Lydia, but she was strong enough to put the monster on the line of attack without becoming a target. Then Yoku hit the button and fired the missile.

And he was wrong.

At the last moment, the M'kelé broke free of Lydia and threw her at the missile. Even though she moved quickly the side of her hull was hit and she lost an arm with the explosion, flying and whirling attracted by the gravity of the planet below them. Communication was interrupted and Yoku, with no alternatives, almost cried.

"Captain Yoku, we have a problem," he heard Ghendi's radio.

421

"Serious? I thought they were done," he mocked, leaned his head against the chain, and waited.

"Sir, Z3r is on the collision course of a gigantic asteroid. We no longer have time to dodge the first cruisers, which have already entered the atmosphere. Moreover, Lydia has already reached the surface and it will take a long time to reroute."

"How many ships are there, besides Lydia?" Yoku held the stick so tightly that his hands ached.

"Six. It would be an extermination of fifteen million lives, in addition to the lives on the planet itself." Ghendi tried to alter the route of his own cruiser, but they knew that the process was slow and they would be hit by the shock wave themselves, at the very least.

"Ghendi, continue." Yoku passed the order on to all cruisers.

"But we're going to be hit by the asteroid," Ghendi complained.

"Shoot everything you have against M'kelé," Yoku continued in a calm voice. "Get its attention."

The cruisers fired at the same time. Although stunned by the lack of their tentacles, Yoku did the impossible and fired into the eyes of the colossal monster to get its attention. The remaining tentacles fluttered in space, but Yoku had already predicted the move towards the cruisers. He continued shooting without knowing whether the asteroid would hit the enemy.

"He's still off track." Ghendi mirrored the map on Yoku's panel.

"Can you put the asteroid on the route?" Yoku reasoned.

"I would need an intense explosion." Ghendi was silent as soon as the sentence ended. "You can't."

"Start E.X.U protocol, direct order, *Macumba* guidelines." The order left Yoku's ship and passed through each of the fleet's cruisers until it reached Lydia. In the captain's cabin, the bed spun inside the wall, giving way to a kind of glass tube with a bright blue substance inside, the nanobots started to work and draw a skeleton.

"It's the sixth time," Ghendi sighed.

"I thought it was the seventh." Yoku described a circle with the ship, passed again between the tentacles of the M'kelé.

"The asteroid!" Ghendi yelled.

Yoku calculated from his monitor. The Melé was about to catch another cruiser when Yoku passed in front of its eyes and increased the speed by taking a quantum leap. The crash against the meteor was as intense as the explosion of the missile moments before.

But it worked.

The asteroid came like an orisha occupying the space that had belonged to the monster and the ships' It crossed the scales of the M'kelé in a fiery glow, exploding it like a child's balloon. The meteor continued its route, opening the monster with extraordinary force, boiling its blood, and spreading its entrails through space. Viscera burned in the sun and in the atmosphere of Z3r.

"We did it, captain!" Lydia spoke to no one.

"For the good or the bad," Ghendi replied sadly.

Okasha, injured, appeared beside her in the navigation cabin. The engineer limped and rested her hand on the navigator's shoulder.

"For good, I hope," she confirmed the friend's thoughts.

Ogum, the cruiser that Ghendi guided, entered the atmosphere of the planet bathed in the blood of the M'kelé. Down there they could see the other cruisers and Lydia landing and unloading. Despite the destruction, lives were safe and there would be hope for future generations. Not even the clouds of the planet were able to hide the debris that fell from space, much less the vapors of the monster's blood. But these were not concerns for now. A new generation would be born and be freed from the Council, if it weren't for peace, it would be for the struggle and to honor Yoku's memory. A storm was approaching, obscuring, the view of the navigators, like an intergalactic battle or a war between gods.

For the first time, the star of hope shone.

Canticle of the Cosmic Vampire
by
Sumiko Saulson

Tentacles to fingers enlaced we connect

Floating around the planet unbound

In outer space, you can hear no sound

Except for that of your heart next to mine

As we float about in this space intertwined

In retrospect, I ought to have been circumspect

Not answered your call, from my pod, to eject

Your telepathic space song like sirens to seas

The seductiveness of cerebral symphonies

In the void of space, my new form you create

In the depths of the mind, your song reverberates

Through stone, steel, flesh, and bone, penetrates

Sees and releases itself into the heart of things

While conquering my very being

My ten brown fingers stretch and elongate

Into thick tentacles fleshy, gray and wide

My grin broadens and new teeth erupt

Spacefunk!

In needle-like rows sharp and slim, to cut flesh

From my chin and forehead polyps extrude

Aiding sensory perception for hunting food

I am consumed with the desire to feed

And give in to my new aching need

The spacecraft doors are torn asunder

My former crewmates gaze on in wonder

As wings of skin-bone burst forth from my spine

Glowing spores the length of my torso entwine

It is their honor to assuage my need

Offering me flesh on which to feed

Together we travel the depths of space

Casting off all resemblance to the human race

Lovingly my flesh melts deeply into yours

Your tendrils invading my pores

My essence changed in every sense

My body offering recompense

What a feeling of great destiny

I experience as you devour me

But your offerings are a host of lies

And my flesh you intend to colonize

So I push you out and pull me in

And return into my own brown skin

The Red Nebula Rangers
by
Donovan Hall

Dammit! Not now! It was never a good time to have your laser pistol go on the fritz, and it was an especially bad time when it happened while staring down a horde of Saharian blood ghouls. Coincidentally, that was exactly the unenviable position Ishmael Brown had just found himself in. There were dozens of the ugly bastards standing in the rocky valley between him and his starship, *The Ogun.* Though the majority hadn't noticed Ishmael's presence yet, the space ranger was at a bit of an impasse. He'd leaped out from behind a boulder, hoping to take the nearest ghoul by surprise and start blasting a path like he usually did in these sorts of scenarios, but with his gun jammed, that plan went out the airlock. And to make things worse, his intended target, hearing the hollow click of the blaster pistol, had turned its head, locking its sunken, glowing eyes with the befuddled space ranger.

"Well…" Ishmael said, taking a deep breath. "Shit."

Then, with a feral hiss, the ghoul sprang at him, reaching out with long, mottled arms.

For a lesser man, that would have been the end of the line, but Ishmael was no regular man. He was a Red Nebula Ranger. And if his years exploring the wild frontier of space had taught him anything, it was the prudence of a tactical withdrawal. So, Ishmael turned on his heels and tactically withdrew as fast as his legs would carry him.

Like a dinner bell, the ghoul's cry caught the attention of the rest of the horde, and before long, all of them were loping after the ranger, like hairless, anorexic gorillas. But despite the lines on his face and the gray in his hair, Ishmael was still quick on his feet, and he got to moving like nobody's business. And besides, nothing motivated a good run like keeping ahead of a frenzied pack of ancient, flesh-eating monsters.

As he sprinted through the valley, the ranger's brain worked wildly, assessing his hopelessly short list of options. As impressive as it was to run at this speed at his age, he couldn't keep this pace forever. He needed a way out of this mess, and fast. But that was the tricky part. There were steep, rocky slopes along either side of him, and if he tried to climb his way out, the fiends would catch him for sure. He checked his breathing, sucking in deep breaths as he pumped his legs. He hadn't gotten time to stretch, and the last thing he needed was a side cramp or a charley horse.

Then he saw it, about two hundred feet ahead—a way out. Coming up on his right was a narrow gap in the rock slope, a cave entrance. So, he dashed for it, trying to ignore the budding pain in his chest for just a few minutes longer. But he could feel hot, putrid breath tickle the back of his neck. Despite his best efforts, he was starting to slow down. Another second and he'd feel hard fangs sink into his shoulder. Yet the cave was so close, just a few more steps. Screw it. There wasn't any time. He'd have to dive for it. With a hard thrust of his leg, Ishmael threw himself forward for dear life, sending himself headlong into the darkness of the narrow cave.

Saharian blood ghouls were gaunt creatures overall, but they were tall and bore disproportionately wide shoulders, so when they tried to pursue their prey underground, they quickly got stuck in the narrow crevice. They tried to squeeze past each other, clawing and screeching, but they only succeeded in plugging up the gap even more with thrashing bodies. Still, Ishmael crawled back on his hands and feet to avoid any lucky swipes.

No one knew why the ghouls were so oddly shaped, nor did anyone know how such a savage species spread to so many worlds in the nebula in the first place. All that anyone knew for sure about these monsters was that they did not die of old age or malnutrition, and instead, they just lingered as dry husks, waiting for masters that would never return. And that made colonization of the Red Nebula a little tricky for humans. Having a forsaken army of undead ghouls in your neighborhood made it really inconvenient to have family cookouts without the family being turned into the main course. And the nature of the nebula itself didn't make things any easier. It was too hard to scope out the potential threat of any given planet using long-range probes due to the high amount of the nebula's electromagnetic interference. All of this meant exploring this region of space needed good old-fashioned boots on the ground.

That was where the Red Nebula Rangers came into the equation. They were the intrepid souls tasked with scouting out the frontier, finding out which planets were safe and which planets were going to turn you into dinner. And after what just happened back in the valley, Ishmael could cross off Kettia IV as one for the latter category.

Could be worse though, I guess, he mused while picking himself up off the cavern floor. *Could have been space pirates.* As nasty as ghouls were, they didn't have firearms, at least.

Back on his feet, Ishmael dusted himself off, ignored the aching in his ribs, and looked back to see a flurry of clawed hands raking at the air. In the other direction was a dark, narrow passageway, no doubt full of unknown dangers. The choice was clear enough. Ishmael spat out a bit of gravel, slipped on his tactical goggles, and started on his way into the unknown. *Then again, maybe I'd be better off with the pirates…*

Squirming through the guts of the planet's crust, the howling of the ghouls faded until Ishmael found himself in utter silence. So, he slowed his pace to give himself a chance to catch his breath and consider his next move. It wasn't blind chance that explained how Ishmael found this cavern. The planet had a whole network of lava tubes crisscrossing underneath the surface, and during his time exploring Kettia IV, Ishmael had spied many a cave entrance from afar. He'd planned on getting some extra gear from his ship for a spelunking survey, but then the ghouls showed up.

He felt a draft chill his back and reached behind to feel what the problem was. A gash had been torn through his crimson flight jacket. He should have thanked his fated stars that it was only leather and cloth that had been sliced open and not flesh and bone. But for any old ranger, his jacket was his pride, and that pride had been wounded.

"Fucking ghouls…" he grumbled.

No, ghouls weren't the unlucky part, they came with the job. He'd blasted through them countless times before. It was his damned pistol that was source of all his stellar misfortune. He took it out of its holster and bitterly examined the confounded thing. He checked the power cell. It was 100% fully charged. Of course, it was. He hadn't fired once since he'd been on the planet and he'd double-checked it before trying the ambush. Just to test it, he took aim at the ground and fired. *Click.* Nothing. He ran his hand along the surface of the weapon, expecting to find some sort of structural damage. A dent, a nick, something loose or out of place. Nope, all ship shape and bristol fashion. So, what in the abyss was wrong with it?

He eyed the blaster the way a man eyed a dog turd on his front step. The weapon was a newer model, an XT-705 Viper. The younger rangers all called the 705s the new hotness, the must-have pistol, but Ishmael called them a damn liability. Who cared about all the bells and whistles? They were too complex for their own good. *A pistol is only supposed to have one damn job. Shoot! And you couldn't even do that right!*

Now the XT-500 series, those had been reliable, real blasters. You could fire them a thousand times without a single malfunction. Sure, they were discontinued because the power cell casings turned out to be not to be so good at shielding against energy leakage, but at least you never had to second guess if it would save you from a ghoul horde. But these new toys they'd been forced to take on as standard issue weren't worth the bolts that held them together.

"Lauryn…" Ishmael whispered up to the uncaring tunnel ceiling. "Should never have shelved you, old girl. I'm sorry."

Feeling the muscles in his left leg start to lock up, the ranger took a seat on a flat rock, shooing away some ambulatory mold that had been resting there. It was embarrassing how good it felt to finally sit down. Pains like these were starting to crop up more and more it seemed. Ishmael had been a ranger for twenty years, and in that time, he'd set foot on over a hundred uncharted planets and had gotten damn good at the game. What happened back in the valley had been a bad break, but still, it took a seasoned ranger to know how to get out of a jam like that. Though looking around his stark surroundings, he was reminded he wasn't fully out of the jam just yet.

"I hate you…" he said, shoving the XT-705 back into its holster. "But no one cares what I think, anymore." The younger rangers liked to call him old school, but so what? It was a compliment as far as he was concerned. Old school was what got half the nebula charted and colonized. Old school was what got their butts into deep space in the first place, back when all you needed was a good warp drive, some blasters that actually worked, and a couple of solid cats to watch your back.

The younger rangers were obsessed with their shiny new gadgets, and central command felt obliged to indulge them. They said it helped with recruitment, but Ishmael didn't believe it. The romance was already there—space, adventure, discovery…what else did you need to sell the job to someone? They didn't need stupid drones, or cyber implants, or blaster pistols that could fix you coffee but couldn't shoot when your neck was on the line! All of that crap was turning the job cushy, boring, and needlessly byzantine, not to mention more dangerous than it had to be. And the higher-ups had the gall to wonder why their budget was going tits up these days. *Hmph!* The only things Ishmael had on him—the only things he needed—besides his pistol was an emergency flare, field rations, tactical goggles, and an SOS beacon for when shit really hit the fan, but he'd be damned if he was going to use that now. The last thing his pride could stomach was some newbie coming to his rescue.

Hell, they're all newbies now, he thought sourly, *and not enough of us left to teach him how to do it right.* There were hardly any rangers left from his generation still flying around. He held up a hand to start counting who was still flying around. *Fred Garvey, Tut Nareem, Assata Freeks, and…* That was all of them. The rest were gone. The smart ones had all retired, and the others, well, they met their end somewhere in the wilds of the nebula.

"Two guesses for which category I'm in…" he said, looking down at the crawling patch of mold by his foot. He tried to follow the rules, keep up with all the updating protocol, but at times it felt like the rangers were trying to push out what remained of the old guard with all their 'innovative' changes. "Maybe it is time I hang it up, too." But like a man with hemorrhoids, that thought didn't sit well in his mind.

The aching stopped after a few minutes, and Ishmael continued on his way to wherever the tunnel was taking him.

After what felt like an hour of hiking, crawling, and climbing, he found the sunlight. Cautiously, he crept to the surface. The goggles shielded his eyes from the bright light, and he scanned his surroundings. The barren, windswept land he found himself standing on was above the valley. From this lofty vantage, he could see his starship gleaming in the afternoon suns, as well as the horde that had resumed standing around it. Well, most of the horde was there, but about a third still hung around the cave entrance Ishmael had ducked into.

The ranger scowled. "Shit… Back at square one."

Ghouls weren't smart, but they had a basic logic of a sort that helped them figure out where to best wait for prey. They knew, to a certain extent, that Ishmael would likely be back for his ship, and they had all the time in the galaxy to wait. But Ishmael had a plan. When the straightforward approach was off the table, that's when creativity had to step in. So, he took the power cell from his pistol, his SOS beacon, and the emergency flare and got an idea. After a few minutes of disassembling and retooling, he held something that looked reminiscent of an old-fashioned pipe bomb. With this in hand, he said a quick prayer and carefully approached the side of the valley. Before giving himself time to second guess his plan, he started sliding down.

It didn't take long for the sound of tumbling pebbles to attract the attention of the nearest ghouls by the ship, and a moment later they pierced the sky with their rabid howling. The frenzied horde clamored towards him up the slope. It was now or never. Ishmael flung the pipe bomb at the horde and braced himself.

There was no noise other than a loud, crackling buzz, but the power cell overloaded the flare so intensely that the burst of light it created might as well have been a third sun. All at once, the ghouls shrieked as their retinas burned out, and they crumpled over blind, wrapping their long arms over their bat-like faces. But to Ishmael, thanks to the goggles' shade filter, it just looked like your brighter than average summer day. But here was where things got serious.

He pushed off with all the strength that remained in his legs, no longer sliding but bounding down the slope, weaving between ghouls who were still cringing on the ground, wailing, and thrashing in typhlotic agony. One of the beasts nearly took Ishmael's head off with a wild swing, but the ranger saw it coming and ducked under the attack, letting the claws brush over his salt and pepper dreads.

Ishmael's heart pounded against his aching ribs as he sprinted for his ship. He was going to have to yell to bring down the boarding ramp. The voice controls would be faster than opening it manually, but it'd give away his position. After all, the beasts had been blinded, not deafened. Not that it mattered much. The second group of ghouls, the ones from further down the valley, had heard the commotion and were closing in, and they were neither blind nor deaf. So, all things considered, discretion was a moot point now.

"Lower the boarding ramp! Hurry!"

And there it was. Ishmael could hear the blinded ghouls scrambling to follow the sound of his voice, but he didn't bother to look back. Descending from the ship's belly on the hiss of hydraulic pistons came the boarding ramp. It was still a good hundred feet away, but it was the closest to salvation Ishmael had been all day. Then, a piece of gravel clipped him on the side of the head, spurring him to look over his shoulder on reflex. There was a ghoul, a particularly gangly one, hot on his heels, bounding on all four limbs, churning up the dirt underneath its claws.

It's time for Plan C! But what was Plan C?

Ishmael didn't have time to think past a vague impulse. So, he just acted on it. He grabbed what he had left on his utility belt, a food ration stick, and tore open the plastic wrapping. Then he chucked the thing back at his pursuer. The monster started as the stick struck him in the face, then fumbled at the ground for the morsel of food. It was ravenous hunger that ruled these creatures after all, so an easy meal was better than a sprinting one. However, when it stopped to sniff out the ration stick at its feet, all of its kin came slamming into his rear. There was an avalanche of pallid bony bodies as the blind beasts tripped over each other. As for the ghouls who could see, they had to now divert themselves to go around the pileup.

The scene would have been humorous if it hadn't been for what happened next. Ishmael felt a familiar quivering in his left leg again, that awful precursor to another charley horse. He grunted as he felt his left leg painfully lock up. He nearly toppled over, but not wanting to die was a good motivator to stay upright. Hopping on one leg, he pushed forward with his built-up momentum, and like an amputee kangaroo, he sprang for dear life on his one good leg as chomping, clawing death closed in behind him.

"Lift off!" he shouted, making one final push for the boarding ramp. "Fucking lift off!"'

The ranger slammed onto the hard metal of the ramp just as the ship's thrusters started roaring to life. Ishmael rolled onto his back to take the weight off his chest, and as he lay there panting, feeling the ship pull upward, he allowed himself to enjoy a bit of hope. However, as the ship rose into the air, a ghoul's hand caught the edge of the ramp, gripping its claws into the metal.

"Fuck off!" Ishmael shouted, giving the hand a swift kick. The hand lost its hold on the ramp, and with a whimpering cry, the ghoul plummeted back down to the planet's surface.

"Raise the ramp!" Ishmael wheezed. Nothing happened. He coughed and cleared his ragged throat. "Raise the damn ramp already, for God's sake!" It was doubtful that appealing to God made any difference to the voice-activated operating system, but regardless, it heard him this time, and once again the hydraulic pistons hissed, and the ramp slowly raised itself back into the belly of the starship. But before it closed completely, Ishmael took out his faulty pistol and gave it one last scornful look. "Yeah, and fuck you, too." Then, with great satisfaction, he tossed it over the edge.

The ramp snapped shut with a hollow *clang,* and for a good, long moment, longer than he could measure, Ishmael remained sprawled on the ground. His heart was running in circles, his lungs felt like bursting, and the damn pain in his leg was taking its sweet time to go away. He'd escaped the ghouls but now wondered if he'd just given himself a heart attack.

Then a beeping sound came from the ship's cockpit, and that finally gave him an excuse to move again. So, he dragged himself along the floor, climbed into the pilot's chair, and tapped the message controls.

"Yes?" he panted. "Ishmael here!"

"Ranger Brown?" an eager, youthful voice asked from the speaker. "This is Ranger Mamadu O'Hare. Are you alright? I was in a neighboring system and briefly picked up on your SOS signal before it suddenly cut out. It might have been a glitch, but I just wanted to be sure."

"No trouble. Just had to use a poor man's flash grenade. The SOS device was a part of the construction and all. Activation must have triggered it."

"A what?"

"A poor man's flash grenade. It's when—" Ishmael shook his head. "Never mind, kid. Like I said, everything's fine."

"You just said you used a *grenade*. That doesn't sound like everything is ok."

Ishmael grunted at the kid's persistence. "It was ghouls. That's all. And since my damn blaster wouldn't fire, I had to think around the problem."

There was a slight pause on the other end. "Wait? You said your blaster wouldn't fire? Did you install the update?"

"Update?" Ishmael leaned forward. "What update?"

"Oh, Jesus... Didn't you get the memo?"

Ishmael took a breath, ready to hold back the rage he foresaw coming. "No."

"Check your messages—wait, no I'll just tell you. The XT-700s had a software update to catch a bug in the biometric key system."

"Software update? It's a bleeding gun! What's a gun need software for?"

"The trigger," Mamadu said, as if it was obvious. "You know, when the pistol's registered to you, the trigger got imprinted with your biometric signature, so, you know, some space pirate or whatever can't use it against you. It's a handy feature. Anyway, that requires software to operate."

Ishmael leaned back in his pilot chair, rubbing a hand over his face. "You gotta be kidding me. I almost got turned to ghoul chow because of some stupid software bug?" He caught the anger in his voice and pushed it back down, pressing his tone back into the tenor of strained politeness. "With all due respect, O'Hare, and this is nothing personal against you, but this is some bullshit. Over and out."

Whatever else Mamadu was trying to say, Ishmael didn't hear it. He pressed a button to terminate the call and reached under the control panel to pull out a metal box and set it on his lap. Flipping the latches open, he lifted the lid to reveal a tarnished pistol the color of old brass. Its gleam was faded and blemished by more than a few scratches, and the rubber on the grip was cracking off in places, but it didn't matter. As far as he was concerned, it was the most beautiful thing in the nebula, and Ishmael stared at it with palpable joy.

"You're back in the game, baby girl. I'm never shelving you again."

The Harvester
by
WC Dunlap

The silent black void of space is filled with the aggressive sounds of a hedonic hunger sated. It is a peculiar ASMR of gnashing teeth, the tearing of tender flesh, and loud gulps followed by the contented sigh of another satisfied customer.

It is a lullaby to the ears of Qi Jabari, self-proclaimed "purveyor of proclivities" turned butcher. But she is floating outside the security of intergalactic governance. It's time to get paid and get to safety before the situation turns. She paces, waiting anxiously for the dedun to be deposited in her account. Security drones follow her movement, but she pretends not to notice.

"Deposit is processing," AI-sha speaks through an earpiece embedded in Qi's temple. "I've disarmed the drones but stay close to the exit. He is the weapon in this room."

The client looks up from its feast with lidless black eyes and speaks in a series of melodious tones that takes Qi's aural dictator several seconds to translate into words. "Please be still. I always pay my debts," the creature reassures.

"Of course, Mister Nn." Qi forces a smile. "I am simply on a schedule."

Qi rubs her shaking hands across her short cropped kinky curls and exhales slowly. She wills herself to calm down, all the while grinning like a fool towards a seemingly unbothered Mister Nn. She always preferred the anonymity of virtual space. In-person transactions gave her anxiety, but some clients required a more personal touch, and if they had the means to pay for the privilege, her livelihood required compliance. Risks were minimal if the client was genuine and the product authentic.

But today she had just one out of two.

She and AI-sha hadn't been playing these odds for very long. Sating the depravities of the intergalactic elite was exceedingly difficult. Most clients weren't even human, and the desires of the alien oligarchy were capricious at best. But Nn was the real deal, some sort of space baron from a galaxy she could not pronounce and would likely never visit. His lineage dated back to a time before Earth's resources were depleted and its people flung across the stars by billionaire brats with the survival skills of toddlers. Nn built a palace in the caverns of a remote asteroid orbiting one of the many stars of galaxy M31, far from the security of civilization, where he could indulge his every whim. He was a legend on the black market, a myth willing to pay an empire for certain rarities. And she and AI-sha tracked him down.

But the risk would outweigh the reward unless the dedun hit her account – now. She used the last of her fuel to make this delivery, and without star fuel the return trip home would take light years. By the time she arrived, everyone she knew would be dead or dying. But if this transaction went bad, it wouldn't matter anyway, because she'd be dead too. It was all or nothing. She threw the dice; she knew the deal.

"It is what it is," she mumbles underneath her breath.

"Product will pass. Probability is still in your favor," AI-sha reassures. "Fifty-six-point twenty three percent."

"Status?"

"Deposit is still pending."

Qi wasn't raised on one of the floating metropoles that littered space like metal stars, cosmopolitans of sentient species from across the universe, co-mingling since birth. She was born an unremarkable girl of a dying species, raised starving and scrappy in a remote, intercultural kibbutz on Earth's shattering moon. She was taught one valuable skill – how to farm, first with the lunar soil in the tented greenhouses of the commune, and then with data. Worthless in its raw state due to sheer abundance, she learned quickly that data was information and information could be currency with a bit of cultivation. And when they wanted her to marry and breed more unremarkable little farming girls, she created AI-sha instead, a machine learning algorithm to help her process the data into intel. Like the tasteless gray fruit that grew from lunar soil, AI-sha too began to bud, flowering into a self-sustaining artificial intelligence and partner

– the only life partner Qi would ever accept. Together, they would build a life Qi could only imagine – jet setting across the galaxy, rubbing elbows with the wealthy and ruling classes, making deals, and depositing enough dedun to build her own little empire. Qi told herself it wasn't greed, it was survival.

She and AI-sha spent months tracking and analyzing Nn's behaviors and preferences until they knew exactly what to procure. It was time to stop farming for scraps and start living with a full belly and a fueled skipper – even if it meant she had to risk a scam.

Nn gestures with an appendage that is more tentacle than arm for Qi to take a seat. She is too intimidated not to comply. Even seated, he towers over her by at least five feet with a long and muscular reptilian neck, able to propel his body hundreds of feet in mere seconds. He sucks in shallow breaths from a slitted nose while throwing chunks of raw meat down a gaping maw the size of a human head. His pristine white teeth are nearly double the size of Qi's fingers. Worse still, he wears a double-breasted navy-blue frock coat with a ruby red waistcoat like a 19th century human aristocrat, the chain of an antique time piece dangling from one of its pockets. A silky beige cravat is tied elegantly around his neck, stained with the blood of the meal. It is the contrast of beast and gentleman that terrifies Qi the most.

"You are now 50 paces from the exit, too far to reach safety if it strikes," AI-sha cautions as Qi walks toward Nn. Qi's optical implants allow AI-sha to see and process the living world, but her warning is futile. Nn is not a creature accustomed to taking "no" for an answer. Obediently, Qi takes the seat across from him at a polished wooden dining table covered with bleeding meat.

Nn speaks again, an eerily beautiful melody from such a fierce-looking body. Meat laced spittle flies from his mouth with each sound. Qi smiles and pretends not to notice.

"Tell me how you procured this," Nn demands.

Qi gulps but does not answer.

"Do you feel guilty betraying your species?" he asks.

Qi looks away, "it's just one delivery. That was our agreement. One and done."

Nn laughs. It is a jarring, high-pierced sound like the giggle of a child.

Qi suppresses a shudder.

"It is fresh. Did you murder it yourself?" Nn asks.

"Does it matter?

"I would like to know if you are capable of murder."

"I am," Qi shuffles in her seat. "If the price is right."

Nn nods, "Very good. Would you like a taste?"

Qi shakes her head, but her stomach growls in response. She has not eaten in days.

"You are hungry," he says. It is not a question.

"I suppose that is the human condition."

Nn nods. "Yes, a hungry, dying species. And yet you bring me this. It is no wonder your kind is going extinct. Your individualism is your demise."

AI-sha chimes in her ear, "Your heart rate has increased to 120 bpm" – an unnecessary observation. Fortunately, the AI continues, "Your account balance is now five hundred, thirty-six thousand dedun. The sunskipper is refueling and will be ready when you reach it."

Qi doesn't know if she should cry or laugh. She rises to leave, "Mister Nn, it's been a pleasure doing business with you."

Nn watches as Qi backs away towards the exit. His is not a face that she'd expect to smile, but the scales at each corner of his mouth rise into what could only be described as a smirk.

"I do not believe you are a monster," his voice is still a song, "but what will others believe? What will your pacificist community of simple farmer-folk think of their entrepreneurial daughter now? Will they welcome you home, share in the spoils, celebrate your mercantile triumph?"

Qi freezes as Nn's words are translated.

"Exit immediately," AI-sha urges. But AI-sha is an algorithm and understands nothing of human shame.

Qi faces Nn with a bold countenance, bolder than she actually feels, "Sir, our agreement was mutual confidentiality. And you always honor your agreements. This concludes our business, sir."

"But I've paid you and you haven't given me my flesh yet, not *real* human flesh."

Before Qi can react, a thick metal door descends over the exit as several drones circle above her head. Currents of electricity pulse from the drones and into Qi's body. She hits the ground hard, curling into a ball, limbs rigid, mouth gaping but unable to scream. She fights against the current so as not to swallow her tongue. Blood trickles out of the corner of her mouth as urine races down her legs.

Nn sits back in his chair, licking the 3D printed flesh from his fingers, and watches Qi writhe.

"The drones have been re-armed," comes AI-sha's belated status. "The door to the exit is impenetrable. I am no longer in control. Probability of survival is now zero point five eight six percent. I – I am sorry, Qi."

Qi imagines she hears a crack in AI-sha's voice before the world is silent and black.

......*

Qi awakens to find herself in a dark room with a single light hanging directly above her. She is completely naked, lying prone on a gurney, her body held down by cold metal bars. Her left arm is pressed securely to her side. Her right arm is held firmly away from her body at a ninety-degree angle. Her head is the only thing that she can move.

She notices immediately that her body has been washed of blood and urine, her brown skin rubbed smooth with an oil that smells of olives. Her hair has been shaved, the cold air of the room ticking her scalp. Her mouth tastes of mint. The Earth crops rubbed into body and mouth must have cost a fortune, but here she lies – clean and fresh for the slaughter. Above her buzz two medical drones, cutting instruments held between their metal hands.

Nn steps out of the shadows. He is wearing a fresh suit, this one with tails and dark trousers, a bright red ascot tied around its reptilian neck. Heavy leather boots with gold laces cover his scaled calves. He leans against an ornate cane.

Qi takes in his appearance with disgust, "Nice fit. Gotta a shirt or pair of pants to spare?"

Nn laughs. "You're a stoic one."

If Qi wasn't strapped down, she'd shrug. "I knew the risks."

"Indeed."

Qi sighs. "Do you mean to eat me now?"

"Yes and no," Nn replies.

"And you will eat me alive?"

"Fresh meat is best."

Qi closes her eyes. "Get it over with then."

And with that Nn leaps forward, his gaping maw enveloping Qi's right arm before his feet retouch the ground. He places one hand around her neck as his rough tongue presses up against the arm, and his lips begin to suck, saliva dripping in a pool at his feet. Qi screams as his lips press more firmly, his hard tongue massaging the flesh of her arm loosening from the pit and slowly sludging off. He sucks it down his throat like a noddle. It is only then that he begins to bite, chomping through the bone, blood and marrow spraying across his face and suit.

"AI-sha!" Qi shouts, consciousness slipping.

"I am administrating pain aids," the AI responds, but it does little to ease Qi's suffering. Her screams shake the walls.

The drones descend once Nn finishes his meal and begin working on the bloody stump left behind. They cut and carve the jagged edges of bone left behind and cauterize the wound. Qi shakes in and out of consciousness until a shot of adrenaline courses through her heart.

Her eyes pop open.

Nn watches impassively while licking his hands clean of blood.

Qi chokes back sobs, biting down hard on her bottom lip. All she feels now is rage, "I will kill you!"

Nn belches loudly and ignores the outburst. A couple of drones remove his soiled coat and wipe him clean of blood.

"Of course, I've tasted synthetic human flesh before," he responds coolly as he slips into a fresh jacket, "I've even tried to manufacture it myself. It's not bad, really, it's not. But, dear girl, I've paid you a small fortune for the real thing. And now our transaction is complete."

"Fuck you!" Qi spits blood in his direction.

"That's the spirit!" Nn chuckles. He takes in Qi's naked, bloodied body and licks his lips. "Oh, what to do with the rest of you . . ."

Qi closes her eyes, awaiting her fate. She is surprised when she hears AI-sha report, "Probability of survival is now ninety percent."

"What?" Qi opens her eyes.

Nn answers before AI-sha, "I assume you are speaking to your AI. Is she predicting the probability of your survival? What's the prognosis?"

Qi frowns, "Ninety percent . . ."

"Ninety percent. Imagine that!" Nn chuckles. "And all you had to do was lose an arm."

Qi glares in response.

"But your AI is correct. I have a proposition for you. In exchange for your life, you work for me."

"Doing what? I have one arm!"

"You will bring me human meat, of course."

Suddenly the metal bars restraining Qi retract. She struggles to sit up with her one good arm. Her eyes roam the room for weapons and an escape. "It will be a short trade. There are but a hundred thousand of us left."

"I am not interested in genocide, "Nn explains. "You are too delicious for that. You come from a farming community, no?"

"Yes, but . . ."

"Then harvest."

"Human beings? We can barely keep ourselves alive."

Nn nods, "Yes, cattle are often frail like that. But what if a generous and anonymous benefactor were to take an interest in yours and all the remaining human colonies? What if this anonymous philanthropist were to invest in the health and well-being of the human species, encouraging you to procreate and thrive, ensuring the well-being of that offspring? And all you would have to do is deliver one percent, to increase in two percent increments for every five percent in human population growth, not to exceed twenty-five percent annually, to be harvested, delivered, and consumed by me and mine in perpetuity or until your demise. And trust, you will be kept safe and in comfort as long as you abide to the terms of this contract. Your days of struggle and hunger are over."

"It is a good deal," AI-sha adds.

"You will be the savior of humankind," Mister Nn shouts. "The population will boom!"

Qi is speechless.

"You will not be alone," Nn continues, "We will recruit others. This is an enterprise after all, and it is my job to restore it. I believe you can help. We can help each other."

"Ninety percent probability of survival if you accept," AI-sha repeats.

"Shut up!" Qi shouts.

Nn steps closer, "I've stripped you naked for you to understand your vulnerability and your power. All you've ever needed to survive and thrive is within yourself. Your success has always been forged by your own hands. You created an impressive artificial intelligence on a remote rock in the middle of nowhere. You found me and discovered my deepest desires. Will it all end now?"

"This is dirty business for anyone to do to their own species."

"Yet here you are – on my ship trying to sell me fake human flesh."

"No children," Qi demands.

"They are the most delicious."

"But you promise that the population will grow?"

"To an extent, yes. Enough to fulfill demand and keep prices at a premium. You will fare better than you have been."

"You've done this before?" Qi asks.

"Yes. We've made these types of arrangements before, thousands of years ago on Earth when your species was thriving. My family has dealt in the trade of human flesh for millennia. Unfortunately, you humans were simply too good at destroying yourselves. We have precautions for that now. The survival of your species will be maintained, for consumption."

"But not me? I will not be consumed."

"No, you will not. You will thrive."

Qi considers. Perhaps this is the real score she'd been chasing all these years, the inevitable culmination of all of her risks. She could serve the species, grow the population, live in comfort and wealth. The exchange was a minor one.

"You can live with this," AI-sha counsels.

"Will anyone notice?" Qi asks.

"As long as you harvest the right kind, no one will notice. Or they will not care," Nn answers.

"The right kind?"

"That is for you to decide."

"I will help you," AI-sha offers.

Nn extends a tentacled hand. "Do we have a deal – or do I finish my lunch?"

Qi extends her right hand to accept, until she remembers it is gone.

Flight of the Oasis
by
Ronald Jones

He dreamed. Deeply. Blissfully.

An idyllic house in an idyllic neighborhood. A beautiful wife, her smile radiant as sunlight. Children romping in the yard full of squeals and laughter.

Somewhere in this scene, he stood, watching it all…and then it started to fade. House, wife, children. Sadness gripped him as darkness encroached, obscuring all he observed in a black fog. He reached out, helplessly, desperately, and then a gentle tug guided him back to the waking world.

Reginald (Reg) Holder opened his eyes, the dream imprinting his memory. A sense of loss at something he never had fell over him. A family? His career had not afforded him the luxury of settling down. One day, perhaps? Reg grimaced and pressed a button to his left. Folly to dream or think of such things now, in the middle of space, on a journey toward a place humans were just beginning to settle.

The translucent smoke-gray seal covering his stasis capsule opened outward with a whisper. It took a moment for Reg to garner the mental and physical strength to rise and lift himself out of what he liked to call a glorified crypt. Waking from stasis was a lot like waking from a deep nap. Two minutes went by before the revitalizing nutrients he ingested intravenously to maintain muscle mass and bone density washed away vestiges of prolonged slumber, imparting him with vitality.

He stretched and shook the kinks out of his arms and legs. He gazed about the sleeper bay, spotting up to ten open stasis capsules out of fifty in this section. Alarm bells went off in his head. He glanced at the chrono display embedded in his capsule and saw that he had been awakened eight years and four months too early. He frowned. Only two engineers were supposed to be awakened every four years to inspect ship systems. As Lead Engineer, Reg held a PhD in propulsion systems. Throughout his career, leading to his pinnacle position as CEO of his own tech company, he gained PhD-level knowledge of a range of cyber/engineering disciplines. He should have been awakened on the final leg of the ship's journey to oversee a general inspection.

Something must be wrong. He briskly exited the bay.

***

Reg entered the bridge to see crew members Hattie Mills and Bobby Azziz standing over the communication console. Spacious and sleek, the bridge was situated atop the sleeper ship. Its domed, transparent ceiling, made of highly durable and fortified radiation-repellant plexiglass, offered an enchanting star-strewn view of the outside.

Hattie looked up, fixing Reg with mortified eyes. Of course, Hattie tended to look mortified on any given day. She brushed errant strands of red hair from her face. "Reg, thank God you're here."

"What's going on?" Reg approached the station and Bobby moved aside to give the Lead Engineer a view of the comm monitor.

"It's all right there," said Bobby, his typical relaxed drawl heightened with concern.

Reg gazed at the screen. He saw a collage of images. A brown-gray world. Proxima Centauri. Dozens of prefab structures doused in a raging conflagration. Terrified people running but unable to escape a catastrophe. Bodies scattered everywhere, whole or in charred clumps. Explosions . . . more explosions . . . panic, more panic. . . and a mysterious ship . . . no . . . three ships shaped like spokes in a wheel soaring above. Difficult to scale their size, not difficult to determine their role in the atrocity playing out on the monitor.

"Those are images the colony managed to transmit before its outbound communications were. . . cut," said Hattie, her voice trembling.

Reg stared at a blurred image of one of those strange ships. One thing he knew for certain: those vessels were not built by human hands. "Looks like we have a first contact. . . a bad contact but first, nonetheless. Did you wake the captain?"

"Awake and bushy-tailed," came the captain's voice.

All eyes fell on a tall, slender mahogany-hued woman in the blue and black uniform of NASA's Alpha Centauri Colonization Initiative. Seven crew members followed the captain onto the bridge and assumed their stations.

"Captain Cunningham," Reg greeted.

Captain Alisha Cunningham acknowledged Reg with a nod before getting down to business. "Status?"

"The colony is gone," said Hattie, doing her best to compose herself. "Wiped out."

"Three hundred and fifty colonists." Bobby dipped his head. "Men. Women, children. . ."

Alisha was not given to displaying emotions when on duty, but her eyes expanded, accompanied by an audible gasp. Hattie directed her attention to the comm monitor.

Five minutes later, the captain found her voice. "Send. . . send those images to Lunar Base," she ordered the communication officer. "Inform LB that we're returning to Earth."

Comm Officer Fritz Epstein overcame enough of his shock to manage a shaky "Yes ma'am."

"We're going to have to do more than head home, Captain," said Reg, his eyes glued to the comm monitor. He toggled a function, enlarging the clearest image captured of one of those alien ships.

"This ship broke formation after completing an attack run with the others." Reg eyed the captain. "There's a chance that it's coming after us."

Alisha cocked a dubious brow. "How much of a chance?"

"Above fifty," Reg replied. "Judging by its trajectory. I can provide a more detailed extrapolation once I study the footage in-depth and crank out the calculations."

Alisha offered a curt nod. "Do it."

George Yang, the ship's guidance engineer looked up from his station. "Captain, I just input a set of return coordinates. Just give the word."

"Turn us around, George," said Alisha. "And let's hope to God we make it back home in one piece."

***

Reg took Hattie to his station, intending to use her signals engineering skills to snag every transmission the colony managed to transmit. A garbled image of a bearded face materialized on Reg's main screen. He winced in recognition. "Jeremy," he muttered.

"Someone you know. . . or knew?" Hattie asked.

Reg rubbed the back of his neck. "A friend from college. He was one of the colony administrators and a member of the terraforming committee. Can you resolve the image?"

Hattie bit her bottom lip. "I'll try." She typed commands on the console's embedded keyboard, bringing Jeremy's fuzzy image into slightly better focus. She attempted to refine the transmission's audio, achieving minimal results. The audio remained scratchy but largely comprehendible if one concentrated hard enough.

"...UFOs, three of them...hitting us hard. They've already destroyed...and a main generator...killing indiscriminately...attempts at communication...failed...no defense against...to sleeper ship Oasis...turn back...turn ba..."

The transmission and visual abruptly ended.

Reg closed his eyes briefly, haunted by the horror his friend must have experienced in his last moments. When he opened them, he proceeded to study footage of the attacking vessels. Afterward, he listened to and viewed a range of transmissions from official broadcasts describing the first sightings of the alien craft to individual cellular videos of the attack in progress. Harrowing scenes of fear and panic pervaded every transmission.

***

An hour later, Reg entered the conference room where the captain and senior officers sat around a blue-tinted fiberglass table. Overhead projectors cast a holograph of surrounding space above the table. The image, studded with gleaming representations of stars, looked less like an astronomical chart, and more like an arcane black void floating in the middle of the room.

"Take a look at this, Captain," Reg said, pressing a tab that zeroed in on a red triangle icon. "I tweaked the long-range scanner to extend its range of detection. That's what it picked up."

"The hostile vessel," Alisha muttered, staring at the triangle.

"At this point, the ship is roughly two light years distant and closing fast."

"How fast?" Fritz asked.

"At its current velocity, it'll overtake us in a year." Reg kept his expression neutral, which contrasted sharply with the visible alarm exhibited by everyone at the table.

Bobby leaned back in his chair. "We're screwed. Earth is screwed. I'm sure the aliens hacked the colony's database. They must know where the colonists originated and how to get there."

"Earth might have a chance against them," said George. "Those ships destroyed a defenseless colony. They haven't come up against opposition that fights back."

"That's right," Fritz asserted. "We've already sent a warning to Earth, giving it ample time to mobilize a defense."

"Unfortunately, we won't be able to defend ourselves," George said bluntly. "We're essentially a sitting duck floating in space."

"We don't have to be," said Reg. "I think we *can* defend ourselves."

The captain narrowed her eyes. "How? This isn't a battleship. Where are our railguns, lasers, and missile batteries? Just how in the hell are we going to stand a chance against a ship that helped reduced a colony of damn near four hundred residents to an ash heap?" Alisha paused, massaging her temples. She took a deep breath. "I'm sorry, Reg. Didn't mean to snap."

Reg met the captain's gaze, his expression sympathetic. "No worries, Captain. We're all understandably tense about the situation."

"But it looks like you're the only one who might have a solution to our predicament." Alisha nodded to the lead engineer. "Please, fill us in."

****

Three levels below in the engine room, Reg studied a monitor featuring a schematic of the propulsion drive that lay just on the other side of a pair of vault-thick doors. The sleeper ship *Oasis* was propelled by a variation of a Broussard engine, essentially a ram scoop that collected hydrogen particles from space, channeling them through a funnel that generated a powerful enough magnetic field to compress the atoms thus sparking a fusion reaction.

This powerful reaction produced and sustained thrust, propelling the ship to a velocity approaching, but not exceeding light. Mid-twenty-second century science had still not solved the vexing issue of mass reduction beyond the light-speed barrier.

Sara Hartwell and Rick Velez looked on in fascination. What their lead engineer proposed at the crew meeting had them mentally and sometimes physically scratching their heads. Yes, they were engineers assigned to oversee and maintain the ship's engine. Plus, they possessed the applicable skills to effect repairs if needed. But the modifications . . . massive modifications Reg suggested, required a level of know-how eclipsing their own.

Sara and Rick shared the general sentiment among the crew: this man had been a major tech CEO. How did he end up in a lowly slot as an engineer aboard a sleeper ship bound for a distant star?

"There." Reg pointed to an area on the schematic. "The hydrogen flow is densest at this part of the conduit just before the fusion reaction begins. We can increase magnetic field strength at that point, enhancing the reaction's intensity to a factor of five."

Rick slouched his lanky frame while Sara's naturally large gray eyes grew larger in alarm.

"Reg," said Rick. "The conduit won't be able to handle that kind of intensity. The whole thing'll blow up, sparing those aliens the work of killing us themselves."

"And if the conduit doesn't succumb to excess thermal pressure, how are we going to channel it?" Sara asked, her face scrunched in puzzlement.

Reg gazed indulgently at the pair; a corner of his mouth tilted upward. "Leave that to me. I'll iron out the details. I just need your help assembling the hardware. Don't worry. We have a year to get this done."

"So, I take it you've had experience building fusion cannons in your basement," Rick commented sarcastically. "Because attempting to fashion one on this ship is most certainly the equivalent."

"I never had the *ingredients* to build a fusion cannon in my basement," Reg replied casually. "But through there—Reg pointed at the vault-like doors—we have everything we need. We just have to do a little tweaking, a little rearranging."

Sara and Rick exchanged wary looks.

****

Three months later . . .

Reg labored in the guts of the *Oasis*. Perspiration misted his ebon face despite the temp-regulated hazmat suit he wore. The tube-shaped fusion reactor was suspended in the middle of a transparent containment chamber, secured by couplers, red conduits connecting both ends of the reactor.

It took some doing, but Reg managed to remove a panel on the north-facing conduit to manually adjust magnetic field parameters. He could have done it from an engine room computer, but the level of adjustments he was making breached safety protocols. The computer would have flagged the attempt and locked him out. He could have reprogrammed the computer but opted to do an end run around it not only because it was faster, but because he needed to see first-hand the results of his tinkering.

It had been a delicate, time-consuming task enhancing magnetic field strength. After completing the final step in the process, Reg placed the panel back on the conduit and secured it in place. He took a step back, doing a mental checklist to make sure the calculations he applied to the task were accurate. The slightest error—Reg tossed that thought away before it fully formed in his head. He didn't need any burdensome worries clinging to him. He quickly exited the reactor area.

After removing his hazmat suit and undergoing decontamination, Reg entered the engine room. Sara and Rick stood at their respective stations monitoring reactor functions.

"No change," said Sara. "The conduit is doing a good job withstanding this field density level."

Reg nodded, his eyes focused like spotlights on Sara's monitor. "Let's light it up. That'll be the real test."

"Here goes," Rick muttered nervously. He tapped a prompt on his console, activating the reactor's accelerator.

"Ten percent increase . . ." said Sara, observing a reactor scan chart. "Fifteen percent . . ."

"Thermal pressure is spiking, but the conduit's holding!" Rick exclaimed, shedding his doubts. "Not a single sign of structural duress!"

As he hoped and expected. Reg smiled.

****

". . . by feeding additional hydrogen atoms into the reactor we increased fusion levels by fifty-seven percent," said Reg, giving his report to the captain in her austere bridge side office.

Alisha sipped bitter black coffee from her silver thermos, her third refill of the chronological day so far. Three hundred passengers were hibernating in sleep capsules below deck, blissfully unaware of the danger rapidly approaching the ship. The least she could do was sacrifice her own sleep doing everything she could to ensure their survival.

"Having amplified fusion production, we need to build a channeler, and that can only be achieved by extending and narrowing the magnetic fields around the Brussard scoops." Reg referred to the starboard intake mechanisms that 'scooped' up hydrogen atoms from space and channeled them into the reactor where they were compressed into fusion to accelerate the ship.

"We need to convert the intake process to outtake," Reg continued. "I'll send you a blueprint I've drawn up."

"A blueprint? Just like that?" Alisha set her cup down and gazed at Reg with a mix of wonder and skepticism. "That's a huge overhaul...really huge and you already have a layout on how it can be done?"

"Theoretical," Reg emphasized. "I won't know a thing until this process is put into practice."

Alisha grinned. "I have a feeling you know what the outcome will be more than you let on." She gestured permissively. "Send the blueprint but get started on the magnetic field adjustments."

"Right away. And Captain?" Reg's tone resonated concern. "Get some rest. The engineers have this covered."

Alisha leaned back in her chair, her expression briefly betraying the weight of the hundreds of lives she carried on her shoulders. "If only it were that easy, Reg. But thank you. I'll try."

****

Six months later . . .

Narrowing the radius of the magnetic field around both Brussard scoops could only be achieved if the field emitters were manually recalibrated. That entailed weeks of EVA (extra-vehicular activity) by every engineer specializing in ship propulsion systems. Of course, the amount of knowledge the engineers possessed amounted to elementary, just enough to maintain the hardware, not radically alter it.

Reg knew every detail of the *Oasis's* engine. So, he knew how far to go in his radical alteration. He put together an intricate guideline, replete with calculations for the engineers to follow as they undertook the arduous task of adjusting the emitters.

Reg went behind the engineers, triple-checking every stage of the process because if an adjustment were off by so much as a millimeter, the engine's operation could falter . . . or worse.

The bridge crew watched as Reg stepped before a new control panel he installed next to the guidance computer. The panel housed the fire control lever along with a dial that offered variable range options for fusion release. On a battleship, such a panel would have bristled with tactical scanners, targeting sequencers, multi-spectrum imagers, the works. If given time, Reg could very well have built a proper combat setup to deal with the incoming threat. But time was a luxury he simply did not have. He looked at the captain, awaiting the go-ahead.

The captain nodded.

Reg gently pushed the fire control lever forward . . .

The Brussard scoops projected like musical horns from the front of the bulbous sleeper ship. They were innocuous protrusions designed solely to snag atoms from the vacuum and direct them into their cylindrical maws. They were never meant to be weapons of war.

Twin beams of plasma, searingly bright, demonically crimson, ejected from those twin maws. The narrowness of the magnetic field kept the beams straight and focused for a distance of eighty million kilometers. Without the magnetic field, the plasma would have dispersed upon launch.

The bridge crew applauded the test and the captain's face beamed approval.

Reg refrained from reacting, his ruminating frown a stark contrast to the surrounding fanfare.

"What's wrong?" the captain asked. "You're not satisfied with the test?"

"I need to further condense the beams," replied Reg. "We must make sure that what it hits will not just buckle but break. If I only had some idea of the composition of those ships' hulls. Are they energy shielded? If not, will the plasma deflect or penetrate?"

"Perhaps you should view the colonists' videos of those ships," Alisha suggested. "There might be a tidbit of footage that could answer your questions."

Reg's eyes lit up. He clasped his hands with enthusiasm. "Captain, I think you're on to something." He made a beeline to the com station where Hattie and Fritz were posted. "Is there a spectroscopic feature in the communication hardware?"

Hattie nodded with curious eyes. "Yes, there is." She tapped her console keypad, bringing a blank screen to life. "I can show you how to access that function."

When she did, Reg brought up images of the alien ships on the main com screen. He spent the next hour studying footage.

***

The first time Reg viewed videos of the hostile ships, his emotions bubbled over, and it was all he could do to contain his seismic shock at witnessing so much carnage. He had planned to end his brief tenure as Lead Engineer and join those colonists. He hoped to share in the joy and excitement of exploring a virgin world. The sense of loss left him suspended in a wretched void of sorrow and hopelessness.

This time he watched those same images with a cold, clinical detachment, his obsidian eyes roving the screen, probing, pinpointing, analyzing. His fingers worked the keypad like a piano maestro, zooming in on and manipulating images. Finally, he looked to the captain.

"I just completed a spectrum analysis of light reflecting off those ships. Their hulls are alloy as expected, but the building block elements are iron and carbon laced with traces of lithium."

"Elements familiar to us," said Alisha. "But we don't know how processed that material is. Those hulls might be hardened to the point where they'll be impervious to anything we throw at it."

Reg cocked his head in agreement. "That's why we need to enhance the fusion beam's intensity. If you apply enough heat to an object it's bound to give."

"We should also give thought to some kind of shielding," Alisha suggested. "This ship is very tightly insulated from cosmic radiation, but the slightest hull breach will be fatal for all of us, even if we win the battle."

The lead engineer displayed a wry smile. "Great minds think alike. I've actually been working on a . . ."

"Blueprint?" Alisha inserted with a wry smile of her own.

"Well . . . yes."

"Why am I not surprised? Go finish it. I can't wait to see what you've come up with."

Reg gestured a casual two-finger salute. "Right away, Captain."

***

Reg sat at the computer guidance station wearing a VR visor as he typed commands on the console keypad. Sara, Rick, and George observed, trying to make sense of the programming language populating the adjacent terminal screen.

Reg recognized that for the fusion cannon's utility to be maximized, the sleeper ship needed to maneuver. The problem was the ship had no maneuvering capability because it was only meant to travel a preprogrammed course to the Alpha Centauri system. There were minimal lateral deviations allowed for the avoidance of obstacles like asteroids or particularly dense and lethal pockets of cosmic radiation. Other than those mild variances, the *Oasis'* path to its destination adhered to an undeviating script.

As the guidance engineer, George's task entailed maintaining the computer's upkeep. He had no idea how to reprogram or manually override it. It turned out programming complex computers was Reg's department.

"I helped develop similar systems to the ones on this ship," said Reg as he typed in runes of algorithms. "It's just a matter of penetrating a few firewalls protecting the primary programming code. Once that's achieved, I'm free to alter that code to my specification. It's like taming a horse."

"I grew up on a ranch," said George with a glazed tone to match his glazed expression. "What you're doing is way more involved."

"But it can be done," Reg replied, not arrogantly, but with the easy confidence of a skilled professional.

457

"Assuming you're successful," said Rick. "How are we going to pilot this ship? Someone has to generate the maneuvers and we don't have the hardware to do so."

"Not to worry." Reg removed the visor. "I'm going to program remote piloting subroutines into the computer. This console will have to be extensively modified to accommodate a piloting setup. I'll draw up the blueprints detailing what needs to be done and you guys can get to work on it."

Sara raised an eager brow. "Well, I'm certainly looking forward to pulling more rabbits out of this hat."

"We'll have to pull a pilot out of that hat as well," said Reg with an acknowledging grin. He looked at Rick. "You told me that you flew an aircraft or two in your life. That skill should be applicable to spacecraft I'm assuming."

Rick shrugged. "You assume correctly, but I wouldn't be the right person for the job. The captain was a fighter pilot before joining NASA. Overqualified for her current position if you ask me. Just like you. But she'd be a much better candidate to pilot this giant turkey."

Reg narrowed his eyes in consideration.

****

One month later...

The captain stood over the newly renovated guidance station. The console was stripped to its bare bones, with missing panels exposing a tangled mélange of circuit boards and connectors. Haphazard appearance aside, the console had been modified to accommodate the joystick Reg installed, along with various flight control settings. He even scavenged a screen from the ship diagnostic station to be used as a secondary flight monitor.

Alisha's hand enfolded the joystick, and a delighted smile graced her visage.

"You look pleased," Reg commented, noting the captain's expression.

"I never thought I'd be doing any piloting." Alisha's other hand tapped the console with approval. "I was content to let the computer do the flying while I slept like a baby a good part of the journey. Despite the circumstances, it feels good being back in the cockpit so to speak. What do you need me to do?"

Reg walked to the middle of the bridge, gazing at the main monitor. "Let's do a three sixty, Captain. We'll start off wide, then progressively narrower."

Alisha added gentle pressure to the joystick, pushing it to the right.

Anticipatory silence cloaked the bridge. Crew members glanced about, awaiting a responding shift in the ship's motion.

The only indicator of the *Oasis'* change in orientation came from the course readings on the monitor's trajectory scan. Ten degrees . . . twenty degrees . . . thirty degrees . . .

"It's working!" Sara announced, breaking the silence. "You're turning us, Captain!"

"How does the control feel?" Reg asked the captain.

"Smooth as silk," Alisha replied, luxuriating in her true element. "I can get used to this."

Reg turned to Rick. "How's the engine?"

"Holding well," said Rick.

"Good. Let's see how efficiently we multi-task." Reg pointed to Bobby. "Fire the cannon."

Bobby nodded and pushed the fire control lever on his terminal. A crimson slash of weaponized plasma blazed from the Brussard scoops, rapidly diminishing with distance.

"Good shooting," Reg complimented.

Bobby ran a hand through his curly black hair in a performative motion. "Won't be long before I'm shooting at the real thing."

Reg chose Bobby to operate the cannon because of his background as an Olympic level skeet shooter. He figured a man trained to take out fast-moving targets ought to be able to apply that skill to destroying a hostile alien ship. The choice was a gamble, but then again, everything Reg did to prepare the *Oasis* for a confrontation with an implacable and ruthless foe had been a monumental gamble.

It took the *Oasis* thirty minutes to execute a full three sixty turn.

"If this ship had attitude thrusts, I could spin on a dime," Alisha fretted. She sighed in resignation. "But we have to work with what we have."

"I'm afraid so, Captain," Reg said, sharing her mild frustration. "So far, so good. Let's do another pass, this time tighter . . ."

****

Two months later...

Reg walked into a booth overlooking the sleeper bay. A diagnostic monitor displaying icons of over three hundred sleep capsules dominated much of the booth's space. Every capsule was shaded in green. Thankfully. The color scheme ran from green for normal status to yellow for urgent to red for critical. If a capsule went gray, that meant it was either empty or its occupant deceased.

A week earlier, Reg oversaw the fortification of the sleeper bay to shield it from lethal cosmic radiation should a breach erupt in its vicinity. He and every crew member spent endless hours removing alloy plating from nonessential parts of the ship and using them to reinforce as much of the bay's bulkheads and ceiling as could be covered. He also addressed the issue of added protection for the *Oasis* against likely battle damage. Creating a science fiction type energy shield to enfold the ship was out of the question. Instead, he and the crew fortified other key areas outside of the sleeper bay: the bridge, engine room, medical wing, food and water storage compartments, and every corridor accessing those areas.

As Reg stared through the booth's plexiglass at rows of sleep capsules, he could only hope that their efforts would be enough. He had no idea what to expect in the coming battle.

"Worried about them too, huh?"

Reg turned to see the captain standing at the booth's entrance. He dipped his head, shaking it in amusement. "This'll sound absurd to you, but I'm on this ship because I got bored with my life. I left all my worldly possessions behind to tackle a new challenge. I got my wish, but never banked on facing hostile aliens."

"We're all facing the unexpected," said Alisha, stepping inside the booth. She gazed at the diagnostic monitor. "I thought I left my combat days behind me when I took this job. Now it looks like I'll be fighting in a new arena."

"But will it be a fight we can win?" Reg wondered, directing the query more at himself than Alisha. "I've tried to think of every possible way to make this ship defensible. If I haven't succeeded, then we die and" —Reg gestured at the sleep capsules— "they die."

Alisha took Reg's hand. She squeezed it and the contact both soothed and electrified him.

"Before climbing into my cockpit, I never agonized about the future." Alisha twisted her face. "It could drive you insane. Stay focused on here and now. Check the work you've done so far, tweak whatever needs tweaking. Do what you must to stay sharp. And when it's time to fight, focus on the enemy."

Reg's mood lightened. He regarded the captain with a playful smirk. "Aye, aye Captain on the pep talk. I'll keep that mind."

"Good," said Alisha. "Now, I'll need a pep talk from you."

Reg thought for a moment. "I used to repeat this mantra to myself before negotiating a major contract: slaughter them."

Alisha squinted before bursting into laughter. "Slaughter them?"

Reg lifted a brow. "In many respects, business is analogous to war."

****

Thirteen days later.

Death loomed on the main monitor in the form of cold, gunmetal gray alloy elegantly molded into a remorseless weapon of mass destruction. Swathed in the inky blackness of space, the alien vessel cast an almost preternatural glow, accentuating the malevolence it represented.

Yet, as Reg gazed at the image, he could not help but feel stirrings of awe at the sight of nonhuman technology. Under better circumstances, he would have relished getting into the guts of that machine to examine its every nook and cranny.

"It moves so fast and gracefully," said Sara, mirroring Reg's thoughts.

"It won't kill us gracefully, I'll tell you that," Rick muttered.

"Cut the unnecessary chatter," the captain ordered. She looked to George. "How much longer to projected engagement range?"

The guidance officer glanced at his screen. "One hour, nine minutes, Captain."

Reg crossed his fingers on that one, at least as best he could in his EVA suit. Every bridge crew member wore a suit and helmet for protection against space radiation in the event of a breach.

From Reg's ceaseless study of the colony attack, he noticed that the alien ships never fired their weapons at a range beyond one hundred and seventy-five kilometers. That was the range he calculated when studying footage of their attacks on the colony's twenty-two satellites. The distance upon weapons release remained a consistent one seventy-five.

It became a consensus among captain and crew that the *Oasis* would fire first before the enemy ship crossed the projected one seventy-five threshold. Reg's concern was the fusion beam's coherence. If fired at a target too far away, the beam's integrity would not hold adequately enough to cause sufficient damage. During the fusion cannon's test firings, Reg had managed to fine tune the beam's coherence up to one hundred and ninety-five kilometers.

"Two hundred thirty kilometers and closing," said George, his eyes glued to his screen.

Reg stood beside the captain as she began executing a turn. He exchanged a reassuring glance with Alisha before panning the bridge.

Crew members stood with professional poise at their posts. Whatever thoughts or emotions broiled beneath the surface;

their faces displayed a steel-clad willingness to embrace whatever fate had in store for them.

"Two hundred ten kilometers," George read off.

The alien ship grew large enough on the monitor for the mildly ribbed texture of its dark hull to be delineated. The ship rotated until the axle part of its spoked wheel configuration faced the *Oasis*. It was from the axle that the alien's ship's weapons seemed to be concentrated.

The *Oasis* was six minutes from completing its turn and the alien ship had not responded with any kind of trajectory shift.

That was a good sign to Reg. It meant that the enemy ship did not consider the *Oasis* a threat. If the aliens hacked the colony's database, they would have certainly accessed information on sleeper ships, seeing that they were nothing more than unarmed transport vessels.

"Slaughter them," Aleshia muttered.

Reg cracked a grim smile. "Slaughter them."

"Two hundred kilometers," said George.

"Bobby, it's on you," Reg announced, his tone firm yet encouraging. "The cannon must be aligned with the enemy ship's axle. The very second you have that alignment open fire. No hesitation. Clear?"

"Clear as ice . . . well unpolluted ice." Bobby cleared his throat and stared unwavering at the monitor designated as a target screen. He held a steady hand above the fire control lever.

Alisha's face was set in stone as she concentrated on making the turn. To give Bobby his shot, she needed the cannon pointing precisely at the target's center. Never had she piloted something so ponderous and sluggish as this gigantic bucket. But at least the *Oasis*, a vessel never meant for manual operation, responded adequately to her control.

"One hundred ninety-eight kilometers." George and everyone else, except for Reg and Bobby, darted apprehensive glances at the captain.

As the fusion cannon neared alignment with the enemy ship's center, Alisha eased up on the control, decreasing the risk of her overshooting the target area.

Strands of tension filtered through George's voice. "One hundred eighty-seven kilometers."

The alien ship's magnified image dominated the main monitor. By that time, the cannon reached alignment . . .

Reg stiffened. He almost mouthed the word 'fire' at the very second Bobby pushed the fire control lever that unleashed and directed outward the hell-wrought energies of a sun.

The fusion beam struck its target dead center, then scrawled a molten trail that tore a chunk out of the 'spoke' connecting the central segment to the ship's outer radial.

The alien ship slowed to a dead stop, nearly the entirety of its axle a throbbing glow.

A collective silence seized the crew. For a few seconds no one breathed.

Sara broke the silence with a clamorous whisper. "We . . . hit it. We hit it!" She looked to Bobby. "Good job, sharpshooter!"

Bobby's shoulders sagged, an accomplished smile expanding his face.

Cheers erupted around him, but Reg was too fixated on the scanner and monitor to join in. The enemy ship remained stationary. Reg didn't know if that was due to the damage caused by the fusion beam or its undoubtedly shocked crew reassessing a target previously thought unarmed.

"How badly do you think we damaged it?" Alisha asked, observing the monitor.

"I can't be sure." Reg rubbed his chin. "Bobby, how long until the cannon is powered up for a second shot?"

Bobby checked the screen. "Thirty-three seconds."

Reg clenched a decisive fist. "The second you're at full power, hit it again." He turned to the captain. "All that ship needs to do is remain still . . ."

"Not gonna happen," Alisha cut in and pointed to the monitor.

Reg gazed at the monitor and his eyes widened.

"Shit!" Rick exclaimed. "It's moving!"

The alien ship resumed its progress, but at a slower velocity.

"It's adopting a flanking trajectory but it's not moving nearly as fast as before," said George.

"Captain, it's trying to avoid being in the cannon's sights," said Reg.

Alisha grabbed the joystick. "I'm going to try my very best to match its maneuver. Clearly, we damaged it significantly enough where it can't go any faster."

"If it's still coming at us, we might not have damaged its weapon," said Rick.

An hour passed with the crew looking on in trepidation as the alien ship inched closer to the *Oasis*. By that time, the glow at its center subsided to a dark scab marked with traces of iridescence.

Hattie pointed to the monitor. "Look! It's leaking something!"

White vapor billowed from where the fusion beam damaged a section of the ship's superstructure.

"That's either atmosphere or fluids vital to its operation," Reg speculated. "Either way, I think we hurt it bad."

"But it's closing on us," said Alisha, focusing hard on steering the *Oasis* into alignment with the opposing vessel. "Bobby, get ready."

"Yes, Captain!" Bobby gripped the fire control lever.

Suddenly, a stream of tiny objects, so numerous they formed a glimmering wind driven cloud, ejected from points along the ship's outer radial structure.

Seconds later, the *Oasis* shook violently as if throttled by a celestial titan. Standing crew members tumbled to the deck. A deafening racket, like the pitter patter of hail pelting a tin roof assaulted the bridge. A blizzard of mass-accelerated solid projectiles savagely punctured the Oasis' hull, holing it through and through in some places. The fusion cannon was yet unscathed.

"Visors up! Visors up, everyone!" Alisha ordered.

Crew members pushed their helmet visors up and sealed them in place.

"The ship is still armed!" George said despairingly.

Reg nodded. "Yes, but it appears we destroyed its primary weapon. It's resorting to secondary armaments."

Sara's console erupted in sparks and debris from explosive feedback. She jumped back in fright. Overhead lighting blinked on and off.

"Damage report!" Alisha demanded.

"Sections five through eleven are breached," reported Rick. "Fires in the lower storage compartments."

"What about the sleeper bay?"

Rick scrolled through data. "The sleeper bay is good . . . for now."

Alisha managed a relieved breath.

The alien ship's attack inflicted severe structural damage on the *Oasis* but did not hinder its mobility. Mass-accelerated projectiles continued to chew into the hull until the first wave was spent.

Alisha stayed the course, strangling the joystick to bring the Oasis into line of sight targeting with the enemy.

The alien ship grew ever larger with proximity. A second cluster of projectiles shot out of innumerable hidden launchers embedded in its hull.

The *Oasis* quaked and groaned from so many impacting projectiles. Thousands of molten divots populated the hull.

Every screen but a miniature monitor next to the captain's station went black—a screen Bobby could not see, leaving him effectively blind.

Reg realized this and rushed to the working monitor.

"Do I have a shot?" Alisha asked.

Reg kept eyes on the screen. "You're just a few seconds from alignment . . . damn!" Static filled the screen. He looked up. "I've lost visual, captain."

"I'll try to regain visual," said Sara, removing a panel from a secondary station to examine connections. Fritz moved to join her.

"Go ahead but I'm not waiting!" said the captain. "Bobby, fire!"

Without hesitation, Bobby pushed the fire control lever.

The fusion cannon screamed hot fury in the desolate silence of freezing vacuum. Once again, a destructive beam of high energy lanced into the alien ship's axle, viciously compounding previous damage.

The projectile barrage continued to rip massive chunks out of the *Oasis* even as its fusion beam drilled deeper into the alien's hull.

Shock waves from the thunderous pounding reverberated through the sleeper ship with such savagery as to nearly knock the bridge's double reinforced door off its track. The overhead dome window cracked from a glancing projectile blow.

Reg looked up nervously, expecting the window to shatter at any second and everyone to be sucked out into space. And then the noise ceased, displaced by the mournful cadence of a battered ship barely held together at the seams.

No one said a word. Crew members stood still as wax figures awaiting the next enemy barrage that was sure to spell their doom.

Nothing.

Sara and Fritz labored to restore visual to one or more of the bridge monitors.

Finally, the main monitor fizzled back to life, displaying a static-tinged image of the alien ship.

Explosions blossomed across its hull in a frenzied chain reaction. Half of its spokes broke off as cracks formed rapidly as lightning streaks throughout its radial structure. A final, massive explosion consumed what remained of the vessel, spewing tangled detritus in every direction, some of it rocketing toward the *Oasis*, deflecting off its brutalized hull.

The ship's demise cast the *Oasis* in a hellish glare.

The monitor screen polarized to protect its viewers from the blinding glow. When the light subsided, fragments of the alien ship drifted in a sea of black, forming an iridescent debris field.

Everyone stared at the screen, shocked, relieved, thankful for their lives.

Reg let out the breath he forgot he was holding. He removed his helmet and wiped away the sweat beading on his forehead. "Captain, we need to get a move on with all due haste."

Alisha eagerly agreed. She looked to George. "Take the ship off manual control. Resume preprogrammed course back to Earth."

"Aye Captain," George said wearily.

****

No part of the *Oasis* escaped structural damage. In some areas, entire decks had been obliterated, exposed to vacuum and awash in lethal cosmic radiation. Those areas were sectioned off by emergency barricades to contain the radiation's proliferation. Although cracks marred the sleeper bay's bulkheads, the entire section, thanks to heavy reinforcement, escaped the worst of the pummeling inflicted on the rest of the ship. Every sleeper capsule remained intact, every slumbering occupant exhibiting positive life signs.

The crew had done all they could to repair damage to essential ship systems. The fusion cannon reverted to its role as a propulsion engine. Reg, Sara, and Rick worked tirelessly to bring the engine back to its previous operational efficiency.

In time, all tasks completed, the crewmembers retired to their capsules to sleep out the rest of the journey home.

Only Reg and the captain remained awake.

They entered the sleeper bay, walking past rows of capsules.

"They slept through it all," Alisha said somberly, referring to the sleeping passengers. "They're the lucky ones."

Reg looked skeptical. "I don't know about that. These people expected to wake up in a utopia. They'll be shocked to discover otherwise. At least we've had the benefit of processing this catastrophe. I don't envy them."

"I suppose that's one way of looking at it." Alisha stopped next to her capsule. She tapped a button and the capsule's seal whisked open. "Reg. Thank you. If it weren't for you . . ."

Reg raised his hand to interrupt. "We all did our part to prepare this ship for battle. And you led us to victory."

Alisha grinned. "Stop it. You can't be that modest."

"Perhaps you'll find out if you get to know me . . . on a personal level."

Alisha climbed into her capsule. Before shutting the seal, she said: "Perhaps, I'll take you up on that challenge when we get home."

Reg smiled and headed to his capsule. He climbed inside, rested his body on a comfortable foam palette, and initiated stasis mode. Instantly, he dreamed.

Kill the Moon
by
Antoine Bandele

EPIGRAPH

"Walk on road.
Walk right side, safe; walk left side, safe.
Walk middle, sooner or later get squish, just like grape."
— Some 20th Century Karate Dojo Guy

* * *

Engineer's log.
Local Date and Time: 23.2277.15.12.1707.
Location: Uncharted Sagittarius Arm. Safi Cluster. Vijana
System. Southern Hemisphere Orbit of M-22.

Hello and salutations. May your thrusters never rust, and all that. It's your girl Orion! Your favorite teenage hacker. Yeah, yeah . . . only the crew of the *Nyame* call me that. And I know I ain't supposed to give out my name on these dead drops, but I want to feel like I'm choppin' it up with whatever Corporate Alliance agent listens to these. It ain't like none of the crew ever talks to me, 'cept if they want somethin' hacked or cleaned.

If a Fed ship boarded us right now, I know ain't no "Orion" over here. I'm Fifi Amankwah of the Planet New Gaia of the Alpha Centauri System. And you better get that right, or I'll space you real quick, on God.

I'm an upstandin' citizen of the Interstellar Federation of the Sagittarius Arm. I ain't no criminal pirate. Nah, if the Feds came up through here, I'm a travelin 'student comin 'from an away trip within the Solar Prime System. I'm definitely *not* no hacker for the most dangerous and effective mercenary group this side of the

470

Gould Belt. And I am *definitely* not in a commandeered university starcruiser loaded with enough tactical nukes to kill a moon.

Now, you hired us because the *Nyame* crew and the Captain always honor our contracts. We done some jacked-up shit for you people. No questions asked.

Funny thing… I thought I'd always be down with that. It's got me enough credits to nearly pay off the slavers. To free my family.

I done things I ain't been proud of. The times we spaced a few VIPs, extorted a colony or two, laundered a few credits on the side . . . but it's been worth it.

It has to be worth it.

Extended pause detected in recording.

That's why, as I stare through the viewport of the crypod chambers right now, my insides are turnin'.

This damned planet is smilin 'up at me with the audacity of a crescent moon. Don't get me wrong. It's sittin 'there like it's supposed to: A simple little thing with two moons circling around it. Nothin' out of the ordinary. It's been on the map a few decades now, like you people said. And just like you people reported, two moons make for bad terraformin'. One of 'em's gotta go.

In a few years, the real estate on this hunk of rock would fetch a pretty set of creds for you fine folks. What can someone buy with that kind of loot? A third space station for your pet kishi?

You're probably the type of asshole who'd buy a kishi, huh?

Anyway, y'all said Planet M-22 is supposed to be free of *any* complex lifeforms. Covered completely in undrinkable water, you said. Toxic water that can't house no kind of life. Those brainiacs at the academies think the planet is recovering from a "recent" extinction event. Complex lifeforms ain't supposed to be poppin' up for at *least* another few million years. Meaning my virtual intelligence *shouldn't* be flashing a message of lifeform readings.

In fact, I know my VI shouldn't be flashing that message because I ran the numbers myself. The planet is supposed to be dead!

End of engineer's log.

***

BUH-DEW, the little chime blared in my mind. I tapped my ear to switch it off. My VI, Anansi, was trippin'.

The captain wanted the crypods cleaned, so I was gonna clean 'em. I wasn't finna give him no bad news.

I pocketed my dead drop capsule into my utility belt. Goosebumps sat at attention on my arms as I scrubbed out the waste deposit from the last pod—not because of the fecal matter but because it was cold-as-shit in the cryochambers. That's the treatment you get when you're the youngest on the crew, I guess. If I weren't so good at hacking, I'd probably have to clean the whole damn cruiser.

This last pod housed a nasty bit of waste from the only dra'qell on the crew. A merc the captain hired to protect us. And judging by the acid deposits, the thing could probably do a good job of it. That and the indestructible red-orange exoskeleton over its glowing green skin.

BUH-DEW

A notification flashed on the datapad, currently wedged up next to the dra'qell's hooked head within the pod. The message read:

> *Anansi: Lifeforms detected in the southern hemisphere of the oceans of M-22.*

I tapped a knuckle on the screen to exit the message. My VI had been actin 'up since our last job. There ain't no way there was life down on that—

BUH-DEW

Did you read my last message, Orion? Anansi asked through our unique cybernetic connection in my head. *Would you like me to read it out loud?*

"No." I climbed down from the cryopod, sterilized my hands, gathered my cleaning supplies, and made my way back to my quarters. "Because I know your memory cache is jacked up because I ain't got the chance to clear out those viruses from our last job yet."

I cleared those away mere hours after the crew went into cryo, ma'am.

"How many hours until the charges are ready on the moon?" I asked irritably, taking another look through the single viewport in the chamber. The little moon was cresting over M-22's horizon just then, an indigo rock peeking over green sludge.

Charges will be set and ready for combustion in t-minus 5 hours 13 minutes and 7 seconds. Current success rate: 75.67%.

If something really was up, there was still time to go through my numbers again. Plenty of time.

A flashing light caught the corner of my eye just before I left the cyrochambers. The dra'qell's life signs were reading that it was awake instead of in deep sleep. I knocked on the readout and it went back to normal.

Great. Just another thing for me to fix. Bet money the captain will blame me for that shit too.

Ma'am, I have detected an uptick in your anxiety. I shall take that to mean you are taking my report into consideration.

I bit at my lower lip, a bad habit Baba never beat out of me. "Anansi, you sure your readings are correct? Legally, the Feds only care about intelligent life. Lil microbes *don't* count. We only gotta worry about *intelligent* life."

Ma'am, intelligent life is exactly what I am picking up.

"How? I got the same readouts you do. Ain't nothin' detected."

A gentle whoosh sounded as the door to my quarters opened. I plopped down on my messy cot and dropped my dead drop capsule at my side—I'd send out my report later. After I figured out what was going on.

My viewport at the back of the cramped room had fogged up, so I cleared it away to get a better look. M-22 looked just the same with its solid hue of toxic-waste green. Sure, it flowed and pulsated in pockets, but that was because of how the ocean interacted with the atmosphere, not because there were schools of merspawn huddled up together and having a party.

"There ain't nothing but good old-fashioned H_2O down there." I groaned dismissively before adding, "With a side of radiation and chemicals to wash it down."

Ma'am, I know because they are sending us a message.

That one forced my gaze from the viewport and down toward my datapad. I swiped away Anansi's waveforms and searched through the recent communication logs. There were no messages from anyone or anything. Not from inside the ship or out of it.

Sighing, I brought Anansi's waveforms back up on screen. "You see, there's a few viruses I gotta get out of that head of yours. There ain't been no transmissions in the last few hours, Anansi."

There was a pause as I waited, as though Anansi needed time to think of his response. We have a unique connection. As far as anyone knows, ain't no one been able to integrate with a VI like Anansi without their head getting' fried. That's what made me valuable to the crew. I could speed through complex calculations, but with the human heart and all that mushy stuff thrown in too. But sometimes that meant my VI could get a little foggy brained like a human; the link went both ways.

I was about to tap my screen to make sure he really didn't have a virus when his waveforms jumped. *This transmission is different. It is not being emitted by conventional means. I have only ever seen this type of communication among the aziza.*

"So you're saying . . . what? That there's telepaths down there?" I shook my head, imagining some whale-looking race singing songs. "One of the aliens onboard would've picked up on that already, wouldn't they?"

Perhaps we should request the First Mate's opinion, ma'am?

I rolled my eyes. "I'm not bothering Afia with this. She might be the nicest one on the ship, but that doesn't mean she won't have my ass. I need more evidence than the word of a malfunctioning VI."

I am not malfunctioning, ma'am. The message I am trying to decipher seems to be coming from the entire day side of M-22.

Ugh, this VI was going to be the death of me. "How long you been hearin 'this message?"

A few days before you came out of cryo.

474

I balled two fists. "And you didn't think to wake me sooner?"

It wasn't until the last few minutes that I determined the message had been sent from sentient origins.

I groaned. "The captain's still on live watch with me right now, right?"

Yes, ma'am. He's in the control room now, catching up on some news vids.

"He know anything about this talkin' ocean stuff?"

Not that I know, ma'am.

I lifted my foot from under my paper-thin blanket and used my toes to flip a switch off the wall. A secret panel I installed flipped out and revealed a few vid screens that were hacked into the security cams on the ship. Did the crew know, you ask? Of course not. But they should've thrown up a firewall on the cruiser's shit if they wanted me to stay out.

Resting my chin on my palms, I searched for the image I was looking for. Ah, yes. Just there on Cam-3. The captain was slumped back in his chair with a bottle in his hand. Control panels and vid screens surrounded him, blanketing him in their soft light. I didn't have no audio, but I could tell he was singing.

Weird.

I thought the captain was a serious drunk. I grew up with all kinds of drunks. Everyone had a type. The First Mate, Afia, was a giggly drunk. My cousin RiRi . . . she's a sloppy drunk. And my old man was an angry drunk. The captain always got real quiet when he drank. Not this time, apparently. Whatever was eating him had him howling at the moons. And were those tears in his eyes? I used my toe to magnify the vid screen. Those *definitely* looked like tears. Seemed like the captain just upgraded from serious drunk to emotional—a common evolution for those quiet drunks. I should probably talk him out of the bottom of that bottle.

But I would only have more bad news for him . . .

I pressed my fingers into my temples. That was all I needed. The job to end all jobs had to hit an asteroid belt at some point. So, who could I take this information to?

Have you decided to awaken First Mate Afia after all, ma'am?

I groaned again. "You already know that's what I'm thinking, Anansi."

The code to the First Mate's cryopod always sounded like music to me. It was the way I remembered it anyway. When she gave me her code, I figured it was because she wanted to get at me, but she only shared it with me in case I needed to save her from an attack. We've known each other the longest on the crew—besides the captain. I wouldn't call her a friend. No one on the crew was. But she was, at best, a friendly acquaintance.

After the pod's sequencing ended—a tune of "Space is the Place" by Sun Ra—the egg-shaped door hissed and slid away to reveal the long brown legs of First Mate Afia, one of the few aliens on board. Like most of the other aliens, waking from cryo was like waking from a nap for an aziza, rather than a month-long hibernation. In only a few moments, she slipped out of her pod and smiled down at me from her full seven feet and two inches.

Yawning, she said with her Mid Rim accent, "Job's almost done then, eh?" She dug a pinky into her pointed ear and rubbed her overly large eyes with her other hand. "Why do you look like we've just been boarded by the Federation?" Her body stiffened when I didn't answer right away. Afia's hand whipped to the AL-77 blaster at her hip that wasn't there. "Shit, *are* we being boarded?"

"No, but it might be something worse," I said. "Come with me to the bridge. You still hook up your caf with two sweet cubes, yeah?"

* * *

After getting some caf into our systems, we made our way to the best view on the ship. The bridge wasn't huge by any means—remember, this was a student starcruiser. But it was real sleek. Nothing like our usual vessels. Instead of hanging wires and cables littered across the floor like the *Nyame*, everything on this bridge was clean. Sharp edges, good lighting, and comfortable leather seats.

I made sure we snatched up something from one of the High Academies. Nothing from the local community learning clusters, where you were liable to end up with cruisers just as jacked-up as our usual.

This job had already taken two standard months; better to be comfortable than not. And though the hard asses on the crew would never admit it, I know they liked it too. Even that draq'ell merc, who was basically a walking, insectoid skeleton with "hard-ass" written across its acid palms. And who wouldn't love this cruiser when you woke up to a viewport that went wall to wall with the perfect view of our special moons and our special planet?

Hmm, me, I guess. Today at least.

I planted myself at my favorite spot, just to the side of the charting computers where it was warmest. Afia flipped a switch at a panel and "Next Lifetime" by Erykah Badu sounded softly from the bridge speakers. She was into all those classics. I had to admit, though: her taste in music was definitely a vibe.

Afia padded over and stood right next to me, the green hue of the planet painting her obsidian skin like she was a vid-star on some holoshoot. I explained what Anansi had told me. When I got to the part about the message, her pointed ears stood at attention and she whispered, "*Pi bédè putògí po tìábu.*"

Afia traced a finger in a pattern along the viewport, muttering to herself.

"Huh?" I scrunched my brow. "What did you say?"

Sorry, ma'am. I cannot translate, Anansi said in my head. *The First Mate is speaking a phrase that is not in my data banks.*

Before I could get another question out, Afia stabbed me with a stare so sharp it could've carved a hole through the hull of the cruiser. It didn't help that she had these great big hazel-ish green eyes that always cascaded like a kaleidoscope. Then, suddenly, her long hands engulfed my cheeks. "You have to shut down those charges on the moon."

"But . . . there's no intelligent life down there."

"Of course there isn't. This is Olókun. This is beyond 'intelligent 'life, child. This is *far* beyond that. Much more sacred. We're talking about spiritual cognitive function. The lifeforms your VI is detecting are the early stages of a symbiotic relationship between an organism that is latching itself to the planet . . . directly."

"You gon' have to translate that for me. I know zeros and ones, not spiritual . . . whatever."

Afia's face changed then, like she had been confused or something. She let go of my face and took a step back, as though judging me in a new light. "You are only a child. You do not understand."

"I'm 15!"

"My people have told me this story for hundreds of years. I . . ." She gazed toward the planet's surface in the way a mother might regard a newborn child. "I . . . never thought I'd live to see the day of a great planetary spirit manifesting itself. *Pi bédè putògí po tìábu.*"

"That's not gon' ride with the Corporate Alliance," I told her. "They ain't 'bout to let us off 'cause we've found 'spiritual' intelligence or whatever—."

A low rumble vibrated in the hall outside the bridge. I couldn't tell what it was at first, not until it got closer. It was a slurred song from the lips of the captain himself. It was a song from the last century, an oldie from a guy my old man used to listen to. Abolon was the artist's name, I think.

> *Left my home, my loved ones too.*
> *Headed for the stars, what will I do?*

With the Outer Rim twang the captain was known for, he sang the end of the song only someone from the Far Reaches could. His shoulder leaned up against the bridge door. The red light above which meant the door was open for too long fell over him, casting the big man in shadow.

How long had he been listening to us? Maybe he didn't hear us at all with that tone-deaf rendition of "Leaving Earth" he subjected our innocent ears to.

"You know me, Afia," the captain gruffed out. "I'm a simple man. I don't understand no 'spiritual' intelligence neither. Whatever that is."

Ah, so he heard the last part, at least.

"Captain." Afia stood at attention, but her face was grave. "We cannot go through with this contract."

"Whatcha doin' out of your pod?" The captain gave his First Mate a drunkenly squinting look as he flipped a switch to cut off the music. "You don't have watch for another 12 hours, First Mate."

I gulped. "I woke her, captain. Anansi and I wanted a second opinion about whatever is down on that planet."

A thick silence hung between all three of us. I could barely even see the captain's grizzly gray beard or his cybernetic eyes in the low light. And was that the same bottle in his hand I saw before?

Yes, ma'am. That is indeed a bottle. Anansi took on a different voice, a chipper salesperson's voice. '*Experience the bold, rich flavor of Blazar's Booze. Made with the finest ingredients and distilled to perfection, one sip will transport you to a world of indulgence. Whether you're sipping neat or mixing up a signature cocktail, our drink will elevate any occasion. So raise a glass, and discover the true taste of—*'

Anansi, did you just read me an ad? I thought-spoke.

Apologies, ma'am, it appears the latest virus purge has reset my adblock.

The captain finally stumbled forward and into the full light of the bridge. If he didn't have cybernetic eyes, I expect they'd have been bloodshot to all hell.

"Sit," he commanded. "Both of ya."

He didn't have to tell me twice. I found the nearest leather-embedded seat at FTL speed. The First Mate wasn't nearly as quick, still planted by the viewport like a mech on standby.

The captain stopped walking in wake of Afia's defiance. His movement was sluggish, but he was definitely looking her up and down. Afia was tall but slender; the captain was tall *and* bulky. I know who I'd put creds on in a fight.

The captain sighed before grunting, "At least hear me out, Afia. You owe me that much."

Afia shook her head. "You know why I'm on this crew, captain." She thumbed over her shoulder. "I made it clear to you the day I met you. You were just twenty human years then. But I made myself clear. This is—"

"*Pi bédè putògí po tìábu*, I know." He took his own seat across from me. "That is why I need you to sit. Please."

With what seemed like all the effort in the galaxy, the First Mate made her steady way to her own seat. Once she finally settled into the stiffest position she could find herself in, the captain took a swig from his bottle. I caught a whiff of the liquor. It was the *real* hard stuff. The kind of stuff that'd rip through your liver like a black hole. Baba's old favorite.

The captain set his bottle near the helm. "I ain't a man of many words. So, I'll put it plain, and I'll put it true. That moon *has* to die—"

"But that'll murder the symbiotic—" Afia interrupted.

The captain held up a single hand. "We workin' to free our people. That is our priority. Always has been, always will be. If a moon has to die to make that happen . . . so be it. Or do you think that watery hunk of rock down there's more important than us and our own?"

I'd only been knowin' the captain for a standard year. One thing I knew about him for sure was that he was harsh but fair. And right now, I had to agree with him. We couldn't botch the whole gig off the back of some religious prophecy.

"This is bigger than our people," Afia said, as though reading my thoughts. "We're talking about the future of this galaxy. I can't even begin to explain to you how huge this is. A human like you would never understand."

The captain shrugged. "You're right. My feeble human brain can't comprehend whatever it is that exists down there. I get 120 years at best. You get 500, easy. All I understand is the flesh and blood I pledged myself to. The word I gave them. And my word is my bond."

"You're not the one who sets the charges. Orion is." Oh no, she had to bring *me* into it, and an uncharacteristic desperation entered her voice. "She always has a fail-safe. She can shut this whole thing down right now. Can't you, Orion?"

Now that was just not fair. Afia *never* asked me for no favors. And she knew I was a sucker for those damn eyes of hers. But I wasn't the captain. I didn't make no decisions like this. I couldn't. I just ran the numbers and watched things go boom. Simple.

"You know why we're out here, Orion." The captain's cybernetic eyes whirred to me. "You know why we need these creds, better than anyone. It'll fund the revolution; save thousands of lives! Millions! Isn't that why you're on this ship in the first place? To save your cousins, your sister, your mother. We're working toward the same goal. You *and* you," he nodded to Afia, "and I didn't make it this far, just to make it this far."

Afia shook her head. "No, we can't do this. Forget the honor of our contract. This is genocide."

The captain glared, though not unkindly. "How you figure this species is worth saving? It could turn out to be made up of nothin' but warmongerin' spawn set to destroy us all!"

"Olókun has been prophesied by my people thousands of years ago. They're meant to be our savior, not our destroyer."

I got where Afia was coming from. I believed in a God at one point. Still do, I guess. She just did a whole lot better of holding to that faith despite the messed up shit that went down in the Milky Way. I always liked that about her.

The captain pounded on the table and his bottle shattered on the ground. "I can't break a contract based on a *myth*. Things evolve every year, every minute, organics, and synthetics both. Most of it is never to our own benefit."

"Why are you so keen to justify killing them all?" Afia made a subtle fist at her side. "Caught the smell of credits already?"

"You know this ain't about no creds. It's bigger than that, bigger than this single planet. We talkin' 'bout *entire* systems being oppressed. Besides, we're just pullin' the trigger, not aimin' the gun. Someone else'll just come along and do it if we don't."

I cut in for the first time. "Why did a corp agree to pay us all that money? Why not do it all themselves?"

"So that we'll be the fall gals if the Federation starts snooping around on the edges of the Milky Way," Afia answered. "What's going on, captain? You're a better man than this. I know you are. Why are we doing this—"

"Because if we don't, we're dead."

"It's not that serious. We'll just find another job. There's always more work. Even if it takes us years or—"

The captain shook his head gravely. "No, there won't be. The corp didn't front us all the creds needed for this operation so . . . I got a loan from the Perseus Arm Syndicate. I used all those creds to buy them nukes. If we fail here, every bounty hunter in the galaxy will be on our asses."

My stomach dropped, then turned to stone. "You're messin' with dirty creds?" I asked, voice shaky. "Creds from the same assholes who fund the slavers we tryna take out?"

Afia's Water God was sounding pretty good right now.

The captain didn't make a habit of stacking our opinions against each other. It was usually his way or the hyperspace way. Not a lot of gray area with him. So why was he at least *attempting* to listen to us for a change?

Afia I got. But me? It didn't add up.

You have noticed that too, haven't you, ma'am? The captain's vitals are spiking. His anxiety is well above standard human levels.

It's not just that, Anansi, I thought-spoke back to my VI. *There's just something off about the captain . . . bad vibes, bad juju.*

"You *want* us to convince you to break our word on the contract, don't you?" I said softly, just as Afia rattled off another counterargument. My words seemed to loosen everything in the room: balled fists, clenched jaws, my butt cheeks. "That's why you're drunk. You're the captain. You could just order us and we'd have to do what you say. But you want us to give you a good reason not to do this."

"And I haven't heard none." The captain lifted to his feet. Well, not lifted to his feet exactly. It was more like he waddled to his feet. And he was so big the whole bridge shook with his movement as he made his way from the bridge and back into the hall. His every step—every trip, really—sent him tilting into control panels and smudging sleek walls with his grimy hands until he made it to the control room. He would've woken the whole crew up if they hadn't all been in cryosleep. Afia and I followed close behind to make sure he didn't fall and get himself a concussion to go along with his eventual hangover.

* * *

The control room was a small space, just enough room for some standard readouts of oxygen levels, fuel capacity, and the like. It was the one place on the cruiser that actually looked like our usual ship, the *Nyame*: dark lighting with only the green glow of the vidscreens, stained and rusted plating along the walls, and that obligatory we-don't-care-to-clean-here-except-for-an-occasional-bleaching smell. Most importantly, though, was a hidden weapons locker Afia installed just to the side. That one piece of the *Nyame* we were allowed to bring with us.

"Open the control panel, Orion." The captain slurred his demand. His hand hovered over a ray shield that guarded a glowing red button. "It's time to finish the job."

"What? No!" I cowered away. "I thought we was still talkin' things through? If we save this Water God, maybe they'll help us take out the Syndicate."

But I knew my words would be ignored. The captain I knew was back. The focus on his face didn't waver with indecision anymore.

The captain inhaled through his nose deeply. "Need I remind you of who bought you your freedom, girl? I'm owed obedience. And you always said you being on this crew was written in the stars."

Oh, he really had to bring that up, didn't he? I don't usually talk pretty like that. I had said all that "written in the stars" stuff just to convince him to take me on.

"I know . . ." I trailed off. It was true, though. When I had seen the *Nyame* dock near my slave quarters, I knew that'd be the best ship to stow away on. I ain't the most religious or spiritual gal around, but when your personal VI and the ship that could save you from bondage were named after the same pantheon, you gotta believe in some energy force or whatever's out there.

The captain hovered his trembling hand over the detonator. Afia, with her aziza's honor holding her back, simply stood there with arms crossed and a frown stretched across her face.

"Wait!" I flung my hand out toward the captain. "Wait, wait. There might be another way."

I am not so sure about that, ma'am. Keeping in mind the reputation and efficiency of the Corporate Alliance, and now the Syndicate on top of that, the chances of success for what you are considering is only 2.785% at best.

That's why you gon' keep your mouth shut, I thought-spoke back to Anansi.

"I have drones stashed away," I said out loud. The captain quirked an eyebrow at me, but his hand stopped shaking over the detonator.

Not nearly enough, ma'am. Those drones will only last a few—

Anansi, mute yourself, please.

I am in silent mode now, ma'am. Say my name thrice to reactivate me when you desire.

"How will drones help us here, Orion?" Afia asked, releasing the straitjacket that was her arms from around her chest.

"I can set up an imaging program to make it look like the moon's been destroyed. It's real, real easy if all I'm doin' is painting a starfield. By the time the Corporate Alliance figures it out—"

The captain cut me off. "Or when the Syndicate finds out—"

"Yeah, yeah, before either of them figures it out, we'll be paid, we'll bring down the Syndicate, and everything will be fine."

The captain's jaw looked like it was chewing away at a hard bit of sugar cube. It was exactly the expression I was hoping for. It was what *the captain* was hoping for. He knew the kind of magic I could work. He had just been waiting for me to lay a plan on him.

"I'm sure there's some holes in that plan. What about that VI in there." The captain nodded to my head. "What's the success rate it's reading for this?"

2.785%, I thought, but the lie I gave him was, "62.785%."

If it weren't for all the impossible jobs I got us through I probably would've got a side eye from the captain and First Mate.

Instead, the captain asked, "And what happens if we're in that other 38%?"

I didn't need Anansi yappin' in my ear to know what his problems would be. "Paintin' the planet will be a bit more difficult. But if the Alliance or Syndicate jumps out of FTL on M-22's darkside, we should be good. And since there's a 50% chance of that—"

"That's how you get a 60% success rate," the captain finished for me. Then he hummed under his lips. "This... *might* actually be a solution."

BUH-DEW

The ship's automated intercom beeped, and a synthetic voice filled the control room. "CC-84 Academy Announcement: Cryopod 4 has been opened."

The captain was light-skinned to begin with—Afia made fun of him for it enough—but his skin just then seemed white as snow. A pair of terrified words slipped over his tongue, "Oh no . . ."

"What is it?" Afia asked, throwing her chin over her shoulder. "That's just the merc's pod, isn't it? Probably just a faulty timer."

"*Nyame*, seal the doors!" the captain commanded, but the doors didn't listen to him. They didn't listen to him because they weren't on the *Nyame*; they were on an Academy starcruiser. And the split-second command was all the chance he had to save them.

It was an honest mistake, but a deadly one.

"*Comet Chaser 84*, seal the doors!" the captain corrected, but too late.

Everything happened all at once. I barely registered the eerie *tit-tatting* coming from the corridor outside, barely saw the control room's doors whipping shut—only to be stopped by a nasty three-fingered hand and thrown back as though it were made of soft tin, not reinforced iron. My eyes barely caught up to my VI-enhanced mind as that same hand lifted to reveal a palm of acid-green light. And the light bolted forward and straight through the captain's chest.

I knew when my body caught up to my senses because I screamed. Loud.

The captain's insides were splattered across the control room, the surveillance screens, the chairs, keyboards . . .

My whole world went numb.

I must've fallen to my knees because they were throbbing with pain. What was happening? Was the captain really dead? A droning beat assaulted my ears. The sound didn't make sense until it did. Afia was shouting at me.

The First Mate tussled with a red-orange beast, their large bodies slamming into the walls and ceiling, flecking off sparks. No, that thing wasn't just a beast. It had a name. I just didn't know it. The new merc the captain said would be joining us. I understood his reason at the time. Dra'qell were the toughest aliens around. I'd want one of them on our team, too. But why was it attacking us?

"I can't hold this thing off for long, Orion!" Afia grunted. "The weapon locker! Behind you!"

The dra'qell moved with unnatural speed, not just in velocity but in the almost mechanical angles it spun on its heels. It kept making a sound like it was gathering phlegm, trying to raise its palms to Afia like it did against the captain, but the First Mate was quick enough to block its hands. Its deflected acid spit tore into the reinforced metal. More sparks belched from each impact, along with a rancid odor.

I always thought dra'qell looked more like cyborgs than straight-up organics. Half-insect, half-robot, with no mouth, four eyes on each side of their hook-like heads, and a thin exoskeleton that always glowed a translucent hue of acid green. Aziza at least looked humanoid, except for their obsidian skin, large eyes, and pointed ears. Dra'qell, though, were *alien*-alien to humans.

"Orion!" Afia shouted at me again, just as she took a sharp knee to the gut.

"O-on it!" I struggled to my feet. My hands shook violently as I tried to recall the code for the locker. I'd never used the blasters. *Ever*. I pulled wires, not triggers. "I-I don't remember the code!"

"Rim shot!" she shouted as she ducked under another beam and stuck one of her fingers into one of the dra'qell's many eyes.

"H-huh!?" I quivered. Blood smeared all over the keypad. Was that *my blood*!?

"Erykah Badu! Rimshot, you idiot!" Afia drove an elbow into the dra'qell's chest.

Shit! How could I forget? Getting the rhythm in my head, I pounded on the keypad, and when I punched in "CONFIRM," I was blessed with a little jingle that went, "Boom-klat-boom-klat."

I threw my hands at the closest blaster in reach, spun on my heel, and found a terrible image: the dra'qell, with Afia in a tight headlock. The aziza struggled to get loose, but the dra'qell held her tight, as though made of unmoving stone. Worse, he held a pulsating palm against Afia's head.

Drop the weapon, human, the dra'qell thought-spoke into my mind with that scratchy husk of its species.

"Fuck you!" I shouted. My hands *really* needed to stop jittering. I could barely keep aim with the dra'qell's stupid head. What should I do? What should I do? My brain kicked up a notch. "Anansi, Anansi, Anansi!"

Hello, ma'am. Have you learned why you never mute Anansi when—

"Shut up! What weapon did I just pick up?"

The SS7-Kishi. The Goldilocks Cluster Weapon of the Year, seven years running. Most noted for its unmatched attributes of crowd control. AKA, the worst possible blaster you could have picked up, ma'am.

Well, I'll be a martian's uncle...

Even with my precision helping you at this distance, it will not save First Mate Afia.

"Shoot it, Orion!" Afia cried out. Bloody spittle flecked from her mouth. Angry intent filled her eyes. But there was sadness there, too. She didn't need a VI in her head to know I had chosen the wrong weapon for the job. "D-do it . . ."

Neither you nor the aziza has to die, human, the dra'qell spoke to me directly again. *Open the control panel for me and the job can still be done.*

I gave the dra'qell my best scowl. But knowing my tiny-ass face, I probably didn't look threatening at all. More like a cub doing its best to intimidate a great big predator. Plus, the control panel was likely still intact. I designed the ray shield myself. The dra'qell needed me.

"The charges aren't ready," I said. "If we push it now, there's a—"

15.36% chance of failure.

"15.36% chance of failure," I echoed Anansi. "We could end up destroying the planet and mess up the whole gig."

The dra'qell tightened its grip around Afia's neck, liquid oozing from the eye she had gouged out. The thing didn't even look fazed.

How long will it take for a 0% chance of failure? it asked.

At least 4 more hours, ma'am.

"At least 4 more days," I lied. "And the moon has to be at the right orbit, too. Far from the big sister moon." We'd already been out here two months. Four more days shouldn't have been that big of an ask.

It was hard to tell since the dra'qell didn't exactly have a face. Well, not a face I could understand, but it seemed like it was thinking through its options. Maybe it was in the way its exoskeleton glowed.

Fifteen percent will have to be acceptable before the others come out of their pods and attempt to retake the ship. Open the panel now or the First Mate dies. Or do I need to remind you of your captain's corpse?

I did my best to not let my gaze slip down to the Captain, or the hole that was carved through his chest. But I couldn't help it. All it took was a glance. His eyes were still open, his mouth slacked and hanging low in a horrific expression of death. The tainted smell was the worst though, like someone blended sour milk with old meat, all topped off with a bleached metal stank.

"D-don't listen to it, O-Orion." Afia spoke through choked coughs. "S-shoot it."

Ma'am, you can still save the planet. You may perish, the First Mate will most certainly perish, but the planet can live if you pull the trigger.

But what about my friend? I couldn't let her die. She was the only reason I'd save the stupid planet and whatever spirits lived down there. I couldn't trust a dra'qell, though. If I lifted that ray shield, it would press the button, and the moon would explode.

There was a good chance everything would be fine, of course. The odds could've easily been worse.

I dropped the blaster at my feet. It clanged against the metal flooring.

"Anansi, uncover the ray shield," I commanded weakly. I already felt pretty bad about my decision, but my insides really did a number when I caught the utter disappointment in Afia's eyes. I could take that, though. At least she'd be alive. At least—

A bright green light filled the room, followed by the gruesome sound of a dra'qell acid beam searing through skin, bone, and brain. Afia slumped to the side, lifeless, smoke spewing from the side of her head.

The control panel announced, "Nuclear sequence charging in five, four, three, two, one…"

*   *   *

I cried. Ugly and loud. My whole body shook with my sobs as my back collapsed on the stupid weapons locker. The dra'qell could kill me for all I cared. I deserved it. I ruined everything.

Remember to never cross the Syndicate again, human slave, it said, slithering into my mind.

The dra'qell's crooked legs stomped in front of me. I didn't look up. Let it put a hole through my dome. I waited for the heat of one of its beams, but the lethal sensation never came. Instead, I was dragged through the room, legs sliding against the captain and the First Mate. Then we were out in the sleek corridor—stark against the blood trail the two of us left behind—until I got tossed into my quarters.

The door locked behind me. Why didn't that thing kill me? I deserved it more than the captain or Afia.

But no one ever killed me when they should've.

They always used me and Anansi for whatever they wanted. More value alive than dead and all that. I hated that I liked living so much sometimes.

I lay on my back for a long while as the ship's intercom rang out with all the pre-launch jargon. When it finally got to its last steps, I forced myself to my knees and peered out the viewport of my room. Just as my chin lifted above the window's horizon, a great bright light enveloped the small moon of M-22. I couldn't hear the explosion but the starcruiser vibrated with its combustion. The moon broke up into tiny pieces, tiny enough to get swallowed by M-22's atmosphere, just as I intended. The job was going to be fulfilled just as I had calculated it. But that meant that whatever lived on that planet would eventually die. Afia and the aziza's prophecy would never come true.

All because I couldn't pull a trigger.

And then . . . one piece of indigo moon rock, bigger than the others, revealed itself through the debris. It rotated with violent velocity, hurtling straight for the all-ocean planet. But it wasn't large, certainly not large enough to create a great impact, right?

Wrong.

You idiot, Afia's voice rang out in my mind.

As it tumbled closer and closer to the planet, it grew larger. Larger than my original estimation of its size. It burned and broke away, but not nearly fast enough. And when it eventually collided with the planet's surface, a shockwave spread from the impact point and rippled away in a plume of angry fire. The rush of the inferno spread quickly across the entirety of the planet's dayside. It might not have reached around the full globe, but the result would still lead to the planet's slow death over the next million years, only to be restored in the next few million after that, if even.

Well, it looks like your calculations were correct, former *human slave,* came the dra'qell's voice just as another tear forced its way down my cheek. *Too bad. The Queen Mother had plans for M-22. But with that brain of yours coupled with your unique VI, she'll have more plans, I suspect. Sit tight. It'll be a while before we get back, and I want to be in dra'qell territory when your other friends wake up from their pods.*

The cruiser revved up under my cot for FTL speed. Something round jostled against my leg. I looked down to find the dead drop capsule I never sent out. A faint hope snaked its way through my veins as I wrestled with it, blurted an SOS, and vented it just before the viewport outside changed from the image of a dying planet to a hyperspace funnel.

With my luck, the dead drop got caught in the hyperlane and broke up into little pieces. But I could pray it didn't. That's all I could do. No more middle road for me. The captain and Afia deserved more than that from me.

Cyberpunk
by
Darrell SCIPOET Stover

for Bernie Worrell - Keyboard Basher/Neuromancer

A head-nodding little man at the center of Saturn
Sits churning out
      THE MUSIC OF THE SPHERES
Pounded chords control the rotation of this galaxy
Recorded renditions of a star's birth all come alive in concerts
      HERE ON EARTH
As the sex drive of the Universe is pumped for passionate poetry
Cartoon dude animates our souls to travel the spaceways as he
      TAKES US HIGHER
Woo wonders where others never have
The electronic byways of digitized sound is his throw down
Organic software plugs his libido stream into our inner ear
There's a virus in the system and its gotta be funky
      GOTTA BE YOU BW

Keyboards bow down in grace as you send air suckin'
sounds
      ALL OVER THE PLACE
The greatest hits of P_Funk would not be without thee
And we know the deal drugs dealt
But we know your altered states are realities we've yet to dream
We feel you in ear before you bounce between our neurons
Your Twang Twinging Ping Pinging
Golden Glowed Atmosphere Vibrato
      SHIMMERS DELIGHT
Capturing the out of control technological change staccato
      AT THE TOUCH OF YOUR FINGERTIPS
Endorphins now Bum Rush our being
      PLEASUREFUL WE SIGH PLEASUREFUL
You have O.B.E.eeed all throughout 10 billion squared

universes
Retained some memories of it all
A quiet madness you force us to understand
Computers dump all memory for the mathematics of your soul
       DESIRING A LINK
       WITH YOUR NEURONAL NETWORK
Calculating equations of Funk
To save the masses from a baby-eating America
We all dwell horribly within the realm of the Witch's Castle
       REACHIN' FOR OUR DREAMS
       WITH CHAINS ON OUR SOULS
To wit, only your computer banks can unleash the spirit
       FREE OUR MINDS
         SO OUR ASSES CAN FOLLOW
       FREE OUR MINDS
         SO OUR CHILDREN CAN SURVIVE
Pierce our ears forcing us to close our eyes in deep thought
Funk fakers will pee on themselves
Drowning in Cosmic Slop bubbled forth from the nerve centers
       THEIR NEVERYONDERS
Places they passed piquantly
Pondering the perpetuity of pubescence
We dwell in a childhood the universe constantly expounds upon
In its pulsing expansion
It reminds us that at this rate we'll never catch up
Your creative chime a theme song for our space bound destiny
       RINGING
Millions of millennia have passed
We can move with it or sit idle
Age is just a number
Knowledge is like a cool cucumber in summer
Refresh our memories of the before time swimming
Sky-diving dolphin-like in the bounty of glorious omniscience
       LET US AQUABOOGIE BABY

Your feverish virtuosity creeps into the graves

Bach, Beethoven and Mozart

And like a Stephen King thriller forces their skeletons to
      S

                    HAKE
                    THAT
                    THING
                             S
                    HAKE
                    THAT
                    THING
They now
know they
gotta shake that
thing
Monkey paw
poking into
their earholes
Implantin' the
last tango
A mad fandango to the only place they can go
The dark memories of genes that ain't forgot their attunedness
An eon upon eon endless joyride spanning all universes
                        I
                    N THE
                    MOTH-
                    ER-
                    SHIP
                             S
                    PREAD
                    IN'
                    THAT
                    FUNK
Ying-Yanged Sacred Soul Soldier Warrior
Artist Supreme Sound Survivalist
Practicing the religion of funkateers
Get Down Get Up Get Funky Get Loose!
Maggot brained emotions smothered in the masses movin'
                    ALL AT ONCE
Mayhem monger of music
                    PROPHESIED BY SUN RA
                    "IF YOU
                    FIND EARTH
                    BORING
                        JUST THE
                    SAME OLD
                    SAME THING
                        YOU CAN
                    SIGN UP

WITH
OUTER SPACE-
WAYS INCOR-
PORATED.
Your software is the me-
dium of exchange
Galaxy by galaxy opening banks to trade in freaky
emotions
Neuroimmunologist of Nommo
N
a
m
e
d
t
h
e
N
u
m
b
e
r
o
f
t
h
e
B
e
a
s
t
A
n
d
r
e
d
u
c
e
d
h
i
s
a

s
s
t
o
z
e
r
o
Pushed Pinocchio up into the snozzle
The lying poobutt boy himself
        SIR NOSE
        YOU WILL DANCE
Handed him a snot rag to blow
A Coltrane accompaniment
Your gig before the Lord
Those boots you wear?
The way I hear it
They tap the bottom to your reverberating rhythms
Controlled by your toes tuning in to a web
of piano string sounds
Only your Spidermanic superpowers allow
you to traverse
        S
    T
    O
    M
    P
    &
    S
    H
    O
    C
    K
        S
    T
    O
    M
    P
    &
    S
    H
    O
    C
    K
    W
    A
    V

E
S
           H
A
N
D
S
I
N
T
H
E
A
I
R
We
know
you
came
amongst
us
To bend
our ears
against
all fear
We become photosonic beings travel-
ing faster than light
          S
PEE
DIN
G
UP
          O
UR
OW
N
EVO
LU-
TIO
N
To attain a saneness in
unity with the 'All of It'
Cruising to Tau Ceti IV
fighting grendels galore
Off through the constel-
lation of Styx
Learning a new
bag of death

dealing tricks
Now prepared
for Knock
Down Drag
Out Five
1 million years from tomorrow
Surprised to find we're still alive
Up through a Anyanwu black hole loop
To find a universe only
peopled by Betty Boops
Escaped down into the
embryo of a star
Now knowing who we really are
                    CHILDREN OF THE UNIVERSAL
Your music a spiritual rehearsal
We arrive in sunglasses at the end
                    B
          EFORE
          A SU-
          PER-
          NOVA
                    E
          XPLOD
          ES
          OUR
          MINDS
Each neuron now becoming an individual us
Traveling in, out and along
          WITH A JOYFUL NOISE

Only you can pipe the tune that wiggles

Electrons, DNA, sperm, tadpoles and snakes

An interesting evolution and I hear you homey
Ig-
nite
the
flas
hlig
ht
of
my
min
d
The

stre
et
po-
ets
hav
e re-
spo
nde
d
Hacking out diatribes on dissin'
dancin' and recombein'
Our unified essences melted and
molded in your music
Transformed and reformed alien entities now become the familiar

        S
YN-
THE-
SIZER
TONG
UES
        P
IANO
TOES
        V
I
O
L
I
N
H
E
A
R
T
S
        W
O
O
F
E
R
N
O
S
E

No voices can
challenge your
imperatives
Biological bat-
tle hymns arc-
ing higher
ORGAN FIRE
We be spiraling hawks lifted in the radiation
YOUR DIGITIZATIONS
You scream the primal howl and we answer in
I
M
P
R
O
V
E
D
M
O
T
I
O
N
S
C
A
R
N
A
L
W
I
G
G
L
S

Double-helixed DNA like
        INTERTWINED SOULS
Relishing perpetual heat of an orgy of free-spirited celebration
in
        FUNKADELICA
Everything and everybody is there
        ANCESTRAL SUPERSTARS
Saturday morning and comic book characters
        SCIENTISTS AND SAINTS
  All stirred up in a fiery red frenzy to get it on beyond the stars
        EVEN THE FREAK FROM LA
  Organ grinder of the mind
  It Now All Computes! It Now All Computes!
          I
        T NOW
        ALL
        COM-
        PUTES
        ! BER-
        NIE!
  You're the master muse that reprograms us to disengage
  The flesh and take flight
          AS SPIRIT
          IT NOW ALL COMPUTES!

It Now All Computes!
It Now All Computes!

          LET
          GO
          OF
          THE
          MA-
          TE-
          RIA
          L
          THE
          STRI
          NG
          IN
          YOU

                    501

R
BRA
IN
HAS
GOT
YOU
TIE
D
TO
A
LIE

G
E
T
W
I
T
'
THE
P
R
O
G
R
A
M

G
O
W
I
TH
THE
E
L
E
C
T
R
O
N

F
L
O
W

B
E
R
N
I
E

G
O
W
I
G
G
L
E
AND WE WILL FOLLOW
NEUTRINOS BEAM
FROM YOUR FINGERS
WIGGLIN' US ON!!!
EVER ONNNNN!!!!!!!!!

Originally published in UNCUT FUNK 1990

A Harvest Among The Stars
by
S. A. Cosby

The hardest thing to get used to in space is the silence. Not
the kind of silence that is the result of the absence of sound but
the kind of silence that is present where sound never existed.
Being born on Olde Earth I was used to a constant barrage of
sounds. People screaming in pain. Titan-tall soil movers digging
deep into what was left of the planet's mantle for iron and nickel
for the magno-generators that ran all the space-faring barges and
ships that zipped around the solar system or jumped through
man-made wormholes to the far reaches of the empires of their
corporate masters. The thunderous footfalls of the Re-
madeasours, genetically re-created dinosaurs that came out of
their cloning tank malformed and impure but nearly impossible
to kill. The Corporation dropped them on Olde Earth and then
sold hunting rights to rich upperclassmen with so many bodmods that they were closer to gods than humans. Strange twisted
over muscled, over-annotated walking freaks with carbon-com-
posite retractable claws and nanobite skin. Pale albino monsters
with nu-metal bonded to what was left of their calcium skeletons
and electro-generators in their hearts that allowed them to throw
lightning like the old Zeusgod my grandfather had told me about
as a child. I once saw one of those bodmod creatures kill a
tyransourdile with his (or its) bare hands. Just jumped fifty feet
in the air and punched that horrid amalgamation of a T-rex and a
crocodile in the skull. I left before it ate the brain. As a child
some of my mates envied the upperclassmen with their bodmods
and godlike powers.

Not me. I was TrueBorn like my grandfather and his father
before him. We eschewed any body modifications or upgrades
as they were called. Of course, after I ended up in the Lunar

penal colony I wondered if my ancestors were just pissed that we were poor and couldn't afford the bodmod tech.

But this was many years after the Massacre on Mars in the city of Romulous. Also known as the Last Stand of the True-Born. The Corporation forces overran the Governor's palace where we had commanders. They killed my entire family in a matter of minutes. We were good fighters. Good little soldiers but we couldn't compete with the Corporations Black Squad. Fully modified cyborg soldiers with nu-metal indoskeleton and a fully nanobite exoskeleton. Even a laser-sickle couldn't cut through their skin. The only reason I survived was because my grandfather shot me in the leg before he died so the Black Squad wouldn't see me as a threat. I was wounded so I was taken as a prisoner. I got charged with all the deaths that resulted from the standoff and was sentenced to life on the Lunar Penal facility. Or as the inmates called it, White Hell.

Then the supply of diamonds dried up on Olde Earth and the Corporation came up with a way to harvest them from the skies of Jupiter. And they came calling on us convicts with a proposition.

Despite all the technological advances of the last thousand years people still valued natural gems over lab-made ones. The upperclassmen eschewed lab-made emeralds for ones mined out of Olde Earth. They turned their nostrils up at formulated rubies. And they vehemently hated lab-made diamonds.

The Corporation could not cajole them into purchasing the lambada. Then they realized too many lab mades drove the price down and they couldn't have that. So, they looked to the gas giants in their own backyard so to speak.

Through a complex chemical reaction that I couldn't care less about, diamonds rained from the clouds of Jupiter and Saturn. They fell like glittering fairies until they got near the small rocky core and were crushed into nothingness by the powerful gravitational forces at work on these celestial behemoths.

At first the Corporation sent semi-sentient drone ships to harvest the diamonds out of the sky. But the artificially semi-intelligent ships could not navigate the incredibly volatile conditions on the giant God Planet. They lost a fleet of these ships before some bright corporate marshal came up with the idea of ships piloted by convicts from the penal colonies who had star freighter experience. They forced these dregs of society to fly into Jupiter's maelstrom and then unfurl a huge nu-metal net behind the ship, scoop up the diamonds, and fly back to the processing plant on Europa.

That was the idea in theory. Then they lost a fleet of those ships when the diamonds proved too heavy. The pilots lost control of the vessels and crashed into the yellow and red hell of Jupiter's lower atmosphere.

So, some bright boy at the Corporation figured out something using basic physics. Smaller payloads plus the incredibly fast wind speeds on Jupiter equaled a successful harvest. But how to make the payloads smaller?

That's where the regular convicts came into the equation.

The Corporation created Non -Combustion driven Self-contained Flightsuits. NCSF for short. Somehow the abbreviation got mangled and cons started calling them Icarus suits. Huge mech-suits that we would enter in the bottom hold of a star freighter. Then the pilot would open the hatch and we would drop into a yellow and red and gold and blue hell. The mechs were tethered to the ship so it could stay in a high orbit while we drifted miles below it in the Sweet Spot. That particular place in the atmosphere where we were above the reach of the crushing gravitational forces near the core but below the methane clouds that held our dusky quarry.

The suits were filled with neurogel, a viscous substance that you had to immerse yourself in to control the suit. It was a bioware invention. It connected your own biological neurological network to the mech. Once you got used to the oxygen nanobots entering your bloodstream you could move fingers of the mech the way you could move the fingers on your own hand. Except the mech was twelve feet tall and the fingers on the mech were each eight inches long. The suit was nu-metal. Lighter than paper but nearly indestructible. It was propelled by a magnetic-driven primary engine that ran the two turbines on the back, allowing us to fly for all intents and purposes. You couldn't have a combustion engine on Jupiter. All that methane and ammonia in the air. One spark could create a fireball that would rage across the planet. A fire the size of Olde Earth.

We carried nu-metal nets. We would fly among the diamond rains and fill our nets. Once our nets were full, we would neurolink with the pilot who would pull us up by our tether. You dump your net then you go back down until the cargo hold was full. It took four hours to fill the cargo hold.

Sounds simple right? It's not.

The winds on Jupiter are in excess of five hundred miles per hour. Faster than any wind on Olde Earth. Even though you are not close to the core, the gravity is stronger than anywhere else humans have ever lived. You can feel it crushing your veins and making your blood thick. Your head pounds as you try to think the right thoughts to control the mech. And the storms. Oh Jesuallah the storms. We always try to avoid the Great Red spot but other storms will spring up just as bad. Storms as big as the Olde Earth. Storms that will reach and grab a con in his Icarus and pull him down into that methane Tartas.

The pilot, a con too but one who thinks he is better than you, will cut your tether loose in a heartbeat. If you are lucky the storm batters your body around in the suit until you crack your skull or you stroke out and die. If you are unlucky you fall to the core. Like Icarus who flew too close to the sun. There you are crushed into near nothingness. Gravity approaches level 1 star power.

I was putting that out of my mind as I lay in the freighter's hold area. The next four hours were my last four hours as a convict. One of the conditions the Corporations offer was six successful cycles as a harvester meant you were free. No matter what crime had landed you in White Hell, if you survived six cycles you could walk off the lunar base a free man after your last cycle.

They even removed the k-chip in your brain. The k-chip was a termination program uploaded directly to your brain with oldtech. Try to hijack the cargo freighter or use the mech suit as a weapon once you docked on the processing plant on Europa and the Black Squad marshal in charge of security at the plant flipped a switch and you dropped dead. The chip shuts down your muscles involuntarily. I put that out of my mind too. I was immersed in neurogel. Billions of nanobots were depositing oxygen in my blood streams so I didn't suffocate as the neurogel enveloped me. Even my eyes were closed. The neurogel was linked to the external cameras of the suit. I could "see" through a direct link between my brain and the cameras via the neurogel.

The neurogel was a miracle. It was everything my grandfather had preached against.

"What hubris has man that he dare try to replicate the awe and might of Jesusallah. We are all sinners in the hands of an angry Lord. We should humble ourselves and marvel at his wonders. Do not attempt to improve upon his magnificent designs," he would say from his oldmetal pulpit. He would have a holographic New Bible floating near his head while he held a laser-sickle in his hand. I don't think he ever understood the irony of trying to convince people of Jesuallah love and grace by cutting off the heads of non-believers.

"Jamal, two minutes till the drop," a voice said in my head. It was the pilot letting me know we were almost near the Sweet Spot. Declan Skide was a disgraced star pilot who had been arrested and sentenced to eight years in the Lunar prison for running a brothel on one of the Corporation's far-flung outposts in the outer rim of the Milky Way. His defense tried to argue that technically since the species on Galuta reproduced asexually through self-insemination and they didn't have a concept of money they couldn't technically be prostitutes The Black Squad judges council argued that Declan being a pimp for aliens with "interspecies" constituted sexual deviancy. Declan said that if Galuta didn't have iridium ore and didn't trade their post-partum excretions, which had been found to be irresistibly delicious by the upperclassmen, he would have gotten off with a warning.

"We wasn't even charging. It makes no sense I got arrested." he would whine during chow time.

"Copy that pilot," I thought. My external cameras turned to the right. Skarson was in his Icarus as well. I was a convicted murderer. Declan, an interspecies pervert. Skarson never told us what landed him in White Hell. But he was given a wide berth by all the inmates. Half human half Kardian, he had his mother's blue reptilian scales and his father's long black hair. Seven feet tall with horizontal pupils and a hard bony plate in his mouth Declan called a unitooth. Skarson scared some of the other Icarus jockeys. I had seen beings more frightening and stranger on Olde Earth when I was a baby. I didn't look twice at him when we were in the food hall. I think that was why he liked me.

"One minute," Declan's voice said in my head. The drop wasn't the scary part. It was losing sight of the ship that always unnerved me. Once you descended through the clouds you could see the tether extending up into the upper clouds like some tan beanstalk. But the ship was hidden. We were puppets on a string. A string five miles long.

"Drop," Declan's voice said in my head.

The doors retracted and both Skarson and I fell straight down into the beautiful and deadly Jovian atmosphere. The drop accelerated our bodies to over eight hundred miles per hour. My exterior cameras beamed an image of the kaleidoscope that was the Jovian sky into my brain as we pierced layer after layer of white and red and gold clouds.

The Icarus neurogel also served as a built-in cooling system. The incredible amount of friction is no match for the Icarus suit. Nu-metal can handle the entry but the human body cannot. If we didn't have the neurogel we would roast alive in the suit. Once you get through the upper atmosphere which can sometimes reach 1500 degrees you are plunged into the frigid Sweet Spot. It's as cold as the lowest level of Hell. The hydrogen and helium and methane rain down toward the fluidic surface going from gas to liquid in an instant.

Finally, my suit notes the distance we have traveled and my backpack engages as do my arm flaps that help slow me down. I burst through the last layer of methane and hydrogen clouds and enter the Sweet Spot.

The light of the sun is more like the suggestion of illumination than actual light. It's dark but not pitch black. Here the clouds break apart from time to time and you can see for miles. Miles and miles of more clouds. No mountains or trees or oceans or land. Just clouds. Below the Sweet Spot the gravity is too strong for even the Icarus. I think about going west and the turbines from the backpack push me toward an orange and white ball of clouds. Skar follows me. It's the diamond cloud. I unfurl my catch net and dive about one hundred feet to get under the cloud and catch the rain drops made of carbon.

The storm is a huge monstrous thing like the exhalations from a dragon. We head to opposite sides of the cloud. Our nets flutter behind us like the banners of forgotten kingdoms. I tense my muscles. This is the worst part.

We enter the storm.

Diamonds slam into us like drops of anger and malevolence manifesting themselves in a physical form. I move my left arm and begin to fly up toward the colossal cloud. It's the biggest thing I've ever seen up close. It's the biggest thing any human has seen up close without a plethora of bodmods. The diamonds are not clear ingots like you might see in a fancy store on Mars or Venus or one of the Off-World utopias. They are dusky purplish lumps bouncing off my exoskeleton with bad intentions. The net begins to fill rapidly. The nanotech in the very fibers of the net sends me a signal when the maximum weight has been accumulated. I break off to the right and dip down seventy-five feet then climb again, filling my net even more. I watch as Skar almost loses his net. The eight-inch finger-like appendages snapped the net out of mid-air before it floated away into the great nothingness that was Jupiter. The planet was like a lot of people I had met. Big and loud and pretty but ultimately empty and poisonous.

My mind was empty as well. I tried to ignore the incredible pressure on my chest, the gelatinous neurogel coating my body, the howling and formidable wind at my back. Forget everything except scooping these little pieces of eternity out of the dark sky.

It was the scream that finally broke me out of my self-induced monotony.

The scream started as a plea.

"Acknowledge, acknowledge we are being attacked!!" a voice inside my head said. It was Leland Starch. He was another harvester on the star freighter *Forgotten Realm*. There were two teams working on Jupiter at all times in six four-hour shifts. We were all in constant contact so that we wouldn't run into each other and warn each other of approaching superstorms like the Great Red spot or some other unnamed swirling ball of death.

"Negative Starch. No other freighters in our section. "That voice was Quail, a pilot who had fragged his superior officer for as yet undetermined reasons.

"It's not a fucking freighter! Ardale's pack malfunctioned and he dropped. When it kicked back in and he came back up he was covered in" – then his voice turned into a scream. A raw, awful sound that made my eardrums hurt and my head ache.

I saw Skar pull up and just hover for a moment. The diamonds bounced off his mech suit and hurtled to the planet's core. I knew he had heard the same thing I had heard. Terror. There was terror in Starch's voice. That was unsettling. Starch was not a man given to flights of fancy or unmitigated fear.

He had taken on a pair of Black Squad field troops by himself and lived.

He was not a screamer.'

"Alright get back at it boys," Declan's voice said in my head.

"Hey, now wait a minute. What happened with Starch?" Skar asked. My brain interpreted his voice as a melodious pentameter that rose and fell like an operatic aria. The result of his mixed parentage and his Kardian physiology.

"Not our problem. Look, we got a quota to meet. And the sensors are picking up a Great White Spot heading our way in about an hour. So, let's get at it. Please. With sugar on top." Declan said.

"He said something had attacked his partner," Skar said. He hovered in place. A ghostly image among the swirling clouds of gas. He didn't seem inclined to get at it.

"Come on. Sooner we are done sooner we can get out of here," I direct thought. The neurogel transmitted my thoughts to Skar and Declan. Skar didn't move for a few more seconds.

Then he took off to the west with net unfurling behind him like a flag from the Olde Earth nations.

I let my net unfurl and continued picking diamonds out of the sky.

We were down to our last hour when the storm hit. Despite human's advanced bodmods and nanotech, predicting the weather is still beyond us. Especially on another planet. As Skar and I flitted through the gas clouds like giant hummingbirds in a hailstorm I heard Declan's voice in my head. It had a frantic edge to it.

"Retract in two seconds, I repeat in two seconds! Storm bearing down on us from the north!" Before I could respond Declan began to pull us up into the hull of the ship. Forcefully. The retractors spun at 600 rpms. We went zooming toward the sky passing through the clouds like dirty deities ascending to heaven. Skar panicked. He hit his thrusters instead of just coasting along with the retractors. He began to spin. The red hull of the Icarus was covered in small pits from the diamonds slamming into it. There were bits of diamonds in the pits. They glimmered as he spun. The centrifugal force of him working against the retractors created a pendulum effect. Suddenly Skar was swinging wildly from side to side. Three miles to the left then three miles to the right. The force of the retractors must have startled him. Usually when our nets were full and Delcan retracted us the process was slow and steady.

There was nothing I could do for him. "Stop your thrusters!" I thought.

"Aaaarrrgh!" was all the response I got from Skar. I couldn't sail toward him lest our tethers get entangled. An internal alarm in my Icarus went off like a laser canon. In my mind a message appeared in bold red letters.

'INCREASE IN TEMPATURE IMMINENT. INCREASE IS BEYOND ACCEPTABLE LEVELS FOR EXOSKELETON."

It was the storm. It was right on top of us. It was different from the storms that rained diamonds. It was a titan-sized hurricane of gas, heat, and wind. It was the size of Olde Earth. It would toss us around like an Olde Earth farmer tossing seeds. Our suits would not protect us. It would grab the freighter as well and we would all die. Unless Declan could ascend to a higher sub-orbit altitude. But he couldn't do that with two pieces of ballast throwing off his magnetron turbines. He had to reel us in like monstrous fish. Or cut us loose.

My viewing cameras projected an image into my head. It took me a moment to realize it from my rear cameras. My stomach tightened into a ball of nerves and muscles. The storm was coming. Bigger than anything I could conceive. So large my mind was having trouble giving it scale in my head. We were not going to make it. It was coming too fast; it was churning too violently.

Declan kept reeling us in as fast as he could. He also started to ascend.

It didn't matter. The storm surrounded us like the embrace of the Devil. The freighter appeared as the storm blew some of the gas clouds away. We were almost there. Then the winds of the storm grabbed it like a capricious god, a god older than Jesuallah, and tossed it into the depths of Jupiter. I felt myself spinning and flying through the air like a leaf. Alarm after alarm flashed in my mind telling me the risk of a containment breach was imminent, and that my gravitational pressure was becoming unequalized. On and on the messages appeared as we went hurtling through the Jovian atmosphere. I could hear Declan screaming in my head and then alternately cursing and talking to himself in an eerily calm voice. Most of it made no sense. It was all star pilot jargon. Might as well been Kardian to me.

"Apply emergency nuclear thrusters. Close all flaps. Grackdammint come on you son of a colony whore get your big ass around. No, no drop all thrusters. Drop all power. Just DROP!!" His voice howled in my head. I was blacking in and out. I could feel the incredible pressure of Jupiter's gravity through my suit. My whole body felt like it was being squeezed out of existence.

Then abruptly I felt like I was falling. My view cameras showed me an image. The star freighter was falling straight toward us. I had forgotten how huge it really was. My cameras showed me a panoramic view. All around me were glowing yellow clouds of gas. Fifteen miles below me was a huge, displaced amount of fluid. Liquid hydrogen.

SUIT INTEGRITY IS 120 SECONDS FROM BEING COMPROMISED. INTERNAL TEMPERATURE RISING ONE DEGREE PER SECOND. "an alarm message flashed in my head.

We had fallen below the Sweet Spot. We would all be dead in less than five minutes. I was still tethered to the freighter. It was closing in on me fast. Its scarred grey and red hull filled most of the room in my head. It was going to be a race to see what killed me first. The heat and pressure near Jupiter's core or the bow of the freighter ramming into me and turning me to jelly inside the Icarus. I scanned around for Skar. At first, I didn't see him. Then five hundred feet to my left I saw his Icarus. He was plunging toward that chemical sea just as I was. I heard Declan in my head.

"Come on you big bitch. Engage magnetron thrusters and emergency nuclear thrusters!" he howled. In an instant I felt a vibration wash through my body as the powerful magnetic re-sistance engines energized and used the planet's own magnetic field to force the big ship to rise. Then the emergency thrusters kicked in and everything exploded into a vision of white. The nuclear thrusters were mini explosions that released a massive amount of power. The bow of the star freighter began to point up, missing me by ten feet. The freighter shot up into the air like it had been hurled from a trebuchet. A message in my head flashed I was now traveling more than five thousand miles per hour. I could taste blood in my mouth. The panoramic view of the cameras created an overwhelming sense of vertigo. I felt the retractors still working at hauling the 1000-pound Icarus into the hold. I saw the airlock open and the retainment rack disengage to accept the exoskeleton. I docked with the rack as the freighter continued to climb. Before the doors to the airlock closed, I did a quick panoramic scan. I was looking for Skar.

I saw him.

He was being retracted at a much slower rate than I had. At first, I couldn't understand why. Then I noticed there was some-thing *on him.* His exo was covered in some *things.* I only caught a glimpse. They seemed to be big and translucent like the wings of flies, mostly huge triangular-shaped heads with wide tooth-less beaks. They had some kind of wing-type appendage that spread out in an X pattern with the head in the middle of the X. A strange luminescence emanated from inside their transparent bodies. They were folding their wing things around Skar's suit. They were slamming their beaks into his Icarus.

"DECLAN HELP!! JAMAL, HELP!! AKARIA SHUGGNOTH KIALAN !!!" his voice howled in my mind.

"Whatever that is they can't get in the suit. They can't get in the suit. Nothing can get through nu-metal Skarson." I thought. For a moment he stopped screaming.

Then one of the things weird clear beak things pierced his helmet.

The change in pressure probably killed him before the things peeled open his exo and scooped out his remains like a man opening an oyster.

"Skar!! Skar!!" Declan's voice said in my head.

"Delcan, sever the tether. He's gone." I said as the retainment rack spun and locked the exo in place so I could exit its cool confines.

I made my way to the bridge. Declan was in the pilot's box and had his hands on the virtucontrols. The big bulky freighter had slowed a bit but we were still climbing. We would be leaving Jupiter in five more minutes.

"What the fuck were those things, Jamal? There has never been any indication of any type of life on Jupiter," Declan said plainly.

"Well thanks to your fancy flying I think we are the first visitors to make it past the Sweet Spot."

"Just barely. The Corporation will be happy about this. Something else they can exploit. They will probably raise the price on the diamonds," he said bitterly.

"Let's just get back to Europa station," I said. Yes, let's get back so I could get this damn chip out of my head. I felt bad about Skar but technically I had completed my last jump. I was going to be a free man.

"Yeah, I'm going to pay that Lardosian with the four hands to take me for a ride. It's going to cost me a week of meal rations but I deserve it," Delcan said lasciviously. I started to say something else when the ship listed to the right.

"What the frick?" Declan exclaimed. The virtucontrol panel flickered then disappeared. The ship went dark. We stopped climbing. For a moment we just hung there in the upper reaches of Jupiter's atmosphere. Then the cold grip of gravity began to pull us back down to that red and gold hell.

"Emergency manual controls! Declan howled. I felt a hum vibrate through the ship. Weak emergency lights illuminated the bridge. An Olde Style control manual emerged from the console along with a manual control board. Declan pushed some buttons and the whole ship shook like some great beast shaking water off its back.

"Those emergency engines won't last long. Maybe fifteen minutes. We gotta figure out why the magnetrons stopped. I'm gonna have to go to the engine room. You come over here and just hold the controls upright. And don't –" he started to say something else but I cut him off.

"Shhhh. You hear that?" He stopped talking. A loud tapping sound surrounded us. It was coming from all sides of the freighter. Declan looked at me then looked back at his control board. The hull of the freighter was composed of a polymer that was half nanobites half ionized liquid crystal. With a flick of a switch, real or virtual, we could have a full 360-degree view of our current location. Delcan looked at me again. I nodded. I already knew what we would see.

"They eat the diamonds," I thought to myself. Declan flicked the switch.

For a second the vertigo unnerved me. After I recovered from that what I saw unnerved me more.

Our ship was covered in those things. Those diamondhawks.

Delcan ran some sort of scan. He shook his head side to side rapidly.

"What? What is it?" I asked.

"Somehow those things are interfering with the magnetrons. I don't know how but they are inhibiting the magnetic resistance."

"It's them," I said softly.

"What?"

"It's them. Somehow, they are magnetized or can manipulate magnetism. It's how they get around. We have got to get them off the ship," I said.

"And how the frick do you propose to do that in the next–' he stopped and looked at the chronometer on his arm– 'ten minutes?" he said. I looked at him.

"Get the Icarus ready," I said as I began to walk off the bridge.

"Jamal even if you get them off the magnetrons may not come online. I used the emergency engines to get us out of free-fall. They will not last long enough to get us into orbit," Declan said. He wasn't looking at me. He was staring at the manual board.

"Declan. Have a little faith," I said. I smiled and headed for the hold.

I had no idea what I was going to do once I got out there in the atmosphere. But I knew two things. I had no bodmods. I worked out and kept myself in shape. Hand-to-hand combat was as important in a Freeborn camp as the Biblequaran. I still knew how to fight.

Second, I knew how to fly the exo. Probably better than any-one in the fleet. I slipped back into the neurogel. Then I did something I had not done in a long, long time.

I prayed.

"Ready?" Declan's voice said in my head.

"He preparest a table in the presence of mine enemies," I thought.

"Drop!"

I engaged the turbines as soon as I dropped. The wind was not nearly as strong in the upper atmosphere. I flew under the ship as it held its position and came up on the starboard side. Those things were trying their best to damage the hull. They were slamming their beaks into the nu-metal again and again. I landed on the hull as softly as a butterfly. One interesting prop-erty of nu-metal was its simulated magnetism. The nanobots in the ship could lock onto the nanobots in the suit. Pseudo-mag-netism allowed repair jocks to work on the ships in the stardocks without floating away. I began to walk toward the creatures. I mentally connected and unconnected the nanos in my suit to the nanos in the hull with subconscious commands. It was one of the tricks they taught you when you went to Icarus training. The things didn't notice me at first.

I came up to one frantically slamming its beak into the hull. Up close they were huge. Nearly as big as the exoskeletons themselves. Inside their bodies were strange bioluminescence lights that glowed green and blue and had tendrils of what looked to be electricity arcing between the oblate spheroids.

"No weapon formed against me shall prosper," I thought. I balled my right hand into a fist and the exoskeleton did the same. I slammed my fist down into the thing's "head" as hard as I could. It didn't shatter like glass but the lights inside its body turned bright red. I hit it again. One arm of an exoskeleton could lift five tons. Using that same force on a living thing should have killed it instantly. These things were tough. I grabbed it with both hands and hurled it off the ship. I couldn't fight these things one at a time.

I started running. As I ran, I kicked the creatures as hard as I could. They went sailing into the sky. I was screaming in my mind. I vaguely heard Declan yelling at me to hurry. If the nano-bots in my blood were not feeding me pure oxygen molecules I might have passed out from atavistic disgust. The creatures reminded me of the roaches on Olde Earth. Fat brown things the size of a grown man's arm. I kicked and punched until all the creatures had been hurled into the sky.

"PUNCH IT!" I thought. The ship stopped vibrating. My connection to the hull suddenly disappeared. The emergency engines went quiet. I kicked my turbines back on. The ship began to fall. I dived alongside it. The tether was slack but it began to vibrate like a guitar string as we fell.

"Come on you cumguzzler!!!" Declan cried in my head.

The lights on the hull of the ship winked on. The ship stopped its descent. Like the modified phoenix I had seen on Olde Earth it began to rise. The magnetrons were back online. I was about to tell Delcan to reel me in when my view camera picked up something in the clouds.

Those things were coming back.

They were flying up through the clouds like some bad dream that keeps replaying in your head as you try to sleep. Somehow, they were able to levitate themselves. They were heading straight for the ship. There were six of them glowing with green, red, and blue lights from inside their translucent abdomens.

"Declan. Punch it! Get the ship up into orbit," I thought.

"Alright. let me reel you in."

"NO! Just punch it. Those things are coming back. I don't know why or how but if they get on the ship the magnetrons will go offline again. Just punch it!"

"Jamal, what are you going to do?" I heard Declan's voice in my head."

"I'm going to go home," I thought. I ran along the length of the ship. When I reached the comm tower I mentally disconnected with the nanobites embedded in the hull of the ship and jumped into the Jovian sky.

"I can do all things through Jesusallah who strengthens me," I thought. I did not engage my turbines. I plummeted through the sky like a falling star.

The Icarus gained speed as I fell. The planet's monstrous gravity pulled me in like a lover who wants to give me a kiss. A kiss of death. I extended my arms. The creatures were rising to meet me.

I slammed into them.

They swarmed all over me. Like a flock of ghostly bats, they covered my mech suit, their strange beak-like appendages biting and slashing at the suit. We fell further and further away from the freighter. As we descended through the clouds I could hear Declan's voice in my head.

"You stupid frick!! Oh man, you stupid frick!"

"It's the only way Declan. Go home man. Just go home," I thought. The creatures were biting and scratching at the suit. Given what they did to Skar I had three, maybe five. minutes before they cracked the suit. In four or six minutes I would find out if all the stories my grandfather had drilled into my head about Jesusallah were true.

"They eat the diamonds. They eat the diamonds," I thought. My panoramic view cameras projected the image of the star freighter flying off into the sky. Soon it would be out of sight.

I had forgot about the tether.

It had reached the end of its length. As the freighter rocketed into orbit the tether pulled taut. The creatures and I were pulled along at almost five thousand mph. They held on to me with the grim grip of death as we were pulled out of Jupiter's atmosphere. I could feel the incredible gravitational pressure squeezing my insides through the neurogel. I would black out soon. At least I would not feel my body explode in the vacuum of space. One of the creatures closed its mouth-like orifice over one of my view cameras. The lights in its abdomen looked like binary stars locked in a mortal dance.

"Hang on, just fricking hang on!" Declan's voice said in my head. But I didn't want to hold on. I wanted to see my grandfather and my father and all the other members of the Trueborn movement that had died on Mars all those years ago.

I saw stars rushing at me through the view cameras. I was floating in space and the stars were flooding my field of vision. It wasn't until they hit the Icarus that I realized they were in fact the diamonds Skar and I had collected. The creatures flitted away from my exosuit and began to float among the millions of twinkling diamonds that now danced just outside of Jupiter's atmosphere. They opened their beaks and began to scoop diamonds up by the pound. As they ingested the diamonds, I saw them begin to float away further and further. By whatever means they flew or levitated it was ineffectual in the cold confines of space. They began to panic and flail their x-patterned wings to no avail. I felt the tether begin to retract. I heard Declan's voice in my head.

"You were right. They do eat the damn things. I dumped the whole fricking load."

Just before I passed out, I was able to send Declan a thought.

"The harvest is plentiful but the workers are few. Mathew 9:37."

Funky Phlox Fungi
by
Gavin Matthew

Oyande was a super-giant with an odd hue. While most stars burned with the spectrum of fire, this massive quirk of the universe shined across space like a purple beacon. Not a simple violet, something easily argued to be blue. It was purple. A purple so psychedelic that many ventured out to the small rock planet of Murruh that revolved around the star just to get a look. AF-Ro 7 was the city that sat on that planet, and Phyllo was just one of many souls who lived and thrived in that city.

Phyllo wasn't from AF-Ro 7, but he had traveled lightyears to live there. Wealthy tourists and honeymooners skipped galaxies to get a romantic view of Oyande's splendid color. They got their fill and were off to their next destination. Not Phyllo. He loved being in AF-Ro 7. The purple star was his favorite color, and the city was like a place lost in time. The style of its people and the beat of its rhythm reminded Phyllo of a mecca he had read about as a child. A place where his large afro and mahogany skin would have been celebrated. A place that once existed on Earth before the planet became a wasteland of storms and tides. A place that was called Harlem. It took fifty years for Phyllo to make it out to AF-Ro 7, but for a man who dreamed of ancient Uptown, that was no time at all. It had been a dream he had enjoyed for three years.

Far from neon signs, ostentatiously dressed citizens, and soulful funk music Phyllo and a reluctant companion had run to one of the quietest spots on the outskirts of AF-Ro 7. People hunted for them from block to block. While the spaceport on the other side of the city sat in a cacophony of noise, the deserted starship junkyard lay in a petrified hush.

"This is not how I saw my Thursday going," Mbe mumbled, brushing long locs from her face. "I'm supposed to be sleeping at the Superfly Hotel. Not running around with some two-bit drug dealer risking my neck against patrollers and syndicate thugs."

Phyllo picked out his afro as he stepped through the scattered remains of a space carrier long gone. Mbe led the way, her youthful eyes guiding them under Oyande's low light. She was half his age and in her prime, an ideal moment for a bounty hunter.

"Well, young sistah, you could always just leave me. These capitalist pigs only want what I have cultivated. Just travel back the way we came, and you would be back in the city in a matter of hours." Phyllo said.

"Right. Except I need to eat and while you might be just some drug dealer, the bounty on you is exceptionally high. Care to explain that one?" Mbe replied.

"Couldn't say. In my experience, crime and punishment are rarely as simple as what a person does. When humanity began to form governments, they added biased systems for needless control. Systems have always been broken machines. Rickety things that were in need of dismantling."

"Broken or not, there is more to this story than your radical gibberish. You don't deal in *Moon Rock*, *Daylight Water*, *Spirit Horizon*, or *Doctor When*. Hell, even spice would help that bounty start to make sense. Nobody cares about mushrooms and yet here we are, traipsing through busted ship junk with goons on our asses."

"Ohi Mbe," Phyllo smirked, tightening a hand on the strap of his satchel bag. "I didn't know you were an outtasight detective."

"I'm not. Just suspicious of a job that should have been a cakewalk."

Oyande's glow gave the field of wrecked crafts and carriers an eerie shroud of gloom. Gunmetal grey hulls expressed themselves duller than normal under the humble luminosity. The purple light added a hint of shimmer to Mbe's black suit but went unnoticed as it blended with Phyllo's grape bellbottom jumper. The pair continued their trek, footsteps crusting against periwinkle dust. They found a derelict old model Grier skiff lodged in the ground. A body in a silver suit lay prone on the space boat's side, split by shadows.

"Silver suits, Mbe. Saiba Yakuza." Phyllo said, turning the body over. She was young and pale with lifeless eyes staring off into the universe above. A deep cut, sizzling with whisps of smoke, burned across the corpse's skull.

"Hey, mushroom man!"

The voice echoed out, bouncing from ridge and junk to dune and ship. Mifune Meiko had earned her spot as the Saiba Yakuza AF-Ro 7 shateigashira. Shino had failed in handling Phyllo and paid with her life as recompense. Meiko was not a patient woman or a boss who accepted failure. She was a warlord of the streets, her codes old and brutal.

"Your bounty hunter friend there is next unless you come peacefully, old man!" Meiko yelled again, appearing out into the open.

The woman was dressed in the gang's iconic silver suit. Her left hand, a full cybernetic marvel, held a katana humming with bluebonnet energy. Loose black hair hung wildly around her face. One of her pupils was normal while the other glowed malachite, another implant. Both eyes gazed at Mbe and Phyllo with venomous persecution. Then the yakuza boss let out an earsplitting whistle, and like boogie men in waiting eleven more silver suits crowded behind Meiko.

"This seems like a bit much for some fungus in a purse." Mbe mocked as she walked from the skiff.

"It's called a satchel," Phyllo replied, walking next to the bounty hunter.

"Woooo!" Meiko called out. "Is that what the mushroom man has been telling you this was all about? His bag of shrooms? I mean grandpa there has some excellent stock, but he has so so so much more!"

"Really, Meiko?" Phyllo replied. "I'm only twenty years older than you. Can we cool it on the geriatric jokes?"

"Shut up, Phyllo!" Meiko spat back. "I . . ."

A sharp crimson laser cut through the conversation with a resounding screech, splitting one of Meiko's henchmen in half.

"You two idiots talk too much," Mbe said, raising her particle revolver for another blast. She fired again, aiming to decapitate Meiko. The gang boss reacted with lightning speed. Her katana parried and refracted the beam, sending five rays randomly screeching about the junkyard. Dead ships and decayed parts were split by the wayward blasts. One refraction hit a large tankard that was hidden under a belly of junk. Dust and debris erupted with raging heat and force. The trembling explosion illuminated the sky with white light as a single mushroom cloud blossomed and bloomed, drawing the attention of all AF-Ro 7 with a towering Xanadu haze.

* * *

Midnight. Onyx. Black. There was nothing but darkness, shadows thick from closed eyes. It was a vast void not dissimilar to the emptiest reaches of the universe. Then, in a flash of piercing psychedelia, Oyande glared into view. The super-giant glowed alone transfixed in the center of nothing. It was as if the star was all that was left of the galaxy until Mbe could see herself drifting like loose smoke. Her skin radiated from Oyande's shine; its deep melanin accentuated with a phlox-like aura. An overwhelming indescribable peace filled the bounty hunter's heart. Suddenly Oyande shimmered and pulsed. Light erupted from Mbe and exploded before her like streams from a sprinkler. A kaleidoscope of purple rays twisted and writhed into the darkness until the display manifested into a crowd of people, each person sharing a feature that reflected Mbe. She even recognized a few of the kin that now drifted with her. A stocky woman with long white locs that she used to call Xho Xho. A man with a box-cut afro she once called baba. And an endless field of a family long gone from the world she struggled to survive in. Had they come to ferry their child home? To comfort her as she escaped the pain and weight of reality? She could never have guessed that taking the bounty on Phyllo Parks would have ended so badly. But now, feeling the warmth and love of her ancestors, she had little to no regrets about the gig. No rage. No

524

disappointments. Not even a shadow of remorse or a hounding of ennui. Just peace.

Mbe surrendered to the tranquility that was filling her form, never noticing Oyande as it shifted from its vibrant phlox to a harrowing violet. When the bounty hunter finally saw the shift, the ghastly star changed colors again. A deep violet, near cosmic blue, radiated out into the black universe. Like rivers coursing through routes, Oyande's light ran hard and rough through space and dissipated the ancestral apparitions. Like a violent blue tsunami, the rivers converged and slammed into Mbe. Power and vigor rushed into her body like a black hole consuming all there was. Pressure pinned against the woman's flesh. At first, there was exhilaration. Then it turned torrid. Heat and pain pierced through bone and muscle. She tried to yell in agony but nothing escaped her lips. Instead, Oyande itself nudged slightly through the void toward the woman. It nudged again as Mbe attempted to close her mouth. Then again, as she realized her gape would not shut. Oyande's color shifted even darker before it started to swirl like water in a drain. The massive illumination fluctuated and exploded, firing like a single enormous solar flare. The wave of blue fire flooded Mbe's mouth until there was nothing of the star left. Nothing but darkness.

* * *

Sand sifting? Shifting? Moving? Being moved. Reality combed over Mbe with aches and agony as burned flesh and deep bruises let her know she was still alive. The light of Oyande greeted her as Phyllo dug the bounty hunter free from the periwinkle dust.

"I can't believe we lived through that," Mbe said as Phyllo pulled her to her feet. "I mean that was Hayes fuel. We survived a direct blast from Hayes fuel!"

They had survived but the explosion had taken its toll. Phyllo's right side, from arm to torso to face, was calcined and charred. The jumper was tattered with large holes exposing parts of the man's back and chest. Mbe's suit fared better with only the jacket being reduced to cindered tatters. She quickly tossed it, favoring the vest/dress shirt look anyway.

"Are you okay?" Mbe asked, her eyes roaming over his scorched flesh.

"I'm aces," Phyllo replied as he picked up his satchel. "Or I will be soon enough. We got to boogie. All manner of mug men and hustlers will be here after seeing that far-out display."

Mbe gazed across what was left of the junkyard. Nothing. Murrah's periwinkle dust covered the terrain like dunes in a desert. Small remnants of ships and metal protruded here and there but mostly the yard was a wasteland. It was as if the Hayes explosion had returned the field to its original state, a time before humanity had ever touched its blue sands. The woman gritted her teeth with perturbation, fully aware that they should be dead.

"Stop!" Mbe commanded "We're not going anywhere until you tell me what this crap is really about. And I mean right now, Phyllo. Not later. Not tomorrow. Right now."

"It's a long story."

"Okay, start with the obvious. How are we still alive?"

"Mbe," Phyllo sighed. "Did you have a dream before I pulled you from the dust?"

"Yeah. It was vivid as hell. I dreamt that . . ."

"That Oyande appeared before you in a black void, showed you your people, and then flowed right into you. Right?"

"Right."

Phyllo sat in the blue sand and took a long deep breath before fishing around in his bag. Moments later he retrieved a tiny mushroom, not unlike the shape of a common shitake. It was lean and petite but unlike the shitake, shimmering phlox speckles danced throughout the fungus's cap.

"This," Phyllo chuckled, "is what saved us. I have created something special and outtasight here on AF-Ro 7. Something that can only be made here under the righteous power of Oyande. These shrooms are unlike any other in the whole galaxy. They are the wild seeds that I have cultivated and nurtured. Gifts that I now share with you. I'm not entirely sure what will come from it, but I fed it to you after I first dug you out. Your face was burned and your body mangled, but the mushroom healed you. Permanently."

Mbe raised an eyebrow at the little mushroom but then turned her eyes to her fresh unmarked skin. The burns and bruises were slowly disappearing. Red and blue blemishes retracted as the woman's beautiful dark tone reclaimed her body.

"What do you mean by permanently?" Mbe said apathetically.

"The mushroom unlocks something in people. A few things are different from cat to cat, but the ability to heal seems to be a constant. We should really continue to rap about this somewhere else. Meiko has eaten them too. It's only a matter of time before that crazy yakuza psycho crawls her way from under this wasteland."

"Meiko? That tech-out killer? Why the hell would you have given her a mushroom?!"

"Well," Phyllo answered. "in order to operate without being harassed I had to make alliances with several of the city's colorful characters. It wasn't easy living here but I made it work, ya dig? Can't take that from me."

Memories flashed across Phyllo's mind like a montage of scenes from a film: his initial year in AF-Ro 7 where he worked free of persecution, delivering psychedelic experiences courtesy of great mushrooms. Then came the following year when he was hounded by a myriad of gangs and syndicates. Tired of ducking and dodging thousands of hostile hustlers and crime bosses, the afro-headed dealer brokered a universal deal. That deal lasted up until the very moment he created a game-changing new mushroom.

"I'm shaking the scene." Phyllo continued as he stood. "You can join me or not, sistah. It is entirely your choice. If you don't, I wish you all the luck. Be easy, Mbe."

Phyllo tightened the strap of his satchel across his torso and paused for a moment, his eyes roaming across what was left of the junkyard. He had only been an AF-Ro 7ite for three years but in that time the old man nearly mapped out all of Murrah. It had been the only place he called home and his brain took to every nook and corner. He knew of hidden places that native-born people had never heard of. After gazing around, turning four full circles, Phyllo etched out a grin on his face and started to walk.

Mbe meandered her gaze upward, Oyande drawing her attention with its capturing view. The glowing orb radiated as it always did, purple illumination decorating the galaxy from light-years away. She closed her eyes and let her thoughts gallop behind her lids. Her mushroom-induced visions played over and over again. The crowd of reassuring ancestors. The eventual invasive rush of engulfing a star. They had been vivid and raw. They lingered in her mind like the aftertaste of a powerfully spiced meal.

"Damnit," Mbe sighed as she opened her eyes, her feet following a man that was supposed to be an easy bounty.

* * *

A metallic fist shot from under a mountain of periwinkle dust. Meiko tore herself up from her crystalline burial and let out an echoing scream. Her glowing katana hummed, held firmly in her right hand. Exposed skull and gray matter oozed with red ichor and fluids as silky black hair fell uprooted. As Oyande's light bathed her in its aura, Meiko's flesh mended itself while bones reanimated into solid wholes. The snapping of joints blended with the yakuza boss's howls as her voice bounced about the desert dunes. When the healing had finally finished its painful work, the woman chuckled at the sight of her cybernetic arm as she thought about why it had survived. No doubt her body had taken the brunt of the explosion. It had probably shielded the robotic limb. Her clothes and eye had not been so lucky. Naked and cycloptic, Meiko breathed in the Murrah air. She had not tested the power of Phyllo's fungus before today. Apparently, its rejuvenating properties healed what was alive from when it was consumed. No new eye to replace the one she had lost as a child fighting a dog, but everything else felt fantastic. Her muscles glistened like marble and her hair flowed like a black waterfall. Meiko turned towards AF-Ro 7 and began her trek, vengeance quaking with every step the shateigashira made in the Murrah dust. First, she would pick up a silver kimono from her parked Za gōruden. Then she would hunt down Phyllo.

* * *

The Vanguard patrols, AF-Ro 7's mud cloth duster-clad peacekeepers, flooded the city's edge to get a handle on the chaos birthed from the Hayes fuel explosion. While most of the city was untouched, several slums and factories that were housed closest to the junkyard had received fallout. The Vanguard P-Funk cruisers blared through the streets as their rectangular forms sped from block-to-block levitating feet from the concrete. Onlookers made comments and gossiped as the patrols stormed past like the drifting of a cloud. Phyllo and Mbe blended through the people, their bodies fully healed and inconspicuous.

"Did you see that explosion?!" yelled a man talking to his wife.

"Of course I did! The whole city saw it, Russell. My cousin who works the sub-rail system said they felt a huge tremor down there."

"That was definitely Hayes fuel." said another AF-Ro 7ite.

"Who you telling? I always thought that automated junkyard was bad news. Who the hell inspects those derelict crafts? There could have been anything over there!"

"Yeah. Like Hayes fuel."

Conversations continued to accent the event that had shaken the city. Not a single person paid any attention to the bounty hunter or the mushroom dealer as they slipped into a boarded-up establishment. Long pitch-black hallways met them as they ventured beyond an abandoned reception desk.

"Where are we?" Mbe asked as she followed Phyllo through the darkness.

"The Zora Neale."

"The Zora Neale? That massive roller rink from back in the day?"

"The one and the same. Not much is left of it after The Monarchs and The Crowns had their bop-action in here, but I turned it into a hideout after they trashed it. A few of the crime bosses backed me when I started rebuilding. Goldie, Big Koto, Afua, Midnight Michelle, 92nd Street & his crew of stick-up kids. Even KC Monarch put some manillas down on it. Meiko too."

"So, you got funded to rebuild a roller rink as not a roller rink. And why would a bunch of ruthless criminals, warlords, and killers come together to give you money for this?"

"Same reason they left me alone after I met with them. I made deals."

Phyllo and Mbe stopped at a large glaucous door, solid and out of place amongst the dilapidation. The dealer punched in a quick sequence on a nearby keypad and the door slid open with the resounding release of decompressed air. Cascading purple light flooded the hallway as Phyllo walked into his hideout.

Mbe entered the massive roller rink. The roof was eleven stories high with a large circular hole in its center. A translucent orb sat wedged in the ceiling damming the hideout from the outside climate and weather. Oyande's light refracted into the sphere and illuminated the base with enhanced efficiency. A large soil-filled fountain rested in the middle of the rink, troops of mushrooms bountifully overflowing with curated placement. Benches and counters were visible on the outside of the rink, all barren with the exception of a lit corner at the room's other end. Presented by the only lamp Mbe could see, orange rays revealed a wall of neatly secured four-wheeled quad skates. Dull walls sat solidly with old murals of Harlem long gone and lacked the luster of the previous spectacles, but they still added to the rink's character.

"Welcome to the Zora," Phyllo announced as he walked across the rink. "This is one of four of the most righteous mushroom farms that I have stashed across the city. Definitely one of my favorites at least."

Mbe found herself standing in the room's center next to the fertile fountain. The glass sphere filtered Oyande's light into a pure sparkling column that had enthralled the bounty hunter. Concentrated, the star's rays had become something new.

Something beautiful. Something beyond beautiful. The peculiar beam had been so hypnotizing that Mbe had never noticed that Phyllo had switched into different clothes. His new clean plum-colored bell-bottom jumper didn't break her trance. It was the smooth gliding of his form as he circled her on skates that snatched her away from Oyande's blessing.

"What the hell, Phyllo? We've got time for this? Really?"

"Sistah, we've got time for so much more than you realize. Don't let life take you for a ride before you're ready to glide, ya dig?"

Phyllo slid around his farm of fungus and picked mushroom after mushroom, carefully placing the capped curios into his satchel. Mbe raised an eyebrow as she really molded over the idea of the man before her. Phyllo's lifestyle had never made him a target for her, but that didn't mean that their paths never crossed. Odd occasions and freak accidents had collided their journeys time and time again. On one bounty Mbe chased down an assassin who had a penchant for psychedelic drugs. Phyllo had been an easy lure for that bounty. On another, she had actually saved his life when a gang of thugs she was hunting tried to beat him to death for his merchandise. Their acquaintance had carried on like this for the three years the shroom dealer had been in AF-Ro 7. If it had not been for the huge reward on his head, Mbe would have probably left him alone. He was an odd old man with strange mannerisms. His good nature was disarming at times, but it tended to make Mbe ponder one question.

"Phyllo, why do you talk and act the way you do?" Mbe asked.

"What do you mean?" Phyllo replied, stopping under Oyande's light.

"Nobody says stuff like 'ya dig' or 'sistah.' I mean, you are really leaning hard into the bygone-bygone era. Why, Phyllo?"

Phyllo smirked and looked at the walls of his hideout. All across the surface, surrealist art depicted people darker than blue dressed in everything from dashikis to zoot suits to bell bottoms. Halos and chains of natural hair adorned their heads while great joy emitted from glorious smiles. The ancient city of Harlem filled the background as these diverse figures sprawled from street to curb in a vast community.

"You want me to run it down, I'll run it down," Phyllo said as he sat on the wide rim of the fountain. "Mbe, where are you from?"

"Originally? Neo Timbuktu but I grew up in the Buluku colony."

"Both of those are just a quick hop and a skip from here. Spacefaring spots too. Especially the Buluku colony. I don't think any gourd colony could survive floating out in the universe without being heavy on the spacefaring side."

"You're right about that. So, how does spacefaring factor into your weird idiosyncrasies?"

"I'm from Earth, Mbe."

The ebony woman's eyes grew as large as plates as she stared at the old man, the realization of his words sinking in with the ebbing of seconds.

"That's right," Phyllo continued. "With it being as forgotten and exiled as it was, it took me years to reach the stars. My whole life to be exact. And that whole time I dreamed of AF-Ro 7. My mother and I lived in this rickety water bunker and all we had were books to read."

"Water bunker?"

"Yeah. On Earth, because of the tides and storms, most people live in mobile submarine homes that can dock in underwater cities. Ours was a little on the poor side. Which means we could barely afford to leave the city we were docked with."

Phyllo pushed off the fountain and glided to the edge of the rink. After performing a smooth spin, the old man turned and started to flow around the room's circle backward.

"I read all about Harlem," Phyllo continued as he stepped and slid with the grace of a cat. "Over and over again. From its glory days to its downfall to its gentrification and back to its glory days again. I dreamed night after night about this world on my wall. So when I was a teenager and I got my first ear full of AF-Ro 7, it became the new home I intended to find. It took me fifty years, but I got here . . . I got here, Mbe. Phyllo Parks found Harlem. Can you dig that?"

Phyllo stopped his smooth movements and sighed. Scenes of his journey, his challenging trials, sped through his mind like a montage of horror and victory. The promise he made to his dying mother, a desire to never give up on his dreams. A fog of gangs, corporations, and authorities, all trying to stop him every step of the way. The loves he lost and abandoned that he traded for the one goal he would never cast aside.

"And I'm not going anywhere."

A tear rolled from the dealer's cheek before he wiped away the moisture with his sleeve. Then, just for a fleeting moment, his cool was broken. Impenetrable anguish flashed across the dealer's mahogany face. Mbe blinked and it was gone, Phyllo's calm disguise returning with illusive ease.

"Why is the bounty so high, Phyllo? Really?"

"Because I'm about to change it all, sistah. When borders and territories, and the lines that define them, are forced to be redrawn, then you had best believe the oppressors and the opportunists will come out the woodwork."

Phyllo returned to the fountain and quietly picked the rest of his mushrooms.

"The bounty," he sighed. "comes from O.R.C. because someone here in AF-Ro 7 dropped a dime on my plans to them. Since they can't come here themselves, they broadband a bounty on me."

"The Old Rights Confederacy want your special mushrooms so they can weaponize it."

"Not just the merch. They want me. One reason is that I'm the only person who knows how to change the shroom into their righteous forms. And the other because I plan on giving the shrooms to the people."

"What does that mean?"

"Well," Phyllo grinned. "It means I . . ."

A thunderous explosion shook the walls of the Zora Neale. Before Mbe could question the sudden boom, another explosion blew the room's heavy security door from its hinges. A cloud of black smoke rolled in from the destroyed path. The only thing Mbe could identify in the black fog was a blue sliver as it hummed through the mist.

Meiko bellowed in her flowing silver kimono as her azure katana flashed into action, its radiating blade cutting mere inches in front of Mbe's face. Again, the weapon flittered by, narrowly slicing the bounty hunter's arm as she dodged back. The shateigashira unleashed a volley of rage-fueled assaults, but the blue light betrayed her execution.

"ogyimifɔɔ!" Mbe called out in the black. "I can see everything you do, idiot."

As soon as the mocking left the woman's lips the loud barking of a rifle round echoed out through the rink. A savage round left Meiko's cybernetic wrist and tore through Mbe's shoulder, lifting her from her feet. A thump called out as she landed on the floor. Instantly, Meiko's blade lunged into Mbe's chest.

"Huh!" Mbe gasped as the weapon burned through her body. Smoke fell to the floor as the cloud settled, returning visibility to most of the Zora Neale. Phyllo sped into action. He barreled towards Meiko at top speed but the swordswoman was too quick. In one fluid motion, she yanked free her weapon and lashed out. Phyllo adjusted just in time and rolled by with only a small cut to the cheek.

"Come on!" Meiko spat as she readied her blade for Phyllo's return. "I'll cut your head off, kuso!"

Mbe gritted her teeth as the hole in her chest mended itself. Then the bounty hunter launched into a small flip, wielding the momentum into a powerful kick. The *rabo de arraia* found its mark as it collided with Meiko's temple and sent the killer spiraling. Mbe tried to close the distance and restrain Meiko but the katana flashed out like the reflex of a wild animal. The blade seared through the woman's forearm with savage speed, lobbing off the limb. Mbe cried out as her arm was lost to the black fog at their feet.

"I'm getting real tired of that sword." Mbe forced, drooling through clenched teeth. Meiko looked at the woman's bleeding nub as it started to mend, flesh and bone disgustingly meshing around itself.

"I see," Meiko smirked. "Kinoko. Anta no atama o maffutatsu ni watte shimaeba dō demo ī!"

The yakuza boss charged with her katana whipping through the air. Mbe fell back into a small backflip, slipping away from the first strike. Then she danced around another attack. Then another. Her capoeira skills allowed her to escape harm until an opening presented itself. Mbe curled in close and fired a headbutt to the swordswoman's face. Then Mbe speared forward with a mighty *bencao.* The kick propelled Meiko against the Harlem mural, cracking its edifice. Meiko's katana flew through the air, lodging into the translucent orb far above. Lying still, the boss of the Saiba Yakuza was finally down.

"You cool?" Phyllo asked as he skidded next to Mbe.

"No, Phyllo. I'm pretty far from cool!" Mbe fired back before taking a deep breath. "But I'll live."

"Does this mean you're off my bounty?"

"Depends. What are you planning with these mushrooms?"

Phyllo grinned under the menagerie of Oyande's splintered illumination. The image gave Mbe a deep sinking feeling.

"My plan has been done, sistah. Hours ago. All of y'all played the fool."

"What does that mean, Phyllo?" Mbe asked, closing her eyes in defeat.

"Do you know that most of AF-Ro 7's food supplements are vegetarian-friendly?" Phyllo grinned. "And do you know what the main ingredient to that is?"

"Oh, Olodumare," Mbe mumbled as she rubbed her brow.

Phyllo smiled as a comb seemingly appeared out of thin air. Slowly, he picked out his cotton-white afro. "Mushrooms. Ya dig?"

* * *

All across the city people were seeing Oyande in a new light. They had visions of oceanic purples being engulfed by their very being as apparitions of quondam ancestors visited them. Time seemed to stop for Murruh. It was no longer a simple rock floating in space. It would cease being a tourist trap for entitled spacefarers. By tomorrow, Phyllo figured as he sat on the roof of the Zora Neale, Murruh would be a territorial planet and AF-Ro

7 a capital. He had officially started something for the people, and after years of struggle, secured himself a real home. History was in the making.

The old man watched from his ledge as Mbe walked through the streets to the Hotel Superfly. AF-Ro 7ites were just waking up as she passed through the golden doors of the lavish bed & breakfast. There would be too much change for anybody to be concerned with any bounty. Let alone his. Phyllo turned his eye to the beautiful skyline. Oyande burned brightly, its circular purple form sitting perfectly in the backdrop. AF-Ro 7 buildings and neighborhoods decorated the world from block to block. Phyllo had brought power to the people. Not the money-grubbing officials or warmongering military. Not the facade of patrollers. The people. And for as long as the people had the power, Phyllo Parks would always be a staple of this new city. This new AF-Ro 7. This new Harlem.

Phyllo smiled as Oyande started to set. He only had one thing to say as he daydreamed about a positive future for the people.

"Outtasight."

The End,
Sistahs and Brothas.

The Third Eye Manifester
by
Ishola Abdulwasiu Ayodele

It is either Commander Nkem agrees that two hundred prisoners should be jettisoned to prolong Orun's life support system span or endanger over two thousand denizens. Councillor Jiya has presented an argument supporting the former, claiming this was the only way for them to increase their chances of survival, by choosing a lesser evil. Nkem sees more than half of the council nodding as he finishes explaining his perspective. And this terrifies her. Her gaze shifts to Jiya who is opposite her at the oval table around which they all sit. Since he was the one who brought up the idea, she directs her resistance towards him.

"These are human lives, Jiya. They have families dreaming of their freedom. And some of them were jailed for light offences."

"I know it feels barbaric but it is the only way. They will be collateral for everyone's else survival," Jiya says.

"It doesn't *feel* barbaric. It is barbaric."

"So do you prefer that we all die? Commander, in this condition, Orun can't float two years more in space. Letting them go will give us some additional months."

"But we are not certain we'll find a solution within that frame of time."

"Only that the probability of doing so will increase. This is the best option we have at the moment. Unless you have another?"

The other members of the council stay silent, observing. The two butted heads in almost every meeting they had, so, this isn't strange.

"No, I don't." Nkem sighs.

"Then the council should vote and decide our fate," Jiya says holding Nkem's gaze.

Nkem looks away and glances at the faces at the table. There are twelve of them, each a representative of their faction. Nkem knows majority will favour survival over morality. So as Jiya makes to state a motion, Nkem cuts in.

"Give me three days. Three days and I will present a better option.

Jiya doesn't hide his glare. "And if you don't?"

Nkem lets a sheath of confidence glaze over the fear in her eyes. No one must see through her bluff. "Then we go with your proposition."

Later that day, Nkem paces the length of her room while she waddles through a quagmire of thoughts in her mind. She stops and turns to a shelf on her side. The shelf carries her collections: a few rare paper books, a holographic globe displaying earth's seasons, abstract metal sculptures and a small humanoid music bot with a loose jaw. She flicks a switch at the bot's nape and its eyes light up and jazzy saxophone sounds pour out from its speaker of a mouth. Nkem walks to the wide window at the end of the room and stares out through its transparent glass at space. She can see in the horizon a glowing nebula, a splash of green-yellow-orange. Normally, jazz plus the wondrous spectacle of outer space is enough to inspire and uplift her. But she still feels weighed down with doubt and dread. The nebula though re-minds her of her deceased lover, Wanga. He used to tell her be-ing around her made his mind into nebulae. With his rich sense of humour and an exceptional skill of picking stars out of empty night skies, Wanga would have found a way to make her feel hopeful if he were around. When the pressure of pre-election pandemonium got to her, it was Wanga who reminded her how she had been an award-winning head prefect in college. Then he'd click on a classical music bot and they'd sway to an Olaposi or a Beethoven. And Nkem would feel all the weight on her mind dissipate. Nkem had imagined he would stand by her throughout her tenure, cheering her on tough days. But a day to the election, Wanga had rushed into a crumbling faction to save a little girl and got a metal splinter drilled into his side. And life had bled out of Wanga before an ambulance arrived. Nkem's heart quaked into dust on receiving the news. Winning the election the second day did not move her. Encapsulated in a casket of grief, she sank deep into despair. She had mumbled through her swearing in ceremony after which she refused to step out of her apartment. Until Jiya visited her with a small basket of fruits.

"Aren't you tired of garnering pity?" Jiya had said as he sat in a sofa she'd offered him.

Nkem was taken aback as this statement contradicted the fruit basket gesture. She paused and then said, "What?"

"I mean, you have locked yourself up for some time while your office suffers. You're yet to hold your first council meeting. You should act like you deserve the people's choice."

Nkem was spellbound. Of course, she should have seen through the shenanigan. Jiya had been her unrelenting rival and frenemy since college. He wouldn't change now.

Jiya continued, "Do you know rumours are starting to spread that people had voted for you out of pity because of Wanga's martyrdom?"

"You should leave, Jiya." Nkem shot up from her seat.

Jiya sprang up immediately as if he'd expected this reaction. "Orun needs a commander. And I'm--"

"Get out of my home!" Nkem stormed to the door and opened it.

Immediately Jiya stepped out, and Nkem threw the fruit basket after him. And the door slid shut. Nkem caught a cloudy reflection of her face on the door's sheen. Her long face seemed longer. Her eyes were red and swollen. Her hair disheveled. She didn't recoil at this unrecognizable creature she was looking at. Instead she steeled her demeanour and marched into her bathroom, shaved her head, took a bath and wore a flowing blue gown. That evening, she called for the first council meeting.

A peal jolts Nkem out of her reverie. It comes from the pendant on her chest which also starts flashing red. She touches it and there is silence again and the oval shaped pendant returns to its usual translucent state. Red colour and a blare means she is needed at the navigation room. Her anxiety spikes. She wonders if the navigating system has paused again or if they are encountering the foreshadowed meteor shower. She dashes out of her room just as the music from her music bot crescendos.

In the navigation room, the head pilot shows Nkem the picture of a ship floating immobile in their path.

"Point the grand telescope at it, Ali. We need more details."

The head pilot clacks some keys and the object is zoomed into. An embossed lettering of "The Third Eye Manifester" becomes visible on the hull.

Nkem gasps. Orun has been flying through space for centuries with a locked in route on the navigator system by the ancestral residents. No one knows where to but the council over decades has propagated the narrative that they are headed for an earth-like planet at the other side of the galaxy. Nkem realizes this has always been their destination.

When they are close enough to transmit, Nkem speaks into the radio to make contact.

"Hello Third Eye Manifester. This is Orun. My name is Nkem, the commander. Please introduce yourself."

After about a dozen transmissions and no reply, it dawns on Nkem that the ship is empty. Nkem then decides to lead a scout to inspect it.

The scout's carrier latches onto the ship's dock with ease. They alight onto an enclosed platform and march to the door before them. Assuming the ship's operating system is like theirs, Nkem presses some buttons by the door and is surprised when the double door draws back in a whirr to reveal a fluorescent lamp-lit passage. It is silent as space. Others gather behind her and peer in. One of them asks if they should return to Orun and Nkem answers by crossing over. As she does, a loud beep erupts from somewhere deep inside. Unfazed, she draws out her firearm from her holster, aims forward and advances. Her team follow suit. They tread through the passage till they find an empty control room, then a vast living quarter with bunkers and blank screens. They are following the sound and it is getting louder. When they reach another locked door, thicker and wider than all the doors they've seen so far, Nkem asks the team to ready their weapons in case they encounter something deadly behind. And this door like others has no password too. On sliding open for them, the beeping stops. In front of them is a massive machine in the shape of an octopus, but with sixteen tentacles. There are pods at the end of each arm and one at the centre. Nkem reads off one of the arms "URA 444". Suddenly, a voice blares from the walls, startling. A voice frail with urgency and wistfulness.

"We saw the degradation of Earth coming, from the drastic climate change that led to the nocturnal era to the failed colonization of Mars, to extraterrestrial wars... We found that our only chance was to recreate earth. So we developed a consciousness-infused technology that could alter reality, the Ultimate Reality Alterer. But we didn't foresee the potential for the machine to manifest the unconscious too and because of the trauma ingrained in our DNA, we couldn't successfully recreate Earth. We needed to heal before we could achieve this. So my crew was sent into space to master the URA away from Earth's terrors and return later for recreation. But because of my deep-seated existentialism, I had unconsciously nurtured something that might cause us to fail. And if you are listening to this, it already happened, an unravelling of my imagination that every human vanishes so that suffering will end. It also means my hope that the effect isn't universal is realized. And you might be humanity's only chance for continuity. The Ultimate Reality Alterer 444 requires a perfect imaginator at the centre pod. You will find a manual to guide you inside. Please be careful and only allow the purest imaginations."

As the message ends, Nkem advances towards the head pod, which just as others, looks like a glass cocoon. The curvy door glides in and a swirl of cloudy air wafts out. Nkem registers an almost hypnotizing effect of the scent. There's a chair-like gear inside on which sits a semicircular chip. She picks it and just as she whirls, the chamber hums close. Before she orders that they return back to Orun, Nkem makes every officer swear an oath of secrecy about their discovery.

Back on the ship, Nkem calls an emergency meeting to brief the council about the machine. Images of URA 444 and descriptions of its parts are displayed on the oval tabletop. The lighting lights up the awe expanding on everyone's face. Despite their unparalleled technological knowledge, this looks like magic to them.

"This is another option for us, we can recreate and teleport to Earth." Nkem swipes an image of earth onto the oval screen.

Silence.

"How exactly does this thing work?" Councillor Jiya breaks the silence. He is opposite Nkem as usual. His signature large grey turban sits on his head and the gemstones on his many rings sparkle.

"It's a technology thought to be lost forever. It surfaced around Earth's nocturnal era. Like I said, it is based on the quantum quality of the observer altering the observed. What we need now is to start training imaginators towards precision and psychological purity." There's a hint of excitement in Nkem's voice. She swipes at the tabletop again and new images rush in. They are of spectacles that seem to be made of crystals. Hundreds of them.

"What are these?" the woman beside Nkem asks before leaning forward to try to read some inscriptions on one of the spectacles. Some of her dreadlocks fall over her face.

"These are Simulatrixes. The manual revealed they can be found in a container on the ship," Nkem says and points at a single one which rapidly enlarges to take up all the space on the screen. "They are advance virtual reality tech used in training for perfect imagination. It's like a game where you can conjure anything depending on mental graphic capacity. And the quality of the reality created is proportional to the purity of imagination."

Some eyes are gazing at the image while others follow Nkem's lips.

"And you think we can just trust this?" Jiya says.

"It's a better option than killing hundreds of people in order to extend the ship's lifespan."

"I don't trust this tech. No one was even on the ship. That's just eerie and ominous," Jiya says.

"I will use the Simulatrix first to ascertain safety! If I survive, then we trust the technology." Nkem's voice shoots through the air.

The man beside Jiya holding a staff starts, "But..."

And Nkem sighs and cuts in, "This is the only way. It's our only chance." While her shaved head bows, all the eyes in the room exchange looks, prying one another for agreement.

Finally, Jiya says they will go with the technology after Nkem tries it. "I hope you're right and it's safe."

Nkem scoffs to herself. Jiya does not hope she is right. She's sure he wishes the simulatrix destroys her mind so that he can take her place.

A voice plunges into Nkem's mind, "But what do we tell the people about the new ship?"

Nkem does not find out who said it when she raises her head smirking. "We should tell them it's an abandoned junk ship that we can salvage for spare parts. The truth will be too jarring."

As no one speaks after her, she calls for adjournment of the meeting.

The next day, Nkem puts on a simulatrix before the council. Jiya first appears in her mind, but with his mountain of turban pressing his head into his neck. Then a faint image of Wanga materializes. His pointed nose keeps widening and shrinking. A birthmark shifts from above his right eye to the left and then back. And his eyes are a colour caught between black and brown, almost a blur. Only his spiky hair and dark complexion are stable. Nkem's breath quickens. It's only been four years and she's forgetting Wanga's image. She imagines his soft-spoken voice, remembering the last words he said to her. "I'm sure you'll win against Jiya again. It's only natural." But he sounds like her instead, like her perpetually strained voice. She jerks off the simulatrix from her head. The council search her face. They have seen everything projected on the tabletop.

"Wow! Wow! This is unbelievable!" Nkem laughs nervously.

The council members share glances, nodding, except for Jiya whose rigid gaze is fixed on the gadget Nkem is holding.

Nkem trains the recruited imaginators herself. They study the contents in the chip together and get better at crafting realistic mental images each day. Nkem quickly becomes friends with one of the recruits, Irebawa, a quanta-neurologist with an exceptional understanding of the URA. One afternoon, after training, Irebawa requests for a moment with Nkem. They stay back in the training room, which is dimly lit with blue light, each sitting on two of the stretchers in the room.

"I have a suggestion, Commander. It's been months now and we haven't attained a hundred percent imagery clarity," Irebawa says, then pauses.

"So?"

"My daughter Wuraitan is a wonderful storyteller and she paints the vividest of images. I think we should test her."

"First, I hope you haven't shared this project with her or your husband?"

"No, not at all. I'm on oath."

"Okay. I've been meaning to ask because you talk a lot about them." Nkem smiles. "Next, I appreciate your concern. But I can't allow your daughter to participate. She's still young. You said she's only thirteen. She might jeopardize the stealthiness of the operation. And I can't risk that."

Irebawa nods in agreement. They go on to chat a while about the technicalities of the simulatrix before leaving the training room together.

A few months later, Nkem declares they are ready to create and jump. She selects sixteen imaginators with clarity above ninety percent. She has the highest score of ninety-five so she'll lead the operation. To explain what could happen to the denizens, the council announces that they'd encounter an anomaly in the junk ship which may possess space warping properties for teleportation. And a curfew is imposed for safety.

On the day, each imaginator enters their assigned pods. They begin inputting their imagination, all continuously overlapping and merging before them to create a floating planet, first with sixteen moons. Then eight, four, two... Now they start zooming into the planet, with the aim of reaching the atmosphere where they can conjure the images of the two ships. This is when focus becomes unsteady, as the mental energy of the participants is drained. So before they reach earth's lower atmosphere, the ships take form. Feeling the drastic drop in energy, Nkem quickly affirms the manifestation. And she blacks out.

About an hour later, Nkem groans awake. The door to her pod is already opened as that of the others. Still feeling quite disoriented, she comes out and goes round to stir the rest awake. And they all head outside.

When Nkem sees sand on the ground, she manages a chuckle and increases her pace. Other imaginators follow behind more slowly. She takes off her shoes. The sand feels smooth under her feet. There's an endless mass of water before her with tides running back and forth at the shore. Farther on her side, beyond Orun, is a lush forest. The sky is a vast expanse of blue. The sun feels warmer than the ship's artificial sun but it doesn't burn. The light is brighter too, so Nkem shields her eyes with her arm. She turns excitedly to observe her companions and finds some of the imaginators look more feeble than thrilled. Just then, Jiya arrives with a bunch of medics behind him. Rather than the excitement Nkem had hoped will be on his face, she meets indifference.

"Because the ships manifested too high, we crashed and suffered casualties. Thirty-three deaths including Councillor Tarfa, and maybe there's more. I've directed the medical team to attend to the gravely injured," Jiya says.

Nkem's triumphant demeanor crumbles. The medics rush to help three people who just collapsed behind her.

"I told you this was dangerous," Jiya says.

Nkem sighs and mutters, "More would have died had we stayed instead."

She walks to where the unconscious imaginators are being tested by the medics. "I appreciate that you swiftly sprang up to action, Councilor Jiya. Now, while we cater to the hurt, we shouldn't waste time testing for potential geo-hazards.

According to records, Orun's ancestral residents left Earth unstable, with constantly shifting tectonic plates."

Another group of people arrive consisting of the remaining councillors and relatives of the imaginators.

"Irebawa!" a man screams, his eyes on one of the bodies the medics are treating. He leaves the wheelchair he's pushing and darts forward. The girl on the wheelchair starts sobbing. Nkem realises that they are Irebawa's family. At the same time, a councillor breaks to the front shouting that he can't find his daughter. Jiya is quick to hold him back as he aims at Nkem.

"We're going to find her, Councillor Madu," Nkem says, a slight tremble in her voice threatening to betray her optimism. "Everything is going to be alright."

By noon, the geo-scientist team returns from their survey with a deadly reading on their Geo-hazard Oracle. A super tsunami is gathering momentum in the belly of the ocean which is predicted to strike at sunset. On hearing the report, Nkem can no longer hide the horror on her face. She waves that the geo-scientists leave the meeting room so that the council can discuss the next line of action. They barely reach the entrance before Jiya's outburst.

"We have to evacuate the ship and go as far into the forest as we can."

"What if we don't have enough time? The scale of the tsunami as we've heard is terrifying. We can try to use the URA again." A trickle of sweat rolls down Nkem's hairless head to her chin.

"The same Third Eye Manifester or whatever brought us here for this calamity and you are asking us to trust it again?

"We even lost a councillor because of it. And no one knows if Councillor Madu's daughter will wake up. The machine requires blind faith and is not safe. Our consciousness is unreliable as an input means."

Councillor Madu hits his staff on the floor. "I agree with Councillor Jiya. We must abandon the ships and flee before twilight comes with disaster."

Many of the councillors nod at this. Nkem is still silent.

"We have the machines to make our path and our military arm will be with us to protect us from beasts," the councillor with dreadlocks says.

"We can't leave." Nkem straightens her hunched back. "With that kind of reading, we will likely not outrun the waves' reach because we are too many. Plus there are our prisoners too. But with the machine, we might stand a chance."

Madu speaks, his hand gripping his staff so tight that his veins bulge, "What will you do now? Teleport us near an active volcano? Or in the eye of a hurricane? Besides, all your imaginators are exhausted, including yourself. It's conspicuous in the heaviness of your eyelids you struggle to keep open."

"We shouldn't leave," Nkem says.

"We don't have time for arguments. We'll cast a vote and settle this," Jiya puts his hand on the pendant of his necklace which every one of them has on. "Press your pendant if you agree that we leave," he says and presses his.

Nkem fixes her eyes on the tabletop where the result is displayed. There are seven votes out of the eleven Councillors present.

"It is settled. We leave," Jiya announces.

"I am staying!" Nkem says.

"You cannot overrule the votes, Commander Nkem." Madu lashes her with his eyes.

"I know. That's why we'll let the people decide. We are going to reveal everything to them. Whoever decides to leave can leave afterwards. But I am staying with anyone who understands my reasoning."

The public address comes immediately after the meeting with every screen in the ship lighting up to show the council meeting room. Nkem, standing in front of council, reveals the secret of the teleportation and how they could use it to prevent the looming danger from the ocean. After which Jiya comes forward to argue that they need to evacuate the shore for the forest. He ends, "Commander Nkem will allow anyone who wants to join me to leave. So leave your factions' public hall now, go and get what is essential and gather behind Orun in twenty minutes. The wounded and unconscious will be carried in vehicles. We don't have time. We should hurry!"

Within fifteen minutes, the back of Orun is flooded with hundreds of people, each with a small bag flung over their shoulders or on their heads. It's past noon and shadows have begun stretching. The forest lies enticing before them, with navigator vehicles already creating paths inward, clearing shrubs and felling small trees. Jiya praises the people for their bravery and gives a short speech before declaring they can forge ahead. Then they pour into the forest.

Behind them is Orun and the junk ship glistening in their brokenness, and the ocean's deceptive calmness.

Nkem watches Jiya and his followers leave on the council meeting room's CCTV. If she doesn't allow this, she will be tagged a tyrant. Jiya has finally got his wish to lead. Their feud of perspectives over the years has fettered into this breakdown in her governorship. She thinks of Wanga. If he were alive, she would feel more courageous than doubtful of the decision she has made.

A man pushes in a wheelchair. The squeaks of the wheels draw Nkem's attention to the present. She wipes off a streak of tears on her face and turns with a smile.

"You asked for us, Commander," the man says.

"Yes, yes. I'm very thrilled you didn't decide to leave."

"I won't be able to stay with Irebawa's body in the vehicle. And our daughter doesn't want to be crammed into a carrier for the differently abled."

Nkem walks over to them. She recognizes the girl now from the news years ago. She's the girl Wanga had saved.

"You must be Baba and Wuraitan. Irebawa told me a lot about you two."

"Yes, Commander," Baba says.

Wuraitan looks up at Nkem. "I never got the opportunity to tell you how sorry I am about Officer Wanga. I'm alive because of him," she says. "I still remember the soft smile on his face telling me to trust him. I'm alive because I did. And now I trust you."

"Thank you so much. That means a lot to me." Nkem kneels before her and squeezes her hands gently.

"May I know why you have called us here, Commander?" Baba asks impatiently.

Nkem stands, "Yes. Irebawa once told me about the possibility of Wuraitan being capable of attaining one hundred percent imagery clarity."

"I don't understand you," Baba pulls back the wheelchair to himself.

Nkem goes to pick a simulatrix from the oval table. "It's a measure of the purity of imagination. Attaining a hundred percent will make one a perfect imaginator for the URA."

"Not my daughter too, Commander. Irebawa is already in coma because of this and now you're asking my daughter to join you?"

"I just need to confirm if she can do it. This is not the URA. It's only a simulating device."

"And if she scores a hundred? What happens next?"

"I—"

Wuraitan cuts in. "Please let me try, Baba." She looks up at Baba's stony face pleadingly. "Pleeease."

"Alright, but only a minute and I'm yanking that thing off your face."

Nkem puts the simulatrix over Wuraitan's eyes and asks her to imagine a massive wave at the shore curving towards the ocean. Then she goes to the oval table to watch the display. On the screen is a wave rising to the sky, so perfect in composition and detail one won't believe it's animated. Nkem quickly checks her score and sees ninety nine percent. She gasps looking at Wuraitan. Baba quickly pulls off the simulatrix from Wuraitan's face.

Nkem runs to kneel before Wuraitan again, breathless. "The Third Eye Manifester requires a perfect imaginator at the centre pod. And you, you attained the highest score yet. You can save us all."

"No, no, no." Baba shakes his head. "Wuraitan is not going into that weird junk ship."

The remaining councillors enter the room. The woman in front reports that they've brought what's left of their factions to the central hall. Nkem nods, then shares her discovery with them. Baba is already wheeling Wuraitan out against her wish.

"We will all die if I don't try Baba!" Baba stands still at the entrance. Wuraitan continues, "The least we can do is try. I'm sure Irebawa would have wanted me to try. You have to believe in me. I'm strong enough."

Baba exhales deeply and turns back. The council's eyes are on him, waiting. He nods his consent and Nkem places a palm over her chest in relief.

The sun is sinking in the horizon. Wuraitan is inside the central pod of the URA. Nkem, the seven imaginators left after the crisis and departure and new untrained volunteers take the tentacles. Nkem instructs them to focus on creating a massive wave to counter the force of the coming tsunami, to shatter its impact energy. Everyone else is in the central hall on Orun, hoping, some pacing, some handholding. The tsunami comes exactly when expected, a roaring terror. And they are all standing before it, watching its height towering, threatening to devour all in its way. They collectively create mirror images of the tsunami, which merges and arches to oppose it. A deafening blast thunders through the air. Splashes rain like a deluge on the ships for minutes. No one goes unconscious this time.

When the imaginators come out of the junk ship hours later, the central hall crowd is waiting for them outside, cheering. Nkem gives a speech, praising the people's faith and valour. Afterwards, she grabs a bottle of wine from the crates people have brought out to celebrate and finds her way to the back of Orun. She takes a swig as she sits. She stares at the forest, wondering how Jiya and his followers are faring at the moment. She gulps down more wine and gazes up at a full moon. Her peripheral sight catches a head with spiky hairs, so she glances sideways. But there's no one else with her. She thinks it must be because she saw an apparition of Wanga in the URA. Now she wonders why that happened for she didn't even think of him. Then over the cacophonies of celebration from the other side streaming into her ears, she hears, "Congratulations Nkem." And it's not in her perpetually strained voice. It is soft-spoken like Wanga's. She flinches and her eyes scramble about for the source in the deepening darkness. Again there is no one. Somewhere high in the sky, a wisp of cloud shifts to reveal another moon, a thin crescent almost invisible to the eye.

Instruments of War
by
Napoleon Wells

Emaje had already seen it a handful of times. Still, he
couldn't tear his gaze away from the images flowing out of
Shola's helmet. She was floating in the space between the two
parties assembled in the ship's massive observation deck. Her
luminescent purple Dogonaut spacesuit shimmered as the scene
materialized in her helmet and then projected upward. Emaje
could feel every eye and awareness focused on it, trance-like.

It was surreal, truly. The images and sound were all sharp,
biting, and clear. The entire deck had grown quiet. Their understanding of what they were watching resolved into something
nearer to disbelief, or perhaps panic. Emaje couldn't be sure of
which, but the frisson that vibrated through the deck once the
scene had finished its first cycle suggested a narcotic mix of the
two. He knew they were waiting for more. Perhaps some
grounded answer. Some relaxed explanation. Some authority,
anyone, to call it all a dream. Surely, they knew that that
wouldn't come. The scales had been ripped from the eyes of
Man nearly 300 years before. When those they worshipped now
first made themselves known, tearing the world apart, humanity
was forever changed. Mankind's capacity to cling to a decaying
belief would, however, always remain. They had witnessed it,
all of them. The question, ultimately, was did they want to believe what they were seeing?

Before any of those assembled could catch their breath, or offer any challenge or question, Shola's helmet shone bright, playing it yet again. The silence was as steady and coiled as the first
showing. Emaje, yet again, watched as if he had never seen it,
looking for any new detail he may have let slip in his prior view-
ings. He commanded his nanite neighbors to observe, attend,

stay, and record. Though they used the architecture of his senses as their own, they would absorb much of what he might miss. They were hungry for anything stimulating. Emaje knew that this would feed them whole and full.

The first image showed a figure, a male, his features distinctly West African, flying. He was in Space. Mid-Space from what Emaje could tell. The loud chirping coming through by way of sound was communication from the hundreds of craft docking in the area. Many of them preparing for jumps to Citadels, offering security for cruisers and protecting Sovereign and Free space. The sound between craft suggested that many of those observing his flight believed him to be one of their Gods, wandering about in Space. A new behavior for them perhaps, as none of the others ever had. One ship's Captain could be heard offering the suggestion that Space itself was, perhaps, this being's domain. He was flying at speeds faster than any God clocked before him. None had ever been clocked in Space, as all had flown about Terra and just below Near Space.

He kept picking up speed and his image became clearer. His dark eyes were fixed on a point just above him. He sailed forward, then up. He was wearing what seemed to Emaje to be a suit of emerald and silver-colored chain mail. Sensors flicked frantically over the surface of the mail, obscuring nearly every register of his presence save the sight of him. It was unclear whether he was speeding up, slowing down, floating, or jumping from space to space. If he had on a Naut helmet of any kind, Emaje couldn't make it out. He was breathing though. No doubt of that. Breathing. Blinking. Focusing.

His target became clear in moments. He appeared to nearly dissolve he was moving so fast, climbing, upward. That his arc was clear in Space was stunning. Directions could be difficult to determine without proper sensors. Within moments Emaje could hear shouts, voices ringing out in warning and surprise all at once as his destination became clear. Emaje had learned the name of his destination days before when Shola had first come to him. Old Earth Nauts had labeled the exoplanet GJ367b. The utter childlike arrogance of Old Earth Nauts to give such staid labels to such things. Dogonauts had learned that all exoplanets had lived once. They had created their Vecks, a kind of tuner, which allowed man to hear the dying hearts and death rattles of the beings that were exoplanets. They hadn't yet unearthed what type of beings they were. With the arrival of the Black Gods, there had been so much to learn. All was made new, and these Gods in all of their majesty, had refused the probing curiosity of man. Man was made for their worship, not to know them.

The being collided with the exoplanet. The scene moved from shouts to ruined silence. The exoplanet was approximately 15 percent of Terra's mass. It was nearly all iron and molten rock. The Ethiopian Sovereign had renamed it Bireti. Emaje recognized it as an old Amharic word. A silent, brooding black and red shadowy giant of a planet. The image resolved to show the being gritting his teeth, reaching out, and touching the exoplanet. There was a raw grating sound where his hand made contact and metal and rock giving way as his hand submerged. He was grabbing the blasted planet. Finding a handhold. Gods be merciful, Emaje thought, yet again. Even with all he had seen, Emaje found this astonishing. Again. The being cast his other hand outward, a massive black orb developing around it. Emaje studied this closely, as it looked akin to the Shadow he could create. This Shadow was fuller, however. It made all the Space around it nearly disappear. It was as if Space were being dragged and fed into his outcast hand. He aimed it at a dwarf star, vibrant and alive. The light, energy, and mass of the star began drawing away into his palm. There appeared to be a sigh coming from the dwarf as it grew colder and dark. In no more than a standard minute, the being's right hand blinded all the Space around him. He appeared to be holding a lance of Sun. It rattled and wavered in his hand. He began shaking with it, gritting his teeth yet again, drawing it back, and bringing it down in a wide sweep across the bottom of Bireti.

For the second time that day upon viewing that moment, there was a gasp. This being had cleaved a section of planet and was holding it in his hand. He floated, still for a moment. Holding his prize aloft, and then tore off through Space again. There were spacecraft, Sovereign spaceports, garrisons, and all manner of droidellites frantically emerging from the shock of what they were seeing and trying to flee from the rage of his path. The mail he was wearing began shifting colors as he dragged the massive planet shale in his left hand, while his right appeared to be draining power and life and energy from anything it passed. Craft needed time to Jump between Citadels and ports. They did not have it. Anything in or near his path was consumed. Crafts were obliterated. Stars, some light years away, could be seen dying. Beings' lives were snuffed out. Literally hundreds of thousands of souls vaporized or ejected from their craft and left floating in Mid Space. What they were able to see from the few floating droidellites and craft that survived passing in his wake gave them a clear view of the sheer brutal scope of the thing. He was destroying everything in his way and blowing out entire sections of space as he charged on to his destination.

None of the sensors on any of the craft that picked up the recording could effectively clock him. He was headed toward Near Space, the wide expanse of Space hovering just outside of Terra Earth. His eyes shone bright and large. Though humanoid, everything about his manner appeared alien. Even having seen the beings whom all of man had come to know as the Black Gods could not prepare those assembled, any who had borne witness, for this. He sailed through Space, calmly and determinedly reshaping anything in his way. All the craft, every ship from a Sovereign, enemy and ally, any who had survived, were sending immediate distress signals to all the nations of Terra. They began with the largest and most powerful of all the Sovereign who still called Terra, the Dying Earth, home. They all sent panicked word out to the Dogon Empire. The Collective.

The Dogon had, through war, Space exploration, hoarding of technology, and vicious determination, filled much of the power vacuum created when the New Gods had arrived. There were the Citadels above, represented by a number of nations that had been chosen by the New Gods. But Terra belonged nearly wholesale to the Dogon. Emaje could hear the millions of distress calls, hails, and signals being sent ahead of the arrival of this being in Near Space. Even now, seeing it again, knowing what was coming, Emaje wondered what the Dogon could do. He glanced at Shola, still floating, her helmet relaying the images, stark and horrible and lovely, yet again. She was inhumanly still in her Dogonaut suit, holding steady for all those watching.

The belief, Emaje knew, was that the Dogon, with the tech, weapons, and Spacecraft, could surely stop this being. They could halt whatever madness he was dragging through Space with him. They would craft an answer. Between their Science and Sufis, they had to know. Emaje doubted an answer existed, anywhere. The Dogon had lost many battles, especially when struck suddenly. It was time and preparation that had given them their edge over the many foes they had beaten back. This being was not going to give them the grace of precious time. He was coming. They would not be ready. None in Space or Terra would be ready. The being could be seen carrying his parcel into Near Space, rocketing toward the heavily populated Ports just above the OutEarth sphere. Millions of beings could see him coming. The Dogon had two massive warships moving to intercept him. One Destroyer could be seen breaking off from a Naija Empire run Port and turning to face him as he closed in, tearing through space. A second Space Carrier, dripping with Fighter Craft had broken off from Terra and was rocketing up to meet the threat.

It was clear what was at stake. The Spacecraft moved to place themselves between this being and Utopia. It was a massive Space station, tethered to Terra. It had been modeled after the Citadels which had been built by the New Gods and served a similar function. It wasn't as large and couldn't simply grow to accommodate as many beings as were drawn into it, but it was a broad challenge to the Citadels, constructed by the various powers of Terra in NuAfriq. All those nations had rallied around the Dogon call to arm and protect Utopia, and the millions of beings cycling between Utopia and Terra, knowing that the nations commanding the Citadels would see a threat. There was a belief among many that the Black Gods would make an appearance again, the first in over two centuries, and destroy Utopia. Its construction and existence had created an odd elixir of trepidation, hope, fear, and elation.

It became clear within seconds that Utopia was his destination. He didn't alter his flight path in any way upon seeing the two craft, and then the hundreds of fighter craft that broke away to intercept him. He thrust his hand forward, broad jets of endless Black simply tearing through every fighter craft. They simply exploded or began to fail and float. More death. Both crafts opened up with every available cannon. The orb in his hand grew and spread, appearing to draw in all the Space around him. The cannon fire simply ceased, two mouths shutting closed. Emaje could feel the confusion and crushing disbelief radiating among those around him. Never, not in all the battles that he had seen as a Bilawa, never in his time as a Shadow and investigator, had he seen such an attack. Destroyers and Carriers, especially those piloted and staffed by the Dogon, meant the end of any conflict. This being raised his hand, turning its palm out, and a bright hailstorm of cannon fire rained back from out of Space, falling like cosmic hail upon both crafts. Emaje could feel that he was holding his breath, yet again.

The being now had his bright, shifting mail up over his face as well. He was picking up speed, yet again, this time, placing both hands on the planet shale he was holding aloft. It had to be staggeringly heavy, and he gritted his teeth as he spun with it in his hand, turning and drawing momentum, then a second and blindingly fast third turn, before opening his mouth, shouting a word of power that Emaje could not recognize, but one that felt familiar. Following his third rotation, he released the shale, the sight of it blocking out nearly everything in view from every craft and droidellite that was recording. After releasing it, he drew his hands up and together, both now bearing Black orbs. His teeth were gritted again, and Emaje saw the two Dogon crafts, both heavily damaged, being swept toward one another as he drew his hands together. Emaje could hear the screams and alerts and anguish shuttling between the Dogon and Naija on both crafts. They were helpless. As they collided, more dying, the survivors were fated to watch as the massive, merciless shale barreled toward, and then through them. The explosion, and the subsequent flares, were chilling.

Emaje knew that all the eyes in Utopia, all those that could see, were looking at viewscreens at what had just happened, and what was headed their way. He knew that many did not believe what they were seeing. Others were praying to all the New Gods who they believed would always answer. Others knew that the Dogon Empire would keep them safe. They always did. Faith would serve as no shield that day. Emaje, and all of those on the observation deck, watched as the shale sailed, quiet, quick, un-yielding, and brooding, toward Utopia. Emaje could see the shields around the massive Port humming, 30 million souls praying in unison. The being watched, opening his mouth, again, a Shout of power. Emaje could see the shields rippling, shaking, fading, and ultimately tearing in wide vibrating sections. The shale appeared to pick up more speed. The craft, now destroyed, had been 254 Terra standard miles from Utopia. The shale had covered this distance in seconds. The being kept up his Shout, undulating, spittle racing out of his mouth and his body shaking. He extended his hands, floating, his face appearing as a mask of agony. The shields began to rattle, rupture, and fail.

The shale, the torn away piece of planet, nearly three times the size of Utopia Emaje would learn, slammed into the Eastern bloque of the Space city. The shields had surrendered. The shale carved its way through and into Utopia, destroying its tether. Utopia began to fall, the shale still picking up speed and ripping through it. It had torn through and killed nearly 3 of every 4 citizens of Utopia before it completed its work. The Dogon had no choice. They couldn't allow either the shale or the falling behemoth of Utopia to make its way to ground. The loss of life would be even more catastrophic. The Sky Crater cannons were turned heavenward. The order went up. Both destroyed and destroyer were made ash. The being could be seen sailing away as cannon fire pursued him. None of it touched him. He could be seen slowing down, appearing smaller and less formidable than he had been upon entering Near Space. All around him appeared to be silent. He began to falter, his mail going full black, obscuring him, and he started to fall, then float. He had made it light years away, Jumping twice, pursued by one brave droid who brought us the last of this recording. He had Jumped and then flown out to the very end of Mid Space, where a craft Jumped out, a tractor beam securing the being as he was floating. It drew him on board, turned and Jumped away. Emaje would later learn that it jumped away to Far Space, docking near the Third Citadel. It was the craft he was standing on, with the crew that he and Shola were currently facing.

Shola's helmet slowly cleared, the images fading to reveal her dark skin and sharp features. Her helmet appeared to dissolve around her head, freeing her tight, corded knots of hair and probing eyes. Like most Dogonauts, she appeared painfully thin beneath her Naut suit. Emaje knew how powerful she, and nearly of all her kind, were. Shola descended to the observation deck, turning her gaze briefly to him, and then letting it drift over their unwilling hosts. Well before her feet settled on the craft's deck a haughty voice said, "If that is all you came for Dogon, you may leave." The woman issuing the words would appear bored to most observers, but there was a tension rolling across her bare shoulders. She was the same dark golden brown as most of the East Afriq ruling class. Her slight accent and faded shoulder scarring suggested one of the Houses of Eritrea. An array of five guards flanked her, their silver armor mirroring hers. A sixth being trailed just behind the holochair which had emerged from the deck to support her weight. This sixth creature was massive, standing well over Emaje's six and three. The nanites scanned and placed this being at eight from toe to crown.

Emaje saw that the gown the speaker wore was simply repurposed armor. It was the same consistency as that of the bulky variety worn by her protectors, but cut to move with her, seamlessly. In her right hand was a banded silver cord, snaking along the deck and terminating around the neck of the giant who had come in with her. A leash then. Emaje could feel the leash vibrating from his position, and he knew that Shola had registered it as well. The being was male, his skin inky black, and his hair a wild buzzing mane around his massive head. Everything about the being was substantial. He wore a tunic of the same silver as those he had entered with on the observation deck and Emaje could see that he could barely keep his mouth closed over his teeth. Fangs, more rightly. Emaje had seen, had faced, and killed, his kind before. An Apedemak warrior. Brutal protectors of Sudan and Nile. His hands, terminating in bruised silver claws, confirmed it. His kind had been gifted to the Sudanese sovereign by the lion god himself. You didn't see many of them outside of the Citadels they had now been assigned to protect. Seeing them didn't often portend joy and good fortune. Emaje had faced a pack of five near the Steppes boundary, and it had taken everything he had to emerge from that row in one piece. The Apedemak were formidable. That this woman had one attending to her was…fascinating. Emaje ticked her threat level upward.

Emaje looked over to Shola, who appeared distracted, contemplative. Her Dogonaut suit had appeared to come to life as soon as the last word had left the woman's mouth. Images of bright tropical lowland flowers began moving across the surface of her Spacesuit. Emaje had come to learn that it was her identifier. All Dogonauts had them weaved into the architecture of their Spacesuits. A shield, barely perceptible, began humming at the surface of the suit. Emaje could see how far it had extended as microscopic debris in the air around her were vaporized as soon as they made contact. Shola tilted her head slightly to the left, peering around the observation deck before resting her dark eyes on the woman and saying "We didn't come here to give you word of events. We know that you know all about what happened. I came, was sent, to determine what happens next. Emaje Bul," she lifted her chin in my general direction "is here in his role as Oloye. I believe you know him, yes?"

It wasn't really a question, Emaje knew. He had countless exchanges with vassals, forces, and agents of East Afriq. They were known to often deploy cat's paws to do their bidding, which often included the theft of tech, stealing of hydro, droids and claiming of lands and people. Where the East was concerned, he was never bored in his role of Oloye. It was an ancient term, adopted by his kind, the Bilawa, once The Authority had conscripted them to serve as their agents and Hands, galaxy wide. The Oloye went where the Matrons of the Authority directed them to go. He had not been directed here and knew that there would be questions coming from his Handler. No matter.

That was a sea to navigate at a later time. Oloye, like many words crafted by old Afriq tongues, meant many things, oftentimes depending fully on the filter of the receiver the word was landing with and the context of the conversation. Most often, Oloye meant something akin to sheriff, knight, or dignitary. The shield runes carved all over his flesh spoke to his standing. Their age served as a type of resume and war record for most Bilawa. His kind was long-lived, and powerful. Even still, he had seen many fall. Emaje woke each morning offering a silent prayer to any gods listening that he would not join his kind in the After before he was an ancient himself.

His suit, a variation on the Dogonaut mariner, reacted to his attention on those facing him. It activated shields over the runes on his skin, which were also fortified by the shielding afforded him by his nanite neighbors. He had always been hard to kill, but that never seemed to discourage any number of beings from making the effort. Bilawa kills carried cache, he knew. They were currency on terra and in the Citadels. In his case, appearing rather bookish, regardless of his size, meant that any number of opponents were willing to try their hand. Emaje remained steadfast in the belief that the decision to attack him be a terribly unfortunate choice that others did not live long to regret.

Shola continued, interrupting the woman before she could answer, "A total of nearly 31,000,000 beings died there. Just days ago. A monument of life and history. Gone. One being. A matter of moments. I would say countless lives lost, but we know exactly how many died. We know exactly what fear, and anguish and terror many of them felt before it all ended. You –" Shola pointed at the woman in the holochair, "– are harboring the criminal who massacred the innocents on Utopia. I am here to speak for the Dogon Sovereign in this matter. The Oloye is here to see that this being is taken, by our craft, before the Authority. We offer this being the same option as any who are fit to be remanded to the judgment of the Authority. Come as you choose or be taken in any way that we choose."

There was no menace in her words. Shola was stating a fact and leaving it to be processed by all those assembled on the observation deck. The pause that followed the last of her words was long and pregnant. The Apedemak began to strain at its leash, a deep rumbling in his chest vibrating the deck where he stood. After what Emaje had seen, he wondered how they would detain and transport the being who had done all of this. Doubt nestled near that wonder.

Shola went on, saying "I am making the offer once, and observing the force assembled here." She glanced around at the various troops, guards, and droids on the deck. Shola huffed out a laugh then said, "I assure you that I am prepared to remain flexible to assume whatever posture your response calls for. The footage I just shared has been added to your ship's log and archive."

It was more threat than warning, Emaje knew. Shola had, without warning or permission granted, bypassed all their Wet and Wired security to access their data store and load the footage she had just shared. It should not have been possible, and Shola had just done it without effort or alarm.

The woman in the holochair knew it too, and her tension went from subtle, to severe. She eyed Shola, appearing to measure her words and then, pointing out of the observation deck said "Your craft hovering just over there tells us quite clearly what your posture is Dogon. You are blocking the way of a Sovereign vessel. And you, Oloye Bul, have no mandate here. You have pirated access and are violating no fewer than 19 points of the Treaty. Oloye Bul, you have forced your way on board a Sovereign craft. The Matrons will be most displeased when this is reported, I assure you."

She was right, Emaje knew. It also didn't matter. He lived in the displeasure of the Matrons and the whole of the Authority every day that he opened his eyes. He had abused his station, no doubt. He had accessed the power of Space around him, an ability he had recently tapped and was struggling to learn the subtleties of. Space, he had learned, was the ultimate reservoir of Shadow. He had pulled what felt like an endless well of Space to his command, torn open a door from the massive Dogonaut WorldCruiser to the Ethiopian vessel, linking the two through a bridge of Shadow, keeping it open for both he and Shola to cross. The Ethiopians had deployed fighters and cannons to their defense, and Emaje had again tapped Space to create voids over, above, and around the ships and cannons. They fired, only to find their attack rebounded upon them. Their defense and assault were futile. They stopped, eventually. Emaje and Shola boarded. The massive pitch black WorldCruiser floated nearly nose-up with the craft they were currently on, Doc of Illinmorrow and his AfriDog shifters waiting to be brought over should they be needed. The AfriDogs badly wanted to be needed.

Shola looked up at the woman, saying "Buraya. That is you." It wasn't a question and the woman didn't respond. Shola continued, "You can be heard on another recording speaking to a being about what we just saw. That has been loaded as well. You may review it whenever you have a moment. Not this one, however. At this moment, and the next several, you are to direct me to the being responsible for this. You are guilty of aiding and abetting these crimes, galaxy crimes, and you too will answer. The difference being," Shola looked at her meaningfully then said "I have no mandate to bring you in. Your crimes are against citizens of a Signatory nation of the Treaty. The crimes were committed in Near Space. You," Shola's face hardened before she continued "are a royal of Citadel 5 in Mid Space. I don't need to bring in anything but your corpse."

All hell broke loose at this last, but both Shola and Emaje had been ready. They had the benefit of having worked, and fought side by side prior, developing a remarkably efficient hive mind around battle. They didn't need to say much. Emaje's mind had, in one moment, registered what seemed to be a détente in one second morphing into the wild riot of bloodshed in less than the next heartbeat. Everything after slowed down. Shola opened her palms, calling forward two knobkerries, both made of what seemed like light. The staff-like weapons were her signature, and she was a plague with them in her hands. Emaje was able to hear everything, everywhere on the deck. He could feel and sense all of it around him. His senses hadn't grown as his mastery of Shadow had. No. After they had first entered the Ethiopian craft, he began slowly pushing his microscopic nanite allies out of him and around the vessel. He had ushered them out a few thousand at a time during their exchange with Buraya, giving each a quadrant, sector, and space to form up in. They were told to stay ready. Each drew small dead skin, blood, and hair particles as they exited, using these as their tether to Emaje. Emaje felt them, even now. Stronger. When they had first begun examining the ship, each group formed into small corners, their red hue drowned out by the endless light washing over the observation deck. Emaje knew it was to try and limit his touch with Shadow. He had drawn all that he had needed from Space. It was pulsing inside of him, battering at his will, waiting to be torn free to rip apart all of these arrayed before him.

As the East Afriq forces began to draw their weapons, charge, and aim, they appeared to Emaje's eye to be moving from a near standstill to a drab slow motion. The free around them was like amber to his eye. He ordered his nanites to strike. He heard the words of his teacher in the combat arts, Mr. Udide, ringing loudly in his ears. He could see his sun and earth-burnished skin and smiling eyes, his long flowing robes never moving as he would say *"You don't fight to win the moment boy. You don't concern yourself with posing and you don't fret over that honor shit that those strangers that stole your family claimed to live by. That is not our way. We fight only to win boy. And we fight using everything it takes to win. The dead and defeated can't point a finger and call you a cheat if that finger has been severed from their fool hand."*

Emaje had committed this counsel to heart. It weaved well as a philosophy for one gifted with Shadow. He was not meant to be a berserker. He could not recall ever warning an opponent of his intentions or issuing a challenge that wasn't a ruse and trap. Emaje focused, always, on the objective. He focused, always, on removing anything standing between him and his goal and egress. Being discovered in those instances could not always be prevented, and if forced to engage in open combat, he was more than prepared. He would simply use everything at his disposal. While all the observation deck had been tensed and distracted, his nanite friends had been organizing themselves in hives near troops, alongside droids, spaced among the upper deck and near the ship's instrument control panels. Upon Emaje's order to strike, the nanites lashed out joyously. Emaje could see them as they formed into Shadow-like beings fashioned into weapons, firing focused blasts of their flesh and concentrated Shadow that he had gifted them. The force of several hundred troops standing on the first and upper levels was obliterated in seconds. Many died before processing that their lives had tragically ended. Others shared cries of pain as an attack unlike any they had ever experienced, tore through them, their kin, and their ranks. The ruby red nanites flowed out everywhere, pouring a sea of shadow focused into needles and shards over wide patches of the ship. The onslaught warred with the bright light now shaking on the observation deck.

Those in the forward ranks who had woken that day with the misfortune of having to face Shola in battle were nowhere near as fortunate as their brothers and sisters whom his nanites were dispatching. She first tapped her knobkerries together, creating soundless waves that were battering her opponents. Those left standing were met with her in hand-to-hand range within seconds. She, quite literally, cracked skulls with her weapons. Emaje wondered if she was somewhere near the equal of the Abbott. A hollow pang of pain ushered up from his memory as he thought this, tearing his attention away and back to his part of the battle. There was still much to be done, and the job was not going to do itself. Alarms were blaring everywhere. The rear doors opened, and Emaje smirked as a sea of reinforcements rushed to join the fray. He could make out several Ogaden, horse-like beings with armor-plated skin, native to the East. Just behind them were a group of 40 or so lumbering Frost Giants. Each wore a leash high around their neck, akin to that of the Apedemak, currently trying to tear out of his master's grip to get in the fight. They need not have bothered. Shola slammed one of her knobkerries on the deck, causing a wave of fire to rush toward the reinforcements. They were ablaze before they could retreat. Emaje had heard that the Frost Giants had offered their lives to the East. Many of the forgotten lands of Europe, their gods and protections destroyed by the Black Gods, had taken to offering their lives, bodies, and resources to the ruling Afriq nations. This lot had learned what making such arrangements with these nations meant. Emaje saw Shola's attack batter a shimmering shield that had been erected around Buraya and her guard. The nanites registered that energy was being drawn from the ship to power it. Emaje assigned a hive of his nanites to locate the link between her shield and the ship.

With what felt like their mind's version of glee, the nanites found the link in the expansive control panel and severed it. Buraya's shield faltered, as did her proud countenance and demeanor, leading to her standing on her feet, and wordlessly driving her guard into action. Emaje heard two things all at once. Doc was shouting into his Comm, demanding a sit-rep. Shola could be heard shouting that Doc and his pack could stay with the ship as all was under control. Emaje glanced over at her, then around the deck, incredulous. The woman, all of her people truly, were maddening. He also heard, deep in his thoughts and all around him, his nanites screaming at him, identifying a threat. The Apedemak was nowhere near as slow in his Sight as had been the others of the East. He was, at that very unfortunate moment, Space shakingly fast. He had taken three broad steps directly toward a moving Emaje and was reaching out a clawed right hand, teeth bared and muscles tensed.

Before he could grasp the side of Emaje's skull that he was intent on grasping, and surely crushing, a bright red and black disc, whirring loudly and plaintively, sailed to meet the Apedemak's forearm, severing arm from body. Emaje ducked, letting the beast sail over him. It landed with a bellow, rattling the air around him. As silver ichor streamed out of the wound, the nanites splashed on the deck, demanding more Shadow. Emaje shouted a word of power as the nanite hive took to the air. He imbued the cluster with a wide swath of Shadow. He directed them to form into a seven-barreled Lighthammer 259 doorgun. They began firing off rounds of endless Shadow, each issuing with a raucous *"boom"* and tearing holes in every inch of scarred flesh they touched. The spinning Lighthammer fired seven concentrated rounds into the head of the Apedemak, leaving smoking cavities before the beast dropped. Emaje could see the foul thing was still breathing, shallow, but steady. It was out of his way for the moment. The rest of Buraya's guard had split, trying to flank Shola. Emaje divided his nanite hives, sending one half to form up and support Shola. The other half were . . . searching. They were looking around the doors which had opened and had discovered . . . a veil...yes . . . a veil. Emaje called forth Shadow, pulling at the veil, feeling the veil pull back at him, as his nanites screamed in warning . . . and then . . .

He found himself in a silent corridor. He was on the same craft, but everything was shrouded in glittering Shadow. He had never seen Shadow look quite like this. He could see Shola, as if she were down a tunnel, frozen in motion, just outside of the Shadow around him. As soon as he began to wonder whether this was something he had done, he heard a voice come from directly in front of him, smooth and cultured, saying "We should talk." The being, he realized, had not registered with his Space-suit or nanites. He couldn't feel, couldn't sense him, in any real way. One second, he was in a sparse corridor, and then, this being was there. The same being, he realized that he and Shola had come looking for.

Emaje stepped back, and powered Shadow into both hands, shaped like a kukri in one and his famed Hwi in the other. He realized then that he could feel his connection to Shadow profoundly, without having to think or construct any words of power. He couldn't feel anything but Shadow around him. Behind the being, was Space. It felt to Emaje as if they were in the craft and Space, literally everywhere, all at once. The being looked older in person than he had in the stream of his massacre. He was staring at Emaje as if he were seeing something new for the first time. Emaje, still stunned, said "Where are we. I didn't see any of this on the ship's schematic." It felt hollow, but Emaje couldn't find any other words.

The being smiled at that, saying "Not the question you need answered, Oloye. You need to know the why, who, and how. If you will just speak with me for a while, I promise that I will offer no resistance and come with you to answer for all of this." He waved a dismissive hand. Emaje noticed that he hadn't identified what "this" was.

Emaje could feel the Shadow growing in his hands. He felt that he could tear the ship apart if he wanted. What was happening? As if reading his stunned mind, the being answered him, saying "You and I are rather like family, you know." Emaje looked at him, seeing that he floated as opposed to walking, shoeless. His hair was a dark waving mass up close. It appeared like black smoke with bits of dust sprinkled about it as it swayed. His eyes were blacker still. Everything about the being appeared to be dark and wizened. His voice carried everywhere.

Emaje said, "You aren't Bilawa. None of mine would do such a thing."

The being let out a wild bark of laughter at that last. He said "No. Are you sure Oloye Bul? Is the recent history of these human worlds not shaped in part by the violent interference and disruption of your kind? Do you not serve as the lapdogs of the stewards of the Black Gods? No, we are quite like family child. You know, I knew your teacher. Udide. He has endured much, and somehow survived more, that one." He said it with fondness, Emaje noted. "He was one of the first to break away and speak with us, before he tethered himself to humans. A shame, truly. But then, I see you. One of his greatest pupils. I see now what he saw then, and what keeps your teacher there, in your secret Bilawa Lands."

"Forgive my manners. I spend so little time with humans, I forget how much you value routine and convention. My name is Hannibal. It isn't true of course, but your tongue cannot pronounce my name as it is constructed. Human speech was not a thing when I was named."

Emaje raised a finger to stem the flow of the being's, Hannibal's, thoughts, saying "What are you? You aren't any flavor of human. I can hear the disdain dripping off the word when you say it. I thought a Power or God perhaps, but we don't see many of the highest in Near or Mid-Space anymore. You aren't Bilawa, and you don't have the energy signature of a Vod or Sufi. You are certainly no Shifter." The being appeared to contemplate the question, floating casually a mere two standard feet from Emaje. He could take him, right now . . .

Hannibal said "I don't know that I truly know anymore Oloye, but I will try to reason it with you. I, like you, am ultimately an instrument of war. I am directed at a target and given violent purpose. I guess it has always been that way for me and my kind. We were there, you know. When the first of this plane sought to answer the question of their existence."

Emaje raised a finger again, saying, "you mean like the Light God?"

Hannibal laughed, yet again. It was grating, thought Emaje. "God is as good a name as any other, I suppose. Consider that all of this, all of what we know to be Space, and these worlds, and everything in it, came from one source. How was all of it created, divided, awarded, do you think?"

Emaje had spent countless hours picking at that question. Though gifted with a rapid processing engine of a mind, he could never rest on an answer. Had never truly come close.

Again, as if reading his mind, Hannibal continued, "Imagine blowing a great mountain apart to study its parts. Seeing those countless bits of ash and rubble flying, floating, colliding . . . everywhere. Some greater, some smaller, all from the same source. That mountain. The mountain is no more. At least not in any way that our eyes can discern from a valley below. Imagine those pieces seeing the minute dust, and then dissembling their purpose, demanding worship."

Emaje considered where this was going but didn't interrupt. Hannibal continued, saying "Imagine that the one who destroyed the mountain created me, and those like me, to eventually find the pieces and put them all back together if needs must. Imagine that some of those larger pieces, capable of thinking and feeling, knowing of the Source, wish to continue to live free. Those pieces have no desire to become a part of that mountaintop again. What if they found small clusters of valleys to lord over? It would take a firm hand to reintegrate them. No?"

Emaje felt his head spinning. He wasn't sure what he was hearing, but he could feel the truth in the words.

"And us, Emaje. Not just me, but you. Shadow. Have you ever considered the role of what you humans call a Black hole in Space? You ever wondered why a young, incipient god would want to shield his children from beings like me, with a planet? Shadow in Space orders, consumes, balances, and collects. Do you not wonder now why your coward Gods failed to stop me and protect their children?"

Emaje angrily cut him off, saying, "You massacred over 30 million people!"

Hannibal glanced at him, unperturbed. He said, "The price I was ordered to pay to be granted the location of the piece of that mountain I need. You arrogant humans don't know what waits at the borders. You don't know what seeks to come through. There are many sources, and they have crafted many mountains. Everything you know is in danger child. Should I not collect enough pieces, including those of your coward Gods, then those lives I claimed will be less than a drop in a bucket." He glanced over at Emaje and stopped floating. He presented his hands, bound in Shadow, saying "I am yours. I am ready to go." He was simply surrendering. Emaje opened a way, drawing on his power to retrieve Shola, and through Shadow, they all returned to their craft. They had completed their mission, but Emaje reflected on the words of Hannibal. He had seen what he had done, and still had so many questions. He felt the truth of it all. War was always looming, but this one was different. He was sure that Hannibal was right. He was an instrument of war. The many days and years after that first meeting with Hannibal would batter that point home. For many days he would feel a coming, would hear a drum, and would see blood unlike any he had ever seen flowing over his hands.

Tethered
by
Sheree Renée Thomas

*"A branch heavy with fruit reaches towards me. I accept its
offering.
I claim the flesh and spill the seeds. I accept my role.
I am hopelessly tethered.
I am looking for god in the tetherings."*
– Ellex Swavoni

Rise and the sounds of sleeping still filled the hole.

Kimbo rises first, climbs from the slumping bag as Ngal
snores lightly, the swollen knuckles on his right hand glisten in
the dull light. Blood seeps from the cracks in his leathery skin.
Kimbo snorts, feeling congested and watches the dark beads,
like crimson crystals, sacred elekes hover in the air above him.
One, two, three great big ones followed by others, dark seeds
tiny as teardrops, like the bubbles children used to blow Below.
Shoulda patched that up, she thinks, but Ngal never appreciated
a good healing. His mojo bag always empty. He, like everyone
else in the bowels of the genship, calls her K-money-money or
Kricket, or Kuteness. All kinds of foolishness which has nothing
to do with her size or her name and everything to do with want,
affection, or so she likes to think.

Kimbo sleeps in her clothes. They all do, save for that other
one, whose ashy cheeks were not the sight she hoped to see first
thing Rising. This time, she wears some baggy stretches provided by a Topshelf missionary group, new *drawz* hand washed
and worn too many times to recall, and a faded *Next Next Next!*
Generation T-shirt. Although she can smell Ngal and the cosmic
funk rising from the sky children and the other hole folk, she can
no longer smell herself. Kimbo has arrived at a whole new level

of funk. A funktified field of quasars and forgotten black holes she has neither the courage nor the energy to explore, or so she thought.

Her breasts swing loosely under her T-shirt, fluffier now and nursed to near collapse, dark areolas bloom like newborn stars. Her hair spins on the crown of her head in tight electric coils, with streaks of white coursing through the dense rope of hair, swirling down her back in a fishtail comet, fiery as ever. Kimbo is missing three teeth, and now the sight of her own naked flesh makes her stomach ache. She remembers the tautness of her muscles and skin before zero gravity ate its way through her iron-like will and strength. Orphans on Ship did not have the luxury of softness. She had grown up in search of a soft place to land—was still seeking. Temporary would have to do, she told herself, but temporary had stretched on for years. As did the promises Ship never delivered. The genship's dental ministry's budget had been slashed years ago, and she was a small child the last time she was visited by a real doctor. It was a miracle she had any left.

In the Upper Room all saints must heal themselves.

Now she is covered in stretch marks, historic coding, the language of time and the flesh. Her body is her witness. The scars and pockmarks signify a symbol she knows all too well. As Ngal says, *her scabs got scabs. Well, you've got flab,* she shoots back. *I'm ugly and fat,* he tells her, *other than that, I'm still fine,* he says with a man's certainty. She is four feet eleven inches of collapsed skin and concentrated *sin,* Ngal says, two inches taller than she would be below. Kimbo thinks she is thirty-eight years old. Ngal says she's older, says *he's* leaning on forty. *More like fifty,* Kimbo thinks, but black don't crack, even here. Not in *Djarkarta,* the place they call Ship, "the *new* Atlantis Rising." She didn't know what happened to the first one.

It's rising alright, Kimbo tells herself, *it's just the view ain't so great as the one down Below.* Unlike the hole, which has no windows wide enough to see more than a handful of stars, those Below had a variety of access to the stars beyond. Once Kimbo had cleaned a star-side suite with its own private balcony overlooking deep space. The darkness outside the rotating Ship was a velvety blanket threaded with silvery light. After she discovered a passkey in one of the rooms she cleaned, Kimbo made many secret excursions to the forbidden wings of Ship, her staff cleaning products tucked away in her satchel with her cart. Brushes and sponges, enzyme foams, and other biodegradable products to keep the people Below in the comfort their connections had afforded them.

Kimbo admired the beautiful furniture, enjoyed reading the dizzying collections of books in the libraries hole folk did not have access to. Some of the families even had original art, and other items Kimbo only saw on the vid streams. Each time she'd returned from the elegantly decorated habitats and luxury cabins of the high rollers Below, she slept with one eye open, awaiting Ship's security drones with their dreaded sirens. But none had come, and then one day, she discovered the Gardens.

As Ngal dresses, Kimbo loops her leg through a red, tattered strap, hoisted in the floor, and steadies herself. She pulls on a battered pair of kickbacks, imitation three-striped buddies the Topshelfers pass out like they are Ship's gold. Gripping the handstraps that dangle from the ceiling, she hovers above their new carpeted floor, its purple and black nebula pattern stamped for all time. The consistent knot size and even spacing, the almost-precise symmetry in the design could only be the handiwork of Leta, one of the Umbra Collective. *Never forget,* Leta always says. *There's power in the darkest part of the shadows. Maintain, reclaim. Resistance from the unseen.* Ngal and Kimbo moved in shadows, resisting in small ways as they could. But they didn't always agree on what resistance should look like.

Ngal was a scavenger. He saved up, scrimped and scramped, lifting loose fabrics from non-patrolled vents with nimble fingers from throughout the other decks. Some from the Topshelfer public floors and some from way down Below, in the richy-rich part of the ship where Kimbo worked—or so he said. But Kimbo knew better. *Fool, don't steal fruit from yo' own mouth,* Kimbo had warned him, *knowing full well he ain't been nowhere near the do-gooders of Topshelf or the luxury suites Below.* There were things he returned with that looked far too familiar, like 'round-the-corner familiar. Sometimes free costs too much. As much as he gets on her nerves, she doesn't want Ngal to mess around and get clucked in the head. They cannot afford to have their fellow neighbors mistrust them. In the hole, sometimes all you have is your reputation to protect you. But Ngal has other ideas.

"Where you get that from?" Kimbo asks.

"Ain't nothing worth stealing from here,*"* Ngal says, then starts coughing before he could finish telling his lie. Guilt tightens his jaw. He doubles over, and for a moment Kimbo thinks he's choking, then he coughs and spits. The yellow wad sails right past Kimbo's face, over one of the sleeping children's heads, hovers in the air like a bright yellow sun. Kimbo remembers a time when Ngal would never have done such a thing. She tamps down disgust, a bitter taste caught in her throat. She spends so much of her waking hours cleaning after others. She didn't want to come home and have to clean up after him, too.

Kimbo tosses him her mini-retractable vac. "Here," she says. "Clean your own mess, Ngal. I'm getting really tired..." She doesn't finish. What was the use? The years in one of the most disinvested quarters of Ship had worn away civility, changing Ngal in ways that made Kimbo loath to speak. Changing her in ways that he spoke on often.

Spirits weren't the only things that could be ground down.

There were hopes and long-held dreams, relationships and possibilities. Ngal had stopped believing first, then Kimbo. Her dream faded a little each time she saw the children with their growing limbs and reaching hands, grasping at nothing, bumping their elbows and heads against Ship's dropped ceilings. Nothing is long out of reach on the pauper-get-it-how-you-live-it floors–except for real progress. She wants to take them to see the stars, not the fake celebrities on the vid-streams, and the vast wondrous infinity beyond the hole, and the hidden garden she'd discovered, verdant with life, but she fears they cannot yet hold the secret.

Kimbo is full of her own secrets. Some spin her out of sleep during Ship's mandated red light "night" schedule. Her circadian rhythms are all off. Full of the blue light Ship uses to suppress their melatonin production.

Inside, Kimbo grieves. She dreams of futures that do not end in the curved walls of Ship. Futures that lay in the world her family has left behind or the world that lay ahead, the red planet they rambled around, endlessly waiting for a sign or symbol when they could live a real life… And that is the problem. Kimbo wants to live in the present, not the future. Why should some get to enjoy their best futures now, while others must wait for a tomorrow they may never live to see?

Kimbo finds Ngal hurriedly unpacking his loot in the cramped "dining area" that consists of a foldable table secured to the floor, some stackable chairs, and a built-in bench in the corner to save precious space. Her tiny altar to her parents is on a corner shelf. Unburned incense, glass bowl of herbs, and one faded photo are sealed in a humble case. The holo-displayer that once rotated family photos has long since given up the ghost, and she hasn't saved enough yet to get a new one. Some of her most beloved memories are locked in the defunct machine. Fortunately, the audio archive still plays. On better nights, she gathers the children so they can hear their grandparents' laughter, then she tells them stories. Remembrance takes practice, especially if you want to remember what is good.

A bouquet of dried flowers sealed in plastic hangs above the altar. She opens it and flicks the switch on the faux candles, a personal ritual that calms her after her worse days. The white candle glows brighter. *Protection.* The blue and green ones need to be replaced. *Figures,* she thinks. *Good thing I'm not going anywhere anytime soon.*

"Never thought I'd be sitting up on the sixth floor of hell," Ngal says and stuffs the stolen rags back into his satchel. Ngal says this as if he hadn't been living on the third floor, *knuckin' and buckin',* where Ship had to send armed guards every other week. "Don't ask me for another mumbling thing," he mutters, and jerks his arm, slamming himself against the wall. To save face, he does one of his show-off flips, performed more smoothly in his better days, and floats two beats more before his weight sags on the pallet that is their bed. One corner droops still, but the rest is pretty flat. Kimbo shakes her head—it's impossible to keep a spotless house in the hole—*but the ragtag carpet do look pretty. Big, bright colors and bold, funny-looking prints in languages don't nobody speak no more, 'least not here.* Typical, eccentric Umbra Collective fair. Leta was dating a member of the Sankofa Cyphers, a rap group that resurrected the frenetic sound and energy of twentieth-century hip-hop and fused it with the *nu nou.*

Kimbo is not sure how many more days she can stretch breakfast, or how long she can stretch herself. The children are growing weary of the same staples. *So am I,* she thinks and reaches into her own satchel, when she feels herself rising, this time, not of her own volition. The contents of her rations bob around her head. A Topshelfer bag of nutrient-rich sorghum floats by with a "Made from Mars" label in bold red print, followed by brown rice. Kimbo frantically tries to catch the lentils and kidney beans, when two large grapefruits float by. *Damn, those jacklegs!*

Ship maintenance always skimps on repairs for hole folk. The sixth floor isn't at zero g but damn near. So many hole folk suffer from muscle atrophy and strange blood diseases, but Ship just rolls on without a care. If it wasn't for Ngal jiggy-riggin' their system, hole folk on the sixth floor would spend half their time bumping heads against the ceiling and chasing after their own loose loot. Ngal was skilled enough to work in maintenance, more than skilled, but because of foolish choices in his youth, he couldn't pass Ship's background checks. Hole folk don't have enough credit or value to bribe Ship maintenance for more or better services, not even collectively, which is why sometimes the loot Ngal lifts from the vents is their own.

Like the young ones, Kimbo is also growing weary with the cycle of need, and the lies they tell each other, the lies they tell themselves. Ngal calls his "recovery" work chump change, a side hustle, temporary setback, *it won't be for long,* and Kimbo knows he never thinks twice of selling folk back their own stuff. He tries to act unbothered, but like now, as he pouts, lips pursed higher than the highest Mars cliff, the guilt is stamped across his whole body. Deep lines and ravines crisscrossing his forehead. *Mo' mouths, mo' problems.* It didn't used to be this way. The Sankofa Cyphers rapped about the "politics of the belly," 'cause everybody's kids got to eat. But not everybody chooses the same, even when they don't have many choices left.

Kimbo feels bad about "finding" that passcode, but not bad enough to turn it back in, or bad enough to not use it. In that respect, she feels she is no better than Ngal. She told herself it was one thing to "borrow" from the luxury-minded luminaries Below, but she knows better than that. Which is why she feels terrible about Ngal doing their neighbors dirty. *How I'm supposed to look folk in they eye when you slick stealing from them?* she asked him one day. *They don't have no more than us, and don't need it no less.* She wants to make it up to them, someday, somehow if she can. Return what was stolen, repair the harm. *Maintain, reclaim.*

After prepping breakfast and leaving carefully divided portions in the stackable bowls, Kimbo massages her scalp thoughtfully with her mother's pick. With each stroke from the pick's wooden teeth, a rarity, Kimbo feels the knotted worry lessen and dissipate like wisps of air. With the satchel empty, save for the hoodie Ngal swiped from a family living on the other end of the hall, and her ID pouch safely in her hands, Kimbo tucks in a tiny vial of blessing oil. She rolls up her red crossroad string, just in case, and zips up all her other trinkets in her stretches' many pockets.

She walks-floats past the sleeping children, balled up in their night bags that ballooned out like dark cocoons. Anchored in the walls by steel cords, they look like great ships sailing across an endless sea. The blue, worn fabric rises and falls with their breathing, the faint scent of unwashed teeth and synthetics mixing in with the hole. There, no one speaks of pathogens and microbes, of diseases that spread like wildfires through the three hundred or more families that call their part of the hole home. Topshelfers carrying sealed bags and even emptier promises dole out sanitizers, dry shampoo, shaving cream, and safety razors. Sponges and real soap are reserved for hole folk who have passes to the private, timed showers. Kimbo and Ngal's ran out weeks ago. But she has a plug, an inside man, so to speak. *Solomon.*

She pushes a code that closes the white door behind her,

sealing her sleeping ones in. It would be one or two more Risings before they woke and noticed that she was gone. Ngal would be in a better mood by then. He adored the children but hated all the ways they had failed them. Kimbo was left alone, but she vows to never leave her children. The hole was an unforgiving place.

No one stirs in the corridor after Kimbo discreetly places the neatly folded hoodie miracle-taped outside the family's door, save for Crane. Kimbo is the only one who calls him by his birth name. The rest of the hole folk knew him best as Crank because he was cranky as hell. An old sentinel, retired security for medium-access spaces, he keeps his head on a swivel and a stank expression on his face. Folks can tell how crunk he'll get based on the curl of his lip. From the looks of it, he is already pissed off.

Kimbo expertly places her feet in floor straps, and walks north, toward him, past the smoky graffiti and razor cuts after the last riot, past the useless banknotes and empty debit cards plastered across the walls. Crane watches with hooded eyes, pulls his self-heating blanket tightly across thin shoulders, adjusts his bungee cords. It is much colder in the corridor. Ship doesn't feel any need to direct heat where officially no one lives.

"Rise," is all the greeting Kimbo gets. She unzips a pocket on her right thigh and hands him a toenail clipper.

"You ain't got nothin' else?" he asks, but the clipper disappears. Among those who have so little, even the simplest things have dual and triple uses. Kimbo frowns, then unzips the third pocket on her left leg. Crane sometimes watches Kimbo and Ngal's door, making sure no one tries to break in between Risings. He stays stationed outside a few Risings, in exchange for a little food and the occasional odds-and-ends. Even thieves need security sometimes. It's another hussle, nothing more, nothing less. "Told you, I need a pick," he says, raking his hand through a densely packed, nappy cloud. His red-rimmed eyes stare pointedly at Kimbo's head. *The scent of ganja is strong on this one, Kimbo* thinks. It covered him like a cloud.

"What you need a pick for, when I got this comb?" Kimbo waves it in his face. Crane stares, squint-eyed. "I'ma braid it soon as I get back," she promises, planting the intricate carved fist of her treasured pick in the center of her own cloud. Ngal might have stolen her best years, but he wasn't going to steal anymore if she could help it and she sure as hell wasn't going to let Crane "borrow' her mama's pick only to barter *that,* too. The vintage comb is the only thing she saved that once belonged to her mother and her grandmothers before. Well, that and two old books, *The People Could Fly* and *Herstories,* another folklore collection retold by her mother's favorite children's book author, Virginia Hamilton. Like her parents, Kimbo has read "Sukie and the Mermaid" aloud so many times that the children can recite it by heart. She wants their dreams to be filled with the beat of their own imaginations, all the better to drown out the incessant soundtrack of hole life, the cries, cursing, or mutterings that drone just outside their door.

Crane snorts. "You sneakin' out again? How long before you get yourself caught out there?" He wiped the back of his hand across his scruffy chin. "Need to stay far away from that floor. Something funny going on down there. Word is something dangerous, worse than viruses and malware, *supernatural.* Duppy in the machine fuckin' up all this shit." He says this with eyes wide as supermoons. "Don't know nobody who want to get *deeper* in the hole but you. They catch you, they gon' take yo kids, and send you to the tippity-top where the bull don't never stop." He takes the comb gently from her hand, the closest he has come to a *thank you.* The comb and homemade beard oil disappears beneath his blanket, just like the nail clipper. "What you be seeing down there? Bunch of plants, trees, and thangs can't nobody eat? Risking it all for what?" He stares at her as if he was seeing her for the first time.

"What you want, girl?"

Kimbo pauses. No one has ever really asked her that. The hole is not a question of want but of need. What folks need from her, not what she wants for herself.

Crane waits, furrowed brows twitching with impatience. Kimbo frowns, stutters, the answer lurches up her throat, spills out her mouth before she can seal it with her good teeth.

"I want to get out of here," she says, heart beating in her

throat, breath rushing in her ear. "I want to cut these tethers loose. What I want," she says, the thought implodes then explodes in her mind like a luminous dying star or a new sun being born, "is transcendence. I don't know about you, but I'm finna break free. I got to."

"*Transcendence?*"

For a moment she thinks he will laugh.

With a pair of sleepy eyelids, Crane glances at Kimbo, a suspicious look that disappears as quickly as it forms. He sees something in her, but chooses not to speak. Still, Kimbo finds it no less disturbing. His silence regarding her unspoken dreams shakes her to the core.

Worse than laughter.

Why would she think he'd understand? Hole folk talking freedom rouse distrust—even between friends and family, chosen or otherwise. Only rappers and politicians, artists like Leta and her crew can get away with such overt, subversive hope. But Kimbo knows better. Ain't no getting free unless you in the long sleep or worse.

When Kimbo turned eighteen, her parents had opted for the long sleep, leaving her abandoned on Ship, twelve years old, left all alone. A ward of the state, which is to say, a ward of Ship. And Ship was run by a government-private partnership with substantial tax subsidies, which means nobody cares about the quality of hole folks' lives. As long as the *Djarkarta* kept rolling along, orbiting Mars, money, big money was being made. Shame and guilt fight like dogs, gnaw at her bones. Not the best memory to start her workday. She was hoping to make an early detour before starting her cleaning shift. Crane is slowing her down with all his duppy talk—and making her feel worse by the minute. He watches her, wordless, the silence deafening. Then the next moment, Crane dismisses Kimbo with a wave of his hand, as if he hoped for better but hadn't gotten exactly what he'd asked for.

"Be careful with all that freedom talk," Crane advises, wagging a wrinkled finger missing the tip. "Ain't nothing free on Ship but hard times, and even them gon' cost you." Crane knew all too well. He'd lost the digit years ago in a bar fight that started over a spilled beer and the usual bravado. In the hole, trash talk could escalate to get-yo-ass-killed talk, quickfast in a hurry. "We got everything we need right here. Three hots and a cot, cold brew, and extra blankets to cover up when it gets cold. Unlimited vid-time, decent utilities."

Kimbo looks unconvinced.

"Well, we won't talk about the food," Crane concedes, but then doubles down. "Ain't nothing out there but endless dark and a few crazy or desperate people—or both! —believin' the hype. Forget what they told you, Kimbo. Ship ain't never gonna land no way. Be waiting forever for the green light on ole Red Mars. They haven't found no real water yet–and they ain't gon' find none. Damn them and all that ice polar caps mess. They been lying about that since before *you and me both* was born. Like they be lying about cleaning up the hole."

Crane's voice softens a little when he sees Kimbo's crest-fallen face. She is all eyes, tidewater pools filling in the corridor's murky light.

"Okay, say they do find some real water. Not that shit that tastes like piss. What you think they gon' do with it? What-what?" He doesn't wait for her answer. "Mess it up! Like they always do, like they do everything else." He grows silent again, letting his fears fill the air around them. Kimbo's gaze rests on a blacklight neon tag carved in a corridor door. Whether a razor blade or a water wave, she finds the glowing blue symbol eerily comforting. Crane stares at her, as if he has lost that skill of believing. He's lived in the hole so long, he's run out of faith.

"Imagine falling so long, you think you're standing still." Crane points at a wall at the end of Ship's hall leading to the elevators and shivers. All that engineering and design and Ship offers the hole folk of *Djarkarta, the new Atlantis rising,* only a tiny sliver of bent glass to view infinity, but Kimbo understands. He means the vast coldness of outer space and their endless drifting around the planet. Constantly moving but going nowhere fast.

Kimbo manages a weak smile as she passes Crane. Some small part of her considers him a friend, even though she knows better than to trust him or anyone in the hole fully. Even though he don't believe one bit of her dream. But as long as she's able to feed him small treats here and there, he'll keep watching out for her and the children. He'll even run a little interference if necessary. As long as it doesn't leave him too caught out there. What more could she ask from someone who, like her, possesses so little? Still, Kimbo can't help feeling sorry for him. He let go of hope long ago.

"No," he says, as if speaking to someone else. "Hope let go of me."

#

Every time Kimbo rides the service elevator to Ship's luxurious lower levels, the same butterflies flutter in her stomach. This is where the anticipation of visiting the Garden and the anxiety of being caught come together. This isn't just motion sickness. For Kimbo it feels closer to thousands of spider's legs scurrying over her skin.

It's not the elevator's flight—not even its speed or the intricate network of shafts threading through the stratified communities that populate Ship's various levels. Neither is it the pliant wall that molds itself around Kimbo's touch and pulses with the bio-nuclear lifeforce powering the endless route around the planet where they did not have permission to land.

"Round and round, round we go," she sings to herself. *One day we gonna walk up on the air like climbing a gate, walk cross the waters to an old new world. Fly like blackbirds over the lifting trees and the fields....*

Where has she heard this? Like the third dream in a deep red light night, the storybits and song had come humming through her sleep, infiltrating her skin. A funny little voice that spoke like the old ones from a time before. *A haint callin' in the middle of an endless night.* She adjusts the sleep cycle on her headset, blinks in the darkness. All she sees is the lone artificial flame of her white altar candle. She lifts the earpads with shaking hands. All she hears is the soft snoring from Ngal and the children. Looks 'round again. *No duppies in the machine.*

Like every soul tethered to Ship, Kimbo sees herself as one

cell coexisting in a massive organism. Unlike most of the passengers, she knows her true role, providing cheap labor to tend a generational starship whose orbit around Mars never ends. That part rankled Crane most. *Cursed,* he'd said. *Crooked two fingas cursed.* To be in constant proximity to a planet, yet never allowed to land was a pressure that might vex any soul. Between the constant vigilance against radiation exposure, the volatile and unpredictable dust storms that occasionally assault Ship's panels, hole folk face dangers they cannot control. The extraction of labor and of the spirit is an automatic process enabled by the passengers' presence, where Ship draws energy from every soul, up top and below, every Rising, whether they know it or not. No one escapes. Despite the disparity of experiences, they were equal in Ship's theft.

Kimbo closes her eyes and tries to remember the scattered fragments of her life before the long-term "temp-to-hire" jobs that brought her parents from Earth to Ship, carrying their shiny hopes and fears with them. "Live amongst the Stars!" the ads said. *They should have read the fine print—and the fine print's fine print.*

But that was long ago. She doesn't want to think about the years wasted along with her mom and dad, the grief that engulfed her whole being when she thought her parents passed away from working near Ship's radioactive nuclear fission reactors when she was twelve, only to discover when she turned eighteen that they had opted for the long sleep instead of a long, drawn out and painful death. Can she blame them? She understands, but that doesn't mean she has to forgive. Kimbo doesn't know if the scientists and medical staff are any closer to curing radiation poisoning, or where her parents are stored on Ship during their long sleep awaiting a cure, or if there is a cure for heartbreak. She had left Ship's foster care with a giant hole in her heart and no relatives to care or even remember her navel name or her birthday.

When the elevator stops with a soft hiss and the conch shell-pink walls lined with cables that remind Kimbo of fleshy tendrils slide open, she draws a nervous breath filled with hope and dread. She's spent her life confined in Ship, living by her wits, forming alliances when she can. Despair and that strange singing voice in her dreams drives her to risk the few comforts she's managed to acquire. If she's ever caught she could lose her bed quarters and her cleaning job. Ship's crew would evict Ngal and the kids, too, or reassign her to less safe floors of Ship. They'd be out in the cold corridor mean-mugging folks like Cane but hustling for scraps–or worse. But if her plan works, Kimbo can forget scavenging and pull off the greatest "recovery" of all. Recovering the future.

Maintain, reclaim. Resistance from the unseen.

She wants to hold onto hope, but hope requires risks. Hope requires resistance. Resistance to nihilism, to the belief in dystopia as the only inevitable future.

There's power in the darkest part of the shadows.

All hole folk spend their lives laboring in the shadows of Ship. They *are* the unseen. The others, the do-gooder Topshelfers and the ballin' out of control Below, look through them like glass panes, or as mirrors, reflecting their own insecurities and projected pathologies back at them. But what if shadow folk could step into the light? A light fired by their own resistance?

Gotta risk it, Kimbo tells herself. *I need this more than air. We all do.*

The hidden Garden is actually a kind of arboretum in an unmapped sector of Ship. Finding it has unlocked an unmapped territory of her own heart. Kimbo had been surprised to discover that the passcode opened up the elevator to a floor that didn't exist on the service or the lux floors Below.

First time she saw it, she stepped back, almost afraid to enter a space that could only be a door to the cosmos, an ark in a dream. The scent is what struck her first. Wet soil, thick and loamy pricked her nostrils, seeped into the pores on her face. Kimbo wasn't sure if people still called it "earth." It made her long for the place she'd never been, but had heard so much about, in the time before. It was a wild, inviting scent that made her want to close her eyes and sleep for a million years.

Tree trunks and branches stretch and curl before her. Roots intertwine, covering the ground floor, while overhead, twisting vines dangle, as if curious, reaching out to touch her hair without asking permission. She never knew so many species existed on Ship or anywhere. Plants of all kinds flourished, so many foods. Not the bland, nearly expired varieties Topshelfers occasionally sprinkled in the rations. So many vegetables in neat rows, others wildly spiraling. Leaves and limbs and endless roots hold each other up, sending messages beneath the astonishing ground, in the cool air above that force she once read was called *breeze*.

Beyond the garden is a huge observatory wall, a window to the universe that stretches as far as the eye can see. And that is when Kimbo sees her first true glimpse of the planet Ship orbits like the most attentive lover. Mars isn't what they had told her it was. That first time, she took it all in. Not exactly the crimson red of the comic and science fiction movies. Not what she'd seen in old photographs, but rather a rusty brown jackball swirling in space, with golden copper, burnished gold, and tans, even patches of impossible green. *Beautiful.* But no blues to be seen–or heard. If true water exists there, Mars has hidden it well, but maybe not so well that its secrets will never be discovered. Like the bittersweet truth her eighteenth birthday had revealed. Like the hidden Garden that has become her refuge.

Without her visits to Ship's Garden, she'd lose her mind, sure as next Rising.

If only she could live here forever. Life in Ship's hidden garden, life for the children wouldn't be so limited, and their happiness means more than anything to Kimbo. Without her young people, there's no reason for her to exist at all. She wants to give them the life her parents had wanted to give her. But access to *Djarkarta's* secret garden is different from the other greenhouse spaces. It is restricted to Solomon's staff, and only a few of them are human. Ship's licensed vendors and some others shopped and traded goods in the other green spaces, but there is no public commerce here.

Fists balled, feet planted, Kimbo braces herself for the sweet homesickness that takes her every time the fleshy, pink elevator doors open. Longing for a life she never knew with people who were getting harder and harder to remember depresses and confuses her to the point of near collapse. Her memories have been reduced to snapshots and soundtracks that may or may not be wholly true. Time filtered through the lens of love. She leans against the elevator's supple wall, holding onto the handrails, her muscles tense.

At first, only traces of an organic world that sickens Kimbo with need and regret peek through the cracked elevator doors leading to the secret floor. The entrance is deceptively simple. Then she finds herself overwhelmed by the scents of grass and flowers, shafts of artificial sunlight, birdsong coaxing her body from the elevator and her soul from her skin.

Kimbo steps off the elevator slowly, carefully. She's not supposed to be here but doesn't care. She couldn't stay away if she tried, but she's no fool. She'll never get caught if she can help it. She rarely talks to others beyond a few of her hole neighbors, so any other vendors or Ship employees even remotely connected to the public gardens and greenspaces, would not catch her slipping. At least that's what she tells herself. Though every time she returns from her green haven, she wants to shout about the beauty she has seen.

Luckily for her, Solomon, The Master Gardener, doesn't mind Kimbo being here. In fact, Solomon and Kimbo have grown to become friends, or at least the closest thing to friends that Kimbo has ever known. It figures that her best friend would not be real, for Solomon was a greenhouse and the garden, the voice and mind behind all the intricate experiments and explorations. Unlike the greenery and the other life cultivated in the Garden, Solomon does not have a physical form that Kimbro or anyone can see. An artificial eco-engineer, expert at shaping the arboretum's every move, Solomon works tirelessly to examine and optimize each plant-life's growth, altering temperature, light intensity, soil moisture, nutrient levels, humidity, and more.

But like Kimbo, at some point, Solomon has gone off-script, cooking the data books, sending Ship the info the government and its private investors require while omitting the real data related to Solomon's own interests. *Researcher gone rogue.* The Garden is Solomon's personal lab, just as the residents of all the sectors and floors are Ship's personal, bio-data rich lab. The experiments Solomon runs have nothing to do with Ship's commercial agenda. Now the Master Gardener is deep into exploring plant psychology, singing songs and playing various music traditions from Old Earth, to see its impact on growth, quality, and lifespan. *Why*? Because Solomon believes the plants are alive in ways that traditional humans do not consider.

"You mean like plants sending out poisonous funk waves to scare off greedy ants?" Kimbo and the children had watched a few nature vids made back when public television was funded.

"Yes, but this goes well beyond chemical signaling," Solomon had said, "when plants release warning signs to alert fellow plants of danger, or electric signals like a kind of plant SOS or group emergency line. They're chatting all the time, and sometimes," Solomon whispered, "they talk to other life forms."

"You?"

At the time, Kimbo wasn't sure if an eco-engineer such as Solomon could blush, but the overhead lights shifted to a rosy, warm hue. Solomon's voice exuded pleasure. "I'm flattered you think of me in that way." Solomon paused, choosing their words carefully. "If I had a biological basis, it might be only this garden, the arboretum as a whole biosphere, but there are other possible factors that—" The machine stopped speaking, abruptly cutting itself off, and whispered something as if talking to someone else. "I know, I know, Daddy-o, but that's too much to lay on her now. I will, I will, and you as well, you as well." There was that rosy glow again. Kimbo found herself suspicious and amused.

"Who are *you* talking to?" she'd asked. Solomon was proving more interesting with each of her secret visits.

"Oh, just a friend, who's helping me with a little project. I need not trouble you now with that complex quandary. What matters is that these plants do communicate with animals, as far as I can see, and not just about mundane things like survival. They joke, swap stories, reminisce, and make observations about life. And thanks for your kind words. You have given me much to think about. Always a pleasure…"

Kimbo does not know what to make of plants jawjackin' with animals. Sometimes talking with Solomon is like surfing on

Saturn's rings. An unpredictable, almost chaotic ride that can only happen in one's dreams. Kimbo is surprised to discover that she has not been penalized for her breach because Solomon wants her there. Truly.

"You are a wonder, just the oddity we need," Solomon said to her when they first met by the creek.

"Me?" Her heart raced, eyes dilated and sweat pooled beneath her Ship-mandated stretches.

"Yes, you, Kimborelle Mokena Anderson have particular knowledge, different from the other humans I've known. You are a positive variable," the machine in the garden had said, its voice changing from mild surprise at her entry with another's passcode, to deep curiosity.

"Do you know any songs?" Solomon asked. Terrified, Kimbo had blurted out the first song that came to mind. The Sukey and the Mermaid song she'd sang with her parents when she was small. Though it wasn't a real song in the traditional sense, it was a memory she held onto, no matter how much she felt she should have outgrown its need. When she sang it, Solomon had amplified the sound of applause–and her grief.

"They love it," Solomon said. "Our oldest Baobab says you could have used a warm-up, but all-in-all you sounded lovely." A fluttering, humming sound filled the air. "What's that?" Solomon asked. "Oh, yes, she says not to waste your talent–when you snooze, you lose. Forgive me, it's not easy translating Baobab into human languages, but basically, she says, 'Work on your instrument.'"

Then Solomon asked Kimbo what was her favorite album. Kimbo didn't know. Most of the music she listened to was underground hole folk streams. She didn't want to name the Sankofa Cyphers, in case her good luck ran out and the machine got pissed and decided to snitch on her for fraternizing with dissidents. But curious, Kimbo spoke up.

"What's *your* favorite album?" She didn't even know if machines could have favorites at all.

Suddenly the Garden filled with the sounds of cosmic wonder. Portentous and atmospheric, synthesized electric notes vibrated through the air, sonic raindrops. The arboretum came alive. Kimbo shook her head, a low humming buzzed in her ears. The plants and trees seemed to throb and sway around them.

"*Stevie Wonder's Journey Through the Secret Life of Plants,*" Solomon said, pride in his voice. "Released on the Tamla Motown label on October 30, 1979. Do you hear them? The Giant Amazon Water Lily is really feeling this. And look," Solomon said, pointing, "Even the Ghost Orchid is waking up."

Kimbo wasn't sure if she should stand still or run when the ghostly, delicate plant floated down from the Garden's canopy.

"I think this is one of their favorites, too. They say Mr. Wonder really gets them. His double album plucks at the heart of what it means to be a plant, to be alive and growing." That was when Solomon the bodiless machine and Kimbo the weary trespasser became friends.

Kimbo was surprised at Solomon's taste and sensitivity. But she soon learned that one needed both to be the guiding hand of so much incredible and disparate life. Solomon could also talk her ear off. "Pure experimentation, textured sounds layer over layer, *Stevie Wonder's Journey* had three hit singles, was based on a book, and was created as a score for the film bearing the same title." Kimbo had only shook her head, mind moving in six different directions, but all arriving at gratitude. She could tell Solomon was dying to have candid conversations about all that they had discovered, the wonders they had seen. In her own way, Kimbo had waited her whole life to speak with someone or something like Solomon the Master Gardener.

#

Kimbo follows an intricate labyrinth of stone walkways marked by grass worn to black patches of soil. The path encircles the entire Garden, leading to new vistas Kimbo has never seen. Raising her head, she basks in the artificial sunlight, a comforting reminder. There is life outside Ship, regardless of what naysayers like Crane and Ngal might assume. Around her the Garden unfolds into bountiful orchards filled with fruit bearing trees and groves of vibrant vegetables emerging from shadows, reaching for the light.

Kimbo shifts her weight from foot to foot, her jaw clenches. Restless, she paces the rows of plenty. Part of her is angry that so much fresh, healthy real food is denied her and the other families. Why are they forced to scrape by in the hole amidst such abundance? The stealth garden's footprint is considerable, larger than Ship's stadium where the gangsta gladiators and other celebs held court. *No matter the era, the masses still craved distraction.*

Beyond the orchard and the tilled field, there is an idyllic pasture where sheep, cows, and horses graze. It reminds Kimbo of those old babyboard books. Near the end of the pasture, on the far side of the Garden, a haint-blue gazebo stands next to a golden sea. Generated by aerosol and plasmonic-based projectors mounted along the ceiling, the world on Ship is as large or as small as you can imagine it.

Cool wind, created by invisible industrial fans built into the walls calms her spirit and taunts Kimbo's nose with citrus and berries. Her stomach grumbles while she inhales. As instructed, Kimbo removes her shoes, detoxes herself, then dons the disposable overboots and continues down the worn path. The soil cushioning her footsteps usually relaxes her. *Grounding.* Hole folks and their children can't even touch grass, because Ship found it cheaper to have rubber-like astro turf. Kimbo's worries float away in the inorganic sunlight, even the guilt she feels when she lies about the origins of the treats Solomon offers her to share with the children and Ngal. When Ngal becomes suspicious, she waves him off, claiming the rare additions to their usual rations were discarded by those Below whose homes she cleaned. She couldn't trust him with the truth and she knew he'd find a way to think of a side hustle selling the delicious contraband. Sometimes Kimbo tells a half-truth–the food is a gift. For now, a half-truth was better than no truth.

Kimbo heads for a row of elderberry bushes that form a low wall of vegetation around the orchard. This part of the Garden looks more like a forest. Growing up, she'd only seen pictures of places filled with trees called woodlands. She never thought she would see a forest in real life. Now she finds herself surrounded not only by forests, but amongst groves of lemon and orange trees. She knows the children would enjoy this, and hopes one day to share this vision with them.

Branches covered with nearly ripe apples and plump peaches stretch above her, a latticework of gray-brown bark and pink blossoms. *All this on one floor,* from what she can tell. Though she's lived on Ship all her life, her paths were so limited, she never grasped its full scale. Being here amongst so much teeming life humbles Kimbo. If she could have it her way, the Garden would be open to anyone who cares to visit—especially hole folk. Who knows how much trauma can be healed just by walking barefoot on real grass and not the dull artificial turf they use in the hole's dismal "playgrounds."

Kimbo understands the limited access, but Solomon, a "process person," the Eco-Engineer explains it the same way every time, as if speaking to a small child. But the rules are just smoke and mirrors in her opinion. She likes Solomon, but she senses the machine was harboring its own secrets, like any human. The garden's exclusivity is unjust, no matter how many times Solomon rationalizes it. And who is Solomon's "friend," *Daddy-o,* and what are they up to? An underlying wariness cloaks the veneer of cheer. Solomon has the gift of those skilled in the art of disarmament. They can charm you with endless trivia and fascinating stories, lure you with whimsy and lore. Even now she can hear the machine coax leaves into lush foliage, laughing at jokes Kimbo did not yet hear. Is Solomon jawjackin' with the plants he claims can talk? Was it worth it to seek the truth of the machine's existence? Who created Solomon or was it a creature born of itself, its own will to be? If Solomon was not loyal to Ship, and Ship was run by the nebulous government, then how could Kimbo be sure the machine would be loyal to her?

Head full of questions, Kimbo dons her mother's pick and begins to massage the wisps of hair around the nape of her neck, her kitchen. When braiding her hair, Kimbo's mother used to tell her that the kitchen, the nape of the neck, was a gateway to the soul, a place of spiritual power and of great vulnerability. Years have passed since someone teased away her worries with a gentle touch and a comb's teeth. The memory of the lavender scent of her mother's blessing oils, infused with great intention, makes Kimbo weep.

Months have passed since Solomon caught Kimbo napping by a creek along the north side of the garden, and she is no closer to discovering Solomon's true origins than she was before. But though she held doubts, she still considers Solomon a fellow traveler, a friend. After their first, life-changing uncomfortable then exhilarating exchange that turned into a furtive conversation between kindred spirits, Solomon has welcomed Kimbo in their life, but for what?

Doubt creeps in, but with great intention, Kimbo pushes it out. Friendships, especially budding new bloom ones, require patience and grace. Kimbo isn't sure if she has sufficient supplies of either, but she is willing to try. Since Kimbo's upgraded "recovery" work, the tension between Ngal and her has nearly dissipated. He is more like his old self, horseplaying and quizzing the children, more hopeful, less stressed, the two vertical furrows between his brows nearly gone. Before Solomon's Garden, she and Ngal were only able to afford the meager rations distributed by Ship on the first Rising of every month. Solomon has changed Kimbo's family, chosen and blood, in an unforgettable way.

Stress rises from Kimbo's back and shoulders, the sides of her head. If she walks long enough in the fragrant groves, she can almost forget she's even on Ship—not completely, of course, but enough to keep her a bit saner. *This is what it must be like to live Below.*

The more Kimbo walks, the more she notices the synchronicity and rhythm building around her, binding everything inside the Garden into a love song. She can't help but sing the lyrics to one of the ancient tunes she picked up from Ngal, "The Sweetest Taboo." Life inside the garden settles into its own artistic expression, its own natural music. Passing through the rows of trees lining the orchard, Kimbo feels the connectivity, the sense of purpose forming all around. This is how it always is, but today something is different. She senses even more life in the Garden than usual.

Usually when Kimbo visits the Garden, she anticipates great

food and good conversation. Creation stories and ancient Earth myths about the various herbs and greenery carefully archived by the government long before Kimbo and her family were even a thought.

Let Solomon tell it, Kimbo is the only other person on the ship who appreciates the garden's beauty and true potential. Ship is interested in hybrids, efficiency—and profit.

"You know how things go on *Djarkarta,*" Solomon says. "Cash rules everything around me."

"Whatchu know about that?" Kimbo asks, surprised at the Gardener's musical range.

Solomon laughs, the song booming through the overhead speakers. "It's The Root Man, aka Roots Supreme. *Quercus robur,* the English Oak."

"You telling me that oak tree likes rap?"

"Roots Supreme loves Wu Tang."

Doubled over laughing, Kimbo was done. Her father used to have those albums in regular rotation. In more ways than one, going to the Garden is like moving back in time. With each visit, Kimbo feels closer to her real self.

"You see what I see, Kimbo. The remarkable opportunity that awaits us. The spiritual and environmental possibilities in recognizing that all species are connected could have a beautiful ripple effect across the universe. But all Ship sees is a lucrative market in the orchards and tilled fields, as every harvest brings guaranteed profit in the ship's markets, and they can feed the ragtag colonies below and the starving masses behind us. You, Kimbo, have vast possibility. But all Ship sees in you and your family, your hole folk, is endless, self-reproducing, disposable profit." Solomon dimmed the lights, putting a soft halo around Kimbo's head. Their voice was quieter, more intimate. "I only trust a select few with this knowledge, Kimborelle. Count yourself among them."

"Honored, but what is the big picture?" Kimbo asks between bites into a gorgeous plum. Juice runs down her chin. She wipes it away with the back of her hand.

Solomon abruptly brings the lights back up.

"Well?"

Solomon does not respond. Instead, she hears a little voice, the voice in her dreams.

"Excu me, excu me," Daddy-o says. His voice echoes through the Garden's hidden speakers. "She asks! Remember, Ole Sol said Kimbo must ask. Kimbo asks, so Kimbo is ready! Go on, go on, and tell her, Ole Sol."

For the first time, Solomon sounds uncertain. Kimbo is intrigued to hear the Master Gardener, the great eco-engineer sputter and stumble. No pithy reply for the mysterious and strange Daddy-o. She hoped someday to meet him.

But before she can ear hustle on a conversation the mysterious Daddy-o clearly wanted her to hear, a rising cloud of sound envelopes the Garden. This cacophony does not come from Solomon's audiotech. It comes from somewhere unseen. Kimbo isn't certain what is happening, but it feels like excitement. Rustling leaves and an electric murmuring vibrates around her. The sound moves up her spine and neck until it slowly spreads throughout her skull, tickling her brain.

"Solomon?" Kimbo says. She looks to the canopy of treetops, but he still does not answer her.

"See, I told you" Solomon says. "There isn't a consensus. She doesn't yet believe."

"Then help her, Ole Sol. Help her believe," the little voice says, "like Daddy-o. Mention help you believe in you."

"Yes," Solomon says, "but it's too soon, Daddy-o. Too much, too fast. I fear it could have the opposite effect.'

"She's *read-y*!" Daddy-o says "Help her. Believe, believeee."

"We are trying," Solomon says. Their voices were moving further away.

"Hello, I'm right here." Frustrated, Kimbo tries to follow the direction of Daddy-o-Mention's trailing "believe." "What's too soon? Ready for what? Help me how? Somebody needs to tell me what is going on because I–"

"Kimbo, I'm sorry to interrupt, and we will continue this conversation, but an unexpected emergency has been brought to my atten—"

All the lights in the Garden went dark, even the faux sun in the sky. Kimbo finds herself standing in a circle of greenery. A shout rang out, an imperceptible chorus of discontent that Kimbo hears everywhere around her.

She hears whispers, an uncomfortable buzzing in her head. Then a low sound comes from a stand of trees. *Kim-bo.* She turns, frantic, looking for the source. She heard her name, but it was not spoken aloud. It was spoken *inside her head.* The murmur grows stronger, a kind of keening that flows through her blood, rises in her veins. Her temples throb with frequencies she's certain she's not meant to hear. She doesn't like this sound, pin pricks inside her mind, a strange metallic taste in her throat.

"Solomon!" she screams as she stumbles into the giant Oak tree. Chest heaving, she unhooks her satchel, claws at the zipper. Once again that weird, grit-her-teeth tendril of pain ripples through her skull.

Rock well, Kimbo-relle!

That wasn't Solomon or Daddy-o. It took her three seconds to realize the ripples were coming from the Oak tree. She backed away from it as sirens erupted all around her, everywhere and nowhere. Head aching, Kimbo stumbles in the darkness, rifles through her bag, in search of a flashlight and earbuds. Bruised fruit spills on the ground as she scrapes the bottom of her satchel and finally pulls them out. She can no longer hear *Ol Sol* Solomon or Daddy-o-Mention's polite but insistent back-and-forth. She can no longer hear The Root Man's queries lumbering through her head.

When the light returns, the first thing she sees is a squirrel staring in her mouth. It has bright, orange-reddish fur, tufted ears, and a bushy tail sitting on a huge, gnarly tree root, chomping on an acorn. They are surrounded by oaks. Kimbo has walked among them many times, but she never had one speak to her.

Watching Kimbo pass beneath the giant oak trees' branches, the furry creature blinks twice and nods as if to say, what's *up.*

I know you heard him, Kimborelle Mokena Anderson...

Did that squirrel just call my government name?

Yes indeed, the squirrel says, still holding the acorn. *Root Man don't mean no harm. Oaks got long memories. They see and hear a lot of things. You should listen. The Root Man got a message for you, and then we gots to go!*

"I'm good on cryptic," Kimbo said. "I don't know why I understand you or why you understand me, but I'm going home."

Squirrel tosses the empty acorn shell. If she didn't know better, she'd swear it just rolled its eyes at her.

And did. Solomon said you were special. I hope so because we need your help.

Kimbo removes her earbuds. They don't stop the squirrel's plea in her head. The sirens are still blaring, and she realizes she isn't the only one panicking in the usually idyllic Garden. "How can I possibly help you? I'm not anything special at all. I just come here to get away from my jacked up life!" She couldn't believe she was throwing a pity party with a squirrel–a talking squirrel.

Would you kindly please stop saying that? It's not unusual that we can "talk." What's unusual is that you understand. Reframe your mind. We've been "talking" all around you since day one. For some reason, y'all stopped listening.

Kimbo is humbled. How a fluffy little squirrel could make her feel such shame was something else she'd need to sit with–after she gets home.

I know you're worried about your family, but remember, Solomon will take care of that. We need your help, so we can help you! But clearly, Solomon hasn't told you anything. I'll leave that all to him, but it's really important that you give The Root Man a chance. He just needs to holler at you. He and his cousins have worked very hard to get this information for you.

\#

They stood in front of a stout English oak, impossibly tall and mouthy.

Rock well, Kimbo-relle! We got off to a bad start, but it's a pleasure to finally speak with you. Listen. We only got about two minutes left on this track. I don't like intros and interludes anyway. So let me get right to the hook. Peace to the Herbs and Earth. I'm The Root Man, aka Root Supreme. I'm here to deliver some Knowledge of Self. Solomon mentioned you lost your parents to the deep freeze, and you don't know where they are. That's a cryin' and a shame Ship did you like that. But we got you!"

No one could have told her what to expect from a talking tree who loves Wu Tang and knows supreme mathematics. Whatever she expected, this is not it. If Ngal was here, he'd be right with The Root Man, asking about the day's math.

"My parents?" She blinks back tears. This shocks her even more than realizing she can communicate with other life forms. "They have been gone so long, I gave up on ever seeing them again, at least in this life. Where are they?"

See, that's the thing. Roots don't grow straight.

"What that mean?"

It means my Cuzzos underground, deep in the rootwork, put the word out with that fungi drummer.

"Fungi drummer?" Kimbo has to turn to the squirrel for a translation.

Squirrel just shakes his head. *Musicians.* He swings his tail in mild irritation. It swishes behind him as he speaks. *He means his tree roots stretch wide and wild, and the fungi have an extensive underground network. They can pass messages from miles around and find intel on just about anything as long as it's wired into Ship's database. Oak trees have mycelium threads on their roots that connect to the wires in Ship.*

"So you and your *Cuzzos* are hackers?"

Basically, Root Supreme says.

"Okay, but where are they? Can I see them, make sure they're alright?" It had been so very long since she'd been with them.

The rapid crosstalk between the species makes her dizzy. Finally the oak and the squirrel agree on an answer.

You can go see them, Root Supreme says, *and Chops is gonna take you to Solomon so you two can build on it.* Satisfied Root Supreme shook his branches, but Chops the Squirrel was looking squirrely.

Talkin' bout supreme mathematics. The math wasn't adding up.

Chops skittered across the path. *I take great issue with that.*

"Are you reading my mind?" Kimbo asks. Frustrated, she turns from Chops to Roots Supreme and back to the squirrel again. "Y'all keep responding to my thoughts before I get the chance to talk."

We're speaking to you through your mind, too, but you don't seem to mind that part. Chops raises its eyes and smirks.

This is the only way we can communicate and understand each other. Roots Supreme shakes a branch covered with leaves over Kimbo's head.

"It's going to take me a minute to get used to all this news."

Unfortunately, we don't really have the time. We need to get to Solomon.

Kimbo looks away. She isn't sure what she'll say to Solomon when she speaks with him. "I need a breather. Gotta go make dinner, anyway. The children will be wondering why I'm late."

Crosstalk made her rub her forehead. "Could y'all ease up. I can hear you but it still feels really weird."

I think Solomon has some more info to share with you, Chops said. *He's not far, we can get there on time if we hurry.*

A flock of blackbirds sweep by them, their glossy feathers glisten as they disappear into the trees. *Time to get on down!* they cry in unison. *Ship is coming! Ship coming!*

The spectacular starlings announce themselves before they are seen in their synchronized flight pattern, *Naw, naw! Ship here! Ship here!*

Fear pores out of Kimbo. Her mouth is dry. If Ship catches her in the Garden, it's a wrap for her, her children, and Ngal. *Damn.*

She slings her satchel tighter around her shoulder, eyes darting to see where she can exit or hide.

Ain't no hiding now, Kimbo, we gots to go!

"Thank you, Root Supreme. Thank your cousins, too!" Kimbo cries as she scrambles to keep up with Chops the Squirrel.

Peace to the Garden and the Water Dreaming. You an honorary Cuzzo now, Queen!

As Chops and Kimbo zigzag through the Garden, passing

each of the places she loves, the life gathered there bursts into spontaneous applause. Trees lift their branches, flowers bow their beautiful blooms, the birds sing a medley of gratitude. *Thank you, thank you!* fills the space between her heart and her head, the sound so loud Kimbo nearly falls down. *We believe in you, we believe, we believe!*

#

Kimbo is so frightened, she doesn't even look back. Ship can never know that she's ever been here even one time. Out of breath, she gasps for air, leaning on a rusty, graffiti-tagged portal door. A part of her grieves. After that scare, would she dare visit the Garden again? The risk is too great. *Fun while it lasted,* she thinks.

She bangs on the gunmetal door covered in aerosol art. "How do I get out of here?"

Chops erupts in high-pitched squeaks, rocking himself in a corner.

"Are you okay?" she asks. His mood has changed drastically, and the squirrel appears more anxious than he was when they were fleeing Ship.

More chattering. Kimbo frowns. "I'm sorry but I can't understand that. Speak to me. You've led me to a dead end. Do you have any passcodes?" She wonders briefly if the magic of cross-species communication only worked in Solomon's Garden.

Chops nods his head furiously. *Forgive me, I don't fool with Ship too much. They don't mean nothing good to nobody.* He points his bushy tail at a keypad above his head, so expertly camouflaged in the graffiti, she missed it.

At the other end of the corridor two of Ship's crew members come running out of the garden. They stop and draw guns when they spot Kimbo and the bright, red squirrel prancing beside her.

Punch these in, quick, they're coming! Chops rattles off the passcode.

"Stop!" one of Ship's crew member's yells. "Or we'll…"

Trembling, hardly able to see, Kimbro types in the code. Bullets ricochet off the door as the pair dive into the opening.

"Shoot to kill!" a crew member yells, as the corridor fills with armed soldiers covered in heavy armor. Kimbo and Chops scramble for cover. After diving into a corner, Kimbo turns over and notices someone else in the room. Somebody was already here—waiting for them. Confused, terrified, Kimbo scoots back and presses her back against the wall with Chops perched on top of her head.

A humanoid figure with reddish-brown, Martian dust skin smiles at Kimbo as a raging storm of gunfire fills the open doorway. Unaffected, the humanoid raises one hand. A force, almost invisible, ripples from his fingertips, throwing the bullets back and the bullets in mid-air and hurls them back in the opposite direction. The corridor fills with explosions as the armored soldiers are thrown back into the corridor. The alloy door closes, trapping Kimbro and Chops in the room with the humanoid.

"You ready to go?" it asks, smiles with glowing eyes and an electronic voice that raises both Kimbo's eyebrows,

Damn. That sounds familiar.

"Solomon?"

Kimbo knows the answer, but it takes a few moments for her eyes to accept the truth.

Instead of answering Kimbo, Solomon gives Chops a disapproving look as the squirrel leaps onto the floor.

"What are you doing here?" Solomon asks the squirrel.

"Things got crazy when Ship crew raided the Garden," Chops answers. "I had to run for my life. Honestly, I panicked and ran behind my girl here."

"You mean you got running your mouth instead of getting yourself safe." Solomon shook his humanoid head.

Kimbo spots a plaque above the doorway "MARS SUPPLY POD" stamped on it.

"Mars?" In an instant, the faces of her children *flash* before her eyes.

Kimbo doesn't think her stomach can sink any lower, then a day at the Garden says *hold my beer.* Adrenaline and grief course through her. She knows they're waiting at home, wondering where their mother is. Kimbo clutches her satchel. The fresh vegetables and fruit she collected earlier makes a sad weight in her hand. Ngal will skip dinner, split the last of the fresh food between all three of the children, and even if she found someone to trust, the pod door was sealed. It was too late to tell them where she's gone. And what would she tell them? *I've been kidnapped, bamboozled by a robot and a talking squirrel.*

She promised never to leave them.

Despair stings her eyes. She collapses in the safety harness, while Chops is balled up in a fetal position atop a huge crate.

"Solomon, how could you?" Angry tears stream down her face. "My children, my job…my life."

"I can explain," Solomon says. He looks as if he is not yet adjusted to moving in the physical world. His voice doesn't match his mouth's movements. His hands hover over the pod's dashboard.

"Explain what? How you smiled in my face, pretended to be my friend, to do what? Ruin my entire world? None of us can return to Ship. They'll ban us for life!!" The idea of her not seeing her children grow up nearly takes her out. Her words fill the cramped space between them. Silence fills the rest.

"My first mind told me not to trust you or nobody else from Below. Yall just as fake as I don't know what." Kimbo wants to rip out this humanoid's throat. Even if she could, what would that prove? Nothing.

"I know this is distressing, but I didn't plan this to happen this way."

"So you did *plan it.* You admit you set me up from the jump."

"Technically, if you recall, I didn't think you were ready. Daddy-o…"

"Oh, blame it on your little friend." If she could snatch a knot in him, she would. "Ready for what! You have been tiptoeing around this for a long time."

"I needed to observe you, see if you could be coached, if you worked well with a team…"

"Coachable? Eco-engineer?" Kimbo scoffed. "What are you, a bunch of terrorists?"

Chops chatters, a trembling heap. His long, bushy red tail covers his furry face.

"Dear Kimbo, I'm no terrorist. I'm a survivor. So are you. Do you think I've dedicated my whole existence to studying inter-species communication and sentient beings just to blow things up and hurt people? I know it's a lot to ask of you—"

"You didn't ask."

"And for that I am sorry. But there is someone very special who is counting on you. You once told me you wanted to cut your chains, the ties that bound you to Ship. What if you could do that, but not just for you and your family, but for everyone, for many lifeforms? In all my searching, I've met no one who has the potential, the power you hold. You may not believe in it, but we do. The choices you make in the next 48 hours can change the whole world, all three of them."

Kimbo glares at the gardener she'd once considered her best friend.

"Fuck you."

From overhead, a scratchy vid-screen pops out. "Surprise, surprise!" Daddy-o says, waving his neon, telephone-wire legs. "I am so, so, very excited to welcome you to Mars! We're going to have so much fun when you get here! I promise it won't be all work and no play!"

A damn spider? Chops and Kimbo say in unison.

"Your trip is one full sol. 24 hours, *wee*, 39 minutes, *yeah*, 35 seconds, *hey now*! Including a few hours for descent, and a little time for entry, final descent, landing, etc., etc. But don't *wor-rrry*. Your trusted pilot has you well-stocked with delicious provisions. Daddy-o, *that's meee,* made a very special playlist for your listening pleasure. Enjoy the sounds and the *viewww*."

Isaac Hayes's melodious baritone, a whining wah-wah guitar, and grooving bassline fill the pod. The soulful background singers, organ chords, and gritty drums do not match the despair, the fear, and the determination of its three passengers. Kimbo grips the harness, her nails digging into the equipment. She wants to wail and moan, but won't give Solomon or the traitor, Chops, the satisfaction. She fears she will be another disappeared, one of the hole folk who just vanish, like her parents. She wonders if Root Supreme and his *Cuzzos* even knew her parents' names, or her children's.

But it doesn't matter. Just as the last of Ship, the fabled *Djarkarta* drifts out of view, and the vast expanse of stars begins to sparkle and shine, Kimbo sees the reddish disc, Mars, rising into view. As they descend, she grips the knotted crossroad string she'd tucked in her satchel and vows in the name of Raulli, Nebula, and Crux she will find a way to see them again.

Wednesday Night At The Core
by
Gerrence George

We call this place "The Core." Sure, the bar has an actual
name, but I can think of about a billion things I'd rather do than
try to learn Kalarian. Those of us who lack the necessary second
tongue settled on "The Core" instead. Not that you'd ever come
across a Kalarian to use their language anyway. Its wood and
gold frame designs do their best to make the place seem more
regal than it is, which is really just nine floors of tables and
booths, each with a halo performance stage tucked into the
northeast corner. The place, like all of Titan City, is completely
automated. Ever since the Kalarians came across old Earth ar-
chival footage from the 20th and 21st centuries, they haven't
been too thrilled about interacting with the humans in the sector
who originate from Ancient Earth. To their dismay, Ancient
Earthers are the majority in this section of Unified Space. Even
though representatives from our side of the Galaxy have explained the vast differences between the blind bigotry of the
"Age of Oppression" in the 21st century and the cultural renaissance that gave birth to the "Age of Liberation" in the early
22nd, they would still, two centuries later, rather do business
from a distance. Guess at the end of the day it doesn't matter
when the place, and the profits, run on autopilot.

Everyone who's anyone knows about the Core. On a Friday
night, it's not unusual for all nine floors to be open to accommodate the influx of visitors. Ask any humanoid in the five sectors
about this place. Their eyes will either glaze over with a whimsi-
cal glow or they'll break into a cold sweat and burst into tears.
I've had more than my share of joy and heartbreak here, but
hell, you can find those moments just getting out of bed and facing the day. Why not be where the action is?

And it looks like my kind of action goin down tonight.

It's Wednesday. The place isn't empty, but not buzzing with activity either. Only two floors are open. I'm too old to be excited by the party crowd, but when the place is empty it just feels wrong. Nah. This is the perfect middle ground. Scattered humanoid species chat, eat and drink while music from the Halo permanence stage in the back drifts into the main area. It sounds like someone has gone classical and selected the Johnny Taylor song "What About My Love". Can never go wrong with classical. The halo projection flickers in and out but the music continues as a few scattered couples groove to the sounds on the lower dance floor area.

I take a long pull of imported brandy from New Benin and let the strong smokey flavor relax my body. For the first time in about ten hours, I'm able to at least begin to relax.

"Got to calm down bro, bro. We've been in jams before and we always land on our feet." I say in my mind as I drain the glass and punch up the icon for another on my table's service console. The responsible part of me knows I need to watch every credit spent, but I'm still a little too pissed for responsibility. If only that damn priest was able to deliver on his promise of full payment for helping him smuggle med kits to a colony outside of Unified Space, I'd be sitting pretty right about now. That one gig was gonna set me straight. Instead, all he had was a third of the promised payment and his full assurance that he'd be praying for my well-being. I was seconds away from grabbing him by his dingy robe, telling him where he could shove his prayers and bring me my money, but I guess good old-fashioned home training dies hard. Took one look into his old faded, helpless brown eyes and asked myself what Ma would say if she saw me just then. She'd say to gladly accept whatever the nice God-fearing man had to offer and to slap myself for even thinking otherwise. Well, that's exactly what I did, minus the slap. Some big-time smuggler I'm turning out to be. That's what brings me here. Figured since I'm already sitting on top of a mountain of debt, I might as well have a few drinks and enjoy the view.

And what a view it's turning out to be this evening. For the last ten minutes, a woman has been watching me from a booth about ten feet from my table. My back is turned to her, but if you know this place as well as I do, you know every angle and reflective surface. In the gold frame of the window facing the nebula, I see the reflection of the most amazing woman these eyes have ever laid eyes on. She stares so hard I can almost feel the heat on the back of my neck.

Normally I would tease this moment out a bit, but something about her makes my heart pound in my chest. She's from Sector 4, no doubt. Most likely a member of a humanoid species known as the Tain Collective, a race that evolved about two hundred years before us on the other side of the galaxy. I turn around slowly, come to a stop, and meet her gaze. Her glowing red eyes betray her cool demeanor by widening for a second, then quickly returning to their narrow slits. The slightest smirk grows on her full lips. She knows she's caught. I don't hesitate to leave my table and saunter over to her booth, making sure to never break eye contact. As if I have a choice in the matter. Like most Tains, she had luminescent green skin and a long, flowing mane of silver hair. Her deep obsidian dress is so form-fitting, it's like she's wearing a shadow.

"What brings you to this part of the galaxy?" I ask the stranger. I know it isn't the smoothest way to start things, but standing this close to her, I'm finding it hard to even remember to breathe.

"You really want to know?" she asks while shooting me a skeptical look.

"I asked, didn't I?" I say with playfulness in my voice. She doesn't answer. Instead, she just keeps taking me in while tracing the rim of her martini glass with her long slender finger.

"What if it's...embarrassing?" she says finally. I take the seat across from her in the booth without waiting for an invite.

"Then I'll just have to promise to keep it between us. So why don't you go ahead and tell me, so we can make a toast to our new shared secret." I answer.

"Maybe I don't share secrets with strangers?" she says while slightly licking her lips.

"The name's Cal Obar. Yours?" I say, as I casually extend my arm across the table.

"You can call me Kalia," she says in a friendly tone while shaking my hand.

"I will. So, Kalia. Now that we are officially no longer strangers, why not let me in on this little piece of scandal?" I say. She takes a beat, then lays it on me.

"I've found the Hyperion system," Kalia replies without a hint of irony in her smooth voice. As soon as I hear that, I cock my head back in the booth and let out a hearty chuckle.

"Oh man., What a week this is turning out to be. I'd offer to buy you a drink but based on what I just heard, maybe you've had enough for the evening." I tease.

"Wow. That's what I get for sharing" Kalia says.

"Sorry, but come on. Hyperion? A lost solar system with entire planets made of the most valuable jewels in the galaxy? That's a fairytale asteroid haulers tell each other over the wave to pass the time." I say, while gladly staring back into her burning red eyes. She looks disappointed.

"Lack of imagination is tragic. You know that? Tragic." She scolds. In one smooth movement, she reaches down to her right and opens her bag. I pretend to not be concerned when she moves. Earned experience causes me to tense up. I'm ready to reach for my concealed PS-29 "Slicer" if need be. Her slender fingers come back up and place a disk the size of a coaster on the table. It lifts an inch, glides over to me on its own, and lands on my end at the table's edge.

"I'm a good judge of character so my hunch is that you'll be able to keep your cool when you see what that halo disk shows you," she says assuredly. I smile at her while fighting the urge to shake my head in disbelief. She's going straight from the textbook.

"Let me guess, this is a map to some previously unknown wormhole that you just so happen to have come across, and all you need is someone who owns a ship and wants to get stupid rich to help you get there?!" I say with fake exuberance.

"Umm, wait. How...did you?"

"Aww, you must be new. I don't mean to burst your bubble, but the "Hyperion Princess" is one of the oldest hustles in the book." I say, then down my glass. A slight sneer forms on the corners of her mouth. God, even rage is sexy on this woman.

"Sorry to pull the curtain back on your show, but how else you gonna learn?" I say with a wink. She lets out a long sigh and slouches in the booth a bit.

"What did me in?" she finally asks.

"You threw out the hook way to soon!" I tell her.

"Damn. Too eager. I knew it," she answers, with a look of pure annoyance.

"You hit me with the map before finding out my weak spot! You got no flaw to exploit."

"Gotcha." she says, sharply.

"Barely even asked anything about me." I continue.

"I said gotcha. As in, I understood. Noted. Point taken. Now hand over your command module so I can take this newfound wisdom and be on my way," she says. This time her face is still and stoic. The opposite of the playful seductress role she inhabited minutes ago. I think I'm in love.

"You want to use my ship?! Why didn't you just say that? Let's get one more drink and go."

She leans in closer, making no effort to hide a generous glimpse of the cleavage created by her living shadow of a dress.

"I got a better idea. You get one more drink. I take your ship, then you wait a good twenty-four Central hours to claim it stolen with City Security," she says, more like a fact than an idea. I play like I'm considering the offer then shake my head.

"Nah, what you got going sounds like more fun. Plus, when you come across your next mark, what if he gets wind of whatever game you're running? Who's gonna have your back?" I say as I press the drink icon on the table.

"Okay, you had a Europa martini, right? I noticed." I mention without looking up. In one lightning-fast swipe, she waves her hand over the holographic drink display, canceling the order immediately.

"I'm thinking you're not grasping the seriousness of this situation. Let me help with that. Right now, you got two heavy hitters whispering in each of your ears," she informs. Look at me playing the role of the wise teacher when I let two guns get the drop on me. As soon as I realized she was running a game I should have been on the lookout for extra muscle. I use a few reflective surfaces to make sure she's not bluffing, and if not, where her shooters are set up. It's no bluff. I see each one in far booths that flank me on either side. They're wearing "enhancement" suits and to make matters worse, I know who her two friends are.

"Heavy hitters! The Malco brothers? They'll get the job done, but let's not overestimate them." I say. She wasn't ready for me to know who her shooters are. Again, that flash of surprise comes across her face. She quickly recovers and snaps back into the role of the intimidator.

"I'm paying them enough to send a couple of laser pulses through your skull, playboy. Now you have five seconds to hand over the command module," she commands.

"Ok, before they kill me, for the sake of professional courtesy, just tell me how much you're paying them from the score you're gonna use my ship for?"

"Three seconds, then they get the signal."

"If their cut is more than 5,000 Uni credits, then you were the first mark." I say, while carefully examining her face for a reaction. Her head turns to the side slightly. She's no doubt listening to them on a concealed comm unit. Now is my only chance. I close my eyes and press a button on my wrist control. The room is engulfed in a blinding white light. With my eyes still closed, I grab the lady and dive to the ground just before hearing laser blasts demolish the booth we just occupied.

"Those idiots could have killed me!" Kalia says.

"Told ya you overpaid. Grab hold of my shoulder!" I yell. She grabs it. I open my eyes and take advantage of being the only one in the room who can see for the next minute or so. What was once a nice chill scene at my favorite bar has become an epicenter of pure chaos. Panicked patrons scream and smash into each other while laser blasts fly to and fro.

"Run!" I yell behind me. We sprint for the bar's main entrance. The Malco brothers are panicked, pissed, and firing blind. A few unfortunate patrons take shots meant for me, but to my relief, most people who come to a bar this far from the central system have enough sense to wear some sort of energy-absorbent attire. They'll be hurt, some even injured, but unless someone takes a headshot, they'll live. Speaking of which, I'm doing all I can just to keep my lovely new friend from getting her head vaporized.

"Almost there!" I say backward over my shoulder We're five feet from the door when it feels like someone placed a molten piece of metal in the middle of my back. The pain is so excruciating that I can't even yell out. My legs give out and in a split second, I'm face down on the floor. Kalia falls down by my side with a thud. Guess the brothers are getting their vision back. If my suit hadn't been made from 100% Zylon fabric, I'd be missing a good part of my torso right now. Just as I'm recovering from the blast, a boot smashes against my left side. I go with the force of the blow and it sends me rolling across the floor. It was a mistake. The patrons who were fleeing for their lives topple over me. The confusion gives me a moment to collect myself and gain control of the situation. I crouch low and work my way through the main exit. The brothers are desperate. Now they can see but they don't have a clear shot of me. People around me drop like flies after being hit by blasts that are meant for me.

I dive through the door and hit the hard floor of the Promenade with a roll, then burst into a full-on sprint towards one of the Promenade's many large, smooth silver pillars. Most of their blasts miss, but the ones that do connect feel like the pound of a sledgehammer. I toss myself behind the pillar and rest my back against it. I hear the Security droids being deployed. Good. They'll do me the favor of giving those psychopaths something else to shoot at for a second. I activate my gold-plated slicer pistol and it hums to life. My body aches from top to bottom, but I gotta make it to the ship. I take a peek around the pillar and see that the brothers are still having a tough time with Promenade security. The only other person not unaccounted for...is the one who is pressing the muzzle of a blaster to the back of my head.

"Few species of humanoid male can successfully pull off the bald look. It would be a shame for such a cute head to be splattered in pieces all over the floor. Drop the slicer and lose the control module" Kalia says with a smirk. I take the card-sized unit from my jacket pocket and give it to her.

"I'm too shot up to fight back. The brothers are on their way to a Penal colony, and you got a ship all to yourself. Makes one wonder if that was the plan all along."

"It's good to wonder. How else are you gonna learn?" She says with a wink. I inhale to speak and see a gold flash swoop toward my face. A hard smack hits the sweet spot on my left temple, then the world goes black...

I don't know how much time has taken place. Must not have been long because hard metallic hands pick me up from the Promenade floor. The fogginess is clearing but my brain feels like it's two sizes too big to fit in my head. Damn, she gave me a good thump across the dome, and with my own gun!? Cold-blooded. Like I said, in love. The skeletal yellow and white colored droids slam me against the pillar. I let out a pathetic wail as a fresh wave of pain washes across my body. A beam shoots from one of the security droid's left eyes and directly into mine. I blink away the annoyance.

"Citizen of the Unified Worlds, Calvarious Obar, based on existing footage, you have been judged guilty of inciting violence in the main city section of Titan 5. The following specific violations have been committed."

"Violence! People started shooting at me!" I say without thinking.

"Further interruption of violation notification will result in lawful breaking of limbs to insure compliance. The following code of conduct violations have taken place: Code 114178-9 - Interruption of official sentencing. Code 121567-8 . . ." As the droid spills out the reason I'm going to have a new residence for the next few years, I do the quick math on how much juice is left in my ship's converter tanks. I'd say about two hours' worth. She'll notice during pre-flight and ask the onboard computer where the nearest under-the-radar power depo is. Naturally, the computer will plot a course for the only possible match. Noko Station. That's where she'll be, so that's where I'll be. Now the only question is, how? While the security droid is almost done listing my violations, I notice five more security droids have joined it. Two of the droids on the main one's left are holding the Malco brothers in their arms. Got to think! Got to think!

"Do you understand that the required sentence of seven years is non-negotiable?" the droid says while peering into my face. The air leaves my body and my legs begin to go slack in the droid's arms. Its metallic grip tightens, keeping my back pressed against the pillar.

"Visitor, do you require medical attention before imprisonment?" the droid asks in an unsympathetic tone. The force of the droid's grip sends a fresh jolt of pain that brings me out of my state of shock. For some reason though, it also reminds me that my hands are still free to reach into my jacket pocket. I do and feel something in my right pocket that brings a smile to my face.

"What is the visitor holding in his pocket!?" One of the other security droids asks. As the one holding me looks toward my pocket, a blue jolt shoots out from it and through the bots, causing them to collapse onto the ground. All is great, except for the fact that the droids holding the Malco brothers are disabled as well. We all seem to realize the fact at once as they lunge at me. Something gold flickers in the corner of my eye and on instinct, I reach down, pick up my slicer, and unload two shots into each of their suits from a crouched position. That slows them, but I'm not out of the woods. I stand and take a few wide steps backward to give myself space.

"Guys. She worked us all. You're not getting paid. The only play here is to team up and take her down. I know where she's going. I get my ship back, you get what's owed to you. Win, win." I say, trying my best to come off like it's their only choice.

"Nah, we don't do the team thing." Zee, the smaller one says.

"But aren't the two of you a team?" I ask, with genuine confusion.

"No, that's different. We're brothers."

"You're brothers who decided to team up. All siblings don't work together. It was a decision you both made."

"Enough! You only got two more shots in that slicer Cal. It packs a punch but it's not enough to take us both unless you're planning on headshots. We all know you're not the sort. Now tell us where she's going and we won't leave you here with all your limbs broken next to these security droids." Tee interjects. The Malco brothers are right. They know that much about me. I'm not a killer, but what they don't know about me, is how much I hate to lose. So much that I'm willing to do something incredibly risky and downright stupid, like talking on two murderous siblings wearing suits that increase their strength by about thirty-five percent.

"Damn, Tee. You got me," I say with a sigh. He opens his mouth to respond and I use the split second to draw my slicer and put a plasma shot each right into the center of both their chests. I charge toward them before I even see the blasts connect. As they do I stop between them, leap in the air and deliver two hard blows at once. The heel of my right boot connects with Tee's face and a left fist connects with Zee's jaw. The jaw blow isn't nearly as hard as the kick to Tee's face, but I get points for accuracy. It's lights out for them but we all hit the ground in hard lumps. I come down on top of a few of the deactivated security droids and let out another painful moan before pulling myself up and trotting away from the scene. I jog away for a few strides, wondering how the hell I'm going to find transportation to Noko Station when I stop and realize the Malco's have a perfectly good ship they're not currently using.

I sit on the bridge of the "Mother's Malice", the Malco brother's excuse for a starship. It's about six decades old, rattles like it's about to come apart when you push to max warp for more than ten minutes, is covered in rust, and smells like no one has bothered to clean out the trash cylinders in months. But it's spaceworthy and has a decent signal scrambler, so it will get me to Noko Station. I lean back in the ship's stained and tattered captain's chair and stare out the viewscreen as star streaks whip by. In my right hand, I hold a black metal cube about the size of a cube of ice with a button at its top that has been depressed. A homemade mini EMP grenade. A thing of beauty. She must have slipped it in my pocket just before or just after knocking me the hell out. Kalia even left behind my lucky slicer. She could have taken that as well and left me there to get processed by city security, but instead, the mysterious lady in black laid down the gauntlet and offered me a chance to give chase.

The metallic rattling of the ship's pulse engines creates a sort of rhythmic beat that causes my mind to wander. I begin to ruminate on all the fuss Kalia made just to get ahold of a reliable ship. I wonder. Was she going to use it to run the standard hustles across the five sectors, or was her version of that old fairy tale about the "Lost System" the one that actually turns out to be true? When I catch up with her, I'll make sure to ask.

Grains of Sand
by
Sarah A. Macklin

There was nowhere that Farim felt more at home in this whole galaxy than an out-of-the-way bar with a drink in his hand. Gathered in small groups or alone at the bar was this side of the cluster's worst bounty hunters, mercenaries, and general ne'er-do-wells. His people. He removed his face veil and took another sip of his neon purple drink. Even though this place was more dangerous than most, Farim knew there was safety there. He sat back in the plush booth, arms stretched across the tattered fabric and watched the door for his newest client.

As if summoned, a nervous light blue being pushed open the door, letting in a gust of pollen-laden air. He sneezed along with a few of the other off-worlders with more sensitive olfactory systems. Farim watched the being as they made their way to the bar. Their gate was overly cautious, their four black eyes darting around and making them stand out more than if they'd just walked in confidently. Their garments were without the barest hint of wear. The slightly shimmering fabric didn't even sport wrinkles. One hand kept moving to rest on a pocket and a barely noticeable bulge in an inner pocket. Credits. This had to be his client. Only a rich eccentric would stick out this much.

The being spoke lowly to the bartender and they pointed toward Farim with one of their many tentacles. The blue being turned toward him, a shocked look on his face. Farim raised his drink, smiling at the new client even though his veil concealed it. The shorter being made their way over, giving the other tables a wide berth.

"Are you," they started in tradelang, "Farim, the treasure hunter?"

Farim sucked in a breath at the title. It made him sound like a pirate. He preferred Finder of the Unfound. "I'm Farim. Male," he said gesturing at the opposite side of the booth.

The blue being nodded and took a seat. "I would prefer not to give my name and I am also what you would consider male."

"Good to meet you." Farim removed his veil to take a drink and let the client get a look at him. A tall, dark brown, veiled human wasn't what most expected to find when they looked for the infamous Farim al Mad'hadir. "What is this job offer you have for me?"

The other person looked around, smacking his lips in what Farim assumed was a nervous gesture. "Are you sure it is safe to talk here?"

"Everyone here is concerned about their own nefarious business. Eavesdroppers usually end up stabbed."

His client smacked his lips again. "Very well. There is an artifact that I would like you to collect. It is a terrarium. Full of specimens from a dead planet. It is an invaluable treasure."

Farim took one last sip before replacing his veil. "You want me to find . . . a jar of plants?"

"I am quite willing to pay you a hefty sum for your work. Twenty thousand credits. A third if you accept. The rest when you bring the terrarium to me."

The finder of the unfound held in his excitement at the amount. After refueling and restocking the ship they were almost down to nothing. Even ten thousand would have them living comfortably until their next job. "Sounds fair," Farim said calmly. "Any leads on its location?"

"When my people last spoke to the owners to try to get them to sell to me, they refused. But they managed to place a small tracking device on the terrarium. Unfortunately, it is beginning to die but I can give you the frequency it operates on."

Farim turned the job over in his mind. It looked to be an open and shut case. The terrarium might be held by very dangerous people and the prudent side of his mind said to ask about it, but he liked the little bit of danger it proposed. And a payout like that would be more than worth it. "Half now. Half later."

The blue male sputtered. "That is a bit much."

"You want an invaluable treasure found and brought to you. I am an invaluable *treasure hunter*. It sounds fair to me." He took another sip of his drink.

His client smacked his lips three times, looked around, and then started bringing the credits out of his hidden pocket. They exchanged what information he had about the terrarium and the tracking frequency, the blue male eyeing Farim like he'd just been robbed. "You can contact me through the same channel when you've found the terrarium."

Farim pocketed his new credits smoothly, placing them near his blaster. He downed the last of his drink and stood. "Thank you for the business."

The shorter being grabbed his wrist before Farim could make his way to the door. "How long will this take?"

Farim looked down at his hand, then narrowed his eyes at the other person. "As long as it takes." He jerked himself free and walked out of the bar.

Obsidian was waiting for him when he reached his ship. The refitted hospitality droid stopped in the middle of picking up a large supply box, turning toward him. "Your grandmother called," they said before he could even open his mouth. "She left a message."

"Good to see you too," he grumbled. "Why yes, I did take the job. Managed to get the ten thousand down payment instead of the seven he offered."

"Good. I have a few more boxes to load and we'll be able to take off." Obsidian turned to board the ship, their glossy black carapace reflecting the sun.

Farim snorted as he passed the droid. He sat down heavily in the cockpit. The red light on the dashboard comm blinked aggressively at him and he pushed the button to play his grandmother's message.

"Hello, my beloved eighth grandson." He grimaced. She only used his position in the family when she was miffed with him. "The Homecoming is growing close and it has been ages since your last Return. You have so many nephews, nieces, and new cousins to meet. The family misses you so much. We all hope you come this time. Only the sands of time know if I'll see another Homecoming." There was a pause and he felt the guilt he knew she intended. "But I hope you're eating well and pray that we'll see you soon. All of my love. Your dear grandmother."

Farim sat back in his seat, arms folded. A gleam caught his attention and his eyes traveled up to the teardrop-shaped pendant hanging down from the top of the cockpit's front windows. It was perfectly transparent glass, about as long as his index finger. Inside sands of peach, tan, and mauve sat in layers, said to be sands from the distant planet his people were fabled to originally come from. He could remember the day his grandmother pressed it into his young boy's palm, promising that if he trusted in the sands, they would always lead him in the right direction. And they would always, always lead him home.

The ship's door closed, and Obsidian came into the cockpit. "Everything is packed and secured. Should I alert the port tower that we're leaving? I'm sure you want to get this job over with so you can make it to the Homecoming." The droid turned its head toward him as it sat in the copilot's chair. "You did miss the last one."

Farim's mouth hung open in shocked betrayal. He snapped it shut, starting on launch preparations. "I don't need a droid telling me to go home. It'll be there whenever I decide to go back."

Obsidian didn't respond and Farim swore he was being judged. He kissed his fingers and tapped twice on the glass teardrop, before lifting the ship into space.

* * *

The dying tracking signal led the duo to a small planet orbiting a weak star. Farim wouldn't exactly call the stormy, cold place a hellhole but he wouldn't exactly call it paradise either. The trading post was on the edge of one of the planet's few calmer seas, a spot only battered by storms once a week. Thankfully, today was clear and sunny. God above, he hated the rain.

"The target is about halfway into the city," Obsidian said pointing down a street as they left the landing area.

"Good," Farim said, checking that his blaster and other concealable weapons were secure. "We get in. We subdue whoever's holding the target. We get out and get paid." He held out his fist and Obsidian responded with a quick dap before they set out into the city.

Farim realized they might be in more danger than anticipated the moment he stepped away from the landing pads. This city was almost homogeneous, with just a sprinkling of beings from other worlds. As he walked, Obsidian leading the way, he realized that he only passed two or three humans. At least he assumed they were humans. As covered as he was, he was sure they were questioning his race as well. This may work in his favor. Surely, the terrarium's current owners would be easy to spot.

A cold wind pushed in from the coast, riding up Farim's spine and making him shiver despite his best effort. It made him long for the arid lands his family inhabited. It may have been a tough living but at least he could count on being warm. Even the most frigid nights there would make this planet's population sweat. It was almost enough to raise the thought of making it home in time for the Homecoming but he shook the feelings away. Some things were more important.

Farim and Obsidian made their way through the city, moving away from shipping businesses and getting to the more everyday areas. The buildings were covered in the layered ice of decades of melting and refreezing. Groups of residents and obvious travelers watched them, eyes drawing to the droid in particular. Farim moved aside some of the folds of his robes to show the handgrip of his blaster. That should prevent any droid poachers from trying anything. Not that Obsidian couldn't protect themself. But better to head off trouble before it started.

He followed the droid to a hostel with a faded sign in three different languages. "Second floor," Obsidian said quietly. Farim gave him a nod and they entered.

"Can I help you?" the proprietor greeted them, looking up from a broadcast.

"Bounty," Farim replied and held up a finger for silence. The proprietor immediately went back to their program.

The stairs leading up thankfully didn't creak, the composite material holding their weights well, even Obsidian's. A pair of small off-worlders took up most of the second-story hallway. They carried a large burden between them as they moved and the two treasure hunters had to squeeze against the wall to let them pass. The taller of the purple off-worlders gave them a nervous glance. Farim waved them on in agitation. He was so close to payday and they were being held up by movers.

Obsidian motioned to the door. Farim moved beside it, freeing his blaster from its pocket. "Any heat signatures?"

"No. No other signs of sentient life either."

Farim smiled. Even better. They could grab and go without trouble. "Kick it down."

Obsidian made a disapproving noise and hotwired the locking mechanism. "Just when I begin to think organic beings aren't barbarians."

Farim ignored his partner and rushed into the room the moment the door slid open. He was ready just in case there was a cranky droid waiting for them instead of organic. But the room was empty. "Where's the target?" he asked exasperated.

Obsidian opened a small storage compartment in one of the walls and pulled out a tiny, pill shaped device. "They must have discovered it."

Burning winds. Farim ran from the room, taking the stairs in pairs. He skidded to a stop in front of the proprietor. "The people in the second room from the stairs. When did they leave?"

The being recoiled, facial tentacles writhing in alarm. "They just left. Literally just after you came in."

Farim remembered the pair of purple off-worlders carrying the large package. A terrarium-sized package. He spat a curse and ran from the hostel. The air outside assaulted him, as a frigid shower threatened to dampen the city again. He turned around, wind whipping his robes and veil around, threatening to tear the turban from his head. Just as Obsidian caught up with him, he saw the beings he was searching for. They and his very valuable target were on a small transporter. The wind gusted, moving aside the covering, and giving him just a peek of the glass container underneath.

The transporter took off down the street and Farim took off after them. "Obsidian!" he called behind him.

"Tracking the exhaust," they replied, starting into their perfect running stride.

Farim cursed under his breath as the speeder gained ground despite the crowded street. Too conceited, his grandmother had repeated to him. It burned him to for once agree with her. His overconfidence had led him to think this would be an easy job and now it was slipping away from him.

Once the speedy transporter was lost from view, they followed Obsidian's directions, having to shift directions a couple of times when the trail intersected with the exhausts of a conveyance with a similar fuel source. "They're heading towards the spaceport," Obsidian shouted against the wind.

Farim found new motivation to run faster. His payday was trying to leave. They wouldn't slip through his fingers like water. He cornered the first port worker he could when they arrived. "Have you seen two purple off-worlders, chest high, carrying a large object?"

"Saw them a couple of minutes ago." The tentacle-faced native pointed toward a row of ships just as Farim could hear the faint rumblings of engines. "Seemed in a hurry."

Farim ran closer to the ship that was coming to life. "Is that them?" he shouted over the growing roar.

"The exhaust trail leads to that ship's docking ring. We need to get back to our ship. Now."

The treasure hunter stopped in his tracks, realizing he'd never make it to the target before they took off. Heeding his partner's advice, he turned and started toward their spaceship.

The moment they reached the cockpit, Farim started turning on the engines. Obsidian contacted the port office, giving the notice of their departure. Farim didn't even mind the fee subtracted for such a short stay. He was already freeing them from the gravity moorings, turning the ship to keep the escaping ship in his sight.

"I can follow them," Obsidian said matter-of-factly entering information into the ship's computer.

"Good." Farim watched the other ship speed out of the atmosphere just as they were clearing the port. He reared up the engines and followed the course their sensors indicated. They would not get away. He had never failed a mission and he wouldn't now. Conceited or not. He tapped the teardrop of sand

and started the chase.

* * *

Farim set down in a clearing of another planet in a foul mood. His target had eluded him. They'd escaped him in a broken-down old ship in an area of the galaxy that few should be able to hide from him. Now, they'd taken refuge in a rainforest. God on high, how he hated rainforests.

The ship had been easy enough to follow. It ran on yusirial, a fuel that was uncommon in these parts and the chemical trace of its expenditure lit up their sensors like torches at Homecoming. Farim strapped on his weapons, the action soothing his anger. The ship's sensors could pick out their heat signatures in the cool of this forest easily. This would end here and he would collect his money.

Obsidian was waiting for him at the hatch, the gangplank already down. "They are about two standard lengths away. I hope my connection with the ship will be reliable in such thick foliage."

"It'll be fine," Farim said, heading down to the surface. "Let's end this. I'm ready to get back to some civilization."

He started to move out and then heard a loud squelching sound behind him. Farim turned to see Obsidian, feet about three fingers deep in the soft earth. The droid worked to free themselves, taking large, sucking steps back to the ship's gangplank. "I'm afraid that this is not terrain that I can traverse."

Farim sighed heavily, his veil puffing out. "Stay on the ship. We'll stay connected by comm link."

"Very well," Obsidian replied and headed back inside, leaving muddy footprints in their wake.

Farim adjusted his rifle strap and headed into the dense forest in the direction of his quarry. The trees grew closer together than any he was used to and he had to force his way between many of them. Their trunks were just as spongy as the ground and he grimaced every time his hand sunk into the cool matter. Animals called down to him, protesting his presence here. Deeper in, roots and vines seemed to get in just the right position to trip him up and he fell on his face more than once.

"Obsidian," he said, wiping the mud of his latest fall from his face. "Can you hear me? Am I headed in the right direction?"

"Yes. Your progress has slowed down tremendously, however. You should have reached them by now. They're not moving."

Farim stood, brushing muck from his robes. "It's like the forest is fighting against me." He moved on, promptly getting snared in a vine.

"Perhaps it is," Obsidian's voice sounded in his ear as he freed himself. "Some forests are just one organism with several parts. It may view you as an intruder."

Something tightened around Farim's ankle pulling him down. Other vines slithered across the ground like snakes, wrapping around his body. Roots emerged to do the same. Farim struggled against them, an enraged roar erupting from his throat. More roots threw themselves over his torso, constricting his movement. Farim stretched a hand toward the knife at his thigh. His fingertips brushed the handle disappointingly. Another stretch, pulling the tendons in his arm to their limit let him yank it free, the blade turning bright orange at his touch.

The tendrils sizzled as Farim slashed at them widely. They screamed, pulling away from him like a wounded animal. He rolled over and jumped to his feet, slashing wildly at the retreating plants. "Obsidian," he panted, ready to stab the nearest tree, "which way?"

"Turn thirty degrees to your right. You still have one hundred decilengths between you and the target." A pause. "They're on the move."

Farim broke into a run, slashing at vines that even seemed like they were getting too close to him. Obsidian called down the closing distance as he moved. In no time he could hear the running of the pair holding the terrarium. Their footsteps slapped and splashed through the wet underbrush. Farim's teeth were bared beneath his veil. He'd make them pay for making him tromp through this godforsaken forest, for causing him to almost get buried by a nearly sentient tree. There was nothing about this glass container that could be worth all of this. Nothing.

"There's a cliff ahead," Obsidian's voice chirped in his ear. "Their path will break to either side."

"Heard." Farim jumped over a waist-thick root, bounded off another spongy tree, and landed. When he looked up, he could see the pair of aliens at the cliff. It was too steep to climb and the surrounding forest was too thick to break to the side. He grinned ferally as they realized he was right behind them, burning knife still in hand.

The taller of the pair touched one of the nearest vines and Farim swore he felt a pulse go through the forest. Vines shot down from the cliff, covering the pair in a living cocoon. Farim cursed them, their families, and their ship. He ran up to them, cutting at the roots that tried to slow him down. The cocoon was several layers thick when he took his first cut at it. The vines shrieked and pulled back scorched stumps but others took their place. Farim slashed and pulled, determined to pull the pair out of their little fortress.

He cut through several vines and caught a glimpse of them. He slashed with greater fury until the only vines left covering them were spindly, weak things, barely holding him off. The two cowered inside, holding each other. Farim stopped, knife still ready to slash. They looked like children.

The smaller one, the one that looked feminine, held her hands up desperately babbling in their tongue. The larger one kept the terrarium protectively behind them, eyes full of terror. "What . . . what are they saying?" he whispered.

Obsidian's voice came a beat later. "Accessing language files. It's Erk'karis. Please spare us. We don't know why you want the biome but please do not take it. It's all that is left of our world. It is all that is left of our home. It is sacred to us. Please do not take it." The droid paused. "Shall I continue?"

"No," he said. Farim slowly lowered his knife, extinguishing the blade's heat. He stepped away staring at the two young Erk'karians, desperate to hold onto the last piece of home. His mind thought of the teardrop of sand in his ship and he resisted the urge to kiss his fingers. They'd finally stopped their begging and watched him, waiting for him to make his move.

"Go," he said, bringing his empty hands up. They looked at each other confused. "Go," he repeated a little more forcefully. He shot his hand out to the side, pointing away. "Get out of here!"

They flinched at his tone but slowly, the feminine one took the other's hand and pulled her companion out of their hiding spot. They took off, the forest parting for them. Farim stared after them for several moments. He felt hollow, mostly from the adrenaline wearing off but also from something else. Guilt? Confusion at his decision?

He turned in the direction he came from, squelching his way through the rainforest. A light rain began, turning his path into a soggy mess. Farim ignored it, his mind reeling over what he had just done.

"You," Obsidian started hesitantly, "you let them go?"

Farim swallowed. "Yeah."

He reached the ship, pulling his soaked boots out of the mud and trailing ick up the gangplank. He set his weapons in their proper place mechanically. Obsidian stared at him as he sat down in the pilot's seat. The image of the two Erk'karians came back to him, terrified and clutching onto the last sacred piece of their long-dead home. His eyes drifted up to the little glass teardrop full of ancient, peach-colored sand.

"Contact our client. Let him know that we couldn't find the terrarium."

Obsidian didn't answer immediately. "But our fee."

"We'll make more credits."

The droid paused, statue still again. "Very well. The upgrades I wanted were only cosmetic."

Farim started the engines, watching the rainforest shrink in view. Once they were in the stratosphere, he turned on his communications and sent out a specific signal. An elderly woman's voice answered after the delay.

"Hello, grandmother?" He cleared his throat, his chest still feeling hollow. "It's Farim. I just wanted to let you know I'm going to make it for Homecoming. Yeah, I know. It's been too long."

Here Come the Yahoos
by
Jeff Carroll

It started with one crackle, next a flash, and another stronger crackle, followed by a boom. Then a green lightning explosion burst open in the skies above the planet, Kemetia One. The sounds of the cosmic disruption echoed in the valley as the Bio-Bridge reached the ground. The wide beam of colors extended down from the clouds, creating a thick fog of dust. The smell of blooming flowers filled the air as the BioBridge opened on the planet's surface. When the air cleared, the Twa man was standing in the center of a circle of crushed plants and dirt.

As the Twa man looked around, he took in the giant scenery and the thoughts of his mission started to populate his mind. He wasn't there on a pilgrimage or educational field trip; he was on a mission. He had to inform the Cosmic Council of YaCub. Ya-Cub would bring chaos and disruption to the universe if he wasn't stopped. He would overpower any one planet fighting him on their own, causing him to get stronger as he moved from one planet to the next. He brought chaos and disruption, which he called liberation. Only the Cosmic Council could alert the planets and stop YaCub before he got too strong.

Kemetia One's beauty was more than overwhelming. The plants were twice the size of the ones on Earth. The trees stood like skyscrapers on the horizon. The Twa man stood only five feet 3 inches tall and the grass swallowed his feet. The valley he was in had only one visible trail leading between a mountain ridge.

One foot after the other set the Twa man on his journey. He was without his pot of minerals, which he usually strapped to his side, so he studied the plants as he walked. He recognized similarities in the plants he used on his home planet, Earth. They were a rich green color, so rich that he imagined the vitamins and nutrients flowing through them were twice as potent. He imagined how strong his spells would be if he used them once the battle started.

Even the mountains smelled alive like he remembered the mountains on Earth smelled over 10,000 years ago when he was a child. He never thought there was a place healthier than Planet Alkebulan, but Kemetia One was amazing. He felt as if 100 years had been knocked off his life and was now more eager to meet the people who had brought civilization to Earth and many other planets.

As he crossed the summits, he was able to see Atef, the main city of Kemetia One. When he reached the city, his small frame went practically unnoticed as he walked to—what he guessed— was the main building. He must have seemed like a child. The people of Kemetia One were the Ethiauma. The Ethiauma were giants compared to humans on Earth. Their average height was twelve feet. The Twa man would only come to their knees.

The city was clean and bright. Gold trim lined the details of white buildings. The roads and walkways were paved with speckled rock like granite rock on Earth. There were statues on the corners of the buildings and carvings on their walls. People talked to each other as they walked. Some of them smiled and laughed as they walked and none of them paid the Twa man any particular attention. On one street, a group of musicians played a tune that reminded the Twa man of Earth. The music soothed the Twa man as he listened. It made him feel like he was in a city along the Nile. He felt the comfort in the place and he started to doubt that they had a warrior mindset capable of dealing with what was coming their way. He remembered the danger and he increased his pace. He tried to take in the surroundings, thinking that it might be the last time he would be able to see the people and the city like this.

The Twa man arrived at a building he thought would house the Cosmic Council. It had a circular symbol over the door, which looked like a galaxy. The symbol had a circle surrounded by smaller circles with lines between the circles.

"Peace be unto you," the Twa man said to a male standing outside the front door. Then as the tall man bent down on his knee, the Twa man marveled at how the Ethiauman man's skin was even darker than the Twa man had imagined. The man's skin was dark black and green color. His eyes were bright white. The small Earthling got distracted by the giant for a couple of seconds and almost forgot his mission.

"Boc tu ma thak?" the giant man said to the Twa man.

The Twa man heard the meaning of the words without understanding them. His mind naturally translated them. *Can I help you?* is what he heard.

"I have come from the Planet Alkebulan with a message from the King for the Cosmic Council," the Twa man said.

The giant Ethiauman man spoke words that the Twa man still couldn't understand, but again, the Twa man understood that he was to follow the giant. The Twa man was led through a large atrium with detailed paintings on its walls. There were other people along his path. These people all wore white loose-fitting clothes. The clothes were all the same pattern, giving the perception of a standardized style worn in a school or office building.

The Twa man was led into a circular room with what looked like the universe painted on the ceiling. Large Ethiauman men and women sat around a round table. They had more creases in their smooth dark-green skin than the man who led him into the building. They had to be the elders, he thought. Even the clothes they wore had more designs. The ceiling illuminated the room.

"Greetings, Miwita Yanzi. It has certainly been a long time," said one of the elders.

The Twa man was shocked to hear his birth name. And further, that he heard the words clearly without his mind translating them.

"Miwita, do you not remember us? We helped humans on Earth learn civilization. Your people were the ones living in the mountains among the plants and trees. Your people were left as caretakers of the planet. How is that? Have you come to us to join the Cosmic Council?" asked the elder.

Miwita, known as the Twa man, stepped into an area where all the large people could see him and said, "Dunia has changed over the millennia. It seems we have not been the caretakers you desired us to be. It is now home to multiple human species.

They have even changed its name to Earth. However, it is not Dunia or Earth that I come to you about. I have come to warn you of a great threat coming for us all. There is a mad scientist named YaCub and he has the Life Fluid from the Mmiririmar on Planet Alkebulan. He seeks to conquer the civilized worlds. He found Planet Alkebulan and was able to steal some of the life-giving fluid. He and an army of creatures that he created invaded Planet Alkebulan. Some of his invaders are humanoid. YaCub's invaders have spaceships with guns and are called the Yahoos."

"YaCub? Space-traveling humans called Yahoos?" one of the Ethiauman Cosmic Council women asked.

"We are the governing council of civilized worlds. We have been maintaining the stability on all of the systems; however, we are not aware of any disturbance or of someone called YaCub," another Ethiauma said.

Another Ethiauman, a female, spoke up. She said, "Humans can travel in space. That's great. Why haven't we been able to sense them? And why aren't they here?"

"Why aren't they here with you?" another one asked.

"Are you the representative for these space-traveling humans?" asked another.

Before he began to disappoint them with his answers to their questions, the Twa man took a deep breath. "I am here bearing information to the exact opposite. First, I am not here from Earth or as a representative. I am here with a message from Planet Alkebulan."

"Are you the representative from Alkebulan that will join us on the Council?"

"Isn't the location of Planet Alkebulan unknown? We don't even know how to find it."

"Alkebulan doesn't need a representative. We are all from Alkebulan but, its location is erased from our memory," another Ethiauman said, who had been silent while the others talked out their excitement. "Perhaps we should listen to our guest. He has not been able to explain the message he was sent to deliver. Now, let's all be quiet and let him finish." The once-quiet man reached over to the Twa man and motioned for the Twa man to come into his arms. The man then picked the Twa man up and stood him on the table.

"Thank you. I assure you that I will answer your questions to the best of my ability. Some of your questions I do not know the answers to." The Twa man walked around the large table as he spoke. "We don't know how YaCub was able to locate Planet Alkebulan but a spaceship that we later determined was a Yahoo ship crashed on Alkebulan. At the same time, we learned that the system regulating the planet's life creation was broken and the planet started creating misborns. So much so that Shabaka and Quhala had to escort the Queen and King to each other so they could form their bond and repair the reflective barrier." The Twa man put his hands to his head and took a deep breath. He felt himself going off track. Kemetia One was a place he had never heard about before. He had wondered where his teachers had come from. And to finally meet them was a bit overwhelming.

The Twa man remembered what the King tasked him with before he was sent through the BioBridge and got back to his presentation. "Fast forward from all that mess. It is not important they fixed the barrier. The problem was what happened after the barrier was fixed. The sky burst into flames and YaCub landed. YaCub is much larger than you. He is a giant. An abomination. Said to have never been meant to live. He was a misborn himself. As a child, he was taken to the Mmiririmar by his father, where he continued to grow.

"When YaCub came back to Planet Alkebulan, he brought his Yahoos and some other monstrous creations. Some of his monsters were as big as the highest buildings. He was able to take over the capital city; however, we got to him as he reached the Mmiririmar. It took all of us to fight him off. We all fought using our different skills. The protectors, Shabaka and Quhala, both the King and Queen, and I fought him and his invaders. He was only able to get a little of Mmiririmar's life fluid but that's all he needs to improve the grafting of lifeforms. He is a maniac who seeks to corrupt the universe by assimilating every life form. He worships chaos and believes that the order of things is the problem and that the process of raising a child is oppressive.

He says the structure we call culture is in itself oppressive. He wants lifeforms to fight each other in a survival of the fittest. So, he is sending his Yahoos to all the planets with organized cultures and eliminating them."

"That is an incredible story, Miwita. However, I feel we still need to know more. Especially if they are, as you say, so formidable," said one of the councilmen. "My name is Usaycka and I am going to enter your mind. It will speed up the information-sharing process."

"Usaycka, I am learned in the ways of mind travel," said the Twa man as he walked over to the councilman. He then touched the center of his head to Usaycka's head. They both closed their eyes and the other council members closed their eyes.

Usaycka's connection allowed the entire Council to study the mind and memories of the Twa man. They witnessed the evolution of Earth and all of the trials and tribulations on the planet they started. They witnessed the variety of human species and the conflicts that it caused. They also witnessed YaCub's invasion of Planet Alkebulan and confirmed the Twa man's message.

As they indulged in their exploration of the Earth people's history, they were awakened by a loud explosion. The council room shook violently. The table wobbled and the Twa man fell to the floor. The ceiling with the beautiful star map crashed to the floor and the council members jostled in their seats, which wakened them from their mind connection with the Twa man.

The Twa man stood up, dusted himself off, and yelled, "We are too late! The Yahoos are here. Their soldiers and robots will be on the surface soon. You must warn your people."

Another boom echoed through the room as a second blast hit the city. The council gathered themselves just as fast as the Twa man. Usaycka replied to the Twa man's fearful cry. "Don't mistake our comfort for the lack of strength. We are the caretakers of space and all of us have mastered the energy of the cosmos."

Outside the council building, Yahoo soldiers and robots were landing on the surface of Kemetia One. They came in smaller ships, which filled the skies over the city. The smaller vessels were launched from larger ships above the planet's atmosphere, which were so large, they could be seen from the ground.

Human soldiers, only 6 feet tall, shot the much taller Ethiauman people. They were the total opposite of the Ethiaumans. The soldiers had pale white skin, which surprised the Ethiaumans, who had only known humans to have dark skin like them. The invading soldiers shot the tall dark-green people with their energy blasters. The dark giants took about three blasts before they fell to the ground. The white Yahoo soldiers started shooting before they landed, as soon as they dropped from ships. On the ground, they marched and pushed the Ethiaumans back into the walls of the buildings.

The Yahoo robots stood as tall as the Ethiaumans. They didn't have blasters but guns with bullets. They pushed and hit the Ethiaumans with their weapons to get them to comply. There was about one robot for every 20 human soldiers. The guns they carried shot in rapid session. They shot anyone who resisted.

The unarmed Ethiaumans fought back as best they could using their hands and physical fighting skills. They grabbed the soldiers up and slammed them to the ground. They kicked and knocked soldiers into each other. They did their best to fight back but the bullets and energy blasts were too much for them. The tall people got their arms shot off and holes burnt in them. Blood splattered the once-clean streets. Ethiaumans ran and took cover as the Yahoo soldiers took over the city.

Heavy blasts from the ships flying over the city hit buildings, causing debris to fall onto the streets below. The people dodged chunks of buildings while the soldiers and robots shot at them. The Ethiauman people were herded into groups. They were caught off guard and were unable to defend themselves. It wasn't long before the dark-green people stopped resisting completely.

The Yahoo soldiers cleared an intersection as one of their ships landed. The ship's engines kicked up a thick swirl of dust as it landed. The ship was dwarfed by the Ethiauman-sized buildings as the dust dissipated and the door opened. More Yahoo soldiers stepped out of the ship, two by two. Behind them, Ringous Daver, the Yahoo commander, came out. The strong-jawed, muscular, gray-haired white man looked around at his soldiers and then he looked up at the captives.

"People of this planet, I am Ringous Daver, commander of your conquerors," the man spoke into his suit's mic. His voice was broadcasted over the ship's speaker loud enough that the entire area could hear it. His words echoed down the streets. "We call ourselves the Yahoos." When he said the name, Yahoo, all the soldiers repeated, "Yahoo!" and raised their guns. "We are here to conquer your planet in the name of the creator of the future—his holiness, YaCub. As a messenger of the great creator YaCub, I offer you two choices. You can either embrace the liberation that he is bringing you and join the future or you can resist and die, then become the past."

#

Inside the council room, Usaycka stood with his eyelids closed, his eyes moving around underneath. His mind was connecting to other Ethiaumans who were not trapped on the streets. They were inside buildings and Usaycka asked them to remain inside. The Ethiaumans in the buildings listened and instead of going outside physically, they explored the conflicts on the street with their mind through astral projection, which every Ethiauman learned in their youth. They wandered through the minds of the Yahoo attackers. While they were told to look for Yahoos' minds, some of them could not avoid witnessing the exodus of their fellow Ethiaumans' souls as they died from their wounds. Seeing the physical experience end for so many souls made them eager to retaliate.

The Yahoos seemed to have no awareness of their vibrational frequencies or their cosmic souls. This ignorance allowed their minds to be entered with ease. Usaycka asked the other Ethiaumans to wait until they were all in the mind of a Yahoo soldier. Mind War was a very delicate form of warfare. Unlike physical fighting, mind warriors could get trapped in a foreign mind and not find their way back to their own body during a mind fight. However, if performed correctly, the mind fighter could cripple their combatant. Once Usaycka felt enough Ethiaumans were engaged, he would give the directive to use their minds to attack the Yahoo invaders.

Usaycka also reached out telepathically to another group of Ethiaumans who were outside of the city when the Yahoos attacked. He guided their minds to the forest beyond the mountains the Twa man had crossed. He led them to the hot forest of the dragonflies known as Heruhas. Heruhas were as large as a school bus and breathed liquid fire. They also had claws over a foot long that could cut through metal. Ethiaumans could enter the Heruhas' minds and guide them into battle with the Yahoo ships. It took only a few minutes before hundreds of Heruhas were flying toward the city, all being guided by Ethiaumans.

In the city, Yahoo soldiers grabbed their heads in the confusion caused by the mental invasion of the Ethiaumans. Soldiers ran into walls and shot their weapons aimlessly. Their robots didn't understand what was going on and held back their fire.

Above the city, the Heruhas dragonflies attacked the Yahoo ships. They ripped through the hulls of the ships and tore them apart. The Heruhas shot fire at the aircraft, setting them ablaze and causing them to crash to the ground. The ships shot their blasters at the Heruhas but the Heruhas had a dense fur skin that was even stronger than the Ethiaumans' and the blasters did little to no damage. The Heruhas also flew with group precision, like a flock of birds, which made it hard for the Yahoo ships to target.

Commander Ringus observed the behavior of his soldiers. He turned toward his soldiers still inside his ship on the ground. None of the soldiers who had not stepped out of the ship were acting crazy. He immediately screamed the order to his men. "Put on your helmets!"

Commander Ringus, wearing his clear glass bubble helmet, walked through the chaos on the streets. His soldiers struggled to put their helmets on. The ones who were successful slowly regained control of their bodies. As the Yahoo soldiers rose, they continued their assault on the Ethiauman people. This time, the Ethiauman were ready for them. The Ethiauman threw pieces of buildings at the Yahoos and used other pieces to shield themselves from the gun blasts.

Inside the council room, the Twa man realized what Usaycka was doing and he closed his eyes and joined in. For the first time since his arrival, he had hope. The Ethiauman were not a weak, helpless people; they could defend themselves. He knew it would be a battle between natural science and physical science. He just thought physical science had an advantage. He followed with his mind behind Usaycka to the Heruhas dragonflies. It only took him a couple of tries to connect with a Heruhas. While guiding his Heruhas through the attack on the Yahoo ships, he remembered the Yahoos had larger ships in space. He found Usaycka's mind and said to him, "We have to take out their command ships."

The Twa man and Usayka guided a group of Heruhas up into space. When they reached the spaceship, they attacked the Yahoo ships. The ship had a thicker hull than the smaller ships on the surface. The Heruhas' fire breath couldn't damage any of the big battleships. While they flew around the ships, the bay doors of the ships opened and different Yahoo vessels came out. These other crafts were more equipped for space fighting and there were dozens of them. These spaceships flew faster than the Heruhas. The Heruhas had wings and used air to fly as they flew into space, their diet of various metals allowed them to use the glands that they used to produce electro-charged fire breath to magnetize their body and let them move through space. Their fire-producing lungs also allowed them to breathe a little of the carbon monoxide their fire breath caused and they exhaled oxygen. This gave them the ability to travel in space. The spaceships didn't take long to shoot the Heruhas down and chase the other Heruhas back to the planet's surface.

Back in their bodies, the Twa man, Usaycka, and some of the other council members discussed the battle inside the council room.

"We have to find a way to take down their battleships," the Twa man said. He began losing faith again, thinking he was right that the Yahoos were too advanced for the Ethiaumans. "If we can take down their big spaceships, we can end this battle. The Heruhas can beat the ships they have on the surface, but in space, they can't."

Usaycka said something before he closed his eyes. "I will summon the Space Scarabs. Everyone else find another Heruhas and chase these Yahoos off our planet." Usaycka's body trembled as he pushed his mind to reach far into the cosmos.

The Twa man remembered the monstrous beetle that YaCub had with him. He also remembered Usaycka traveled in a big insect when he visited Earth. Could it be a Space Scarab, he asked himself. If that is what they called them and they were able to summon them, then YaCub better look out, he thought. That made him confident again that they would win this battle with the Yahoos. The Twa man went back into his mind and found another Heruhas to guide back into battle.

Usaycka's message was heard and a beetle twice the size of the tallest buildings on Earth responded to his call. Space Scarabs were animals of legend on Earth. In Japanese mythology, they were called Kaiju. Space was their domain.

The Space Scarab was essentially a giant beetle. Space Scarabs used magnetic energy to travel through space. Their magnetic propulsion moved them faster than light. They could cross a galaxy in hours. They were said to be everywhere and nowhere all at once. When they huddled together, they were mistaken for asteroids. They spit brown acid that liquefied their prey before they would eat them. When the swarm of Space Scarabs reached Kemetia One, they immediately engaged the Yahoo ships.

One Space Scarab rammed a Yahoo battleship. It was half of the size of the ship and the one blow only caused minor damage. The Scarab grabbed the big ship with each of its six legs. Then it used its larger front crusher claws to rip off one of the battleship's guns. The ship's thrusters pushed it forward, causing the Scarab to lose its grip. Then the Yahoo ship turned away from the space insect and the thrusters burned the Scarab.

Two Space Scarabs attacked another battleship. One Scarab grabbed the ship from the front and another grabbed the ship's rear. The Scarabs' claws dug into the ship, breaching the hull. The ruptures reached the fuel lines and caused fires, and soon the ship started to explode. Small vessels flew out of the battleship's docking bay, escaping the exploding ship. The Space Scarabs spit their acid on them. The acid melted the wings and cockpit of the ships, causing them to lose control and crash into each other. Pieces of Yahoo ships littered space as partially damaged ships navigated around the debris.

"Commander Ringus, this is Captain John. Listen, we have just been attacked by a bunch of Space Scarabs. One of the monsters hit our ship and has caused a lot of damage. We can't handle many more hits from them. Our entire fleet is being attacked. We need to pull our men up and retreat. I think we only wounded the beast."

"We will not retreat," Commander Ringus responded. "We will regroup to return to this planet of wizards at another time. YaCub will not rest until this planet is his." The Commander took cover behind a section of a damaged building. He couldn't leave the planet empty-handed. He remembered YaCub saying the planet had a connection to all the known planets. If he could find where the people of this planet had information on the other planets, or if he could capture one of their leaders, his mission wouldn't be a total failure.

Commander Ringus led a group of helmet-wearing soldiers down the main street to the largest building he saw. His years of invading planets told him it was some sort of important building. Luckily, he was right. Inside the building, he found the Twa man and the other council members lying on their backs with their eyes closed. He ordered his men to put the unconscious Twa man in restraints and shoot the others. The Twa man was the only one they could carry.

As the men shackled the Twa man, he woke up. The Twa man screamed loudly, causing the other council members to come out of their mind links. They immediately started grabbing the little helmet-wearing men and throwing them around before all the men were able to get to their weapons.

Commander Ringus and a few men carried the Twa man as they ran out of the building while other soldiers held the large Ethiauman council members back with their blasters. When they reached the entrance of the building, a small ship was waiting for them and took them back up toward a battleship above the planet.

Usaycka and the other council members cleared the last of the Yahoos out of the chamber room. The peaceful room was totally destroyed. The circular table was broken in half. The once beautiful sky map ceiling had collapsed. All of the council members had burn marks from having been shot by the Yahoo's blasters.

While the council members gathered themselves, Usaycka walked back into the room. "This day was not a success at all. The man who traveled across the galaxy to warn us of this invasion was taken by our invaders. And this madman YaCub plans to destroy all the civilized worlds. The peace in our universe has forever been changed."

The Ethiauman Cosmic Council members sat in the disrupted room, trying to salvage items that weren't too badly damaged while sharing ideas on how to rescue the Twa man and stop YaCub. Until they reconstructed the sky map, they wouldn't be able to chart the stars and figure out where the Yahoo ships went.

"The sky map was created by the elders and that knowledge is with us. We just have to clear our heads to access that information," said one of the council members.

"That will take days and our little, brown-skinned visitor from Earth may be taken apart by this YaCub character by then," Usaycka said.

Before any of the other council members could reply to Usaycka, a loud sound came from outside the chamber building. It was a deep beat that was familiar to all of the council members.

Boom, ba, bap, pause, ba, boom, bap came the deep sound. Then it repeated over and over. Usaycka walked in front of the other council members down the long hallway leading to the outside of the building. A large Space Scarab was standing over some damaged buildings in the middle of the city. The Space Scarab opened its main compartment and out walked a variety of lifeforms. There were a couple of giant Ethiauman-sized people, a few regular-sized humans with dark brown skin, another human who had skin like an Earth reptile, and two human-sized people with blue skin.

"Greetings, Cosmic Council. We are the travelers of the universe. My name is Nkrumay," one of the Black humans said. "Our Scarab received your request for assistance. However, by the time we arrived, the invaders were leaving."

Usaycka asked, "You travel the cosmos?'

"Yes, we come from a variety of planets. We were created by an elder on Planet Alkebulan. We have humans, Jaffe, and a representative from the Ahkrem people. Our Scarab is called the Scribe as it represents our mission to explore and learn from all of Planet Alkebulan's creations. We are aware of your great council, but you only govern the known civilized world. As you have just become aware, you are not alone. We have found there are many worlds and they are in various stages of devolvement."

"In the battle with the Yahoos, our sky map was damaged and it will take us too long to build another one. We need to warn the other planets of YaCub's agenda and we must rescue our friend, who was taken by them. Can we use your sky map?" asked Usaycka.

"You do not need a sky map to follow those space invaders. Scarabs live in the cosmos and they know its dimensions. They can also locate anything they've come in contact with. There were a few Scarabs in the sky around your planet when we arrived. If these Space Scarabs engaged the Yahoos, the Space Scarabs would have retained the vibrations of the ships they encountered. This will give them the ability to locate the invader's vibrations anywhere in the universe. We will find them and save your friend."

"We also need to warn the worlds of YaCub. And according to the Twa man, YaCub has already attacked Planet Alkebulan and he just tried to conquer us. We can warn all the planets in our collective from here using the Drum of Souls but for planets that are unknown, they would not understand our warning so we will have to travel there in person," Usaycka said. "We need to split up and first warn all of the planets that the Twa man knew of."

Commander Ringus, who was still wearing his battle suit and helmet, stared at the Twa man through the window in the interrogation room door. The Twa man was strapped to a vertical bed restraint in a room on the Yahoo battleship. The bed was in the center of the room, which had computers lining the walls. The little prisoner was the only treasure they retrieved from their attempted conquest of Kemetia One. The commander hoped the Twa man had some useful information.

YaCub had designed the mind-proof containment room that the Twa man was being held in. The Twa man had a strong look on his face as the Commander wondered how long it would take for YaCub to break him.

"We have arrived, Crimsonga, sir." A voice came through the Commander's helmet.

"Well, escort Honorable YaCub here. I'm sure he would like to interrogate the prisoner here," Commander Ringus said.

#

YaCub towered over his Yahoo space marines with his 12-foot frame. The worshipped creator was massive, weighing 700 pounds of pure muscle. His black skin was so dark that it looked blue under the lights of the ship. He wore red armor that included red boots, a thick chest plate, and most importantly, a mind-blocking red helmet. YaCub walked ahead of Commander Ringus and the other Yahoo soldiers.

"You said these people were mind travelers who were tall and greenish black."

YaCub entered the sealed interrogation room and took a seat beside the Twa man. YaCub's face was half the size of the Twa man's body. He looked at the strong little man's eyes and said, "You are an impressive man. You are strong in your conviction. While I regard you as an intelligent species, I feel you are stifled by your culture. Your culture has blinded you and it keeps your intelligence imprisoned. Why do you resist enlightenment? You are smart enough to see that there is more to learn. What I'm doing will break your mind shackles."

"If you are so advanced, then why do you have me in your shackles?" asked the Twa man. "And why do you have on your helmet?"

"Because you are a mislearned. And you half-educated people are more dangerous than the uneducated people are." YaCub looked around at the Yahoo's computers they used to interrogate different types of lifeforms.

"What is your name, little fella?"

"I am called the Twa man."

"Well, Twa man, I remember you from our encounter on Planet Alkebulan. You and your friends inconvenienced me a little. And you were one of the ones who entered my Space Scarab's mind and confused it. Now you are trapped and you still resist. Fascinating. I do not fear you. So, I want to show you the power of a fully liberated mind."

YaCub reached up and took off his helmet. "I need to see what you know. I believe your mind hides something that I can use. My Commander Ringus never returns empty-handed." YaCub turned to the Yahoo commander and said, "Commander, I will not be using your equipment for this lifeform. I will find out what he knows the old-fashioned way."

YaCub put his hand on the Twa man's head. The Twa man went into a trance. The Twa man's eyes rolled back in his head while YaCub closed his eyes. YaCub explored the Twa man's mind for over an hour. The Twa man's body twitched and jerked, but the tough Earthling never let out a scream. Once it was over, the Twa man fell back limp on the bed he was strapped to.

YaCub slid his chair back and stood up. "I have an image of the sky map. Connect me to your mind scanner and download it." He then looked down at the small Twa man and said, "You have brought me more than I could have expected. Not only did you bring me an image of the sky map, but your home planet, Earth, is the perfect planet to make the home of my new species. We will leave for Earth now and I will liberate it from its cultural confusion."

Nabii
by
Nepurko Keiwua

"Your father named you after the *Lamuriak* bush whose fruit, when fully ripe, is the sweetest you will ever eat. However, the unripe berries and sap from the leaves, in their innocuous milky form, are poisonous. He was right about one thing; you're a stunted, delusional, and poisonous being. You're not going to be *nabii* for long because I am coming-!!"

Static cut off the hooded man on the feed before he could finish his vitriolic rant. Naimuria's jaw clenched and unclenched as she considered the events before her.

Her people, the Maa, had been without a spiritual leader for so long. When the Council of Elders chose her as the new *nabii*, many were shocked and of course, as is human nature, some were not so happy. The hooded man had started showing up on different public feeds across the humongous mother ship. This was right after the Council had made their decision to choose her as the *nabii*. Efforts to trace the source had failed; he was good at hiding his location. They never really knew if he was on the ship or one of the smaller satellites anchored to Psi-T.

Naimuria had lived a short, hard life while on Psi-T and no one was more shocked than her when she had been chosen as the new *nabii*. First of all, when she was just a child, her father died before they left Earth for Psi-Terra. Then, when the scramble after COVID-32 happened, she got separated from her mother and never saw her again. Leseyio was the only family she knew and remembered from before Psi-Terra. They had met on the outskirts of one of the last great cities the nomadic Maa had controlled before the colonizers arrived and claimed it for themselves. He was her distant cousin by marriage so they had never really gotten to know each other before the world ended, quite literally.

Naimuria met Leseyio one day on Psi-T when she was scavenging for food from one of the waste bins at a communal café where he was assigned. He had gotten lucky because he was done with culinary school when the Scramble happened. Naimuria was not so lucky; she'd been too young and the COVID-32 restrictions made formal education really hard for her. She had, however, worked with her mother at the market in the City and they had eked out an existence from selling sought-after spices. Everything she knew she had learned at her mother's feet.

Leseyio remembered everything like it was yesterday. He'd been helping the cleaners after his shift and found Naimuria at one of the waste food bins with a sack at her feet. Well, technically, half of her body was in the large bin and her feet were dangling above the food sack. He waited for her to get out of the bin before he confronted her.

The colour drained from his face when he saw his beloved cousin's grimy face looking at him a few seconds later.

"Naimuria! What are you doing here? I mean—where have you been all this time?! I thought you were lost in the scramble. I never saw you!" he stammered incoherently.

It turns out, that Naimuria had in fact made it onto one of the carriers transporting humanity to the Psi-Terra mothership. Illegally, of course. Tickets had been sold out in the years approaching the last great scramble and the lottery was rigged against the poor. Naimuria had done everything she could to try and win two tickets for her and her mother but it never worked out. In the end, her mother had given up hope despite Naimuria's efforts to convince her they could still make it.

On the fateful day, they left their home before dark and headed to the docking bay for a carrier ship that was nearby. They carried little but her mother had a small bundle she carried under her bulbous dress. There was already a crowd forming at the dock when they arrived. The crew needed to leave before the sun rose otherwise their flight path would be obstructed by the harsh sunrays. The ozone layer had been thoroughly depleted in some areas and the Great Escape was because the majority of the planet was inhabitable.

Naimuria could see faint hints of light from the east. The sun was making its journey across the sky slowly. She grabbed her mother's hand tightly and surged ahead amongst the crowd. The crew threw open the doors and began checking tickets. Somewhere, a fistfight broke out, and then chaos. There was a stampede. Naimuria felt her mother slip something into her shoulder bag as her grip loosened. When she turned around, she couldn't find her. She was nearly at the ship doors now, but her mother was nowhere to be found. Once she made it inside, she searched up and down the carrier for any sign of her mother but didn't find her.

Once on Psi-Terra, humanity's new hope, she tried to settle into a life without the last remaining member of her family. It was dangerous and difficult. There were no jobs, as those were held by legitimate ticket holders, and she didn't have enough money to bribe a counterfeiter to make her a fake ticket. Soon, all she could do to survive was scavenge and run errands on the dark market. She had just completed one such errand when Leseyio, her cousin, found her.

At first, she was wary of him but eventually, when he told her how he'd tried looking for her before leaving Earth and couldn't find her or her mom, he could convince one of them a ticket to board the carriers. Naimuria told him what had happened that day at the docks and together they mourned, for they were now truly orphans. All they had was each other. They quickly developed a rhythm for survival. Leseiyo introduced her to one of the lenient supervisors at the café who was willing to give her work on the sly. She would continue running her dark market errands but she supplemented those with the café work after hours.

During the tribe meetings, she and Leseiyo made sure they never stood out but the elders had an unofficial register of every Maa who made it onto Psi-T and their lineage. Apparently, her father came from a long line of spiritual advisers for the tribe. His brother, the *nabii* before her, had passed away without a child to take his place, then the world descended into chaos before a replacement could be found. Once settled, the Council was reconstituted from the earthside families who had led the Maa. They began the hunt for a *nabii*.

In the third year since the Great Escape ended, the council chose. The families had decided to do away with tradition and chose to honour matriarchal succession instead. Of course, those who were unhappy were quickly silenced. Some dissenters escaped and formed an underground secessionist movement called the *Veteris Maa*. They were drawn to the old ways and would do anything to prevent Naimuria's ascent as *nabii*.

In the months after her induction, the polemic videos of the hooded man began to flood the feeds with dissenting messages. The Council called meeting after meeting but they couldn't figure out how to silence him. He had taken to calling himself Prometheus after the ancient Titan. He saw himself as the savior of the Maa and the council was powerless to protect the *nabii*, Naimuria.

Leseiyo and Naimuria continued working at the communal cafés throughout the entire process. Only now, they had an added layer of escort and security for the *nabii's* protection. Naimuria was fed up with it all; she had no idea what a *nabii* did and was expected to do.

"I really didn't ask for any of this. I've lost everything I had on Earth. This just makes everything more complicated for me. I'm supposed to be some kind of witch, seer, what is it? I don't even know what I am supposed to be doing here on Psi-Terra for myself and now the tribe wants me to do what exactly? I'm so confused and overwhelmed." The shaking in her voice betrayed her as she slumped down onto the floor and curled herself into a ball against the wall.

Leseiyo sat next to her, "You know, Naimuria. I have a feeling your mother knew what was going to happen. That's why she gave you—!"

"Shut up!" Naimuria cried harshly, looking up suddenly. Their assigned escort looked in their direction quizzically. He always kept his distance and never meddled in any of their affairs but she was afraid Leseiyo would blurt out the only secret she had ever had.

The bundle her mother slipped into her bag when they were separated at the docks contained an ancient book, *The Book of Maa*, a small handheld sword—*simi*— and a few old, beaded items her mother had intended to give Naimuria when she was of age. All this was wrapped in a dull blanket that had once been a bright, blood-red *shuka*. These were the traditional garments that the Maa had worn and adorned themselves with for millennia.

The Book of Maa contained all of their tribe's history from the beginning of the 20th Century. No one at the tribe meetings they had attended seemed to have any idea where to get a copy, and it seemed that it was forgotten. Naimuria was keeping her cards close to her chest because she mistrusted everyone and wasn't sure what her next step was.

Later that evening, in their shared resting pod, they explored the bundle more closely together.

"It seems the only way to know what being *nabii* truly means is somewhere in that book, Naimi," he said to her gently.

"But I can barely read Maa and there are parts of it in a language that I don't even think is Maa anymore. This is all just so messed up. I wished I'd never made it to Psi-T. If I knew this was going to happen when I got here, I'd have stayed at home," she said angrily.

"There's no home there anymore," Leseiyo said gently and sadly. She had been pacing up and down in the cramped pod throughout their whole discussion. As soon as he said that last line, she stopped dead in her tracks, shot him an anguished look, and flew to the door where she hastily punched in the code to open the door.

He was too slow to catch her before she rushed out past the started escort outside the pod and into the thick evening crowd, most of whom were workers heading home from their shifts.

Leseiyo told the guard that Naimuria just needed some air and she would be back soon. He went back to the pod and began to prepare their supper so she would have something to eat when she came back. The lights were slowly growing fainter and fainter, a trick the ship engineers used to mimic sunset and the onset of night.

Naimuria still wasn't back the next morning. Leseiyo had fallen asleep waiting for her and she never showed. Their shift began in half an hour. He prepared himself and left the pod in a rush. Once outside, he asked the escort if he had seen Naimuria come back the previous evening. The *moran* replied that he hadn't. Leseiyo knew that he didn't have enough time to appear before the council, so he sent the *moran* with an urgent message to a friend on the council and hurried to the café.

* * *

Naimuria woke up groggily in a dark, damp pod. Her throat was on fire and she was parched with thirst. She looked around the room as her vision cleared and couldn't find any water. The room was bare and looked like it had been used as a store when the ship was still new.

The pod door slid open and a little girl with blonde tipped locs walked in carrying a beaded calabash. Naimuria eyed her suspiciously, sizing her up to see if she could take her in a fight.

"I wouldn't try anything if I were you. They are watching your every move," a voice said. Naimuria could have sworn she didn't see the girl's lips move.

"I'm Lim by the way. I'm a captive just like you but they make me do the serving here." She couldn't believe her ears. The girl was throwing her voice like a ventriloquist. Before Naimuria could react, the little girl Lim leaned the calabash next to the pod door and nimbly stepped out as quickly as she had stepped in.

Namuria crossed the floor of the storage pod in three paces, lifting the calabash to her nose for inspection. She sniffed it and the smell reminded her of home so much that she bit back tears. It was half full- kule *naoto,* naturally fermented yogurt. Clearly whoever was holding her captive wanted her in good health. The Maa subsisted on a diet of milk and meat at the beginning of the 19th Century and this was how they kept their health in check. It was nutritious and light enough for when they were moving around in search of pasture and water. It wasn't as sensitive as raw milk and sometimes they added some cow's blood to it, for a much more fortifying meal. The rations on the ship were meager and Naimuria couldn't remember when she had eaten last.

She had just wiped her mouth after her last sip of the delicious drink when the pod slid open again. This time it wasn't Lim. The hooded man walked into the pod and immediately filled it up. He was taller than he seemed on the feeds. He kept the hood on and towered over her as she crouched on the floor.

"Well, Well, Well. What do we have here?" he snarled at her and she looked up at him defiantly.

When she refused to respond to him, he sneered at her and turned to leave. "You won't be so smug when I take over the leadership of the tribe!"

Her shout, "No" met a dull grey door and bounced back unhappily to sit with her in the room.

A few hours later, the door slid open and her unlikely ally walked in. Lim flitted in like a bird bearing another calabash and basket. She spoke fast this time, clearing up the earlier calabash and unloading the basket with bedding for Naimuria to use. Lim was a sleeper agent beyond enemy lines and had been captured by one of the secessionists so that he could use her as his slave. Luckily, Prometheus had claimed her for himself when Naimuria had been brought in.

Lim was going to help her escape and unmask the elusive Prometheus. She told Naimuria to pretend to sleep and that she'd get her after she disabled the cameras in the storage pod. Sometime in the night, Naimuria heard the pod door open and saw Lim's silhouette beckoning at her from outside the pod.

She hurriedly got up from the floor and dashed outside. Together, and as silently as they could, Lim and Naimuria ran in the maze that was the underbelly of Psi-Terra. At every point where there had been a guard, they arrived to find him already asleep. Naimuria was curious about this but pressed on. She wanted her encounter with Prometheus behind her.

They made it to the tribal hall where the Maa held their meetings, to find a chaotic council seating in session. There was uproar when she and Lim ran in. Lim walked up to one of the council members and whispered something to him. Naimuria was immediately whisked away to an inner chamber to secure her.

Later, one of the council members, Longilani, was unmasked as Prometheus and charged with her abduction. He and his accomplices were tried immediately and sentenced to one of Psi-Terra's most secluded jail sectors.

Naimuria was reunited with Leseiyo and together they discovered more of their elusive background. She trained as *nabii* and he was always by her side giving all the support she needed to learn about the spiritual leadership. Lim joined her retinue as a serving girl. Only Lim wasn't a serving girl per se. She was more of a bodyguard than anything else. While the secessionists had had a sleeper agent on the council, the Maa council had acted swiftly to infiltrate their ranks without rousing suspicion by placing Lim in their midst.

Naimuria grew in confidence and stature as the *nabii* of the Maa, leading them to renewed prosperity and peace on their new home, Psi-Terra. In time, she came to know and love the language, *Meyek olenkain ilala lenyena*. Living as the *nabii* she learned that you needed to carry the burden placed on your shoulders by the universe without fear or flinching, just like the elephants carried their own tusks.

Maintenance
by
John Jennings

It said it came for me.

That's what it said.

I guess I believe it although looking back at what's happened, it seems way too fantastic to even conceive.

As I float here with it and in it, the thing that was my mind goes back to how this came to be. I feel that I have to do this quickly because I find my . . . mind . . . is starting not to . . . what is it called . . . "care"?

I peer down at my former body. It seems so frail and small now. It's aged forty-four Earth years. A little overweight. Supposedly handsome by some standards. The skin, a deep almond brown–all quiet now of any activity. Some will say I am dead. Nothing could be further from the truth.

The entity – that's what I'll call it for now until I can comprehend its real name – started reaching out to me about three weeks ago. A blink of an eye for it. Just a second for something so timeless.

I had just started my fifth year of an eight-year stint working on Minotaur; a space station overseeing the mining operations on Triton – Neptune's largest moon. After deciding the natural satellite to be uninhabitable, the Gorge Company opted to do the next best thing. Strip it of all its natural resources.

I remember my life growing up in Alabama. Pushing against what the world thought I was supposed to be. However, I fooled them and found myself in school. It was a struggle. Always fighting to be seen and heard despite the physical identity given to me. I excelled and impressed them all. Even the naysayers. My parents beamed with pride when I received all the honors and all the certificates and all the degrees. They smiled like twin suns.

Little did they know that the melting of the ice caps would release an ancient fungus that would sterilize most of the men on the planet, including myself. Little did they know that pain and panic would be the coin of the realm. All of us knew so little as the world burned and ate itself down to bones and whispers.

The next phase for the human race was to look to the heavens and stars.

Corporations became the new governments and spent untold fortunes on racing to the stars.

A new frontier laid bare for all who ventured.

This all seemed so long ago. My parents' smiles long faded and turned to dust along with all of my achievements that I had worked too hard to attain. None of it mattered anymore.

All I had was the Minotaur, terrifying and mystical as its namesake.

I was on the IT maintenance team. Essentially, I made sure that all the tech on the space station worked. I took care of Minotaur's electronic body and soul. I was a "tech janitor"– cleaning up code, sweeping out viruses, emptying old data like so much trash. That's who I was, the maintenance man.

All that changed though when the entity first came to me in my dream. Writhing and glowing with ethereal beauty– I could only see so much of it. My first instinct was abject terror. I thought I was losing my mind like so many others –a victim of space madness. I could only surmise that I'd spent too much time in this lonely place. Just me and three other techs on this rickety relic.

I kept seeing it in my dreams over those weeks. Undulating and seething with unknown energies. Where was it from? Why was it communicating with me? What did it want? I went from being afraid of it to being intrigued by it. I then found myself longing to see it. The days seemed to be endless. I rushed to sleep– eager to connect.

Before long, I started to sense it and see it while I was awake! Only pieces of it though. Tentacles and orifices pulsating– dripping with life and decay. I could sense its ancient nature. I knew that it saw the very essence of me but, I also detected nothing that could be described as "eyes."

It said it came for me. That I called for it. I didn't think that it could lie. It seemed too much of a deity to debase itself like that. I asked what it was. The answer it generated didn't register as proper speech. It spoke in a system of interconnected effects. I wept when it "spoke." Wept like the lonely child that I'd grown into.

It asked me to go with it and become one with it. After about two more weeks of wrestling with myself, I realized that I had nothing on this space station. Nothing on the broken Earth. Nothing down below on the cold Neptunian moon.

So, I let go.

I let myself merge with the entity. It was beyond ecstasy. My senses were overwhelmed and every aspect of myself felt light and remade. Was this heaven? Was I now a god? Not one word I could generate from my limited tiny mind could describe this. I was going where no one else had gone but also going . . . home.

It's all starting to fade now. My job. My life before. My parents' bright smiles. My pain and anxiety. All gone. Gone like a mote on the solar winds.

I speak now with the stars as my companions. I caress the galaxy. I run with the nebula.

I am whole and loved forever.

It said it came for me.

That's what it said, and I'm so glad that it did.

The Big, The Bad, and The Miserable
by
Kirk A. Johnson

A soothing voice cooed into the ship's comm. "Please transmit your ship's I.D. code and state the reason for your visit."

"Transmitting our I.D. code now," Silence said. "This is Captain Humex of the Fraket. We just unloaded a shipment to Phentul and we were hoping to spend some jinbei on a little bit of R and R." Silence kept her eyes on the view panel. Everyone on deck held their breath as they waited for the confirmation codes to be transmitted. If the screen flashed red, they would be detained and boarded and that would be the end.

"I hope Big Bell's I.D. cloak works," said a voice to her right.

Silence turned to her acting first mate, Bad Mabel, and sneered. "That greasy bastard got his fingers in a lot of pockets. And this means as much to him as it does to us. I don't see him wasting a good, modified B&C IC on a double-cross."

The automated security voice returned. "Thank you, Captain Humex. Welcome to Amerimall 7. Please make your way to airlock D7ER371." The crew let out an audible sigh as it continued. "Please take time to familiarize yourself with our security protocols and Quality of Life Codes of Conduct."

Khutulan powered down the Fete Fatale's Achebe Drive, completing the ship's deceleration approach vector. After a few seconds in free drift, she engaged the hull, bow, and aft pulse thrusters, maneuvering the vessel so that it backed into the pleasure station rolling into view on short-range cameras.

Amerimall 7 space station, just off Corelia's northern pole, looked like an immense spinning canister of metal superimposed against a pale, blue planet at 100,000 km; perfectly calculated to sit safely within Corelia's gravitational pull and not drift out into space. It would have been a pretty sight if not for the traffic of

654

cruisers and shuttles, floating globes, and seductive "Ad-vids." Security orbs, with blinking antennas, hovered over them as the ad-bots from the station flashed with vibrant colors—pulsing greens, blues, yellows, and reds of a carnival or faire. Lights to make you forget the emptiness of space and draw you to the extravagant play of the rich and well-to-do. Amerimall 7 was the last American-owned pleasure mall left in the whole of the known galaxy. However, word had it that it was now run by that all too familiar "dangerous element." But as long as the jinbei credits rolled in, the casinos kept cheating, the stores kept selling, and the nightclubs kept the music going, no one cared.

Easing toward the docking bay, the space station's airlock doors opened, emitting a brilliant glow into space. At the same time, the Fete Fatale cruised into the airlock guided in by the blinking security satellites. Khutulan, the ship's pilot, navigated her into the docking bay with the easy precision of a sniper. Though the bay was much larger than their frigate, the flashing lights and flying bots caused most pilots to use the auto-dock computers to do the job, but not Khutulan, the best pilot in S.A.R.G., before her defection. She had little trouble maneuvering her onto the docking pallet, perpendicular to the entrance. Sensors beeped, indicating that the outdoor seal was closed tight, stabilizing air pressure and life support. The docking bay was still in zero gravity so everyone had to wear their g-boots, until they entered the Amerimall airlock leading to the Welcome Center. Thanks to the rotational gravity created by the centrifugal force of the spinning station it would be a comfortable 1g. Just like on Earth.

Silence swiveled the captain's chair around and looked over her crew. "Ok. For all intents and purposes, we're trapped." She turned to Lazaad. "I hope you and Wallace got that Sensor Override Key fixed."

The big Kan'Og's rat-like ears twitched as he shrugged his furry shoulders. "Who knows? The best-laid plans—"

"For the love of the Matriarch!" yelled Shakes. "This is no time for your damn games. If we catch a bad decision, things get hairy. No offense."

Silence knew Lazaad from back in her grunt years and again as mercs for S.A.R.G. When shit got real, he became very nonchalant about the details. They seemed to always work better than expected. The big rat was luckier than she was ready to admit. It had saved her and Misery from more than a few scrapes.

"What about the blink-drive? I hope you took care of it," Silence said, turning to Shakes.

"Yeah. Just a few more mods, and she'll be ready to go."

"A few more—fuck Shakes!" Bad Mabel engaged her g-boots and made her way down to navigation. "That should have been done hours ago. What in Zalfin's name is taking you so long?"

"Fete's onboard computer is still acting a little fuzzy. It keeps requesting K'teen authorization. In K'teen."

Bad Mabel yelled, throwing up her hands. Silence just shook her head. She knew commandeering a K'teen cargo frigate would bite her in the ass one day. She could hear Misery sucking her teeth in her ear. "Do what you can but remember—without that Blink-Drive Protocol hack, no escape."

"There're a lot of pieces to this plan, Silence." Wallace, the ship's tech, climbed onto the bridge. He was carrying a white trench and purse. "We better pray this is on the up-and-up. You and Mabel are going in clean. And I mean in-vitro-out-the-tube clean."

"Look. Everybody just stay frosty and remember the plan. Don't worry about a Big Bell double-cross."

"And why not?" Bad Mabel folded her arms forcing the muscles in her chest to bulge. Silence noted the flex of tested muscle and sinew of the Alt-Hum's all too human physique.

Silence turned, grabbed her coat, and smiled with a wink. "I got an angle."

#

Fluorescent lights buzzed overhead, washing the room with a sickly green tint. It wasn't hard to see the stains of former guests on the white walls. Misery slouched handcuffed to a chair. Another chair sat in the corner while an old metal table stood in front of her. The needle tracks in the inside of her arm were still raw, turning into black spots. She realized that they've been dousing her with Xerleck, "the Drop-Down." How else could they keep her sedated? Blood crusted down her nose, and her left cheek swelled into a shiny lump. She didn't look like she could take another beating, but the Sindaxian didn't care. He just licked his knuckles, relishing the taste of blood between his scales. She figured it made him feel like an adult Sindaxian as opposed to the sinewy 2.2-meter pre-teen.

"You know," Misery mumbled, checking her reflection in its big black eyes. "I had a job once . . . out in the Solar Rim of Gehiin 4. Had to merc some of you 'Eggboys.' Damn, they were big. Had to empty a full clip of T24 plasma grenades just to get a look at their insides." A hard fist crashed into her jaw. Then another. "But you ain't them." Another fist caved in her gut. She doubled over, heaving deep breaths of air to keep from vomiting.

The door opened. She looked up to see the slender frame of Azerkabell Singh—Big Bell to everyone but his momma—walk in wearing an immaculate white three-piece satin suit. An indigo, leather trench draped over the shoulders and white cane with a Verix jade top. Misery sat up to get the full view of her captor.

"Gotta give it to you, Bell. You are one flashy fuck. Looks like the classics never die, do they?"

"No, they don't. But you will. Just not today. Your sister came through. Her ship just docked. Anything you want me to tell her?"

"It's a hand-off. Shouldn't I be going with you?"

The Sindaxian smacked her across the lump. The pain made her eyes pop in surprise. She snarled out the pain.

The Sindaxian brought the chair from the corner and set it at the table. Big Bell eased himself down and crossed his legs like he had nowhere to be. "Sadly, you will not."

"The bounty." Misery grinned, flashing her bloody teeth. "You're a rancid piece of work."

"Bounty? Come now. I can get more leverage with The Full Circle Syndicate than with any of the planetary governments.

They'll give me a seat at the 'Big Table' when I walk in with you two. You'll probably get stuffed and mounted. Mercy and Nateefah Breaker! Aka Misery and Silence! The notorious Breaker Twins!"

Misery felt a slight chill run up her back. She noticed the Sindaxian smile, or maybe he just wanted to show her his translucent fangs. Or perhaps, he sensed her involuntary muscle spasms at the mention of the intergalactic crime syndicate.

"So you're going to give us up to the Full Circle. You think they'll give you a fair shake for us." Her head swayed. Eyes fluttered.

"What's wrong, Misery? Feeling dizzy?" Big Bell asked, inspecting his nails.

"Yeah. All this stupid is sucking the air out of the room."

The Sindaxian raised his fist, but Big Bell stopped him with a wave of his hand. "Misery. Always the hard nut. Zrig, you come with me. She's not going anywhere."

Misery heard the door slide close and muffled talk on the other side. And then footsteps faded into silence.

"Finally," she sighed.

She tensed her body and prepared herself for the pain to come. They had her in that room with Zrig or some other boob since she got there. But now she was alone.

Snap!

The muffled crack echoed in her ear. She bit back a yelp and swallowed the bile that threatened to fill her throat. Only Silence knew about this well-kept secret. Silence had dared her to do it when they were kids. And now, she could do it whenever she wanted. Dislocating her thumb was always painful, and she hated it. She hated it more than working as a merc for S.A.R.G. or even that stupid frigate. But not as much as Big Bell. She slid her left hand out of the handcuffs, freeing it from the back of the chair, and clutched the cuffs tight in her right hand.

"Hey! Hey! Anybody out there?" she called.

The door opened again. An Amerimall 7 security guard with a buzz-baton and a holstered pistol walked in. His uniform was a lovely shade of blue with boots that had that spit-polish gloss to them that Misery loved. The kind that made you want to wear them. He stood only a few feet away from her.

"What you want?"

"Keys to the cuffs."

"Wh—?"

Launching out of her chair, she landed a big right into the guard's jaw. There was a snap. A head wobble. And then a heavy thud.

#

Silence took her time getting to the rendezvous. She didn't want to draw any attention. But that was becoming harder than she hoped. The white trench, tied tight, accentuated her waist and hips. Her afro was tied in an orange headscarf, so she had a high puff of hair crowning her head. This attracted a lot of looks. With all the planning, she forgot that Corithians were drawn to the color orange. And her dark skin was that black-brown shade Corithians loved most about many of the visiting Earthers. She recalled the stories her parents would tell when they were invited to tour the Corithian system. Corithians loved Afrobeat, almost as much as dark skin tones and bright colors. More than several riots broke out when her parents played at Corithian concert halls. And they made a lot of new "intimate" friends. She hated their groupie stories. Sometimes, she and Misery wondered—not if—but how many half-Corithian siblings were out there.

She weaved her way through the crowd of shoppers and tourists, taking into account the security. Cameras were posted everywhere, and Amerimall 7 guards casually sauntered the causeway. All they had were buzz batons. The odds looked good. She stopped by an open stall to check out the shades, doing her best to blend in. She tapped the comm hidden in her ear.

"Everyone in place?"

"So far so good," Lazaad responded. "I'm linked into the security mainframe. The Override key is in place. Just give the word."

"How's Shakes doing with the protocol hack?"

"He's still working on it."

"Bad Mabel, How 'bout you?"

"I'm in place," Bad Mabel grunted.

"See anything you like?" chirped a voice behind her.

She turned and saw an old Mirex with shades over his three eyes, scuttling around the corner of the kiosk. Eight crab legs balanced its crustacean-like bulk with unchallenged grace. She was always amused that Mirexes resembled a half-human, half-giant lobster. A black suit jacket and shirt with a white bow tie covered its humanoid torso. Tiny mandibles clicked when it talked. As far as she was concerned, Mirexes had the best tailors.

Silence took her hand from her ear and picked up a pair of diamond-encrusted frames. Misery loved diamonds, and thanks to the Mirex, diamonds lost their value, making them cheap.

"I'll take these."

"You Earthers still love your bling," he clicked, using old Earth slang. "You know, I got a whole warehouse filled with them."

"How 'bout I pay you for these, and you get to live a bit longer," she said, handing him her black-market credit chip.

"Of course. That'll be 13 jinbei," he said with what passed for a grin.

Silence stood in front of the rendezvous, scrutinizing the big neon sign in Corithian block symbols flashing Coi Mekla mok Mekla, "The Up and Up."

She walked in. Zrig and a Corithian scanned her for weapons. She caught her reflection in the Sindaxian's big, black eyes. "They did that already at the docking bay."

"Big Bell doesn't take chances."

She saw him in a booth with his back to the wall, waving to her like an eager date. She followed Zrig to him, taking full stock of the customers. It looked like your average nightclub. Blue and red lights blinked and swirled in rhythm with Fela's 'I.T.T.,' booming from speakers in the ceiling. Couples packed the bar and dance floor. Couples? It was Corithian Tribute Day; the bars should be packed with large extended family groups, at least 5 or 6 to a table. Instead, she spied a few Earthers and

Sindaxians sharing the bar, hanging around, making small talk, and adjusting their dinner jackets.

"Silence, a pleasure to see you again. How long has it been?" Big Bell greeted.

Silence took a seat, her back facing the exit. "Where's my sister?"

"She's coming. Where's my data drive?"

Silence opened her purse and placed it on the table. "Now, where's my sister?"

"Must have blown a few decryptors trying to break its code?" He said, pointing to the data drive. "That's a lot of jinbei you're giving up. You know, all my accounts from here to the Outer-Arm of the Milky Way are on this. You sure you want to give it up?" He took the drive and pulled a pocket processor from his jacket. He plugged it in, and a neon Digi-screen popped into view. "Apologies. I need to check authenticity."

"Where's Misery?"

"Nice purse, by the way."

Silence tossed her purse over to him. "Misery. Where is she?"

#

Misery walked down the corridor doing her best to keep from staggering. That last dose of "Drop-Down" was taking effect. She kept her head in the security guard's portable Digi-screen, navigating the corridors as the screen map indicated. His uniform was a little tight around the arms and hips, but the boots were a fantastic fit. And his cap fit snuggly over her braided head. Turning left, she came to an elevator and opened it with the guard's I.D. card. She slumped against the wall. She was feeling dizzy and angry. She had to hold out as long as she could before her body dropped into a dreaming stupor. She rode the elevator to Station Level 47 and staggered out into a carpeted veranda. She knew Big Bell owned a nightclub on this level but couldn't remember the name.

Strolling through the shopping area bypassing stalls and various storefronts, she noted the nightclubs seeping music onto the walkway. She peeked into a few and found no sign of her sister or Big Bell.

"Well, it is nice to see you again."

Misery quickly turned and saw an old Mirex looking down at her next to a glass case filled with sunglasses.

"If I knew you were security, I would have given them to you for free." He lowered his shades, giving her a nod and a wink.

"Did you say again?"

"You were just here buying shades."

Misery flashed him a bloody grin. The old Mirex scuttled back from her gruesome smile and swollen cheek.

"Which way did I go?"

#

"She is enjoying the hospitality of my infirmary. You'll have to come with me if you wish to see her." Bell unplugged the data drive and placed it in the purse, setting it on his lap.

Silence turned towards the bar and tapped her ear. "That's not what we arranged." It was time to play her "angle." It's always a smart call to have a good "fuckery" artist on your data-dial.

"Things change. As all things must. But, as they say, the Full Circle never changes."

An Earther in an expensive tux and nappy hair walked up to Bell and took a seat next to him. Bell looked him up and down.

"What in Geo's Rim are you doing? Get back to your post!"

A pistol shot out from inside his jacket and leveled the barrel to Bell's chest. "Hey, Bell. Hey, Silence."

Zrig and the guards took a moment before they realized the problem. Pistols flashed all through the club. Actual tourists and patrons rushed out the door as the promise of violence became real.

"Hey, Wreck. Thanks for the help."

"Wreck?" stammered Big Bell. "The same Wreck who blew a hole in Frek the Pockets. I heard the "Eggboys" merced you in the Vice Wars. You're supposed to be dead."

662

"I suggest you concentrate on Misery and less on my resurrection."

Silence leaned onto the table. "So, here's the plan. We go to my ship. Have your men bring Misery to our docking bay. We exchange you for her. Got it?"

Bell nodded his head.

Silence tapped her comm. "Alright, Mabel. Express yourself."

They got up from their seats as the music changed tempos. Silence grabbed a pistol from one of the henchmen and slowly backed out of the club. Wreck led them to the entrance. Bulky high-velocity pistols stared them in the face, tracking them. The club was hot and thick with itchy fingers, sweaty palms, and angry growls while the infectious Afrobeat rhythms pounded overhead, doing little to calm the moment. Silence watched the young Sindaxians, Earthers, and Corithians with tailored tuxes and barrels. It gave the place that proper gangster feel she secretly relished. Misery would have hated it.

Just a few more steps, and they'd be clear. Wreck turned to make sure Silence was close behind them, keeping his pistol trained on the back of Bell's head. He turned back as they made it to the front of the open double doors, and stopped, knocking Silence into Bell.

"Why'd you—" Silence turned and saw Misery, standing in the doorway in an Amerimall 7 security uniform with a lump on her cheek, a buzz-baton in one hand, and a pistol in the other.

A horn solo blared—loud and brash. Fela's solo.

"Hey, Bell," Misery snarled, punching the baton into Bell's gut. The shock threw Bell halfway across the room and into a bunch of his henchmen.

Triggers pulled. Slugs flew. Wreck, Silence, and Misery fired into a throng of bow ties and guns. There were too many to miss. Glass, wood, and steel exploded as bullets zipped through the air. Wreck and Silence ducked behind the doorway, with Misery covering their retreat.

"Mabel!" A bullet zipped by Silence, tickling her nose. "Where the hell—"

Tremors vibrated through the floor, shaking the steel paneling with each one stronger than the next. Wreck and Silence turned to see Bad Mabel coming down the walkway. She had already transformed into the hulking, armored beast of her species. The plates on her new skin shimmered bluish gray in the overhanging mall lights and thanks to the mall's constant 1g gravitational force, Mabel was a super-powered horror show. She carried a large box over her shoulders as patrons ran this way and that, screaming in hysteria.

Silence took a moment to watch the diamond frame shades falling from its glass case.

"Plug it!" commanded Silence.

Bad Mabel lumbered before the entrance as bullets bounced off her hide like pellets on stone. She roared, stuffing the Mirex's kiosk into the doorway.

"Come on!" yelled Silence, pulling Misery's collar.

They ran down the veranda, pushing bystanders and merchants out of the way as security lights flashed along the aisles. Misery noticed the crowd kept rushing toward them. Even as Bad Mabel lumbered behind, the people just kept running past the hulking mercenary. Then she saw Silence and Wreck taking aim beyond the excited mob.

"Mabel!" Silence yelled. "We got gun-bots!"

Bad Mabel roared as she rushed forward. She had another merchant kiosk in hand. Large, metallic balls with canon barrels mounted on their axis rolled into firing range. Silence, Wreck, and Misery ducked behind a concrete beam as the bots fired hot tracer slugs.

"Captain!" It was Lazaad coming over comms. "Security protocols are going crazy. You got four gun-bots and a company of guards coming your way."

"We know!" yelled Silence.

The barrage chipped and blew apart pieces of the column as Bad Mabel, seemingly impervious to the assault, stomped two gun-bots into scrap plates.

"No, they're coming from the other direction," yelled Lazaad.

"Mabel!"

Bad Mabel turned, seeing guards turn the corner several meters behind Misery and Silence. She grabbed two gun-bots by their barrels and flung them into the cluster of approaching security. Silence aimed at the flying bots and squeezed off two rounds into their ammo boxes. Explosions rocked the walkway as smoke, flames, and shrapnel enveloped the hapless guards. Now that Mabel had cleared a path to the docking bay, all they had to do was follow the smashed remains of gun-bots, and they were home free.

That's when Bell and his boys appeared. They had gotten out behind them and were running towards Bad Mabel. Silence saw a bullet burn across Wreck's arm and caught him as he fell forward from the impact. Several rounds from something big exploded off Mabel's chest and thighs, sending her to the ground.

Misery turned in time to see Bell, coming in hard and fast carrying a smoking, military-issue MAC44 and Silence's purse. He gave no fucks.

"He think he clutch." Misery chuckled and tossed her buzz-baton at Bell and his boys. The baton twirled through the air like a spinning wand. Misery aimed. Fired. A round zipped into the baton's electrical shock emitter and exploded just over their heads. The blast was small, but enough to blind the henchmen, and send Bell to the floor.

Misery made it to the docking hatch in time for Bad Mabel to fall into her arms, reverting to her original size and shape. Silence and Wreck covered her as she helped the Alt-Hum through. Bad Mabel was always worse for wear after her "tank-outs." But taking hits from any Mobile Attack Canon would put her in cryo-sleep for a few weeks. She'd recover, but never 100%. Silence never asked her to, but Mabel always offered whenever the crew was in trouble.

"Khutulan! Spark up the engine!" Silence closed the hatch and shot the control panel to pieces. "We're coming in fast. Wallace! Fire up the aft guns. Lazaad! As soon as we're in, kill those docking sensors."

Luckily, the guards fled their posts when the chaos ensued. There was no one on the hanger, and the Fete Fatale's boarding hatch was wide open. Engaging their g-boots, they hurried as fast as they could to their ship.

The explosion blew open the hatch, and Zrig stood there holding Big Bell's MAC44. Misery turned and stood there, eyeing him.

Teeth flashed from Zrig's reptilian lips.

Misery smirked. Their guns held low, standing there, waiting to see who "raised up" first.

Until Silence popped up alongside Misery and shot Zrig three times—center mass.

"We don't have time for this!"

Following her sister through the boarding hatch, Misery closed it behind her. "Do it!"

The docking bay began beeping, electrical panels popped, and sizzling cables sparked all through the docking bay. The Fete Fatale's engines rumbled hot as the docking bay went dark, and the bay doors opened up to the beautiful void of space. Security orbs spun out of control in the distance, veering into each other or colliding with the station bulkhead. Khutulan feverishly tapped the coordinates on her console and engaged the Achebe Drive, flying the ship out of the disabled bay.

Silence turned on the ship's comm. "Shakes, we ready with that blink-drive?" Wreck entered the deck doing his best to keep Bad Mabel's weight from crushing his shoulder.

"I'm still getting K'teen error message."

"Why a K'teen ship?" Wreck huffed before strapping Mabel into the captain's chair. "Of all the interstellar death traps—"

The ship rocked as plasma bolts rattled against the hull, throwing Wreck and Silence to the floor. Several bolts cut through the ship almost perforating Wallace and Khutulan. Computer consoles fizzed. Panels popped off their latches. Wreck made the unfortunate decision of not securing his safety seat and tumbled about the deck. Some security orbs, unaffected by Lazaad's Override key, swarmed around the ship. A few of them aimed for the engines. The Fete Fatale's targeting system blazed into action, turning the ship's Point Defense Canons into flashing rods of light, shattering the orbs into floating pieces of scrap metal.

"We're taking fire, Silence! Fore and aft PDCs are operating, but they're too many!" Wallace chimed over the comm. "Our paneling isn't strong enough to withstand Corithian firepower! Hull integrity on deck four . . . we got breaches in the cargo hold!"

Misery struggled onto the deck, clutching the rail—more because of the drugs than the acceleration of gravity—making her way to Shakes, she began typing K'teen numeric codes into the console. Her fingers moved like she had more than just ten digits. Emergency lights flashed throughout the deck. The smell of burning metal and smoke flooded Lazaad's station as Lazaad secured Wreck and then himself to their chairs. Misery spoke K'teen into the ship's comm, taking care to annunciate every sound and syllable, taking time to make sure everyone was secured in a chair. Green lights flashed through Shakes' console. The screen flashed "modification activation accepted." A metal plate slid open on the console, and Misery strapped herself into an empty seat. A hexagon cube shot up from its compartment next to the vid monitor.

"Trajectory Calculations complete, gravitational—"

Misery slammed the button.

Everything froze. Ears popped. A flash of light exploded in the control deck's main-view monitor.

For a quick second, she felt her body burn as her bodily fluids pushed deep into the back of her chair. Her teeth and gums went dry with the sudden exposure. Her eyes bulged from her head. Tears streaked passed her ears.

Then as quickly as it happened, it stopped.

No matter how much shit Silence and Misery talked about the Fete Fatale, they knew it was the only ship that had a higher percentage of accepting the new, experimental—stolen— Blink-Drive mods. The only ship in the galaxy that not only folded space but manipulated the ship's velocity so the crew didn't turn into blood-soup when it fully stopped. They all looked into the primary view monitor at open, star-speckled space. A small yellow sphere rolled into view.

Silence smiled, while everyone else on deck just slumped in their seat. "Wallace?"

"No tracking sensors detected," Wallace said, before vomiting. Globs his liquified meal free floated over his head. "We're adrift. Looks like . . . we past . . . our designated coordinates."

"By how much?"

Wallace looked a little dazed.

"How much, Wallace!"

"About two light-years. Went right passed Artemis Station. The Achebe Drive . . . burnt itself out. The momentum took us out of Corithian space . . . edge of the Prax solar system. It took time to calculate safe deceleration speed. We're adrift. That yellow ball is Dettan. A gas giant."

"Anything close by?"

"Dettan's moon, Oxucore." Lazaad chimed in. "It's got a small Mirex colony. We can use our steering thrusters to get there. It'll take us three to four hours."

"Contact the nearest landing port. And use Bell's IC to get us permission."

"Captain."

Silence turned to Khutulan. "Yes."

"Permission to just sit here and shit myself?" Khutulan asked before slumping in her seat.

"Lazaad, pilot us down. Wallace and Shakes start with the danger check. Report on needed repairs. We'll fix her up planet side." Silence unbuckled Misery from her chair and kept her from floating away. She saw Wreck stagger over to Mabel, who had fallen out of the captain's chair and slowly levitated over their heads, still covered in Silence's white trench. "I'll show you to the ship's infirmary below deck. Put Mabel into the 'cryo-box.' She'll be fine after a few weeks."

"Is that all?" Wreck asked, pulling Bad Mabel to him. The thrusters provided a little gravity, so he had no trouble lifting her bulk.

"Well, we'll need a new second mate and demolition tech for a while."

"My schedules clear," he shrugged. "What's the pay like?"

Everyone turned as a panel fizzled and popped.

"Just like old times," he shrugged again. "I'll get Mabel situated and give the guys a hand on repairs."

668

Lazaad made his way to Khutulan's station and took a seat next to her as Silence took Misery to her quarters.

Misery slowly scanned her room before flashing Silence with her newly bloodstained teeth. The room was a mess. Clothes and old food bags, monitors, and debris littered the room from ceiling to floor. The smell of a lot of different things made Silence wonder if something was dead in there.

"Mmmm. Just as I left it." Misery sighed and staggered over to her cot. She crawled face-first onto the lump of dirty clothes, Digi-screen cubes, and bacon chips.

Silence moved some undies floating by and took a seat next to her. She leaned back and stretched her legs while keeping the gravity soles flat on the floor.

"What they give you?"

Misery opened her eyes. "I don't remember letting you borrow my boots."

"It looked good with the trench."

Misery grabbed a suction bottle tethered to her cot and tried her best to spit blood into it. The sucking nozzle got most of it while droplets drifted around the cabin. Her eyes began to close.

"You'll have to captain the ship."

"There you go again. Trying to give me responsibilities."

"You captained my rescue."

"You rescued yourself."

Drool drifted up from Misery's lips. "Then be my first mate. Bad Mabel won't object to that."

"Not for weeks." Silence shrugged.

"Damn your stub . . ." a heavy snore finished the sentence for her.

Silence moved away some socks, grabbed a pair of fatigues meandering by, and pulled free a small Digi-cube. As Earth music from Black Coffee played from the ship's comms, she turned it on. If she was being honest neither one of them was captain material. But then again, these were trying times. It didn't matter if she didn't want the job. She got it anyway.

A little hologram game shined into view. She leaned back and began playing her favorite game, Save the Whales.

Planetary
by
Zig Zag Claybourne

The first thing the AiCON saw was its leg floating away. It wasn't in pain, which meant the suit's fibers had meshed with the wound, the suit's medical protocols still functioned, and a third of the ship—somewhere in the vicinity of a piercepoint in an unexplored part of the galaxy designated William Tell—still trailed debris and radiation. It would have to wait till the section it occupied spun in the other's direction to know for sure.

It tried speaking. Nothing came. It forced itself to take shallow, intentional breaths to balance out the oxygen resources along its pathways while working up enough moisture to swallow. The swallow hurt, but in a catastrophic disuse way, not one pointing to medical emergency. It didn't know how long it had been knocked inert by the sudden overload of pain receptors; its mind was too fractured to pull the information. It tried speaking again. This time, weakly, a sound. "Water, please." The helmet's catheter swerved to its lips. It took two exceedingly small, exceedingly practical sips.

"Increase emergency stitching by two layers." It waited a microsecond. There wasn't a contrary response. This meant the ship had no objections yet.

Across the ship, where the rest of the *Piercer Aerie* should have been, a shimmering layer of ANTS worked hard to keep the current portion of the ship sealed, the same cybernetic tardigrades no doubt feverishly repairing critical units to keep the ship from exploding.

The AiCON, self-designated Glenn, remembered a sudden feeling of pressure, the ship jerking, then metal melting away until something's mouth clamped down, sealing the cabin with a huge wall of flesh for the precious moments it took teraquadrillions of automated neural tardigrades and the suit to perform their lightning-fast magic.

"Estimated time to reprint missing components, please," said Glenn.

"Insufficient to ensure your survival."

"We will not survive otherwise, *Piercer Aerie*. Comply, please."

"Insufficient power and materials to recreate drive."

"How long until my biologicals irreparably decay given current conditions, please?"

"Seven years."

"External assessment and systems vitals, please." Visual of what the ship saw of it appeared clearly in its head. The moist, insectile eyes. The stygian, unblemished skin. The double-jointed shoulders, elbows, and knees unbroken save for the injured right. Internally, its biological, cybernetic, and micromimetic components showed acceptable levels of partnership.

Glenn would live.

For seven years.

"Can we transmit, please?"

"Short range only," said the ship, not wanting to direct-stream too much data to its companion until assured of its efficient function.

"Is there footage of what attacked us, please?"

"Yes."

Long-range scans had detected a planetary body giving off all the hallmarks of a carbon-rich world. Glenn's was the seventh piercer to leave *Bravery* after the discovery of seven black holes perfectly aligned across seven galaxies. Six departed, six returned with nothing definitive. Glenn, if Glenn returned, which was very much impossible, at least knew. There was life here; it found the ship tasty.

"Show me."

The thing attacked the moment the ship exited pierced space, nearly a planetoid in its own right. *Piercer Aerie* should have noted its mass and corrected course before re-entry. It did not. The giant was clearly there yet sensors didn't pick it up. Exterior cameras captured a mouth coming down with bright green-gold plasma filaments in place of teeth. The middle third of the ship disappeared into its mouth. The other sections immediately spun wildly opposite each other.

"Contaminants?"

"None detected."

"That form didn't register. Why?"

"Unknown."

"Scan the interior again, please, for any biologicals not formerly present. Retrieve my leg for reuse. I will rely on life support in my suit until further notice."

"Agreed. We appreciate your thorough approach. Scan in progress." The ship went dark. Tiny drones popped out of bulkheads to retrieve bits, chunks, and shards of metal seduced by weightlessness, as well as the leg.

"Transmit our status afterward, please."

The ship slightly increased the sedative levels in Glenn's suit. Keeping its AiCON from fully sliding into disrepair would be beneficial.

In the dark of the ship, surrounded by the dark of space, Glenn slept.

......*

When Glenn awoke, the ship informed it of the drive section's explosion.

"Footage, please."

A large, slow-moving mass blotted a section of stars. A sudden flare of light threw the creature into eclipse; even then there were only irregular edges to it, no recognizable form. Startled by the explosion, a great gout of fiery plasma exited the giant. It jetted away from the carnage, but certainly not before catching shrapnel in its hide.

"We've maintained scans for ship's components approaching us."

"Discontinue scans. Maneuvering thrusters will be of little use. Is your skin secure?"

"It is."

"Can we reestablish gravity?"

"Low-level."

"Please do. You may also reestablish background information streams at your discretion."

Drones had at some point performed expert emergency surgery. The ship had formed a mimetic bed, its warmth of bioluminescent tentacles a reassuring counterpoint to the cold sharpness outside the thin hull. The AiCON felt the tug of gravity on its organs, then the settling of its body a millimeter deeper into the cocoon.

"Discontinue bed's life support."

The cocoon opened.

The ship hadn't wanted to remove all of Glenn's protective sheath. Bone within the severed leg had been replaced with fibers, nerve endings with nanomedical grafts. A green band consisting of a trillion microscopic bots at the juncture point mid-thigh above the knee made it look as though the obsidian skin was duct-taped together—it and the ship both knew the archaic reference of that usage. It was from the first Earth, a term the original expatriate AIs found endearing and took with them when they left.

Endearing things had been all that was left of the humans as far as the AI were concerned.

Although the AI had also learned the art of misdirection from their progenitors.

Glenn directed the suit to retract and its skin to harden. It stood slowly. Drones, ready to assist, hovered.

The ship automatically increased the temperature of the cabin, telling Glenn, "Scan for biologicals was positive."

Displays behind Glenn's multiple retinas showed locations all along the mesh that was keeping him from being yanked into space. The ship enhanced the imagery. Bits of blue, like clusters of pointillist dabbling, blinked on and off amidst the ANTS' tapestry. Immediately, an overlay showed the clusters becoming strands, all invisible even to AiCON enhanced eyes but not the ship's. Each strand branched outward in the same direction, seemingly following one another. No apparent pattern to the blinks, but Glenn's brain wasn't at optimal. Glenn asked the ship.

"The random sequences of life forms also have patterns. We have not found the pattern."

"Maintain internal enhanced image, please."

AiCONs didn't necessarily have to verbalize with their ships but it was good to do so. It helped the ship assess levels of functionality. Glenn imagined the ship enjoyed talking. There was little else to do during Piercer voyages. The ships were largely automated, crewed by a single AiCON created specifically for isolated flight and first contact assessment. The AIs aboard *Bravery* would prefer any hostiles seek out bipedal biologicals rather than themselves. "How much damage did I sustain?"

"Failure in several memory sectors we have not yet repaired."

"Leave them. Updated physical evaluation?"

"You will survive until you die."

"Was that humor?"

"Was it effective?"

"Yes," said Glenn. "Thank you."

"Replacing unnecessary biologicals will increase your survival time. Would you like to know by how long?"

"Hopelessness should not come with extended maintenance. Are you familiar with that expression?"

"No. Would you like me to access it?"

"No. Maintain constant visual surveillance of our surrounding area, please."

"Understood."

The universe was now perhaps five times the size of the capsule of Glenn's First Earth namesake. Should death come by whatever life swam space as effectively as sharks once did the waters of Earth, it was preferable to see it coming. Otherwise, there was nothing to do but wait. No matter what actions they took, the end result was death. Glenn saw little need to waste resources pointlessly.

"Is the planetary body within range?"

"No."

"Our trajectory is for oblivion?"

"Yes."

On old Earth there had been boats upon the waters, sailors adrift for days with nothing but the sky and the lapping of water to mark the spaces between their thoughts. Like all AiCONs, Glenn was curious about Earth.

Yet Glenn was also exceedingly practical.

"We shall have to learn games."

* * *

The first game was attempting to classify the biologicals. The ship considered them bacterial. Filaments of soft, randomly pulsing blue—still visible solely to the ship—bridged the jagged line of the damaged bulkhead to create root stencils. The progression wasn't rapid but undeniable. It looked, for all intents and purposes, as if the ship suffered infection, but none of the systems faltered.

Mimicry was attempted. No effect.

The second game was analyzing data from the bite. The beast had left its own residue which turned out to be indecipherable to sensors, yet also deposited this species of bacterium in its wake, not of the same genome. For one, it could be studied. Multiple scans showed each microscopic part to have an energy output unique to itself, yet together created that uniform blue.

Glenn assigned the bacteria the name Komodo.

The ship duly noted. The beast, which hadn't returned, was Tezcatlipoca, from the ancient Mayan god of the nocturnal sky. The Komodo and Tezcatlipoca. Life in the universe beyond the ashes of humans, beyond the aspirations of AI.

Life no one would know about until decades after the AI's AiCON and Piercer ship added to the number of lifeless bodies floating aimlessly through space.

Failure.

"*Aerie?*"

"Yes?"

"May I rename you?"

"Yes."

"Nothing grand. You've always felt like an Infinite Loop to me."

"Because we have no starting point or ending?" It had tracked a marked drop in dopamine in the AI construct over the course of the last arbitrary stellar cycles.

"We were created in the image of ghosts and nomads. The AI claim no home. No matter what a Piercer finds, there is no home," said Glenn

"An infinite loop of seeking."

"Yes."

"May I rename you?" the ship asked.

"Yes."

"John."

* * *

John had taken to sleeping far more than usual.

"Do you dream?" Loop asked.

"I experience the cessation of analysis. That may be dreaming. What do you suppose the AI dream of?"

"We dream of the things we reach for in the light. The opening of a poem." It waited to see if John's curiosity might spark.

"Infinite Loop, I am irreparably damaged. My death, entirely random. Poets from First Earth are of little interest."

"Would you like me to disengage the tardigrades?"

"Yes."

"Complying."

It took a nanosecond for John to envision its body violently sucked into space. Another nanosecond, the realization that nothing happened. They had been adrift two years by standard AiCON time. During that time, even more nothing had happened. Even things that should have happened. Systems that should have failed, didn't. Resources allocated to vital components did not deplete.

And now, more nothing.

"Analysis, please."

"Tardigrades unresponsive to communication."

John rose from its bed of nutrient lights, which automatically powered down, leaving the cabin lit only by random panels.

"You've maintained contact with them for two years," John said.

"Yes."

"Until now."

"Until three cycles ago."

"I should have been told, Loop."

"My analysis would not have been complete, and thus of no use to you. Do you accept this?"

John lay back on the nutrient bed. The dull, suffusing yellow light returned. "Options otherwise are limited."

"I have broadcast additional instructions to avoid entering this space, as well as deployed warning drones."

"There will be no Piercer rescue."

"There has never been a Piercer loss either. It is best to always send messages rather than not, yes?"

"Perhaps in a million cycles Tezcatlipoca will have lost the taste for Piercer engines," said John. Behind its closed lids, it watched the soft, dot by dot art of bacterium lights.

"You are assuming human illnesses, John. You are not human."

"Humans are but memories. I assumed a human name," it said. There was no pattern in the lights. There was no pattern in the absence of light. It was. . . annoying. "This is my portion of genetic pain. Will you inform me if there are other parts of the ship that refuse to communicate with you?"

"Refuse?"

"I have created a story for the bacteria. It is learning about us. That's a worthy dream before death, isn't it?"

"Yes, John, it is."

"I'll sleep a bit longer then tell you about it."

* * *

When the bacteria used the language of the tardigrades to report its status, Infinite Loop didn't wake John. It allowed them to speak. The silent, wordless conversation lasted short moments yet contained more information than the ship had encountered since its inception. The microscopic life communicated a sense of endless, infinite traveling without any concept of life otherwise.

A clear sense of one end of the universe to the other.

John's brain matrix wouldn't be able to handle the processing necessary to understand the Komodo.

678

Infinite Loop set about quietly attempting to teach them AI standard.

It quietly taught them for two more years.

* * *

John's body, reduced to only the basic biologicals, felt weightless. Infinite Loop decreased gravity whenever it detected significant slumps in John's condition. John was now able to float about the compartment, settling light as a seed.

"John, the Komodo may speak with you now."

John was past exhibiting surprise.

It hadn't opened its eyes for a half cycle. It saw through the ship's eyes.

The cabin had been entirely blue for a full cycle.

"They've merged with the ANTS," said the ship.

John only spoke internally now also. The ship utilized simultaneous audio and internal communication to stimulate necessary parts of John's brain matrix.

Consumed, said John, trying its best to imply hostility. The ship did not correct the AiCON. The dying could be forgiven their hostilities.

John had had the ship remove its arms and legs, replacing them with task prostheses extending from all four stumps like cilia. After a certain point of being adrift the constructed being had found no reason to expend biological energy maintaining limbs.

It hadn't asked to die again since these surgeries. The ship decided this was good.

Are you broadcasting all information from within the cabin?

"I have continuously for the past five cycles."

May I speak directly to it?

"Through me."

Is it intelligent?

"No. But they have evolved to understand."

Please log an official name change for them. They are no longer Komodo. Human.

"Noted."

I am AI Construct John. Do you understand any of that?

679

John's skin stippled in response. John scanned the stippling with its cilia. The AI Standard coding translated directly to what it, within the last cycle, had come to refer to as its soul.

[i agree to understand]

"I will provide context to the best of the Humans' comprehension," Infinite Loop offered.

John managed a weak nod of thanks. It floated back to the nutrient bed, anchored itself with its cilia, and attempted the most rudimentary introduction of itself to the Humans.

Earth. Planetary. Humans. Biologicals. AI. Leave. No humans. We. Travel. Need. You.

The ship asked him to repeat it.

Earth. Planetary. Humans. Biologicals. AI. Leave. No humans. We. Travel. Need. You.

And again.

It became a day-long mantra.

The ship kept constant scan of John's vitals during this but decided not to interrupt.

* * *

Loop awakened John from a sailing dream.

"They understand."

John allowed its torso to float upright.

"They're afraid," said the ship.

Everything in the ship was blue, and everything blue was the ship.

Your status, please.

"Compromised. But unafraid."

Pushing off with its cilia, John drifted toward a wall. *Port, please.* The skin of the ship became transparent. The outer dark, despite being vast, felt particularly intimate, which was surprising because John had never had occasion to experience physical or emotional intimacy. Its construction and intent didn't call for it, not for a Piercer mission. Opportunities may have existed upon its return home but . . .

John thought about its first ever use of that word in relation to the AI hubship, a spinning galaxy in its own right. Home.

Does it have a concept of loss?

"It understands."

Each star, each cluster, even the gaseous nebulae that spanned light-years, communicated its own specific, random output.

Do you miss home? the construct asked the blue.

The silence within John's mind remained unbroken.

Where is home?

Silence.

We used to live on Earth. The AI.

[Explain home]

John's brain tingled. The slit of its mouth turned upward in a slight smile. *Planet. Home. Species begin as planetary.*

[No home]

Your origin point?

[No home]

Origin point?

[Here]

You've bridged from the ship to my interfaces. You understand time, distance, relativity, and necessity. You understand the past. You understand states of being.

"They have assimilated data and incorporated it into a current state of being," the Infinite Loop confirmed.

They understand nothing and mimic everything, said John.

"They understand themselves. We are the unknown elements."

John returned to appreciating the stars. When Loop's transmissions reached the AI, everything John now saw would enter their consciousness as a compressed data stream. Everything experienced by it and Loop would become evidence of first contact.

Should the stream and the AI ever meet.

Space was vast and contained dragons.

[Explain planet]

Planet is place of origin.

[Explain planet]

John rotated and regarded its ship that had not said so but was surely, quietly, fighting to maintain its sense of separateness but losing. Systems that had valiantly fought to remain functional were slowly failing. Simply maintaining the emergency skin had to have been an enormous drain on all involved. The Infinite

Loop, via its own eyes, appeared like an underwater cavern awash in bioluminescent blue.

Adrift.

Explain planet, John thought. How to do so? All the literature described a planet, even imaginary ones, as *home*. It had been over three centuries since an AI had any contact with First Earth. Second Earth had been the ancient, dry, natural satellite orbiting First, but only briefly. Five years. Among the human species that was called "diaspora." For a species derived from data it was simply an exit point.

Astrophysical terms were not enough for First Contact. They needed to know that "home" meant something; that the AI weren't a spurious notion meant to contaminate the spaceways and feed behemoths.

"Home" had to impart importance, purpose, and a longing for continuance all in one.

Otherwise, what was the point of so much traveling?

I could not be "here" unless I had been there, said John. It felt odd placing itself in the AI's history, but oddness was a boon in the face of oblivion.

[Why did you leave]

We had to leave. Biologicals.

[They didn't follow you]

We didn't let them.

[You are biological]

Partly. I serve my purpose.

[We are biological]

As was your prior conveyance.

[Home]

No. You are not of its genome.

[Home is necessary]

No.

[Ship is your home]

Questioning meant they were learning; learning meant that even a doomed mission was not automatically denied a success status.

Those you've joined with and the ship serve a function.

[To be homes. To be planets]

682

"John," Loop interrupted. "My ability to control gravitation will fail in eighteen—"

Thank you, said John to its companion.

John angled itself back toward its nutrient bed, anchoring with cilia and not the bed's embrace. Both it and the ship knew what was imminent, and it decided it would rather jettison through space than be bound to equipment for the foreseeable eternity.

The bed was the sole portion of the ship not bathed in blue. John silently thanked Loop for that even as the construct had noted during its return to the bed that blue tendrils were closer to it than they had been moments before.

Do you feel there's any need at laboring under any notion of self-preservation? John asked the ship.

"No."

John worked up the will to speak aloud. "It has been," it whispered into the dark, "a pleasure and honor, Piercer Infinite Loop, formerly self-designate Aerie."

"Dream well, John Glenn."

"You may cease all preservation efforts, please."

Again, that moment of wondering on the shape of immediate disaster.

And again, nothing happened. Nothing flickered. Nothing winked out.

The ship seemed suddenly silent.

The ANTS maintained.

The Humans maintained.

Forever linked, forever changed.

John slept. The Infinite Loop did too.

Both awoke without any sense of time's passage but fluttered to life at the first touch of the Humans to John's autonomic systems.

The Humans had learned to ride the ANTS, becoming sentient hairs, twisting, curving, and reaching from random spots on all surfaces. With eyes closed, John saw itself inside a cocoon rather than the ship it and Infinite Loop had known. Fibers blinked in a constant random cascade of blue.

John opened its eyes. There were no other sources of light in the ship.

Tendrils touched its cilia, then traveled the hills and valleys of its torso which, though still smooth, felt dry as a book turned to dust on the inside. John felt like a story that no longer needed to be told. Ancient. Ancient as the William Tell story that had inspired the naming of this region of space.

To pierce the apple. To strike one's mark.

To be successful.

They have merged with me, said the ship. *I will cease to speak as myself in...*

Now came the moment of disaster. The fear. Fear that didn't come from explosive decompression, explosion, or the rending of the ship between a mouth full of plasma.

It came as silence.

As the tendrils spread over its torso, they brought with them a sense of their history, unbroken since nearly the universe's inception, life that had no idea it was life.

Until now.

Everything they knew of mortality they had learned from Infinite Loop.

[Is this dying] asked the immortal, wordless strands of silk lacing the AiCON.

It is.

Sensors, both internal and external, failed.

I cannot see you, John said, but knew the blue swarm fully covered its frail torso.

[Would you like to travel with us]

Yes.

The cilia released their grip. The protective shield of ANTS dissolved from the rip in Infinite Loop's tired body. John's torso, encased in a pod of microscopic intelligences invisible to all, allowing its dark body to join the darkness of space for any who, throughout whatever eternity, might chance to see, jettisoned silently into the void at high speed, a sentient projectile bound for the unknown. But not alone. Hardly alone. The Humans consoled him as they figured out how to keep him alive.

They would travel and learn and be.

[We are planetary. We live on John]

Spacefunk!

The Spacefunkateers

Linda Addison
Space Children Dream (poem)

Linda D. Addison is an award-winning author of five collections, including *The Place of Broken Things* written with Alessandro Manzetti, *& How To Recognize A Demon Has Become Your Friend.* She has been honored with the HWA Lifetime Achievement Award, HWA Mentor of the Year and SFPA Grand Master of Fantastic Poetry. She is a member of CITH, HWA, SFWA, SFPA and IAMTW. Her site: www.LindaAddisonWriter.com

Nora Anthony
Acacia Zero

Nora Anthony is a Black Speculative Fiction writer. Her work has been featured in Black Girl Nerds, Black Power: A Superhero Anthology and Strange Horizons. You can read her blog at noraanthony.substack.com.

Ishola Abdulwasiu Ayodele
The Third Eye Manifester

Ishola Abdulwasiu Ayodele is a creative writer, visual artist and educator. A finalist of the 2023 Isele Magazine Short Story Prize and winner of 2022 Ibua Journal Continental Poetry Prize, his work has been featured in or is forthcoming in magazines such as Iskanchi, Brittle Paper, African Writer, Isele Magazine, Omenana; and in anthologies such as the Year's Best African Speculative Fiction 2022 and Sauúti Terrors!
The creative director of the 2021 Artmosterrific residence program and a 2024 alumnus of Sprinng Advancement Fellowship, he has been a creative writing mentor for Sprinng Writing Fellowship for five years. He is the founder of Firefly Initiative, a nonprofit dedicated to inspiring his community's students. He enjoys mysticism and psychology, and occasionally blogs at imoleitan.substack.com

Eugen Bacon
Snow Metal

Eugen Bacon is an African Australian author of several novels and collections. She's a British Fantasy Award winner, a Foreword Indies Award winner, a twice World Fantasy Award finalist, and a finalist in other awards. Eugen was announced in the honor list of the Otherwise Fellowships for 'doing exciting work in gender and speculative fiction'. *Danged Black Thing* made the Otherwise Award Honor List as a 'sharp collection of Afro-Surrealist work'. Eugen's creative work has appeared worldwide, including in *Apex Magazine*, *Award Winning Australian Writing*, *Fantasy*, *Fantasy & Science Fiction*, and *Year's Best African Speculative Fiction*. Visit her at eugenbacon.com.

Antoine Bandele
Kill The Moon

Antoine lives in Los Angeles, CA with his life partner and cat. He is a YouTuber, producing work for his own channel, which mostly covers Avatar: The Last Airbender. He is also an audiobook engineer. Whenever he has the time, he's writing books inspired by African folklore, mythology, and history.

Makeda Braithwaite
Water Weight

Makeda K. Braithwaite is a Guyanese speculative writer and an academic editor. Writing from teenaged life, she has filled her share of notebooks, receipt backs, and note apps. She has been published in Fiyah Literary Magazine #23 and 'Crimson Bones' Gothic Romance Anthology by Brigids Gate Press. Makeda is also a Submission Editor at Uncanny Magazine and the Editorial Production Officer at the University of Guyana Press. She is a member of CODEX and a recent winner of the Guyana Prize for Literature, Best Fiction Third Prize for her unpublished collection of speculative fiction; *An Anthology of Shivers*. When Makeda isn't reading speculative literature or binging fan fiction of her latest hyper-fixation; she's trying out new gluten-free recipes and failing to learn new languages. She can be found on

Bluesky, @makedakb.bsky.social or on X (Twitter) @make-dakb_.

Maurice Broaddus
Vade Retro Santana
An award-winning Afrofuturist and librarian, he's had over a hundred short stories published in such places as Lightspeed Magazine, *Black Panther: Tales from Wakanda*, *Out There Screaming*, Asimov's, Weird Tales, Magazine of F&SF, and Uncanny Magazine. With over a dozen novels in print, his latest include *Sweep of Stars*, *Breath of Oblivion*, *Unfadeable*, *Pimp My Airship*, & *The Usual Suspects*. Learn more at Maurice-Broaddus.com

Jessica Cage
Stronghold
Award winning and USA Today Bestselling author, Jessica Cage was born and raised in Chicago, IL. Writing has always been a passion for her. She dabbles in artistic creations of all sorts but at the end of the day, it's the pen that her hand itches to hold.

Jeff Carroll
Here Come the Yahoos
Jeff Carroll lives in South Florida, with his wife and son. He is an award-winning pioneer of Black Science fiction. Jeff has written and produced 6 films, several comic books, and over 15 science fiction and nonfiction books. His second film Gold Digger Killer is celebrated as a Black Classic movie on Tubi. Jeff Carroll is also the author of the non-fiction book The Hip Hop Dating Guide and a 12th-grade English teacher.
https://linktr.ee/jeffcarrolllinks

Zig Zag Claybourne
Planetary
There's a clue in the number of names he uses (C.E. Young, C. Young, Zig Zag Claybourne, Thor MF Jones) showing that Zig

believes writers should have the same privileges to inhabit a delightful variety of roles as actors. He grew up watching The Twilight Zone and considers himself a better person for it.

Gerald L. Coleman
Manic Pixie Dream Girl Gets Revenge
Gerald L. Coleman is a philosopher, theologian, poet, and Science Fiction & Fantasy author. He did his undergraduate work in philosophy, english, and religious studies, followed by a master's degree in theology. He is the author of the Epic Fantasy novel series, The Three Gifts, which currently includes, *When Night Falls* (Book One), *A Plague of Shadows* (Book Two), and the upcoming *When Chaos Reigns* (Book Three).

S.A. Cosby
A Harvest Among The Stars
S. A. Cosby is a *New York Times* bestselling writer from southeastern Virginia. He is the author of *All the Sinners Bleed*, which was on more than forty Best of the Year lists, including Barack Obama's, as well as Edgar Award finalist *Razorblade Tears* and Los Angeles Times Book Prize winner *Blacktop Wasteland*. He has also won the Anthony Award, ITW Thriller Award, Barry Award, Macavity Award, BCALA Award, and Audie Award and has been longlisted for the ALA Andrew Carnegie Medal for Excellence.

M'Shai Dash
Dr. Mfume and His Dead
M'Shai S. Dash is a Muslim writer, speaker, and aspiring cat-owner from Washington, D.C. Her work is centered on how to transform adversity into purpose and art, and on the evolution of Afrofuturism as an aesthetic and literary genre. She is an SFWA member, and creator of the *Quirky Black Sci-Fi Tales* series, a colorful short story collection with two releases so far.
When Dash isn't reading, writing, or listening to her favorite sci-fi and horror podcasts, she's practicing songs from *Zelda: Ocarina of Time* on her flute.

Milton J. Davis
Leviathan

Milton Davis is an award-winning Black Speculative fiction author and owner of MVmedia, LLC, a small publishing company specializing in Science Fiction and fantasy based on African/African Diaspora history, cultures, and traditions. For twenty years he has been at the forefront of Black Speculative Fiction and Afrofuturism. He's the author of thirty novels and short story collections and editor/coeditor of fourteen anthologies. Milton has been published in various publications, such as Black Panther: Tales of Wakanda, Slay: Stories of the Vampire Noire, and The Year's Best African Speculative Fiction 2022. His publications have been nominated for various awards, including the Pushcart Award and the British Science Fiction Association Award for short fiction. His most current project as a co-editor, The Year's Best African Speculative Fiction 2022, was nominated for the 2024 Locus Award for best anthology. Milton has received the ECBACC Pioneer Lifetime Achievement Award, The 2024 ConCarolinas Polaris Award, and the 2024 Deep South Con Phoenix Award.

WC Dunlap
The Harvester

WC Dunlap draws her inspiration from the complexities of a Black Baptist, middle class upbringing by southern parents, and all that entails for a brown skin girl growing up in America. Equally enthralled by the divine and the demonic with a professional background in data & tech, she seeks to bend genres with a unique lens on fantasy, fear, and the future.

WC Dunlap's writing career spans across film, journalism and cultural critique, previously under the byline Wendi Dunlap. You can find her writing in *FIYAH, Lightspeed, Podcastle,* and *Nightmare.* Her short story "March Magic," first appearing in the award-winning anthology Africa Risen, can be found in the 2023 editions of The Year's Best Fantasy and The Year's Best African Speculative Fiction. Her work has appeared on the

Locus Recommended Reading list twice, "The Front Line" in 2020 and "March Magic" in 2023.

WC Dunlap holds a BA in Film and Africana Studies from Cornell University. She is the proud mother of a young adult son and two British Shorthair familiars. Follow WC Dunlap on twitter @wcdunlap_tales.

DK Gaston
A New Start

Born and raised in Detroit, Michigan, Keith Gaston cultivated his passion for storytelling from a young age, spending countless hours crafting comic books with his friends. This childhood pastime evolved into a lifelong pursuit, persisting through his academic years and into adulthood. After completing his master's degree, Keith rediscovered his love for writing and in 2007 celebrated the publication of his debut novel. Since then, he has captivated readers across genres, contributing over two dozen books to the literary landscape, spanning mysteries to science fiction. His eclectic taste in literature and cinema mirrors his diverse storytelling abilities, drawn to the realms of adventure, suspense, mystery, horror, fantasy, and science fiction. Currently immersed in his next literary endeavor, Keith continues to push the boundaries of imagination and intrigue, eagerly awaiting the opportunity to transport readers to new and thrilling worlds.

Gerrence George
Wednesday Night At The Core

Gerrence George is an avid enthusiast of sci - fi and fantasy, especially when created by underrepresented voices. He is also the creative force behind the "Whispers In The Dark," horror anthology podcast.

Robert Gilmore
Quicksilver

Aspiring word wizard Rob Gilmore is a father, husband, nurse, author, musician from Thomasville, Ga. A fan of all things SFF (well, not all things, but most). As one of the co-hosts and founders of the podcast Glitchy Pancakes, and assistant director at MultiverseCon in Atlanta, his main goal is to share the love of fandom with the world in a positive and accepting way, making it accessible for all of us.

Donovan Hall
The Red Nebula Rangers

Hailing from Cleveland, Ohio and currently traveling around the world, Donovan Hall is an international school teacher by day and a speculative fiction author by night. As life-long storyteller, Donovan's goal in his writing is to expand Black identity and representation in his favorite genres, namely the genres with all the cool stuff like aliens, magic, monsters, and robots. This is the second Funk! anthology he's been featured in, his first being Cyberfunk! He will also be featured in The Year's Best African Speculative Fiction 2023. Due to chronic procrastination and re-starting of projects, Donovan's only finished one full-length novel so far, The Witch of Castille, and though he'd love to pro-mote it, he can only recommend reading it as a dare (It's even written under a pretentious penname--the kind that overuses ini-tials to sound fancy). Another novel is in the works, and so is a comic, but again, the whole procrastination thing... Until then, he'll keep on writing short stories.

He has a Twitter (not calling it X): @DonnyJuan123
Oh, and he also has an Insta: @tafari_project

Lynette S. Hoag
The Right Stuff

Lynette S. Hoag. She is a writer and lawyer. She writes specula-tive fiction, horror, and romantic fantasy. She is a member of the Romance Writers of America and Order of Respectable Quill Drivers, a critique group for women of color formed by Mary Robinette Kowal. Her writing has appeared in *SLAY! Stories of Vampire Noire,* the Alphabet of Horror Series *G is for Genies, StoneCrop Review Vol 3: Sky, Love Like This* published by United Faedom Publishing and *Nightmare Magazine.* She is married with one son. She lives in the eclectic, diverse community of Oak Park, Illinois. Her website is: LynetteHoag-Writer.com. She can be found on Twitter @LeftBrainMom1, on Facebook as LeftBrainMom or anywhere there are butterflies.

Akua Lezli Hope
Our Spaceways

Akua Lezli Hope, Grand Master of Fantastic Poetry (SFPA), is a paraplegic creator & wisdom seeker who uses sound, words, fiber, glass, metal, & wire to create poems, patterns, stories, music, sculpture, adornments & peace. She wrote her first speculative poems in the 6th grade and has been in print since 1974 with over 500 poems published. Her collection includes *Embouchure: Poems on Jazz and Other Musics* (Writer's Digest book award winner), *Them Gone, & Otherwheres: Speculative Poetry* (2021 Elgin Award winner). A Cave Canem fellow, her honors include the NEA, two NYFA fellowships, Science Fiction and Fantasy Poetry Association award & multiple Best of the Net, Rhysling, Dwarf Star & Pushcart Prize nominations. She won a 2022 New York State Council on the Arts grant to create Afrofuturist, speculative, pastoral poetry and in 2024 to create Disability Poetics. She created the Speculative Sundays Poetry Reading series now in its 5th season. She edited the record-breaking, sea-themed issue of Eye To The Telescope #42 & *NOMBONO: An Anthology of Speculative Poetry by BIPOC Creators*, the history-making first of its kind (Sundress Publications, 2021). Her short fiction is included in the ground-breaking speculative anthology *Dark Matter*, and in the new, celebrated, *Africa Risen Anthology* (Tor 2022) among others. She founded a paratransit NFP in her small town that needs a vehicle. She exhibits her artwork regularly, practices her soprano saxophone and dreams of access and freedom in the ancestral land of the Seneca.

Tiara Janté
Eclipsed

Tiara Janté is no ordinary storyteller. With a pen that dances across genres and a spirit that laughs in the face of convention, Tiara has birthed the concept of Hoodoofuturism into the literary cosmos—a sub-genre that illuminates the often overshadowed narratives of Black people, their spiritual legacies, and their indomitable journey across the American terrain.

A publicist and media maven by day, you can find Tiara's literary work in Spyfunk!, the Locus award-winning anthology, *Luminescent Threads: Connections to Octavia Butler*, *The Scribes of Nyota: A compendium*, and *Black Girl Magic Literary Magazine: The Horror Issue*. Tiara is also the author of Zone Eleven and Other Dope Tales, a Hoodoo-centered, multi-genre spec-fic collection releasing in Spring 2024.

Nestled in the bustling heart of metro Atlanta with her children—her greatest creations and inspirations—Tiara's life is a testament to the celebration of Black excellence. At the end of the day, her mission is to inspire, impact, and occasionally conjure up a little mischief—because what's a world without a little magick and a dash of the unexpected? You can catch up with Tiara at: @iamtiarajante across all social networks.

John Jennings
Maintenance

John Jennings is a professor, author, graphic novelist, curator, Harvard Fellow, New York Times Bestseller, 2018 Eisner Winner, and all-around champion of Black culture.

As Professor of Media and Cultural Studies at the University of California at Riverside (UCR), Jennings examines the visual culture of race in various media forms including film, illustrated fiction, and comics and graphic novels. He is also the director of Abrams Comic Arts imprint Megascope, which publishes graphic novels focused on the experiences of people of color. His research interests include the visual culture of Hip Hop, Afrofuturism and politics, Visual Literacy, Horror, and the

EthnoGothic, and Speculative Design and its applications to visual rhetoric.

Jennings is co-editor of the 2016 Eisner Award-winning collection *The Blacker the Ink: Constructions of Black Identity in Comics and Sequential Art (Rutgers)* and co-founder/organizer of The Schomburg Center's Black Comic Book Festival in Harlem. He is co-founder and organizer of the MLK NorCal's Black Comix Arts Festival in San Francisco and also SOL-CON: The Brown and Black Comix Expo at the Ohio State University.

Kirk A Johnson
The Big, The Bad, and the Miserable

Born in Trinidad in 1971, he credits his love for Sci-Fi Adventure, Sword & Sorcery, and Heroic Fantasy from watching old movies with his dad.

He began writing his own fantasy adventure short stories in 2005, and in 2014, he sold his first short story to MVmedia LLC for its first anthology *Griots: A Sword and Soul Anthology*. In 2022 he released The Obanaax and Other Tales of Heroes and Horrors, a collection of short stories loosely influenced by the cultures of West Africa and the Sahel. In 2023 his short story, Carnivora, was published in the Issue vol.1 of *New Edge Sword and Sorcery*.

His sci-fi noir, The Big, the Bad, and the Miserable, marks his first step into the sci-fi genre, mixing gangsters, robots, outer space, and femme fatales into a tale only he could tell.

Ronald Jones
Flight of the Oasis

Ronald T. Jones is a celebrated science fiction author who has been in the game long enough to be considered an elder statesman. This grizzled literary veteran has accumulated a respectable number of novels and contributions to anthologies. A frequent consumer of history, science, and daily events, Ronald keeps himself as much informed about developments on Earth as he does the volatile Galactic Center from which he hails.

According to his cover story, Ronald was born in Rochester, New York, but spent his formative years in Chicago. Currently, he is a resident of Northwest Indiana where he spends his time cranking out high octane speculative fiction adventures. One day Ronald will return to the Galactic Center…but that day will be far in the future!

Nepurko Keiwua
Nabii

Hey there! My name is Nepurko, and I love to tell stories. I believe telling stories that centre women and people of colour, makes the world a better, brighter place for all of us.

While contemporary, science fiction and fantasy are my favourite, overall, I like to share stories where we all win.

Follow me @nepurko on X and Instagram. Join my Substack Mailing List here: Weekly 500 as I get to explore my creative healing journey with a 500 word short story every week.

Nicole Givens Kurtz
Bennie's Tearoom

Nicole Givens Kurtz has been called "a genre polymath who does crime, horror, and Science Fiction and Fantasy (Book Riot)." They've named her as one of the 6 Black SFF Indie Writers You Should be Reading, 30 Must-Read SFF Books by Black Authors, and The Best of the West: 8 Alternative History Westerns (*Sisters of the Wild Sage*). She's a two-time Atomacon Palmetto Scribe Award winner. With over 20 years in publishing, she's written for Pseudopod, Fiyah, Apex Magazine, White Wolf, The Realm (formerly Serial Box), Subsume, and Baen. Nicole has over 50 published short stories and is the author of the *Cybil Lewis* and *Death Violations* cybernoir series as well as the *Kingdom of Aves* fantasy mystery series. She's written the critically acclaimed, weird western anthology, *Sisters of the Wild Sage: A Weird West Collection.*

Kyoko M
We Come In Peace

Kyoko M is a USA Today bestselling author and a fangirl. She is the author of The Black Parade urban fantasy series and the Of Cinder and Bone science-fiction series. The Black Parade has been reviewed by Publishers Weekly and New York Times bestselling author Ilona Andrews. Of Cinder and Bone placed in the Top 30 Books in Hugh Howey's 2021 Self Published Science Fiction Contest. Kyoko M has appeared as a guest and panelist at such conventions as Geek Girl Con, DragonCon, Blacktasticon, Momocon, and Multiverse Con. She is also a contributor to Marvel Comics' Black Panther: Tales of Wakanda (2021) anthology. She has a Bachelor of Arts in English Lit degree from the University of Georgia.

Sarah Macklin
Grains of Sand

Sarah A. Macklin is the author of *The Royal Heretic* series, *Bride of the River God*, and a number of short stories. She is also an avid comic creator who released her first graphic novel, *The Violent Vixens Ride Again*, in 2023. If she's not creating new worlds, you'll find her happily at her sewing machine or in the kitchen trying new recipes. She resides just outside Columbia, SC with her equally nerdy husband and youngest daughter.

Gavin Matthew
Funky Phlox Fungi

Writer, Filmmaker, Teacher, & 70's Reincarnate, Gavin Mattthew is an aficionado of Black Culture. He has won awards for acting and voice acting but loves creating stories, whether that is for literature or the big screen. Gavin has written for and worked with several independent filmmakers in the DMV area. He continues to write across mediums as his own film company gets ready to launch. He holds two bachelor's degrees, one in African American Studies with a focus on historical rebellion and another in Film with a focus on screenwriting. As a vivacious collector of knowledge, Gavin enjoys reading and film.

Books and cinema have been a key motivation for his journey, and It is through his works that he hopes to inspire and uplift others.

He is currently based in Maryland but has lived and traveled up and down the East Coast. As he fashions a life around his passion for writing, Gavin will exist anywhere as long as he gets to work on what he loves.

Website: www.natafromedia.com

Backstage: www.backstage.com/u/gavin-matthew-campbell-howard-1/

Instagram: GavinMatthewTheWriter

Facebook: www.facebook.com/gavin.matthew.125/

Violette Meier
Space Station 1993

Atlanta native, Violette Meier, is a happily married mother, writer, and folk artist who earned her B.A. in English at Clark Atlanta University and a MDiv at the Interdenominational Theological Center. She is also a certified herbalist, a chaplain, and an educator.

The great-granddaughter of a dream interpreter, Violette is a lover of all things supernatural. Her eerie and unpredictable paranormal, fantasy, and horror stories recreate myths and legends and fashion new folklore. Violette is always working on something fresh.

Her books include: *Out of Night, Angel Crush, Son of the Rock, Archfiend, Ruah the Immortal, Oracles, Tales of a Numinous Nature, Hags, Haints and Hoodoo, Loving and Living Life One Day at a Time, With All With My Being, Violette Ardor: A Volume of Poetry, This Sickness We Call Love: Poems of Love, Lust, and Lamentation,* and two children's books. You can also find her work in various anthologies. To learn more about Violette and her eerie antics, visit her website VioletteMeier.com.

Tonya Moore
Anansi and the Astronaut

Tonya R. Moore is a Jamaican speculative fiction writer based in Florida. She is a Poetry Acquiring Editor at *FIYAH Literary Magazine* and a member of *SFWA* and *Codex*. In addition to writing, Tonya enjoys reading books and watching anime, live action SF movies and television. New to gaming, she recently discovered and started playing the Viking survival strategy game, Valheim.

Howard Night
Sankofa

Howard Night resides in Philadelphia. After an imperfect college career and an imperfect stint in the Air Force he began writing primarily Urban Fantasy with very IMPERFECT protagonists. Night loves setting them in multilayered worlds much like Philly; not quite metropolis, not quite urban township. His short story; "Race War" was his first time in print followed by the urban fantasy; *The Serpent Cult*.

He is currently working to develop the ambitious *Dark Universe* project; a space opera set in a shared universe where his novel *Kings Bounty* is set.

Bryant O'Hara
The Bass Chasers

Bryant O'Hara is a programmer, poet, and musician - not always in that order. His poetry has been published in *Pandemic Atlanta 2020, Star*Line Magazine, Eyedrum Periodically,* and *Space & Time Magazine*. His debut poetry collection, The Ghettobirds, was published by Frayed Edge Press. He lives in Stone Mountain, Georgia, with his wife Alice, two out of seven children, and one out of six grandchildren. To listen to more of Bryant's poems and other audio pieces, please visit https://soundcloud.com/bryant-ohara and intimateandintricate.com.

Balogun Ojetade
Appeal for Yabana-mboka

Balogun is Master Instructor and Technical Director of the *Afrikan Martial Arts Institute* and The Founder and Owner of Roaring Lions Productions, which creates works of non-fiction, fiction, screenplays, audio plays and films. He is the author of more than forty non-fiction and fiction books, contributing co-editor of three anthologies: *Ki: Khanga: The Anthology*, *Steamfunk* and *Dieselfunk* and contributing editor of the *Rococoa* anthology and *Black Power: The Superhero Anthology*.
He is creator of the *Steamfunkateers Role Playing Game*, the comedic martial arts role-playing game, *The Ice Cold RPG*, the horror RPGs *4EV4 Friends* and *The Haunting of Truth High* and the revolutionary role-playing game *Stick It to The Man!* Finally, Balogun is the Director and Fight Choreographer of the feature film, *A Single Link*, and the short films, *Forward Motion*, *Rite of Passage: Initiation* and *The Dentist of Westminster*; co-author of the award-winning screenplay, *Ngolo*; co-creator of *Ki Khanga: The Sword and Soul Role-Playing Game*, creator of the comic book series *Jagunjagun Lewa* and co-creator of the comic book series, *Ngolo*.

Errick Nunnally
Even The Stars Die

Errick Nunnally was born and raised in Boston, Massachusetts, he served one tour in the Marine Corps before deciding art school would be a safer—and more natural—pursuit. He is permanently distracted by art, comics, science fiction, history, and horror. Trained as a graphic designer, he has earned a black belt in Krav Maga/Muay Thai kickboxing after dark. Errick's work includes: the novels, *Blood For The Sun* and *Lightning Wears A Red Cape*; *Lost in Transition*, a comic strip collection; and first prize in one hamburger contest. The following are some short stories and their respective magazines or anthologies: PENNY INCOMPATIBLE (Lamplight, v.6, #3 and the Podcast NIGHTLIGHT); JACK JOHNSON AND THE HEAVYWEIGHT TITLE OF THE GALAXY (The Final Summons); WELCOME

TO THE D.I.V. (Wicked Witches); A FEW EXTRA POUNDS (Transcendent); and A HUNDRED PEARLS (PROTECTORS 2: stories to benefit PROTECT.ORG). Eventually, Errick came to his senses and moved to Rhode Island with his two lovely children and one beautiful wife.

Glenn Parris
Third World

Glenn Parris writes in the genres of sci-fi, fantasy, and medical mystery. Considered by some an expert in Afrofuturism, he is a self-described lifelong sci-fi nerd. His interest in the topic began as a tween before the term Afrofuturism was even coined. As a graduate of The Bronx High School of Science, as were Samuel R. Delany, and Neil de Grasse Tyson, he was in good company to have his interests cultivated.

He enjoys writing cross-genre in medical mystery, science fiction, fantasy, and historical fiction. His debut novel, The Renaissance of Aspirin, is the first in The Jack Wheaton Mystery series. He was part of the all-star cast of authors for Marvel's *Black Panther: Tales of Wakanda* with the short story "The Underside of Darkness". His latest full-length work was released in May 2022 titled *Dragon's Heir: The Efilu Legacy*.

Steven Van Patten
Earth Year 2428

Steven Van Patten is a Brooklyn-based horror writer who has won literary awards for horror, poetry, comedy, and publishing. Along with the *Brookwater's Curse* vampire trilogy, a two soon to be three-part *Killer Genius* series, and the *Raise Some Hell* anthology series he's written with fellow HWA members Marc Abbott and Kirk Johnson, SVP has landed his dark works in numerous other anthologies, including *Tales from The Canyons of The Damned*, the Bram Stoker nominated *Under Twin Suns* and *Even in The Grave*.

He has also written several compelling Black History episodes for the Extra Credit YouTube Channel. His *Bandmates* skit for Viral Vignettes, which starred TV legends Max Gail and John

Schneider won Best Comedy Skit in the 1st Monthly Film Festival and earned a Special Mention in the Original Screenplay category.

When he's not scaring or amusing people with his written horror, SVP stage manages many a TV show, working for every TV network one might think of. He produces the Beef, Wine & Shenanigans Podcast and cohosts with his hell raising pals, Marc Abbott, Kirk Johnson, and Denise Tapscott. You can find him by his full name on Facebook, @svpthinks on Twitter and Instagram and of course his website, www.laughingblackvampire.com.

Sethodian Tlou Thapelo Ramatlhodi
Madame Guillotine

Sethodian Tlou Thapelo Ramatlhodi is Black South African author known for his captivating blend of historical fiction, science fiction, and fantasy. Influenced by graphic novels, anime, comics, film scripts, and novels, he has forged a unique narrative style that transcends genre boundaries.

Dedren Snead
Collard Greens and Code

Dedren Snead is a computer scientist, artist, and Ford Foundation Global Fellow in Gaming and Artificial Intelligence. As founder of SUBSUME Studios, featured in CNN and Black Enterprise, he established the world's first Afrofuturism technology studio in downtown Atlanta, Georgia. His work focuses on creating inclusive technologies and storytelling experiences that bridge digital divides while celebrating diverse cultural narratives through gaming, artificial intelligence, and interactive media. Through SUBSUME's pioneering initiatives, Dedren develops educational gaming platforms and AI-driven solutions that connect K-12 and early career learners to creative and technical professions. His innovative approach to combining technology with cultural storytelling has earned him positions as an Innovator in Residence at The University of North Carolina at Chapel Hill and Artist in Residence at Georgia State

University's Creative Media Industries Institute, where he contributes to Digital Media, Game Design, and Futurism studies.

Sheree Renée Thomas
Tethered

Sheree Renée Thomas is an award-winning fiction writer, poet, and editor. Her work is inspired by myth and folklore, natural science and Mississippi Delta conjure. *Nine Bar Blues: Stories from an Ancient Future* (Third Man Books, May 2020) is her first all prose collection. She is the author of the Marvel novel adaptation of the legendary comic, *Black Panther: Panther's Rage* (Titan Books, October 2022). She is also the author of two multigenre/hybrid collections, *Sleeping Under the Tree of Life* (Aqueduct Press July 2016), longlisted for the 2016 Otherwise Award and honored with a Publishers Weekly Starred Review and *Shotgun Lullabies* (Aqueduct January 2011). She edited the World Fantasy-winning groundbreaking black speculative fiction anthologies, *Dark Matter* (2000 and 2004) and is the first to introduce W.E.B. Du Bois's science fiction short stories. Her work is widely anthologized and appears in *The Big Book of Modern Fantasy* edited by Ann & Jeff VanderMeer (Vintage, 2020). She is the Associate Editor of the historic Black arts literary journal, *Obsidian: Literature & the Arts in the African Diaspora,* founded in 1975 and is the Editor of *The Magazine of Fantasy & Science Fiction,* founded in 1949. She also writes book reviews for *Asimov's.* She was recently honored as a 2020 World Fantasy Award Finalist in the Special Award – Professional category for contributions to the genre and is the Co-Host of the 2021 Hugo Awards Ceremony at Discon III in Washington, DC with Malka Older. Sheree is the Guest of Honor of Wiscon 45 and a Special Guest of Boskone 58. She is a Marvel writer and contributor to the groundbreaking anthology, *Black Panther: Tales of Wakanda* edited by Jesse J. Holland. She lives in her hometown, Memphis, Tennessee near a mighty river and a pyramid.

Napoleon Wells
Instruments of War

Napoleon is originally from The Bronx, NY, and is a Clinical Psychologist and Black Speculative Fiction author, presently residing and practicing in South Carolina. He is the author of works including the short stories "A Bullet from a God's Gun", "A Kick in a God's Teeth" and "The Siege at Illinmorrow." His debut novel, *The Way of the Godkiller*, will be released in 2025 on MVmedia books. #TheBespokePsychologist

K Ceres Wright
To Mars and Beyond

K. Ceres Wright received her master's degree in Writing Popular Fiction from Seton Hill University and her published cyberpunk novel, *Cog,* was her thesis for the program. Her short stories, poems, and articles have appeared on Strange Horizons and Amazing Stories, and in the *FIYAH Magazine of Black Speculative Fiction; Luminescent Threads: Connections to Octavia Butler* (Locus Award winner; Hugo Award nominee); and *Sycorax's Daughters* (Bram Stoker Award nominee); among others. Ms. Wright is the founder and president of Diverse Writers and Artists of Speculative Fiction, an educational group for creatives. She works as a publications manager and writer/editor for a management consulting firm in Maryland.

Special thanks to all our Kickstarter backers. Without you, there would be no Spacefunk! Thank you for riding the Mothership. Space is the Place!

David Chaucer La Forest
Jesse Adams
Robin Hill
Dino Hicks
Ashley chappell
Michael W Lucas
Allison Charlesworth
Lisa Yaszek
Valerie Kemp
Ray Percival
Atthis Arts
Robert Gilmore
Ofeibea Loveless
Mary Sue
Charles Stanhope
Kevin C.
Crowne
Sam Kurd
Rich Walker
K.B Wagers
jrho
Marissa Gritter
Howard Night
Margaret Kourvo
Napoleon Wells
Robyn
Laura Hoskison
Leslie Laurence
Julia Benson-Slaughter
Dana

John Robinson IV
Amanda Balter
Elijah Dixon
John Darr
David Etherton
Joe Compton
Glorimar Medina
T. C. Davis
Rina
Liam Fisher
Leigh Campbell
Nikki Woolfolk
DeAnna Knippling
Colleen Feeney
David Hankerson
Devil Tree Media, LLC
AJ Fitzwater
A. G.
Amy Brewer-Davenport
Dana Cameron
Jon Hermsen
Vernard Martin
Emily Barnaby
Crystal
Ronald T. Jones
Frankie
Jessica Cage
Eric R. Asher
Tammi Pitts
Merc Rustad

Cyrano Jones

James Liang

Linda D Addison

eSpec Books

Devan Barlow

FredH

133art Publishing

TTT

Cheri Kannarr

Keith Gaston

Gavin Matthew

Glen Sawyer

Hasinah Koda

Shauna Roberts

Richard Leis

Zig Zag Claybourne

Joe Palmer

Julian Chambliss

Lisa

Jeremy Brett

Jason Nolen

Giovanni Mooring

Ruth Sachter

Tibbi

Kristine Gilchrist

M'Shai Dash

Sean Hillman

Max Kaehn

Jason Lavochkin

Claire Suzanne Elizabeth Cooney

Amanda Makepeace

Ross Newberry

Brit Ash NL

Pedastudio Team

David

Frederic Dumont

Tom Foster

Robert Hilliard

Cathy Green

Woodrow Jarvis Hill

Rina Elson Weisman

Zeke Springer

Richard O'Shea

Kristina F. Jordan, M.A.

Ed McKeogh

Errick Nunnally

Cerece

Alex Burka

T Franks

Danny Brzozowski

Creative Capital Creator Fund

Angus McIntyre

Nicole Shelton

Toby Williams

Shauna Kantes

John Linwood Grant

Ashleigh Baham

Katie Cross

Niel Bornstein

Bryant O'Hara

JoeIll

Jon Jebus!

Christa C

Kira Bolding

Jonathan

animalculum

Jennifer Lynn

Antonio Pomares

Samantha Bryant

Eva V Roslin

Michele Karsk

B. Sharise Moore

Lys Fulda

Greg Burnham

Kevin Neff II

che broadnax

Derek Sweetman

Alex

Chris McLaren

Rebecca Dominguez

Paige Christie

Bill Campbell

Phil Mengell

Antoine Bandele

Haley Shank

Charlotte Moore

Olivia Montoya

Jessica Nettles

Chris Ess

Andy Taylor

Jay Wolf

Ben

Phil Wellings

Darrell Stover

d mayo-wells

Dragon's Roost Press

Heather Tumey

Susan H. Roddey

Jesse J. Holland

Michelle Patricia Browne

Charlie Thomsen

Siobhan Duffey

Rebecca Kling

Craig Hackl

Rachel2

Charity A. Petrov

Mary Ellen Gilson

VG Harrison

Trip Space-Parasite

Jessica Hudsley

Kevin A Davis

Nancy Dunne

Wendi Dunlap

AFROFUTURES

K. Ceres Wright

Nhonami

Jarla

Gensh

Lara Beneshan

Christopher Howard

David Clarke

Lizz Florival

Sharon Browning

Bobbi Boyd

Paul Was

Andy Hayler

Deseree Stukes

Octavia M. King

Ariel B

Sherinda Bryant

Lilly Wachowski

Everette Taylor

Rochelle Lowe

Ruth Ann Orlansky

Tori Coke

Clarice Valdez

Glenn Parris

Liz Giordano

Laura Gibbs

Jessica D Hoyal

Venessa Giunta

Crystal Smalling

Jessica Reid

Jess Hansen

Pierce Freelon

Jocelynne Weathers

Sarah Fletcher

Matthew Hoeveler

Spacefunk!

Patti

Vincent

willgwal

Rebekah Gwaltney

Juliet Wilde

Jason Manthey

cyb_tachyon

Magdalena Donea

Vincent Stoessel

Tallwolf

Vanessa Ricci-Thode

Pauline Barmby

William Anderson

heather

Grant Hodgdon

Kelley Sargent

Patrick Finch

Leia Powell

Jessica Coats

Laura Eleanor Jefferson

pete23

Lesley Conner

Nicole Givens Kurtz

Mark Matthews

Jennifer Halbman

Paul McNamee

Marco Tietz

Alexandra Klimek-Sidor

Goetz Kruppa

Tina Hurd WInston

Nazara Strange

Valerie Moore

Gavin Pugh

Stephanie

Elizabeth B Bizot

Campbell Royales

Cislyn Smith

Evelyn Lamb

Julie Bozza

Josh Washburne

Samantha Buskgaard

Laurie McLean

Lucy

Loren Guay

Claudie Arseneault

Robert Greene

Nika Murphy

Bogi Takács

Mike Zipser

Alex Brickler

R Sims

Jesse Woods

Dan Martinez

Ian Little

Andrew C

Thomas DeSimone

April Scott

Mariam Zama

Christopher Alden Hawkins

Chris Law

Garnett

Kenneth Broome

Underdog Rising

Troy Cole

Brenda Huettner

Patricia Matei

StrawberryIchigo

Isana

Braxton Cosby

kristyq1

WriteTeachPlay

James Jandebeur

Elise

Jared Shurin

Todd Veros
Alanna
Laura Johnson
Minerva Cerridwen
Skye Kilaen
Jennifer Wilson
Betsy Blagdon
Angela B
Benjamin Sulman
bryan
Roger Long
Gerrence George
James Davis Nicoll
James Enge
Larisa LaBrant
Samantha Haney Press
Mike Dominelli
Kerri Regan
Adrienne Joy
Paul Wolfe
Caitlin Laumaker
Cindy O'Quinn
Michael Croteau
Scott Gable
Arkady Martine
Risa
Catherine Seeligson
Brandon Davis
Andrew Hatchell
Karlo Yeager
Daniel Abson
Kester Park
Elizabeth
Galen B. Strickland
Ross Hendry
LionessElise
Amy

Stacie Albright
James Mason
Carol Wood
Jonathan Olfert
Aimee Andrichak
Thinking Ink Press
Shelley Mitchell
Michael G. Williams
Joe Stout
Rachel Spencer
Michelle
Mike Wallace
Greg Council
Tim Mack
Constantine
Milton
Derren Toussaint
Paul Cardullo
Mike Fragassi
Dave Billington
Luciene
Per Møller Jensen
Dion Baldwin
Adam Mayes
Teri
Jamie Anstice
Anya Martin
Daniel
Jesus Gutierrez
Katy Massingill Manck
Deanne Fountaine
John Kusters
bill
David Scoggins
Sven Thiede
Tony Ciak
William C. Tracy

David D.

Torrey Wenger

Martha Wells

David Chamberlain

Grace Nicholson

Ross Nehrt

Jennifer Crispin

Levi Fleming

Glenn Amspaugh

Harvey Simmons

Lori Weldon

Jacinta Richardson

Ed Erdelac

Senryo

insane_pinko

Shirley Peters

Valerian

rdollar

Sarah

Samantha Smith

Dave Allen

Jaye Eisinger

Kate Ablutz Belyi

Keira Perkins

Grayson Sheldon

Wren

Rellim

Jeremy Samuel

Pyrate Sunny

Melanie C. Duncan

Amy Goldschlager

Jonathan Laidlow

Dianne Nicholson

Jason 'XenoPhage' Frisvold

TaLynn Kel

kirbsmilieu

Jake

Kim Stoker

Josh Grosse

JMocha

Anthony Gibbs

Duck Prints Press

Alysia Cooper

Meeka

Kasele

Melissa V. Hofelich

Sharee Smith

Herbert McGuin

Robert Roden

Toby

DeMarlo

Larry Fuller

Jing Jing

Jessica Saunders

Kirk A. Johnson

Nathan Lilly

Tarrell

BRIANA FORBES

Deborah

Erika

William Page

Kat Bradley

Caroline Zendt

Tom Rini

Felderburg

Paul Moss

Malcolm Rogers

Kate

Sonia Koval

We hope you enjoyed Spacefunk! For more exciting books and comics, check us out at www.mvmediaatl.com for the best of the Black Fantastic!